STORM & SHELTER

A Bluestocking Belles with Friends Collection

GRACE BURROWES   MARY LANCASTER

ALINA K FIELD   BLUESTOCKING BELLES

CERISE DELAND   CAROLINE WARFIELD

JUDE KNIGHT   RUE ALLYN   SHERRY EWING

Cover Design by Jude Knight

ePub ISBN: 978-1-3932358-4-2
Mobi ASIN : B08L9X3TGF
Print ISBN: 978-1-7332450-2-9

CONTENTS

FORTUNE HUNTER WINS THE PRIZE

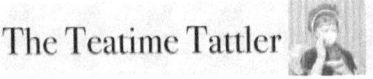

Dear Reader,

Has your Faithful Correspondent met Fortune's Favorite?

It has been noted by a member of the ton currently staying at the Queen's Barque in Fenwick on Sea, that shipwreck survivor Mrs. Simon, who is recovering at the inn, bears a striking resemblance to the well-known beauty, heiress Miss Letitia Lovell. On the other hand, no one claims to have ever seen the mysterious Mr. Simon among Miss Lovell's many suitors.

We must offer Mr. Simon our heartiest congratulations upon his good fortune—which we are assured is considerable!

AN IMPROBABLE HERO

MARY LANCASTER

An Improbable Hero
By Mary Lancaster

A runaway heiress, a mysterious stranger.

When Letty's ship founders in a violent storm, she forges a rare bond with her rescuer.

Simon is a troubled man on a final, deadly mission—until the spirited yet soothing Letty makes him question everything. Hiding in plain sight among the refugees at The Queen's Barque, Simon is more than capable of protecting them both. But when the floods recede, can either of them say goodbye?

CHAPTER 1

Letty had never been truly afraid in her life before. She realized that within moments of stumbling onto the heaving deck beneath one wildly swinging lantern. At once, rain and wind drove into her, trying to push her below again. A horrible creaking sound of breaking wood screamed above the noise of the storm.

"We've been blown back against the rocks!" one of the sailors shouted at the captain, who was peering over the side, until he slipped on the now wildly sloping deck.

"I can see that!" the captain yelled amid a string of curses. "We're going down! Man the boats! Abandon ship!"

"The boats have no chance in seas like this!" someone shouted at him. By the lantern's weird, swirling light, she saw he was not dressed in sailor's garb, but in an incongruous morning coat, with an open overcoat billowing over the top. Another passenger?

"No chance here either!" the captain said brutally.

"Who the devil is that?" the passenger demanded. His eyes glowed intermittently in Letty's direction. "Damnation, did you bring another passenger aboard?"

"She paid for her passage!" the captain said, urging his crew to hurry with the lowering of the boats.

"Well, you took her money, damn you, so look after her!" the passenger commanded, clinging to the rail as he made for the other boat. He didn't look back.

Letty, realizing all at once that her great adventure was about to end in disaster and drowning, staggered across the deck, fighting the wind and the chopping of the ship. There was no contest. She would have fallen and been washed over the side if the wind hadn't held her up long enough for the captain to seize her and drag her toward the second boat, which was now in the sea with several sailors, being tossed around like a lump of seaweed.

The ship screamed again and listed.

"Go!" yelled the captain, thrusting her at the rail.

It was the other passenger who grabbed her, clamping her to his side. The wind or the currents were trying to spin the tossing boat away from the ship.

"Close your eyes," the other passenger shouted, and then she seemed to be flying through the air, only to land with a jolt on something that heaved beneath her more horribly even than the ship's deck.

The sailors were trying to row away from the ship. But there was even less light now to see where to aim for in the maelstrom. The sailors heaved the oars with all their might. Even her fellow-passenger, who seemed to have taken her under his wing, added his weight. They made progress away from the ship, heaved and tossed on the massive waves. Her whole body felt numb from the battering of wind and rain. She had never felt so useless, so utterly helpless. So resigned.

The end of my great adventure. If I'd stayed with my aunt, I would at least live...

Imminent, terrible death certainly changed one's priorities.

She fixed her gaze on the other passenger who felt, somehow, like her one link left with the living. Because he had helped her, because he was closest to her. Because he was still trying.

However, it seemed inevitable when the huge wave seized the boat, tossing it high and tipping them all into the angry, swirling sea. Apparently, she wasn't numb at all, for the shocking cold of the water smacked her, filling her mouth and nose, consuming her.

In moments, I will be dead and gone. It will all be over.

In sheer panic, she lashed out with arms and legs, refusing to give in. She was rewarded with a brief, blessed gulp of air and then the sea caught her once more, dragging her down.

But then something else scooped her up, a human arm that seemed, temporarily at least, even stronger than the sea. She emerged coughing and gasping, clamped to someone's side.

A man's voice was yelling, "Hold on!" Her hands were dragged across something hard, a jagged object. Wooden. Part of their boat, or the ship, perhaps "Hold on!"

Her scrabbling fingers found a grip, and clung, and she saw that her savior was her fellow passenger. A ridiculous sense of safety washed over her.

"Look, we're close to the shore and being carried in that direction," he shouted in her ear, and indeed there were lights in the distance in a long, uneven row. "We'll live if you don't let go."

We are close... We will live... It was that *we*, that connection with another still living soul that gave her the strength, the courage to cling on, even to gasp out, "Thank you!"

The sea heaved around her, carrying her and her companion where it willed.

"What's your name?" she panted, because they seemed to be tying each other to life.

His head turned in the darkness. There was a distinct, baffled pause. "Simon."

"Letty." She even risked sliding her hand across to touch his. It was as close as they could come to shaking hands.

A sound like laughter escaped him, though it might just have been a gulp of breath. "Honored to live or die with you, Letty," he said.

And then, the sea hurled something against her head. The darkness fuzzed in an explosion of pain, and the last thing she remembered was his hand slamming over hers as she fell into nothing.

When the world came back, it was blessedly still. She was lying on her front with one cheek on something soft and gritty. Sand. Rain battered down on her.

Not dead.

She opened her eyes, and the pain in her head made her wince. She was shivering uncontrollably, but she recognized the face bending over her in the lantern light. Simon, her savior.

His lips curved. "There. I knew you would live." He reached out, gently brushing the damp hair from her face. His hand lingered on her cheek. "Take care, my Letty, and have a happy life."

Then she saw only his boots as he stood, and other men took his place, with kind voices and supporting arms, helping her to battle up the beach to scrubby grass and a covered wagon. A wonderfully dry blanket was flung around her shoulders.

As they helped her inside, she saw sailors she recognized already there. She looked anxiously over her shoulder for Simon, but she could not see anyone at all.

Horses began to draw the wagon forward and the pain in her head screamed with every jolt, distracting her from everything else. Standing water splashed up from the wagon wheels as more rain lashed relentlessly down. At one point, only seconds after they had passed, the hillside crumbled, tumbling into the road. An instant later, another farm wagon shot past them, driven, surely, by two young boys, one of whom was staring over his shoulder.

What a bizarre night... This wasn't quite the adventure she had sought.

From nowhere, laughter tried to fight its way out, but she swallowed it down again. She had a feeling it would turn to tears.

The wagon, with rain battering against its tarpaulin, fought its way through a straggling village, to a large, sprawling inn. There, more kind hands helped her from the wagon and through a front door where, for the first time in hours, neither wind nor rain could touch her.

For a second, she and the surviving sailors stood in a damp huddle, staring about them, for the inn was full of people, some eating and drinking, some asleep on benches, some rushing around on clearly urgent business.

A huge, hairy dog lying before the fire stood up and trotted toward them. As it sniffed her, she patted it without thought. It looked gratified.

Letty blinked and turned to the sailors. "Where did he go? The gentleman from the boat?"

They shrugged, more interested in their own current misery and in the fearsome dog now sniffing from hand to hand. It looked as if it could eat a man in two bites.

"They were fished out of the sea." The words were spoken by the man who seemed to have led their rescue to a harassed-looking woman in a mob cap. "They'll need dry clothes and the lady has a head wound."

At this woman's direction, a younger woman supported her upstairs to a chamber containing a bed and began to help her peel off her wet clothes. Another brought a rough chemise and a gown that was too large. By virtue of their warmth and dryness, they felt finer against Letty's skin than the most expensive silk. But she didn't think she would ever stop shaking.

She was no sooner dressed than a man came in and cleaned and dressed the wound in her head. It prickled, though she was too exhausted even to ask what he was doing. Every muscle in her body ached. Her fingers and nails were torn. The doctor looked at those too, bathed and anointed them.

"Thank you," she whispered.

He grunted. "Sleep. It may be someone else has to share the chamber with you, but I'm afraid you must put up with it for tonight. Tomorrow, I hope, will be better."

"No chance," muttered the young woman, pulling back the bedcovers for her. "The roads are blocked with landslides or floods and it's still raining. Where else can anyone go?"

Letty didn't care. She crawled under the covers in all the newly donned, wonderfully dry clothes. All she wanted was warmth enough to sleep. Her last conscious thought was that if everyone came here, then Simon must be here, too. Somewhere.

⚜

She woke to daylight and the throbbing of her head. She had stopped shaking. Wind and rain still battered against the windows, although perhaps with less force, and, when she rose warily and opened the shutters, the sky was still wild and dark.

Her plan was in ruins. She had to assume her remaining money had been lost with the ship, and she had no means of reaching her uncle in Brussels. Yet to return to London was unthinkable. Of course, she might not have a choice. Her guardians in London were bound to catch up with her... Though perhaps they would assume she had been drowned when the ship foundered. The hope cheered her, although it still left the problem of money. Perhaps she could work at the inn, or somewhere in this village where she would not be known.

Doing what? she asked herself.

She sighed, turning away from the window. Someone had rinsed the salt water from her clothes and hung them to dry from hooks. A warm wool shawl had been left over a chair and she gratefully wrapped herself in it before pinning up her hair as best she could with the pins she found on the dresser. Then, since her stomach was rumbling, she went in search of sustenance. Although she had no idea how she would pay for it, she felt quite unequal to making a new plan on an empty stomach.

Descending the stairs, she was confronted by a sea of people, most of whom looked up and regarded her with varying degrees of curiosity. Many were clustered around tables consuming breakfast. Delicious smells of fried ham and sausages made her mouth water.

"It's the poor young lady who was shipwrecked," an elderly female said to her companion in a clearly audible stage whisper.

"Oh, miss!" exclaimed the young woman who had helped her undress last night. Her hands were full of used crockery. "We didn't know you were awake. Sit yourself down and I'll bring you luncheon directly."

Luncheon! She must have slept longer than she knew.

"Sit here with us, my dear," invited the elderly lady, patting the chair next to hers. "What a terrible time you must have had!"

Letty smiled politely and sat, looking around for Simon, her savior in the storm.

"I am Miss Haddow, and this is my sister, Mrs. Pickering," the old lady said, offering her hand.

Letty shook it civilly and stood to offer her own to Mrs. Pickering across the table. "I'm Letty—" Aghast, she broke off, for she had almost revealed her true identity, which would make it only too easy for her guardian to find her. "Letty Simon," she blurted, adding the first name she could think of that wasn't her own.

"Miss Simon?" asked Miss Haddow.

"Mrs.," Letty said recklessly. After all, it was the perfect solution. Her guardian would not be looking for a married lady.

Her companions looked surprised.

"But where is your husband?" Mrs. Pickering wondered.

"Alas, I have lost him in the storm," Letty said.

"Oh, my dear," Miss Haddow said in quick sympathy, clearly misunderstanding.

Mrs. Pickering leaned forward. "There is always hope. People are still out looking for survivors, though it is so much more difficult now, with the roads flooded, and so many needing help. But someone will be sure to find your husband."

At least she did not say *your husband's body*.

Letty tried to smile hopefully, while seizing the coffee set beside her by the maid. A large plate of ham, sausages and toast quickly followed and Letty set to with enthusiasm. Breakfast or luncheon, it was tasty and very welcome.

"But while I remember, you must watch what you say," Miss Haddow confided. "Don't mention to anyone—apart from us, of course—anything you do not wished splashed across the scandal sheets that call themselves newspapers." She lowered her voice. "Rumor says there is a reporter from *The Teatime Tattler* here at the inn, so discretion is essential."

Letty looked uneasily about her once more. Everyone here seemed to be at least middling folk or even of gentle stock like her companions. But any of the men present could be the *Tattler*'s employee. And she really didn't want any word of her presence at the inn to reach London.

"Where are we?" she asked helplessly.

"The Queen's Barque Inn," Miss Haddow replied, "in the village of Fenwick on Sea."

"It feels more like Fenwick *under* Sea," Letty remarked, glancing out the window at the still raging storm, and then around the bright, newly painted walls. Despite its air of age, the house smelled new and clean.

"Brewster—the innkeeper—is working on it," Mrs. Pickering said, as though guessing Letty's thoughts. "He has recently inherited the place and has entirely refurbished this wing to begin with. He means to attract quality guests for purposes of sea bathing. They have a very pretty beach here, though I don't suppose you saw..."

"No, we came ashore further up the coast," Letty replied quickly, shuddering in spite of herself. She frowned. "But where is everyone else? I don't see the sailors who were with me."

"I expect Brewster put them in one of the outbuildings," Miss Haddow said.

Having consumed the coffee and half of her meal, Letty politely excused herself and went in search of further information. Discovering the girl who had helped her last night, scuttling toward the stairs, she held her back.

"What's your name?" Letty asked her.

"Becky, miss. Becky Brewster. My father's the innkeeper."

"Oh, good! Then you'll be able to tell me—are these *all* the people staying here? Do you have others sheltered elsewhere?"

"We got folk all over the building, miss, even in parts we thought weren't habitable! You looking for anyone in particular?"

Letty was at a loss as to how to describe him. He was more an impression in the darkness. Strength and determination and curiously cold, hard eyes. And yet kindness. Without him, she knew she would be dead.

"A youngish gentleman, rescued from the sea with me," she said lamely. "His name is Simon."

"Don't think there's any such here, miss, unless he's with the sailors next to the storeroom?"

"Where is that?"

Becky nodded toward the front door. "Just across the courtyard. I'll send a message for you, if you like."

Letty drew the shawl up over her head and hurried toward the door. "No need. Thank you, Becky."

"You can't go out there, miss!" Becky protested. "Weather's still foul!"

"It can only be a step," Letty said optimistically.

Becky gave a shrug. "Third door on your left."

The wind tried to whip the door out of her hand, but she managed to pull it shut behind her and hurried through the still driving rain, counting the doors to her left as she went. At the third she knocked long and loudly until a vaguely familiar man pulled the door open and gawped at her.

She slid under his arm, leaving him to close and bolt the door.

Several sailors gazed at her in amazement from heaps of straw. Some of them clutched mugs of tea and, from the scattering of used plates, they had eaten. None of them was Simon.

"Are you all well?" she asked. "Have you seen anything of your fellows in the other boat?"

"We're all fine, ma'am," one of them said impatiently. "Don't know anything about the captain or the others."

Awful to think these other men could be dead. With an effort, she wrenched her mind back to the matter in hand. "And the other passenger? What became of him?"

The sailors all shrugged.

"He went off on his own," one of them volunteered. "Ran ahead of us like a man in a hurry. Ain't seen him since."

Letty frowned. Then he really wasn't at the inn. "Thank you," she said. "And for everything... before. I'm glad you men survived at least. What will you do now?"

"Nothing we can do till the storm dies down. Then find another ship."

Letty shuddered at the very thought of being aboard another ship ever. "I salute your courage," she murmured and departed, hurtling back to the house, where she dragged off her shawl and shook it.

"Bless you, miss, you've never been out in this?" a man in an apron exclaimed as she leaned on the door and bolted it again.

Letty guessed he was the innkeeper. "Only for a moment," she replied. "I was looking for someone. Where else would survivors, or stranded folk, take refuge?"

Brewster scratched his head. "The vicar might have taken people in. Maybe the manor house. We'll know more when the storm dies down. But if he came to Fenwick, he can't have gone far. The roads are flooded and blocked with landslides."

Letty thanked him and returned to her chamber, which she had not, fortunately, been obliged to share. Someone had built up the fire, so she huddled in front of it, gazing between the flames and her still drying clothes while she tried to make plans.

Ideally, she would have liked to know that Simon was safe and well, and to say goodbye to him, but he seemed to be the sort of man who could take care of himself, and she should not consider him.

She was stuck here until the storm abated. After that, if she could dredge up the courage, she might be able to take a ship here, if the harbor was large enough for vessels sailing to the continent. If not, she could perhaps go to Harwich. If her guardian followed her to Great Yarmouth, where she had boarded her previous vessel, he would surely not look in Harwich... would he?

On reflection, she doubted this village was big enough to hide her, so she would have to go somewhere.

How, with no money? she scoffed at herself.

Perhaps she could borrow from the kind ladies she had eaten with? Her uncle in Brussels could easily pay them back once she had explained matters.

After an hour, she was driven by loneliness to seek out company, and found Mrs. Pickering and her sister in the upstairs parlor. By then, the wind had abated somewhat and the rain had lessened to more of a drizzle. Her optimism restored, Letty asked about the harbor.

"Only a few fishing boats," Mrs. Pickering replied disparagingly.

"Do you suppose one of them could take me down the coast to Harwich?" Letty asked hopefully.

"If you paid them well enough," came the sardonic response. "And if there wasn't a ship just run aground there, blocking the way out."

Letty sighed and mentally struck another idea off her list. Still, if there was no way out of Fenwick on Sea, there was no way her guardian could get in either. While fending off the questions of the curious with vague half-truths, she accompanied the other ladies to the main room for a light tea. And then worried again about paying for it.

She was working up the effrontery to ask Becky if her father would allow her to work off her account when a commotion at the outer door heralded a blast of cold air and voices. A moment later, a very damp and bedraggled figure strode into the room, scanning the gawping occupants in one penetrating sweep of his eyes.

Letty's heart soared. "Why, it's *you*!" She jumped to her feet and hurried toward him, a smile splitting her face. "I thought I would never see you again!"

The man's eyes flew to her, hard as she remembered them and cold enough to freeze her to the spot. "Who the devil are you?"

It felt like a slap in the face, and not just because of the deliberate rudeness. Anger fought its way up, along with a desire to punish. For somehow, she was sure he had recognized her at once.

She laughed, an odd, forced sound that she hoped would fool everyone. "This is no time to joke. You know perfectly well I'm your wife!"

CHAPTER 2

S imon Jarvis recognized her immediately. In fact, one of the
reasons he had followed the voices into the room was to assure
himself she was safe. He hadn't expected her to leap to her feet and
rush to him. He certainly hadn't expected her face to light up in such
dazzling welcome. He couldn't ever recall anyone being so genuinely
pleased to see him, and he was undeniably thrown.

His first instinct had been to ward her off. "Who the devil are
you?"

Only then, for the first time in years, he had felt guilty because of
the open hurt in her eyes. With a flash of those same, pained eyes, she
had swept the feet from under him.

"You know perfectly well I'm your wife!"

Worse, the entire room full of guests and inn staff must have heard.
So much for discreetly blending into the crowd.

He regarded the gleam of triumph in her rather beautiful blue eyes.
He could humiliate her with denial—which would serve her right—and
appear to her a heartless scoundrel. Or, since there was nothing to lose
at this stage, he could play the game and see where it led.

He smiled, seized her around the waist, drawing her against his
damp body, and kissed her full on her soft, shapely lips.

"A bad jest," he admitted as blood and outrage flooded into her face. "Now show me where I can change out of these wet clothes and tell me all about your adventures."

Her rigid body jerked against his arm as he hurried her toward the stairs and for a moment, he thought she would throw caution to the winds and slap him. That she didn't, impressed him.

In fact, her body relaxed and moved of its own accord up the stairs.

"I'm so glad her husband has found her," came a loud stage whisper from the room below. "She was so anxious about him, you know."

Was she, by God? What the devil is she up to? He let his arm fall away with odd reluctance, and followed her along the passage to a door at the back of the house.

With her hand on the latch, she paused, and glanced fleetingly over her shoulder at him. He gazed back. At least she knew enough to be worried. But she straightened her shoulders and opened the door. He followed her inside, closing the door behind him, and leaned one shoulder against it. She walked across to the window, where she turned to face him from what she must have imagined was a safe distance.

She wore a dress that was too large for her. Her hair had been inexpertly pinned and was escaping in several places. She looked like an extraordinarily beautiful street urchin.

"I'm glad you're not dead," she blurted.

Whatever he had expected, it wasn't that. "Why?"

She blinked, almost started toward him, then stopped herself and sat on the window seat. "You saved my life. It would not be fair if you ended drowned on the marsh or buried under a landslide. Where did you go?"

He eased his shoulder off the door and strolled further into the room, unbuttoning his coat. "To the harbor—which is blocked by another wrecked ship—and then to find a way out of the village to Harwich or some other port. There isn't one except across the marshes, which I don't know well enough to risk in such weather. I found an empty cottage to shelter in for the rest of the night, then went to look for a way out of the village to Harwich or some other port. I came here to sit out the storm and find a horse."

"You are in a great hurry. Do you have an important appointment in Ostend?"

"Ostend? Why would I have an appointment in Ostend?"

"Just an assumption since that was where our ship was bound, and you seem so anxious to go."

He frowned. "We were not bound for Ostend. Who told you that?"

"The captain, when he took my money for the passage."

Greedy scoundrel. "Well, I expect you would have ended up there eventually," he said vaguely.

A discreet knock at the door heralded a girl with a pile of clothes. She beamed at Letty, and laid them on the bed. "I daresay they're not what you're used to, sir, but they'll serve while your own dry."

"Thank you," he murmured, watching her leave before he sat on the rickety chair and stretched out one leg. "Well? Are you going to perform the wifely duty of removing my boots?"

"Not unless you can't do it yourself," she retorted, although she softened it almost immediately by adding, "Are you not ill from wearing those wet clothes all night?"

"I didn't wear them all night," he said, pulling off his own boots, then casting his waistcoat on top of his already discarded coat. "I stole a horse blanket. I even had a fire of sorts."

As he tugged at his shirt, she hastily turned her back. He smiled wryly. She really was an innocent and, from the way she talked, she was undoubtedly a gentlewoman. Which threw up a lot more questions.

Stripping off his salt-crusted pantaloons, he said, "You had better tell me what you were doing alone on that ship, and why I am suddenly your husband."

"The answer to both questions is the same," she replied. "I am running away and I don't wish my guardian to find me. He will not enquire for a Mrs. Simon."

With a hiss of laughter, he kicked his drawers in the direction of the pile and reached for the dry clothes on the bed. "So, I am Mr. Simon?"

"I didn't know if it was your surname or Christian name," she said apologetically. "I just happened to be thinking about you at the time."

Her open and apparently genuine care disconcerted him once

more. "Because you were afraid I was dead?"

"Or at least that I would not be able to thank you for saving my life."

"There is no need," he muttered, pulling up a pair of shabby and somewhat baggy breeches. "It was you who saved us both."

She jerked around, frowning with incomprehension. At sight of his semi-naked person, color flooded into her face and the clear question forming on her lips died. Instead, she said, "What happened to you?"

Deliberately, he finished buttoning his breeches before reaching for the dry shirt. He thought of turning his back and letting her see the scars there, too, but he suspected she was disgusted enough. "You don't want to know."

He pulled the shirt over his head, and met her gaze.

She said, "You mean, you don't want to tell me."

It surprised another breath of laughter from him. "Perhaps. Why are you running away from this guardian of yours?"

She sighed. "Because he wants me to marry his son, my cousin George."

"And what is wrong with Cousin George?"

"He has bad breath and stares at me."

"I expect his breath comes from toothache and he stares at your beauty to distract himself from the pain."

"Bah," she said derisively. "And you needn't be so flippant."

"Flippant? I was attempting to show matters from the perspective of my fellow man. In any case, I fail to see why you need to run away like a heroine in a bad melodrama. Just say no and promise you will keep saying it even at the wedding."

"I did. My uncle Kent assured me his clergyman will not care."

Simon's hands stilled on the buttons of his coat and he glanced up at her. "Really? Why is he so determined?"

"He wants to keep control of my fortune. Although it's my belief he has already spent it and is afraid of the fact becoming generally known."

Outside the pages of a romance, Simon had never heard such nonsense. And yet there was still something about that guileless face— perhaps the same thing that had inspired him to fight for both their lives in the sea—that suggested truth. If she was a liar, she was the best he had ever encountered. And God knew he had met many.

"What is there in Ostend?" he asked abruptly.

"My uncle—my other uncle, Robert Lovell. At least, he went to Brussels, partly because his son, my cousin Henry, is with Wellington's troops gathering in the area."

"I see. You would rather marry Henry."

Her mouth fell open. "Of course, I would not! He once pulled the head off my doll. Besides, he is already married to someone not quite suitable, which is the other reason my uncle and aunt went to Brussels. But they were always kind to me and, if I explained what my Uncle Kent—my guardian—is about, they would welcome me."

"And scare off the malodorous George?"

"Exactly." Apparently pleased by his understanding, she smiled upon him, forcing him to look away before he succumbed to his baser impulses. "But instead of being safe with the Lovells in Brussels, I am trapped in Fenwick on Sea where my Uncle Kent could easily catch me as soon as the road is passable. He might have followed me to Great Yarmouth by now. So, I'm trying to be harder to find by pretending I am not Miss Lovell but Mrs. Simon."

"Simon is my Christian name."

"Do you have objections to using it as your—*our* surname?"

"No." He had, after all, used many that were a lot less familiar.

"Good, because I could tell you were not pleased by my ambush downstairs."

"You took me by surprise," he admitted. "And to be frank, I do not wish to be saddled with a wife, real or imagined."

"Then we are in accord, for obviously I am escaping the annoyance of being saddled with an actual husband. We only need to be "married" until we leave the village."

He sat in the chair once more. "You are courting ruin, you know. There seem to be a number of people here of your own world. They could easily know you, or run across you later on."

"That is true," she allowed. "And I have to warn you, one of them might be a journalist from *The Teatime Tattler*, which is a gossip-mongering—"

"I know what it is," he interrupted grimly. Not that such a paper would pay any attention to him, a nobody, but he was more comfortable in the shadows, well away from the curious and the prying. He seemed to have walked into a hotbed of minor annoyances. "I can see why you wished to use a different name and title, but what if your guardian or Malodorous Cousin George simply walk in, as I did, and see you?"

"Well, they can't until the roads are open," she said reasonably. "Though I suppose they could be first and carrying the news with them. Hmm... I suppose we shall just have to hold to the pretense that we are married until they go away."

"Then you'll be ruined in your own world," he said brutally. "How will your Uncle Lovell welcome you then?"

"With open arms when I tell him the truth," she replied, although a little frown of fresh worry was forming between her brows. "Besides, I can say that the marriage lines were lost in the storm or that you later died or abandoned me or something, Though I don't like to lie."

His lips twitched. "Perhaps it would be simpler if I just killed George and his papa?"

Her eyes sparkled for a moment, as if she was genuinely considering it, prompting him to ask in a quite different voice, "Have they hurt you?"

"Oh, not beyond the odd slap behind my aunt's back," she replied distractedly. "But no, I don't *think* they would stand up to you. You are quite frightening when you choose to be, so perhaps you could just intimidate them so that they go away. I should hate you to be hanged for murder."

"I wouldn't be, but never mind. I'm just as glad not to kill them. However, I have to warn you, if you truly don't like lying, you are miring yourself in deeper with every moment."

"I know," she said regretfully. "I'm sorry. I should never have said you were my husband."

"Well, we shall just have to get away from here before your guardian arrives. And if you ever run into anyone from the inn, you can pretend you've never seen them before and know no one called Simon. If you say it with enough belief, they will believe it, too."

"You sound as if you speak from experience."

"I do."

She gave him a long look that warned him she was perceptive and highly intelligent, in spite of her current pickle. A wealthy girl without friends, alone and in someone's power, was no less to be pitied than one of lesser birth. Both had to use what meagre resources they had to survive. And Letty, despite knowing nothing of the world, would have got herself to Brussels—eventually—if it had not been for the storm and Captain Lambert's belief he could sail through it. Simon had to admire her determination.

Clearly no longer afraid of him, she came closer to pick up his discarded clothes. "Shall I give them to Becky to rinse?"

"No." Standing, he took them from her and spread his shirt and waistcoat out on the hearth to dry. Then he took his notecase and purse from his damp coat and transferred them to his borrowed, too-wide one. "They are already ruined."

When he glanced at her again, she met his gaze with a look of open speculation.

"Do you have money?" she asked.

"Now you *do* sound like my wife."

Her eyes widened. "Oh, no! Of course, you *are* married! I am so sorry—"

"I'm not," he interrupted. "I meant like *a* wife. But yes, I have money. How much do you want?"

"Just enough to pay my passage to Ostend. And my account here."

"Naturally, your husband will pay your account here," he mocked. This was where he should promise to escort her to Ostend, on whatever vessel he could find. But the words were too eager to be spoken, alarming him, and he swallowed them back. "We'll sort out your passage too." He turned away, striding to the window which looked out over the stables to the sea, then walked back to the door. "I'm starving. I'll get Brewster to send up some food. Do you want anything?"

He had to go all the way to the kitchen to find any of the staff, which was certainly enlightening. He could hear two maids gossiping before he even reached the door.

"Yes, but Becky, you've been looking after her," one cajoled. "You must surely have some ideas about her. Didn't you think her reunion with her husband odd?"

"It's their business," another girl replied.

"Yes, but—"

"Girls!" bellowed the innkeeper's voice. From the blast of cold air and the banging door, he had just entered from the outside door. "More work, less gossip!"

The innkeeper erupted from the kitchen in front of Simon, and was brought up short.

As Simon made his polite request for sustenance, he reflected ruefully that the rumor mill was already going at full tilt, and that it was out of his hands or Letty's.

⚜

Letty spent the rest of the day in Simon's company. As the wind dropped and the rain finally went off, they donned outer garments and ventured outside. With only faint irony, he offered her his arm and she laid her hand in the crook, although it made her feel odd, claiming an intimacy she had no right to. However, splashing through the puddles in the inn yard reminded her pleasantly of childhood games and she allowed herself to relax. Above them, seagulls squalled and played in the wind.

But beyond the village, the road looked more like a river in both directions, as far as the eye could see.

Letty gazed in dismay. "We won't be going anywhere today."

"Or tomorrow. There was never any chance of that."

"Horseback might be possible, or a carriage, but I suppose we don't even know what's under the water."

"And then there are landslides to clear."

Some element, almost of relief, in his voice, made her glance at him curiously. "I thought you were in a great hurry to leave. Even after almost drowning at sea, you were looking for another way to cross."

He shrugged. "It was my duty to try. It seems I'd rather fail and be married instead."

"Most people would be proud of marriage to me," she said humorously. "I am, you must know, a considerable heiress."

"Not if your wicked guardian has stolen your fortune," he pointed out.

"Then I shall have to marry for love. Or become an old maid, which might be preferable because then I could live alone and consult no one about what I do. Providing I have enough money left to buy a cottage."

She considered the merits of each course until he said abruptly, "How old are you, Letty?"

"Nineteen."

He drew in a deep breath but said nothing, merely turned away from the river of water, and they splashed back to the inn.

They took dinner informally, in company with the other guests, who were comparing stories of how they came to be stranded. Inevitably, their own shipwreck came up. Letty was happy to let Simon describe the terrifying ordeal in vague and humorous terms, intervening only once to insist he had saved her life.

"And which ship was that?" a man half-way down the table asked. "It seems several got into difficulties along this coast."

Letty cast him a covert glance, wondering if he was the reporter from the infamous *Tattler*. It was impossible to tell.

"The *Santa Ana*," Simon replied.

With difficulty, Letty kept her face expressionless as she returned to her food. Their ship had not been called *Santa Ana*, which, surely, any discussion with the sailors next to the storeroom would confirm. But then, refugees had been trailing into the inn in such numbers and mingling groups that there was no reason to assume they had been on the same ship as Simon and herself. And the name might certainly repel her guardian's curiosity at a later date.

"Thank you," she murmured below her breath as they followed some of the others into the parlor. "I would have blurted out the real name and landed myself in the basket."

"And me."

"Why? Who are *you* hiding from?" she asked, distracted.

His lip quirked. "Malodorous George."

CHAPTER 3

Foolishly, it was only when others began to retire to their own chambers for the night that Letty realized the full consequences of her deception. She had to share her bedchamber with Simon.

Nervously, she almost jumped to her feet, afraid to look at him as she bade her companions good night. When he did not at once follow her, she didn't know whether to be relieved or annoyed, for she wanted their sleeping arrangements to be clear.

Hastily, she removed the borrowed gown—a simpler matter than usual since it was so large—and wrapped the generous shawl about her chemise for decency, just in case he came up too quickly.

By then, she had decided on the best solution and hastily removed the top coverlet, the bolster and a couple of pillows from the bed. Using the pillows as a mattress and the cushion from the window seat as her pillow, she then rolled herself into the coverlet on top, and found it surprisingly comfortable.

In this way, he could have no compunction about taking the bed, which he deserved when last night had been a lot less comfortable for him than for her. And at the same time, he would not mistake the boundaries of this marriage pretense. Not that he would, she was sure, but the human male was an odd creature, and there was something... *overwhelming* about Simon...

She could not help wondering about him. He spoke like a gentleman and yet more than once he had referred to *your world*, as if it were not also his. He could have been a cit or a manufacturer, she supposed, or even someone of the lower gentry who did not move in such refined circles. But somehow, he defied all those categories. Which was fine with her. She was happy to accept him as he was, her kind friend who had saved her life.

And yet he claimed *she* had saved them both, she recalled drowsily. She wasn't sure what he meant by that either. She would ask him tomorrow.

Footsteps moved along the passage. Voices murmured goodnight, and her bedchamber door clicked open and shut. Huddled beneath the coverlet, she kept her eyes closed and her body still, though her heart beat a wild tattoo.

"It's me," he murmured.

Still, she kept the pretense of sleep. In a moment, she heard him moving about the chamber, the splash of water in the washing bowl and the creak of the mattress. The lamp by the bed went dark.

She smiled beneath her cover and relaxed slowly into sleep.

Distress filtered through her dreams. Not the terrifying sense of drowning that had troubled her slumber last night, but rather someone else's pain.

She snapped into wakefulness, disoriented, anxious. Of course, she was at the Queen's Barque and sharing a bedchamber with Simon. She could hear him moving in the bed on the other side of the room, his limbs, his head swishing erratically against the bedding, though his voice made no sound.

"Simon?" she whispered. "Are you ill? Are you hurt?"

He did not answer. Nor could she see anything in the darkness, but his head continued to thresh on the pillow. Alarmed she scrambled out of her nest and reached for the flint to light the candle on the hearth.

Armed with the light, she rose and hastened toward him.

Beneath the bedclothes, he rolled, curling into a ball. His face was contorted into a grimace of agony, though his eyes remained shut. Her breath caught. Surely that was a tear squeezing from the corner of his eye.

Involuntarily, she reached out and touched the teardrop with awe and helpless pity.

He jerked, his hand flying out to seize hers. He bore it down on the pillow so hard that she almost dropped the candle in her other hand. His eyes were murderous as he snatched for her throat.

"Simon, it's me," she gasped.

His reaching arm dropped. He flung her hand from him as if it burned. "Go away."

"Of course," she murmured, stupidly hurt. "But tell me first, are you ill? Is there anything I can do?"

"No." He swallowed as though searching for civility. "I must have been dreaming."

"Were you drowning?" she asked sympathetically.

A harsh sound that wasn't quite laughter broke from him. "Not I. Go back to sleep." He turned his head away from her, holding himself so rigid she was afraid he would shatter.

"Can't I help?" she asked.

He squeezed his eyes shut.

She could only pad forlornly back to her own makeshift couch, where she lay listening to his breathing which sounded quite peaceful and even, as though he had gone straight back to sleep.

Only, she was sure he hadn't.

A few minutes later, he proved her right by slipping from the bed. She heard the creak of the mattress, a rustle of cloth and the soft thud of feet on the floor. A black shadow moved through the darkness toward the door.

Instinctively, she leapt after him, bumping into the chest of drawers in her hurry. "Wait! Where are you going?" She tripped over something, possibly her own too-long chemise, and seized hold of him at the same moment as his arm swept around her waist to steady her.

There seemed to be a bundle of clothing between them, held in his free hand.

"It seems I am not cut out for marriage," he said sardonically. "I would rather sleep alone."

"Where?" she demanded.

He shrugged. "In the parlor, or the tap room, I don't much care."

"But they will say we have had a quarrel and gossip. Think of the *Tattler*..."

"I would really rather not."

"Actually, I don't care about that at the moment either," she admitted, "I am trying to persuade you to stay."

"Why?"

"Why?" Actually, she didn't know. "Because there is no need... it's comfortab— You don't need to run away from me. I am your friend."

It was too dark to see his expression but she was sure she had taken him by surprise.

"Friend," he repeated with derision. "And what do you think a friend should do in this situation? Whatever you imagine this situation to be."

The grip of his arm had altered subtly. She was only too aware of its heat and strength, the intimate touch of his fingers at her waist. "Give you comfort," she blurted, because she knew that was what he needed even if he would neither admit or accept it.

A breath that might have been laughter stirred her hair. "Oh, I hoped you would say that. And what would you do to comfort me?"

"I don't know," she admitted.

"Well, I can help there."

The clothes between them slipped to the floor as he changed position. She gasped as his fingers slipped up her throat, sending wild, delicious shivers the length of her spine. Before she could grasp what any of it meant, he took hold of her chin and his mouth found hers.

Too shocked to move, she let it happen. And by the time she realized the danger, her lips were parted and trembling under his, and her whole body thrilled to the novelty. The enveloping darkness felt curiously hot.

"What a sweet distraction," he whispered against her mouth as he swept her closer. He seemed to be wearing only his shirt, flapping loosely over unbuttoned breeches, and the intimacy overwhelmed her. She flung up one hand to clutch the shirt at his back, to steady herself as much as to pull him away, but somehow her hand tangled in the linen and she touched hot, velvet skin.

Distraction indeed. Her hand flattened over smoothness and ridges and undulating muscle, and the world tilted as he lifted her in his arms and strode to the bed.

As he laid her down with dizzying speed, his mouth left hers at last. An inarticulate sound of protest escaped her. The exciting heat of his body had gone, though one of his hands gripped her shoulder, then stroked gently across her collar bone to her throat.

His breath tickled her ear, sparking a slew of fresh sensation. "You are a sweet girl and a heady distraction. But perhaps I am not yet quite lost. You sleep in the bed."

His hand, his presence, slipped away. Covers were drawn over her dazed body, but she did not feel the touch of his hands. It seemed he could see in the dark for he moved confidently away from the bed and an instant later, she heard the sounds of him wrapping himself into the nest she had made for herself.

Dazed, she stared upward, wondering what on earth had just happened. Her heart gradually slowed its hammering, though she seemed to still feel the thrilling pressure of his lips on hers.

Innocent as she knew herself to be in matters of intimacy between men and women, she understood she had been in danger, that she had narrowly escaped it only because he had chosen to let her. But it hadn't felt like danger. And lying there alone in the darkness, she was conscious chiefly of disappointment.

She turned over, pressing her face into the pillow, and realized it smelled of him. A smile flickered across the lips he had kissed. She liked that smell, manly and salty and clean... She liked his presence only yards away, and the memory of his closeness, even if, together, they were too much to allow sleep.

That was her last thought before she drifted into slumber.

When she woke, the pillows and coverlet were back on the bed and there was no sign of Simon. Hastily, she rose, washed, and dressed in her own clothes and opened the shutters to see what the weather was doing. It looked to be a pleasant spring day, until she lowered her eyes from the sky to the ground. The inn yard was still saturated, the road in the distance still like a river.

The briefest of knocks on the bedchamber door caused her to turn just as Simon strolled in. He, too, was dressed in his own clothes, although they appeared somewhat water-stained and misshapen. Somehow, it detracted nothing from his presence.

"Breakfast is about to be served," he said cheerfully. "Shall we go down?"

"Oh, yes, I am starving."

"There isn't much sign of the water receding," he said regretfully. "Though I believe they're trying to shift the ship blocking the harbor. I've had a word with her captain about passage to the continent, but, according to that fellow Danville who's been hanging around, it isn't exactly a respectable vessel. If you care for such."

"Was our ship respectable?" she asked bluntly, for in retrospect the captain had been too quick to take her money and according to Simon had no intention of sailing directly to Ostend.

"In its way."

It was on the tip of her tongue to ask him where exactly their ship had been bound, and why he was going to Europe, but by then they were on the stairs and could easily be overheard, so she wasn't surprised when he changed the subject to impersonal matters.

After breakfast, since the sun was shining, she accompanied Simon on a walk, splashing through the village streets to the harbor to watch them try to right the grounded ship. By tacit consent, neither mentioned their encounter in the dark, or whatever nightmare had begun it. Not that Letty had given up. She was merely biding her time. For the moment, it was easier not to dwell on the kiss.

Returning to the inn, they found Mrs. Brewster in barbed conversation with another lady, who curtseyed when she caught sight of them.

"Mrs. Fullerton," the innkeeper's wife introduced her friend reluctantly. "She's housekeeper up at the manor house. Mr. and Mrs. Simon were shipwrecked and rescued further up the coast. They just made it here before the landslip."

"What good fortune after bad," Mrs. Fullerton declared, her eyes avid.

"Does your presence mean the road is passable once more?" Letty asked eagerly.

"Oh, no, we are some distance from the road. The path to the village is monstrously muddy, but we made it on foot."

"We?" Simon pounced. "Then your master, or some of the servants accompanied you?"

"Alas, no, sir, the master is not currently in residence."

"Nor likely to be," Mrs. Brewster muttered.

Mrs. Fullerton ignored her. "Friends of the family sought shelter with us when the storm was brewing. They felt the need of exercise, and to see if they had friends among those staying at the Barque. And, of course, I had heard that Mrs. Brewster was struggling with such a full house."

"Not in the slightest," Mrs. Brewster said sharply. "But I'm not sure I can supply you with food for your guests, Mrs. Fullerton, since I shall need all our stores for my own."

Simon, with a speaking twitch of his eyebrows in Letty's direction, strolled off to the taproom, leaving Letty to extricate herself from the civil quarrel, which she did by retreating to her chamber to remove her bonnet and cloak.

She took a little time to brush and repin her hair, an art at which she was improving. Then, aiming to discover if any of her fellow guests had a novel they might lend her, she went in search of company.

And there, in the first floor parlor, she almost walked into her guardian.

Simon sauntered into the taproom in search of information and a way out of Fenwick —preferably a separate way from Letty since her proximity was disturbing his peace, his privacy, and his resolution.

In the tap room, Brewster was serving ale and brandy to a couple of stranded guests, as well as to two gentlemen he didn't recognize.

"Here's one of the shipwrecked gents," Brewster said to the newcomers, and to Simon, "What can I get for you, sir?"

Simon asked for ale and bowed amiably to the newcomers. One was a young man, not above five-and-twenty, with a petulant expression and a red-striped waistcoat that rather dazzled the eyes. The other was, perhaps, on the wrong side of forty, soberly yet impeccably dressed.

"How do you do?" the older man said languidly to Simon, who immediately picked up a lingering French accent in his speech. "Allow me to introduce myself. I am the Comte de Gascard."

There were many such aristocratic refugees from France in England. They or their parents had come to escape the Terror of the revolution and were at least as much invested in the defeat of Bonaparte as everyone else in Britain. Simon had even found some of them useful in the past. Yet the presence of this man at the coast, at this moment, when Bonaparte had escaped and was already in Paris preparing to meet the alliance gathering to dethrone him —again... It made Simon's neck prickle.

"Simon," he murmured, offering his hand. One could learn a lot about a man by his hand. In this case, Gascard's was neither clammy nor of the "wet fish" variety. But there was no warmth in the grip and his hand slid free after the barest minimum for civility, to indicate the younger man beside him.

"My friend, Kent," he murmured.

Kent? Could this be Letty's cousin? Casually, Simon offered his hand once more. Kent was probably no younger than he, but he had a spoiled look about his sullen mouth, a certain petulance about the eyes that spoke more of thwarted adolescent. Even his handshake was given somewhat grudgingly, while his contemptuous gaze swept up and down Simon's water-damaged clothes.

"How do you do?" Simon said amiably. "What brings you to this part of the country?"

"Visiting friends," Kent said. "Torrential rain drove us onto the back roads, which turned out to be a mistake, and we had to seek shelter at the manor house. Now, we're trying to make sure my cousin is safe. She may have become separated from her friends in the storm."

"That must be worrying for you," Simon said sympathetically. He glanced between the two men. "But at least you have an ally to aid you in your search."

Kent curled his lip. "Gascard is in search of his own friend."

"You *also* became separated by the storm, *monsieur?*" Simon marveled.

"Not so much separated as kept apart," Gascard explained. "We were to have met at Great Yarmouth. A young man on his own. Perhaps you came across him there? His name is Jarvis."

The prickles at Simon's nape were almost a pain. Only years of dealing with such surprises kept his expression even, but that the Frenchman named him was disconcerting in the extreme. Was his purpose betrayed? Was Gascard an enemy or an ally? Since he wanted neither at this moment, he said politely, "I don't recall the name, but then I did not linger there. You should ask Brewster."

He drank his ale.

Kent straightened and said abruptly, "This is a waste of time. I'm going to find my father."

"Yet another separation," Simon observed.

"Only by a somewhat creaky staircase," Kent said distastefully, "You," he added, pointing at Brewster. "Show me to the upstairs parlor."

Brewster gestured to a maid who was sweeping up very slowly at the back of the room.

"I'll take you," Simon offered, setting down his ale. He thought the maid looked disappointed. "I'm going up in any case." In fact, he could not get there fast enough. If Letty had gone to their chamber and run into her uncle...

Gascard, fortunately, remained in the taproom. Simon was quite prepared to fend off both Kents with physical violence if necessary, but a third man who may or may not have been his enemy was a complication too many.

CHAPTER 4

Harland Kent, Letty's guardian and her aunt's husband, stood just inside the doorway, listening politely to Mrs. Pickering and her sister chattering away about their fellow-guests. But Letty barely heard the words. At the first terrible sight of him, she whisked herself back out of the room, her heart hammering.

He didn't see me. His back was mostly to me. Surely, he could not have seen...

Through her shock, she heard footsteps climbing the stairs, and the welcome sound of Simon's voice. Sheer instinct drove her toward him, as though to her only safe harbor. But although he was talking amiably to the man behind him, his expression was both appalled and warning.

"Kent, do mind your feet on these treads," he said. "I'm sure the wood is rotten..."

Kent! She spun around in immediate reaction, realizing George must be the man behind him. With her back to him, she would have fled along the passage to her own chamber but, without warning, her uncle Harland walked out of the parlor and stopped dead.

A smile of utter relief and unseemly triumph flashed across his face.

"Letty," he uttered fondly. "Thank God."

Letty threw her head back, glaring at him. "Uncle," she said coldly.

Harland closed the door behind him. The smile had quite vanished. "If you have things, fetch them," he commanded. "You will come to the manor house with us."

"I will not," she uttered. She dreaded the inevitable public scene, but not as much as the alternative. Half-turning to keep her back to the wall and have both Kents in her sight, she suddenly found Simon beside her.

"I see I don't have to present you to my wife," he drawled. "Letty, is this your uncle?"

"Wife?" George uttered in horror.

"Don't be stupid, George," his father snapped. "She has clearly duped this man. Of course, they are not married. How could they be? Sir, you have my apologies if my minx of a niece has misled you. She is underage and cannot be married."

Letty cast Simon an anxious glance, but he only smiled, apparently unconcerned. "Of course, she is married." He took her hand, proving the intimacy and, with a rush of understanding, Letty laughed.

"Of course, I am. The whole inn knows it, too, including the reporter from *The Teatime Tattler*. You won't cause a scene, will you, Uncle?"

Harland's eyes narrowed. His lips thinned.

"Disgusting little harlot!" George exclaimed, just before Simon hit him squarely in the mouth.

Letty gasped with more wonder than outrage, as George staggered back against the wall.

"You may write to her with your congratulations," Simon said contemptuously, retaking Letty's hand.

Harland's eyes spat with fury. "I have the law behind me, sir! And I will use the full force of it against you!"

"If you wish to drag your family's name through the mud, you must of course do so," Simon said politely. "Certainly, it is the only way Letty will ever return to you. Good day."

And with her arm through Simon's, they strolled away as though from a mere morning call.

It was only then, as she realized neither her guardian nor George were following, that she began to shake.

"Oh, Simon, that was so brave of you," she whispered, as he opened their bedchamber door.

"No, but it seemed the only way to deal with things. No wonder you ran away from them. And you're right. Your cousin does smell."

A choke of laughter escaped her. "Oh dear, do you think everyone heard?"

"Probably not. And your family would be stupid to spread it around. Still, it would be as well to be gone before they involve the law."

"I suppose you can't punch the law in the nose," she said regretfully. She smiled up at him somewhat tremulously. "No one has ever stood up for me like that before. Not even Uncle Robert."

For an instant, he seemed disconcerted. Then he released her. "I'll always stand up for you," he muttered.

"Like a knight in shining armor," she said lightly.

His smile was sardonic. "Very tarnished armor. I'm no knight, Letty. If you're to have any chance, these fools need to be silenced and you need to be with your other uncle. And I should probably die on the voyage."

"Providing you don't *really* die, I shall be a very romantic and tragic widow."

"I'm only sorry I won't be around to see."

She laughed. "I shall tell you all about it!"

⚜

Simon took no chances. When he left her to make sure the Kents and Gascard had vacated the inn, he bade her lock the chamber door behind him. For it was quite possible the Kents had waited to see which room was theirs.

However, it seemed the visitors from the manor had all departed, and, since no one looked at him as though accusing him of abduction or fortune-hunting, he could only assume the Kents had remained silent and no one had overheard the little contretemps outside the parlor.

He half-expected the incident to have frightened Letty into

hysterics and depression, but he should have known better. Although it had undoubtedly upset her, her spirits seemed more buoyed up by victory. If anything, she rejoiced in his physical violence against her cousin, which led him to speculate somewhat grimly on the abuse she had borne under her guardian's supposed care. However, she did not volunteer the information, and he did not ask. He merely vowed that she was never going back to them while he was alive.

She even laughed with unmaidenly glee over the implication that their marriage was consummated. The joy, of course, was in fooling her uncle. If only she knew how close he had come last night to sacrificing her to his own distraction, comfort, and sheer, blind lust.

"Which is why I have to die en route to Europe," he said austerely.

"So long as word does not get back to your family and upset them."

He shrugged. "I don't have a family."

All the same, her words got him thinking. Apparent death could be as good a way out for him as actual death. Less honor, perhaps, but who was he to complain of that at this stage of his life?

Far from being disastrous, the brief squabble with her family seemed to bring Letty and Simon closer together. Dangerously, he did not even seem to mind. He was almost resigned to sleeping in the same chamber as her, even with the risk of dreaming...

It was not difficult to persuade Letty to take the bed tonight. It seemed she trusted him now, and so he turned his back and tried not to think what she looked like as she undressed.

"Tell me," he said from the window, "are you acquainted with a French *émigré* called the Comte de Gascard?"

Her feet pattered across the floor and water splashed in the washing bowl. "I don't believe so," she replied at last. "I don't recognize the name. Why?"

"He was in the taproom, appeared to be a friend of Malodorous George."

"Perhaps he is not the sort of friend my aunt would allow me to meet."

"Did you go out in society?" he asked curiously. "Or did they keep you close in the house?"

"Oh, no, I have had two London seasons. I was even the rage in some circles. But somehow none of my most promising suitors came up to scratch. My uncle said they were fortune hunters, but I don't see how you can say that of Lord Kittering, for everyone knows he's as rich as Croesus and will inherit more besides."

"Then your uncle dismissed them all? In favor of George?"

"I suspect so. But if there was gossip on that score, it never came to my ears. It wouldn't, of course," she reflected. Her voice became muffled as she dried her face. "Perhaps you heard something?"

"My dear girl, I hardly move in your circles."

"Why not?" she asked clearly. She must have emerged from the towel. Her feet padded back toward the bed and he imagined her slim, shapely body swaying beneath her chemise.

He swallowed. "Bad luck, bad birth, bad life."

"How can you say that?" The bed creaked as she climbed on and lay down. "You speak like an educated gentleman."

"Anyone can learn to speak in any way they choose."

"Is that what you did?"

He turned to face her. "Yes."

She lay on her side with her cheek propped up on her hand, regarding him. With her hair loose about her shoulders, she had never been more beautiful, more desirable. "I don't believe you."

"My dear, I was born in the gutter," he said harshly. "I grew up stealing coins and baubles and lace handkerchiefs from people just like you."

If he had meant to appall her, he should have been disappointed, for she only smiled. "I don't believe you. At any rate, you don't do such things anymore."

"No, that is true," he said bitterly. Striding toward the washing bowl, he dunked his face in it and scrubbed himself dry. "Turn off the lamp."

He undressed partially, in the dark, and lay down with his clothes right beside him and his dagger under the pillow.

Years of difficult and dangerous situations had taught him to sleep lightly and react quickly to any disturbance. Which was how he had come to seize Letty so roughly last night. Of course, she should never have got so close to him before he woke, but it had been an exhausting couple of days.

The second night in her company was different. He was better rested, ridiculously comfortable about her presence, and alert. He woke to faint, but continuous sound. It came from the door. Someone was trying to turn the key from the other side.

Grasping the dagger from under the cushion, he rose from his bed of flattened and scrunched pillows, still in his shirt and pantaloons, and crept silently across the room to get between the bed and the door. He already knew which boards creaked, where every obstacle stood.

The key clicked softly and an instant later, with his eyes accustomed to the dark, he made out the slow, wary opening of the door. A pale light glimmered from a shaded lamp, carried by a man. A man with a long dagger in his other hand. Grimly, Simon tightened his grip on his own weapon.

From the widening crack of the opening door, the intruder must have first seen Simon's makeshift bed, rumpled, with the pillows looking like a curled-up body.

In the bed, Letty breathed with the evenness of sleep. Simon wondered if he could end the matter without waking her. She need never know anything about it. Except, of course, he was curious and needed to know.

With no servants to consider, the intruder must surely assume the makeshift bed was occupied by the male of the couple. Simon's fear was that he would turn toward the four-poster with the intention of stealing Letty away. Mind you, Simon doubted she would go quietly. She would bring the whole house down on them. All the same, Simon had no intention of allowing their intruder to get anywhere near her.

And apparently the intruder had the same thought, for after listening intently and no doubt hearing Letty's comfortable breathing, he moved straight toward Simon's couch without even glancing in the other direction. It soon became clear why.

The intruder dropped to a crouch beside the pillows and raised his dagger, stabbing repeatedly. His other hand jerked with the motion, flickering light over his face. And it was neither of the Kents.

Which probably meant Letty was in no immediate danger.

Interesting.

Simon moved forward, uncaring now about silence, for the intruder had finally realized his dagger met no resistance. Feathers floated in the air from his murdered pillows.

Swinging around, the man raised the lamp, just as Simon kicked his other hand and the feathered dagger flew through the air to land with a clatter on the floor.

***

Letty woke with a start to the sounds of scuffling within the chamber. She sat bolt upright and, by the pale glow of a lamp on the floor, beheld Simon struggling with a complete stranger. She had the curious impression he was trying not to wake her, as though that were just as important as dealing with a violent intruder.

She leapt out of bed, instinctively charging to Simon's aid. She even swiped up the washing jug as a weapon. Only then, she noticed Simon didn't seem to be in much need of assistance. Although the other man swung vicious punches, Simon swayed to avoid them or blocked them on his arms. And then, as though he now had the measure of his opponent, he fought back with lightning speed. Two swift punches to the jaw upset the intruder's balance before Simon kicked his legs from under him. He was on top of the man the instant he hit the floor, pressing a wicked-looking dagger to his throat.

Letty's mouth went dry. Perhaps it was a trick of the lamplight flaring over his face, but Simon looked suddenly like a stranger. Cold, merciless, cruel...

"Well?" he asked his victim casually. "Did Kent send you?"

The man glared. "Of course not! Do you imagine I am for hire? I am the Comte de Gascard!"

Gascard? That was the name Simon had asked her about last night. George's friend. Did Simon imagine her uncle and cousin would send a man to kill him? Just to free Letty for marriage once more? That was ridiculous.

"You just tried to murder me in my sleep," Simon said dryly. "That doesn't say much for Gascard's honor."

"You mistake. It speaks of your miserable crimes. You are not worthy of an honorable death!"

Simon must have known she was there, rooted to the spot, the jug still poised in her hands, but his gaze never left his captive. "And why is that?"

"Don't pretend ignorance. I am aware of what you do, of where you are bound and why."

The point of Simon's dagger nicked the Frenchman's throat. "And how exactly have you learned this?"

Gascard's lips stretched into a grimace. "You are known in France. I have relations in France."

"And they have given you a way back," Simon said thoughtfully. "Kill me and you can go home at last. I hope Bonaparte was going to return your ancestral acres."

"I'm sure he will," Gascard murmured.

A faint movement of his left hand caught Letty's attention. While he held Simon's gaze with defiance, his fingers curled around the hilt of another dagger on the floor.

"Simon!" With the warning cry, she leapt forward at last and dropped the jug on Gascard's head.

It didn't even shatter. But Gascard's eyes rolled up in his head and his fingers loosened on the dagger. Simon reached out and removed the blade before, slowly, raising his gaze to Letty.

"Thank you," he said politely. "I had the matter in hand."

"I know. He had just given you the excuse you needed to kill him." She understood that now. She thought she understood a great deal more.

His eyes were steady. "I don't need an excuse. I'll kill him now without a second a thought."

"No, you won't," she said with certainty. "Once, perhaps."

Those eyes, so cold and hard and alien bored into hers, shocking, frightening. Her one hope lay in the fact that he was *trying* to frighten, to stop her asking questions he didn't want to answer.

"I'm an assassin," he said deliberately. "I don't fight duels with my victims."

"But you didn't kill him when he was defenseless."

"I haven't killed him *yet*," he corrected. "I needed information." A hint of almost helpless fascination softened the ice of his eyes. "Am I to understand you... er... wielded your jug to save him from me?"

"I don't know." She dropped to her knees beside him. "I think... I think I was trying to save you."

"He would never have raised the dagger."

"I know," she whispered. "And you would dream more."

His head snapped round. For an instant, anguish stood out in his eyes before he veiled them. "You are mistaken," he said casually. "If I dream, it is of my own dangers."

She let that go, for now. "Who did he think he was protecting by killing you?" But she already knew, and it was confirmed by the flickering smile on his lips. "Bonaparte himself? Dear God, is that even *possible?*"

He shrugged. "Probably not. But it seemed worth the risk to prevent Europe erupting in war once more."

"How would you even get near him?" she wondered, then shook her head impatiently. "It doesn't matter. War is surely a terrible thing, but who decides preventing it is worth *your* life, your soul?"

He tried to laugh. "My *soul?* Oh, that died a long time ago. No one considers it, least of all me."

"I do." She caught his hand, now free of daggers. "Simon, who wants you to do this? Surely no one in government would be so dishonorable as to order such a thing?"

His smile was spontaneous this time, softening his eyes, and he actually lifted their joined hands to his lips and kissed her fingers. "You are very naive and very sweet. People like me do the dishonorable things so government hands appear clean."

"They order you to do these things because you were born poor?"

"To be fair, I was caught stealing. I was given a choice of taking my chances with the law, or accepting an informal position—a smattering of education along with tasks for which I am eminently suitable." He drew his hand free, adding with harsh deliberation, "I am an assassin, just as he implied. You need not pity me."

"How old were you?" she asked intensely. "When they offered you this choice."

He shrugged. "Twelve? Thirteen? I don't recall and it doesn't matter."

"But it does!" she exclaimed. "You were a child!"

"I was a child already going to perdition," he retorted. "They gave me purpose."

She searched his eyes, which slid away from her gaze. "Once, perhaps," she guessed. "But it is destroying you."

"Don't be dramatic." He rose quickly, and pushed his feet into his boots before striding toward Gascard once more. "Be so good as to open the door. Unless you want to spend the rest of the night in his company."

"Where are you taking him?" she demanded, hastily throwing her gown over her head.

Simon hefted the unconscious man over his shoulder and straightened. "Doesn't it seem to you that he smells of horse?"

Letty twitched her nostrils. "Perhaps."

"Then his horse must be somewhere. Close the door behind me."

Letty had other ideas. Cramming her feet into her own boots, she grabbed her cloak and his coat, snatched up the lamp and followed him.

"Afraid I'll kill him?" Simon murmured as she softly closed the inn's front door behind them.

"No. I'm sharing the adventure," she replied with dignity.

He stood very still, listening, and then set off toward the inn gate. Trotting after him, she thought she heard what he had, the faint shifting of a horse's hooves. He turned right at the gate, moving toward the row of cottages.

He put his finger to his lips. She nodded, but touched his hand in warning, then darted forward to spy out the land. There, in the shadows at the side of the church stood a man holding the reins of two horses. Cousin George.

His stance spoke of impatience, but he clearly hadn't heard her approach. She hurried backward, almost bumping into Simon and his burden, who must have been growing heavier by the instant.

"It's George," she breathed. "Two horses. I don't think he's armed."

Gascard let out a groan, but, though it alarmed Letty, Simon seemed to have given up on surprise. He merely strode around to the side of the church and up to the horses.

George jerked round to face him, and Letty raised the lamp, blinding him in the sudden light. He threw an arm up over his eyes, while Simon dumped his burden unceremoniously, face down, across one saddle.

"What the—" George sputtered. "What have you done, you damned fiend?"

"Saved you making a fool of yourself," Letty snapped. "Your so-called friend is a Bonapartist spy."

George laughed angrily. "Idiot girl! There's no such thing. Besides, he's a gentleman, even if he's French!"

"Gentlemen don't break into people's bedchambers to murder them," Simon said, turning his attention to George. "Nor do they call my wife an idiot."

George backed away from him. "You're both idiots," he said wildly. "And we know damned well you're not married! You've had no time."

"Actually, we were married on board the ship," Letty said with sudden inspiration. "By the captain. Before he died in the storm. You shouldn't come here again or we'll expose you as this traitor's accomplice."

George laughed with more contempt than humor. He even made a grab for Letty before Simon seized his collar and yanked him away, and twisted one arm behind his back. With that, Simon searched his pockets, throwing a purse and some keys into the mud, followed by a handkerchief and a folded document which he handed to Letty.

Intrigued, she opened it up and held it under the lamp light. She laughed. "It's a special license to marry. You are too late, George. I'm already married to Simon."

"Goodbye, Cousin," Simon said, with a mocking bow, and offered his arm to Letty. Together they walked away and back to the inn.

CHAPTER 5

It was a long time since Simon had been afraid of anything. Even his latest task, to assassinate Bonaparte, had held no fear for him. He had fully expected to die in the attempt, which would have been a blessed relief in many ways. To die knowing he had saved so many. A recompense, perhaps, for the lives he had taken.

But Letty... Letty brought a new fear he had never contemplated. A fear of her closeness, of her understanding. Of her contempt.

Yet she clung blithely to his arm, even after they were beyond her cousin's vision. There was no disgust, no fear in her eyes as she smiled conspiratorially up at him. He looked hastily away.

Neither spoke until they were back in the bedchamber. She set down the lamp and lit another candle before throwing off her cloak.

"I thought that was rather clever of me," she said, "to say the ship's captain had married us."

"It's a myth, you know. He couldn't really have married us, even if we had asked him."

"Really? Oh well, I daresay George and my uncle don't know that. I'm sure they will give up now in any case. Especially if—" She broke off, biting her lip and gave an embarrassed little shrug.

He sat on the chair to kick off his boots. "*Especially if* what?"

"Well, it just struck me when I saw the special license. I daresay you don't wish to be married but I can't help thinking it would be better than continuing to assassinate people, even men like Bonaparte who clearly deserve it."

His jaw dropped. "Are you suggesting we *actually* marry?"

"Why not?" she asked lightly.

For a moment, he was speechless. "There are so many arguments against it, I don't know where to start. In fact, I can't think of one *for* it." Dear God, was that actually hurt in her face. "Letty, I am not just no one," he got out with suppressed violence. "I am a bad man without morals or convictions or—"

"No, you're not," she interrupted.

He blinked. "What makes you imagine that?"

"Your dreams. You are suffering for what you've done and, in any case, I think you did it for the greater good."

He stared at her. "I didn't. For God's sake, Letty, I'm no hero."

"You saved my life."

"It was as easy as saving my own. It means nothing."

"Nothing?" she asked wistfully.

He dragged his gaze free. "Nothing."

She was silent a moment, then crouched before him and pulled off the boot he was kicking at half-heartedly. "I don't believe you. I think you should retire and look after your estates and your people."

"I don't have estates and people," he said irritably.

"You will if you marry me."

A breath of laughter escaped him before he could stop it. "You are incorrigible. Besides, I thought your uncle had spent your fortune."

"I doubt he could really have spent *all* of it."

He sat back, frowning at her. "And you think, because of the life I have led, I should crown it all by marrying you for your wealth?"

"No. I think you should marry me because you like me. And because I like you."

Deliberately, he reached out and wound his fingers in her hair. "You don't like me. I'm just a species you haven't encountered before."

"If that was self-deprecation," she retorted, "I believe you have met my uncle and cousin?"

His grip tightened involuntarily, tugging her head back. Immediately, he loosened his fingers but didn't release her. "You deserve better. You will find better. But not in me."

She rested her arm on his knees and his blood surged. "We have not known each other very long," she said seriously. "But I feel something when I'm with you, a... an affinity. I think you feel it, too."

"That's physical desire," he said cynically, "and trust me, you can feel it for any low-life in the right circumstances. It doesn't make for happiness let alone—" He broke off with an irritated shrug.

"Love?" she suggested. But perhaps she knew he would never acknowledge the existence of such a fantasy, for she carried on immediately, "Then it was desire that made you kiss me?"

"And made you like it," he retorted.

She smiled and blushed at the same time, which was curiously enchanting. He had the rare feeling of being out of his depth. Well out. She made no effort to free herself. Indeed, one finger traced distracted patterns on his thigh. And she had no idea of the danger she was in. Or perhaps she did.

"I'll make a bargain with you," she offered at last. "If you kiss me again and can then look me in the eye and tell me you do not care for me, I will never mention marriage again."

She had no idea who or what she was dealing with. He smiled cynically, and bent over her, drawing her to him with the hand still tangled in her hair. Her breath caught. Her fingers curled, grasping the fabric of his pantaloons as her lips parted in anticipation.

Dear God, this is insanity. I can cure her, but how do I cure myself?

By reminding himself of what he could not have. He covered her mouth with his and kissed her with tender, sensual grace.

She flung her free arm up around his neck, clinging as her mouth opened wider, responding to every caress of his. Behind the sweet, eager innocence, he tasted passion, strong and intriguing. She was no child, but an intoxicating woman ready to be awakened. By him. He had to swallow a groan, but still he allowed himself precious moments longer, kissing deeper and deeper until the delicious illusion came to him that she was in command here. That he was hers.

It all added to the pain as he forced himself to draw back and stare deep into her eyes. "I want you," he whispered. "But I don't care. I will never care."

It should have devastated her. Her hurt should have stabbed him through the heart. But, incredibly, a smile flickered in her eyes, curved her soft, kiss-swollen lips. "Liar," she whispered back, and kissed him.

He was, it seemed, only human. He hauled her onto his knees and returned the kiss with aching fervor. Her body was trembling and pliant in his arms. He could do with her as he wished. And he wished intensely. With any other woman he would have gladly taken what she offered, but Letty... her very belief in his goodness, faulty as it was, stayed him.

He lifted her in his arms and, just as last night, laid her on the bed. Only then did he drag his mouth and body free and cover her. He sensed her bewilderment as he strode to the damaged pillows and covers. In a cloud of feathers, he wrapped himself in the coverlet and lay down beside her on the bed. Separate and yet close. He didn't know why.

Perhaps because it seemed to comfort them both.

Neither of them spoke, but her breath gradually evened and lengthened, and he let himself bask in her nearness. Worse, unobserved in the darkness, he let himself imagine that different life she so foolishly offered him. No more killing. But not a useless life either. If she had estates, she had people who worked on them, tenants who lived on them, people who needed direct help. A different responsibility...

And her by his side, a laughing, loving, constant companion. A different kind of ache joined the frustrated desire in the pit of his stomach. An ache of longing for that life. For her.

And since she was asleep, he let himself say it, in soft words she'd have had difficulty hearing even awake. "I will make a bargain with you, Letty Lovell. If you still want it when we leave this place, I'll marry you."

But he underestimated her again. "For my fortune?" she countered immediately.

Laughter hissed between his teeth. "For your fortune," he agreed.

There was movement beneath the covers. Her hand crept across the pillow to his, and he let his fingers curl about it.

Gladness seeped into his soul, along with something very like wonder.

Five days later, Letty gazed out of the bedchamber window. The sun was shining. The standing water had drained away from the fields and the roads. The landslips had been cleared. It was time to move on, and Letty didn't want to go.

Her heart was heavy because Simon was in such a hurry to leave. He had gone in search of a carriage to take them to Great Yarmouth. From there he would escort her to her uncle in Brussels. They had talked a good deal over these five days and he had at least admitted she was correct that his "work" was destroying him. He meant to tell his superiors so and had no intention of even trying to carry out the impossible task of assassinating Bonaparte in France. Or at least, so she believed.

But then, she had believed he was falling in love with her and, despite their long, frequently bantering talks and the ever-increasing closeness she sensed, he had given no sign of that love. He had not kissed her since that memorable night they had scared off her cousin and a French spy, and she had proposed marriage.

Over-bold, she told herself ruefully. He was a man who had been around the world, and no doubt known many beautiful, fascinating and sophisticated women. Why should she, naïve and ignorant, appeal to him beyond the moment? It was just that, when she had thought his life threatened, she had acknowledged the terror of loss, recognized the novel feeling rising in her like a tide. Friendship. Care. Tenderness. Love.

They had lived this week very much in each other's company, but as she had fallen deeper in love, was it not more likely that he had grown increasingly bored? Not that he had seemed to be. But he was too anxious to be gone, to be done with all of this and, no doubt, with her.

And Letty didn't want it to end.

The door opened abruptly behind her and she swung around to face Simon.

"Oh! I didn't see you come back."

"I came around the front," he said cheerfully. "A chaise will take us up at two."

She nodded, trying to smile as he came across the room and lounged in the window seat beside her. Unexpectedly, he took her hand, gentle fingertips closing over her wrist. Her gaze flew to his face, searching.

"So, we are leaving this place and it is time to keep my word." The pad of one finger moved back and forth across her veins, sparking fire within her. His lips quirked, and a look that was surely triumph flashed in his eyes. "Do you want to marry me, Letty Lovell?"

She tilted her chin. "That rather depends."

His breath caught. "Yes, you always surprise me. On what does it depend?"

"On whether *you* want to marry me. I said a lot of things that night."

His eyelashes swept down, veiling his eyes. Why had she never noticed before that they were so long and thick? Many a woman might envy them.

"Do you wish to take back your words?" he asked lightly.

"No," she admitted. "But I want to add to them." She took a deep breath, staring at him until he raised his gaze once more. "I care for you. I love you. But I would rather never see you again, I would rather die, than bind myself to someone who was unwilling."

"Unwilling?" He stared back at her. Several expressions chased each other across his face and ended in a flickering smile. "You love me. I only had the nerve to ask because your pulse gallops beneath my fingers." He raised her hand and kissed the inside of her wrist, letting his lips linger.

She couldn't breathe.

"Dear God, Letty, there is no one like you," he said hoarsely. "I am a man of no birth and nefarious occupation and your only condition is that I am willing? Don't you know you are my only comfort? My peace? I don't even dream when I lie beside you. But it seems I would accept all the dreams all the time, just to see you smile when I'm awake." He took her face between his hands and she gasped at the fierce passion in his face. "I adore you, and I am at your feet, whether you want me or not."

Her stumbling words vanished under the sudden onslaught of his mouth, and, with a sob, she threw her arms up around his neck.

"I'm taking that as a yes," he whispered against her lips. "What a pity we can't just use George's special license and be married by the vicar here."

"We could elope to Scotland."

"I thought of that," he admitted. "But it would amount to social ruin for you."

She sighed. "And people would say you hurried me into marriage for my fortune."

"My sweet, they will say that, whatever we do," he said cynically. "I think our best bet is still to take ship from Great Yarmouth and reach your uncle as soon as possible. Let him arrange everything. Of course, he may not like it much and I can't say I would blame him." Suddenly, his eyes were serious again. "I will be a devoted husband, Letty, but it will never be easy for you, being married to me."

"I don't care," she said with perfect truth.

Simon laughed and tugged her to her feet. "Come then, if you're brave enough."

THE END

๑๕๖

I expect, like me, you are wishing Letty and Simon well as they set out on their new life together! Hopefully, they will manage to avoid scandal —which is more than can be said of the ladies caught in my Season of Scandal quartet, who have to fight for the return of their reputations and to bring down the trickster who ruined them. Escape with Hazel and fall in love with the enigmatic Sir Joe in Pursued by the Rake— learn more about this fun series on my website wwww.MaryLan-caster.com

SOCIAL MEDIA FOR MARY LANCASTER

You can learn more about Mary Lancaster at these social medial links:

Website: http://www.MaryLancaster.com
Newsletter sign-up:
https://landing.mailerlite.com/webforms/landing/e2p7c6
Facebook: https://www.facebook.com/mary.lancaster.1656
Facebook Author Page: https://www.facebook.com/MaryLancaster-Novelist/
Twitter: @MaryLancNovels https://twitter.com/MaryLancNovels
Amazon Author Page: https://www.amazon.com/Mary-Lancaster/e/B00DJ5IACI
BookBub: https://www.bookbub.com/authors/mary-lancaster

ABOUT MARY LANCASTER

Mary Lancaster lives in Scotland with her husband, three mostly grown-up kids and a small, crazy dog. Her first literary love was historical fiction, a genre which she relishes mixing up with romance and adventure in her own writing. Several of her novels feature actual historical characters as diverse as Hungarian revolutionaries, medieval English outlaws, and a family of eternally rebellious royal Scots. To say nothing of Vlad the Impaler.

Her most recent books are light fun Regency romances.

Website: http://www.MaryLancaster.com

NEW BRIDE ESCAPES HUSBAND

The Teatime Tattler

Dear Reader,

Among those sheltering from a dreadful storm in the Queen's Barque Inn in Fenwick on Sea, has come a new bride, the lovely Lady S.

She arrived in a hired hack (of all things!) with her little dog... but without her husband! So soon after the nuptials, too.

As all are aware, his lordship, a revered hero of the Peninsular Wars, did not enjoy wedded bliss in his first marriage! This new marriage, to a bride of the merchant class, appears to be another debacle.

I ask you, why would the new countess leave her husband? And why hare off to Fenwick? Did the new couple quarrel? Over what? Does she seek someone else? Alone? Who can it be?

LORD STANTON'S SHOCKING SEASIDE HONEYMOON

CERISE DELAND

Lord Stanton's Shocking Seaside Honeymoon
By Cerise DeLand

She is so wrong for him.

Miss Josephine Meadows is so young. In love with life. His accountant in his work for Whitehall. Her father's heir to his trading company— and his espionage network.

Lord Stanton cannot resist marrying her. But to ensure Wellington defeats Napoleon, they must save one of Josephine's agents.

Far from home, amid a horrific storm, Stanton discovers that his new bride loves him dearly.
Can he truly be so right for her?
And she for him?

CHAPTER 1

Tuesday, March 28, 1815
Stanton House
Grosvenor Square, London

As Russell Arthur Fenwick Downey, the sixth Earl of Stanton, glanced around those seated at his dining room table the night before his second wedding, he understood the myriad permutations of the saying, to marry in haste and repent at leisure.

He inhaled, stealing himself to suffer the rudeness of his mother and younger brother. He could name each anew, dubbing Mama Stuffy and his brother, Clifford, Dandy. Opposite them in every way sat his fiancée, whom for her kindness in spite of them, he would name Merciful. And since he was to be the most fortunate man in the Realm after he wed her tomorrow morning in her father's house, he would call her Beloved—and thankfully, joyfully, at-long-last His.

For after tomorrow at nine o'clock, he would know the rewards of having waited until long after she'd come of age, this sprightly woman of twenty-four who laughed so easily and who had reminded him just yesterday afternoon that she was a perfect match for him.

"A trader's daughter?" Her large grass green eyes had twinkled at him in mirth. "I know maths better than I can recite your ancestry, dear sir. Plus," she said, marveling as she held up her wooden darning egg and worn sock upon it, "I am expert at mending clothes."

He'd assured her that her skills at such were most welcome in his house, where her good cheer and boundless energy for life had mended his heart and his belief in the rightness of the human spirit. God knew, he had proof—too much—of the other.

"Where do you go for your wedding trip?" His mother finished her *blanc mange* and Russ could count the minutes until this blasted meal was done.

Josephine's fork paused at the question.

"We've postponed any trip, Mama."

The Countess of Stanton stared first at her soon to be daughter-in-law, then at him. Did she suppress the haughty smile that tugged at her lips? "Why would you do that?"

His left eye twitched. The old injury caught him in times of stress. This certainly was one as he could take bets at White's that she saw how he adored his future wife but would not bed her until she appeared eager for such a union. But he could not let his mother intimate it, lest he harry her to the street and her carriage, not to return until he righted the problem.

"Napoleon, my lady." Josephine reminded his mother of the scourge of their days and nights. "We are beset with grave matters now that he's returned to France."

"Stanton's challenge I do understand, Miss Meadows." His mother trained her dour brown eyes on his. Like a crown, she wore her pride in his position as adviser to the Secretary at War. Though she suspected, he doubted she knew his full role as advisor to the Army Commissariat for supply of Wellington's Army in the Low Countries. But she was being purposely obtuse on this point of the wedding trip, solely to embarrass his future wife and snidely to ridicule her father. "Surely, Stanton, for your wedding, you might take a few days to become better acquainted?"

Ah, and there is the rub. From my mother, no less, who knows I met my fiancée six years ago, but who wants to drive a wedge between us. He massaged his left temple. "Josephine and I have agreed that we will retire to the country house in Bury St. Edmonds after we have defeated the man."

His brother Clifford snorted. "That may take years."

"I doubt it," Josephine replied with such speed and assurance that both his relatives glared at her. Women, they believed, particularly daughters of merchants, were not worthy to claim such opinions. But because of her commanding position in her father's company, Josephine was. Neither was she cowed by their shock. Instead, she took a sip of her own muscat and smiled at them. "Napoleon has little with which to carry on the fight now. Fewer soldiers who are willing to die for him. Worse, he has little money to fund them."

"You've read, Mama, I'm certain, that Louis and his court have fled Paris. And wise of him, he had presence of mind to take the French treasury with him." The Army Commissariat's courier, who arrived from Ostend yesterday, expected Louis to reach there today or tomorrow, trailing an immense baggage train behind him. Gold bullion, all hoped, would be among the contents.

"I would bet they took the crown jewels, too," Josephine added on a chuckle. "Worth fourteen million francs. Can you imagine?"

His mother tutted. "You have this from your father, Miss Meadows?"

"No, Ma'am. I do not." Josephine's sharp gaze glanced off Russ's.

That fact she'd had from her own courier, one of the last to sail from besieged Calais. She'd shared the news with Russ earlier today when they'd met in her father's offices in Dawson Street. Her father's deteriorating health had turned Josephine into the head of Meadows Trading Company. Her father's suggestion before Christmas that Russ ask for Josephine's hand was occasioned by her father's worries over her future and his deteriorating health. Russ had taken the man's advice not only because Meadows had indicated that his daughter would welcome the union, but also because Russ had fallen in love with her on the first day he'd met her.

"I do hope you are not delaying any travel because you are ill."

"No," was his clipped reply.

His mother's concern was a dry declaration that posed a question beneath. Russ knew what it was because his mother had demanded an answer to this last week. Then, she'd not been so subtle.

"Why did you acquire a special license to marry her?" His mother had asked him after he'd appeared in her drawing room and announced his impending nuptials. "The wedding was set for June."

"Her father fears his imminent demise. He wishes to see his girl married."

"To you? Of course, he would! A marquess for his lowly cit."

Biting his tongue, he readied to take his leave. "Excuse me, Mama. I have urgent business."

She shook with anger. "No other urgent reason for this date?"

He fought to contain his ire. "None."

She'd sniffed. "I don't suppose you'd tell me anyway if she were *enciente.*"

"Good day, Mama." He was fed to the gills with her opposition to his marriage. "Come to meet her next Tuesday evening for dinner. I've invited Clifford up from Brighton. Attend only if you wish to be civil."

Without waiting for her reply, he'd spun for the foyer, her butler, his hat and walking stick.

That she was here tonight and rude was testament to her tenacity to ruin this union.

Yet he would never let that happen.

"Shall we adjourn to the drawing room?" He shot to his feet. The others followed. "We must have an early start tomorrow."

CHAPTER 2

J osephine stood when Stanton returned to the drawing room after showing his mother and brother to the door. In hopes to appear nonchalant, she gave him a cheery smile. But the tensions at dinner aroused such fear in her. "I'm not good at hiding my feelings. I hope I did not offend your mother."

"She was the one who offended you." He took her cold hands in his warm ones, the corners of his appealing mouth turned up in consolation. "I know how intimidating my mother can be. Allow me to apologize for any discomfort."

"Oh, Stanton. She does not want to like me. I am so unacceptable." *I am her nightmare.* "She wished for you a young woman of more stature than I."

His long fingers crushed her fidgeting ones. "She has little acquaintance with marriage for the sake of affection."

So, she would not understand that I marry for the sake of love. "She does not know how to excuse me to her friends."

"Once they see how kind and quick you are, they will love you."

As you do? The question, ever on her mind for more than a year, burned through her. When he'd proposed Christmas day, he'd not declared his affections as more than that. Admiration for her fealty to her father. Respect, perhaps, for her business acumen. But as for desire? She'd seen it in his gaze once, twice, when she'd caught him studying her at dinner or over the company records. What would she do married to a man who thought of her as a friend? What she wanted —no, required—was a love that burned and invigorated, that nurtured and enriched. True, she'd glimpsed that only twice. First, between her parents and lately, between her friend, Margaret Alders and her new husband, Vernan Alders.

"I will work to make it so." She had to voice her greatest worry. "But your mother wonders if I have shamed you."

"You and I know that is not so." He caressed her cheek with the warmth of his palm. She tipped her head into his touch, wanting more than this from him. "In your work, you understand truth from fiction. Let that be your guide here with my mother. She does not realize what a diamond you are, my dear. When she sees how happy you make me, she will drop her opposition."

"I'm glad you are certain," she said with more humor than she felt. Indeed, Josephine doubted that the Countess of Stanton understood happiness. The lady was a creature of her noble lineage and the strictures of the *ton*. Bitter, too, though Josephine had no idea why and considered it prudent not to learn.

She sought to turn the somber tone of this conversation. "But I would like it to happen, you see. Certainly, before our third child is born."

He chuckled and stepped nearer, drawing her for the first time against his tall firm form. She wound her arms around him, happy for the embrace that she'd yearned for these past few months. Tomorrow, she could do this freely. She went a step more and rested her head against his chest. Beneath her cheek she felt the strong vibrations of his heart. Oh, that she might have that beat for her. Tomorrow and every day henceforth.

The very hope had her pulsing with desire. With her eyes closed, she could see him. Would see him until her last breath. His startling height, his impressive breadth, his coal black hair disheveled on his broad brow as he stood invincible in his portrait upon the dining room wall. He, daring, in his dashing blue jacket with yellow facings, the crimson and gold cords of his busby glowing brightly, the hero who took down the French at Benavente, Lieutenant General the Earl of Stanton of the 10th Regiment of Light Hussars. His face in that portrait was unscarred, without the white line from mid-brow to temple of the blow that gave him headaches and required he use a quizzing glass to improve his sight in that left eye.

He backed away from her, but kept her hand. "Come. I've something to show you."

She could have sworn his bright blue eyes danced, declaring enticing things.

Up the grand main staircase he led her, round and round, to the second floor, down the long hall, past one set of double doors to the end. There he paused before another set.

He opened both wide. "Your suite. Or rather, soon to be."

She gazed upon a sitting room, big as her bedroom in St. James's Square. And nearly empty.

"Furnishings are sparce. The two Hepplewhite chairs you may change, of course. The floor needs rugs. Come in here." He led her into the chamber with a door ajar to a smaller room, most likely her boudoir. Here before her stood only a gigantic clothes press and smaller French lingerie chest, both of Rococo design and most likely very old. But there was no bed.

She swung, her mouth open to ask why not.

"I ordered my housekeeper and butler to prepare a list of items the room needed for you. They did, but I must say I failed to choose anything."

"You're busy," she said in quick excuse for him.

"That's not it at all."

"No?" Dare she hope he intended to take her to his bed? Tomorrow night? And all the nights thereafter?

He threw out his arms in frustration. "I did not know what to get for you. What you'd like."

I'd like to sleep with you.

"I want you to have everything you desire."

The lump in her throat grew large.

"I want you to choose. You have excellent taste."

"Do I?" she asked, wistful, charmed and so unaware he had ever noticed any details about her person.

That gave him pause. "I know you do. From the green gowns you favor that turn your eyes to emerald and the pinks that accentuate the blush in your cheeks. You are quite stunning."

No one had ever called her stunning. "Thank you."

He looked at a loss, this man who had commanded hundreds, fought his opponents to the death and now ran the logistics of supplies that would either make or break the Duke of Wellington's forces against the little Frenchman who would not stay in exile.

She got her wits about her. "I didn't expect you to go to such expense for me."

"Money has no place in marriage. Not in anyone's. Not in ours."

"I agree. And for this, I am delighted to do it." She smiled and spun, arms out, in full circle to welcome the joys of her marriage. Then she went with her impulse and took two steps toward him and, on her tip-toes, reached up to kiss his lips. Briefly. Too briefly.

He clutched her upper arms and as she stepped away, cleared his throat. "I want you to be comfortable. And happy, Josephine."

"As I will work to make you happy, Stanton."

"You'll make me delirious if you use my given name."

She tipped her head to and fro. "I must practice."

"Say it now, then."

"Russell."

He cocked his right brow. "Russ."

She let her eyes dance. "Russ."

"I want this for you, my dear. A completely new start. I owe it to you and to myself. Changing whatever relics of the past that now do not apply to our future."

"I wish to be your loving helpmate."

Once more, he reached out to her and this time, stroked the backs of his fingers down her cheek. "As I will be yours. I am determined to be a good and willing partner, Josephine. Tomorrow I repeat words made by man, meant for God and others. To many who say them, hear them, they are useless. A sign, merely, of lawful commingling. A seal of financial union. I swear to you my words bear none of that. None."

"Nor will mine." *Ever since I first set eyes on you, I have wanted you for my own. Sans title, money, land.*

His sky-blue eyes grew stormy with new happiness and old pain. "Hear me, Josephine. Please, as this revelation is new for me. But I will tell you. I do not wish to belabor you with old sorrows but I will have you know this about me. This, which few have ever learned from my lips." He seized a breath. "My first marriage was no union of like minds or pleasures."

He had never spoken of his first wife to her and she doubted to her father, either. While the gossip about the late Countess of Stanton was sparse, the lack of information irritated Josephine, especially now that she had accepted his proposal of marriage. A woman who valued an abundance of facts in her work, she knew the past would be vital to understand... and just as vital to avoid duplicating.

He stared at her. "I married my first wife out of duty. Friendship among our families and land that marched beside each other's led to an expectation that she and I marry to seal the union of affections. From childhood, I never questioned it. Neither did Henrietta."

Torment sluiced over his brows and he dropped her hands as if they burned him. Josephine swayed toward him, the magnet of his touch, the hurt of his rejection had always drawn her toward him no matter where he strode.

He took up a stance near the mantel, an Adam's creation of stark white. His severe black dinner attire created a pillar of harsh contrast to the alabaster. His hand to his lips, the swipe of his fingers across his mouth gave her notice that he meant to continue in this dark vein of remembrance.

"Growing up together we thought we knew each other. Certainly, we valued the same things, didn't we? The same friends. The Berber horses our fathers raised. The hunt. Poetry." His pause sent a chill up her back and the hair on her arms lifted. "She wanted to marry young and quickly. Her father had died and her older brother had married. She wished to set up her own house. I agreed to that, to everything. I was free. A carefree lad. Randy, actually. And I had the money. Why should I not marry and indulge us both, eh?

"But I did not see that my agreements were one-sided. I wanted the city. She wanted the country. I wanted the work of Parliament and my friends who worked at Whitehall. She wanted the solitude of her dogs and her roses. When I heard the call of the cavalry and the need to defend my country, she did not approve of my decision to join the Hussars. She demanded I return home and give her babies, days of idling in gardens and reading and pulling deadheads from rosebuds."

He ran a hand through his hair. The thick mass rumpled wildly around his aquiline features. "She ordered me not to join, not to leave her alone in the country. I refused. For the next few months, she ran hither and yon about the country. Without word of her whereabouts, she kept me guessing. She also kept the *ton* in ripe gossip. She led me a merry chase. When I learned finally that she had returned home to the Hall, I went there and confronted her. She was wild. She bargained with me. She'd stay in one place if I quit the service and came home to her. She required a constant attendance I could not give her. When I refused, she turned... ugly and took an andiron to me. I bear the scar."

Josephine's mouth fell open. She'd never asked how he'd acquired it, assuming it was a battle scar. "Oh, my dear."

He swung toward her, the horrified look upon his face warning her off. "I left her that night and never returned. I went off to Portugal and Spain, and learned first-hand the delicate art of supplying thousands of men and animals on the march in a foreign land. A year later while I was there, she died of catarrh. I had her buried in her family's crypt. Six years ago, when I returned home to England, I had the Hall in Bury St. Edmonds stripped of all she'd put into it. Since then, I've had a few essential rooms redecorated. That house, too, awaits your kind touch."

He'd told her last week that he'd written to tell staff there that they would arrive at a future date for a wedding holiday and that she would attend to the renovations.

He threw her a wan smile. "When I married her, I was twenty years old. She was eighteen. I thought I knew her. She said we were... cut from the same cloth. Ah, but what does one know at eighteen?"

I knew I loved you. That first afternoon, when my father brought me into his offices and introduced his friend, the dashing creature who ensured soldiers had uniforms to clothe them, blankets to warm them, beef to sustain them, shot and rifles and cannon and boots.

"I am sixteen years older now, Josephine, and I do hope much wiser. I see in you, my dear, much that resembles my own temperament. You love people and your work, your father and young brother. You see joy in living and cultivate it. I want to make a good husband to you, Josephine, and I promise to give you the best of me."

No declaration of love, but she would take it. "Thank you, Russ. I do not marry you lightly. I've had suitors."

His face broke into a rueful smile. From the looks of it, he welcomed the change to a lighter topic. "I know you have. Many, I would say."

She took his good humor and wished to build on it. "I refused them all."

"Good prospects they were, my darling."

At his use of that endearment, she noted progress in his regard of her. She tipped her head. "You knew, did you?"

He grinned. "Your father and I are very good friends."

She flowed nearer to him, her hands flat to the silk of his waistcoat. "I was never attracted to any of them."

"I often wondered why. They were young. James Caffrey of Hammond Lane was only twenty-five when he asked for your hand three years ago. And what's-his-name English? Thomas English is rich as Midas. Clothier to His Majesty's Army makes him a good catch."

She toyed with a button on his waistcoat. "Youth and money have their charms but I was not enchanted."

"Your father was astonished you refused."

Years ago, he was. Not lately. "Many times, he asked me why. I'm shocked he told you about their proposals."

Russ reached for her, his large sure hands cupping her cheeks. "Your papa sprinkled details like lures to a treasure. In truth, I heard more from my friends, tidbits of gossip that you would not have any of them. And I rejoiced."

Her heart pounded with his admission. "I wish I'd known."

"Do you?" He hooted, hugged her close and kissed her forehead. "Minx! With every man you refused, I could not keep up with the parade."

"Surely, sir, you can count to five."

He guffawed. "Miss Meadows! Your father counted eight."

"That many? How complimentary!" She wrapped her arms around his waist and drew back to admire the man who would be hers at last. Here in this noble, honorable, hard-working creature was all she had ever desired of love. "I wanted only you."

He blinked, the shock of her declaration making his words sound unrehearsed. "No, surely."

"Most definitely. From the day I strode into Papa's office and he introduced me to you as your personal private accountant."

"Josephine," he pronounced her name as if he were reading a hallowed passage from the Bible. "Sweetheart, you were—"

"Young. But never cloistered. I'd met men, of all ages, for years. In trade, we women are not kept in tidy little confines sipping tea, my darling."

Her statement—perhaps even her own endearment—induced him to crush her close. "You do not marry me because your father wishes it."

"Or because he fears he dies soon. No. I marry you because finally you asked me."

"Josephine—"

"Russell Downey, hear me. I marry you because I want to be your wife."

He gasped and took her lips in a happy declaration of a devotion and yes, a passion that set her on her heels.

He took his lips away all too soon and she nestled into the crook of his shoulder.

He spoke against her ear. "Come. I will accompany you home. I wish to assure your father I am not stealing you away like a highwayman."

She laughed, rejoicing at the results of the evening. "I will always run away with this thief."

"You try a man, my darling. Patience we must have until tomorrow."

She pecked him on the lips. "Tomorrow." She'd almost said, we shall never part. But prudence and his revelations of his first wife cautioned her that binding him to her in any way could resurrect his old torments and destroy all prospects they had for a happy future.

CHAPTER 3

Wednesday, March 28, 1815
No. 16 St. James's Square, London

"That's just so, Sayre." Her father waved away his valet, who put the finishing plump to her father's bed cushions. "I am perfectly situated. You may leave until the ceremony. There you are, Jo, my girl! Come in, come in!"

The overzealous servant contemplated that far longer than most would, then he exited the sitting room and closed the door behind him.

Her father put on a valiant show of strength as he lifted his arm to bid her closer. "What do you think? Am I presentable for this morning?"

"Dashing, I say." Josephine hurried to her father and placed a kiss on his forehead. Sayre had worked his magic, attiring her father in his best linen, a Spitalfields silk maroon waistcoat and grey frock coat, topped with an elaborately tied cravat. What the man could not eliminate were the white lines of pain around Papa's mouth.

"Horse feathers! Not as ravishing as you, my girl."

Her little Blenheim spaniel Rose scampered around her feet,

yipping in agreement. She was excellent at imitating the emotions of Josephine and her father.

"Oh, that dog!" Her father made a shooing motion at the creature he adored as much as she. "I hope you're leaving her here for a few days?"

"I am, sir."

"Don't need her in your bed after today," he said, in half serious tones.

She pressed her lips together in laughter and shook her head.

"You have better things to do. I told Rodgers to leave you be. And I do hope you repeated that he's to handle all business at least until next Tuesday."

"I did." Fergus Rodgers was her assistant in the company, a trusted employee of her father's for over a decade. Now he was her man. "He agreed only in dire straits would he seek me."

"True. I will keep track of *Aries*."

Their very special cargo on that brig headed from Ostend to the port of Deal was one both of them wanted to monitor. Josephine had given in to her father's insistence she relinquish all details of that vessel's arrival for her honeymoon week. Still she was concerned. Their prime Paris agent had sent word via another of their informants last week that she'd sail on their next vessel out of Ostend. The only one due out of that port in the past five days was the *Aries*—and Josephine prayed to God *Madame Argent* made it safely to the ship and to England.

"Ah, ah! Do not scowl at me, girl. Fergus will be on top of this. Now turn around! Around again!" Her father chuckled and began a coughing streak that bent him over in his massive four poster.

"Papa!" She helped to ease him backward to his pillows. "Let me talk. Water? Tea?"

"Whisky," he croaked.

She'd long since given up casting him a rueful eye over this special palliative, but handed over the glass that was on his night stand. He sipped it slowly, sighed and sank back. A phantom of his former burly self, he nonetheless continued to live in his head. A man of quick mathematical calculations and perceptive geographical computations, he had built his business on his acumen learned in Italian ports. Ten years ago, he'd brought his family to London and opened his business near the East India Docks as a profitable merchandise mart trusted by the Government to service its Army on the Continent.

She glanced about the finely appointed room with ornate plastering and woodwork, the artistry of one of the most noted architects in London. The room, the entire house on the south side of prestigious St. James's Square was a testament to her father's financial success and his understanding of human nature.

He scrutinized her with narrowed eyes. "I like your choice for your wedding. More green than blue, it does justice to your auburn hair. And your mother's pearls in your coiffure. That maid of yours can do miracles. She needs a better pay, what do you think? Stand back. Stand back. Twirl once more. I wish to imprint you on my mind. Like your mother. So like her." He swallowed loudly but the moisture on his lower lids told her of his sweet memories.

"The pearls are a precious gift. I thank you, Papa."

"A young lady needs a memento from her family to help her remember who she is, who loved her first."

"I need no reminders of that. I have lived it with you each day of my life and I am grateful. I take that with me to my marriage, Papa."

"I've no doubt. You were always a good girl, Jo. Smart and wiser than your years. You will do well with Stanton."

The grin that welled up inside her felt glorious.

"I see you agree!" He chuckled and began a new coughing spree.

"Oh, I do not want you to exert yourself!" She helped him to sink once more into his cushions.

"Tell me sour tales then! Happiness makes me laugh." He cupped her cheek. "And I am so happy for you. He is what you want, isn't he?"

"He is."

"More than any other you ever met?"

She arched a wicked brow at him. "More, and well you know it, too!"

"Indeed. For years, I've watched you eye the poor fellow like a starving woman over a tasty treat."

"Oh, you make me sound mercenary." She shushed him and took up the chair near his bed. Arranging her skirts, she pinned him with a testy gaze. "You told him how many proposals I'd had."

He barked in laughter but did not, this time, cough afterward. "An astonishing lot!"

"He didn't need to know!"

"Of course, he did. Any man needs to know his competition."

"None were his competition."

"So I began to realize..."

"Then you do understand that this is no missish infatuation I feel for him?"

"If you'd told me at age eighteen that you had to have him for your own, I would have warned you against him."

"I came to understand that," she admitted.

"He was not a proper mate then for any woman. He had... suffered."

"I had heard rumors, but last night he told me more."

"Good. He is not a man to hide things. But he is discreet, else he would not consult on such dire needs as supplies to France."

"That I detected these past six years you've worked with him. You knew more about him personally than I ever could. And I did not want to be wrong in my choice of a husband." She lifted a shoulder. "If indeed an earl so much more worldly than I would look upon me as... acceptable."

"He bears no prejudices against class."

"That makes him unique among his peers and creates problems for him. Who knows if any of them will accept me? And I would rather live without him than ruin his reputation. But I—"

"What?"

"I am selfish, Papa." She gave a sad little laugh. "You might not think it, but I am."

"I've never seen it in you. How can you say that?"

"Because when he proposed on Christmas, I wanted to wed him that day, that hour. I did not want him to leave or change his mind. I wanted him as I always have and could never refuse him."

He grinned. "Well, then! I would say you are well-mated, my dear child. And I am thrilled for you. Happy for myself, too, that I leave you in the best of care."

A knock at his door had them turning.

"Enter!" he called.

Sayre appeared on the threshold to the bedchamber. "Sir, the vicar has arrived."

"Good! Tell Master Theodore we're ready!" Her brother at fourteen was a keen young man even snappier at maths than she had ever been. He merited a special tutor for his brilliance with algebra and three others for art, architecture and history. "He's to join us now too, Sayre."

Hesitating in the doorway, the valet eyed her father like a bird of prey.

Sayre had strict instructions from her father's physicians not to move him from his bed. Papa had argued repeatedly with his valet and with Josephine, but had succumbed to his own weakness to rise.

"Yes, yes, Sayre. I see your look. I will be docile. Bring the vicar up. Stanton and his family, too, when they get here. No ceremony other than the one we're to embrace, eh?" When the man disappeared, he smiled at her. "Are you ready, Jo?"

She stood and brushed her skirts, nervous, joyful. "Oh, yes, I have been for six years."

Stanton House
Grosvenor Square, London

Russ took a last look at himself in his dressing room mirror and assessed the fellow reflected there who would appear to be—as a dandy would say—all the crack. New coat, new waistcoat, new breeches. He snorted. *Daring of you, old man, to fall in love with a young lady who deserves so much better.*

Yet he could not deny how magnetic Josephine Meadows was to his soul. He'd shocked himself when first he admitted to himself he liked her. That had been days after he'd met her six years ago in her father's offices. She was so fresh, so alive that he forced himself to discount his attraction as improper. As years wore on and she continued as his accountant, he wrestled with his admiration for her talents and his delight in her effervescent humor. He told himself he was a satyr who needed a good romp with a woman who knew what she was about in bed—and he'd tried that diversion. To little avail. And here he was marrying her, unable to keep himself from wanting her with him in all ways a man can enjoy a woman.

"You've done me proud, Tipton." He flicked the ends of his cravat and nodded to his valet. "I shall stand up as much younger than my years."

"You *are* young, my lord." His valet—with him seven years now—thought him a self-induced reclusive. The truth was, he'd always enjoyed smart company, but only learned to welcome it socially after working with Josephine. "And you deserve her, if I may be so bold as to say."

"You are a jolly fellow, Tipton. And I can be so delighted with the world today that I can even agree I deserve her." *Long may I live to show her what she's done for my belief in the goodness of humans.*

He tugged on the points of his blue and white striped waistcoat. "My frock coat, Tipton."

A minute later, he took the stairs down but halted on the landing.

Forester, his butler, was just closing the front door upon Simpson Walters. His assistant at Horse Guards, Walters had been with him as sergeant in the Hussars and, four years ago, had mustered out with a leg injury. Upon returning home, he'd found Russ at Whitehall and asked for a position. As luck would have it, Russ needed an additional man and he had hired him instantly.

"Forgive me, my lord." Walters worried his hat in his hands. Rain dripped from his hair, his nose, his clothes. He swiped it away. "News from Gravesend. A word, please?

"It's bad. I see it," Russ said when they were sequestered in his library and he'd handed over a generous pour of brandy for his man. "What's wrong?"

"We've had a messenger up from Gravesend this morn. Winds at Deal are blowing hard. The Frigate *Mercurius* and the fleet of transports with it were put back. The *Rosario*, too, with General Lord Hill on board, remains in port."

All had been bound for Ostend, the best port open for troops and supplies since Napoleon had closed Calais and Dunkirk the other day. "Any arrivals from Ostend?"

"Aye, my lord. Two packets yesterday safely in. But another that was due yesterday is in trouble. A lieutenant of the *Templar* out of Bombay says he saw a vessel blown north west, trying to right itself. Its main mast was gone."

"The name of it?"

"In the storm he couldn't see. No wonder. Our runner in Gravesend says that even the huge *Princess Charlotte of Wales*, the outward-bound Indiaman, lost two anchors and cables last night in the gale. So violent it was, she's put back to Deal as well."

Wellington would not be happy with the delay of his reinforcements for his northern army. At last count, the Duke had thirty thousand men north of Lille, but currently Whitehall had no idea how many the French had in their garrison there. The Russians and Austrians who had sent their forces home after Napoleon had abdicated last April, were on the march back, expected to add another one hundred thousand to the fold. Still, they had to hurry.

From Russ's calculations—and information from Josephine's network of spies, they concluded that Napoleon could raise half a million men within two months and put them in arms. That worried Whitehall and they sought news of the Frenchman's recruiting abilities to man his garrisons, especially in the north of France. They did know the emperor lacked sufficient stores of ammunition, uniforms, artillery and especially cavalry horses. Yet the tiresome Corsican was a wily opponent. With one speech he could rally the French to madness.

"Bad news indeed. And the *Aries*?" That supply transport owned by Meadows Trading Company had sailed last week to Ostend with a cargo of beef, biscuits, gunpowder and tobacco vital to keeping the British Army fed, armed and sane. Returning bound for Deal, *Aries* was ordered to come home brim full of French refugees. "Is she in port?"

"Not yet, my lord. But if she sailed early enough, she might've missed this storm." Walters brushed back his dark wet hair.

"Send our man from Gravesend back to Deal today for news. Hellish weather to keep him out, but can't be helped."

"Yes, sir."

If Fergus Rodgers, Josephine's advisor, had word of this storm and the fate of the *Aries*, he'd run straight to St. James's. Josephine would take it poorly.

He certainly did. This was a bad blow to his hopes for his wedding day. Hers, too.

"Thank you, Walters. Keep me informed."

The man looked skeptical. "My lord, it's your wedding day."

Russ nodded, unable to summon some cheerful statement to console the man or himself.

So much for the adage he'd concocted, to marry at leisure and enjoy at leisure.

❧

Her new husband remained far too quiet in the carriage, rubbing the twitch of his eye as he stared out the window into the gloomy gray day.

"Rethinking your vows already, my lord?" Fortuitously, his coachman paused in the streets, so Josephine rose up and switched sides to sit next to him. Then she took his gloved hand in hers.

He barked in laughter. "Never, my dear wife!" He grinned and pulled off her glove, then kissed the back of her hand. "Forgive my bad humor. Business plagues me."

"I, however, am on holiday from business. May I lure you to do the same?"

"Lure on, Madam!"

Ah well. She had risqué ideas about that, but that should wait, should it not, for tonight?

"Did you enjoy breakfast? I asked Cook to make the fruitcake of cherries and plums for you." His mother and brother hadn't thought the celebration worthy of remaining for more than the champagne. They'd left soon after the toast to the new couple. "I hope it was as good as your own Cook."

"My dear wife, my Cook is now *our* Cook. And yes, I did enjoy your father's cook's fare. I should be telling you how I enjoyed the entire morning."

"You should indeed." She settled into the sumptuous leather squabs. Everything about this morning's wedding had been deliciously comfortable. The way she'd refused to be offended by Russ's mother's and brother's chilly formalities with her father. The way her husband said his vows with eyes only for her. The way he led her away from others down the hall and whisked her into the small parlor to kiss her at leisure with heat and heart. "So, until you are ready to share your thoughts on our wedding, dear sir, I will tell you how I enjoyed the morning."

"Despite the surliness of my mother."

She bit her lip and let her eyes widen in answer.

He let out a laugh. "And the airs of my brother."

She merely stared at him.

Russ turned her hand over and kissed her palm, a warm generous homage it was, too. "I adore you, Countess Stanton."

Not quite love yet, but she would take this tender bit, too.

"I shall take advantage of your suggestion," he said and lifted his arm to curl around her shoulders and bring her close. "They've gone now. Not to bother us again until Mama needs money and my brother needs a recommendation to a hatter in Brighton."

She settled into the welcome hollow of his embrace. This was such a good indication of how their relationship might become more amorous. "He does like fashion."

Russ lifted her chin, his gaze encompassing her hat, which he dispensed with and threw to the seat opposite. He chose one loose tendril near her ear and rubbed his fingers down the strands. "I like your hair uncovered. Free. I like the pearls today, too."

She quivered; her breath caught with his compliment. "My mother's. Papa gave them to me yesterday."

"A generous man," he said as he smoothed her hair behind her ear. "I have gifts for you, too."

"Marvelous! When do you give them to me? I am a greedy creature!"

"The devil, you are!" He hugged her close and the whole carriage boomed with his laughter.

"Really I am. When do you give them to me?"

"Tonight."

She took her time letting him see the fullness of her desire for that.

"Scamp!" He kissed her madly on the mouth and she flowed against him, her hand cupping his nape. Gasping, he broke away to trace her bottom lip with his thumb. "Ah, Josephine, I will trade any gifts for kisses like that."

"You don't have to, Russ. I would beggar myself to have yours."

His features fell to desperately decadent lines. "You are the most enchanting woman."

In love with you. She found her voice. "So, I needn't sell my wares to gain any kisses?"

"I shouldn't like to bankrupt you."

"Your price, sir!"

"That depends. How many would you like?" he asked, his voice a wreck.

"Innumerable."

"In that case, my darling," he brushed his lips on hers, "let me buy them all."

CHAPTER 4

F orester opened the door to them with bright congratulations. Their outer garments dispensed with, he and Josephine stood as the full array of servants lined up for introduction to their new mistress. Josephine had met the butler before and seen a few of the four footmen at service in the dining room, but not the eight others who served her husband. With a word for each person presented, Josephine offered her promise to all of them that she would be as easy to make happy as their lordship.

"You are such a diplomat, my dear," Russ said as that formality came to an end.

She would have demurred but Forester leaned close to Russ and said, "Sir. Mr. Walters is in the library."

Alarm flashed over his face, but he turned to his wife with a soft smile. "Business, my dear. Forgive me. Come, I'll walk up to the first floor with you. Do continue. I believe your maid arrived earlier, did she not, Forester?"

"She did, sir. My lady, if you wish to refresh yourself, I know your maid has been sorting your wardrobe."

Josephine put a hand to Russ's sleeve when he would have left her at the landing. "If there is anything I can help with, do summon me."

"I will, darling." He pulled her close and kissed her lips, the warm sorrow in his brief embrace some solace for his necessary departure.

His wedding day was not the one to have a disaster at sea! Dammit! He had planned a leisurely afternoon and evening with Josephine. Conversation, reminiscences of childhood, the little revelations about oneself shared with a spouse, dinner and... more. Now, none of that. Not today.

He girded himself for her disappointment. His own was gargantuan, but he had to press on. She would. Yes, she would—and would not take it amiss.

He climbed the stairs to the next floor with anger for the fickle winds of fate that could drive them all to sixes and sevens.

When he opened the doors to his sitting room, he halted. All the air in his lungs drained away. His new wife had been in the process of walking from his bedroom into the sitting room and the light from the far windows shone upon her figure in silhouette. A sylph in diaphanous pearl French silk, his wife paused upon the threshold and his observation of her earthly charms struck him to the quick.

"Forgive me," she said and spun for the bedroom. "I'll return!"

She took a few minutes, long enough for him to encourage a particular part of his anatomy to display much less enthusiasm for hers. Even at that, he worried and found himself taking a chair opposite the fire to cover any tell-tale evidence that might affront her.

When she reappeared, her waist-length hair still flowed over her shoulders like a cape in the vermilions of a thousand autumn maple leaves. But she'd donned a Ch'ing mandarin-necked forest green brocade dressing gown over the translucent chiffon that was her wedding night gown.

"I took the liberty of ordering supper to be served here. I told them I'd ring when you're ready. But..." She strode closer and brushed the lock of his hair from his brow. Her fingers were an angel's balm to his worries. With solemn ease, she took the chair opposite him and arranged herself as if no shock had occurred to her own system when he saw her nearly... practically... naked. "You've talked with your visitor for over an hour."

Her gaze met his squarely. This before him was his associate, Josephine Meadows. Correction, Josephine Downey, née Meadows, charming woman, beautiful beyond mere words, able to add long columns of numbers or nautical distances, sans ink and paper. "Whatever it is, it's bad, isn't it?"

There was no sugar-coating the problems. "Terrible."

She tipped her head and folded her hands serenely in her lap. "What can you tell me?"

This was the twenty-four-year-old who bought beef on the hoof for the Army barracks here in country and who recalled precise ballast loads better than he. Here before him sat the current head of Meadows Trading Company, that entity now thirty-two years in business, with offices in London, Deal and Dover. Thirty-two years ago, her father had opened his business with a partner out of Genoa. They had developed an extensive network of correspondents throughout the Mediterranean and regularly fed information to the British espionage agents. Meadows had come to the attention of Whitehall seventeen years ago when he relayed intelligence that the French were loading particular types of barrels at Leghorn. Such items were useful only if ships needed to traverse shallow waters. Whitehall saw that this meant Napoleon would invade Egypt and they sent Sir Horatio Nelson to harry the little man. In one stroke, Meadows had not only helped destroy Napoleon's dreams of empire in Africa, but secured his own place in Whitehall's intelligence network.

When Josephine assumed total control over the company four months ago, she assured Whitehall of her continuing dedication to delivering covert information to the Government. While Russ was not directly involved in her company's espionage information—nor did he ask or need to be, he coordinated efforts with her and benefitted in his own work from her network's excellent source of information. She had agents in Paris—one *Madame Argent* very well placed—who provided her and him with detailed numbers. This included such vital statistics as those numbers of soldiers under arms, rioters in the streets, the defenses of northern French garrisons... and even how much gold the little French despot had to spend on recruiting reluctant Frenchmen to sign up for his infantry.

Russ trusted her implicitly with everything. News of troops and transports. Facts about his unpleasant first marriage. And now, even his heart. But this disturbing news, on their wedding night, riled him to tell her. "We've got a troop transport out of Portsmouth run afoul by a brig that stove in her bows. The bowsprit's broken, too. She's leaking. A hundred or more troops injured. Fourteen crew dead."

She stared at him, painstakingly assessing the damage. "You must go."

Less than an hour later, she kissed him goodbye with all the resolve of a businesswoman and the sorrow of an hours'-old bride.

He cupped her cheek. "I'll meet with the Prime Minister at Whitehall and return as soon as I can."

"And I await you in there." She tipped her head toward his bedroom.

He pressed her tightly into his embrace and rocked her. "Forgive me this departure."

She did, of course, excuse him all. But as the hours ticked by, she rued her loss of her groom. Not much served as substitute, however. Though supper was filling. The wine smooth. The brandy smoother. Alone, none of it had any taste. After that, she told Jane to go to bed.

The fire in the grate was high. The night was cold and chilly, though the rain outside had stopped. But storms in the Channel were nothing new. Nor were stories of ships tossed by them, but with so much at stake in this new assault against Napoleon, she was disheartened.

She sighed, wishing she'd brought her little dog with her. Or even her work. She'd left her ledgers of yesterday's arrivals locked in her desk in her office in St. James's. Perhaps a book! An adventure! She'd begun one last week titled *Waverley* by some man with the impossibly funny name of Jebediah Cleisbotham.

Sliding her hand across the cold marble of the mantel, she admitted to herself she was taken aback by the change in her wedding night. She'd hoped for a delightful evening, a consummation of all her years of yearning for the noble Earl of Stanton. Unafraid and welcoming the physical joining of him to herself, she pushed back the disappointment that made her frown and ponder how and when she might become his wife in deed as well as word.

Idle now, she trailed her fingertips over the ormolu French clock on the mantel and the Murano glass vase on the sideboard. She was never idle, without a task, a project, a job to do. On this wedding night she had planned to enjoy herself. Alas.

She roamed her husband's bedchamber, searching it in detail for him. He was everywhere. In the sturdy masculine mahogany linenfold paneling of his dressing room. In the careful white muslin drape in his toilette room. In the handsome wainscotting of his master closet. The fragrance of his lime and anise cologne hanging in the air. The precise march of his boots and shoes across the racks. His superfine frock coats hanging from molds, the breadth of those shoulders no match for the symmetry of his body and the lure of his embrace.

She touched one coat, the wool a silken texture that sent her away in search of anything to distract her from the sorrow of being alone on this of all nights.

She plunked into the overstuffed chair and sat to dream of the company she missed tonight. Next to the chair upon the table sat a book of poetry.

She picked it up and opened it to the page he'd marked by the leather band. She grinned. Her husband might be a tower of integrity and restraint, a force to be reckoned with in the Government, but he evidently had taken to reading the love poetry of that noted cavalier, Andrew Marvell. The words of *To His Coy Mistress* had her chuckling.

Who would have thought her rational, stoic-looking husband would like this?

> *And now, like am'rous birds of prey,*
> *Rather at once our Time devour,*
> *Than languish in his slow-chapt pow'r.*
> *Let us roll all our Strength, and all*

Our sweetness, up into one Ball:
And tear our Pleasures with rough strife,
Thorough the Iron gates of Life.
Thus, though we cannot make our Sun
Stand still, yet we will make him run.

She let the book drop to her lap. Watching the flames dart behind the grate, she vowed that, when she had the chance, she would do her part to make her husband's Sun stand
still.

She needed a different book. Anything to divert her. Help her fall asleep. The *Orations of Cicero* would keep her awake. She'd admired Caesar's *Gallic Wars*, but not the old bombastic Roman orator.

She made her way down the winding staircase to the first floor and had just gained the library when she heard a pounding at the front door. She paused, listening to the footman who was on night watch tonight rattle the locks and grumble at the untimely intrusion. Voices floated up the stairs. A man called and he sounded worried, urgent. She hastened down the hall. The servant took the steps up. As he turned the landing for the second floor, she gained the top of the staircase.

"I say, Barns?" She wrapped her dressing gown closer about her. "It is Barns, isn't it? Do you wish to speak to me?"

"Aye, milady. A caller for you."

After ten at night? Not a good sign. "Who is it?"

"Says 'is name is Rodgers."

Fergus? Her man was not to bother her tonight. Yet here he was. "I will see him. No need to bring him up. I will go down." Whatever had driven her man here would not wait on ceremony.

Nor did he. She barely reached the bottom step when he said, "I come from St. James's, Miss. Er... my lady. I went straight there, I did."

She waved a hand. "Do not worry about formalities, Rodgers. You saw my father?"

"Asked for 'im, I did. Woke him. He told me to come. Sorry, milady, but—"

"It's serious. Yes. What is it?"

"We've our runner up from Deal." Runners dashed up from the

coast on a regular basis to alert her and her staff to arrivals, departures and those plans that changed for whatever reason. Only a disaster would compel Rodgers to her so late at night. And with the approval of her father on this auspicious evening, too.

"And? His news? Is it the storms in the Channel?"

"Aye, milady. Our sloop out of Newcastle, bound for Ostend, had to change course and put in at Deal midday. Blown off, she was. No mizzen, ye see. Takin' water."

"Men lost?" That was the worst when men died. Meadows Trading hired on seasoned sailors, paid them well, so when they lost men, they lost the finest.

"No'm. They didn't. But Captain Torrens tells he saw our *Aries* in distress off the coast of Yarmouth. Listing, she was. He couldn't see the main mast what with storm ragin' so hard."

"The *Aries* was bound home out of Ostend." She clenched her hands together. The *Aries* most likely had priceless cargo aboard. Meadows Trading Company's prime agent in Paris.

"She was, Miss."

Josephine had dealt with crises similar to this. Ships blown off course, especially in the Channel or North Sea, were not uncommon. Most survived, even if they came in to port damaged.

"Any other of our arrivals delayed?" She had to know the full of the current problem. The fate of her Paris agent was a horrifying mystery, which said nothing of the fate of the other passengers on board, most of them refugees from Napoleon. If her agent were lost now with that woman's most vital information, Josephine did not know how she would rightly calculate new quantities of beef and boots and gunpowder for the Allies.

"None, milady. All due in are safely in."

"Thank you, Rodgers. Have you had supper?" He was a tall, strapping man of thirty or more but he shivered like a child in this raw weather.

"No, milady."

She went to the bell pull. "I'll have the butler show you to the kitchen. You eat before you go. I assume my father sent you here in one of his carriages?"

"Aye, he did, ma'am."

"Good. You'll take it to the office and tell our runner—" She frowned, her mind awhirl with plans of how to learn about the fate of the *Aries* and all aboard. "Tell everyone, I'm for Yarmouth. Any future word of *Aries*, then you send a man north to me."

He did not argue. He knew better. What Josephine decided, she never wavered from.

She ran a hand through her hair, estimating travel times from London to the north east town of Yarmouth. "I'll be at Stanton Hall in Bury St. Edmonds by tomorrow sometime, depending on weather. Then I press on to Yarmouth. I must discover what happened to the *Aries*."

CHAPTER 5

He arrived home after two, chilled of mind and body. His hat, coat and walking stick turned over to the night footman, he went for the stairs and his new wife.

But his man interrupted him. "My lord, Lady Stanton is not at home."

"What?" An old pain sliced through him. His eye twitched. Silly, he thought himself done with women who fled suddenly in the middle of the night. Like ghosts. Like a particular ghost, this was. But reason countermanded old fears. "Why? Her father? Is he not well?"

"I dunno, sir. One of her men come to call earlier. Roberts or—?"

"Rodgers? Yes." That man was her assistant. If her father had taken a poor turn, a servant from St. James's would have come to fetch her. That she'd gone because of business eased his woes. Yet, because of what he'd been through tonight with transports lost and men dead, his worries doubled. The hideous storms in the Channel and North Sea had been brutal. "And? What?"

"They talked. He left, she dressed, then she called for the brougham, my lord. She said to tell you she had to see her father."

"How long ago?"

"Just after ten o'clock. But Bagby came home about an hour ago, sir. She sent him. Told him to go to bed."

"Did she say how long she'd be?"

"No, sir. Gave him a letter for you, she did."

"Do you have it?"

"I put it upstairs in your sitting room, sir."

He took the stairs at a run.

By noon the next day, Josephine sat fretting as her Meadows coachman and groom attempted to roll the heavy coach from yet one more muddied lane. Though the rain had stopped over an hour ago, her servants would not let her, her maid or her dog Rose out while they struggled. A six-hour ride had become ten.

She huddled in her winter wool coat, glad she'd seen fit to wear it. The early morning ride out of London had proven bone-chilling. The roads northeast were so drenched that she might have considered swimming to Yarmouth. Her little dog, Rose, snuggled into her blankets on the backward-facing seat, sleeping through the occasional downpours and the endless gut-wrenching ruts in the roads. Not so for Josephine's maid, Jane. The poor girl, who was ever valiant, had climbed into the Meadows's traveling coach last night with her at one o'clock, bleary-eyed. The deluge had not improved her spirits and, judging from her cough, not done anything for her worsening health, either.

"When we make the Hall, I want you to remain there, Jane."

"No, Ma'am. I will na'."

"You cannot come. Your health is more important than you accompanying me."

"Lord Stanton and your father will turn me out if I do na' go."

"And I will hire you back. Rest. Do not worry," she said and the maid took her word and settled back into her uneasy slumber.

Josephine eyed the gun case beneath the opposite seat. She had her blunderbuss and her skills with it. Her Meadows coachman had his larger one. Although it was up underneath his seat, she doubted the powder in it was dry enough to fell a mouse. In her own valise, she had packed her own tiny muff pistol. A French affair with Sèvres china handle and gold trim, the weapon was one of a pair her father had bought from a French *comte* whose estates and income were lost to him in the Terror. His family executed by the guillotine, the man now sought to become a proper Englishman.

Those who had stayed in France to embrace the new Republic, changing their allegiances to retain what rights they had to land and their homes, had found it just as hard going. That included her *Madame Argent,* as they called her in the Company. *Madame Silver*, her best agent, close to the Bourbon court, was just as trusted among the Bonapartes. For the past five years, even through the Bourbon Restoration and now the Bonapartist, *Madame* had obtained the most sensitive and reliable information about everything from the restored king's gluttonous diet to the numbers of soldiers in various regiments. How the woman managed such a transition from *ancien regime* to republican to Bonapartist was unimaginable—and invaluable to Whitehall.

The lady was an asset whose worth Josephine could not count so much in British lives saved as in the guessing games the British did not need to play. Expediting *Madame Argent*'s flight from Paris on short notice had been easy. Perhaps too much so. She'd simply declared her intentions, sent word through the network, learned of Meadows ships lately leaving Ostend and headed there. Josephine knew not how, but simply that they had to find her. If she were on the *Aries*, she must be hidden away from the man who years ago had put a bounty on her, mystery as she was to them. Joseph Fouché, Napoleon's chief of Police, was not known to leave off pursuit of an enemy whose life and activities he wished to extinguish.

Josephine shifted, uneasy, as she gazed at the whirling grey clouds. She fought not to think of Russ, wondering how he'd taken her scribbled note telling him of her departure. Her apology for leaving on their wedding night. She hoped that he imbibed the urgency of her mission in her clipped words. He did not know much about *Madame Argent*. The fewer who knew, the better. He, like Josephine, did not know her real name, her home or what her connections were to Republicans and Imperialists alike. He knew that the woman had been her father's agent before Josephine's—and that all of her information had been of incalculable value.

With hopes *Madame* was alive, that if she'd sailed on the *Aries,* that it too survived, Josephine meant to save the woman and the vital bits of intelligence she could relay in this last desperate fight against the little emperor they had to defeat.

Stanton Hall
Bury St. Edmonds

Russ climbed down from his traveling coach and hurried into the foyer.

"Bloody weather, Firth." He pulled off his gloves, then handed over his hat, coat and walking stick. With a hand through his disheveled hair, he glanced about the serene Wedgwood blue and white foyer. This country home was one he rarely visited these past few years. He'd been too busy in London. As a boy, he had loved the house, the rolling fields, the forests thick and dark, the solitude away from his feuding parents. "Sorry to rush in on you without warning."

"To have you with us, milord, is never an inconvenience. We had fair warning you'd follow when Lady Stanton arrived yesterday."

"Is she here?" He didn't expect her to tarry here, but one could never predict travel times during inclement weather.

"No, sir. She left us this morning." His butler here in this house had been with his family since Russ could remember. Once the major domo in his London house, Reginald Firth and his wife Maribel, the house-keeper, had retired here more than nine years ago. They kept it up to snuff, and he had every right to believe that they had responded to the surprising arrival of the new Countess of Stanton with an aplomb indicative of their years of service. "She was bound for Yarmouth, sir."

"Yes. I know."

Firth looked relieved at that. The butler had known Russ's first wife, who'd appear at odd times and hie off here or there, never having told Russ or the staff where she'd gone or when or why.

"What time did she leave?" He had to estimate her arrival in Yarmouth. He wanted to be there for support if news of her agent's survival were bad.

"After eight, my lord."

"Early, that."

"Yes, sir. She wanted to leave earlier but that Meadows coach of hers is in disrepair. Problems with the wheels. Her coachman and groom are ill. Took a deep chill, they did. Her maid, too."

"And my wife?" Russ had never known Josephine to take cold, but there was always a first time. "Is she sick too?"

"No, sir. Not that I could see. Hardy lass."

"Yes. Very. So, if the Meadows coach is down, how did my wife travel?" He hoped to God she hadn't attempted to ride. Nor to go without a groom.

"She had us order a hack from town."

Not the most comfortable conveyance. Still. "She's alone?"

Firth gave him a smile. "With Billy James up in the box, sir."

The James family had run the best stables and smithy in Bury for generations. "Ah. A good man."

"She took her little dog, too, my lord."

He had to smile. "Rose."

"Sir?"

"The Countess's spaniel."

"Happy little bit."

"She is, until she comes upon a man she does not like." Then she barks until he is removed from her sight.

The old butler drew his hoary brows together. "Mayhaps then, she's a good protector."

"Indeed." *And I will join her in that effort.* "Hot coffee for me, Firth. Porridge or stew. Something bracing from the kitchen for my coachman and groom, too. Then we're off. But first, where is the Countess's maid?"

"Upstairs sleeping in milady's dressing room."

"Come. Awaken her for me. I wish to speak with her briefly." He motioned for the butler to precede him up the stairs. "And the maid's name? Refresh my memory, Firth."

"Jane, sir."

CHAPTER 6

Yesterday's rain had gone but thunder still threatened. Lightning danced along. The horses spooked at the harsher bolts, but kept to the road.

Josephine hated to keep Billy James on the cold harsh task, but what alternatives did she have? She had made a commitment to preserve and protect Papa's network and for this, his finest asset, this woman who had brought them word of the decisions of Napoleon's councilors since long before his abdication, she could not fail.

The coach slowed.

Rose raised her little head and sniffed the air. If they were encountering anyone, Rose would tell her mistress whether they were friend or foe just by the smell of them.

Josephine clutched her little pistol, insurance against chaos.

Billy James rapped on the roof. "Road's under water, ma'am. Slow going, 'ere. But a farm's ahead. I'll ask about them's that's docked. I can see two brigs anchored off to sea. Royal Navy I bet. Hard goin' in this." She'd told him she had to learn the fate of a certain ship. He'd accepted her explanation for continuing her journey in such foul weather.

"Ask whomever you meet if they've heard or seen the ship *Aries*."

He led them around a bend and stopped before an old grey stone cottage.

Josephine overheard his conversation with the woman which, according to their raised voices, did not progress well. She was testy. James was persistent, asking what she knew of ships and road conditions.

He ran to the coach and pulled the door ajar, his jolly round face nearly obscured by the bulk of his knitted scarf. "No new ships docking in past two days, she says. But two shipwrecks, she told me, ma'am. On the coast, near the church, she says there's an inn."

"Good! Let's put in there, if they've room. Did she know if there are survivors of the wrecks?"

"I didn't ask."

"Still we must go and get out of this chill!"

"Aye, ma'am. Not far."

When he pulled into the courtyard of a tumble-down inn, Josephine checked her pocket watch. It was only four-twenty but the grey storm clouds made it look like nine or ten at night. They could go no further tonight. But James was jovial still when he stopped the hack and yanked open her door.

A quick glance at the far cluster of cottages told her the village had seen better days. So had the half-timbered inn. A sign dangling from precarious straps flapping to and fro in the sharp wind denoted this was The Queen's Barque.

Josephine hopped down, Rose under one arm, and pressed money into her coachman's hand. "A bit extra for you and your kindness to me on this journey. You keep this."

"Thank ye, ma'am."

"I do see the inn has a stables and a coach house. Please get rest and refreshment for yourself and the horses. I pay for it all."

"Aye, ma'am. Yer kind. I'm off to it!" He handed over her little valise to the tall thin fellow who came running to greet them.

The sprawling establishment spoke of past glories during the reign of the Tudors. As Josephine hurried inside and up the stairs, the place looked clean. On the first floor, the inn opened up to a gathering room and a huge bar. By wafts from flames in the huge fireplace, she was instantly warmed. A giant dog, a hulking mastiff with odd floppy ears, bounded up to her, sniffing Rose. Her little pet regarded the huge mutt with a dainty sniff of disdain followed by a wag of her tail.

"Hector! Off with you!" The man who carried her bag threw Josephine a smile. "Mr. Brewster, at your service, ma'am. The Queen's Barque, about to be restored to greatness."

If that was so, Josephine applauded his ambition, for the inn needed as much money as skill to renew her faded beauty.

"A meal? A room, ma'am?"

"Yes, thank you, sir. Your best room with a fireplace, if you have it." From the corner of her eye, she saw a few people in a common room huddled near the big hearth. The aromas from the kitchen to her right made her faint with hunger. "I see you've a full establishment. I would ask for a beer here in the gathering room, if that's possible, within minutes."

"Of course, Ma'am. Your name, ma'am?"

She leaned close to him, discretion appropriate for her mission. "I am Lady Stanton." So odd it seemed to say that, when in many ways, she was not yet that particular person.

"Milady." He shifted her valise to his other hand and pulled his forelock. "Come with me." He led her up the main stairs to the bedrooms. "We've not had so many in our inn for years. Happy to. Happy to. We've even a gent from London. One of our maids says he writes for a London newspaper. I told her to suggest to him that he write about our inn. Bring more visitors, you see, and make us well known. Rich, too."

"Really? How nice." Her feet were frozen. When that happened to her, a chest congestion was not far behind.

"She says he told her he's here to catch flies and spies."

Horrified, she gasped, then quickly covered it with a short laugh. "How amusing." It damn well wasn't, but she could not agree with such a truthful concept as that. "I understand this storm has brought damaged ships to your shores."

"Aye, ma'am. Limping into the harbor, they are. We've had to drag up from the beach more'n eight poor souls gone overboard."

"Eight?" Her heart skipped a beat.

"Four of 'em dead. Drowned."

"Oh, that's awful. Awful. And... and the others?"

"Others?" He opened the door to a simple but serviceable room with rough-hewn wooden bed, wash stand, cupboard and screen.

"Yes. The other four? Do they still live?"

He scratched his head. "Far's I know, ma'am. They're lying in an old wing. Our vicar tends 'em. Had his start setting bones and so on."

"I see. I see. Are they cogent?"

He frowned. "Co—?"

"Awake? Aware?"

"Not sure. You'd have to ask him. Our vicar, that is."

"Where is he?" She had no experience dealing with delirious patients. And she had to admit now that she was here, she felt a twinge of fear. But she had to march on, didn't she? So much depended on *Madame* and what information she brought with her of Napoleon's readiness for battle.

"He was downstairs a few minutes ago. Talked to my wife, he did. He may have gone off to see the people from the carriage accident in another part of the inn."

"I'd appreciate an introduction, if you would, sir."

"I can." He assessed her with narrowed eyes. "You think you know these castaways, do you?"

What to say? Yes? And give herself away? No? And sound like some ghoul who liked looking upon those afflicted by nature and God? "I'd like to help him."

"Ah, well. There you are!" He went for the door. "Come down when you can. I'll get your supper out for you. Beer, too."

"Thank you. And for my coachman, also, please give him whatever he wishes."

"He'll be with the others then in the stables and sleep in the loft. We'll provide well for him, we will."

"Thank you. His name is James. Billy James."

"Right you are, my lady. Right you are."

"Sir? On second thought. If you would put out a pitcher of beer or wine for me to take up to the survivors right away. I'll take them that and water, bandages. Supper, too."

"Aye, my lady. Good of you. Come along when you're washed, eh? I'll give you goods to take to 'em."

"I will reimburse you for your kindnesses to them, Mr. Brewster."

"That's good of you, my lady."

"We must help each other in crises, mustn't we?"

Russ climbed down from his traveling coach and made his way across the courtyard.

From the looks of The Queen's Barque Inn, she'd stood much too long against the winds of time and fortune. In the gloom of a charcoal-covered sky, the rough and tumble building was the center of a small village that had seen better days.

"Milord." A tall fellow rushed out to greet him and flung a towel over his shoulder. He was squinting, trying to read the family escutcheon on the side of his carriage. "Honored to have you."

Russ nodded to the man, whom he presumed was the proprietor. Peeling off his gloves, he scanned the steps up to the first floor of the big inn. Old it might be, but inside a welcome warmth flowed around him.

"Come upstairs, milord." The man beckoned. "We're happy to have you."

Russ would be happiest if his wife was here. His coachman had questioned a matron on the coach road who told of ships in distress, damaged, shipwrecks and passengers and crew floating in to shore. "I understand yours is the only inn on the shore?"

The innkeeper paused at the entrance to the gathering room where dozens milled about. "We are, milord."

"Do you have here—?" Russ caught a glimpse of a figure in heavy purple wool descending the stairs, the only sight he'd ever wished to see here or anywhere else in this world or the next. "My wife."

He opened his arms wide.

Josephine rushed to him, one arm going around his shoulder, the other clutching a squirming ball of white and red fur.

"My darling," he whispered and lifted her chin, beside himself to kiss her here, to hell with propriety. "You look well."

"I am. About to be even better thanks to Mr. Brewster's hospitality, too." She pressed her fingers into his forearm, looking here and there, aware they made a bit of a scene. "But I am even happier now that you're here."

He hugged her close, damn the rules. Laughing at the wiggling dog between them and the enormous white muff she held, he nonetheless was able to plant a kiss on her sweet lips. "I had to come."

In her eyes stood tell-tale tears. "I began to regret that I wrote you must not follow me."

"My dear wife, why would I stay away? This is our honeymoon!"

She let her head fall back as laughter shook her to her core. "Oh, how I love you!"

"Do you, darling?" His heart left his chest. Worth riding to the ends of the earth to hear that from her.

"I have loved you for eternities."

That—he caught his sanity—was more than he'd hoped for. In the beauty of her forest green eyes, he saw all the verification he'd ever hoped to have of this, his wife's affections. He'd planned to reveal his own ardor in an appropriate moment on their wedding night. To declare it now would seem like mere reciprocity and the love he bore her was no trifle meant to be tossed at her in exchange for her own heart-felt declaration. He drew her closer, detecting in her body's reaction no slight at his failure to proclaim his affection. His Josephine had declared who she was, what she felt. He would treasure it and her for eternity, and save his own words of devotion for a time and place more intimate than this.

"Oh, Russ." She flowed against him, her expression full of the devotion he'd longed to see she had for him, to the devil with anyone in that room. "I have never loved you more than now that you've come to help me."

He cupped her cheek and brushed his thumb across her tempting lower lip. Dear God, he loved this woman. "I will always stand by you. In this. In all else."

She fought back tears.

He dug out a handkerchief from his greatcoat pocket and handed it to her. "Have you a room?"

"Yes. I arrived only minutes ago." She dabbed at the corners of her eyes. "The hack. The coachman was so kind. Persevering as no other. The rain and the roads are hideous."

"I know. I was happy when Firth told me you'd hired Billy James. I knew he'd take good care of you."

"Milord?" The proprietor had been cooling his heels while they reunited. "Supper for you?"

"Thank you, yes. Beer too." He took Josephine's arm and wound it through his.

She pulled him close, her green eyes suddenly hard with serious intent. "Would you mind, my dear, if you and I had our supper later? You see, there are poor souls who are survivors of shipwrecks up in another part of the inn."

"I see," he said, reading the purpose in her features. "And we should go help them, shouldn't we?"

She hugged his arm and planted a kiss on his cheek. "We must. Mr. Brewster is kind enough to give us supper for them. Do they—?" She turned to the proprietor. "Do they need clean bandages? Blankets? What else might we take to them?"

"I think they have enough blankets. Bandages, no need of, as far as the vicar has said. But supper? Aye, hot food'll do them right. I'll have one of my daughters bring out a pot. Hot, it'll be. She should carry it up. Bowls. And water."

"I told Mr. Brewster we would be paying for the care and feeding of the castaways."

"Indeed, we will," Russ added. "If you've any wine, that, too, sir."

"Aye, milord. Ours is not the finest but you'll find it surprisingly good." He tipped his head toward the gathering room. "If you'll take a seat there, I'll get the kitchen to gather it all."

When they were seated at the wooden trestle in the far corner near the fire, he took her cold hand in his. "What do you know of your ship and your passenger?"

"Go play, Rose." She let her spaniel romp with a huge old dog that looked like a cross between a mastiff and a hound. Then she told him all she knew.

At the end of her tale, her lips quivered. "You're not angry that I left home on our wedding night?"

He hugged her against him. "Steady on, my darling. I read your note and immediately understood and agreed. We will see to this matter first and then have forevermore to see to our marriage, eh?"

She broke then, putting her face to his shoulder and letting out her frustration with her silent tears.

He could not care about the audience they had. She sought him. She needed him. She loved him.

And he now had to help her complete this hideous challenge of learning the fate of her agent. That might be here or in Yarmouth or another town, another shore.

But after that, in all good faith, he would declare that she was and would always be the love of his life.

CHAPTER 7

They finished their beer just as one of Brewster's daughters
appeared with a cast-iron pot in one hand and a pitcher in the
other. Behind her stood a maid. She was shorter and thinner than the
hearty Brewster girl and carried four earthen bowls and a pitcher full
of spoons. But she had a newspaper crammed in her pocket and her
gaze darted everywhere noting all the details of the room. Plus, her
fingers were ink-stained. Did she spend her leisure hours writing? Odd
for a maid to be so well educated that she devoted herself with such
endeavors.

Russ rushed to the Brewster girl's side and reached for the handle
of her stew pot and her thick old mitt. "I'll carry that for you, Miss."

She gave it over with a smile. "But you must know that some aren't
eating or drinking. Too sick."

"We'll offer it all anyway," Josephine said.

The Brewster daughter lead the way through dark narrow corri-
dors. She raised high a candlestick, Josephine behind her, followed by
the other girl. Each held a candle. Russ came last, Rose scampering up
the steps behind him.

The chamber was old, small but cozy and their candles gave a soft
illumination to three bodies laid out around the edges of the room, all

covered in old blankets. A fourth, a woman in rags, sat slumped on a bale of hay, one arm in wooden splints. As Russ met her gaze, he detected her fevered state. A glance at the others told him two more were women and the other, a man. If those three slept or suffered from unconsciousness, he was not clear.

"*Bonjour, Madame*," he greeted the woman.

"Good day," she responded in refined English, suitable for any London drawing room.

Rose scampered up to her, sniffed her hands and feet, then circled the other survivors on the floor. The male did not appeal to her because she sat at his feet and barked sharply at him. He did not respond.

"Quiet, Rose!" Josephine admonished the dog. "Sit!"

The animal whined but sank to the wooden floorboards with a huff, her nose twitching near the man's bare feet.

Russ approached the lady with the splint. "Allow me to introduce myself."

She coughed and waved an impatient hand at him and Josephine. In the dim light and in her disheveled condition, he could not detect her complexion or the whites of her eyes. Nor could he say how old she was or how healthy or disabled apart from her broken bone.

"I am Lord Stanton and this is my wife."

"Good of you." Her voice was a rasp. "I am Emily Norton. Mrs. Trenton Norton, of Norton and Stokes, formerly of Chantilly."

Russ smiled politely, noting she claimed her home was that small town north of Paris. Had she sailed on the *Aries*? Might she be *Madame Argent*?

"Oh, ma'am!" Josephine took her limp hand in her own, solicitous for the woman's infirmity. "I am the owner of Meadows Trading Company. My father has spoken often of you and your husband. You deal in French fabrics and lace."

The lady gave Josephine a weak smile. "My, me. Meadows. Odd. Fate is odd, eh? I remember your father. Met you once when you were ten or... eleven? Where were we? Genoa? Can't remember. Can't. But oh, you do look like your mother, you do."

"You knew her?" Josephine grinned at the news. "Marvelous! Oh, ma'am, we're here to help you return home. My husband and I are so horrified to hear of your travails at sea."

"What's your given name? Joan? Jean?" The lady coughed but leaned forward to examine Josephine more closely.

She told her.

"Ah, yes. The bright child. The one who added numbers in her head." She coughed again, fighting a deeper liquid disturbance in her lungs.

Russ knelt before her. "You've a broken arm?"

She let Josephine feel her brow. "Lucky I don't have more, eh?"

"Are you hungry? Thirsty?" Russ motioned for one of the young girls to approach.

"Yes. Thank you. I'd like that, I would."

"Mrs. Norton." Josephine stroked her hand. "Tell us what happened to you. And if you know, what of these three, too."

❧

"We were on a ship." She gulped, her voice frail. "Out of Ostend."

Russ directed the Brewster girl to pour water into an earthen mug and gave it to Mrs. Norton.

"The name of it?" Russ asked.

She sipped the water. "*Aries.*"

"Oh, ma'am." Josephine burst with delight followed by dread at her revelation. "Is it sunk?"

Her eyes told tales of nightmares beyond her ability to describe. "Oh, yes. We were struck by lightning and the ship listed. It was... I swear to you I've no idea how I'm here. Or you, for that matter." She coughed, bent over with the force of it.

Josephine asked for a mug of wine. "Try this. It will soothe your throat. We should get her warm brandy, Russ. That will help."

The woman waved her quiet and pressed a hand to her throat. "Listen to me. All on *Aries* are gone."

"All?" Josephine wanted to scream at the possibility. "Are these three not from the *Aries*?"

"We four? Yes. But others?" She shook her head, weary. "Gone. There were others here... I think. Six? I do not recall."

Josephine realized the lady was confused. Understandable in the circumstances. "Yes, Mrs. Norton, there were other survivors but they've died."

"Nooo." The woman sagged with grief. "When?"

"I'm not certain," Josephine told her and stroked her good hand. "The innkeeper told me there were four more who washed up here. Did you see them come ashore?"

The woman shook her head, but gazed around the room as if she might suddenly find the others sitting there. "Four more? I cannot be sure."

"Might you have known any of those onboard who survived or—?"

"My maid," the woman said and tears sprang to her eyes.

Russ handed her his handkerchief.

She took it eagerly, wiping her cheeks. "She was a good girl. Very good."

"I am so sorry, Mrs. Norton." Josephine knew how dear a servant could become. "Do you have family in England? Anyone you can go to?"

One of the women stirred upon the floor, moaning and curling into a ball of misery.

"My sister in Brighton," Mrs. Norton went on and wiped her nose. "I've not seen her in four years."

"Have you been abroad all that time?" Josephine asked, nonchalant about her question.

The woman's red-rimmed eyes narrowed on Josephine, her demeanor at once wary.

Russ stiffened.

"I have," she said simply and for a moment, pressed her lips together.

Had she said something wrong? Russ noted she did not elaborate on where she'd lived during that period. Certainly, an Englishwoman in trade could not have been in Chantilly for four years. Not in her role as yard goods merchant. Yet the woman was not volunteering the information that would clear the cloud from her name. Nor should she. Not to someone she'd met minutes ago.

Russ took the woman's mug from her, giving no indication of his concern about her revelation. "Let me give you more."

Josephine pointed to those upon the floor. "Do you know these three persons, Mrs. Norton?"

Russ wrapped the woman's shaking hands around the mug of red wine.

"Them?" She drank, much too quickly and coughed. When she had her breath, she pointed at the man. "Not him."

"And the ladies?"

"Sad, those two." She stared at the two bodies curled up into ragged woolen blankets on the hay strewn floor. "I'm shocked they still live."

"What?" Josephine gazed at the two who faced each other. The younger one who moaned had stopped but her eyes were now open. "Why?"

"They argued like cats and dogs from the minute we left Ostend."

"Did they travel together?"

Russ noted that their soiled and torn attire told him little of their status.

Mrs. Norton frowned over that. "Probably."

"Do you know their names?"

"That one," she said as she pointed to the older woman, a silver blonde who struggled to breathe, "is Madame. Madame la Duchesse, that one called her."

Russ looked more closely at the duchess. *Madame* meant nothing of any import. Josephine's *Madame Argent* could have adorned herself with any name in the world.

"And the other one?" he asked Norton. The second woman was lithe, and once probably quite regal with sharp features with long hair. Matted and tangled with sea water now, her hair showed signs of the glorious color of autumn honey.

"Madame du Tourneville."

Two women, one perhaps five years older than the other. One

silver-haired duchess, one golden. One with an honorific, one with a specific name.

"Had you ever seen them before you saw them on board?" Russ asked her, his gaze upon the two on the floor.

"Never." Mrs. Norton took another swallow of her wine. "You have stew? I'd like some, if I may. When they came before with food, I could not rally to eat."

Josephine nodded. "Of course. Do you know how they fare? Have they been awake or talking when you've been awake?"

"That one, yes." She pointed to the golden-haired woman.

Madame du Tourneville, the younger of the two women on the floor, stirred and pushed herself to a sitting position against the wall. Bleary-eyed, she cleared her throat. "I'd like to eat too, *s'il vous plaît*."

"Of course." Russ noted her English was good, but tinged with French pronunciation. He held a bowl while Brewster's daughter scooped stew for her and Mrs. Norton. When the pot and pitcher were empty, he dismissed the two maids. "We'll take care of them here. You should go and help with the other guests."

The two castaways ate and drank with more eagerness than they should have. After a few minutes, both struggled with swallowing and coughing.

At long last, Madame du Tourneville surrendered to her infirmities and sank against the wall. Her hand lax upon her spoon, she sighed. "Who are you?" she asked Josephine and Russ. "Not... not... *proprié-taire, non?*"

Russ introduced himself and Josephine to her. "And you are?"

"Madame du Tourneville. Cousin to Madame la Duchesse de Saint-Aubin."

"And this is she?" Josephine gestured toward the other lady upon the floor.

The young woman nodded, listless. "I have served her for many years. She wished to leave now that the Bonapartes return. We are a family originally from the Gironde, never trusted by royalists or imperialists alike."

"Do they rise again now against Napoleon's return?" he asked. Since the Terror, those in the Gironde near Bordeaux had fought against any who tried to rule them. Any news of their rebellion would be welcome in Whitehall to those who hoped that Frenchmen rose *en masse* against the returning Corsican.

"They do. Unhappy as ever," Tourneville told him with bitter resignation.

Josephine took the cups from both ladies. "Rest now. I will return later and bring you more to eat and drink."

Later, as she and her husband took the stairs down to seek their own supper, she worried. "We may never know if any of those three are our *Madame*."

"But wonderful of you to remember Mrs. Norton."

"Papa speaks of her and her husband often. He lost track of them after the Treaty of Amiens ended." That temporary peace between Napoleon and Britain began in 1802 and lasted barely more than one year. "When Papa heard nothing, he wondered if they'd been swept up by the French police and he was very sad. I know that Mr. Norton was part of Papa's network."

"Bears asking her about her past. But for now, we will eat." He curled his arm around his wife's waist and led her to the bar room. "Later, we will return. Perhaps with time and sustenance, they all will feel better and we may learn more."

CHAPTER 8

Over their own bowl of stew and wine, Russ and she made acquaintance of a few among the many stranded travelers. From them they learned that all roads to the inn were now closed. One woman talked of seeing a land slide and escaping its force just in time.

The owner of the inn, Mr. Brewster, said the high tide would come in early at three or four in the morning. "I pray it does not come so far up that we are endangered."

"Has it ever?" Russ asked him.

"My father said in the eighties, it took out a few cottages on the other side of the dunes."

"But not the inn?" Russ added.

"No, milord. Not us. We've been here since old Queen Bess. Hope to stay until eternity, too."

The travelers appeared to be strained, trying to do their best to ignore the virulence of the storm. Talking easily with others, making new acquaintances, each seemed cheerful.

Russ recognized no one among the travelers. Josephine, however, spied a lady across the room, whom she'd met years ago at school. She told him she'd like to renew their acquaintance and took him with her to introduce him. Josephine's father often said she had never met a stranger in her life... but tonight, amid the attempt at conviviality in the gathering room, she worried that indeed she had. Both Mrs. Norton and Madame de Saint-Aubin had secretive natures and she could not yet fathom what each concealed. Yet she had to learn.

Though she wished to deny it, the storm added to her dismay, a downpour that beat upon the roof of the old inn and brought even more rain-soaked travelers in from the blustery shore. Lightning crashed and thunder drummed in tune with it. She pressed close to her new husband for warmth and comfort.

He circled an arm around her shoulders and took one hand in his. "My God, you are freezing. We must get you more wine and a hot brick to take up to our bed."

"Oh, no. Please. I will not be a bother to the owner and his family. There are so many here to cater to. Besides, my hands and feet are always cold. Comes of being born in August, I believe."

But he did not laugh. "Let's finish our meal and go up, shall we?"

Much later, they climbed the stairs to their room. Her little dog Rose scampered close behind them.

"I'm eager to return to our castaways," she confided in Russ as he closed their door upon them.

"I see it in your eyes."

"Forgive me, won't you?"

He led her to sit upon the bed and cast his gaze down as he toyed with her fingers. "Josephine, you need never ask to do as you must and leave me—"

He sounded so practical that her heart ached.

"I am not so sensitive as that, because I trust you, my darling."

She put two fingers to his lips. "But we have not had the usual wedding and honeymoon. I left you for business."

He splayed his fingers into her hair and cupped her throat. "As did I, sweet lady."

"Still in all. Dear me, Russ. I want us to be one but—"

"But tonight is not the time for that. You have suspicions of that woman, Norton. I don't blame you. The other woman does not seem blameless, either. And you must learn more." He raised her hand and kissed the back. His mouth was firm and oh so inviting. "There will be a better time. Soon. I want that to be joyous for you."

"And for you," she added with an urgency to convince him.

"Trust me, will you? To be with you as your true love will be the most divine experience of my life. I pray to make it yours."

"Oh, Russ..." She surged toward him and kissed his cheek. "You are so good to me."

"A mere reciprocation for your generosity to me and to all others."

"You are too complimentary."

"Ah, but you are mine to compliment as I wish as often as I wish."

She tipped her head to and fro, a grin upon her face. "I shall indulge myself in that."

He paused, his expression a ripe declaration of his need. "Then I will continue to pamper you. Now," he said and pulled back to gaze down at her attire, "why not wash your face and hands then change your gown? I will serve as maid. Good training, don't you think for the future? And then we shall go down and get one of the Brewster girls to fetch us more wine for the injured in the far chamber."

After she had washed her face and hands and brushed out her hair, she tried to pin it up. "I'm not good at this," she said jabbing pins into the heavy mass.

"Let me help." He took a few pins from her and with surprising dexterity, created a French roll that was tidy but sat heavy at her nape.

"You are skilled at this, dear sir."

"Now who compliments too much?"

She turned and hugged him close. How she hated to leave him.

"I don't approve of you tiring yourself out," he said at last and put her from him. "You've had a long day and I want you to return as soon as you think them settled."

She nodded. "I will do that."

"Though we won't be spending the night as once we intended, my wife, I do want to warm your fingers." His bright eyes danced in mischief. "I also have a special technique to bring blood to cold toes."

She threw back her head and questioned him with a teasing glance. "You apply hot compresses?"

He barked in laughter and crushed her close. "I apply hot kisses."

Her mouth fell open. "In that case, I will be quick."

He locked his wicked gaze on hers. "You do that."

⚜

Josephine hurried down the winding corridor and up the back stairs with a candle in one hand, more candles in her pockets and her jug of wine in the other. Rose followed, her tail wagging. Josephine paused, and in the dim light found Mrs. Norton stretched out asleep, but Madame du Tourneville leaning over the body of the Duchesse de Saint-Aubin. She appeared to be putting something around her throat, but Josephine could not see what it was. As Josephine gained the top of the stairs, the woman fell back. She'd been securing the blanket around the duchess's neck.

"Ah, *vin*," she sighed and threw Josephine a tight smile. "*Je vous remercie.*"

"How is *Madame la Duchesse?*"

She shrugged. "*Le même.*"

The same. Not good. Josephine poured wine for her and waited until she seemed comfortable before handing over the cup. The duchess opened her eyes wide and suddenly, she seemed restless and alert. Mrs. Norton, however, slept with her mouth open. She also snored.

Josephine sat down between Madame du Tourneville and the duchess. How was she to learn more about the two women's loyalties? The younger woman's previous statement that they were from the Gironde told Josephine little of their recent lives. "You and the duchess are of the old regime. Did you return to France when Louis was reinstated last spring?"

"A long story. From the first, the Duchess de Saint-Aubin and all her family sided with the republicans. She remained faithful. Always. The result? Ah, well. Bonaparte allowed *Madame* her chateau. Her land, her jewels." Her tone held respect but also resentment.

Why? "Did the duchess like the emperor?"

The woman rolled a shoulder. "What is to like, eh? Any man with all power eventually becomes an animal."

"Do you imply she did not appreciate all he did for France?"

The woman scoffed. "You could say that, *oui*. She appeared to support him *carte blanche*. Nonetheless, in the past weeks Fouché sought her out."

Joseph Fouché was Napoleon's Minister of Police, a ruthless fellow who changed sides as often as his Minister of State, Talleyrand. "What did he do?"

"Tried to turn us. Took away her son."

"No!"

"Sent him to Vincennes."

The old fort east of Paris had held hundreds of French prisoners over the centuries. Most never saw freedom again. "And?"

"He escaped, but she knows not where. Two weeks ago, her chateau was attacked by mobs and burnt to the ground. Fouché instigated it. If they'd caught her, they'd have carted her off to Vincennes, too, we are certain."

So, Madame la Duchesse de Satin-Aubin might very well be her *Madame Argent*. Well placed to know much about the court. Smart enough to survive all these years as an agent of the British. Wise enough to leave Paris when those in power in the Empire turned against her.

Time to learn how they escaped. "Tell me, *Madame*, about how you were able to survive the ship wreck."

"I cannot remember much. The storm, the wind, the rain, it was..." She circled a hand in the air. "Terrible. I was so... so afraid. We two clung together. So very afraid." Her words came slowly as she relived the moments that showed as horror on her ashen face. "We fell together against others as the ship tossed. This way and that, it went. Out there? Now?" Her dark eyes went round with fear as the sounds of waves crashing upon the shore rent the air. "It is the same, *oui*?"

"Catastrophic. The proprietor says high tide begins to come in over the night. The storm does not stop but builds." Yet Josephine wanted to bring her some hope and comfort. "Are you warm enough? Do you wish for anything?"

"No, *merci*," said Madame du Tourneville.

"Blankets," murmured the duchess.

Happy to hear her voice, Josephine turned to the lady who stared up at her with clear blue eyes. "*Madame la Duchesse*, you are awake."

"No!" snapped her companion. "She has the temperature. She is not well."

But the duchess reached out to Josephine, her long fingers plucking at her like talons of desperation. "*Madame* Stanton— but—but not?"

Why would she ask that? Josephine grasped her hand in comfort. Only if the duchess had overheard Mrs. Norton proclaim she knew her as Josephine Meadows would she wonder about her identity.

"Madam Stanton, *oui*, I am. But a new bride. Formerly Josephine Meadows of Meadows Trading Company." Did her lashes flutter at mention of the company? "I am here to help you get to London. That is, if you wish to go. Do you?"

She crooked a finger at Josephine to beckon her closer. Licking her lips, she tried to speak. "I am..."

Josephine bent close, afraid she might speak too loudly any words that might harm her. "*Oui, Madame.* What is it you want?"

"Water."

Relief swamped Josephine. "I have wine at the moment. Would you like—?"

"*Vin*." The duchess gripped Josephine's hand. "*Oui*."

"Yes, that I can get for you. And another blanket." She glanced around. She didn't know where or how, but she would give the lady her own if she could find no other. "What else?"

The duchess tugged on her sleeve.

And Josephine bent closer.

"Laaaal," was all she could gather from the lady's lips. She stared at Josephine and shook her head once. Then crooked a finger at her again.

This time, Josephine leaned so close, she could feel the duchess's breath on her ear.

"Lille."

This was a city in northern France, a garrison held by the French. Not far from Brussels. How it was provisioned with soldiers, ammunition and food was of prime interest to the Allies of the British. *Madame Argent* had often before sent news of the garrison's strength through the Meadows Company network. Josephine needed the duchess to continue now.

The lady licked her lips. "*Vin, s'il vous plaît.*"

"She's awake?" Mrs. Norton struggled up on one elbow.

Madame du Tourneville fretted.

"No, no," Mrs. Norton said, "I will get it."

"Stay where you are." Josephine shot to her feet. "Both of you, please." She fetched the jug and a cup, poured and returned to sit down at the side of the duchess.

The woman drank eagerly, but a slide of her eyes told Josephine that she noticed the other two women were up and about. The duchess sank to her bed of hay, squeezed shut her eyes and alas, it appeared, would say no more.

Was the duchess wary of her two female companions? If so, why? Was this woman her *Madame Argent*?

"Sleep, all of you. I will remain." She should go down to tell Russ about her decision and her speculations about the two women here. But the eeriness of the storm and her suspicions combined into justifications to remain where she was. He'd told her to use her best judgment. She would. She picked up a blanket from a neatly folded pile upon one trestle and tucked it up about the duchess. "There. Warmer?"

The lady blinked once. "Lille," she mouthed.

Josephine lifted her forefinger to ask for a moment.

The duchess widened her eyes in recognition, then laid down her hand upon the back of Josephine's with five fingers spread. Then she picked up her hand and laid it down on Josephine's with four fingers out.

"Nine?" Josephine mouthed.

One nod.

"Soldiers?" she silently asked.

One nod.

Nine thousand French soldiers in the garrison at Lille. While Wellington currently had thirty thousand assembling south of Brussels.

She smiled down at the duchess and continued to fuss about her with the blanket. "Do sleep now and rest. We are happy here, safe and warm. The storm will subside soon and all will be well."

Her duchess closed her eyes, a serene smile curving her lips. Mrs. Norton finished drinking her wine and returned to her makeshift bedding. Madame du Tourneville sat up, staring at her friend the duchess and at Josephine.

But Josephine was not only relieved but also desperately tired. She settled into a mound of warm hay herself, Rose next to her, and wrapped her wool shawl tightly around her. "Awaken me," she said to all, "if you wish anything."

The storm raged outside. Thunder rattled the old panes in the windows and drummed upon the roof. Josephine tossed and turned away from the others toward the wall. Curling into a ball for warmth, she smiled to herself. Tonight, as the previous two since her wedding, she should have been in a sweet hot bed with her new husband. But she'd done her duty by everyone first. So had he. Comforting, he was. Her love. Soon to be her lover.

At last she let herself drift...

A thump pierced her slumber. She grumbled and turned.

Rose growled.

Another thump shook the floorboards beneath her.

A cry, muffled and urgent, had her opening her eyes. The candles had died. The night was raw with whirring rain and earth-shaking thunder...

"Die, damn you!" A ragged whisper of anger had Josephine awake.

She shot up to her elbow.

Rose barked, fierce.

A figure was bent over the duchess.

At first glimpse, Josephine thought it was Madame du Tourneville. But no. No!

Mrs. Norton knelt beside *Madame* working, kneading, grunting.

"What are you doing?" Josephine scrambled up and lunged for her.

Norton shrugged her off, glaring at her, teeth clenched.

"Stop!" Josephine sprang again, grabbling bits of Norton's thread-bare gown.

Norton pushed Josephine away and bore down on the duchess.

Josephine struggled to her feet and darted full force at Norton. The woman whirled on her, the duchess falling back, gasping as Norton clamped her long agile fingers around Josephine's throat.

She clawed at Norton's grip.

But the woman howled, savage, using her weight to force Josephine to the floor beneath her.

Norton was heavy but not agile—and Josephine summoned a great momentum and rolled her about.

"Stop!" A male voice.

Russ!

"Ahhh!" Norton let Josephine drop and whirled on him.

He thrust her to the floor.

She stumbled.

Staggered.

Would have fallen on top of Josephine but she rolled away in time.

Russ reached for Josephine, pulling her up as Madame du Tourneville leapt toward Norton.

But Norton backhanded the French woman and sent her to the floor. Then she scurried toward the stairs.

"Get her!" Madame du Tourneville shouted as she stumbled over hay and blankets.

But Norton ran, taking the wooden stairs in a run that pounded with each step.

"Sweetheart?" Russ held Josephine by the shoulders and examined every inch of her he could see.

"I'm well! She tried to hurt *Madame*."

Rose ran in circles, barking her distress.

"We must get her, Russ!" Whoever she was, friend or foe, and whatever she knew, the woman could die outside in that storm.

He nodded.

Josephine ran toward the stairs.

He followed.

As Josephine scrambled down to the first floor, she saw only the pale gown of Norton as she rushed out into the black void of the storm.

At the door, Russ shouted above the din. "Stay here!"

"I can't!"

He frowned at her but spun toward the shore and trotted off.

Out in the wind and the rain, Josephine ran after him, instantly soaked to her skin.

The night, so dark, so black, gave no light to any endeavor. Wherever Norton had gone, it would do her no good. Worse, Josephine feared for Russ. And she could not see a thing before her. Not even her hand.

"Russ! Russ!" She called.

She yelled.

The rain stung like needles. The wind howled and raged. Oh, she could not lose him when she had barely even won him.

"Russ!"

She staggered forward and a wall of surf hit her and knocked her down. Her mouth full of briny sea water, she retched and crawled toward the inn on the sand and rocks that cut her hands and her legs. The wave receded; the drag as powerful as the one that slammed her to the shore. High tide. It was coming in and if Russ did not see it, feel it, he could be dragged away. Away from her. Forever.

To the very devil with Norton. Her life. Her crime.

I want my husband.

"Russ!" she screamed so long, so hard she swore that God above could hear her.

Another roar grew louder, louder and she thought she saw a wall of water so tall three men could not equal it. She ran backwards. "Russ!"

A wave crashed before her and in its might, took her down to stones and sand that cut like a thousand knives. A hard shell of fear, she clawed backward on all fours like a crab.

No. No! She would not die here. Not like this.

She got to her feet and called for him again. "Russ! Russ!"

A vise clamped around her waist and bore her up, her toes dangling in midair. The hell of nothingness became the mighty embrace of her husband who bonded her to his torso and walked like Goliath with her in his arms. She clung to him, frantic with joy.

Did it take him minutes or hours or eternities to carry her through the howling dervish of the storm far from the devouring waves? But he did! He did, fighting all odds. He brought her to the shelter of the inn and thrust open the heavy door with a kick to the bottom iron plate. He whirled inside, put her to the wall and stood, his chest heaving, his breath harsh as the wind.

"My darling," he rasped and put his icy hands to her cheeks. Rain matted his dark hair and poured over the stark planes of his handsome face. His worried eyes adored her as he brushed cold wet hanks of hair from her face. "You are safe. Well. Oh, Josephine, my darling. I love you. What would I have done if I lost you?"

He pressed a salty kiss of devotion to her lips.

And with his act and his words, he wiped away the trauma of the night and made her life perfection.

"You love me?" She wrapped her numb arms around his waist and admired the chivalry of this man whom she could not live without.

"I do. I have since first you laughed in your father's office at some silly joke about... God knows what."

"Oh, Russ." Tears leaked out of her eyes.

Her little dog Rose weaved between her legs and Russ's.

Her husband smiled sadly and brushed rain water from her forehead and tears from her cheeks. "Nothing to cry about now, my darling. You have saved that woman upstairs. You are a hero. I should have come sooner. I was remiss. But I wanted you to have your time. You are always so efficient. So dedicated." With each thought, he kissed her cheek or her nose or her lips and started then again. "I love you."

She shivered and let the tears continue, a silent declaration of delight and fear. "And Mrs. Norton?"

"That's her name?"

"It's what she told me."

"Ah. Well." He brought her close, put his chin to the crown of her head and rubbed her back with his huge strong hands. "I believe she stepped into the tide. She won't be back."

And even if the woman did survive, she would not find any place of sanctuary. She could not escape this shore. All roads were closed. And all people on this shore were stranded.

"Here's Brewster," Russ said and turned aside to speak with the owner of the inn.

In quick summary, he told him of one woman's rush into the hell of wind and rain and surf. "I'm taking my wife upstairs to warm her and comfort her."

Josephine had more to do though, especially for the duchess. "I'll change and then go upstairs to check on our patients myself. But if you could do that now, please for me, Mr. Brewster? One of the women attacked another and I hope she was not hurt. I will come to see for myself in a few minutes."

The man agreed and hurried off.

"Forgive me for that," Josephine told her husband. "I am concerned."

"I understand. Come. We will both change and see to your castaways. I think you have more to tell me about them."

"You know me well, sir." She pushed back his drenched hair from his forehead. "I wish to tell you everything quickly and get to the business of being your wife."

"You take care of your castaways, my darling, and I will order up a hip bath and hot water."

"Delightful idea." She kissed his nose, his scar and his mouth. "And after our baths, I will take you up on your offer."

"Oh, what's that?"

"How soon you forget!" she chided him, shook her head and spun for the stairs to their room.

He caught her wrist. "What did I forget?"

"My cold toes, sir! They need attention!"

He chuckled and picked her up to whirl her around in his arms. "Hot kisses for your toes! Madam, every day of your life I shall kiss each inch of you!"

And by one o'clock that Saturday afternoon, the Countess of Stanton, Josephine Downey née Meadows rose up on her hands from the tiny—but very satisfactorily used—featherbed and climbed atop the long majestic body of her naked husband to grin at him.

Their worries over, their two French ladies safe and healthy despite the attack of the other, the Stantons had adjourned to their room for rest and the enjoyment of each other that they had postponed.

She kissed his jaw and traced the firm expanse of his lips. "Now it is my turn, my husband, to savor each inch of you."

He ran an open palm from her throat to her silken shoulder, to her firm breast and then her sweetly rounded hip. "I adore you, Josephine. My world was dark before the moment I saw you laugh. Now you are the sun that lights up my universe."

He chuckled when her cheeks burned with his compliment.

"Does this mean, sir, you are ready for me to kiss your toes?"

He settled back, donned a foolish grin upon his face and flung his arms wide. "I am yours, Mrs. Downey."

She threw back her head to chuckle.

He hugged her close. "Have your way with me, my love."

And then she did.

EPILOGUE

June 22, 1815
16 St. James's Square, London

As the Meadows' butler closed the front door upon the last of their guests, Josephine sank into the open arms of her husband and rested her head against his massive chest. "A glorious evening! Unmatched anywhere!"

Russ chuckled and squeezed her tightly in his warm embrace. "A rousing success as hostess of your first ball, my dear Countess."

"Ah." She looked up into his laughing blue eyes and shook her head. "'Twas Henry Percy arriving with those three captured French Eagles and laying them at the feet of the Prince Regent that did it."

At about eleven-thirty that evening, General Wellington's aide had rushed into the home of Josephine's father during a dinner party. Straight from the Continent, Percy still wore his blood-stained uniform. Much of the *ton* was in attendance, Prinny included, all having accepted the invitation of William Meadows, his daughter, now the Countess of Stanton, and her new husband, the Earl. Her papa, whose health had improved lately, had wished to have the event at his home so that he could come, even if he had to appear in his new wheeled chair. But he relished the idea of entertaining those whom he knew and served so well.

Their one-hundred and fifty-two guests had come because gossip had it that the new Countess and her husband had contributed significantly to the war effort and, out of courtesy and some curiosity, they had discreetly decided to overlook the Countess's background in trade. Details of the Stantons' contribution were scant, of course. Secrets had to be kept, and justly so. But the trio had to be recognized, honored if you will, by Society's polite acknowledgement. The guests, like all others in Britain, anxiously waited for confirmation of hints about three days of armed conflict between the Allies and that horrid creature Boney. Numerous merchantmen and smugglers fresh from the coast had declared a battle had begun June sixteenth in a small town south of Brussels. Therefore, many thought it wise to forget one's worries, if only for a few hours, to dine and drink and dance while one awaited word.

"Ha!" Josephine discarded her husband's compliment. "I, dear sir, had little to do with the joy of the evening. All credit goes to the man who led them in that fight and to the thousands of soldiers and their families who now will need our care and attention, more than our homage."

"Madam, hear me." He threaded his long fingers through her coiffure. "Without your skills and dedication, we would have lacked vital information to send to Brussels. I will not let you demure and ignore the praise that is yours alone."

"*Madame Argent* was more brave. *Madame du Tourneville* as well." Both ladies resided now in a manse in Truro, a gift of the Government for services rendered. There, last week, *Madame Argent* welcomed her missing son, the Duc de Saint-Aubin, who joined her in retirement.

"And now we can rest from our worries about Bonaparte and about Mrs. Norton's identity."

"That woman was wily," Josephine agreed with a stern set of her teeth.

When Josephine and he had described Norton to her father, the man had deduced that person in the chamber at the Barque was the true Mrs. Norton's sister. Mrs. Norton had a younger sibling whom she'd suspected of working with the French, but try as she might, she could never prove it.

"Whatever her game once was," Russ said, "she now lies at the bottom of the sea."

Josephine sighed and swayed against him in fatigue, her breasts in the thin silk of her ball gown abraded by the super fine of his formal black attire. She suspected she'd soon have good reason to tell him about an imminent arrival which he'd conclude was more exciting than the appearance of those three golden prizes of war.

He laughed, a jolly sound, then bent and swept her up into his arms. "How am I so fortunate to know you, Madam?"

"Because you are a wise man," she said as he climbed the marble staircase to her old bedroom that they used when occasionally they stayed the night. "But I do wish you were wiser and did not strain your back to carry me up all this way."

"You're tired," he said simply and stared straight ahead, undeterred by her jibe.

"I am, my love, but you must take care."

"I do." He smiled as he gained the second floor and headed for her former suite. "I take care of you."

At the door, he asked her to turn the knob and swing wide the door. Inside, he shut it and strode straight through to their bedroom. There, he set her to the bed and plucked pins from her hair, earrings from her lobes and, from her throat, the emerald and diamond necklace that had been one of his wedding gifts. As he worked, she unwound his cravat. On late nights like this since their return to London, she sent her maid Jane to her bed early, and he his valet to his. The newly-wed Stantons—it became well known among their staff—often preferred to act as their own servants to each other, their joy in their intimacy a hallmark of the couple's love affair.

He urged her to her feet and she took the opportunity to kiss him. She adored the firmness of his lips, the way he swept his tongue inside her mouth to foretell of the ecstasies to come. Over the weeks they'd been one, she'd learned new and sensuous ways to thrill him and herself. Lingering kisses were just the beginning of hours of bliss spent in his arms. She took his frockcoat down his arms, his waistcoat too, then swept down his braces. "I wanted to kiss you tonight when Percy laid those eagles before the Prince."

He crushed her close and spoke on her mouth. "I saw your glance. I was tempted to run away with you up here."

She threw back her head to laugh. "You rogue."

"I confess I am that." He spun her about and made quick work of the laces on her gown. Then he pushed it to the floor. Nuzzling her neck, he circled his arms around her to cup her breasts. "Wanting you is the challenge of my days."

She chuckled as he turned her yet again toward him and went to plucking at her stays, her petticoat and her chemise. Then naked as God had made her, she flowed against him. "We have never restricted the time when we can come together."

"I find I need you at all hours." He smoothed his big hot hands over her shoulders and down to lift her breasts. They blossomed with heat and longing as he caressed her. She arched backward and sighed as he bent to suck one and then the other into the searing cavern of his mouth. "Oh, you are so very good at that."

"Practice makes perfect," he told her, his voice a dark summons to new delights.

"You are always perfect," she whispered. "You make my sun stand still."

He grinned at her reference to the work of Marvell that they both adored. "You are my sun, my moon, my stars, my heaven on earth."

"Russell Downey, may you ever think so."

"Lie down, madam. I shall prove it."

Hours later, he rose from their rumpled bed, his wife asleep, sprawled in elegant repose, her long red tresses gleaming silver upon the pillows in the moonlight. Fulfilled and unimaginably happy, he went to view the sky through the windows to the garden.

Outside, the night lay before him, a spectrum of blues with nary a cloud obscuring the perfection. That was how he viewed his new life with his new wife. A clear firmament electrified by the bright colors of erotic delights, set to the music of his wife's laughter and her love.

And soon, if nature developed as it should, she would bring him more to grace the rhythm of their days and the harmony of their nights. She had not had any of her monthly courses since they'd married. He knew because they had enjoyed each other every day and night since that morning they first joined amid the storm in the old Queen's Barque Inn upon the Norfolk coast.

He could laugh at life now. She'd taught him how. Led the way, actually. Where once he had little faith in the future, she affirmed it would be bountiful—and he believed. Where once he doubted his choices in the ways of mating and affections, she had swept into his life with her verve and her devotion to everything and everyone she adored—and he followed.

Where once he had worried that he must never again marry, she had smiled at him and he had fallen irrevocably in love with her. Then when he had feared he might again wed and make a poor choice; she had shown him that to love her was no mistake.

He smiled to himself and turned back for his bed and his wife and the beauty of his days to come. In truth, this time, he had married at leisure—and he would enjoy her at leisure for the rest of his life.

THE END

Lord and Lady Stanton's romance represents the essence of what I write in every novel. Solid historical fact about a specific slice of history is my *metier*. Here, the story of ships and troops lost at sea, the preparations for defeat of Napoleon and the last scene where the *aide de camp* to Wellington presents the Prince Regent with the captured French Eagles are facts adapted slightly by me to fit the characters of this novel.

I hope you enjoyed the love affair between Josephine and Russell and that you will read many more of my novels available everywhere.

Do visit http://cerisedeland.com

SOCIAL MEDIA FOR CERISE DELAND

You can learn more about Cerise DeLand on these social medial links:

Amazon: amazon.com/-/e/B0089DS2N2
Facebook: facebook.com/CeriseDeLandAuthor
Twitter: twitter.com/@cerisedeland
Bookbub: bookbub.com/authors/cerise-deland
Goodreads: goodreads.com/author/show/2940404.Cerise_DeLand
Pinterest: pinterest.com/frenchcherryred
YouTube: https://www.youtube.com/
channel/UCba82P_Q1kUrJUVVWoCwJmw/

ABOUT CERISE DELAND

Cerise DeLand loves to write about dashing heroes and the sassy women they adore with her signature poetic elegance and accuracy of historic detail.

Published since 1991 by Pocket Books, St. Martin's Press and Kensington, she's been honored to have her novels chosen by Doubleday Book Club and the Mystery Guild. Plus, she's won nominations and awards for Best Historical of the Year, Best Regency and rave reviews from *Romantic Times, Affair de Coeur, Publisher's Weekly* and more.

To research, she's dived into old texts on dusty library shelves and traveled abroad to visit the chateaux and country homes she loves to people with her own characters.

And at home every day, she loves to cook, hates to dust and tries (desperately) to coax vegetables from her arid backyard in south Texas!

EARL'S DAUGHTER CAVORTS WITH COACHMAN

Dear Reader,

One does not expect to spot an earl's granddaughter cleaning the halls of a provincial inn.

Nonetheless, Lady W. and Miss H. confirmed to this reporter that Miss Patience Abney, currently toiling beside the lowest servants in The Queen's Barque—seen sweeping, scrubbing and even emptying night soil—is, in fact, the granddaughter of the Earl of Montour, cousin to the current title holder.

Both ladies assured us that they were well acquainted with the family. They further volunteered that this same young woman—one hesitates to call her a lady—was dismissed from a respectable position at The Spraggins Charitable Institution.

As if that weren't enough, many here witnessed this personage cavorting with a common coachman. The earl must be mortified.

THE TENDER FLOOD

CAROLINE WARFIELD

The Tender Flood
By Caroline Warfield

Waters cannot quench love; neither can floods sweep it away.
Song of Songs 8:7

Zach Newell knows Patience Abney is far above his touch. But he has
been enchanted by her since she raced out of the storm and into the
Queen's Barque with a wagon full of small boys, puppies, and a bag of
books. When the two of them make their way across the flooded
marsh to her badly damaged school in search of a missing boy, attraction deepens. She risks scandal; he risks his heart.

.

CHAPTER 1

The excruciating pain in Zach Newell's stump of a leg hurt him less than the humiliation of collapsing short of his objective. He could manage the pain, a familiar adversary since Salamanca, but Zach Newell never shirked duty and never fell short. Well, hardly ever. This night, a fierce storm and mud had brought him to his knees—literally.

The two massive draft horses that brought them to safety through the flooded roads rested under warm blankets in a dry stable, groomed and fed, their reward well deserved. Neither had suffered any harm, for which he thanked the Good Lord. As to Zach himself, he had removed the prosthetic leg as soon as the carriage was led up to the stable yard of The Queen's Barque and the door closed on his passengers, cutting off the light and warmth of the inn's interior.

A hired coachman had a duty to his passengers but also responsibility for the well-being of his team and the equipment. In Zach's case, the carriage belonged to his uncle. Fred Newell's carriages for hire were high-end vehicles, a notch above a typical hired hack, and the one he drove was no exception—well sprung, with a clean, comfortable—if not luxurious—interior. He planned to keep it that way.

With the horses well cared for, the tack inspected, and the carriage carefully stowed in the inn's cavernous carriage house, he had time to consider what came next in this stretch of foul weather.

The vehicle and tack would be ready in the morning and the horses could manage the rest of the distance to Great Yarmouth easily. The condition of the roads was another matter. Hatless and coat unbuttoned, in one of the stalls that lined the stable yard next to the inn, he mulled over his options. There weren't many. He leaned his weight on his good leg, his left arm over a crutch, and his head against the neck of one of the great beasts that brought them to safety.

"You served well today, Sergeant Newell." The quiet voice came from behind him. "You ought to be in bed. Rest that leg." Major Mallet, one of his passengers, stood at the stall's gate offering a steaming mug of cider. He stepped in out of the rain.

Zach spun on his crutch, accepted the mug with a nod, and inhaled deeply. *Saints be praised—well spiked with rum.* He let it burn down his throat and bring welcome fire to his belly.

"Thank you for that." Zach studied the major carefully. "I suspect you could use the comfort of your bed also." The major still suffered the effects of time in a French prison. He ought to be spared service, but he seemed fiercely determined to join the forces massing near Brussels, giving a sense of urgency to the journey. Zach didn't blame him.

"Told him so," Major James Heyworth boomed from beneath the carriageway, an opening under the grooms' quarters that provided shelter from the torrent and an outlet to the road. "You, on the other hand, should join me, Newell. The taproom is morose of mood and short on song. We could use one of yours."

That his passengers were old comrades had been an unexpected blessing, though not all memories of the Peninsular War were pleasant. A smile at the memory of campfires and song many miles away across the sea took Zach by surprise. Jamie Heyworth had a way of cheering a man. "Thank you for leading the team that last quarter mile, sir. I'm sorry I fell short." Zach almost choked on the words. He downed the rum-soaked cider.

Before Heyworth could respond, he leapt aside when a wagon careened into the relative shelter of the stable yard with rather more speed than was wise, two boys in the box. The driver, a sodden hat pulled down over his eyes, appeared young and inexperienced.

Zach hurried from the stall as swiftly as he was able, waving them into the carriage house and out of the rain. Two things struck him as the wagon lurched to a halt in the shelter of the barn. The wagon's cargo stirred and shifted under an old patchwork quilt, and the driver, who scrambled down and swept off the ugly hat, was no boy. No lad had eyes so warm and brown, lashes so long, or so glorious a fall of hair; she held him transfixed.

"I need to talk to Mr. Brewster!" The tiny bit of a woman cast wide, frightened eyes up at him as if he could produce the innkeeper. "The road collapsed above town; it gave way and slid down just as we passed."

"If we were two minutes later, we'd've all been tossed into the sea!" The boy who sat with her jumped down beside her. This one, definitely a lad, looked to be fourteen or so.

Mallet set a hand on Zach's shoulder. "I'll alert the innkeeper while Jamie tries to wake a groom. You do what you can for the lady and her, er, cargo."

Zach nodded without looking at his departing passengers, his attention still transfixed on the woman: rum, exhaustion, and a pair of deep brown eyes making it hard to think. One word finally wormed its way into his consciousness. "All?"

He followed her gaze to where the boy pulled back the wet blanket over the bed of the wagon. Five pairs of eyes stared back at Zach, five boys soaked to the skin, and shaken with terror.

"Are we safe now, Miss Patience?" one asked, his voice quivering.

"We are indeed safe, Walter, as I promised we would be," the woman said with confidence. Only Zach heard her add "Thank God," under her breath.

"It's cold," one lad said, teeth chattering.

Zach leaned his crutch on the wagon and grabbed a little body that threatened to teeter over the edge in an attempt to climb down. "I'm Froggy," the boy told him, with water streaming down his face.

Zach grinned at the lad. "I'm Zach and you are wet."

"We all are," the boy said. "The quilt was wet through before we even got to the coast road."

"Made January pee," another added as the older boy pulled him out of the wagon.

Another climbed down on his own. "I tried to keep January warm, but he kept scooting into the corner."

"Come to me, January," the woman coaxed, lifting her arms to the smallest of the boys, a wisp of humanity with white-blonde hair plastered to his head. "We'll get you dry; don't you worry." As soon as his feet hit the ground, January clung to the woman's skirts, adding less salubrious moisture where they were already wet. He didn't speak.

Brewster, the innkeeper, bustled into the barn, concern in his face and voice. "Miss Abney! What has driven you and your charges out at this hour, and what is this about the road?"

"The road along the coast gave way behind us just before we reached Morphew Manor," she said. "Peter saw it happen."

All eyes looked to the older boy, who spoke with a young person's glee at describing horror. "We heard a rumble, and I looked back. Miss Patience were—was—driving so I looked back and saw it. Saw the whole thing. Right behind us. The whole road and part of the hill slipped into the sea. Left a great gaping hole straight down the cliff. Gone, Mr. Brewster. A quarter mile of the road's plain gone."

"Was there another wreck, Mr. Brewster? We passed a wagonload of folks who appeared to be survivors," the woman said.

Brewster cursed under his breath. "Tragedy compounding. Looks like you won't be leaving tomorrow, Mr. Newell. Or much of any time soon, with the coast road out and floods rising behind us on the inland roads."

"My passengers have transport to catch," Zach muttered. *And Napoleon won't wait.*

"Can't be helped," Brewster said. He appeared immobilized, staring at a stable full of small boys.

"We can worry about that tomorrow, I expect," Zach responded. "We best get these lads warm blankets and a place by the fire.

"And Millie." One last boy remained in the wagon.

The woman frowned at the lad. "Norb, leave those dogs alone and climb down here."

"I'll take th' boys to the kitchen until I can figure something out." Brewster said, looking pained.

The woman stilled. "You're guessing I can't pay, but won't turn us away."

"I have to make way for paying customers, Miss Abney. I have already opened up rooms in the old wings for the vicar to use for the injured."

"I understand. I'll keep them out from under foot, and I—Peter and I—can work for our keep for a few days."

Another woman would have collapsed in tears. This formidable sprite may have appeared fragile, but hid a backbone under that fall of glorious hair. Zach suspected she would accomplish whatever she set her mind to. He kept his smile to himself.

Brewster gave a long-suffering sigh and nodded. "Mrs. Brewster would have my hide otherwise."

"Norb, I asked you to climb down." Patience Abney glared at the boy in the wagon.

"But Millie and her babies!"

In the gloom to the rear of the wagon, Zach caught a flash of movement. A closer examination revealed a dog lying on a pile of straw in the far corner. She did not rise to greet him. "Babies?" he asked.

"Four," said the one called Norb proudly.

"There'll be no dogs in my kitchen," Brewster ground out. "One shaggy beast is as much as an inn needs."

Zach lifted Norb out of the wagon over the boy's objection, balancing his left hip against the wagon's side while keeping the flailing legs at arms' length. "You go with Miss Patience and Mr. Brewster to warm yourself. Quick time, now, young sir!"

The boy gazed longingly up at the wagon.

Zach softened his voice. "I'll see to Millie and her family; you listen to the lady."

A sleepy groom descended from the loft and trotted across the stable yard with Major Heyworth on his heels. He didn't require instructions. "Best brush this 'un down," he said with a yawn, unfastening the horse.

"You have quite a squad, Ma'am," Major Heyworth said, offering his arm. "May I escort you—and them—to the kitchen as our innkeeper suggests?"

They all walked toward the door to the carriage house, preparing to bolt through the driving rain in the stable yard to the inn itself. Zach watched them go, mystified by the twinge of jealousy that had lodged in his heart.

"You can bed down upstairs, Mr. Newell. I'll manage this rig," the groom said.

Zach turned to explain the dog and her pups when Brewster caught his attention with a question behind him, his voice trailing away. "One thing, Miss Abney. You didn't explain what you were doing on the coast road at night, and in a fierce storm at that." Zach's hand stilled. He'd been wondering the same thing.

He couldn't make out the woman's quiet answer, but a boy's voice floated back to him. "...and then the roof caved in."

CHAPTER 2

Patience woke in the dark, shaking off nightmarish images of her boys being tossed from a wagon into the torrent, only to be gathered up by a stranger with one leg and kind eyes. While her eyes adjusted to the gloom, she allowed her mind to dwell for a few moments on the safe haven his image provided in the midst of the chaos. The tiny window above her head would have admitted little light even if the sun shone, which it most certainly did not. The pounding of rain on the roof sent shivers through her, bringing back the storm and their narrow escape the night before.

The inn had provided a pallet on the floor of the chamber shared by a maid. Warm, dry, and above all free, she felt naught but gratitude for it. She shook off the horrors of the night and dressed quickly, conscious of the Brewsters' kindness. She planned to seek out the innkeeper's wife and offer her thanks and her services. It must already be past dawn. She had fallen back to sleep after the maids rose, and she knew well that inn servants were customarily at their post before full light.

But Patience had other duties, and the inn would have to wait. Her lads had been taken to the stables to bunk with the grooms, the gear, and the animals. Given their collective gift for mischief, urgency drove her down the stairs, through the kitchen door, to the stables. Boys needed boundaries, structure, and security. God only knew what they'd get up to unsupervised.

She peeked into the loose stall nearest the stairs to the grooms' quarters where the boys had been told to bed down. Their blankets were rolled and neatly stowed along the side, but they weren't there, which sent her sprinting across the stable yard to the carriage house with her cloak held above her head with both hands. She needn't have worried. Soft voices coming from the farthest corner told her what she needed to know. As she approached, she recognized the words. Someone was reading from *The Family Robinson*, the book she'd been reading to the boys before she put them to bed the night before. Before the disaster. Before they fled. Before they escaped catastrophe.

The deep rumbling voice of the reader soothed even Patience, and she paused to listen. Four small boys sat transfixed on a horse blanket on the brick floor near the iron stove that provided heat. Peter stood with his back to the wall, listening as well. Remains of their breakfast were neatly stacked next to the bench on which the reader sat.

Something must have alerted him to her arrival because he stopped reading and rose with a slight inclination of his head. "Good morning, ma'am. I hope you don't mind me reading to your boys."

The man from the night before, the one who soothed frightened boys, the one who offered to care for Millie, stood before her, tall, broad shouldered, and respectful. His reassuring strength that made her want to curl up with the boys and sit near him. *The man from my dreams...*

But something seemed off. Close examination showed her the same overlong hair clinging to his collar. The same lanky frame. The same intelligent face and kind eyes. She wrinkled her brow; this man possessed both his feet and no crutch was to be seen. One side of his mouth tilted up, and Patience felt her face burn at the realization she had been staring.

The boys giggled. "Can't tell, can you," Stump, ever the impertinent one, said. "Foot's wood, ain't it?"

"I beg your pardon, Mister..."

"Newell. Zachary Newell." The deep voice rumbled through her chest. She longed for him to keep reading just to hear it. He gave another shallow inclination of the head. "Don't fret yourself ma'am. Boys are always fascinated by missing body parts."

That statement set the boys off again. "Show her, Sergeant Newell," Froggy urged. "It's amazing, Miss Patience."

"At your ease, men. Ladies don't take to such display like we do. We best watch our behavior before we embarrass Miss Abney."

"You know my name."

"Brewster used it last night. I apologize for making free with it," he said, though the twinkle in his eye belied any regret for a lapse in manners.

"No, no. Not a problem. Froggy called you Sergeant Newell. Are you one of the military men traveling to the continent?"

"Bless you, no. Merely a coachman for Newell's Coaching Services. The boys heard the majors call me sergeant last night. Those officers knew me in another life; we served together." He lifted his left leg and wiggled it. Patience noticed it didn't bend at the ankle. "This works for most things, but not the King's army. It was home for Zach Newell after that."

He didn't need and wouldn't welcome sympathy, so she swallowed her instinctive reply and turned her attention to the boys arrayed around the room. "Where is Norb?" she asked.

"He's with Millie," Froggy said, more mournful than usual.

"Grieved and fretful, I'm afraid," Newell cut in before the boys could say more. "Better to show you."

The dog lay on a pile of straw across the way from the boys behind some boxes. She followed behind him, noticing his graceful gait, with no discernable limp. *And you're gaping at the man like a mooning schoolgirl. Act your age Patience!*

Norb crouched over Millie, making soothing sounds. When Patience approached, he jumped up and threw himself into her arms.

"He's gone," Norb wailed. He sobbed into her skirts.

She blinked up at Newell's sympathetic eyes. "There are only three puppies," he explained. "That's all that were in the wagon. One must have fallen over the side." Lines at the side of his eyes deepened, his kind face expressing concern for the boy as clearly as words might.

Norb pushed himself away, rubbed a fist across his eyes, and glared up at Newell. "No," he shouted. "No. We must have left him. It were that dark in the barn and Hercules likes to wander. I thought he was in the basket with her, but he must have wandered. We left him behind. We have to go back, Miss Patience. We have to. We can't leave him there."

Patience darted a glance up at the man next to her and back to the frantic boy. "Norb, we can't. You know we can't. We're lucky we made it here."

"But Hercules needs his mama. He's just now walking around, but he always comes back and he needs her."

"Weaned?" Newell asked.

She shook her head and murmured, "Almost. But we can't go back." Newell nodded solemnly.

When Patience tried to pull Norb into a hug, he yanked away. "You don't understand. Herc could die out there."

"Oh, my darling boy. We could all die out there if we go back. In any case, the road is gone and the school is a wreck." The thought of the building that housed them wrung her heart, but she refused to give in to despair.

Norb must have assumed the tears in her voice were for his beloved puppies. He hung his head, dejection in his drooping shoulders and downturned head. She reached over and raised his chin, lowering her head toward his. "Hercules is the toughest and most adventurous of them all. He'll be with George. They will manage."

"Do you really think so, Miss Patience?" The boy asked.

She'd never lied to him and wouldn't start now. "I believe it is possible, yes. We can't know for certain." *Though we may have our doubts.*

He gulped back tears, nodding unconvincingly.

"Come now; we all need to talk. Just because we're far from the school, doesn't mean we'll neglect our lessons. What is the name of our school?"

"*The Academy for the Formation of Young Gentlemen,*" the boy murmured.

"And what do young gentlemen do?"

"Young gentlemen do their duty and never shirk, obey rules, study hard, and are loyal." Norb recited the words without enthusiasm.

Drawing strength from the presence of the man beside her, she put an arm around Norb's shoulders and tugged him to her. "Come with me."

The boy did, and Newell fell into step next to her as well. "Who is George?" he asked.

"Our milk goat," she replied, shooting a glance at him to check for laughter.

He bit his lips in an unsuccessful attempt to suppress any such rude reaction. "You named her after the king?" he choked out; dancing eyes transformed his rugged face into a visage approaching handsome—and deliciously irresistible.

Patience couldn't suppress a grin of her own.

❦

What sort of school has a milk-goat named after the King of England? The Academy for the Formation of Young Gentlemen. It sounded more like a lofty ambition than a description of an actual institute of learning. *If these six half-drowned whelps are the sum of her students, it is a paltry institution indeed.* Zach kept his thoughts to himself, curious to see what this fascinating woman would do.

Norb hunkered down next to his friends, and all eyes turned expectantly to Miss Abney—including Zach's. He feared she would send him away. He hoped she didn't, so he made himself quiet, far enough away to avoid disrupting, close enough to observe the proceedings.

She picked up the book he had been reading and set it on the bench. "We don't usually start our day with our story, but today is not an ordinary day, is it gentlemen?"

It most certainly is not.

The boys answered politely. "Yes, Miss Patience."

Gentlemen indeed. Not ordinary for me either. It promised to be much more interesting than he expected.

"How do we usually begin our day?" A rustle of hands raising. "Walter?" the sprite asked, every inch the teacher.

"With our prayers."

"We did that. We said our prayers before breakfast," Stump interjected.

"I'm delighted to hear it. Well done, all of you."

"Peter made us," Froggy said to general laughter.

"Excellent, Peter." She beamed at the older boy. "We may be in strange circumstances, but that is no call to lower our standards or change our schedule."

"We have no classroom, Miss Patience. Does that mean no classes?" Stump didn't keep the hope from his voice.

"Not at all. We must continue our lessons."

"But Miss Patience, it is Saturday," Stump reminded her. The boy sounded pleased with himself.

"What is our duty on Saturday?"

A jumble of murmurs greeted that question. Zach made out "chores," "barn," "muck," and "dormitory."

"But Miss Patience, we can't. We're gone from school," Walter pointed out reasonably.

"Mr. Brewster and his servants have given us food and shelter, at a time when they are overwhelmed. It is already obvious we will not be the only refugees he has to take in. How can we help?"

She raised a hand toward Peter to order him to keep his peace. Zach gave her credit for allowing the younger boys' silence to stretch until they squirmed.

"Stable's same as a barn I suppose," Stump said. "Me and January can muck out the stalls and sweep up."

The grooms will be over the moon for that one. More horses had arrived since sun up. Zach expected to help out himself. Then Norb spoke up and Zach thought he should have seen it coming. "Algernon will need to be brushed, and I suspect the other horses too," the lad said. "I can do that, and talk to them so they're not afraid of the storm. Froggy, want to help me?"

As if conjured by the thought, Ryman, the head groom, sauntered up to Zach, who put a finger to his mouth to suggest silence and slanted his head toward the proceedings.

Walter spoke up next. "If Froggy and the others want to work in the stable, I don't expect they need so many of us in here. I'm thinking they could use a pot-boy over at the inn. I used to help at my Grandfather's public house in Yarmouth."

It was the first any of them had mentioned family. Zach had suspected Patience Abney of running an orphan asylum under the guise of her fancy academy. Her warm smile at Walter had layers of meaning in it.

"Excellent idea, Walter. Well done all of you." She paused and looked from face to face, drawing their full attention. "Routine is good, but remember, this isn't our home. You take your orders from the grooms and other servants about how things are done. Be as useful as you can be. I won't have running and rambunctious carrying on during or after. When you finish working, I want you to read."

She peered directly at Zach at that point. "I stored an oilcloth bag under the seat of the wagon. Did you find it?"

He had. "I took the liberty of unpacking it. The books are drying upstairs in the grooms' quarters by the chimney. There's only a bit of damp and they should be dry by noon. Peter can fetch them."

"Well, then, reading after lunch. You can pay your respects to Millie while I speak to the gentleman in charge. Use the necessary one at a time if you need to and for heaven sake don't stay out in the rain."

"I'm going to need someone on mud-clearing duty full time if this continues," Ryman said under his breath. "I have helpers, do I? I already talked to Peter, here. If he can oversee the cleaning, I can set my men to the welfare of the beasts and some much-needed mending of tack."

Take your orders from servants... Don't neglect reading. What sort of gentleman does she expect to instruct? Zach's curiosity about this school of hers grew. It almost matched his curiosity about the woman herself.

Peter followed Ryman, leaving Zach alone with Patience. He stood a little straighter. Zach generally drew his fair share of admiring gazes from women even after his injury, but this woman's approval suddenly seemed important to him.

"I had best get over to the inn. Mrs. Brewster will be needing all the help she can get. I'll take Walter with me." When she met his eyes, Zach's breath stopped. He wanted to ask questions, wanted to know more about Patience Abney, wanted her near on this dreary day.

He inched closer, but checked himself. *This will not do!* he thought. *She has duties and so do you, Newell.*

"Thank you for your help last night, and for reading to them this morning," she said into the awkward silence, her voice gentle.

"Miss Abney, would you have dinner with me tonight?" The words were out before he thought. "At the inn. After the boys are fed."

She blinked up at him.

"That is, if I'm going to help with the boys, I'd like to know more about them."

"Are you?"

"What?" Her eyes transfixed him.

"Going to help with the boys?"

He shook himself to break the spell that held him. "The majors and I will be off the moment the roads open. A private yacht belonging to some friend of theirs is meant to take them to Ostend on their way to Brussels, and their presence is urgently expected. Until then, Miss Abney, I have little enough to do, and I will gladly help you manage your academy for young rascals."

The smile that lit her face at his turn of phrase ignited a fire in his heart.

She tilted her head to peer at him from under her long lashes. "The Brewsters and their people would be relieved to hear it," she said, and then, "And I would be beyond grateful."

"Dinner?" Her smile still held him in inarticulate wonder. One word was all he could say.

"If we can manage it, yes," she said, pulling her gaze away to call Walter to follow her.

CHAPTER 3

A man accustomed to solitude does not require entertainment. Zach sat on his cot above the stables and listened to the rain pound down while the wind shook the roof and an unfamiliar sensation rattled his soul.

You are alone, Newell, and nobody gives a damn where you are or what you do with free time you didn't expect. You may as well get on with it.

Even his uncle didn't much care, as long as he got the carriage back in good condition; he'd already done what he could for the equipment. He reached between his legs, pulled out his valise and retrieved his journal with a bit of rummaging, flipping to the page he sought, the one with his estimations.

His sister Abigail might put her head up now and again to wonder whatever became of him, but she had five children and an irritable husband. Life would pull her back and she'd forget. Women? There'd been a brief flirtation since his return to Rumford, an innocent one compared to relations in the Peninsula, his limp notwithstanding, but it never amounted to anything.

What brought on the blue devils, Newell? Y've never been a brooder. He intended to use the day to review his accounts to see if some rearranging of his figures might show him a path forward to act on his plans sooner than he originally thought. He tapped a pencil on the page, but his thoughts floated away.

Is it the majors? Seeing Jamie Heyworth, that hey-go-mad officer from Spain, had dragged up memories, not all of them good, but no. *That isn't it.* Transporting Mallet had been pure privilege. The man's legend as one of Wellington's exploring officers didn't fit the quiet bespectacled man he'd picked up in Rumford, but spies could be funny that way.

No. If anything, the majors' presence let him sit a little taller and remember when his life made a difference before it had been reduced to dragging passengers back and forth across England.

He didn't hate the work; he didn't expect to do it forever, either. Zach Newell had plans and dreams. He stared down at the page again. *Ones that matter to no one but you.* He slammed the journal shut.

He ran his hand through his thick hair, making a mental note to get it cut, and considered what sent him into the dismals. The morning started well enough, with Zach jumbled out of a dream deep in the throes of defending himself to discover that the noise he heard wasn't a rampaging French regiment but a rowdy bunch of hungry boys. The memory made him smile.

It felt good to settle the troops down, putting them in good order and—reading them a story? *Admit it, Newell. It was more fun than you've had in months.* For a brief while, someone had needed him. More than that. Patience Abney approved. Her glowing face rocked him to his core.

When he promised her that he'd help, he'd looked forward to earning more of that approval—and to the fun of keeping the inventive imps from trouble. Inviting her to dinner had been pure impulse and a foolish one. He'd been without a woman's company too long; his wits had gone begging with his manners.

But she left, and soon enough, Peter expressed an interest in hoof care. That's when old Ryman attached Norb and Froggy to his grooms to show them proper use of curry combs and brushes—a role Zach had planned to take. Then the head groom led Peter out to the smithy, and Stump—with January as well since the little one stuck to Stump like a burr—took to sweeping with serious intent, needing only the occasional reminder to slow down.

That left Zach on his own. To brood.

An outburst of noise outside, the thing he didn't even know he was waiting for, brought him to his feet and a grin to his face.

He tucked his pencil into his simple waistcoat, and briefly considered donning the heavy coachman's coat that hung above the cot, rejecting that idea. The soft jacket he kept tucked in his valise may have been wrinkled, but it impeded his movement less. It would do as long as he had the sense to stay out of the rain. He stuffed the journal into an inside pocket.

Halfway to the stairs he remembered Miss Abney's books. There were six—a mixed bag of primers, maths, and stories—laid out by the chimney, dry now and in the way of the grooms. He scooped them into their oilcloth bag and started down the steps that led to the stable yard, grateful they were covered.

"Need help, Sergeant Newell?" Stump stood in the rain at the bottom of the covered stairs staring up at him, watching his awkward progress.

Zach cursed silently; he always hoped to get through moments like this unobserved. "I can manage." He wondered if the lad had come to fetch him.

"I can see that. But Miss Patience always tells us that sometimes a man has to take help. Pride can lead a man to tumble," Stump countered. January, at his side nodded in agreement. The lad's eyes missed nothing even as Zach descended, but he never spoke. Another puzzle to feed Zach's curiosity.

"Miss Patience is wise," Zach said out loud while silently adding, *but she underestimates a man's need for his pride*. "Best get out of the rain, young sir. Have you finished your first task?"

Stump raised a brow at 'first.' "We were, but some more folks arrived. Came to ask if I should get clean hay from the loft after I sweep out their mud?"

"What is the racket I heard?"

"Froggy and Norb got into it over whose turn it was to work with the horses, only Bert, the groom with the squirrely hair, told 'em both there's no need and to bugger off and stay out of the stalls and then they—"

Zach caught sight of Bert leading another team, drenched with rain, into the stable yard. "I expect clean hay won't go amiss," he muttered. Stump sauntered off toward the coach house with a cocky tilt to his head, January on his heels, and Zach took the inside passage behind the stalls to search for the two miscreants.

A small rump hung over the half door of a stall and Zach could hear a muffled argument from inside. At his gruff, "What do you think you're doing?" The bent body jerked upward and Froggy scrambled down to the cobbles. "I told him not to do it," he said.

Zach put one hand on the boy's shoulder and peered over the door. "Remove yourself!"

Norb's eyes flew wide, his hands dropped the brush he'd been using, and his mouth began to open and close.

Zach held the stall door open. "Out now. What is your surname?"

"Me? Tucker," the boy said. "But I—"

"Quiet, Mr. Tucker. You were told not to enter a stall without the supervision of a groom."

"But Bert wouldn't—"

"Bert has work to do. You're meant to help, not get in the way. Miss Patience expects you to do your duty."

"Told you so," Froggy said out the side of his mouth, head hung down.

"What is your duty when the work is done?" Zach asked still peering down at Norb.

"Read. But this is our Algernon. He brought us here, even though it were storming fit to blow him off the road. He wanted more brushing. I'm sure of it."

"The grooms decide when you are done, Mr. Tucker. You and mister..." Zach peered at Froggy, still hanging his head.

"Morling," Norb supplied.

"You and Mr. Morling are meant to be reading."

"But the books!"

Zach held up the sack of books, suppressing a grin when the lad's face fell.

After rescuing the dropped brush, the boys trooped after him to the space allotted for the Academy boys in the far corner of the cavernous coach house, slumped to the floor and waited expectantly while he dumped out the books onto the bench. Zach had no idea what might be appropriate for those two.

"I don't read," Froggy said, shame haunting his eyes.

"He's getting better with his letters," Norb said defensively. "I help him. He knows the sounds all the way to L."

"Lamb, ladder, lady..." Froggy said helpfully.

"Well done, Mr. Morling. And you, Mr. Tucker?"

Norb pointed to the primer in Zach's hands. "I can read most of the words."

"Do you know why it matters, Mr. Tucker?" Zach asked. He might not know teaching, but he understood reading.

"It won't matter when I go out to work, so don't tell me that. I'm going to work with animals."

"A skilled groom has to read. What if the horse needs a tonic and he gives it the wrong one because he couldn't read the label?" The idea was a bit far-fetched but made its point. "But that's the least of it. You have a mind, Mr. Tucker. It matters. How do you feel when Miss Patience reads about the Robinson Family?"

Froggy brightened up. "It is ever so exciting. I can see myself on a ship or an island."

Norb shrugged. "I like it."

"That's just one story. When you can read, the whole world opens up to you. Hundreds of books. You can learn what you want, imagine what you want, love what you want. But you have to learn first."

Norb sighed and took the primer. "Want to find the L words Froggy? You find them, and I'll read them."

A bubble of pure joy formed in Zach's chest. He leaned back and beamed at the boys making magic. *If only they knew that's what they did.* He let his thoughts drift until the image of a certain diminutive teacher took hold of his imagination.

Dinner. He would see her then. Anticipation gave spice to his day. He could wait.

CHAPTER 4

"Right quick, Miss Abney. Cook'll have eats for us in the kitchen, but we only have a few moments. We can't rest until we're done." Delilah, the little maid Mrs. Brewster had assigned to cleaning rooms beside Patience, bustled off.

Patience hadn't stopped for hours. Refugees had flooded in, some injured. Once it had become apparent that they would need every bit of space, they had begun opening up the old wings of the inn, left from when Fenwick was a bustling port. The morning's influx had meant Mrs. Brewster needed every hand to lay straw, fetch blankets, and carry water. The maids moved from four rooms to two, packing their belongings with some grumbling, adding two more rooms for less fastidious guests—or the servants of the particular ones.

Her drive to check on her boys outweighed hunger and worry propelled her through the kitchen, where she found Walter packing up lunch for the stable servants and her boys. The cook seemed pleased to let both of them carry it over, sparing the man of all work.

The stable yard, partially sheltered, held off the wind, but it provided only a small bit of protection from rain that seemed to grow fiercer by the hour. It soaked the cloak she tossed over her head and wet her cheeks while she grappled with one handle of a large hamper and sped across to the carriage house with Walter, grateful when they ducked safely inside. Stump took her side of the hamper so she could shake off the rain, and wipe her face on her damp handkerchief. She reached to do the same to Walter, but he jerked away.

"Where are the others?"

"Peter went to the smithy with Mr. Ryman and didn't come back. The others are with Sergeant Newell."

"Even January?" She rarely saw the little one far from Stump.

"Stories, Miss Patience. Couldn't keep him away."

She skidded to a stop at the back of the coach house. Norb sat cross-legged, bent over a book. Froggy, January, and Millie listened with rapt attention while he read.

Millie? Maybe not. She and her puppies were snuggled up next to Norb at least, and he had one arm over her.

What put Patience's heart in her throat though, was the man overseeing the proceedings. Sergeant Newell rose from his place on the bench at her approach. "On your feet, gentlemen. A lady has approached." He put a finger in his own book, the one he had been reading while he watched Norb and the others.

The boys clambered to their feet and all four of them, from the lanky Sergeant to tiny January, gave a polite bow. Stunned, she said the first thing that came to mind. "Lunch is here," which set off a small stampede. The sergeant smiled down at her, and Patience found herself unable to speak in the warmth of it.

She dipped her head, giving in to an inappropriate curiosity about his reading matter. "Shakespeare!"

"Surprised?"

She was not about to admit it. "Everyone loves Shakespeare," she said, pleased she didn't choke on her embarrassment. "Thank you for getting Norb to read. I was afraid he wouldn't leave Millie."

"He helped Froggy with the letter L first, but the younger boys demanded a story, and I decreed one of them had to read it. No *Robinson Family* until the day is done—correct?"

"Correct."

"Norb fussed about the lost pup several times, but, when he got down to reading, it distracted him."

"I was hoping he'd forget about that," she sighed. "There's little enough we can do. We had best go supervise."

"We don't want the locusts to devour the grooms' lunch."

Patience laughed at that nonsense as they walked toward where Walter had set out the lunch. Newell paused by a particularly fine carriage. "Yours?" she asked.

"My uncle's."

When he flipped up the lid of a box built into the boot she gasped. "Books!"

He slipped the Shakespeare into the one empty spot. "Surprised again?"

Not a little embarrassed, she blurted out. "You must like books very much to ship them with you."

The deep small smile of a man content came over him. "'*My library is dukedom large enough.*' My poor room in Rumford is thick with them."

"Prospero," she said.

The glow of his smile swelled into sunlight. "You know *The Tempest.*"

She had the curious sensation that he caressed her with his eyes at that, but he looked away soon enough. He snapped the lid shut and gestured toward the luncheon. "Shall we join the troops and attempt to keep them in order?"

She fussed over January's bread and cheese, cutting it just so. She reminded Walter to drink his milk. She suggested Froggy eat more slowly. All the while, half her mind focused on Zachary Newell, who leaned against a wagon and left the grooms and boys to the luncheon. When she could no longer resist the need to talk with him, she asked him why.

"I'll get something in the taproom later," he said.

"Are you going to leave the boys on their own?"

Consternation pushed his eyes wide. She had wondered if they were gray or blue. It appeared they were both. "I hadn't thought. I best have a bite." Through bites of bread and cheese he asked, "What do you want them to do this afternoon? I have no idea how to teach boys."

It seemed to Patience he'd done a good job so far. She made some suggestions, he mulled them around. "Norb might manage his numbers better if he was counting horses," he said, making her laugh. His next words sobered her. "Tell me about January. He never speaks."

She breathed deeply. "Perhaps later. I have work to do. Send Stump to help Walter with the hamper. The Queen's Barque can keep the two of them busy."

She left less worried about the boys than she had been, and muddled about the man she left leaning on a shabby landau. *A lover of books and small boys. What other surprises lie in store?* A smile sprouted on her face and took root in her heart.

⚜

It had been a long time since Zach Newell had dinner with a lady, and he had never felt awkward before as he did this night. Standing next to his cot in the loft above the stables, he pondered the matter.

Neither he nor Patience Abney were servants of The Queen's Barque, but neither were they precisely paying guests. A lady would require a private parlor, but he believed a woman of Miss Abney's class might dine with a man in a public place without giving offence, and he knew he was welcome in the Taproom after the dinner rush. He didn't believe the Brewsters would object to her joining him, though she labored—albeit temporarily—among their servants. She sent word she was willing.

Why so uneasy, Newell? Hair, coat, and boots all brushed as well as could be managed, he gave a moment's regret for his overlong hair and unstarched cravat, and shook off his bout of nerves. The sight of an umbrella tucked in the corner by the door at the foot of the stairs brought a smile. Some may regard an umbrella as effeminate but, in the persistent storm, he was pleased he didn't have to get wet. He ducked under the thing for the ten yards or so to the inn, then left it at the door for the next man.

Making his way down the central hallway to the lobby, he found Brewster absorbed in his ledger while in an earnest conversation with a customer. Zach approached the tap room, looking about for Patience, but stepped back when two ladies sailed from the private parlor into the lobby and on up the stairs like the queen's barque itself—the royal barge.

Overdressed and overflowing with their own consequence, neither would have drawn his interest when they brushed by—they certainly hadn't drawn Brewster's—if a snatch of their conversation hadn't startled him.

"I tell you, I saw Patience Abney cleaning the room and carrying out the night waste. She didn't see me, thank God. How mortifying that would be. The Earl of Montour would turn over in his grave if he knew that his niece mucked out rooms in a common inn. What will the new earl do if he finds out his cousin shames the family?" This pronouncement by the older woman, decked out in feathers and puce, stupefied Zach.

What followed merely puzzled. The younger woman's voice faded away as they climbed the stairs. "You must know—earl's cousin or not, she already spent time as a common teacher at that charity school in Yarmouth. They let her go, and I heard..." Whatever the viper meant to say was lost, but Zach had heard enough. He struggled to absorb it all, torn between proceeding to a table in the tap room and bolting to the door.

He didn't notice Patience until she spoke. "Planning to withdraw your invitation?" Every line of her body rigid, she stood chin high as if daring him to cry off.

His immediate thought, *of course not*, stuck in his throat because he'd been considering exactly that.

"If the company of the Earl of Montour's disgraceful cousin shames you, then by all means walk away." Her body listed left as if she meant to turn from him.

"Good God, no!" That sort of language had no place in front of a lady, and his discomfort grew, but at least she stopped walking away. He took her hand and pulled her to the side where the Brewsters had placed a woebegone fern in an overlarge pot. In its shadow, he whispered, "If you think I'd take the example of those horrid women, you're wrong."

"Something upset you." Her lips were drawn tight.

"Miss Abney, I had no idea that you were an earl's niece. I would never have presumed, if I had known."

When she wrinkled her brow adorably as if trying to make out his words, he pressed on. "You must see that you are far above my touch." At the word 'touch' he glanced down to the hand that still held hers. He dropped it as if it were on fire, mumbling an apology.

Light rekindled in her owlish eyes. "I never took you for foolish, Sergeant Newell. It is you who do me an honor, asking me to dine."

"Hardly. I don't pretend to be any more than I am, an invalided soldier and common coachman, but if you're willing to share mutton with me, it would be an honor indeed."

The light in those eyes threatened to engulf Zach in its flame. He winged one arm, and, when she took it, he floated along on a river of warmth, pushing aside the niggling thought that, if the viper and her companion saw Patience in his company, she would sink even farther in their regard. He vowed that would never happen.

But for tonight, just for tonight, he would enjoy the lady's company.

CHAPTER 5

re all men oblivious? Charles Remington had been. She pushed the
unpleasant memory of his ill-fated courtship years ago from her
thoughts. Zachary Newell was not a dandified fool.

The server's obvious flirting and exaggerated hip movements
seemed lost on the man, yet the girl persisted in her efforts to
attract his attention. *Alice,* Patience remembered. *Her name is Alice.
Day help, thank goodness. We don't have to put up with her upstairs.* The
girl's not so subtle spite tossed in Patience's direction firmed that
opinion.

A pint of ale arrived, presented with a flourish in front of Zach.
The sherry Patience requested did not. Zach's firm reminder sent the
server off in a huff. He set his drink politely aside to wait.

"What—?" Whatever Patience meant to ask was overridden by his
simultaneous "When—"

They squirmed a little, both uncertain how to begin a conversation.

Finally, Patience got down to it, proving once again how poorly her
name fit. "You said this morning you had questions about the boys."

"I do. But also, about your *Academy for the Formation of Young
Gentlemen.*"

"You think the name is a foolish conceit." Her drink arrived, but this time Alice, who had come under Mrs. Brewster's eyes, didn't linger.

"I think it's ambitious, having met your students, but admirable. Education is vital to boys of every class and station."

He surprised her again. She wouldn't have expected a coachman and former soldier to be such a passionate advocate. "You were well educated."

"Well enough. Better than many."

"But you enlisted in the army." She bristled with inappropriate curiosity about this man, and her impulsivity made her wiggle in her seat. *Did he wish to enlist? Or was he forced to take the king's shilling? Through hunger? Desperation?*

He ignored the intrusion and answered politely. "That I did. I stayed in school until I was Peter's age, but left with a head filled with tales of England's glory and a longing to earn some for myself when I went to defend king and country."

Patience thought of Peter and cringed. "What did your parents think?"

"My mum was gone and my father distracted. By the time he knew, I was on my way out the door. He gave me his blessing, but I never thought he approved exactly."

"And did you?"

"Did I what?"

"Cover yourself in glory?"

"There's little glory in war, Miss Abney, no matter what appears in stories. I did my duty, and I believe I did it well."

"Froggy told me what you said about the importance of reading. Thank you. I've struggled to get that point across, but the boys seem to have taken you seriously."

"Books kept me sane in the army. They still do. I'm grateful for my education. The Cranford School provided scholarships for the sons of the freemen of Rumford, an enormous gift to an eager boy." His eyes studied her face, unasked questions lurking in his expression.

"You're wondering about what that woman said about losing my position."

"I was, yes, and I apologize. It isn't my business."

"It came down to January, but really it had been brewing."

"January? He doesn't speak."

"He never has, at least not since I met him, but I have hope," she replied. "When he came to Spraggins—"

"Spraggins?"

"*The Spraggins Charitable Institution*, founded by a devout mill owner I always suspected of attempting to atone for his sins by molding boys into pious little automatons."

Newell winced. "I suspect you lacked skills in the creation of automatons, pious or otherwise."

"They assumed the daughter of an impoverished vicar would be biddable for them and severe with the boys. I proved a profound disappointment after they hired me to beat reading into the youngest boys.

"Beat?" His horror echoed her own.

"I wasn't informed when hired that my duties included generous use of a switch on those who did not or could not learn quickly enough. Headmaster Bartram and I were at odds immediately. I'd have been gone the first day but for my tenuous connection to an earl." She leaned a bit forward to whisper, "I'm not above using it if I have to. My cousin neither knows nor cares."

"But a vicar's daughter?"

"He was the youngest son in a family of eight. I suspect my grandfather was content to ignore us, snug in our little vicarage at a distance, once he gave Papa the living. I had little enough to do with the manor house as a child."

Their dinner arrived just then, a beaming Mrs. Brewster herself bringing it. "You're lucky to meet our Miss Abney, Mr. Newell. That school of hers keeps her away too much of the time. She's a good friend to the inn and to Fenwick." She patted Patience's arm. "And good of you to pitch in like you are, Patience. Mr. Brewster is that impressed with it. 'Never gets above folks, does Miss Abney,' he said. 'Dun't ask charity even when she deserves it more than most. Willing to do her share.'"

Mortified as the innkeeper's wife waddled off, Patience stabbed a fork into her pork pie.

"Well. You have supporters here, it seems."

"The Brewsters are good folk. They see Fenwick on Sea as the next Brighton—don't laugh! That may sound ambitious, but they are shrewder than you might think. The sea, with proper accommodations, could draw merchant families, and their concern that Fenwick provide refinement and real culture along with recreational activity is to their credit."

"She sees your school adding that air of culture?"

Patience couldn't hide her amusement. "Somewhat. I come once a month to tutor the servants here in elocution and, yes, reading. The Brewsters and some other town folk meet over dinner to talk about projects such as bathing facilities or sailing races in the summer. Folk truly would like to draw musical talent or a theater as well. I like feeling part of it; as if we're building something."

"I'm impressed."

"I won't say you should be, at least not yet. But someday."

Their dinner had disappeared without talk of the boys. When Alice meekly brought tea, casting a wary eye at Mrs. Brewster, they ordered apple tarts, happy to linger.

"You never explained about January," Newell pointed out.

"You may have gathered some of it. An orphaned charity case, a boy that can't or won't talk, smaller even than he is now... He couldn't survive Spraggins."

"You mean that literally?"

"I came upon Headmaster Bartram beating him with a staff as thick as your thumb—tiny January. It's how I met Stump, actually. He was also a charity student and had assumed protection for January. He leapt at Bartram and got beaten around the head for his trouble."

"You inserted yourself into it." He said it with an absolute approval that filled her with pride.

"I did. I got a nasty welt on my cheek for my trouble, but he stopped and ordered me to leave him to it. I refused. He fired me on the spot, making it clear he didn't care who my uncle was. I left and took Stump and January with me."

"You got away with that?"

"It skirted legality, but truthfully the Spraggins so-called school was happy to be rid of the three of us. I sometimes fear the parish might come looking for them, but I doubt it."

Astonishment suffused her dinner companion's expressive visage. "Where did you go?"

"Home to the vicarage. Papa is used to all of us bringing home strays. He might have kept us, but I had ambitions."

"Clearly! You are a wonder of nature, Miss Abney. Did your father help you found your school? I thought you called him impoverished."

"You don't miss anything, Mr. Newell. No. Not Papa. I did something I had never done before. I went to my cousin who had succeeded as earl. We knew each other from childhood, for all we grew up in different worlds. Horace listened politely. Laughed. And let me know his charity had limits. He gave me a ninety-nine-year lease on a small unentailed property just north of Fenwick on Sea, with a paddock, a pole barn and a ramshackle house just big enough for a boy's school on the condition I never ask for more. I haven't."

"And the other boys?"

She shrugged. "Here and there. Walter and Peter were both tuition-paying students at Spraggins, God help them. It wasn't difficult to convince their parents they would be better off elsewhere. Walter's father had assumed he lied about treatment at Spraggins; Peter's parents didn't care, but when the boy begged to join us, they allowed it."

"Did the school object?"

"Shrewd question. They minded losing paying students very much. Bartram never forgave me. When his hints about my honesty didn't turn the parents' mind, he fed rumors of immoral behavior. There was no rush of families to transfer to the *Academy*."

"No wonder the boys adore you."

She waved the comment away. "Nonsense. They are just boys. My job is to civilize them."

That made him laugh. "Cranford was a cozy family compared to Spraggins, but the job of civilizing boys went on vigorously there too. How do you manage it all?"

"Well enough. I have four day-students from Fenwick whose parents pay tuition. Froggy's grandfather pays what he can, and Norb's uncle as well. We raise chickens. The Queen's Barque is a good customer for our eggs. A retired farmer and his wife come during the day to help and I do all the teaching. I would wish for a more advanced mathematics teacher and Latin for Peter, but we get by. I have plans to grow—or did."

Memory of the roof coming down into the boy's dormitory crushed her spirits. God only knew what she would find when they went back, and she couldn't afford to brood about it until the storm abated.

Sergeant Newell—she couldn't help seeing him as a military man— had been a considerate and compassionate dinner companion, but she could see he sensed her mood. He deserved better entertainment for his evening. After a few more desultory bits of conversation, Patience excused herself.

He rose and bowed politely, but didn't offer to accompany her to her room. There would be no point, and she would have refused in any case. She left up the stairs that led to the balcony above the tap room. Just before she turned down the passageway to the chambers beyond, she glanced back down.

He smiled up at her; he had been watching. Her heart did a little dance.

Zach stared at the gallery though Patience had disappeared into the inn's warren of guest rooms, so lost in thought the sound of Jamie Heyworth's voice caused him to jump.

"Come share a pint with me, Newell!"

Ale sounded good. Something stronger sounded better. They took seats at a battered table along the side, close to the bar.

Drink swiftly obtained, the major raised an eyebrow at Zach's choice of rum, especially when he downed it and asked for another. "You look glum for a man who just enjoyed the company of a lovely lady."

"That's the problem. I'm not likely to have the pleasure again."

"The lady looked pleased enough to be in your company. I saw the way she gazed down at you. Your friend from Stratford Upon Avon would have words for that expression."

Zach snorted and took another deep swallow. "If I'd known what I learned just before we sat down, I might not have gone into it."

The major leaned forward, both arms on the table. "Not to her detriment. Our innkeeper finds her unexceptional."

"Well he should. The woman is an earl's niece."

Heyworth's brows rose. "She is? I wouldn't have guessed."

"You shouldn't have to. She should have been well chaperoned in a private parlor not consorting with a common coachman in a public tavern."

"Wait, wait. Dinner is hardly consorting and Patience Abney is not some flower fresh from the school room that must be handled delicately. She appeared perfectly comfortable in the tap room to me. She seems comfortable working alongside the inn servants."

Zach glared sourly into his mug of rum. "She shouldn't be."

The major shook his head. "Needs must when the devil drives in a storm. Even our scholarly friend Mallet helped with horses and carriages this morning."

"Scholarly. Is his Latin decent?"

Heyworth's mouthful of ale landed on the table, setting off some frantic sopping up and choking. "Andrew's Latin, my man, is beyond decent. Latin, Greek, Hebrew. Ran circles around the rest of us. His father tutored private students at Cambridge. We all thought he was headed that way, but he ended up in the army. Why?"

"Miss Abney needs help for Peter, at least while we're stuck here."

"You admire that woman."

"That I do. She has more drive and ambition than most men, and less help." He briefly sketched what he'd learned about her school.

The major let him rattle on until he finally put up two hands to stave off the flow of words. "Now you're planning how she could expand this little enterprise. I'll tell you one thing, Newell. What you said about consorting with a common coachman? You are many things my friend, but common isn't one of them."

That remark seemed to call for another round of drinks, which led, as sufficient amounts of alcohol often did, to shared memories good and bad of old companions, muddy hillsides, and French treachery. When the major called for a song, it seemed a good enough notion.

Tables moved, locals gathered, someone found a fiddle, and Zach Newell put his raw feelings into song. Admire the woman he might, but she was far above his station. He'd treasure the dinner; it was the last one they would share. One song led to another, each more maudlin than the last.

> The bee shall honey taste no more,
> the dove become a ranger
> The falling waters cease to roar,
> ere I shall seek to change her
> Vows we made shall bind me,
> the girl I left behind me.

"Ye're getting all weepy. Go back to *The Jolly Coachmen*," one wag called. "Aye!" and the crowd began, and Zach obliged.

Here's the man who drinks dark ale and goes to bed quite mellow...

"Better yet, Newell. Time for bed," the major said, and Zach saw the sense of it though his eyes had gone blurry. They left the tavern with arms around each other's shoulders singing,

> For tonight we merr-I be. Tomorrow we'll be sober.

CHAPTER 6

The storm raged into Sunday morning, inclining the inn's guests to keep to their beds. Patience, bedraggled and determined after a restless night haunted by visions of a tall man in uniform who alternately hid from her and sheltered her under his coat, ducked under an overhang and then darted across the stable yard.

She roused the boys from their sleep in the stall below the stairs with orders to join her at their meeting place in the carriage house, and bring Peter with them. Walter clambered up the stairs to convey the day's orders to the older boy who'd been invited to the grooms' loft. Sergeant Newell, he reported, still snored on his cot.

Carriages and wagons now occupied every available space, forcing Patience and the boys who straggled after to weave and wander through the maze to reach the corner allotted to the Academy denizens, a luxury really, considering they also took up a stall for sleeping. The space appeared smaller, as if the boxes marking it had been moved in a bit on the two open sides, and perhaps they had. Millie's little family had been moved into their corner, and a rather muddy gig had been pulled forward as far as the wall and now stood right next to them.

Of Zachary Newell, Patience saw no sign; the intensity of her disappointment made her wonder if one dinner had sent her common sense to the Antipodes. She had no reason to believe he had interest in her beyond dinner, and ought to remember the only men ever to show serious interest had been after her uncle's favor, not hers.

Then again, even the grooms were just waking up and seeing to the horses in their stalls around the stable yard. Perhaps he'd appear later.

The boys wandered in, sleepy eyed and quiet, to sit at her feet. "I know things feel strange, lads," she told them, "but today is Sunday. What does that mean?"

"Pudding at dinner," Stump said to general laughter.

She gave him a glance meant as reprimand. "Anyone else?"

"It's the Lord's Day," Walter said, wiggling a bit to get comfortable on the cobbled floor.

"No work," Stump added, leaning back on his elbows and sighing dramatically to more laughter.

Panic shot through her. *If I can't think of work for them, what will they get into? I should have the boys clean that gig, Lord's Day or not.*

"Normally yes. We'll see what this day brings. But first, we give thanks for our blessings."

Heads bowed automatically. Patience began the familiar spontaneous litany, "We thank you for the Brewsters who have been kind and generous."

"Thanks we're out of the rain," Walter said

"And the roof didn't smash us," Peter said.

"We didn't fall into the sea either—thank God for that," Stump added with relish.

"I'm grateful for Sergeant Newell. He has good stories," Froggy said with conviction.

"Now petitions. Who needs our prayers?"

"Hercules is lost and scared. God keep Herc safe," Norb prayed fervently.

"Who else needs safety from the storm?" Patience asked. Boys called out names of neighbors, family members and friends.

"Folks at sea," Walter added, causing a ripple of unease to shudder through Patience. She'd watched the churning waves from the upper story windows the previous day. This morning it appeared as bad.

"Sergeant Newell feels poorly. He needs blessings," Walter blurted out.

Patience blinked.

Before she could ask the question lurking on her tongue, Peter spoke with a wry grin. "I don't think it's serious, Walter. He just needs to sleep off a long night."

I hadn't thought— But Zachary Newell's behavior wasn't Patience's concern. She sighed and began their closing prayer.

"But Miss Patience, you didn't read our Bible story. We were worried about Gideon and those Midianites," Norb interrupted her.

It occurred to Patience on previous occasions to wonder if indulging the boys with the more lurid stories in scripture was quite the best form of spiritual development. It didn't matter. "Unfortunately, we didn't bring our Bible," she said.

"I'll bet Sergeant Newell has one. He puts great store by books," Norb said.

"Well, Mr. Newell isn't here, is he?" she said, her mouth pursed tightly. *Enough about Zachary Newell. Isn't it enough that thoughts of him kept me up most of the night?*

She concluded their little service and led a discussion about how they might have some fun this day. They brought no boards or cards, but Stump believed they could create their own jackstraws, and Peter thought he could draw a board for checkers on the floor with charcoal if they could find pebbles enough to play. Various games involving hiding and seeking came up. Enthusiasm for those died with Patience's adamant insistence that they could not open trunks or enter any of the carriages and coaches surrounding them. Nor were they to climb on them. Or get under where they might tangle in the wheels.

"The inn is big, isn't it? I'll bet there are a heap of places to hide in there," Stump suggested.

Patience felt the color drain from her face. She was almost ready to allow tag in the stable yard in spite of the rain. "You will stay in this space or the stall where you sleep. Play charades. Make up stories. Read. Do not under any circumstances enter the inn, or I'll have you all writing out your arithmetic tables."

Faces fell, but she hardened her heart, leaving to see about breakfast for her boys. In the stable yard, she spied Zach Newell just coming out of the grooms' stairs, but he turned around and started back up.

Her face fell. *He saw me and turned around.* She began to believe she'd given offense at dinner.

The early morning passed without her rascals causing any trouble, but Patience felt compelled to remain in the carriage house with them. Guests arrived, and Patience's heart gave a lift at their approach. Majors Heyworth and Mallet both claimed an interest in the boys' welfare. She didn't doubt their sincerity, but she suspected boredom and a nudge from Zachary Newell to be behind their unexpected arrival. Of the former sergeant, she still saw nothing at all.

After polite greetings, Major Mallet took Peter aside while Heyworth let the boys pepper him with questions about the army. His anecdotes skirted inappropriate once or twice—to the boys' delight— but some of the stories merely confused them, and her boys didn't find his stories as funny as those told by their Sergeant Newell. Reluctant to leave the lads unsupervised with the kind, but unpredictable major, she delayed returning to her work, although she knew Mrs. Brewster needed her. She caught snatches of Mallet discussing Latin studies with Peter while she waited impatiently.

Throughout, Patience couldn't keep herself from glancing between the carriages, hoping Newell would return. She told herself she watched because she trusted him with the boys, because he would take over, and she needed to leave. *Ninnyhammer. Be honest. You're mooning after that man like a schoolgirl.*

"He's shy, you know." Her face burned at the thought that Heyworth had read her thoughts. "At least, he's overly conscious of his 'place.' That's his word, not mine. Army makes a man conscious of rank. We tried to get him to take lunch with us on the way here. He said it wasn't his 'place.'"

"I heard he joined you last night," she objected tartly.

The major grinned. "Well, drinks between old soldiers, you know. Not the same thing. I tempted him with stories and song. A great man for a drinking song is Sergeant Newell."

Perhaps I need to learn some, she thought sourly.

A distant sound and vague disturbance interrupted her thoughts, one she dreaded so much she hoped she mistook it. She tipped her head.

"What is it?" Major Mallet asked, coming to her side.

She picked up her skirts and ran through the carriage house and out into the stable yard. She knew it then, louder there, carried through the storm by the wind, the tolling of the church bell.

"An alarm?" Mallet demanded, blinking rain from his eyes, as men poured out of the inn, the loft, and the stables, putting on coats and oiled cloth capes. Zach Newell stopped in the door to the inn, hesitating only moment before limping toward her in the chaos.

She looked up at Major Mallet. "Shipwreck. It is the signal for a wreck. They'll be organizing rescue."

"Don't even think about it," Heyworth said striding up to them, and glaring at Mallet. "I'll go. Listen to me, Andrew. I know nothing could keep you from the coming fight, but you need to keep your strength. You won't do Wellington any good if you relapse."

Mallet seemed to sink into himself and Patience remembered hearing that the man kept mostly to his room.

Heyworth rushed on. "You and Newell stay here and keep these boys sorted so they aren't under the feet of the rescuers." He grinned over at Newell.

"You don't need a cripple in the way, you mean," Newell growled.

"I mean no such thing, Sergeant. Every man to his duty. We don't all have the same orders. Make sure Major Mallet stays put." He clapped Newell on the back and started toward the street, Peter on his heels. Heyworth glanced back to Patience for approval. She nodded and the boy ran off with him.

Patience, Newell and Mallet stared after them.

"I guess that puts us in our place," the major said.

The word *place* made Patience cringe; she peeked at Newell's face, his pain and frustration plain for the world to see. She wanted to reassure him that she needed him here, but no words came to mind that sounded right. He'd prefer and deserved only the truth.

"You want to go with them," she said at last.

"A man needs to make a contribution," he replied without looking at her. "Sitting to the side when there's need..."

"You aren't!"

He peered down at her then, his expression a mask of sorrow, rain clinging to his eyelashes. "The other night, coming here, I had to get out and lead the horses in. I made it to the turn in the road, and my damn—excuse the expression, ma'am—dratted false foot stuck in the muck. I went down and Jamie Heyworth had to bring us the rest of the way. I'd be no use to them out there."

"But we aren't on the side. They'll bring the survivors here and Mrs. Brewster is already stretched to the limit. I can't do my part unless you help with the boys."

He gave a shuddering breath and nodded. "I can keep your troops in order, that's something. You best hurry inside."

He limped away before she could respond or risk giving him unwanted sympathy.

Beside her, Mallet spoke. "The stubborn fool didn't mention the superhuman effort it took him to get us this far the other night. Our business in Brussels is urgent, as you can guess, and he pushed himself and his horses harder than we imagined possible, until we ran into darkness and the flooded roads. He walked that team at least a mile." He shook his head. "I fear I'm no help with the younger ones, but I promised Peter we'd work on his Latin later—at least until I'm able to get to my transport."

CHAPTER 7

The next hours ran together, streams of worry, fear, and work, blurring into one wide river of exhaustion. Patience hurried between the kitchen, the public rooms, and the older wings of the inn, soothing the wounded, stretching their supply of blankets, spreading clean straw on the floor, serving soup, shoring up sagging window frames, stopping leaks...

She worked alongside the inn staff, and even some generous guests, to care for the flood of shipwreck victims. Lady Stanton was notably helpful, but seemed particularly concerned about a group of French-speaking refugees from an earlier shipwreck.

When Mrs. Brewster, whom Patience had ever known as one of Fenwick on Sea's bulwarks of strength, seemed ready to drop by dark, Patience volunteered to sit up that night in one of the old wings full of recently arrived refugees. She had no time to check on her boys, but she trusted Zach Newell to keep them safe and out of mischief.

Staring into the dark through the interminable night, she pondered that trust. The man carried himself with confidence and even grace when his leg didn't pain him. Tall, slim, and graceful, he still conveyed a kind of strength, the sort that comes from within, the sort a person can rely on to be there when you need him, the sort she wanted to lean into. She instinctively gave him her trust.

But what do you really know about him, Patience?

The mystery of Zachary Newell filled the night between helping refugees with personal needs and worrying the roof might leak. Over their one dinner, he'd let her babble at length about the Academy and how she started it, but had spoken little of himself. He spoke of the army but she couldn't tell if he regretted leaving it. He implied that he worked for an uncle, and struck her as a contented sort of person, but did he want to drive coaches his whole life?

Is he happy? Is the coaching world all he knows or wants to do? Surely not —What kind of coachman fills a trunk with books for his travels?

His care for Norb over Millie's plight, and gentle patience with Froggy—so far behind in his reading—impressed themselves on her. He had Stump's respect too, no small thing.

Perhaps he ought to be a teacher—or a father...

Sitting on the floor and leaning against the sickroom wall, she nodded off on that thought and awoke with a start when one of the maids, sent by Mrs. Brewster, came to relieve her just before dawn. She trod off to her room, knowing she ought to check on the boys, relieved she didn't have to.

Zach will have taken good care of them. She smiled as she drifted off. Sometime in the night Sergeant Newell had become Zach, at least in her private thoughts. When she finally got to her little pallet to sleep, she vowed to herself she would check on her boys the next morning before she was drawn back into the inn and its refugees.

Ducking under the overhang, Zach leaned one hand against the frame of the loose box stall closest to the stairs to the grooms' loft where he slept. The wind had slowed, but thick rain clouds still covered any hope of moonlight, making inspection difficult. He peered into the gloom and cocked one ear to the inside, listening for sounds of fretful boys or incipient trouble. He heard none.

Eyes adjusting to the dark, he could just make out lumps under blankets, enabling him to take silent rollcall. He counted and counted again. There should be five boys sleeping, with Peter upstairs. He counted six. He leaned in further, and found the faint whiff of dog, narrowing his gaze to the more oddly shaped mound that seemed to shift with his movement. Millie and the pups slept with the boys. Miss Patience wouldn't approve, but if that was the most wayward behavior these lads got up to, Zach did. He went to bed smiling.

He rose Monday morning with a lift in his heart. From the sound of the wind on the shutters—or lack of it—the storm had weakened even further overnight. He anticipated a day with his squad of bright lads, one with no boredom and little time to fret over his own tedious life. Even his leg felt better; going without prosthesis since the previous afternoon let the inflammation from the other night mend itself. He strapped the dratted thing in place under his trousers and headed down the stairs. One or two of the grooms had already risen, but Peter slept soundly on his cot.

The scene he encountered in the stable yard upended all his expectation. Patience Abney, fisted hands on her hips, engaged in a heated argument with Ryman, the head groom, while some of the boys milled around her in a soft drizzle, half dressed. Millie whined in the door to the sleeping stall with her puppies at her feet. From the corner of his eye he saw one of the grooms leading Algernon from his tie stall, and alarms went off in his head.

Stump spied Zach and headed for him at a run, the rest of the pack on his heels. "Good thing you're here, Sergeant Newell!"

"What are you lot doing out here undressed? And, Walter, why didn't you fetch me when the lads woke up, as ordered?"

"No time, Sergeant. Miss Patience woke us up when she came to look in on us and found Norb gone," Walter said.

Zach's heart froze. "Gone?"

"We think he's run off after Hercules," Stump told him.

Froggy stared at his feet, and his dejection caught Zach's attention. He lifted the boy's chin with gentle fingers. "Look at me, Froggy. What do you know about this?"

Froggy swallowed hard. "He's been talking for three days that we need to fetch Herc, but you wouldn't listen, and Miss Patience won't go. Yesterday he pestered me about the marsh. I— " The lad choked and swallowed again. "I told him my grandda taught me the marsh is a sponge. It soaks up the rain and the floods so folks can move about on the roads."

"Froggy's grandda lives on the marshes. Froggy, too, when he's not at the school," Stump interjected. "Norb's been pestering him about it."

"Roads through the marsh?" Zach asked.

Froggy nodded. "The back way to town from th'Academy. He knew it was there; I told him what Grandda taught me. It's my fault. I told him." Tears began to flow. "It's only a track, but it's usually above the water. It's my fault; I told him," he went on through sobs, "Now Mr. Ryman says Miss Patience is going to die if she tries it."

Zach enveloped the boy in a hug. "Norb's bad decisions are his own, Froggy. You are never to blame for what someone else does."

He glanced up and saw Peter coming toward them. "Look after him," he murmured to the boy, as Ryman walked away shaking his head and waving his arms to give some sort of order to his men. Zach went to Patience.

For a moment, Zach thought he saw relief and hope in her expression, but belligerence quickly supplanted it. "I'm going after him," she insisted.

"Are you out of your mind?" Fear at her determination drove the words out as anger he didn't intend. "You have no business riding out into the marshes in this weather." He gestured through the open archway between the stable yard and the less protected road where rain sputtered in sudden squalls.

"Who else will?" she shouted back. "Norb is my responsibility. I should never have left them. I should never have trusted anyone else with their well-being."

"He was where he belonged at midnight when I checked on them," Zach spat back, struggling for a grip on his temper. He breathed in deeply, knowing her own guilt lay behind the unintended insult. He went on softly, "We can't watch all of them every moment, Patience." He realized he'd used her Christian name, but had no time to consider or apologize.

She swallowed and put a hand on his arm. "I didn't mean to blame you, Zach, only Norb is gone and in danger and..." For a horrible moment he thought she might collapse in tears, but Patience Abney was made of sterner stuff.

"I was meant to be watching him. It's my responsibility. I'll go after him. You stay here with the boys."

"I won't endanger anyone else." She shouted again, something Zach suspected she rarely did. "I cannot bear having anyone else hurt. And you have passengers. You have your own duties."

He took her hands in his, and leaned forward until their foreheads almost touched. "Listen to me. The worst of the storm is over. I will find him. He can't have gone far on foot in this mess."

"I hope you're right, but I'm going, Zach," she said, pulling away. "You can't stop me."

He tugged her hands back. "Then we'll go together. You are not going alone. I won't permit it."

Ryman had come up behind them. "Thank God, Mr. Newell. She has no business out at all. Please tell her she can't take that wagon on them marsh roads."

Zach nodded. "We'll need sure-footed mounts with good heart and stamina. My uncle's draft horses are the best in the stable, but they aren't mine to endanger. We'll have to take Algernon, but we need another."

Ryman shook his head. "Brewster would usually allow you one of ours, but none of the mounts we have that would be up for it are available. Two're at the smithy for attention and another's ready to foal."

Zach's mind raced. Algernon could carry the two of them, but they had to bring Norb back. *If the rogue made it to the school, he'll have a puppy with him as well.*

"What about the dog cart I saw in the carriage house? Light as it is, that is less likely to get mired."

"If it doesn't get blown off the road," Ryman shook his head. "No, best if you ride. Miss Abney can stay here."

"It is my horse and..." she began.

"She can ride pillion—or I will. The beast can carry both of us. We'll worry about the boy when we find him." Thoughts of walking back on muddy roads caused Zach's stomach to clench in apprehension, but he refused to think about it now. *God sends what He sends. We contrive.*

The fool woman wouldn't give up. "But Zach, your passengers! You have..."

"We aren't going anywhere today, not with the road blocked, and my uncle's horses are snug and well cared for. Ryman can be trusted to take care of the beasts. Give Peter your instructions for the boys. Look, he's come down and needs to know."

She nodded.

"Take a minute to reassure Froggy. He's blaming himself. I'll go explain to the majors—they'll help Peter with the lads when we tell them why we're leaving. I'll be back in a trice."

He walked off before she could object, cursing under his breath at the foolishness of impulsive boys, stubborn women, storms, and his own dodgy leg. He would manage. He always did.

CHAPTER 8

P atience almost believed she hadn't been dry in a month. She rode astride Algernon, her skirts hiked to her knees and her cotton hose clinging, wet and cold, to her skin. The rain that had drenched them as soon as they rode out of the inn's stable yard came and went, but had not stopped entirely.

She might have been miserable, except heat radiated down her back where Zachary Newell sheltered her against the hard wall of his chest and—she blushed to think of it—belly. She held the reins; he held Patience. At least he anchored her in place with one strong arm while his other held up the makeshift shelter of oiled cloth. The oilcloth draped around them, covering Zach's back, her shoulders and his. He had to lean his head down in order to keep hers covered.

Her position was perilous, cold, and utterly scandalous, yet Zach's commanding presence wrapped her in a blanket of security. Even her frantic fear for her missing student was kept in check by his decisive leadership. When she hesitated at the crossroads, worried Norb might have wandered up to the landfall in the direction they came, Zach repeated Froggy's certainty the boy had gone to the marsh. When her companion's sharp eyes found the track before she could pass it, gray and dim in another of the sudden downpours, his deep voice vibrated through her, assuring her the horse would step carefully as long as they went slowly enough.

She quickly saw the impossibility of taking the wagon on the narrow track. One wheel could have slipped into the high water that sloshed onto the track still in places; it would have pulled the whole thing over. The first hours dragged by while Algernon crept forward until she wanted to scream, but the big horse stepped carefully, one foot in front of the other. Until he didn't.

"Hold on." Zach slipped off and retrieved his crutch from the holster he and Ryman had contrived.

"The track has disappeared," she groaned.

"Not entirely. It is merely flooded for a way." He pointed forward and off to the right where the track could be clearly seen above the marsh.

The rain, which had been slowing all day had dwindled to an intermittent drizzle over the marsh, but the waters ran high. "There's no way to see how it meanders over there!" Her heart sank to her half boots.

Zach, leaning on the crutch and grimacing, didn't answer. She suspected that the ride astride, cramped behind her, bedeviled his leg. When he stepped into the flood where the road disappeared, she held her breath, but he surprised her by taking the crutch from under his shoulder and tamping it in front of him.

"Give me the reins," he said, reaching back.

"What—"

"Trust me and this horse." He took the reins and led Algernon, testing the way in front with his crutch every few steps. With every one, she held her breath in terror, expecting him to sink into the marsh. Zach, unperplexed and utterly confident, pushed forward, and her admiration grew with every step. She could never have done this alone.

As if in blessing, the rain stopped entirely just as they came up on the clear track and a momentary dizziness shook Patience, faint with relief. Two strong hands grasped her waist, pulling her off the horse. She slid down his hard body and sank into his arms. He held her momentarily before moving mere inches away while he searched her face. Tender fingers cupped her cheek. "We're safe."

She caught her lower lip between her teeth to keep them from chattering and nodded. It took all her strength and the tattered remnants of her self-control to keep from wrapping her arms around him and clinging to the safety he offered. "But we've seen no sign of Norb, and we have miles to go."

They stood for a while next to the sturdy animal that carried them this far, stretching their legs and refreshing themselves with cheese and bread from The Queen's Barque. The silence became uncomfortable eventually.

"Tell me about Zachary Newell. You have my entire sad story, but I know little about you."

"There's little enough to know, but I'll tell you a bit while we ride. First we need to get going." He returned the crutch to its holster, rolled up the oilcloth, and fastened the saddle bag. "Hold Algernon steady while I mount."

She stood at the animal's head running a soothing hand down his neck, wondering how a man with half a leg missing and no mounting block would manage the thing. She needn't have worried. He went around to the left and gripped the saddle with his graceful fingers, so tender in his touch, but strong when he seized the saddle. He pulled himself up, muscled shoulders rippling beneath his jacket, until his right foot took hold in the stirrup, and threw his left leg, stiff and wooden, over the horse's back.

He grinned and reached a hand to her, pulling her up in front of him with perfect ease. He anchored her against his chest; with no need for their oilcloth, he kept the reins and urged the horse forward. "Now you know a little more about me. Some things can't be managed gracefully," he said. "What else would you like to know."

Everything.

She let her head sink back against his shoulder, and closed her eyes prepared to listen.

Thank God for her questions. The woman's body nestled so close to Zach's made him cross-eyed with longing, yearning for a woman he'd resolved to keep at arm's length, one too far above him for any honorable relationship and too honorable for any other kind.

"My father was a printer, a freeman of Rumsford." He couldn't keep pride from his voice. They'd owned their business and the building that housed it, he explained. It belonged to his brother now. Still, she must see the great distance between a printer's son and the Earl of Montour.

"We lived above it. My brother and I shared in the attic—a great privilege that, to have a place of our own."

"Older or younger?"

"Jeremiah is younger."

"Yet he has your father's place."

Perceptive baggage. "Aye. I had the army career," he said, pleased to keep the bitterness from his voice. His injury and unplanned separation weren't his brother's fault. "I was meant to have a share, they told me. Jer is paying me back a bit when he can." *Rarely.* Resentment and jealousy on the other hand belonged entirely to Jeremiah; Zach did his best to avoid threatening the man's snug life. He'd stayed away completely after Jer rejected one too many friendly overtures.

"And you work for your uncle?" she asked. "Are you likely to take his place in time?"

"Merciful angels, no. He has three sons to squabble over it—and I wouldn't want it."

"What do you want then, Zachary Newell?"

He clamped his mouth shut over the dreams, some long-standing and practical, some more recent and hopelessly inappropriate. "For now, I want to stay dry," he muttered.

She seemed to take the hint that he didn't wish to share any more than that, and they rode in silence for a while before she tried again. "No sisters?"

He embraced the change of subject fervently. "One that made it to adulthood. Abigail is the oldest of us all, married to Ralph, a haberdasher who does well enough in business and is good to her. They have two rambunctious boys and three little ladies who know how to wrap uncles around their dainty fingers."

"You're close to them." It wasn't a question.

"They mean the world. Uncle Fred is kind to me in his way, but Abigail is family. I visit whenever I can." He launched into stories of family dinners, children's shenanigans, and his sister's charities. He spoke until he ran out of steam. "She's a good woman. I admire her."

He breathed deeply, turning his gaze upward. "Look, Patience, the clouds are parting. Dare we hope for the angels coming in glory?" he teased.

"I'll settle for sunshine if it would only stay for several days," she replied, tipping her head back. The movement put her head in the hollow of his shoulder; he savored the fit, content for long moments as they rode along.

Patience straightened up sooner than he liked and said, "You never answered my question."

"Which question?" he asked, though he knew where she was going. *Persistent baggage, too.*

"I got the impression you live above your uncle's carriage house, rather like you do at The Queen's Barque. Are you content with that? What do you want from life?"

Home and family. You. He dared not say either answer. He gave her the practical one instead. "I want to be a shopkeeper."

She bounced up sending a jolt of desire through his genitals. He grit his teeth against it.

"Shopkeeper—with a home above it?" she asked. "What sort?" She sounded genuinely interested. *Can't the fool woman see that a shopkeeper is so far below an earl's niece he has no business in intimate conversation with her? Much less riding along with her nestled up against parts of him where she shouldn't be.*

"Here's the full truth: I want to open a bookstore. I want to own, read, sell, and deal in books and more books."

Her laughter filled the air with music. "I ought to have guessed. I've never met a man as in love with reading as you are."

Zach very much feared he was falling in love with the woman who shared the horse and his most intimate thoughts.

"Is that why you live above the stables? To save money?" She cut to the truth again.

"That is exactly why. I save every penny I make from every trip I take; I add it to what little I left the army with and what little my brother remembers to send me. I have a nice nest egg."

"How close are you?"

"That depends on where I settle. Rents and properties in Rumford aren't as high as London, but much higher than Fenwick." He wanted to kick himself. He didn't want to tell her he'd been discussing Fenwick on Sea with Brewster, who had half convinced him the town was on the rise and he'd do well to open up before prices rose.

He was saved an embarrassing explanation when she pointed excitedly. "The road! We're almost out of the marshes."

So they were. "How far to the school once we reach the road?"

"A few miles. Not long." She sank back, deflated. "We've seen no sign of Norb. I thought we'd catch up with him before this."

So had Zach when they departed. But by the time they crossed half the flooded track he knew they'd missed something—that or the boy didn't come this way. He prayed Norb would be found hiding somewhere in Fenwick, too frightened to go on and too ashamed to come back. He kept his thoughts to himself. "Perhaps he made it to the school. We'll know soon enough."

His doubts and fears warred with a need to protect and reassure—and with a yearning to get a look at this Academy of hers.

CHAPTER 9

I t took Algernon another hour to plod his way home even after they reached the road. By the time they arrived at the gate, clouds had dissipated completely and the afternoon sun shone golden light on the sign over the entrance, *The Academy for the Formation of Young Gentlemen.*

Gazing at her beloved school, Patience wondered how it appeared to the man behind her. Did he see the carefully tended grounds or the peeling paint? She had no time to ponder the questions; she pushed herself off the horse before he could dismount and ran down the lane toward the house shouting for Norb. There was no response.

He caught her at the kitchen door. "Wait for me. You don't know what damage has occurred. Let me see to Algernon and I'll go with you."

"Yes, he's been a hero. Do see to him, and check the barn. I'll be careful." She didn't wait for the objection she saw coming. She flew through the kitchen calling the boy's name. There was no answer. Nor did she find him in the classroom or the front parlor, the walls of which showed water damage. She didn't have time to study it carefully, she took the stairs two at a time.

She gave her room a quick glance, but of course he wasn't there.

She flung open the door to the boys' dormitory and stopped, her heart pounding and her stomach threatening to rebel.

"Patience!" Zach's voice, somewhere in the house, startled Patience from her stupor.

"I'm up here." She remained riveted, staring into the room, and up at the sky where the roof should be. The damage, beyond her ability to fix and her financial means if she tried, left her dumbfounded.

"Look what— Ah. I see." Zach came up next to her. "It's a miracle none of them were injured." The largest beam had come down between Stump's and Walter's beds, but splinters of wood were scattered everywhere. Mattresses and quilts had sponged up much of the storm's wrath, but, where water once pooled on the floors, wide damp stains spread in every direction.

"What is beneath us?" he asked.

"The front parlor. I only glanced, but it's water damaged."

"We need to cover the roof before it rains again."

She stared at spreading stains, the ruined roof, and her boys' belongings, while waves of discouragement crushed her under the immensity of it all. She couldn't look at him until he nudged her shoulder.

"Look what I found," he said, calling her attention from the mess. He held up a wiggling little body.

"Hercules!"

"Hungry, half drowned, and weak, but alive and grateful to see us." The puppy licked his finger as if to agree with his assessment.

"Was Norb—"

"No sign of that rascal. He hasn't been here. If he had, Hercules wouldn't have been hiding in the straw in George's pen."

"Oh God! We need to retrace our steps."

"We can't. Your milk goat is fine, by the way, but in need of milking," he said nuzzling Herc's nose with his.

"We have to! Norb—"

Zach straightened up. "Think for a moment. You said yourself we saw no sign of him on the road, no sign of anyone slipping off the track into the marsh, and no sign of anyone being here. Have you considered that he may have never left Fenwick? That he hid when he realized he couldn't make it and became too afraid to slink back to the Queen's Barque?"

Hope stirred in her heart. "He may be there when we go back." She said it as much to convince herself as to convince him. She'd have no peace until she had Norb under her care. "We must go back immediately. He'll need me and the boys will as well."

"Yes, but not tonight. The sun is already low in the sky. We can't risk traveling across that track in the dark no matter how able Algernon is. Tomorrow, we'll travel in full sun and hope the water will have receded a bit more."

He thrust Hercules into her arms and turned her gently to the stairs. "Let's see what we can find for this fellow," he said.

Herc appeared remarkably fit but undoubtedly hungry. *At least I can care for one of God's creatures... But Zach is distracting me, isn't he?* Another alarm exploded into her maelstrom of thoughts. She spun on the man beside her.

"I can't stay here with you overnight! That would ..." She bit down hard on her lower lip, and breathed deeply to collect herself. "I wouldn't care for myself. I'm far past a marriageable age already. But my reputation is fragile, and the school could be put in jeopardy. That I couldn't bear."

Eyes the color of rain, gray-blue and stormy with emotions she couldn't identify, bore into hers. The scattering of gold flecks in them, and the lines life carved in the corners, held her in fascination.

"You can trust me," he said, the deep timbre of his voice vibrating with determination. "But we must stay. The rest is a problem for tomorrow."

Nothing changed, and yet, at the sound of his voice, everything had. She trusted him—just as she always had—and they would find a way.

⚜

'Far past a marriageable age...' Is the woman mad? How old can she be? And why haven't a dozen men fallen at her feet with proposals?

The sway of her derriere held him transfixed as he followed her down the stairs. He let the pleasure of physical attraction, familiar and ordinary, if inappropriate, settle in. Perhaps it would drive out the fascination that gripped him. *Not for you, Zachary Newell.* The thought had become a chant in his heart.

By the time they reached the kitchen, he feared his desire had become all too obvious. He swept past her to the door. "See what you can find for the little fellow—and perhaps for a ravenous coachman— I'll see to the animals."

"Take the milk bucket," she called, handing it to him.

He almost ran out the door.

Ravenous, Zach? Couldn't you have found a better word, a less suggestive word, a calmer word? He let work distract him from the woman waiting in the kitchen.

Algernon, content in his accustomed stall, happily munching on feed, accepted his ministrations with little more than the flick of an ear. Toweled and brushed, the beast almost sighed when Zach covered him and ran a soothing hand along his neck. "You're a heroic fellow for a gentleman of your late years, Algernon. Well done, sir."

George had more dignity. She stood for milking calmly enough before nipping his arm as if to say, "You took long enough to see to my needs, Worthless Human," and trundling off to butt the gate with her head. Zach led her to a fenced paddock with a rope and left her cropping the grass greedily.

"Did you check the chickens?" Darts of the desire he had been trying to suppress shot through him at the sound of Patience's voice.

He leaned both elbows on the fence and kept his back to her. "You have chickens?" he asked over his shoulder.

"Behind the barn. Follow me."

He did so gladly, happy with the view and grateful she wasn't facing him. *This has to stop, Newell. You promised she could trust you. Doesn't that extend to a ban on ogling her person?* Perhaps not. After an interminable day with her nestled between his thighs, he thought he deserved to ogle. *But no more than that.*

She stopped abruptly, arms out, and he almost ran into her. "The coop is intact! I feared the feathered dears might have been blown clear to Yarmouth." She spun around, joy radiating from her expressive face like sunbeams.

"It's leeward of the barn," he mumbled, turning with a pounding heart to a structure that also survived but less well. "So did that tool shed, but not as well."

She laughed. "The shed looked like that before the storm! I'm surprised it didn't fall in." She nipped into the chicken coop, and Zach walked over to inspect the rickety tool shed.

He listened with half an ear and most of his heart to her announcing to the chickens that their feed had remained dry, cooing over each one, calling each by name. He forced his thoughts to the structure in front of him.

The tool shed had been built from four frames, each nailed in a piece, and then put together. He suspected the entire structure had been built by the boys who got it almost but not quite right. While the shed leaned precariously, three of the four major pieces appeared solid. A door cut into the fourth disrupted the integrity of the piece, bringing both rot and collapse.

An idea took root. "Patience, I could—" His jaw dropped when he turned. The woman who had been cooing over her birds had one by the neck.

She shrugged. "Dinner. We need a good one. And Bertha hasn't been laying for months." She started for the house, then glanced at him over her shoulder. "Don't forget the milk bucket."

Zach leaned against the shed, but it swayed and he stood upright, laughter overtaking him. *Lush and desirable. Brilliant and nurturing. Resilient and unpredictable.* He knew then that he had tumbled completely in love—passionate, all-consuming, and wholly impossible love.

CHAPTER 10

P atience watched the man at work; she'd come out to call him to supper, but the sight of him drove her objective into a ditch. He'd removed his coat and loosened the maroon and indigo scarf he'd worn around his neck all day. His linen shirt, damp and dirty from his labors, clung to his shoulders, muscles flexing beneath the fabric. The sight beguiled her almost as much as his honey brown hair glowing in the last meager light of the setting sun.

She blinked to clear her head. *Speak up before he catches you drooling, you ninny.* "Mr. Newell—dinner is ready." He'd been Zach all day. He'd been close as her own gown all day. He'd been too close all day. His smile when he looked up from his work left her knees week. *This will not do, Patience. Endure the night and let this good man get back to his own life.*

The smile disappeared as if he brought a shade down over it. Patience wondered if he struggled with the same uneasy but consuming awareness she did. The thought excited her; his words didn't.

"Will it keep? If I can finish this much, I can get started early tomorrow so we can be on our way."

This much? It took her a minute to remember why he pulled down her shed. *He wants to patch the roof before we go.* He had told her he thought he could pull the walls of the shed up using a pulley he found in the barn. She thought that possibility dubious, given his injury, but left him his pride, determined to offer aid in the morning if she had to.

"Miss Patience? Do you mind? I can come now if you prefer."

"It will keep. You finish here. I'll heat water; you'll want to wash up." She thought for a moment, and an image brought fire creeping up her neck. "Will you want a bath?"

He went perfectly still. "No," he choked out. He hesitated before going on. "I'll manage—but dirty as I am, I best wash up outside."

It was dark before he came to the door, coat over one arm, and picked up the pan of water she had kept warm while she waited.

"You'll need the lantern," she said. "I can hold it for you."

He let her follow him out, but he took the lantern from her as soon as he set the pan of water on the table that she used for drying herbs just outside the kitchen door. He hung the light on a hook above the table, and reached one hand to unfasten his shirt only to pause. "I'll manage," he said, watching until she left him.

Patience leaned against the closed kitchen door for a moment before going about her preparations. *I'll manage.* He'd said it twice. She suspected Zachary Newell managed most hurdles that came his way. She warmed chicken and vegetables while she waited, heart beating in a rhythm she didn't recognize. She set places for them on the battered kitchen table. There seemed no point in heating up the other rooms.

They ate in silence, bathed in the lantern's glow and firelight. Patience tried to focus on her dinner, but her eyes kept flickering toward the man across the table, studying his face as if it were the map to El Dorado. Smooth planes. Prominent cheek bones. Firm chin. Furrows in the corners of his eyes—hard earned, she had no doubt. Where lanternlight struck his right side, strands of silver gleamed among the brown hair that cascaded to his chin and over his collar. She wondered how old he was.

His face came up abruptly. "Thirty-two."

Oh God, did I say that out loud? One hand covered her mouth. She gulped down the thickness in her throat. "I'm so sorry," she said when she could speak. "That was unforgivably rude."

One side of his mouth quirked up adorably. "We've been traveling companions. Curiosity is normal. How old is *'far past a marriageable age?'*"

Patience rose to collect the dishes. "Old enough."

He grinned and handed her his plate. "Fair is fair, Patience. How old?"

"Twenty-seven, ten years past most girls' come out, not that I had one anyway."

"Why not?"

"No money. No one to sponsor me. No interest! Would you like some tea?"

He looked skeptical about her lack of interest, but he allowed the change of subject, politely requesting tea, picking up a chair, and pulling it toward the hearth. She joined him moments later.

"What do you normally do of an evening?" she asked. As a question, it trod a line between familiar and safe.

"I have two sorts of evenings. On some I fall into bed too exhausted to think after supper. On others I read."

"Do you not socialize?" That one started to cross the line. *Why don't you ask him if he has a lover and be done with it?*

"Rarely. I visit my sister. I occasionally attend a lecture or chorale at church."

Alone? Questions crowded in one after another, each one leading to dangerous ground. She stared into her tea.

"And you?"

Her head bobbed up. "With a half a dozen boarders? Once a month or so, a farmer's wife relieves me so I can tutor and attend the Brewsters' meetings at The Queen's Barque."

His direct gaze intensified and, for a moment, she thought he might ask her a question. If he had one, he thought better of it and sipped his tea.

Hercules woke up from the towel she had placed by the hearth. He trundled over to lap up more milk. They both watched him wander back, where he rubbed against Zach's boots. He set his tea aside, picked up the tiny creature, and began to pet him, long fingers caressing the puppy's back and rubbing his ears. Patience had never envied a dog before; she did now.

Her eyes met Zach's for a long moment before he looked away first. "Norb will be pleased when we bring this wanderer to the inn. What are you going to say to him?"

"After I get done hugging him fiercely, I will bring down the wrath of *The Academy for the Formation of Young Gentlemen* on him."

Laughter erupted from the man across from her. "A terrible fate indeed," he said between guffaws. He slowly grabbed on to control. "What exactly does that wrath include?" he asked, gulping air when he was able.

Patience raised her chin, indignation stiffening her back. "He won't see pudding at dinner for a very long time."

His brows shot up and she rushed on before he convulsed again. "But he'll be more upset to miss our reading times after supper. Banishment to write his arithmetic tables is a fate worse than death."

Zach's mouth quirked up on one side, and he nodded in appreciation, still amused. "A horrible fate indeed."

"Though Stump would argue that the worst is being assigned to privy-cleaning duty every Saturday for a month."

He gasped in mock indignation. "Miss Abney, you are a cruel woman!"

A smile spread across her face and through her heart. "Aren't I just evil? What did they do to disobedient boys at the Cranford School?"

He sobered, but answered. "I was a day student, so cleaning duties —privy or otherwise—didn't apply. I did feel the bite of a hickory switch more than once. It didn't do any damage and my behavior was the better for it."

A hickory switch was miles from Bartram's weapon, but Patience loathed physical punishment, certain it did more harm than good. He must have seen something in her face, because he went on. "A switch, not a staff. At Cranford, punishment was proportional to the offense and meted out fairly. Not all headmasters are as sadistic as the one you encountered at Spraggins. A boy walked away uninjured, with his dignity intact."

"You think I should be harder on the boys?"

"Your job is to civilize the little savages. I think you should use what works best to accomplish that and to teach them to make good decisions. From what I've seen of them, you do that."

The approval she read in his face warmed Patience down to her toes, but she could think of nothing else to say. They sat for a while, Patience sipping tea, Zach stroking the blissful puppy.

Every fiber of her being vibrated with awareness of him close, compelling, completely male, and she couldn't think what to do next. It had been much too long since she enjoyed a man's company. Even then, Charles Remington's attentions tended to wander during their brief courtship, even as he urged her to marry him. When Zach looked at her, she felt like the center of his universe.

Foolish as that was, she allowed his warm regard to inundate her as thoroughly as the sea washed over the marshes. *Just for a moment. Just for now. Just for tonight.*

❦

If I don't move, perhaps this dream will become real. Zach knew the thought for the absurdity it was, but he wished... *So much. To own such a hearth, such an evening every night, such a woman to share it with.*

Domestic dreams had come on him occasionally before, usually after visiting his sister when the loneliness closed in. On nights like this, his other goals—his determination to own a business of his own, his desire to manage a bookstore, his need for success—paled. The dream of family lay under all the rest.

Three days with a troop of rowdies and their exquisite teacher brought needs to the surface—chief among them a place of his own and a good woman to share it with. Impossible dreams tied his thoughts in knots; dreams, dark and as fiery as warm rum, heated his hopes. Zachary Newell was tired of being alone and that was the truth.

Held by light from the hearth and the company that shared it, he didn't wish for a place of his own, he ached for it. He ached for the woman who sat with him in perfect harmony. Desire had bedeviled him all day, until it boiled in his entire body as they sat. He knew better than to act on it. If he acted on the fantasies dancing in his head, he would destroy the very thing he craved. Shared purpose, shared concerns, shared peace drew them together, creating this cocoon of serenity. He intended to savor it.

He forced his unruly thoughts to other things—the roof, the animals, the journey back to Fenwick on Sea—only to run into a ditch when he recalled the trouble that beckoned them. If folks knew Patience spent the night with a man—any man—her reputation would be in shreds and her school in jeopardy. When they realized her companion was a common coachman, it would be worse.

If he were a gentleman, he would embrace the obvious solution. He wasn't. Zach had never envied his so-called betters, but he wasn't a fool. Class mattered. The army taught him that as it taught little else. A coachman did not offer for the niece of an earl. It wasn't done. Marriage to him would make Patience's situation worse not better. Despair nibbled at the edge of his pleasure in the moment. He brushed it aside; it would keep for another day.

He might have sat there all night neither retreating nor acting, but spreading damp on his knee startled him to attention. He took the puppy by the scruff of the neck to finish his business outside while Patience covered her apologies with a hand over her laughing mouth.

He dawdled outside, fetching George who meekly went to her place in the barn, before he scooped up Hercules and carried him in.

"There's a reason dogs don't belong in the house," he said without preamble. She turned from cleaning up their dishes with a spoon in one hand to smile, a sight so adorable it reminded him of his decision. "Herc and I will bunk down in the barn."

Consternation wiped the smile away followed by a rush of expressions so varied and so clear to see that he almost laughed. *Foolish woman ought to be relieved instead of confused.*

For one exultant moment, he realized she wanted him—not just his presence in the house, but him. He recognized it in her parted lips, in her darkened eyes, in the yearning in her expression. He recalled the confusion, and his good sense reasserted itself. "I've had worse quarters," he said.

"There's no need! There's an empty room in the attic. It may be dry. If it is, I can have it ready in a moment."

The silken rope of awareness that tied Patience to Zach Newell drew her to him now, until she stood so close that she could feel the heat from his body, smell the scent of male and hardy soap on him. She opened her mouth to beg him to stay, and closed it abruptly.

"Hercules can stay in the kitchen," she said instead, peering down at the little creature he held like a shield between them with one arm. She glanced up and saw it then, in the pupils of his eyes, wide and dark, and the tightness around his mouth. This man desired her.

Patience understood the look of desire. She had seen it in Charles when he eyed her, and more often when he leered at other women. She'd been right to push that wretch away until he tired of her, deciding her uncle's influence wasn't worth it. This was different, oh so very different, because she also saw respect, honor, restraint.

She reached a trembling hand to his cheek. "No one will know where you sleep, Zach. Retreating to the barn won't help my reputation. You may as well—" She wasn't sure what she meant to say he may as well do. She may have seen desire in others, but she had never before known the force of it in herself, the longing for passion that throbbed through her. It rattled her. Before she could finish, he turned his head to kiss her fingers, and smiled back at her.

"I would know," he whispered. He reached over with one hand to tuck an errant curl behind her ear. "Tomorrow will come, and we'll face what needs faced. I won't add to it."

He turned and left her there, more alone than she had ever been in her beloved home.

CHAPTER 11

George and Algernon made poor company. Zach reminded himself several times in the long night about *worse quarters*. The straw bedding was soft enough, and the vermin few. The blanket Patience ran out to give him provided a kind of warmth; her departure left him chilled at his core. He slept little.

As soon as the darkest night faded to gray, he rolled out and strapped on the wooden prosthetic, determined to cover the school's roof and still get Patience back to Fenwick on Sea by nightfall. He couldn't endure another night here, alone with her but not able to touch her.

He pulled the ladder he'd found over to the side of the house where the kitchen jutted out. He would have to pull the ladder up onto the kitchen to reach the higher roof. Staring up at it, his scheme began to feel even more crack-brained than when he conceived it, but he was determined to try. Preventing further damage to *The Academy for the Formation of Young Gentlemen* had become a fierce need in him, the one need he could act on.

A half hour later the sun had peeked out over the horizon, and Zach had dragged the third and last wall of the shed over to the house.

He peered up again, lost in gloom. He would have to ask her help, no matter what he tried.

"What the De'il do you think you're doing?"

An odd little man had come up behind him. Short and stocky with the hard muscles of a laborer, he had the appearance of a farmer—or a farmer's ox—and he brandished a spade in a manner intended to be threatening.

"Who are you?" Zach demanded, groaning inwardly. The last thing Patience needed was someone she knew seeing a man here with her.

"Miss Patience's friend. What have you done w'th'lass? She has more than them lads to protect her."

"I can't tell you how glad I am to hear it," Zach told him. "She and the boys evacuated to The Queen's Barque when the roof caved in."

The man's widened eyes flipped up toward the roof and he grumbled a muffled curse. "Told her it needed done. Hoped it would hold longer." He studied the boards against the house. "What're you doing with our shed?"

Before Zach could answer Patience came out the kitchen door wiping her hands on a towel. "Banks! I'm so happy to see you well. Did you and Mrs. Banks weather the storm safely?"

Banks peered up at Zach. "I thought you said she were at the inn."

"I was. We—did he tell you the roof caved in? We spent the weekend in Fenwick on Sea, but our Norb disappeared. We thought he'd come here after a missing puppy, but he isn't here."

Zach cursed silently. As she appeared at first light, it must be obvious to anyone they had been here the night before. He tried to glare some discretion into her, but she babbled on while Banks's disapproving frown deepened.

"Sergeant Newell kindly escorted me and thank God he did. The coast road is out above Morphew Manor, and we had to come through the marsh. The water's so high, I don't think I could have managed it alone."

You're babbling, Patience. The less said the better. Banks glared at Zach, but turned up a smile to face Patience. "Good you're here safely, Miss Patience. I came this morning myself to see how the school fared. I'm that sorry to hear about our roof. I was hoping we'd get another year from it." He shook his head. "I'll take a look at 'er, but I fear it'll be beyond me. You'll need to hire a roofer."

"I know. I've known since it happened, though where I'll find funds to fix it is beyond my ken at the moment."

Her dejection tore Zach to shreds. He leaned his head on his arm where it gripped the top of one of the sad pieces of shed he had to work with. "We'll have to worry about that after we get you back to Fenwick," he said. "For now, this will have to do."

She left them after they refused her offer of eggs and fritters, Banks claiming he'd already eaten and Zach insisting he'd have it later.

The little farmer listened and nodded agreement while Zach explained his plan to pull the ladder up onto the kitchen, climb to the top, and attach the pulley to the eaves. Zach put the loop of rope over his head and one shoulder and started to climb.

"You were here all night."

Zach stilled half way to the kitchen roof; he didn't turn. "I was, and, before you ask, I slept in the barn." He pulled himself over and reached down to pull up the ladder. Banks, sober and stern, peered directly up at him.

"It won't matter where you sleep. Folks will talk."

"Not if you don't." Zach pulled the ladder up while Banks held it steady.

"She's not some shopkeeper's daughter," the man called from below. "Her lot expect a man to do right by a lady's reputation."

Visions of his sister shot through Zach on a wave of fury. *So does my lot.* He clamped his jaw tight against an outburst, and breathed deeply for control. "I'm a shopkeeper's son, Mr. Banks, and the lady's reputation matters to me too."

Work put a stop to the issue; the two men manhandled the three large pieces to the roof with muscle and cunning. Zach pulled the first toward the gaping hole, crawling carefully and testing the integrity of the remaining roof as he went.

A whistle behind him caused Zach to jerk sidewise, his heart pounding. He had no idea how Banks managed to get up on the kitchen roof. Zach hadn't lowered the ladder for him.

"It's a bad 'un. She's in trouble for certain."

Zach accepted the man's help without comment. "Pity about this," Banks said. "This school's been a blessing to the neighborhood."

"It's a blessing to those boys," Zach responded.

They dragged the next set of boards over. "It would be a pity if folks shunned her over this," Banks went on.

Zach stopped the work and leaned up on one elbow breathing heavily. "We're in agreement on that. I don't think an alliance with a half-crippled coachman will enhance her standing any, however."

"Half crippled?" Banks snorted glancing at Zach's rigid ankle. "You scrambled up this roof right enough."

"Her cousin would have fits if a shopkeeper dared—"

"That earl? He don't give a damn what Miss Patience does. That's why she needs friends to protect her interest." Banks stuck up his chin to make sure Zach understood she had friends. "There are harpies everywhere, Newell. Fenwick was no different even before they took to calling it 'on Sea' and putting on airs. Folks will notice. Mark my words."

"Hand me those nails."

Banks did.

"I don't know how I would have managed if you hadn't come, Banks." Zach said through the nails he held in his teeth. He took to hammering. Loudly.

The wooden panels pried from the shed covered the hole and managed some overlap, to Zach's relief. He tossed the hammer and pulley to the barnyard and crawled aside so Banks could go down the ladder first. He waited patiently while the older man started down. He estimated it was already mid-morning, and he had some time before he had to get them on their way.

"She's a good woman." The persistent little farmer glared up with a stubborn set to his chin.

"No one knows that better than I do, Banks." Zach's long cold night resulted from his assurance on that point.

Banks didn't move. "Can you read?"

Zach started to laugh. He laughed so hard he fell back onto the roof tiles.

"What is so blasted funny?"

"Is that your only criteria for a suitor for Miss Abney? Literacy?"

"No, but it matters. Her boys need a man who reads."

It struck Zach then that Banks probably could not. "I read." He said, scrambling down after the man.

When he got to the ground Banks looked him up and down, studying his face, and then giving a sharp nod. "You'll do. Tell Miss Patience I'll look in every day now the storm's gone."

With that odd statement he disappeared.

CHAPTER 12

P atience saw Banks say something to Zach and leave. "That was an
odd look. What did he say to you?"

Zach took the wet cloth she offered without looking at her directly
and wiped his hands. "Nothing of import. Go upstairs and check your
roof. I'll be in for those eggs in a bit."

She did, but didn't linger. When she peered up at the ceiling, she
saw no daylight. The boards weren't watertight, but they would do for
now. In a few hours Zach had protected her school from additional
damage, but the roof wasn't her most immediate problem. What on
earth, she wondered, was she to do about the man who worked this
small miracle?

By the time she whipped up a fresh batch of fritters and coddled
some eggs, Zach led Algernon, saddled and ready, out into the yard. He
went back and brought out a bucket of milk, Herc hopping at his
heels, and came into the kitchen without meeting her eyes.

He murmured his thanks and ate in silence so thick Patience
thought she could brush it aside with a hand; all the while, he stared at
his plate and refused to look at her. When she couldn't stand it any
longer, words burst out. "What did Banks say?"

"Nothing we don't know. If he guessed we've been here overnight, other folks will too. He reminded me there are gossips everywhere, even Fenwick on Sea."

It was Patience's turn to pull away. The last thing she wanted was this man forced by loose talk to make her an offer he didn't intend. She cleared the dishes, fussing about the cleaning up, her back to him. "Fenwick won't care. What with the storm and all, the story won't even matter."

"Fenwick might not care—Banks believes otherwise—but the storm brought other verbal vultures to The Queen's Barque as you already know. They will delight in carrying the subject at least as far as your cousin's social circle."

She spun back toward the table. "Horace? He won't care. At least —" she caught her lower lip between her teeth.

"What?" He stood and faced her.

"I don't actually know how he would react if his cronies took the story up. He ignores me, but—" She shrugged.

"Your school matters, Patience," he said, his husky voice taking her breath away.

Standing as close as they were, the intensity of his gaze drew her. His breathing came fast. Her body leaned the slightest toward him before she caught herself and put up a hand. "Don't even think about any obligation you might feel, Zachary Newell. You did me a favor coming here."

His face in the grip of intense emotion she couldn't name, he took a step back. "I'll check the barn one last time. Be ready to go."

Patience groaned. Her heart fell, forcing her to admit she had hoped for a declaration—of affection, of—she refused to think farther than that. She grabbed up the few things she meant to take in a sack, including a jug of milk for Hercules. A sound at the door drew her attention; he had come back and stood holding the door jamb with both hands.

Before she could speak, he crossed the room and pulled her into a crushing embrace, taking her mouth with his until her knees failed and she had only his embrace to rely on.

Insanity born of hope. Zach could think of no other explanation for his behavior. When she responded to his kiss with sweet passion, coherent thought eluded him. One dainty hand slid up his neck and into his hair as if to pull him closer. The other clung to his shirt. He pulled his mouth away forcing himself to gentle the kiss, only to nibble the corner of her mouth and kiss his way across her cheek to her ear.

She groaned and followed his lead, the difference in their height enabling her to kiss his neck just above his collar. An urge to tear his shirt off to give her access shook him, bringing him to his senses. He removed the hand that had somehow migrated to her round little behind and the one around her back anchoring her to him, gripping her by her upper arms instead.

He held her away, but not far, their mouths still inches apart.

"A gentleman would have offered for you first thing this morning, before Banks even arrived. This display of behavior—"

"Are you saying you aren't a gentleman, Zach?" She wrinkled up her nose, teasing him adorably.

His laugh tasted bitter on his tongue. "I'm no man of leisure, wealth or title. Isn't that the definition of a gentleman?"

"If behavior matters, you're more gentleman than all the social climbing fops who thought to pursue my uncle's favor by courting me."

That startled him. It cooled his heated blood like an ice bath. "Is that what happened? Why you aren't married?"

She nodded shyly, dipping her forehead to his chest. "It was long ago."

"Fools the lot of them," he muttered, kissing the top of her head. "Come sit. We need to speak rationally, and I can't with you this close."

She gazed up at him with dazzled eyes.

He had to kiss her again. "See what I mean?" he asked against her lips.

He put the table between them, determined to have that rational talk. "You will have to face down gossips, and this school matters."

She opened her mouth and closed it again.

"You can't argue that point, can you?" he went on. "I know what an education does for a boy, and I've seen how well you do it. The school matters. I'm not without means. I have enough put away to repair that roof and upgrade this crumbling school of yours."

She gasped. "No! Your dreams—"

"Fenwick needs a bookstore. Brewster offered space in his lobby for a stall and a room to sleep in in exchange for work. I have inventory—didn't I tell you my room in Rumford was full? I may not have mentioned that the piles are floor to ceiling, two deep, along all the walls. It would be a start. Staying at the inn, I could court you properly." He felt himself color and prayed she didn't notice.

"You've thought this through," she said, eyes wide in astonishment. She leaned across the table. "You spoke to Brewster about it before we came?"

"Aye, he convinced me Fenwick on Sea has a future."

"You're willing to marry me?" The words were barely a whisper.

"Willing? I had nothing else to do all night but dream of it, lying there wanting you, unable to sleep."

Joy unfurled in her eyes and the upturn of her mouth. "You want me," she said with a spreading grin. "You're not offering out of obligation."

"There's every obligation, Patience, but I take it joyfully." He grinned back. "Besides, if we marry, I won't have to stay at The Queen's Barque. When I live here, I can open a bookstore in the small parlor—and a library for the boys—until we can manage a store in town."

"God knows, you aren't asking for my hand out of greed—I bring you nothing but a shabby house and an entire army of troublesome boys."

"Your work will be my work."

What he saw in her eyes in response humbled him. He sobered then. "You've only known me for a few days, but I've come to love you, Patience. We could announce a betrothal, but take our time with a proper courtship, me living at the inn, until you are sure. My only concern is whether an offer from a coachman will bring you more disgrace than honor."

"For an educated man you speak a great deal of nonsense, Zachary

Newell. It may only have been a few days but I've quite tumbled into love with you. You could never disgrace me."

He gripped her hands and she squeezed his in silent assent. He swallowed the lump in his throat. "In that case, we had better get ourselves back to Fenwick before I prove you wrong."

She looked as if she would argue, but he reminded her they had to find Norb, transport Hercules, and get back to some worried boys. He didn't mention his own obligations to his passengers and his uncle, who deserved a proper resignation from him.

They traveled back along the track in full sunlight, Hercules nestled in a sling attached to the saddle. Zach's never-ending supply of ribald songs, his only defense against pulling her down to the track and making her his in the midst of the marsh, kept her laughing most of the way.

Patience didn't recall laughing so much in her entire life as she did while listening to Zach's songs and silly nonsense. His magnificent baritone kept her fears at bay even as he held her close. She sobered, however, when he pointed to the end of the track and reality intruded.

Algernon stepped eagerly onto the road, still muddy but less than it had been and much more solid than the track through the marsh.

"What if Norb isn't there?" she asked, not expecting an answer.

"Then we'll work with Brewster and Ryland on a search plan," he said, leaning in to kiss the top of her head. "We'll find him."

They were the words of a partner. Nothing in her past prepared her for the sensation of it. *Partner. Your work will be my work, he said—my boys, his boys.*

They rode into the stable yard, deserted in the late afternoon, and Zach urged Algernon to a stop. He slid down and reached up to help Patience dismount. She did. Straight into his waiting arms. He kissed her tenderly, brushed her hair back from her cheek, and smiled against her forehead when they heard Stump yell, "They're back."

Patience buried her face in his wooly waistcoat, "So much for discretion."

He pulled her close, kissed her again, and slid his hands down to take hers. "Look," he said, gesturing with a shake of his head. Six boys stood ten feet away, mouths agape.

"Norb!" Joy, consternation, and relief propelled her into the midst of them, where she grabbed Norb by the lapels, gave him a wee shake and pulled him into an embrace.

"Why are you crying?" the boy protested, trying to wriggle loose. "I'm fine."

She gripped both his arms. "Where have you been, young sir? You have much to account for!"

Before Norb could answer, Zach came to her side, a squirming ball of fur in his hands.

"Hercules!" Norb took the puppy, snuggling his nose into the furry back.

Zach took her hand and looked sternly at the boy. "You frightened Miss Patience and caused her to go off on a perilous mission." At *perilous mission* Norb glanced sheepishly at Patience and dropped his gaze to the dog.

"Sorry, Miss Patience," the lad murmured.

"You didn't answer my question," Patience said firmly.

Froggy pulled on her sleeve. "He were with my grandda, Miss Patience. Grandda found him in the marsh." He tugged and pointed.

They turned, still holding hands, to see old Mr. Morling standing with Brewster and Ryland. Mrs. Brewster, the cook and two of the maids stood nearby. Every one of them appeared to be staring at her hand joined with Zach Newell's. Worse, well-dressed guests, drawn by the disturbance, peered from the door and first floor windows.

Zach cleared his throat. She hoped he knew what to say because she had been struck dumb. Before he could, another man spoke.

"I take it we are to wish you happy." The familiar voice came from behind them, behind the boys. *When did the majors come out of the carriage house?* Absorbed in the boys—and the feeling of Zach's support and security—she hadn't noticed them.

They turned back as one to see Jamie Heyworth's cocky grin and Major Mallet's kind face. Zach lifted her hand and kissed it. "You may indeed wish us happy, Major. Miss Abney has honored me by agreeing to become my wife."

"Marry?" Boys began to talk at once, words climbing over questions, over exclamations.

"Easy lads, easy. First, the proper thing is to congratulate the lucky gentleman and wish the lady happy. Second, to answer your most pressing question, no. I'm not taking your Miss Patience away. I'm afraid you will have to endure my presence at *The Academy for the Formation of Young Gentlemen.*"

There was no room for more attention to Norb's behavior, because Patience was surrounded by her boys rushing to wish her happy as instructed. Zach let go of her to accept the majors' congratulations, leaving her with a peculiar feeling of being disconnected, but she was inundated with well-wishers among her friends from the inn.

Brewster insisted they all come to the tap room for a celebratory toast. Zach smiled down at her, "Are you at ease with all this fuss?"

"Perfectly," she said, taking his arm to let him lead her in. She glanced up to see Mrs. Fullerton, the housekeeper from Morphew Manor, sneering at her. When the woman realized she'd been caught, she flounced away from the window. *Your loss, you old witch. Run to my cousin with it. He's likely to toss you out.*

It was an hour before the celebration subsided enough for Patience to have a quiet moment at a table with old Mr. Morling. She loved the dear old man, and he, in turn, had been proud his grandson could attend her academy.

"I'd gone out to check my traps by my cottage early dawn Monday; still raining but the wind wasn't as fierce. Found the lad on the road a quarter mile up staring into the marsh looking like a scared rabbit. Couldn't find the track." The old man took him home until the rain stopped, when he brought the boy to the inn. By that time, Zach and Patience were well on their way across the marsh, and he didn't see them.

If there were raised eyebrows at the inn, the sight of their clasped hands and private looks reassured the locals. The others didn't matter, not to Patience, not to Zach.

One of the footmen interrupted the excitement soon after when he announced that a sleek sloop was sighted off the coast.

Patience saw the majors rise to their feet. "May I borrow that spy glass of yours, Brewster?" Major Mallet asked. He and Heyworth rushed after the footman to the vantage point on the floor above. She saw a well-dressed gentleman follow them.

Patience followed the crowd to the seashore where they watched the sloop lower a whaleboat into the churning sea. By the time the boat rowed in to Fenwick and a very correct naval officer in a starched uniform jumped out, saturating his perfectly polished boots, the majors had come down, crisply uniformed and followed by two other guests from the inn, the gentleman who had followed the majors, who turned out to be an earl bound for Brussels, and his sister. A footman brought up the rear with their luggage.

"I'm looking for Major Andrew Mallet and Major James Heyworth," the starched-up ensign called.

"You found them," Jamie Heyworth replied, as Mallet directed the footman to put their luggage in the boat. "How did Glenaire find us?"

The ensign grinned. "How does the Marble Marquess do anything? When you didn't turn up in Yarmouth as scheduled, he told the captain you'd be holed up from the storm somewhere snug. We guessed this place likely."

"We were indeed." Heyworth quickly explained the Earl of Hythe's need to get to Brussels and their offer of transportation. The ensign assisted the earl's sister into the whale boat and oversaw the loading of trunks while Heyworth turned to thank Brewster, and Mallet discreetly handed him more cash than required. The two of them approached Zach and Patience.

"It's been a pure pleasure, Sergeant Newell," Mallet said, shaking his hand. He handed Zach an envelope. "That will more than cover your uncle's expenses. The rest is a wedding present."

"Thank you, Major," Patience said, impulsively planting a kiss on his cheek.

"It has been my honor, sir," Zach told him. "You go take care of Boney once and for all."

"That we will," Mallet replied. Patience found his expression profoundly sad.

"Sorry we'll miss the wedding," Heyworth added jovially, giving Patience a peck on the cheek. "You two be good to one another." He strode off and clambered over the side of the whale boat.

The crowd watched the boat row out to the waiting sloop. "That doesn't look like any navy vessel," Brewster sighed. "Beauty of a thing."

"I was to deliver them to meet the Marquess of Glenaire's personal yacht," Zach replied, without taking his eyes from the sea. Patience felt his hand, long fingered and tender, slip up her back, caress the back of her neck, and go around her shoulder to pull her close.

His arm around her, her head on his shoulder, they stood together, gazing out to sea until the ship took sail and disappeared.

"Do you wish you were going with them?" she asked.

"I won't lie. Part of me wants to see the end of this thing. If we don't stop Napoleon now, we'll be at war until our boys are grandfathers." He turned to her then and cupped her cheek, "But I have more important things to see to; making you happy for the rest of our lives."

He kissed her then in the gentle wind to the sound of waves lapping the shore.

EPILOGUE

To Zach's immense relief Patience adamantly refused his offer of "a proper courtship." He didn't think he could have kept his resolution to keep his hands from her if the thing had gone on for more than the three weeks it took to call the banns.

Those weeks gave him enough time to return his uncle's rig, to share his joy with family, and to ship his belongings to Fenwick. Still, three weeks can feel interminable to an eager bridegroom. His wedding, or more to the point, wedding night, couldn't come soon enough to suit him.

Sun blessed their wedding day, enabling Zach to walk to Fenwick on Sea's ancient stone chapel side by side with Mr. Abney. Fenwick's own vicar, Barnabas Somerville, met them at the door. Though still weak from a bout of illness, Mr. Somerville beamed approvingly and showed them to the sacristy. There, Zach paced, waiting.

Zach's cousin Paul, the one likely to inherit the coaching business, joined him. Paul had come to stand up with him, and surprised Zach by filling one of his uncle's carriages with his sister Abigail, her husband Ralph, and their little ones. They brought a polite note of congratulations from his brother Jeremiah, which was more than he expected.

Every time Zach peeked out from the sacristy the church pews were a bit fuller. For a man perishing of loneliness a month before, he found himself awash in family and friends. Villagers and Academy parents filled the pews; some he recognized, others he expected to know eventually. Mr. and Mrs. Banks chatted with old Mr. Morling and a couple introduced to him as Walter's parents. Mrs. Fullerton and Alice, the cheeky little serving maid from the Queen's Barque, both came early, avidly watching the arrivals.

His sister waved from her place next to Ralph. Abney relatives, up for the day, sat next to them. Of the earl, there had been no sign. Zach found that a relief, but some folks appeared disappointed, Alice among them.

Brewster had pride of place behind Zach's family, the seat next to him empty. Zach suspected Brewster's wife assisted his bride. He would remember them all fondly someday, but at that moment he wanted only one person.

"What do you think is keeping her?" he demanded, rearranging his hair with a restless hand. Paul's knowing smirk didn't help his nerves, and neither did the assurance of both vicars that "the bride always comes eventually."

And then she did. Chords on the organ alerted them, and Zach came out to stand in front of the altar, Paul at his side and the vicars behind. Mrs. Brewster scurried down a side aisle to join her husband.

Sunlight shining through the open door gave the entrance a mystic glow, momentarily blinding him. Zach blinked. What had looked like a crowd of fairies proved to be, instead, children. His nieces, bubbling up with excitement, led the procession, industriously tossing flower petals. Behind them marched a troop of boys, Patience's boys, his boys, augmented by his nephews.

He had asked her who would give the bride away, her father being otherwise engaged, and ought to have guessed the answer. Patience, a vision in peach muslin, came toward him between Peter and Walter, them being the eldest. A woman might have rhapsodized over her dress and the flowers in her hair, but Zach had eyes only for her face. The love he saw there filled him to the marrow of his bones.

They said their vows in a circle of loved ones, and allowed themselves to be cheered the length of the village to the inn and universal celebration.

There comes a time at many weddings, when the celebration takes on a life of its own, and the bride and groom feel free to escape. Zach led Patience to the stable yard quietly, hoping to avoid notice.

"Where are we going? I arranged a room upstairs," she whispered.

A chestnut gelding, one Zach knew to possess a strong heart and good manners, his uncle's wedding gift, waited for them saddled and ready. He leaned down for a quick kiss. "This part is mine to arrange," he said.

Still clutching a bouquet of flowers, she stared up at him. "But my... things."

He patted the bags tied to the saddle. "Mrs. Brewster made certain you have all you need." He leaned in to whisper something the innkeeper's wife had let slip. "I hear it includes an interesting nightrail." Her ferocious blush tickled him so much it required a quick kiss.

He mounted using a block, but before he could pull her up with him, the doors burst open and the revelers flooded into the stable yard, led by yahooing boys. His beloved, her face an adorable shade of red, took his hand when he leaned down, and he pulled her up in front of him.

"Is he kidnapping her?" Froggie's deep voice demanded.

As they rode away, he heard one of his nieces reply, "No, silly. He looks like a knight and his lady," to general laughter.

"Where are you taking me?"

He had gone to great trouble to prepare their wedding night bower, but he didn't answer immediately, being too busy reveling in the discovery that holding her across his lap rather than astride in front made her easier to kiss. They turned toward the marsh road at the corner of Market Street.

"To the Academy, of course," he said, kissing her again. "So that we can complete what we started there."

When they turned down the track through the marsh, she returned his kiss so passionately, he had to stop. His little wife pulled away to whisper, "We best stop this so we can hurry to it."

He chuckled and obliged, pleased at how much easier it was to trot across the dry track. She leaned her head against his shoulder and sighed. "I'm not so sure we're finishing anything, though. I think we're just getting started."

THE END

The majors do indeed make it to Brussels. Jamie Heyworth survives Waterloo unscathed, but Andrew Mallet almost dies—almost. He finds healing and happiness with the help of his friends in ***Dangerous Works***. Jamie has to wait a few years before his troubled life takes him to Rome, and his own happy ending, in ***Dangerous Secrets.*** Caroline's Dangerous Series and more can be found here:

https://www.carolinewarfield.com/bookshelf/

SOCIAL MEDIA FOR CAROLINE WARFIELD

You can learn more about Caroline Warfield at these social media links:

Website: http://www.carolinewarfield.com/
Amazon Author: http://www.amazon.com/Caroline-Warfield/e/B00N9PZZZS/
Good Reads: http://bit.ly/1C5blTm
Facebook: https://www.facebook.com/groups/WarfieldFellowTravelers
Twitter: https://twitter.com/CaroWarfield
Email: warfieldcaro@gmail.com
Newsletter: http://www.carolinewarfield.com/newsletter/
BookBub: https://www.bookbub.com/authors/caroline-warfield
You Tube: https://www.youtube.com/channel/UCycyfKdNnZlueqo8MlgWyWQ

ABOUT CAROLINE WARFIELD

Award winning author of family centered romance set in the Regency and Victorian eras, Caroline Warfield has been many things: traveler, librarian, poet, raiser of children, bird watcher, Internet and Web services manager, conference speaker, indexer, tech writer, genealogist —even a nun. She reckons she is on at least her third act, happily working in an office surrounded by windows where she lets her characters lead her to adventures in England and the far-flung corners of the British Empire. She nudges them to explore the riskiest territory of all, the human heart, because love is worth the risk.

Learn more about Caroline at:
Website: http://www.carolinewarfield.com/
Email: warfieldcaro@gmail.com

SCANDALOUS MISS UP TO NO GOOD

The Teatime Tattler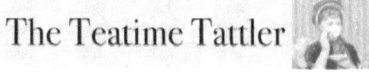

Gentle Readers:

This just in from our Faithful Correspondent at the Queen's Barque in Fenwick on Sea!

Who was the fashionable damsel who entered the inn looking like a drenched field mouse, with no one else to give her countenance but her maid? None other but Miss d.C.

Dedicated readers of The Teatime Tattler will be familiar with the escapades of this particular young miss. She has been a frequent piece of tittle-tattle in previous editions, barely escaping ruination in the past several years. There is sure to be a bit of excitement while she is stuck here.

Which of the several eligible peers also stranded at the inn will she set her cap on? We will just have to wait and see. Knowing her past, anything is possible. Stay tuned for further developments.

BEFORE I FOUND YOU

A de Courtenay Novella

SHERRY EWING

Before I Found You:
A de Courtenay Novella
By Sherry Ewing

A quest for a title. An encounter with a stranger. Will she choose love?

Miss Miranda de Courtenay has only one goal in life: to find a rich husband who can change her status from *Miss* to *My Lady*.

Captain Jasper Rousseau has no plans to become infatuated during a chance encounter at a ball.

Their connection is hard to dismiss, despite Miranda's quest for a title at all cost. What if the cost includes love?

CHAPTER 1

Bath, England
February 14, 1815

aptain Jasper Rousseau surveyed the crowd, wishing he could be anywhere other than this ballroom full of Bath Society. Standing near the balcony door, he nodded to those who strolled past him, although he continued to wish for a hasty retreat. If past experience was anything to judge by, many of the *ton* gathered here tonight would look down on him. He may have enough wealth to be comfortable for more than one lifetime but, without a connection to a title, he was outside of their circle. Not that he really cared. He wanted their investment, not their approval. For the most part, the people in attendance at the Valentine's Day Ball were strangers but some had done business with him. Indeed, somewhere in this room might be the prospective investor he was meeting in the morning.

He caught his mother's eye from across the room and she offered him a small smile of encouragement. He had fulfilled his obligation to her by escorting her to this event. But he would rather be at sea with the planks of his ship beneath his feet instead of in a ballroom with a cravat twisted entirely too tight like a noose around his neck. At least Bath was in close proximity to tomorrow's meeting.

"Buck up, ole chap," a gentleman chuckled next to him. "This, too, shall pass."

Jasper steadied himself. He had not realized his face showed his feelings. "I was just admiring the dancing," he replied before turning his full attention to the gentleman. "Have we met?"

"Lord Adrian de Courtenay," the man said holding out his hand.

"Captain Jasper Rousseau," he replied as he shook the gentleman's hand. His soft French accent caused a flicker in the man's demeanor before he masked the look in a friendly smile.

"A pleasure," Lord de Courtenay said before he, too, surveyed the room. "You're not a regular at such an event, not that I blame you. These balls and rounds of the season can be quite tedious."

"Which is most likely why I avoid them at all costs," Jasper chuckled as if jesting, although in all honesty that reply was not too far off its mark. He was only here because his mother insisted. His parents wanted grandchildren. Jasper had yet to find someone who remotely interested him, let alone tempted him into marriage. He had plenty of time. He was, after all, only thirty. A ball, according to his mother, was just what Jasper needed. "Are you enjoying yourself this evening?"

Lord de Courtenay gave a small laugh. "More so than you, it appears. You look as though you are at a funeral instead of a ball."

"I suppose I have distanced myself from the revelry. My mother would no doubt be appalled." Jasper nodded once more to his mother across the room and plastered a smile upon his face for her benefit. "What about you?"

"I am here with my lovely wife," Lord de Courtenay said, discreetly pointing in the direction of a young blonde lady in a pale pink dress. She excused herself from the group of women she had been talking to and began making her way toward her husband.

"A reason to celebrate on such a special occasion," Jasper answered before taking a sip of his champagne. *Another damn happy couple. The room was full of them.*

Lord de Courtenay raised his own glass in a silent salute. "Plenty of women here would love the chance to dance, Captain Rousseau. Find someone to perform introductions to the lady of your choice and enjoy yourself." With a smirk of encouragement and a wave of his hand, he excused himself to meet his wife, taking up her hand and raising it to his lips.

Lucky man, Jasper thought before he looked about the room once more. He supposed to please his mother he should make at least an attempt to enjoy himself and choose someone for the next dance.

A young woman suddenly caught his attention as she skipped to the lively patterns of the current dance. Dark brown hair was swept up in a pleasing coiffure sprinkled with what looked like diamonds winking in the candlelight of the room. Her gown was pale blue with a pink ribbon just below her breasts. She turned and the look on her face was one of bored indifference, making Jasper inwardly laugh. Had Lord de Courtenay seen in his features what this woman showed to any who cared to gaze upon her?

Jasper continued to view her from a distance. Blue sapphires hung from her ears while a delicate golden chain with the same stones and diamonds graced her neck. He continued to watch, a slow grin spreading, until the dance ended and she gave a small curtsey to her partner.

As she rose, she scanned the room and he briefly wondered whom she was looking for in the overfilled ballroom. Their gazes met and held for an instant on a heartbeat. Jasper raised his glass in a silent toast and her eyes widened before she looked away, leaving the dance floor and melting away into the crowd.

His curiosity roused, Jasper drained the rest of his glass and handed the empty flute to a passing servant. He began to move, casually walking among the throng of people, hoping to catch another glimpse of the young woman who had momentarily caught his attention. His taste did not normally run to young maidens. She could hardly be older than a score of years, he surmised, as he continued searching for her. There she was, near the banquet table.

She appeared thoroughly engrossed in the delicacies before her. She at last took a small slice of cake decorated with a heart and placed the treat on her dish. Jasper took a plate for himself and slowly made his way down the table until they stood next to one another. They reached for a fruit tart at the same time. A gasp escaped her as she mumbled an apology, snatching her hand away from the dessert. She looked up to stare at him, and her mouth opened in an O of surprise, though her eyes twinkled with delight. They stood staring at one another only for a moment, then she rapidly turned away from him.

A sigh escaped him. Under Society's protocol he must be introduced to a young woman before having a conversation with her. He turned around so they were back to back, knowing it was expected of him. He could sense she had not moved to distance herself from him. Was she, too, just as interested in knowing exactly who he was? He held back a smile.

"*Bonsoir, mademoiselle*," Jasper pitched his voice to be heard over the music in the next room and other conversations intruding into their moment together. He swore he heard her breath catch in her throat and he waited to see if she would acknowledge him.

"Good evening to you, sir," she replied, her voice a breathy whisper. She set her plate down on the table as though filling it had been but an excuse to keep her occupied. His near empty plate joined hers and he noticed she had taken a small nibble from the slice of cake.

Jasper waved to a servant, who quickly moved forward to offer the tray he carried. Jasper selected two crystal flutes of champagne before he hesitantly held one of the glasses toward the lady behind him. Her gloved fingers briefly touched his when she accepted his offering and Jasper's heart raced at the contact. How could such a young miss prompt such an intense physical reaction? He didn't even know her name.

"Perhaps you would favor me with the next dance," Jasper said hopefully but, of course, she would decline.

"I am afraid I cannot," she answered and her tone sounded somewhat disappointed.

"Because we have not been formally introduced?" he asked, already knowing her answer.

"Yes," she confirmed before rushing onward, "I'm sorry."

"Perhaps we can find someone who could remedy the situation."

He waited. But instead of answering she placed her glass on the table, her fingers lingering on the crystal stem. He set his own glass down, their hands nearly touching. He swore he could feel the heat of her skin next to his own. He turned slightly to better see her. She looked up over her shoulder. At first, he thought her eyes were a soft brown but after she blinked, he saw that they were, in truth, hazel. His gaze moved down to her parted lips, wondering how they would taste after the champagne she had sipped and the sweet cake she had eaten.

"That would be lovely," she finally answered. She blushed before looking away and Jasper had the urge to pull her into his arms. Not that he would ever embarrass her so. As they both turned to face the room a gentleman came and bowed before her, holding out his hand.

"I believe this dance is mine, M—"

"Y-yes, o-of course," she quickly stammered. As she was led away, she glanced back only once, to smile at Jasper before she once more disappeared into the crowd.

Jasper stood alone wondering about the identity of this mysterious young lady and who, exactly, would be able to introduce them.

CHAPTER 2

M iss Miranda de Courtenay was in turmoil and there was no one she could blame other than herself. She should have never begun to converse with a gentleman to whom she had not been introduced, let alone allowed such a lingering glance. But he had hypnotized her when he all but pulled her toward him with his dreamy green eyes.

Filled with thoughts of him, she missed a step in the patterns of the dance! She quickly caught up to her rightful place in line with the other women. She craned her neck around the room when she dared. Where had he gone and more importantly... who was he? Never had she felt such an instant attraction. And he felt the same, she was certain. Would he seek an introduction? Would he come calling? Perhaps he was a duke or a marquis! An earl, at least—her quest to wed only nobility had been engrained in her every action as long as she could remember.

Some of her actions to that end had been unfortunate, of course. Her horrible embarrassment during the Hollystone Hall fiasco came to mind before she quickly dismissed it. She had known the Grenford brothers were rakes, but she had never imagined they would flirt with a maiden like her without intending marriage.

An inner voice pointed out she had only just been forgiven for her part in the forced wedding of her brother and his wife. Adrian had overreacted. He and Celia had loved one another for years. Adrian should be grateful that Miranda had prevented Celia from falling into the clutches of the marquis who wanted her.

What did it matter that Miranda's motivation was to secure the man for herself? Everything had turned out for the best. For Adrian and Celia, at least. The marquis turned out to be a rake, as well. And how was a lady meant to tell, when these rogues were welcomed into polite society? It was hardly her fault if she continued to be attracted to the wrong men who only had one thing on their minds.

She moved down in the line and acknowledged the man before her as the dancers changed partners. She gulped back a sharp remark when she recognized the Marquis of Wyndham, the despicable man she had just been thinking about.

She dismissed the marquis with a toss of her head as the dance continued and the line moved onward and she was reunited with her original partner. She gave him a brief smile. She had found him attractive earlier in the evening. He was a viscount but, to be honest, that was all she could remember about him. Later, she would need to check the dance card dangling from her wrist just so she could remember his name.

The ending notes of the music echoed in the room and Miranda sank into a curtsey. At her claim she was parched, the viscount went to fetch her some punch, giving Miranda the opportunity to scan the room for the gentleman who had captured her attention. She saw him standing next to an older woman but the lady was unknown to Miranda so there would be no help with formalities from that direction. Still... he had such a commanding presence about him and she admired the dashing figure he presented in his evening finery. Surely, he must be titled.

No man had the right to look so handsome. Earlier, after she had dared to look up at him, she had come very close to reaching up to push back the lock of his blond hair that had fallen rakishly across his brow. She had done enough foolish acts in the past few years, but she had luckily not made a spectacle of herself tonight. That was the last thing she needed. Not when her brother Adrian had only tonight forgiven her for the role she had played in ensuring he wed his lady. Still... A total stranger had her tongue-tied. Never in all her twenty and three years had some man done that to her. What had come over her?

Her eyes followed him when he walked out the balcony doors and into the dimly lit night air. He casually sat back against the marble railing, folding his arms across his chest as though he had not a care in the world. Surely, he was silently asking her to join him. She began to move in his direction, hesitating briefly when the voice of reason demanded she remain indoors. It wouldn't be prudent to allow her heart to rule over her head. She was here to find a titled gentleman as her husband. But perhaps this mystery man of hers had all that she had been looking for. It was possible, was it not?

Right before she reached the doors, she wavered again and looked back into the ballroom. Adrian and Celia were dancing and only had eyes for one another. Even her sister Grace, with whom she had lived since her brother exiled her after his forced betrothal, was deep in conversation with her husband Nicholas. Surely, Miranda would not be missed for a brief moment or two. Throwing caution to the wind, she stepped forward into the shadows of the cool night.

She was not sure what to expect. Being outside alone with a man she did not know was a bold move. If she needed reinforcements, she could easily call out for help, but that would hardly do her reputation any good. It had barely recovered from her last scheme. Society's memory was short, remembering scandals only until something new came along for them to gossip about—or until something happened to remind them. She couldn't afford to give them new fodder to chew on.

She could not resist. Miranda took the remaining few steps until she stood next to him, and he rose to his full height, his hair tousled by the evening breeze. She suppressed the urge to push back the lock of hair across his brow that refused to stay in place. *Oh my, but the man was tall!*

Miranda did not even realize she offered him her hand until he leaned down and kissed the air between her knuckles. His fingers were warm even through the silk of her gloves. How would they feel if her hand was bare? Good heavens! What was coming over her?

"*Mademoiselle,*" he whispered in a husky French accent, causing goose bumps to rise on her arms. His voice was utterly divine!

"Miranda," she said offering only her first name. It was hardly appropriate, but she did not wish to see his disinterest when he learned she was a "Miss" and not a "Lady".

Although it might not matter. Many gentlemen present this evening were on the lookout for a well-dowered heiress to enrich their estate. The man before her could be one of them. Even though she could not attach "lady" to her name, she was still wealthy in her own right... or would be when she finally wed.

Love had nothing to do with what really mattered in life—marriage to a husband within the nobility, one with enough wealth to keep her and her children in luxury. Not for her a boring life as a country matron, with nothing to do or to talk about beyond counting sheets and breeding children. She wanted a glittering life as a Society hostess! It would be an adventure. Or so she had always thought, and she would not allow her heart to rule her head.

She bit her bottom lip before she realized she had done so. The man before her could not know it was an automatic reaction when she was worried. She watched his brow arch in surprise before a grin turned up at the corner of his lips.

"Jasper," he finally replied in return, examining her reaction to his touch. "The evening has become brighter now that you have joined me for a breath of fresh air. Look how the stars above beam in approval that they may gaze down upon you."

Miranda's lips twitched at the compliment. Very nice, though she sensed that he used this phrase often. She realized he still held her fingertips and she reluctantly pulled them away before waving her hand towards the crowd inside. "It's quite the crush this evening. Have you been enjoying the ball?"

"I am now," Jasper replied, leaning back against the marble railing again.

Miranda blushed at his words. Another well planned compliment, or so it seemed. Miranda was used to them. She had utilized them herself enough times in the past to grab the attention of men she had hoped to snare into marriage. Obviously, since she was still unwed, she had failed.

Given her own distrust of his practiced charm, she might need to rethink her approach to wringing a proposal from the peer in her future.

She chanced another glance at him. He watched her intently. "I have not seen you join in with the dancing," she replied softly, before giving him a small smile.

The edges of his lips again crooked upward. He had guessed what her words meant; that she had been searching for him. "Maybe I have not found the right partner."

"There are plenty of women who would more than happily accompany you," she remarked, although a part of her was thrilled he had not danced with another. What would it feel like to dance the night away with him?

"And does that include you, *ma chérie?*" He took a step closer and once more reached for her hand, rubbing his thumb across its back. He pulled her slightly closer to his side and she could sense the slightest hint of his cologne. She inhaled deeply. A pleasant mixture of musk, spice, and something else she could not detect. It was intoxicating, and she swallowed hard at what this man was doing to her.

Silence stretched between them, even the distant melody of music from inside seemingly diminished in Jasper's presence. His eyes continued to work his magic on her, pulling her deeper under his spell. Her breath hitched in her chest and she suddenly found herself unable to breathe. She had done it again... made a horrible mistake. What had she expected when she met a mysterious man alone... in the dark... with all of Society but a heartbeat away?

He was waiting for her answer. She took a deep breath to steady her nerves. "I am afraid that would never do. We still haven't formally been introduced," she finally whispered, while she continued to gaze into those hypnotizing green eyes.

He raised her hand to his lips and kissed her hand. Miranda gasped at his boldness. "Maybe we should just give in to whatever is between us. Surely no one will notice one more couple upon the dance floor." He began gently pulling her toward the door leading inside.

She quickly tugged on his arm. "Good heavens, no!" she replied. "My brother would never approve."

Jasper gave a chuckle and the deep baritone caused her heart to flip end over end. "Brothers generally never do. Why do I sense you tend to try and bend your brother, and Society for that matter, to your will, *mademoiselle?*"

Miranda laughed but her tone sounded strained to her ears. His words were more accurate than she wanted to admit. "Why, you know nothing about me, good sir!"

He shrugged and continued escorting her inside by tucking her hand in the crook of his elbow. "Perhaps not, but let's enjoy our moment together with a dance," he urged softly, while the musicians struck up the chords as if he conjured them to do so for his own personal pleasure.

Miranda's eyes widened, listening to the tune that began in the ballroom. "But the next dance is a waltz!"

"Well... so it is. Dance with me, Miranda. Throw caution away and show the *ton* you care not for their restrictions," he coaxed, holding out his hand for her to take when they reached the edge of the dance floor.

The prudence engendered by the last few months in disgrace melted like snow in the heat of his gaze. She did not think nor did she hesitate when she placed her hand in his. He gently pulled her into his arms and she forgot everything else but Jasper. He swept her into the pattern of the waltz as though they had danced together a thousand times before.

Jasper's eyes twinkled in the candlelight of the room and Miranda could barely contain the smile that flowed effortlessly across her face. She'd had no way to calculate his social position before accepting, and somehow being held in his arms felt so very right. Perhaps she had found her match in this handsome unexpected gentleman.

As Jasper continued whirling her around, she noticed her brother stood at the edge of the dance floor with a frown. She recognized that look and knew the moment the dance ended, Adrian would whisk her away and send her back home with Grace. Her face fell, knowing her time together with Jasper was at an end.

"Someone so beautiful should have only a smile reflecting in her eyes, *ma petite*," Jasper murmured, as they continued twirling around the room. "What troubles you so?"

"My rash decision to dance with you will not go over well with my brother. From the look he is giving me, he knows we haven't been introduced. I'm afraid I'll be escorted from the ball as soon as our waltz is finished."

"My apologies, Miranda, if I have caused you trouble. It wasn't my intention to damage your reputation."

"You are not entirely to blame, Jasper. I could have adhered to the rules that are expected of me," she replied. "I could have just as easily declined."

"I'm glad you didn't, but hope we can salvage the situation."

"I'm also happy I accepted the invitation to dance with you." She smiled up into his handsome face, regaining some of her confidence that Adrian would forgive her impulsiveness.

"I have a business appointment in the morning. Where can I call upon you or leave my card with your brother?" Jasper asked to the dying notes of the music.

Before she could answer, couples began withdrawing from the dance floor and she saw Adrian making his way towards her.

"I must go," she said quickly. "Thank you so much for the dance... Jasper."

"Miranda!"

She could not give in to her desire to have one last look at Jasper when he called out her name. She also wouldn't look back. She had turned her nose up at the restrictions of Society where he was concerned, and she would not make things worse.

She made her way towards her brother who said not a word but took her arm, escorting her to Grace and Nicholas who already held her redingote. Her time at the ball with her handsome stranger was over.

CHAPTER 3

J asper handed over the reins of his horse to a lad who came running to see to his animal. He gave the bay a pat on the neck before his steed was led away, leaving Jasper staring at the four-story brick mansion before him. At Lord Nicholas Lacey's urging, Jasper had ridden over to Batheaston and enjoyed the excursion, knowing their meeting was not far from his own country estate. Once the business portion of the day was concluded, Lord Nicholas offered to show him the rest of his property and perhaps also take in a bit of sport along the way.

As Jasper approached the door, the faint melody of someone on a pianoforte reached his ears. There could be no doubt that whomever was playing the instrument was accomplished. He rapped upon the door and waited only a fraction of a moment before it was opened. The butler stood back as Jasper entered the foyer.

"Captain Rousseau," the man said as he led him to the parlor. "His lordship is expecting you, sir. If you would await him here, I shall tell him you've arrived."

Jasper watched the man disappear quietly down the marbled hallway before he gazed around the parlor. It was richly decorated with mahogany furniture, the fabric of the chairs a deep shade of forest green. The curtains had been drawn back to let in the morning sun but it was the sound of the high soprano voice that caused Jasper to continue forward through to the next room.

The woman sat at the pianoforte with her back to him, not realizing she was no longer alone. A riot of dark curling hair tumbled down her back as if she had forgotten to finish her morning toilet in her eagerness to reach the instrument. Her white dress had small pink rosebuds scattered along the fabric while dainty slippers sat on the floor near her feet. The lady's nimble fingers flew over the ivory keys as if she had performed this song a hundred times or more, because there wasn't any sheet music to guide her. Her voice sang in perfect accord to the melody and, as her hands finished the song, the last strains of the melody faded away into the room. Lord Nicholas was a lucky man to have such an accomplished wife.

"My apologies for interrupting your morning, Lady Nicholas, but that was very well done," Jasper said, giving the well-deserved compliment to the performance he had been privileged to hear.

She quickly placed her feet into her discarded shoes. "You are mistaken, sir, I'm not..." She laughed and turned.

His eyes widened in surprise. "Miranda!"

Her hand went to her throat just as startled. "Jasper! Whatever are you doing here?" She quickly looked around the room as though for a missing chaperone, since they were completely alone.

His brow furrowed at the implications of this chance meeting. "*Bloody hell*..." he swore softly. He mumbled an apology before coming forward. How could he so misread the situation? He had been sure he and the lady before him had forged a connection. "You are the lady of the house?"

Miranda stood, placing a chair between them, looking as confused as Jasper himself was feeling. "What?"

What game had this woman been playing last evening? He knew a few among the *ton* had open marriages but Jasper stayed clear of women who were only looking for someone to fulfill whatever needs their husbands lacked the wherewithal to supply... not that Lord Nicholas gave the impression that he lacked anything at all.

"Lord Nicholas..." he tried again, feeling sick that he had briefly coveted another man's wife. "He's your husband? Is this why you were so vague about your identity at the ball?"

Her eyes cleared and a joyful laugh escaped her. Jasper saw nothing comical about the situation.

"Nicholas isn't my husband, Jasper. He's my—"

"There you are, Captain Rousseau," Nicholas said, entering the room. "I see you've met Miranda."

Her eyes darkened, as though in disappointment. "Captain?" she asked, in a hushed whisper.

Jasper gave a short nod, before turning to shake Nicholas's outstretched hand. "Actually, the lady and I lacked formal introductions last eve." Jasper turned once more to look at the young woman before him. She had turned away while he had been shaking Nicholas's hand but, as she turned back to them, he swore he saw the remnants of tears lingering on her eyelashes.

"Then let us remedy the situation now," Nicholas beamed. "Miss Miranda de Courtenay, may I present Captain Jasper Rousseau. My wife Grace and Miranda are sisters."

Miranda curtseyed while Jasper bowed. "Captain Rousseau," she said, politely, but the fire of the woman he had met at the ball suddenly appeared dimmed.

"Miss de Courtenay... it's a pleasure," Jasper said before the name hit him. "Are you, perhaps, related to Lord Adrian de Courtenay?"

She nodded. "He's my brother. Have you met?"

"Only briefly, last evening."

Nicholas stepped forward, offering Miranda his arm. "Grace was asking for you upstairs. I'm certain you won't mind if the captain and I leave your lovely company while we discuss business."

Miranda stole a glance at Jasper. *Ah... there she was...* His heart leapt at the flash of irritation that briefly lit her eyes. Clearly, she was annoyed at being politely dismissed from a discussion between gentlemen.

"Business? What kind of business?" she asked.

"Captain Rousseau has recently purchased a merchant brig called *The Legacy*. It's docked in London and we're to discuss shipping opportunities that will benefit us both," Nicholas replied as they reached the entryway and he walked her toward the stairs to the upper floors. "Nothing too exciting for such a lovely young woman; it would surely bore you to tears, Miranda, to hear all the details."

"Of course," she replied quietly. Her features stiffened into studied indifference. "I will see to attending Grace, then. Good day, Captain Rousseau."

"Miss de Courtenay." He gave a short bow and watched her head up the stairs to disappear out of sight.

He wasn't allowed any further time to contemplate the woman who had consumed his thoughts for the better part of last evening. Lord Nicholas led him into his study. A reminder Jasper was here on business and needed to keep focused on why he was at Highgrove Manor in the first place. He wasn't here to court a woman, not when he had a new ship to see to and accommodations to be made so he could also take passengers as an extra source of income. And untrustworthy rivals like the Danvilles, father and son, who had bid on *The Legacy* and lost her to Jasper, would love to steal his cargoes. He would leave thoughts of Miranda for another day. At least now he knew where to find her.

CHAPTER 4

Miranda paced the garden path that gave her a clear view of the front door. This morning, she had waited for what seemed like days, instead of hours, for the opportunity to speak with Jasper. When she heard Nicholas saying he looked forward to seeing *The Legacy* next month, she knew the moment was upon her. She flew through the manor to the kitchen and out the back door before she could rethink her actions. Now, with her shawl wrapped around her, she tried to forget about the cold and instead focus on what she really wanted... just one last moment with Jasper.

She should forget him, shouldn't she? Of all the wretched luck! A captain of a merchant ship was not in her plans, no matter how handsome he was. Who would have imagined that the first man ever to really spark her interest would have no title? She had wanted a title of her own since she was a small girl, especially since Grace married their second cousin, the Earl de Courtney, and became his countess. As the great granddaughter of an earl, Miranda was not even an 'honorable'. Just a 'miss'. She wasn't going to be a Mrs., that was for certain. Even her brother was a peer now, inheriting the earl's title when Grace's first husband died. And Grace had gone on to marry the second son of a duke!

Miranda could not give up her dreams of being, at the very least, a countess. Or could she? She shook her head. Forget her dreams of marrying nobility? What a silly notion. A gentleman with a title would be lucky to have her as his wife. It was all she had ever wanted for her life.

She stomped her foot in frustration at the injustice of her situation! Being stuck out here in the country with Grace and her children left her little to no opportunity to convince someone within the peerage to offer for her. Last night's ball would have been a prime opportunity to find her next conquest, but she had failed herself by getting smitten by a pair of mesmerizing green eyes. What was she to do?

After she had seen Grace earlier, Miranda had watched from the upper window of her bedroom overlooking the courtyard as Jasper and Nicholas left on their horses. Even remembering Jasper when he mounted that horse caused Miranda's heart to flutter in her chest. Both men had discarded their cravats but Miranda's gaze was focused only on one. Her eyes had wandered down to the brief glimpse of blond hair at the opening of Jasper's shirt. Fingers tingling, she reached out to the glass pane window as though she could really feel his chest. She closed her eyes briefly as she imagined the texture of his skin. When she opened them again, their eyes met and his smile was truly wicked.

Miranda had jumped back from the window as though burned. How could Jasper be even more handsome in broad daylight than he had been in the candlelight at the ball?

Which, of course, was why she was standing here in the cold waiting for him to leave the manor. She blew air into her icy hands and was just about to give up on this idiotic notion when the door opened. Jasper began putting on his gloves and Miranda heard the distant sound of his horse being brought around from the stables.

Knowing she only had a moment to spare, she rushed from her hiding space around the corner of the house. "Jasper," she exclaimed, loud enough to get his attention.

He looked over his shoulder and smiled before heading in her direction. Miranda drank in the sight of him. He was properly attired once more. She almost preferred seeing him at his leisure instead of the proper gentleman closing the distance between them.

"Miranda," he said, in that unnerving French accent that caused her blood to race in her veins. He gave her a bow. "Whatever are you doing outside in the cold, *ma chérie?*" He took off his jacket and placed the garment around her shoulders. Such a kindness was going to be her undoing, especially when that lock of unruly hair once more fell rakishly across his brow.

The impulse was too great for her to ignore. Reaching up, she moved the hair from his forehead, and he captured her trembling fingers in his warm hands. Keeping his eyes fixated on her own, he bent forward and kissed the inside of her wrist. Dear Lord... her knees almost buckled when his lips connected with her feverish skin.

"Miranda?"

"Yes?" She continued staring up at his face as if to commit every inch to her memory so she would never forget him. From his green eyes to the dark shadow of stubble roughing his square jaw line, she couldn't take her eyes from him. He was just as fascinating today as last evening and perhaps even more so, in a rugged kind of a way.

"Why are you outside?" he chuckled in amusement as though he had known where her thoughts had gone.

She at last remembered herself and backed up a step. He, in turn, stepped forward and continued to do so until they were out of sight of the front of the manor. It wasn't until she felt the brick wall upon her back that she realized she had nowhere else to turn.

"I had to see you one last time," she murmured in a breathy whisper. She leaned her head back just so she could once more stare into his eyes.

"I'm certain our paths will cross often, Miranda, at least when I'm on shore," he said, coming so close she could feel the very heat of him radiating from his body. She almost moaned but as she placed her hands upon his muscular chest, instead a gasp escaped her. Her action was meant to halt him from coming any closer but it had the opposite effect when he pulled her into his arms.

"I don't see how that will be possible," she managed to say, while attempting to hold him off. Her pulse quickened and every fiber of her being craved to be held in his arms forever more. She must remember her goal, and Jasper could never fit into her plans.

"Anything is possible, Miranda. We just need to have a little patience. Time will eventually be on our side. I won't always be at sea." He ran a finger down her cheek, causing her to shiver in pleasure.

"It's not about *time*, Jasper, because all the time in the world won't change anything."

He bent forward until his forehead touched her own. "I know we have only just met but, for whatever the reason, I feel drawn to you. Was I mistaken that you feel the same way?"

Her breath caught in her throat to hear his words. "No," she said honestly. "You weren't mistaken."

He cupped her face so she had no choice than to give him her undivided attention. "Then, hopefully, you'll forgive me if I do something I've been craving to do since last night."

She gulped. *Oh no... please don't let him kiss me.* "What's that?" she asked instead, even though she knew what was coming.

"This..."

His lips gently slid across her own as if testing to see if she would accept the gift of his kiss. She should have pulled away but how could she deny what she herself wanted just as badly? She tilted her head to give him full access to her mouth and, when his tongue slipped inside, Miranda was completely lost. Shivers of delight swept across her entire body until she found herself wrapped in Jasper's arms. Her hands made their way up into his hair and her fingers tangled into the soft length. He deepened their kiss without any protest from Miranda until she thought her feet would never again touch the ground.

How long their mouths danced with one another, she could not say. For one brief instant, Miranda never wanted the kiss to end. She never wanted to leave Jasper's arms or his life. But when a soft moan escaped from her lips, the reality of what this man did to her finally penetrated her numb mind. She broke off their kiss and yet their mouths lingered near as their breaths mingled together. She may want him, but he could never offer her the life of her dreams.

"We cannot continue this, Jasper," she quaked, her voice stricken with grief at what she would lose after he was gone. She gulped in deep breaths of air to calm her nerves. He kissed her forehead before stepping backward to a respectable distance. Miranda had never felt colder knowing what was to come.

"Of course. You made me forget myself," Jasper replied as he reached for her hand. He kissed her knuckles before wrapping her hand between the palms of his own. "Your brother-in-law and sister will be coming to see my ship in a few weeks before it sails. Perhaps you can convince them to bring you along so we might see each other again."

A part of her heart soared with joy at his words but she knew that what had just transpired between them was all they would ever have. She might as well get this part of the conversation over with. Wasn't this why she had initially waited for him? She had already let this situation go further than she had planned. It wasn't right for her to lead him to believe that they could be more than just friends.

She gave a heavy sigh before bringing the edges of his coat closer around her neck. She had never felt colder. "I don't see what good can come from us continuing any sort of a relationship, Jasper. If that was your intent, that is." She refused to look into his eyes but he took that choice away from her when his finger tilted up her chin.

"What are you talking about? Of course, I was implying I would like to continue getting to know you better. I thought you wanted the same thing."

She moved around him so she was no longer backed up against the wall. She lifted her chin, determined in her desire to continue her search for a man with a title. She masked her face into an expression that she'd perfected over many years... indifferent, even haughty. Such a look had turned away many a beau who did not fit her criteria of landed and titled gentry.

"Since we are barely acquainted, you don't know what I need, Jasper. I am trying to tell you that I must wed someone with a title." Her voice was quiet but firm. She wasn't sure if she was trying to convince Jasper or herself.

A sound came from his throat that almost sounded like a wounded animal. "You are not a titled lady yourself, Miranda. My birth is perfectly respectable. Not that I was ready to offer marriage, but what difference does it make if your future husband is titled or not?" he asked. His fists clenched at his side. Was he attempting to hold his disappointment in check? Or was it anger?

"It matters to me! You must see that both my brother and sister have titles. It isn't fair that I am denied an honorific," she burst out. "It matters, Jasper." A sob escaped her. Perhaps that was no longer as true as it had been. The thought of not seeing Jasper caused tears to well in her eyes.

"I see," Jasper replied, his eyes flashing fury. He looked her up and down as though finally seeing her for the first time. When his eyes at last met hers, Miranda was heart stricken to no longer see warmth for her reflected there. "I did not take you for one of *those* women who wish for a title no matter the cost. But, as you said, we barely know one another. The mistake was mine to assume otherwise. My moral compass must be off." A smile cracked his lips as he tried to hide the hurt with a joke.

"Jasper, please..." She reached for him but he held up his hand to halt her progress.

"There is no need for further discussion, Miss de Courtenay. I wish you success in finding a gentleman you believe is worthy of you." He gave her a short nod before taking his leave.

Not Miranda... Miss de Courtenay... A formality that sounded out of place considering what had begun between them... and what she had willingly ended. She went to the wall and placed her hand on the corner for support. Jasper mounted his horse and never once looked back as he left Highgrove Manor.

It wasn't until she had run upstairs to her room and flung herself onto her bed for a well-deserved cry that she realized she still had his jacket. She pulled the garment into her chest as if to will Jasper back to her side. And as her tears consumed the better part of the evening, Miranda wondered if, by letting Jasper slip from her grasp, she might have just made the biggest mistake of her entire life.

CHAPTER 5

Jasper peered at detailed drawings of *The Legacy*, an exasperated sigh escaping his lips. His ship had been plagued by breakdowns. One repair after another was needed and he began to wonder what he had got into. His plan to leave the London docks by the end of the week now seemed elusive. Not when a rudder chain needed to be mended along with one of the main sails.

"Bloody hell," he swore, before reaching for his cup of coffee. He inhaled the bitter fragrance and took a sip before setting the mug down again. "Is this endeavor doomed?"

Gasparel Beaumonte, his friend since childhood, straightened from his own assessment of the drawings. Jasper had hired him as his First Mate or Chief of their cargo. As another investor, Gasparel had also grown leery of a failed operation.

"It seems to me someone doesn't want us sailing out of London." Gasparel raked a hand through his dark curly hair.

Jasper grimaced. "Hugo Danville?"

"I have yet to find anyone tampering with the ship, *mon ami*," Gasparel said, shrugging. "Once the repairs are made, we can continue to load the goods from your warehouse. It shouldn't take more than a few days."

"Unless something else decides to break down," Jasper muttered. "With all new crew members, it's hard to know who is trustworthy and who isn't."

"I'll keep an extra lookout and maybe we can enlist Dr. Roth to aid us."

"Yes. You can trust the good doctor. He's been a family friend since before I was born," Jasper said going to his desk.

"I almost forgot. There's a gent who's looking for work. He showed up right before I came down to your cabin. Says he was previously Quartermaster in the Navy before he was injured and let go."

"References?"

"In order, along with a remarkable military career." Gasparel handed over the paperwork.

Jasper took several minutes to read the documentation before him. "Impressive. Send him in," Jasper replied. He rolled down his sleeves and donned his jacket.

He didn't have long to wait before a knock sounded upon his door. With a call to enter, a middle-aged sailor took off his cap and stood before him. A patch across his left eye gave him a look of a pirate. Surely the man wasn't retired from the Navy due to an eye injury?

"Captain Rousseau," he said, shaking Jasper's out stretched hand. "I'm George Watson."

"Mr. Watson... A pleasure. I understand from Mr. Beaumonte you are seeking employment on my brig."

"Yes, sir, I am."

"And may I inquire why you are no longer in the Royal Navy?"

The man moved the patch from his eye before putting it back in place. "Lost my sight during a battle that included saving the captain of the ship I was serving on. Instead of being grateful, he deemed me unfit to continue on as Quartermaster. I've been looking for another ship ever since. No one seems to want a one-eyed navigator," he grumbled.

"Well, today is your lucky day, Mr. Watson. You will soon learn I am not like your last captain and I value a good man with an outstanding career. The job is yours if you'd like to sign on."

"Thank you for the chance, Captain. You won't regret bringing me onboard."

The two men left Jasper's cabin before returning up deck. "Mr. Beaumonte," Jasper called out. Gasparel finished his instructions to one of the crew before making his way across the deck.

"Mr. Watson has agreed to sail with us. Show him about *The Legacy* and see him settled," Jasper ordered, before he noticed his cook coming from below.

Arthur Dennison was a man of many talents, or so Jasper had learned. His brown hair and beard were peppered with gray but his age did not detract from his merry disposition. Jasper had never met someone who so constantly appeared jolly, causing his belly to shake whenever he laughed, which was often.

"Mr. Dennison. I've vacated my cabin to await my guests. If you could see to a light repast in my quarters, I would appreciate it."

"I will endeavor to make your luncheon acceptable for the ladies who will join you," Arthur answered with a wink.

"I'm certain whatever you provide will be adequate."

Arthur laughed. "Adequate? I can do better than adequate!" he announced before taking himself back down below.

Jasper went to the railing and saw his father's carriage pull up to the docks. A footman let down the step and Jasper watched as his parents began making their way carefully over the gangplank. Once his mother was firmly on the deck, she lifted her chin.

"*Maman*," he whispered, after kissing both cheeks. "Welcome aboard *The Legacy*."

"Hello, son," his mother, Sophie, replied. "Your father has done nothing but exclaim his excitement about this boat."

"Ship, my dear," Tavas interjected with a smile.

"Boat... ship... you sail on it so it's all the same to me." Sophie laughed brightly, with a wave of her hand. "Will you show us about, Jasper?"

"In a moment, *Maman*. Lord Nicholas Lacey and his wife will also be joining us. He's investing in our shipping business and should arrive soon."

Sophie shrugged. "I don't understand why you need investors. We have more money already than we know what to do with." Her eyes traveled around the ship.

Tavas put his arm around his wife's shoulders. "Investors means more money coming into the business, my sweet. More business means further expansion."

"I'll trust the details to you, Tavas," she replied. "In either case, your boat... errr... ship looks impressive, son."

He was about to reply when another carriage pulled up alongside the dock. He recognized the Lacey crest on the door. Lord Nicholas alit first, followed by his lady, who waved from the shore. Jasper returned the gesture, but, when the footman held out his hand for another occupant, Jasper's breath caught.

He gulped hard when Miranda left the carriage. She adjusted her shawl around her shoulders before she looked up. A smile hesitated upon her lips, and Jasper swore his heart betrayed him when it flipped end over end inside his chest.

He may have previously invited her to join Nicholas and Grace when they came to visit *The Legacy,* but he never thought Miranda would actually accompany them, given their last conversation. He squared his shoulders, knowing he could do nothing more than welcome Miranda onboard.

His mother came and took his arm. "Who is she?" she asked, a hopeful expression twinkling in her eyes. His mother had been begging him to marry for the past several years and he could imagine her already planning his wedding to this young woman who might have stolen his heart.

"No one... no one at all," Jasper muttered. How would he ever endure the next couple of hours knowing Miranda was on his ship?

CHAPTER 6

E yes closed, Miranda stood at the bow of *The Legacy* and took a deep breath to calm her shattered nerves. Her pleas to stay at Grace's London town house until they were ready to travel to the coast had fallen on deaf ears. Grace was tired of Miranda's melancholy mood and had told her the outing would do her good. Besides, her sister had insisted, how often did one get a tour of a merchant ship?

How often indeed? Miranda knew next to nothing about ships and generally cared even less about the intricacies of sailing one. It wasn't as though a ship was going to be taking her someplace exciting. When would she ever see Paris? The war with France had lasted most of her life, and she shouldn't be complaining because she was safe and sound on English soil. But somehow, listening to Jasper's deep baritone voice had changed her opinion about being onboard and she had carefully listened to his every word while he took them for a tour of *The Legacy*.

The newly constructed cabins were sparse but would provide passengers with the minimum of necessities. Jasper had explained that, although he and his father would take on travelers, cargo remained their main source of income and all extra space was needed to store their goods. This justified the small quarters. Not that it mattered. It wasn't as though Miranda would ever set foot on Jasper's ship again or see him for that matter. So why did her heart continue to ache at the thought of never seeing him again? She shook her head and reasoned that, if she ever traveled by sea, there were plenty of other boats that could take her wherever she needed to go.

As Jasper continued his tour, he had shown them an open doorway to the lower portions of *The Legacy*. He refused, however, to lead them further below, insisting it was no place to take ladies. Instead, he ushered their group to the far end of the passageway. Miranda had been surprised when the door opened and she saw the spaciousness of the room. Obviously, this cabin situated at the stern of the ship was Jasper's. Light from the windows reflected off the water, bringing rays of sunshine into the room. A small desk sat in one corner. Miranda saw another table where parchments of some kind were still open and a quick peak confirmed they were drawings of the ship.

Everyone took a seat at the table set up for dining in the middle of the room and Miranda found herself sitting next to Jasper's mother, who began chatting away as though they were long-lost friends. Miranda recognized her from the ball last month and learned that his French father had married an Englishwoman. From the stolen glances his parents gave one another, Miranda could assume it was a love match.

A light repast had been provided for them but, while tea was being brought into the room, Miranda did everything in her power not to look over at the large bed set into the far wall. It was near impossible, since she was directly across from this particular luxury afforded the captain. Just thinking of Jasper's tall body stretched out between the linen at night caused her heart to hammer away in her chest. This had *not* been a good idea.

His cook had performed a culinary miracle with the food he had provided, and the repast would have been the envy of many of England's best chefs. Small delicate cakes, finger sandwiches, scones and clotted cream had been set out for them to enjoy at their leisure. Soon conversations began to flow and laughter filled the cabin. Miranda couldn't remember the last time she had felt this content.

Their time in the same room seemed to both drag and pass all too quickly. Still... Miranda continued to steal glances at Jasper whenever he appeared preoccupied with other conversations. He looked so handsome in his dark brown jacket and cream-colored trousers. His white linen shirt contrasted with his deeply tanned skin. His cravat was impeccably tied and a golden chain disappeared into a front pocket of his striped waistcoat. She watched when those lean long fingers took hold of the golden fob before opening the watch to take note of the time. As the piece clicked closed and he returned the time-piece to the pocket, their eyes met.

A flicker of something gleamed in those smoldering jade orbs. Appreciation? Caring? Longing? He was hard to read from across the table. Not that she should worry about what he thought of her. After all... she was the one who abruptly ended their short relationship. She took another deep breath. Just thinking of Jasper caused her nerves to become a rattled mess.

"You look as though you belong here, Miranda." That voice broke into her musings, causing a shiver of pleasure to race throughout her body. His tone was gentle. Might Jasper still care for her? *God help me.*

She turned to face him and realized he was closer than she thought. Her breath caught in her throat before she finally answered him. "Do I?" she asked hesitantly, before she shrugged. "I never seem to really fit in anywhere."

"Maybe you're just looking in all the wrong places." His solemn expression seemed genuinely concerned. Miranda's determination to have a titled man as her husband waned in Jasper's presence. It troubled her, and at the same time she felt guilty. Wasn't she being untrue to herself?

"Perhaps," she replied, quietly. She would concede that something inside her was changing. She wasn't sure if she cared for the changes or not, but she couldn't stand to see the hurt she might cause this man once again reflected in his eyes.

A few locks of her hair whisked across her face and Jasper reached out to tuck the length behind her ear. "Miranda—"

"I must apologize if my presence has made you uncomfortable, Jasper. I tried to persuade Grace to pick me up after they were done here," she interrupted. She gestured at the planks beneath her feet. "As you can see, I failed."

"You are more than welcome onboard. But you're not remaining in London?" The ship chose that moment to sway and, before Miranda's stance could falter, Jasper took hold of her elbow to steady her. Her heart betrayed her yet again when he placed her hand into the crook of his arm to offer his support.

"No, I'm afraid not. Nicholas has purchased a cottage on the coast at Cromer in Norfolk. I'm to accompany them and their children while they look the place over and furnish it. It's part of my punishment for past offenses, I suppose. I'd rather not go into the details."

"Spending time with your family hardly seems like punishment, Miranda."

"I'm glad you haven't heard the gossip surrounding me the past few years. Elsewise, you'd be like the rest of the *ton* and stay away from me at all costs. I'm only really accepted among them because of Grace and Adrian."

He pulled her to face him and lifted her chin. "We may not have known one another for long, but you must know I'm not cut from the same mold as most of society. I've lived by my own rules, and, while I try to remain the gentleman my parents raised me to be, I don't mind taking a risk now and then."

"Like at the ball?" she asked, trying to keep her nerves calm.

"Yes. I thought you also didn't mind occasionally dismissing the convention of men and women of their ilk since you decided to dance with me."

She thought of how a foolish bet with Grace had almost been the ruin of her reputation at Hollystone Hall. A laugh escaped her. "If you only knew..."

"Perhaps one day you shall confide in me. I promise to keep your secrets." His grin was completely wicked, and another piece of her heart melted.

"I just may hold you to your vow, Jasper," she teased, her eyes twinkling in merriment while they jested with one another.

They began to stroll along the deck. Jasper set a leisurely pace as if he, too, didn't wish for this moment to end. It was almost as if their conversation at Highgrove Manor never occurred.

"Will you return for the rest of the season?" he inquired, stopping at the rail opposite where she would leave the ship. Had he planned that they were conveniently hidden from Grace and his parents behind some large cargo roped off and wrapped in tarp?

She tried to still her erratic heart and failed. "My plans are to travel south to visit with my friend Lady Jane Wallace. She and her husband have recently moved to Southwold. She asked if I could come and stay with her during her confinement." A blush heated her face at the turn their conversation had taken. "Good heavens. You must forgive me. I'm such a chatterbox and shouldn't be discussing such matters with a gentleman."

His chuckle told Miranda much. She may have angered him at their last meeting, but there was still something obviously drawing them together with invisible ties. The pull that connected them was hard to ignore and warred inside of her heart. "No need to apologize, Miranda. Believe me I've heard far worse living on board a ship."

He ran a finger down her cheek and she did everything in her power not to lean into his hand. "But certainly, never from a lady, I hope." She gazed up into his eyes and once more realized her mistake when those green orbs twinkled in merriment.

"Only from you, and I still hold you in the highest esteem no matter how much I think your aspiration for a title is misguided."

She wanted to be insulted by his words, but it was hard to muster up any indignation when he pulled her closer, after looking around to ensure they were still alone. "I thought you said your moral compass was broken where I was concerned," she murmured, caressing the edges of his jacket.

"Perhaps it was only a little misguided. I can't help but still feel we belong together." His roguish grin and chuckle were almost her undoing but it was nothing compared to when he quickly leaned down and stole a brief kiss.

"I should go," she whispered, while her lips tingled from the contact of his mouth on hers. She needed to leave him before she completely lost her heart to this man. He would ruin all her plans for a different life.

"I wish you didn't have to," he said, his husky tone once again turning her insides to mush. He leaned forward and brushed his lips against her forehead and she sighed. How she wished he could be more than a mere captain of a ship.

"I wish you safe travels on your coming journey," she whispered, before pulling out of his arms. She took several steps backward and memorized his features. "Farewell, Jasper."

Turning away from him, she began to distance herself from the man who had somehow stolen her heart. But her footsteps faltered when he called out to her again.

"Every time you walk away, you're going to take a piece of my heart."

A groan escaped her, because his words mirrored her own thoughts. She tried not to cry when she turned toward him one last time. "I'm certain your manly pride will somehow survive, Captain," she teased instead. She watched his smile broaden before he laughed.

Dipping into a curtsey, she made a hasty retreat before she completely succumbed to Jasper's charms. It wouldn't take much effort on his part to make her change her mind about whom she should marry.

※

Hugo Danville stood in the shadows of a building on the wharf, pulling several coins from a pouch inside his jacket. He handed them to the seaman standing before him.

"You've done well so far. Be sure to continue to wreak havoc on *The Legacy* and I'll double your pay. Do not fail me." Hugo waved the man off. Their business was concluded.

"Ye can count on me, Gov'nr," the seaman replied before slipping away into the crowded docks.

Hugo pushed off the brick building and began strolling down the docks heading toward the inn he had been staying at. He saw there was a lady leaving *The Legacy*. Rousseau came to the railing and watched her depart. It was obvious the captain must have feelings for the young woman.

Another plan began forming in Hugo's mind, and he chuckled at his own cleverness. As he watched the woman's carriage depart, he hired a hack and told the driver to follow them. He rubbed his hands in glee just thinking of another way to thwart the Rousseaus.

Jasper's heart sank as he watched the lady disappear into the Lacey carriage and vanish away from the crowded wharf. What else could he have done other than to let her go? Again! He certainly couldn't proclaim his intentions, nor could he announce how he truly had begun to care for her. He wasn't ready to give Miranda the leverage of knowing he had so readily fallen for her. Not when she was determined to fulfill some childish dream of wedding a peer.

He supposed he shouldn't have been surprised the lady was after a title. So many young ladies were. But still... the memory of her standing at the bow of his ship with the long ends of her shawl billowing behind her in the breeze was one he wasn't likely to forget anytime soon. The beautiful image of her had engraved itself into his very soul. He had been truthful when he told her she seemed to belong on his ship. If only...

Jasper muttered a curse and returned to what mattered for the time being. He had a voyage to worry about, and he would do his best to forget the fair Miranda. There was no sense in wondering if this budding infatuation with the young lady might bear fruit. She had told him what she wanted in life and unfortunately that didn't include a mere captain of a ship. Maybe he should take up a mistress, but he dispelled the idea as soon as it entered his head. The thought might once have been appealing, but the only woman he wanted in his bed was the one who had just left him.

CHAPTER 7

Miranda stepped into the coaching inn in Norwich and promptly bumped into a gentleman who was leaving. Strong arms wound around her waist to keep her from falling while her hands stretched across a firmly muscled chest. A gasp escaped her when she looked up into his dark brown eyes while a slight grin swept across his mouth. She blinked several times as his black hair blew in the breeze from the entryway. Once she was again on firm ground, he released her.

"My sincere apologies, Lady..." he inquired, giving her a courtly bow that appeared as though it should be given in a ballroom instead of an inn. He waved his arm to allow her entrance.

"Miss de Courtenay," she replied without thinking, leading the way into the establishment with her maid Elsie directly behind her. Elsie was actually Grace's maid but her sister had allowed Miranda to travel with her when Grace felt indisposed and unfit to travel farther than their newly acquired cottage. Her sister's illness must surely have rattled Grace's wits, because she exclaimed Miranda could hardly get into trouble in one day's time. Miranda kept silent, happy for the freedom to continue on her way to Lady Jane's house in Southwold.

The morning was nearly gone and Miranda's only thought was to get back on the road once the coach changed horses. If she was lucky, they could make it to her friend's before nightfall, and she could attend Sunday services in the morning, if Jane felt up to the excursion. A brief gaze out the window at the stormy skies allowed a moment of worry to crease her brow. The last thing she needed was another delay in reaching her destination. It had been raining all morning.

Miranda found an unoccupied table and, after a pot of hot tea and two cups were set before her, she began to pour. She had just handed one of the cups to Elsie when a tall form blocked her view of the window. The gentleman took hold of the empty chair next to Miranda, the sound of wood scrapping across the floor causing Miranda to pause what she was doing. The man had the gall to sit. Apparently, when she bumped into him, he thought this was some sort of an invitation. Her brow rose at his forwardness.

"I didn't have the chance to introduce myself," he said flashing a smile that probably had most women swooning. But she had never been drawn to men with dark hair, and her memories of Jasper quickly flitted across her mind. Perhaps she should widen her scope of the men who usually appealed to her. "I am Hugo Danville. My father, Lord Lansbury, and I are to visit our ship the *Acacia* on business. She is docked in Yarmouth. What brings you to town?"

Miranda set down the teapot, intrigued that a titled gentleman had practically fallen right into her lap, although she was surprised she had not heard of his father. She thought she was familiar with all the peers of England. Perhaps it was a Scottish or Irish title.

The gentleman's tone implied she should be impressed with his announcement he was nobility. She opened and closed her mouth several times trying to form a reply but she had no idea who this man was. She certainly wasn't about to divulge her travel plans.

"Lord Danville," she murmured politely, before placing her hands in her lap. She stole a glance at Elsie who looked uneasy. "My business is my own, sir." She tossed him a look that had left more than one beau running for the door, but such was not the case with the man before her. His grin only widened and she took a sip of her tea to distract herself from this all too handsome rogue. She had the distinct feeling in her bones this man was used to getting his way She wasn't familiar with the title 'Lansbury', but he must be an earl or a marquess, for she had called his son 'Lord', and he had not corrected her.

"Perhaps I could procure a private room so we might enjoy a meal together?" he proposed raising his hand to call over the innkeeper.

She almost spewed her tea across the table. "I should think not!" she managed to squeak out, before setting down her cup. "I do not know who you are, Lord Danville, but I am not accustomed to talking with nor taking refreshments with unknown men."

He leaned back into his chair, his hands forming a steeple when he rested his elbows on the arms of his seat. His fingers went to his lips as he contemplated her before he relaxed.

"I meant no disrespect, Miss de Courtenay. You intrigue me and I only wished to get to know you better." He reached over and grabbed her hand so fast Miranda had no time to react. He quickly kissed the air between his lips and her knuckles, and she was surprised when a sudden blush rushed across her cheeks.

She pulled her hand away and was at a loss for words. This man presumed too much on a chance encounter with an unknown lady. "A gentleman would know the proper way for an introduction to occur, sir."

"Then point me in the direction of your parents so I might plead my cause," he said looking about the room, but Miranda had the notion he already knew she traveled alone.

"I'm afraid that's impossible," she stated, before taking another sip of her tea. She tried not to think of her parents and how they had been gone from this world for many years.

"You look sad and that was not my intention," he declared while worry and concern etched its way across his features. "I pray your parents have not..."

"They are..." Miranda interrupted. "Gone several years now."

"My condolences on your loss, my lady," he said, patting her hand before taking the liberty of pouring more tea into her cup. "I wouldn't have brought up memories of your loved ones had I only known."

"Thank you, Lord Danville," Miranda replied, finally relaxing in his company. He appeared so sincere when he offered her an encouraging smile that she completely overlooked the fact he had introduced himself. She tried not to over think why she wasn't uneasy with the lack of a formal introduction with Lord Danville. Was it only because she assumed he was nobility? This had certainly been her main concern with Jasper when they first met.

"I only wish I had more time to linger in your company. Alas, I am on my way to our ship at Yarmouth and can delay my business no longer. Is there a relative near where I can leave my card and perhaps call upon you at a later time?"

Miranda hesitated in giving out information on where she was headed. Instead, she gave him a bright smile. After all... he was titled and he might be just what she needed to get Jasper out of her mind. "My brother-in-law Lord Nicholas Lacey and my sister are residing in Cromer. You may leave your card there if you happen to travel in that direction."

"I shall indeed make the effort to get myself to Cromer then," he beamed with another bright smile. "I will look forward to when our paths cross again, Miss de Courtenay."

"As will I, Lord Danville," she answered with a nod of her head.

"Ladies..." he said, giving Elsie a wink that caused her maid to gasp. Lord Danville stood but, before he took his leave, he bent down to whisper in Miranda's ear. "I look forward to seeing you again, Miss de Courtenay. I guarantee you shall enjoy *my* company far above anyone else you might meet." He gave a short bow and left the inn.

Elsie set her cup down. "What a horrible man!"

"Nonsense, Elsie. He was utterly delightful, although I must admit I was at first leery when he just assumed he had our permission to join us without asking first."

"You would think that a gentleman would have better manners."

Miranda's gave a light laugh. "Not everyone plays by the rules of polite society, Elsie, and Lord Danville seems to go after what he wants." Miranda tried not to think about why the son of a marquess would be interested in a woman with no title. But no matter... if Lord Danville was interested in her, then perhaps she just might find herself wed to a title after all. Miranda also knew a thing or two about going after what a person wanted. She had been trying to do the exact same thing for more years than she could count!

When the coachman entered the inn to announce they were ready to travel again, Miranda was more than relieved to leave Norwich behind. Luckily, Grace and Nicholas had hired a coach, so Miranda and Elsie had the conveyance to themselves.

But as they continued traveling overland beyond Norwich, she grew more and more concerned. The skies darkened until day turned almost to night. Larger raindrops began pelting the windows followed by huge balls of hail. Not long afterwards the coach came to a halt and the driver opened the hatch to call down they were going to have to detour from the main highway and take a less traveled route out to the coast road due to flooding on the main road.

The weather continued to get worse, and the glimpses of the muddy mess that had once been a road confirmed her gravest fears as the coachman made one turn after another.

She barely made out a sign of a village named Fenwick on Sea before the coach hit a large rut causing the coach to tilt. She let out a scream when she was bounced from her seat. The coach began to list. Miranda strained her ears over the storm to hear the coachman yelling at the team of horses when he yanked on the reins bringing them to another halt. Miranda righted herself and returned to the seat but held onto the ledge of the window. Elsie looked just as terrified as they waited with bated breath for the entire conveyance to topple over at any second.

The door to the coach was yanked open and a torrential downpour began flooding into the interior. Two wet oiled coats were handed over to the women while the coachman quickly explained their predicament.

"We broke an axle, Miss. Luckily we're only a short distance from the Queens Barque. Tommy an' I will 'elp ye and yer maid get to the inn an' we'll come back fer yer luggage an' the 'orses."

Thankful for the walking boots she had on, Miranda welcomed assistance to leave the coach, especially given the slippery mud beneath her. She was glad the coachman knew where they were going, because, with the hood of the oiled coat over her head, Miranda could hardly make out anything as the rain continued to beat down on her.

They finally reached the inn and Miranda saw it was, at core, an old Tudor style building with several wings that looked to have been built in every century since. When they entered, the sounds of conversations seemed deafening, as though all of the countryside were currently residing inside. A voice rang out above the sound of others.

"We have another guest," the man's voice boomed as he flung a bar towel over his shoulder.

A matronly woman began making her way to Miranda, who took off the oiled coat and handed it to the coachman. He hurried back toward the door. As he opened it, an oversized dog with big floppy ears came bounding into the entryway. He began shaking the water from his coat.

The dog cocked his head as if assessing Miranda while she stared into his searching eyes. The dog's mouth hung open and he began to drool, making Miranda wonder if she was his next meal. The animal's head reached her waist, and Miranda began to shake with fear. She stepped back from the dog, which appeared as if it was a mix of mastiff and heaven only knew what. The dog came to sit before her, lifted up a paw apparently so she could shake it and then his plumed tail began to wag.

"Off with you now, Hector," the woman scolded the dog. "No worries, my lady. He's friendly enough but must have escaped the coach house. Will you be needing a room for the night?"

"Yes, if you have something available," Miranda replied, trembling from the cold. "I'm thankful to be out of the storm."

"Oh, you poor sweet lamb," the woman cooed. "I'm Mrs. Brewster. My husband and I run the Queen's Barque. Let's get you up to a room."

"I am most grateful, Mrs. Brewster," Miranda replied.

"We're nigh full up. We still have a vacant room but your maid will need to bed down with the other servants. I hope that won't inconvenience you much."

Miranda's gaze swept the crowded bar where every table was filled. "I'm sure we can make do, Mrs. Brewster. If you could perhaps have a bath sent up, that would be lovely."

"Of course," Mrs. Brewster said before waving towards a young woman. "This is my daughter, Charlotte. I know you're busy, dear, but have one of the lads fetch the tub and have hot water sent up to room number three for Lady..."

"Miss de Courtenay," Miranda replied, once again glum over her lack of a title.

"I'll take care of it, mum," Charlotte replied, before scurrying off to do her mother's bidding.

"This way, Miss de Courtenay," Mrs. Brewster said, before heading toward a set of stairs along the far wall of the room.

Miranda followed behind Mrs. Brewster while the woman chatted on about what in the village might be of interest once the weather cleared, including a Norman church. They hadn't gone far down the hallway before Miranda was shown to a room with modest furnishings. This inn had certainly seen better times but she would in no way complain about the accommodations. She was lucky to have a bed to sleep in tonight, and at least she was having an adventure.

Before long, a tub of hot water was set before the fire in the hearth, with a small meal left within reach of the bather. When the luggage arrived, Elsie left out a nightgown for Miranda to put on once she was finished with her bath. Miranda sunk into the calming hot water and sighed in relief as the bath began to work its magic. She could only wonder what tomorrow would bring. Until the coach was repaired, she would be stranded at the Queen's Barque.

Hugo could not believe his luck! Of all the places Miss de Courtenay could have found herself, it would be the place Hugo was doing a bit of business.

He returned his attention to the men at his table and began discussing the contraband he had for sale. He had been cursing the need to travel in this weather, but it was becoming a most profitable and pleasant excursion after all!

CHAPTER 8

Aboard *The Legacy*, Friday morning gave way to early afternoon with the clouds thickening. Jasper checked the barometer and wasn't pleased with what he saw. "I don't like the look of this," he complained bitterly, before raising his eyes to the thunderous clouds above. "I've got to be the biggest idiot in all of England *and* France to be sailing out into weather like this."

"What option do we have?" Gasparel asked, holding the hood of his oiled coat while the wind tried to wretch it from his hand. "We couldn't sail in the storm earlier this week. If you don't think this is going to blow over, we could delay another day."

Jasper swore. "And miss the delivery date of our cargo? That's really not an option."

"Then we must get underway before the tide is no longer in our favor. Surely we can make it across the Channel without further incident?"

"One can only hope." Jasper scanned the dock and finally saw the carriage he had been waiting for. "Looks like the last of our passengers decided to show up. I'd best go greet them. As soon as they're onboard, along with their luggage, take us out while I show them to their cabins."

"Aye, Captain," his first mate exclaimed, before standing next to the wheel.

Jasper descended from the taffrail and met Lord Hythe at the railing. "Welcome aboard *The Legacy*, my lord."

Hythe extended his hand and the two men shook. "Sorry for the delay, Captain Rousseau, but my sister's maid is not too keen on traveling."

"It happens to the best of us," Jasper replied politely. He glanced at the girl, who looked positively green, and they hadn't even left the dock yet.

"Fliss, may I present our captain, Captain Jasper Rousseau. Captain, my sister, Lady Felicity Belvoir, and her maid Miss Theodosia Conroy," Hythe continued. Jasper contained his astonishment at being introduced to a servant. He'd heard the Belvoir family called progressive in their thinking, and apparently it was true.

Jasper gave a short nod. "A pleasure, ladies, but let's get you out of the rain and into your cabins. You'll at least be warm and out of the elements."

Taking them below, he first showed Hythe to his cabin before opening the door next to his wide enough for the ladies to enter. Their luggage followed right behind them and Miss Conroy all but fell into a nearby chair.

"We may encounter rough water due to the storm," Jasper explained, trying not to alarm the women but it was best they were prepared. "Please stay inside your cabin."

"We'll be sure to do so," Lady Felicity responded, her eyes twinkling. "We'd hate to be a distraction."

He gave them a brief nod before heading down the passageway. Another ladder took him to the galley, where he braced himself on the door frame while addressing his cook. "Mr. Dennison, have a pot of hot tea sent to cabin four for the two women on board. Afterward, it's light rations until we're out of the storm. No sense on a fire breaking out during inclement weather."

A snarky laugh left his cook. "This isn't my first trip to sea, captain. I've got my galley handled. You take care of sailing this ship," he quipped before pointing toward a kettle already heating on the stove.

Knowing he'd done the best he could for the two ladies on board until the storm was over, he returned topside and took a firm grip upon the wheel. If it wasn't for the rain pounding upon his body, he would have enjoyed the moment of getting underway. The recent pitfalls that had befallen his ship were still a mystery; they had yet to figure out exactly who was deliberately causing one thing after another to fail. Sails didn't just get slashed; rudder chains didn't break as though someone had cut through them.

Hugo Danville continued to be in the forefront of his mind. It wouldn't be the first time his nemesis had tried to ruin his business, nor did Jasper feel it would be the last. But there was no longer any time to ponder what Danville planned next. If he had someone in his employ on *The Legacy*, the man would be found out eventually.

Once they left the Thames, Jasper's muscles strained while keeping his ship on course in the open Channel. Roaring winds whipped at the sails as the storm gained momentum coming down from the North. The barometer had not lied.

They fought the wind all that night and on into the next day as the storm built. Approaching the coast—either the port at Ostend that was their destination or any other port that might grant them haven— was too dangerous in these seas and winds. But Jasper did his best to hold position so that he could take advantage of the first break in the weather to deliver his passengers and his cargo to their destination.

By early Sunday morning, the worst was over, though the rain still drummed on the deck and the small bits of canvas he sported to keep *The Legacy* turned into the wind. By noon, he could begin his run to the coast of Europe—further off than it should be if that was England he saw in the far distance between squalls.

As prepared as he was to handle his ship, he wasn't ready when he heard a loud crack. His eyes turned upward to the forward mast and widened when one of the cross timbers snapped. As the lines and rigging also began to give way, the falling spar ripped open another sail in its descent to the deck.

He barely heard the cry ring out when one of his crew got caught in the falling wreckage. Jasper called out orders to rescue him from the debris.

"Mr. Watson," he yelled out to his Quartermaster over the storm. "We make for the nearest port we can find on the English coast. Take the wheel while I head to my cabin briefly to look at my charts."

Once inside his cabin, Jasper quickly scanned the chart laid open before him. Running his finger over the parchment, he assessed any ports to the north. If he was right about how far north they'd drifted with the storm, Yarmouth was the closest port where *The Legacy* could make repairs once it was berthed. He'd head in that direction.

Back on deck, Jasper found out his sailor had sustained several injuries. Other men were in the rigging putting up the sails that were necessary to get them to their new destination. Jasper took the wheel. The ship rocked back and forth with the heavy waves of the channel and Jasper prayed his passengers were weathering the storm.

But it wasn't until he could barely make out the coast that the unthinkable happened... again. The rudder cable snapped. He could only watch in horror as the wind blew *The Legacy* off course and it began to drift further south than Jasper's intended destination. He could hardly make out the shore.

Jasper began to call out orders for jury-rigging a sea anchor, when a sudden side draft caught the ship and the entrance of a river or inlet began to rush upon them at alarming speed. He barely had time to yell for everyone to take hold when the ship slammed into a rocky shoal. *The Legacy* teetered on an angle and Jasper held his breath when it settled.

Chaos erupted among the crew until Jasper took control again, bellowing orders above the wind to check the passengers, hull and cargo. He then began ordering the first of several cables to be strung from the ship to the shore to secure it and its cargo. They'd next need to see to getting the passengers to safety.

Men began readying the skiff to be lowered to the water below. Those who had been injured would be removed first, including Dr. Roth who had banged his head, although he insisted he could still attend the others. Jasper sent Gasparel to inform the passengers to be ready when he returned for them to disembark.

Mr. Watson came up to the taffrail holding a sailor's arm in his meaty fist. "We found our culprit, Captain. Caught him red handed trying to cut through the spare rudder cables on deck."

"Well done, Mr. Watson, but we have no time to question him further at the moment. The passenger's safety and undamaged cargo are our priority. Take him down below to the hold and lock him in a cell," Jasper said, glaring at the man who had caused so much lost time and damage to his ship. "We'll deal with him once the storm is over."

"What if the cells are flooded with water," George asked.

"I'm sure you'll think of something so he is... detained." Jasper waved the men off but remained satisfied he'd have his answers soon as to whom the man worked for.

Jasper went to help with his injured crewmen, praying there were accommodations of some kind in the local village and rooms for a makeshift hospital.

CHAPTER 9

Miranda entered the entrance hall and saw a familiar face. She made her way over to the lady to extend a greeting.

"Miss Meadows, how lovely to see you here among so many strangers," Miranda said cheerfully.

"Miss de Courtenay! What a pleasant and unexpected surprise," the lady replied, before leaning forward and lowering her voice. "Actually, I've recently wed. I'm Lady Stanton now."

"Congratulations on your marriage, my lady," she replied, although inwardly she cringed at the thought of another commoner snagging a title while she remained unattached.

"Thank you. You must be stranded here like the rest of us. Tragedy already struck yesterday when one of the castaways from a shipwreck died in the high tide."

"How horrible!" Miranda said. She scanned the room looking for a vacant table.

"Were you about to take tea?"

"I was planning to. I see a woman alone at a table. Perhaps she will allow us to sit with her," Miranda said, before she began heading in that direction.

"Excuse me, miss. Do you mind if we join you?" Miranda asked, hoping the woman would allow them to sit.

The lady looked up from the book she was reading before her gaze around the room showed all the other occupied tables.

"By all means," she said with a smile, gesturing to the empty chairs.

"Thank you, so very much. I am Miss de Courtenay, but please call me Miranda," she stated before taking a seat. "This is Lady Stanton."

"Please call me Josephine," Lady Stanton replied.

"Miss Eugenia Fynlock." The lady extended her hand in greeting to each of the women.

A serving girl came and took their orders before scurrying off to the kitchen.

Miranda pulled her shawl closer around her shoulders. "We're old acquaintances but we accidentally just met in the entrance hall and decided to dine together. The inn is so crowded. You were very kind to share your table with us."

Miss Fynlock nodded, and the two other women continued their conversations while Miranda began wondering how long she might be stuck here in Fenwick on Sea. She would much rather be sitting in Jane's parlor than in this rundown inn swarming with all of humanity.

But she would rise above her situation and make the most of it, even though she was bored to tears. After all, she couldn't magically fix the coach or drain the floods so she could be on her way, nor could she change the weather. She swore last night she had been waiting for the roof above her head to collapse, given the deluge of rain that had pounded on the window.

One of the ladies interrupted the musings about yesterday's fiasco.

"And I heard that a reporter from that nasty *Teatime Tattler* has taken up residence inside this very inn," Josephine said.

Good heavens... not a reporter from the Tattler, Miranda thought, worrying she'd be the subject of another scandalous article about her. She scanned the room and was surprised to see none other than Lord Danville sitting in a darkened booth with several men. Whatever was he doing here? Despite the weather outside, things were indeed looking a bit brighter with his presence.

"Best be careful of your reputation, ladies," Miranda warned as she came back from thoughts of the handsome man she met just yesterday. "You don't want to end up as the latest tittle-tattle for all of Society to learn about."

The maid returned with a pot of tea and Miranda took the initiative to pour for her newfound friends.

"The information about the reporter is troubling. Perhaps what is needed is a plan to get out of this inn and away from prying eyes and ears," Eugenia suggested.

"Interesting," Josephine remarked, before taking a sip of her tea.

"I'd love to escape this inn for a time," Miranda exclaimed, wondering if Lord Danville might accompany her on the outing. "But the weather is hardly conducive to excursions."

"I agree," Eugenia said. "What if we plan to take an outing on the first good day? The rain is already subsiding. With luck we might go as early as tomorrow afternoon."

"But where?" Josephine queried.

"I was told by Mrs. Brewster when I arrived that the village church is a fine example of Norman architecture and was visited by Queen Elizabeth," Miranda suggested, repeating the information the innkeeper's wife had relayed to her. "She informed me the stained-glass window in the church is supposedly a gift from that noble monarch."

"That's an excellent idea." Eugenia smiled before reaching for her teacup. "My traveling companion is acquainted with Mr. Somerville, the vicar. She assisted him with aiding the injured from this storm. She could ask him if he would guide us through the church."

"Would your friend be Miss Walford?" Josephine asked.

Eugenia nodded. "She is."

"I met her when she was helping the vicar. She has a very tender heart."

"Thank you. I agree. Shall I ask her to speak with Mr. Somerville? I'm sure she'll want to get out of the inn as much as any of us."

"That would be wonderful, Eugenia," Miranda replied while she blushed, thinking of asking Lord Danville to join her.

"Then we are in accord. I will send notes to you both via

Mrs. Brewster when I know the details of our visit to the church." Eugenia began eating their lunch when it arrived.

Miranda was busy thinking of ways to arrange an outing with Lord Danville when she heard a distant bell sounding out an alarm. She didn't give it much thought since she was unfamiliar with the workings of this seaside village. But when a man came rushing into the room drenched from the rain, all that changed.

"Been another wreck..." he started to say, while gasping for breath as if he'd run the entire coast. "This time it's on the other side of the inlet and blocking the fishing harbor. Stuck on the rocky shoal, it is. They've got casualties!"

Men and some women rose from their tables to go to the ship's aide. Miranda returned to the remainder of her tea until a conversation stood out from the group about to leave.

"What's the name of the ship?" someone asked the man, who sat with a cup of hot coffee to warm his hands.

"*The Legacy*," he replied before taking a gulp of his brew. "Never been here before and it's not going anywhere for a spell till repairs are done.

When Miranda heard the wreck was Jasper's ship, she shot to her feet so quickly she nearly toppled her chair. "Good heavens... Jasper!"

She turned to flee the inn when her arm was taken by none other than Lord Danville.

"Why, Miss de Courtenay!" he exclaimed, his eyes twinkling in delight. "Wherever are you off to in such a hurry?"

While on any other occasion she would have been more than thrilled this handsome man was having a conversation with her, now was not the time for an idle chit chat.

"I must apologize, Lord Danville, but you will have to excuse me." She wrenched her arm from his grasp and gave him no further thought.

Running through the entrance hall, she grabbed an old oiled great coat hanging on a peg and thrust her arms through the sleeves. The hood was barely over her head before she was out the door and running to catch up with those who were heading toward the wreck to help.

Her feet sunk in the wet sand of the dunes but this was no time to be worried about her shoes. Jasper might be in danger! She trudged ever onward until she reached the edge of the harbor. A low skiff was bouncing over the rough waves while men with bulging muscles pulled it across the water by a heavy cable. It had just reached the shore when Miranda came up to the boat as it hit the shingle at the water's edge. Two women and a man looked grateful to be on solid ground.

She went to help the women from the small boat and recognized three of the occupants immediately; an earl and his sister, along with *The Legacy's* surgeon, Dr. Roth. "My word, Lady Felicity!" Miranda commented over the howling wind.

Before the lady could respond, her brother came to help his sister's maid. "Miss de Courtenay... we must get Miss Conroy settled. Please follow us," Hythe ordered, putting his arm around the maid's waist to support her. "This is no place for a young lady to be out in such elements!"

"Yes, of course," she answered, even though she stood there in indecision. She should go back to the safety of the inn but, when she saw Jasper's ship at a ghastly angle, her only thought was to see first-hand that he was unharmed.

Another man came to lift the maid in his arms, and Hythe and his sister followed him along the shore. Miranda went up to the men who were ready to once more pull the skiff back over to *The Legacy*. "Take me over," she ordered the men before jumping into the small boat.

"But miss..." one of the men began in protest.

"Take me over now or I'll find a way to get there myself!"

She held onto the edge of the boat and, after a brief argument, one jumped in to ensure she made it over the rough water. She began to doubt the wisdom of her actions as the waves splashed over the sides and rocked the tiny vessel as though the sea would like nothing more than to have it sink to the bottom of the harbor. If she was wet when she first ran out into the storm, it was nothing compared to how she was now as the bottom of the skiff filled with water. Her shoes and stockings were drenched while her petticoat clung to her body like a second skin. But she held on for dear life and before long she was at the side of the ship. Looking up at the ladder she would now have to traverse in order to obtain her goal, she shook any doubts from her head and began to climb.

Hand over hand she made her way up until strong hands reached to pull her over the rail to safety. When her feet hit the slippery deck, she fell into Jasper's arms.

"What the bloody hell are you doing here, Miranda?" he yelled before pulling her away from the railing.

"What does it look like? I'm here to make sure you are safe." She held her chin up and the wind took the hood from her head while rain soaked her hair. His eyes blazed in anger and a curse left his lips.

"Mr. Beaumonte," Jasper called out and the man came running over.

"Aye, Captain?"

"See that the next set of passengers disembark while I take care of this insolent young miss. She can wait for the next boat, since we have those who are injured and need immediate medical attention once on shore."

Jasper didn't wait for an answer. Instead, he pulled Miranda down below until they reached his cabin. Flinging open the door, he pushed her inside and the door slammed shut behind them. Miranda unsteadily made her way over to the stern window, distancing herself from the angry man before her. The ghastly angle of the ship made her wonder once more if she had made a mistake. Would it topple over at any moment? She stood shivering now that she was no longer outside but it could also be from being alone... with Jasper... in his cabin.

But the look he gave her had nothing to do with passion even as her eyes roamed over every inch of his body. He appeared to be fine... at least physically.

His mouth was set in a harsh frown when he crossed the room to her. Taking hold of her arms, he shook her as though this would knock some sense into her. "I don't have time to deal with you. How stupid to be out here in the middle of a storm. Or didn't you think about your own damn safety when you decided on your course of action?" he growled out in frustration.

"I needed to make sure you were safe!" she cried out, thankful he appeared as well as could be expected under the circumstances.

"Why? You made it clear at Highgrove Manor we weren't suited and you were only after some lofty title and the life such a *bagatelle* would give you. Why does it matter to you how I fared?" His raised voice was loud enough to be heard over the wind and waves, probably all the way to the shore on the other side of the inlet. She watched him take in slow deep breaths as though to calm his growing anger.

"Because I still care," she admitted, even while her eyes widened at her admission. Considering she had leapt into a bobbing boat in the middle of a storm just to check on his safety, she should have realized just how much Jasper meant to her. But she hadn't thought of how those actions would look to the outside world. She did that now. She gulped... hard. "I didn't think..."

"No, you didn't," he said. But his anger faded from his eyes as he took time to examine her. "Good Lord, you're soaked to the bone. You'll be sick before nightfall if you stay in those wet clothes."

The angle of the cabin deck obviously didn't hinder Jasper when he easily went over to the trunk at the foot of his bed and pulled out one of his linen shirts. He tossed it on the bed. Before she knew what he was planning, he returned to her side and ripped the oiled great coat from her body, tossing it to the floor. Turning her around, he started to undo the tiny buttons of her gown.

"Jasper," she said trying to distance herself from him without any success, "Stop it this instant."

"Stop struggling!" he warned. "I have no intention of harming you." He pulled her back against his chest. His hands settled upon her shoulders as though to offer some form of comfort before he continued to unbutton her sodden gown.

"Whatever are you doing?"

"Obviously assisting you out of your clothing, my dear. But don't worry... your virtue shall remain intact. As I said, I don't have time to worry over you right now. Not when my passengers and cargo are my priority. Now hold still."

Mortified when her gown was thrown over her head and she stood before him in only her corset, chemise, and stockings, she hid her face in her hands, barely able to understand how she put herself into such a circumstance.

"What will people think if they find out I'm here?" she whispered in embarrassment and horror. She would in no way be able to salvage her reputation after this.

"You should have thought of *that* before you had someone row you out to my ship, *ma chérie*," Jasper murmured before he put a blanket over her shoulders.

The endearment as it left his lips surprised her and, when she looked up into his face, she saw a hint of appreciation in the small smile he gave her. He appeared no longer angry with her, and Miranda wasn't sure if she should be relieved or concerned she was alone with him.

"Put on my shirt and crawl into bed. You'll at least be warm there. I'll come back as soon as I'm able and will take you back to shore myself."

Miranda stood where she was as if frozen while he made his way to the door. "Jasper... wait." She ran across the room and flung herself into his arms and he captured her against his chest. "I'm so thankful you weren't injured during the wreck."

He held her firmly with one arm and her heart fluttered inside her chest when her eyes met his. Something shifted inside her and Miranda knew she would never be the same again. She crushed her lips against his own in a searing kiss that was far shorter than she would have liked.

"What was that for, *ma petite*?" he asked, his smirk cocky.

"It was in case I don't get the chance to kiss you later," she answered honestly, before heat rushed to her cheeks.

A chuckle escaped him before he quickly kissed her again. He set her down and gave her a slight push away from him. "Get into bed, Miranda."

He left her. It was probably for the best. As she pulled his shirt over her own body and crawled between the sheets of his bed, she began to wonder exactly what she had landed herself in. She may have just sealed her own fate with Jasper.

Hugo checked his watch for what seemed like the hundredth time. When Miranda didn't return with the rest of the people pouring into the inn who needed medical attention, he became more than annoyed. He would need to find a way to get the lovely young lady to himself if only to further irritate Rousseau. He was certain he'd come up with some idea before he concluded his business in Fenwick on Sea.

CHAPTER 10

Several hours later, Jasper was finally able to deal with the lady who awaited him in his cabin. He had decided to keep her safe in his cabin until the rest of the passengers and cargo had been seen to. It was probably a mistake to add onto hers—the one that brought her here to *The Legacy* in the first place.

He hesitated briefly with his fingertips on the handle before he discreetly knocked upon his own damn door. When he heard the call to enter, he went inside, not knowing what to expect from the beautiful but unpredictable Miranda. She spouted about wanting a husband with a title, but her actions today said otherwise. She must know her reputation would be in ruins if others learned she was aboard his ship and unchaperoned for hours on end.

She was sitting in the window seat of the stern reading a book she had found and his breath left him at the picture she presented. It was one he always imagined... a lovely wife of his waiting for her husband to return to their cabin. Her hair flowed down her back in a cascade of black curls. She had donned her gown again and it looked a crumbled mess now that it was dry. He noticed she had at least taken advantage of his bed to stay warm, for his shirt was neatly folded and lying on top along with the blanket he had given her. She rose to meet him and rushed to his side.

"You must be freezing, Jasper. Let me take your coat." She helped him out of the oiled coat. "Your cook came up a while ago and left some hot coffee. It should still be warm."

"Thank you, Miranda. Let me get a change of clothes and I'll return directly." He went to the trunk, grabbed a few garments and left to change in another cabin. Once he was dry again, he returned to his quarters.

Miranda quickly crossed to the table to pour him a mug of coffee which she handed to him, insisting he sit at the table so she could set a blanket over his shoulders.

"Mr. Dennison must have been surprised to see you here," he said, watching her face when she blushed, trying to keep his mind off the fact that the buttons of her gown needed to be redone.

She cleared her throat. "Yes..." she barely mumbled, her cheeks flushing an even rosier shade of red that truly became her. "Surprised is an understatement when he saw me in your... errr... bed."

"At least you listened to me for a change. Did you get some rest?" He warmed his hands on the mug of coffee before taking a sip. The hot brew began to work its magic, or perhaps it was the vision before him that was thawing every part of his body. The idea of Miranda sleeping in his bed produced ungentlemanly thoughts. He seemed to lose all sense whenever she was near.

"No, not really," she answered, and her gaze said she truly had been worried about his safety. "I was more concerned with this ship toppling over and whether you were staying safe above deck. What happened, Jasper?"

"The storm and sabotage to the ship." He suppressed his anger and took another sip from his mug, then setting it on the table.

"Who would try to do such a thing?" she gasped.

"We found the culprit, and he's currently locked up in a cell in my hold. We'll interrogate him soon, now that we've ensured all the passengers are safely off the ship, it is well secured so it's not further damaged, and our cargo hasn't been ruined. We've offloaded what was stored on deck in order to allow more room for repairs that are needed topside."

"How horrible someone would try to ruin you in such a way, especially with passengers on board. The loss of life alone would be far greater than the monetary value of whatever you're planning to sell."

"I have an idea who is behind the scheme, but without proof, it's only a hunch." He ran his hand through his wet hair.

"You will be careful, won't you, Jasper?" she asked, taking hold of his hand.

He raised her knuckles to his lips and felt her fingers tremble in his. "Yes, of course, *mademoiselle*," he whispered, running his thumb over her hand before placing a kiss to the inside of her wrist. Her heavenly sigh went straight to his heart. No matter what she claimed, her actions more than told him she cared for him. Why else would she be here aboard his ship?

"I would hate for anything to happen to you, Captain," she murmured, confirming his thoughts. Her voice was like a soft caress over his weary body.

"Miranda..." he began, "we must talk about your presence here."

She jumped up as if she knew what he was about to say. In her nervousness, she began tidying up the cabin, not that there was really much for her to do. She finally stood near the window looking out over the water.

He pushed back his chair and went to her, taking her arms and turning her body into his. He lifted her chin. Pools of tears threatened to escape her eyes and he wished he could take some of her fear away.

"How many saw you being rowed out to my ship?" he asked, already knowing her answer. He had seen for himself how the villagers had come to the aid of his wreck and Jasper was certain Miranda wouldn't have been missed among them.

An unladylike sound erupted from her lips. "Far too many, including Lady Felicity Belvoir and her brother the Earl of Hythe."

"I assume you've been staying at a nearby inn?"

Miranda nodded. "The Queen's Barque. I was lucky to find a room where the roof didn't leak."

"Did others see you rush out into the storm from the inn?" he asked, while skimming his hand over her back. He'd have to do something about those uneven buttons.

"I was having tea with two ladies, but there were more than enough people who also ran to the sound of the bell."

"Maybe you won't be missed then," he said, trying to give her a bit of hope that all was not lost.

"Oh, no!" Her cry rang out in the cabin and she pulled out of his arms.

"What's the matter?" Jasper asked in alarm.

Her lips quivered before she spoke. "There's a rumor circulating at the inn that a reporter from that ghastly *Teatime Tattler* is in residence. If word were to leak to whomever this is that I was here..."

"We'll think of something," he said, but was unprepared when she ran back into his arms. Her head rested upon his chest and he pulled her closer.

"I'm ruined! I've no one to blame but myself for this mess." Her tears began to soak his shirt and he could only whisper nonsensical words of comfort that really were no comfort whatsoever.

"I'm partly to blame for the situation. I should have sent you back to shore with the next boat instead of indulging my need to keep you safe inside my cabin."

She began shaking her head. "No. You're not to blame at all, Jasper. It was my own stupidity that has my reputation now in tatters."

"We can marry and that will solve all our problems," Jasper replied, thinking of the only solution that would allow this woman to remain at his side. He didn't want to lose her to another.

She once more pulled out of his arms and paced the length of his cabin. "Maybe there is hope! It's almost dark. I can creep up the servant's stairs at the inn and make my way to my room. Surely there must be complete chaos running rampant with all those who were in need of medical care? The inn was already crammed full with guests. I can slip inside with none the wiser," she exclaimed happily.

Jaspar became increasingly dismayed as she rambled on about her plan. "Miranda..."

"Yes, Jasper?" Her eyes twinkled in delight that she had solved her problem.

"Did you hear a word I just said?" he asked, knowing her answer.

Her finger tapped at her lip, drawing attention to the mouth that Jasper desperately wanted to kiss. "Sorry..." she replied, apparently lost in thought. "What did you say?"

"Marry me." His words grounded the woman to a halt and wide eyes stared at him from across the cabin.

"Marry you?" she gasped out, her hand reaching for her throat.

"Yes. Marry me," Jasper replied, with a weak smile.

Harsh laughter escaped her. "I cannot marry you!"

"Why not?"

"And trap us both into a marriage neither of us wants? That's no way to start a life together."

"And yet you'd rather have a life with some titled gent? You think that will bring you the happiness you deserve?" he shouted, furious that she would once again dismiss him as an unsuitable husband.

She pointed her finger at him, anger brimming in her eyes. "Don't you dare judge me, Jasper Rousseau!"

He pulled her into his arms. "I'm not trying to criticize you, Miranda. I'm only trying to understand how you can possibly deny the attraction between us that brought you aboard my ship in the first place."

"It was impulsive," she whispered. "A mistake."

"We are not a mistake."

"We are!"

"No, we are not, and I'll prove it to you," Jasper declared, as he once again lifted her chin to meet his eyes.

Bending down, his lips brushed against her mouth, coaxing her to join him in this crazy connection they had between them. His hand came to rest on her cheek and when she leaned into his hand, all her inhibitions seemingly left her. She molded herself into his body while her arms wound themselves around his neck. His tongue skimmed along the seam of her lips and when they parted to allow his tongue to dance with her own, a moan escaped her. He took possession of her, laying a claim that he hoped no one had dared before. Miranda was his and he swore he would convince her that they were a perfect match for one another.

Minutes passed but the world could have swept them away and Jasper wouldn't have cared if time became hours. But with those thoughts also came the fact that he needed to help Miranda salvage her reputation to the best of his ability. He ended their kiss. Their mouths hovered next to each other as their breaths became one. He finally kissed her forehead, holding her at arms-length. When she gazed up at him in wonder, he also prayed that perhaps she had seen reason in his offer.

"Lie to yourself, if you wish, Miranda, but I know the truth of the matter. You care for me or you never would have risked everything to learn of my welfare."

He claimed her lips in one last searing kiss before he turned her around and began redoing the buttons of her gown. Once he was finished, he grabbed the oiled coat she had arrived in while she quickly made an attempt at fixing her hair. She failed, miserably, and only appeared more than ever as if she had taken a recent tumble in his bed. Considering her lips were redder from his kiss, she never looked more lovely.

She headed for the door to the cabin as fast as her feet would take her. "Good-bye, Jasper," she tossed over her shoulder.

He followed close behind. "Only for now, *mon amour*," Jasper murmured before running a finger down her cheek.

"You c-cannot p-possibly think you're g-going to accompany me," she sputtered.

"I will see you back to the inn. This is *not* up for negotiation," Jasper warned.

"I hardly think that is necessary, Jasper," she said, obviously trying to persuade him to change his mind.

"I'll leave you at the inn, but this matter between us is in no way settled. We will talk again, although our conversation may be delayed a few days while repairs are being made to my ship."

For once, she didn't argue with him, and Jasper wasn't positive that a quiet Miranda was better than one who was fighting with him. For now, he let the matter rest.

Under the cover of night, they made their way down off his ship to the skiff that was tied alongside *The Legacy*. Now that the worst of the storm had passed, rowing across the harbor was easier than when Miranda had arrived. The trip over the dunes and back to the inn took less time than he would have liked and with a hasty farewell, Miranda disappeared inside the Queen's Barque.

Jasper could only reluctantly let her go. He would need to trust his instincts about the feelings he knew they had for one another. He prayed what he thought they had wasn't all one sided.

CHAPTER 11

Getting ready for the excursion to the church the next day, Miranda stared at her reflection in the mirror. Did she appear any different than she had a day ago before her world turned upside down? She could no longer dismiss her feelings for Jasper. They had grown into a burning flame. He had offered marriage to save her reputation. She was ruined but she was glad she'd gone to check on his safety.

She had thought her flight up the servants' stairs last evening a brilliant idea. But she had only ascended half way up when she bumped into a maid. Old newsprints went spilling from the girl's hands and they both quickly reached down to gather them. Miranda had held back her surprise when she realized she was collecting old editions of *The Teatime Tattler*. Praying her name wasn't linked to anything inside that gossip rag, Miranda handed her copies to the girl. A gleam of satisfaction briefly flickered in the maid's eyes. Miranda left, mumbling her apologies, and her feet flew to her room, where she remained in hiding the rest of the evening.

But Miranda was not going to stay closeted away cowering like some skittish colt. No! She would face whatever she must, however

Society might ostracize her. She had recovered from more than one outlandish stain upon her reputation. This would be no different.

Elsie finished arranging Miranda's hair for the outing to the church and, after grabbing her shawl, Miranda made her way down to the reception room where she found the other ladies assembled for their trip through the village.

"I'm delighted everyone could join us. Allow me to introduce Lady Felicity Belvoir," Miranda announced, gesturing to the young woman standing next to her. "We wait only for Mr. Somerville, the village vicar, to arrive before departing."

Other introductions were made to those who were unknown to each other in the party, including Miss Verity Walford who was Eugenia's traveling companion. Miranda nodded politely and they conversed until the door opened. Mr. Somerville and another gentleman named Mr. Gilroy entered and were also introduced.

"Ah, Miss de Courtenay. What a pleasure to meet you." Gilroy beamed at Miranda taking her hand and bowing over it. "You and your friends are about to visit the church, if what Mr. Somerville tells me is correct."

Miranda was never one to turn down attention from an attractive man. "We are, sir."

"It's vastly unfair that Somerville alone is privileged to enjoy the company of so many fair damsels. Might I be your escort as well?" He offered his arm to Miranda and Verity.

"By all means," Verity said, murmuring her thanks.

Eugenia turned to Mr. Somerville. "I'm so looking forward to seeing the church and learning its history."

The man offered his arm to her and extended his other to Lady Felicity. "I'm honored by the interest of all of you ladies. Mrs. Brewster has undoubtedly explained that the church, like the Queen's Barque, was visited by Her Majesty Queen Elizabeth, who gifted it a window. In my view, its surviving Norman features are even more fascinating. I'll explain more when we arrive at the sanctuary. Ladies, are you all ready to depart?"

Everyone agreed and they went outside to a day full of sunshine, despite the mud underfoot and the scudding clouds. The walk to the church didn't take long before they entered a beautifully preserved example of Norman architecture.

Mr. Somerville began explaining the details. "The stained-glass rosette window was a gift from Queen Elizabeth. You'll note, from that queen's coat of arms, the lion and dragon rampant in the two lower corners as well as the triple Fleur de Lis and lions supine in the upper corners."

Although the church was indeed impressive, Miranda lost all interest in the description that kept the other ladies entertained until the door opened and Lord Danville rushed inside. Miranda stood her ground as he began making his way toward her. How strange was it that she was no longer excited to see him?

"What a pleasant surprise to see you here, Lord Danville," Miranda murmured, while he bowed over the hand that she extended him. Even though she had wanted to see what could possibly become of a relationship with him at one point during this journey, there was another that her heart continued to long for. The way she felt about Jasper altered everything she used to want in her life. A possible relationship with Lord Danville no longer held any appeal.

"I just learned your group was meeting here and I hurried over to see if I might join everyone and enjoy your lovely company," Danville replied. A hopeful expression flickered within his eyes.

"You are too kind, Lord Danville. As you can see, we are quite the group today." She waved her hand towards the others who continued to listen to Mr. Somerville. "You are more than welcome to join us."

He tucked her hand into the crook of his arm. "If I am honest, I'm really only here to spend time with you, dear lady. I missed seeing your return to the taproom last evening," he began while intently watching her face. "I hope all is well."

"Y-yes, of course. I-I just thought I might be coming down with a cold after being out in the rain helping those who were in need. I decided it was best to keep to my room," she stammered, while returning her attention to the others.

"Understandable. I must admit I was very concerned when you rushed out into the storm. Very noble of you to wish to help with those who were shipwrecked," he said but there was something in his eyes that made Miranda hold back a further reply referencing Jasper.

Instead she turned the conversation away from herself. "I am surprised to see you here in Fenwick on Sea, Lord Danville. The last we talked at the coaching inn, your business was in Yarmouth where your ship was docked."

His eyes narrowed before he quickly transformed his features with a smile that didn't quite each his eyes "A last minute change in plans left me stranded with the rest of the occupants of the Queen's Barque due to the flooded roads. Sometimes my business takes me to places where I don't normally trade. An occupational necessity. My schedule adapts accordingly to the needs of my business, my dear."

His endearment left Miranda with a cold dread in the pit of her stomach. Something was strange with the man before her. Something she hadn't felt when she had met him but days before. Or perhaps it was Miranda herself who had changed. In either case, for once she listened to her inner voice to not encourage any further attention from Danville or indulge in speculations about a future with him.

"I'm certain your shipping trade takes you all over the world," she replied, while trying to disengage her hand from his elbow. He held firm and, unless she wanted to make a scene in a church, she let the matter rest for now. "Now that the storm has passed, I assume you'll be leaving for Yarmouth shortly."

"My business should conclude in the next couple of days. Will you be leaving soon as well?" he asked pulling her closer to his side.

"Yes. I will continue on my journey as soon as the coach is fixed. The driver said the blacksmith here in the village should have it repaired soon."

"Marvelous! We can continue to enjoy each other's company at the inn until our departures," he beamed, with a bright smile.

Before she could answer, their group began leaving the church and she had no choice but to continue to allow Hugo to escort her through the short tour of the rest of the village.

When they returned to the inn, Mrs. Brewster had tea waiting for them and they all took seats at a large table. Conversations swarmed around the crowded room and Miranda sat quietly sipping her tea, not really wishing to make idle chit chat, trying to ignore Lord Danville who insisted on sitting next to her. But when a tall form filled the entryway to the room, her eyes lit up in excitement for the first time that day.

Jasper had arrived, but he hardly looked happy to see her. Whatever was the matter with him now?

❧❦❧

When Jasper saw Miranda sitting next to Hugo Danville, fire erupted in his veins. What the bloody hell was she doing with his enemy? Not that she knew the rivalry between their families, but hostility suddenly overwhelmed him at seeing them together. He took a deep breath and reassured himself he was overreacting. She was sitting at a table with more than enough people that she could call for help if the need arose.

Seeing Danville was a grim reminder Jasper still had to deal with the crewman he had in his hold. Jasper had been so occupied with the needed repairs to his ship, that he had delayed the needed interrogation. He would rectify that soon.

He gave a brief nod of his head to the lady who had consumed his thoughts since he had last seen her. She excused herself from the table and made her way across the room. She gave a short curtsey and he bowed before she held out her hand. The moment he took her fingertips within his own, those same crazy currents raced up his arm. He kissed the air between his lips and her hand, knowing they had the attention of the room.

"You look lovely today, Miss de Courtenay," Jasper said, knowing the need to keep up appearances for the sake of the others.

"You are too kind, Captain Rousseau," she answered. The smile she bestowed upon him set his heart lurching in his chest, making him forget his anger of but moments ago.

"Might we have a private word, Miranda?" he asked quietly.

"I don't see how that's possible, Jasper," she responded softly, "not when there are so many watching us."

"Then let us sit over at the table by the hearth," he said, pointing across the room to the vacant chairs. "We'll still be in the company of others but far enough away where we won't be overheard."

"That should be acceptable," she agreed.

Jasper led her to the table and a maid came with another pot of tea for them to share. She briefly lingered at their table before taking her leave. After Miranda had poured and handed him a cup, Jasper couldn't hold back his concern. "I've been worried whether you were able to get to your room last night un-noticed."

"I'm afraid not," Miranda replied, discreetly nodding to the servant who just left. "I ran into the maid who just served us but there's no need to worry about that now. There's nothing I can do about what happened at this point, and I'll make my excuses to my brother and sister when I return home, if the need arises."

"I'm sorry for the trouble this has caused you," Jasper replied, before his gaze returned to his nemesis across the room. "It may not be any of my business, Miranda, but how do you know Hugo Danville?"

Miranda set her cup down. "You mean Lord Danville?"

Jasper jerked taller in his chair. Cursing beneath his breath, he glared at her. "*Lord?* Is that how he's passing himself off these days?"

Their glances across the room showed Hugo was intently watching them. "He's not titled?"

"Hardly. He and his father have made their money in trade, mostly from the black market. He doesn't move in respectable circles, which is why I was concerned when I saw you seated next to him. How did you meet?"

"At a coaching inn on my way here. He introduced himself, but I was surprised to see him here in Fenwick on Sea, since he had not mentioned his business would take him south. At the time, I will admit, I thought him charming."

"He can put on a convincing façade, *ma chérie*. I can only advise, based on my past relationship with him, that you would do well to stay as far away from him as possible. He can be dangerous, and I would know, since he has been trying to ruin my business for years," Jasper confided.

"You cannot be serious," she gasped.

"I'm afraid so. It's an old rivalry between our families and I think Danville will do anything to further our ruin. I already believe he is the person responsible for the recent accidents that happened on *The Legacy*. We have someone in custody but have yet to question the man. I won't be surprised to learn that Danville paid him to do so much damage."

"I'll be careful, Jasper," she responded, a frown marring her brow. "Besides, I won't be here much longer and see no reason why I would further any sort of association with him. The coach should be repaired in the next couple of days and I understand the roads should be passable by then. I can then be on my way to stay with Lady Jane before returning to Grace and Nicholas's cottage in Cromer."

"Will you be at your friend's long?" he asked, wondering when he would be able to see her again.

"She should have her child any day now; that is the reason why I was in such a hurry to reach her home. I never expected to be stranded here in Fenwick on Sea for so many days," she replied, searching his eyes. He briefly wondered if she were thinking the same thoughts he had just moments ago.

"The storm has been most unfortunate."

"How are the repairs to your ship going?" she asked, confirming that her thoughts matched with his.

"Better than expected, thanks in part to the fact *The Legacy* has been blocking the entire harbor. With the villagers' help, along with my own crew, she should be refloated shortly and we can finish the remainder of the repairs with her out of the way of other shipping."

"And where are you sailing next?" she inquired, before taking a sip of her tea. "I'll be honest and say I didn't pay any attention when I was onboard previously, when you gave us a tour of your vessel."

"Ostend in the Low Country to drop off passengers. I then have other business there that will have me in port for a while.

She gave a heavy sigh. "Then it will be some time before you return to England." She looked so forlorn it about broke Jasper's heart.

He reached across the table to take her hand, despite the audience they had. "Will you miss me," he teased, with a coaxing smile. When sudden laughter burst from her lips, Jasper glowed at the thought he was the cause of her joy. In that instant, he fell more in love with this woman before him.

"I would never admit such to you, Jasper, even if I did. A woman does need a bit of mystery or two about her. How else would she keep a gentleman interested in returning for her?" She looked at him shyly. "You will come back... for me? Won't you, Jasper?"

"You must know I will, Miranda." His husky reply had her blushing.

"I shall look forward to our reunion at some later date."

"Then you'll wait for me?" he asked, hopefully. "No more of this business of wanting some titled gentleman for a husband?"

She stood and offered her hand to him and he once more bowed over it. "You'll have the task of getting my brother to give his blessing first. If you can manage such a feat, then I'll be waiting and our reunion will be all the sweeter."

She mumbled her thanks for the tea and returned to her original party.

As Jasper made his way back to his ship, he began to wonder how many more times he would have to say goodbye to the lovely Miranda.

CHAPTER 12

In the next few days, Miranda managed to have two short and frustrating encounters in the public parlor of the inn with Jasper, when he had reason to come ashore, and to avoid more than the briefest of conversations with Hugo Danville.

Friday morning dawned bright and clear and, after a light breakfast, Miranda and Elsie enjoyed a stroll along the beach. Miranda had learned the coach had been repaired and they would finally leave the Queen's Barque by early afternoon so they could reach their destination with plenty of daylight.

In many ways, Miranda would miss this brief reprieve from the restrictions of her daily life. She had found a certain amount of freedom while she had been stranded in this tiny fishing village near the sea. With the roads opened again, she would return to her normal life and the possible repercussions from any reports in the *Teatime Tattler* of her wild dash to the wreck and her late return to the inn. She could only move forward at this point. There was no changing the past. She would deal with the scorn of Society when she must.

Miranda understood why her moments with Jasper had been so constrained. After all, he was behind his deadline for getting his passengers and cargo delivered, not that it was his fault his ship had become damaged in the storm. But she reasoned that such a delay was hardly good for business, whether he was to blame or not. However, she couldn't resist the urge to have one last look at the man who had stolen her heart, even if it was from the distance of the harbor.

The chore of getting *The Legacy* released from the rocky shoal had been completed, and the ship now lightly bobbed up and down in the gentle waves of the inlet instead of blocking its entrance. Miranda had learned from those who returned to the inn that there had been no damage to its hull, so at least that wasn't something else Jasper had to worry over. The other ships that had taken refuge from the storm could now embark for their original destinations.

From the distance, she watched men climb the rigging as they went about their work, including those who hung from the rear of the ship while they repaired the rudder chain. Shielding her eyes from the sun, she couldn't imagine the courage it must take to climb such dizzying heights. Still... her eyes searched for the one man among many who had crept into her heart when she least expected it. Who would have thought she could come to care for a man so easily or so quickly? They barely knew one another and yet Miranda felt as though Jasper had always been a part of her life, no matter how insane that sounded.

He came to the railing and waved when he recognized her, and she returned the gesture until he once more disappeared to return to his duties. She would miss him terribly, and she continued to ponder how he had made such a claim upon her heart. Miranda only knew Jasper had completely turned her way of thinking. A silly title now seemed so insignificant compared to having someone's love... no... not just anyone's love. It was Jasper's love that had changed her. He made the difference the moment he found her in Bath months ago.

Time was getting away from them. Miranda and Elsie walked back towards the inn. When she saw Hugo emerge from a building with a group of men, she frowned, wondering what he was doing. But it was none of her business, and she would heed Jasper's warning to beware of the man.

Unfortunately, Hugo had other plans, for he ran to catch up with her and forcefully took her arm. "Why, if it isn't Rousseau's little chit," he sneered, no longer keeping up any pretense. "I had thought you all prim and proper but rumors going around the Queen's Barque tell me differently." He began pulling her down the lane toward a carriage waiting near the inn.

"How dare you talk to me like that? Get your filthy hands off me this instant," she fumed, trying to loosen his grip to no avail.

"You're coming with me and, if you know what's good for you, you'll keep your damn mouth shut," he warned, pulling harder on her arm.

"I'm not going anywhere with you," Miranda shouted, but began to panic when she realized Hugo was far too strong. No matter what she did, she was at his mercy.

Elsie began trying to claw his fingers from around Miranda's arm. "You let her go this instant!"

Her poor maid didn't see the backhand landing on her cheek, sending the dazed girl tumbling to the ground. As the two women became further and further apart, Elise's eyes widened in fright.

"Elsie! Run and get help," Miranda yelled out, when her maid was at last able to pick herself up from the ground and dash away.

"Bloody hell," Hugo cursed, as he continued to drag Miranda toward a waiting carriage. When they reached it, he pulled open the door and tossed Miranda inside. She had barely gathered her feet beneath her and was about to open the opposite door, when Hugo jumped inside and took hold of her wrists, tying them together with a rope. He then rapped on the roof and the carriage took off, even as Miranda let out a scream of protest.

"Why are you doing this?" she cried out when she saw his plans to gag her next.

"Isn't it obvious, my pet?" His smile was completely wicked as he put the rag in place so she couldn't answer him. "Rousseau wants you. There's no better reason than that for me to steal you away so he can never have you."

His laughter rang out in the carriage, and deep cold dread consumed Miranda. Only a miracle could save her now from the madman who held her captive.

CHAPTER 13

J asper watched as the crewman who had been held prisoner was tied to one of the masts. The man had confessed more than Jasper had hoped, including his association with Danville, who had hired him to sabotage the ship. Jasper now had proof about how far his enemy would go to cause havoc in Jasper's business. He had found it hard to believe that Hugo would put innocent passengers in jeopardy. The man was even worse than Jasper had believed.

"Mr. Watson," Jasper called, before nodding to his Quartermaster who unfurled a whip at his side. "See that a swift punishment is given before returning this scum to the hold. As soon as we return to London, we'll see that he makes his confession to the local magistrate."

"Aye, Captain," the man said, before the crack of the whip sounded out. Any of the crew who might be tempted to take payment from an enemy in future needed to know what was in store for a traitor.

Jasper heard a shout from the shore. A woman was waving her arms. Alarm froze his face when he recognized her. She had been with Miranda a short while ago.

"Gasparel," Jasper shouted out to his long-time friend before heading toward the railing and a skiff waiting below. "You're in charge until I return."

"What's the matter? I thought we were getting ready to sail."

Jasper pointed in the direction of the shore. "I have a feeling something is wrong with Miranda, and Danville may be the cause of it."

"Here," Gasparel spat, thrusting a pistol at Jasper. "Don't go without something to defend yourself."

Jasper nodded his thanks. He descended the ladder and was soon rowing over to the shore. The closer he got to land, the more frantic the woman became as tears cascaded freely down her cheeks.

"Thank God, Captain Rousseau! You must save Miss de Courtenay," she exclaimed.

Jasper gently took hold of the woman's chin, seeing the red bruise already forming on her cheek. "Who did this to you, Miss?" he asked already knowing her answer.

"It was that horrible man we met in Norwich... Lord Danville. He dragged Miss de Courtenay into a carriage," she began to cry in earnest. "You must save her!"

"You can trust that I will do all in my power to return her safe and sound," Jasper replied, before breaking out into a run, pulling her by the hand. He headed toward the Queen's Barque and burst inside demanding a horse. He impatiently waited in the courtyard while the steed was saddled.

Man and beast became one as Jasper pushed the horse into a gallop in order to catch up with the carriage that had taken Miranda away. He could quickly gain ground, since he would be able to ride faster than a carriage could travel. As long as he was going the right way. Danville had boasted his ship was anchored at Yarmouth; Jasper could only hope they were headed in that direction.

He was relieved to see the outline of the conveyance up ahead of him. Leaning over the steed's neck, he flicked the reins, causing the animal to lurch forward. As he came abreast of the carriage, he peered inside to see Miranda bound and gagged. Anger flooded his veins and, as he came in line with the driver, he pulled out the pistol yelling at the man to stop.

With the team of horses lurching to a halt, a growl of outrage came from inside the carriage. The door was flung open and Danville threw himself at Jasper who lost his grip on the pistol. The two men landed in the dirt and began fighting fist to fist until Danville pulled out a knife. Jasper watched the blade being tossed from hand to hand.

Danville called out to the driver of the coach. "Shoot him!"

"Nothing to do with me, guv. You gents sort it out yourselves."

"I enjoyed taking your little toy away from you, Rousseau," Danville taunted. "She'll make a good whore on some tropical island far from your reach once I sell her to the highest bidder. I'll look forward to the coins that will line my purse with her purchase!"

"You're threatening the woman I care for, Danville. Your reputation with the women you abuse is finally catching up with you. You won't be selling them any longer now that Miss de Courtenay is a witness to your plans for her. I knew you made your money from the black market, but this is despicable, even for you."

"You bastard!" Danville yelled taking a swipe with the blade. "I'll kill you and spit on your dead body afterwards."

"And I'll look forward to seeing you put in jail for what you've done to the young lady and also for the damage you've caused on my ship," Jasper said, and enjoyed the brief flicker of fear in Hugo's eyes.

The two men circled one another. Jasper lunged towards his enemy and was able to knock the knife from Danville's grasp. They once more began throwing punches. Jasper made every attempt to keep his attention on his enemy despite catching a glimpse of Miranda emerging from the coach. She had managed to somehow untie the ropes that had held her captive and was racing toward the pistol.

Danville had just taken hold of the knife and raised his arm to flick the weapon at Jasper when the sound of the pistol rang out. The blade fell from Hugo's hand as he fell to the ground. Miranda stood there holding the smoking gun, with a gleam of satisfaction on her face.

"That bloody bitch shot me in the leg," Hugo complained, holding his injured thigh, unable to do more than moan and thrash.

"You're lucky I didn't shoot you directly in your black heart!" she called out, before she flung herself into Jasper's waiting arms.

"You saved me," he said, taking her cheeks in his hands and examining her for injuries.

"I think we saved each other," she confessed, before kissing him.

"Where on earth did you learn how to shoot a pistol?" Jasper asked.

Miranda gave a hesitant shrug. "My brother gave both Grace and me lessons just in case we ever had need to defend ourselves."

"Smart brother."

Miranda gave a short laugh. "He would agree with you."

"Remind me to thank him when next we meet," he replied.

Jasper gave her a quick hug before taking the discarded rope and tying Hugo up to take to the local magistrate. Jasper would give testimony of what happened and the rest of Hugo's fate would be out of his hands.

Jasper ordered the carriage to return to Fenwick on Sea with Danville secured inside. There was no way he was going to ask Miranda to share the carriage with the snake, bound or not. He jumped into his saddle and held out his hands for his lady. He settled her into his lap and she rested her head upon his shoulder as they made their way back to the inn.

There was quite the ruckus when they returned, since Miranda's maid had alerted everyone about what had happened. Jasper escorted Miranda inside but was surprised when she swept her arms around his neck in a fierce hug.

"You realize your reputation is going to be ruined even further than it was before, *mon amour*, after such a display of affection," Jasper whispered into her ear while keeping her close.

"I couldn't care a fig what they think of me," she replied tartly, before lifting her chin and pursing her lips to receive his kiss.

Never one to leave a lady wanting, he gave free expression to the desire he had been holding in. She was his... they belonged forever together.

CHAPTER 14

Cromer, England
Three Months Later

M iranda sat next to a large picture window staring out over the sea in her sister's cottage. Nicholas's daughter Blanche and his and Grace's baby boy played on a blanket on the floor, making Miranda wish for a child of her own one day... that was if she were ever to marry. She had almost given up on Jasper's return after only three months. How would she ever survive waiting on shore for months on end while her husband was at sea?

"He'll be here soon," Grace said, as if reading her mind. She poured a cup of tea, handing the porcelain to Miranda.

"I wish he was here now," Miranda confessed, with a smile that swiftly faded. Had the man she had come to love forgotten about her?

"Stop it," Grace ordered while her eyes lit up in a mischievous twinkle.

"Stop what?" Miranda asked, not knowing what her sister was talking about.

"Stop thinking Jasper isn't going to return. He loves you. Just be patient."

Miranda laughed. "You, above all people, should know being patient is not one of my strong points."

"Should we place a bet then?" Grace smirked with a knowing grin.

"Our betting days are over, Gracie," Miranda said throwing up her hands. "I've learned my lesson."

"If you're certain..." Grace let the challenge hang in the air.

"I am," Miranda answered, setting down her cup before following Grace's gaze out the window. A lone gentleman was walking along the shore and as he came closer, recognition lit Miranda's face. "He's here!

"Well, go on then. Don't keep your man waiting for you," Grace urged. Miranda ran from the house, down the back stairs and out onto the sand.

She had never been so happy to see anyone in her life and, when Jasper recognized her, he also began running. If she had been paying better attention, she would have seen Jasper's ship anchored off the shoreline just as Grace had.

"Jasper," she called out, before she jumped into his arms. He began twirling her around and around on the sand.

"Miranda!" he rejoiced before setting her down on her feet. "How I have missed you."

He bent down and his lips touched her own. Miranda wanted nothing more than their kiss to last forever more. She gave everything she had into their kiss leaving him no doubt how much he had been missed.

They began walking along the shoreline hand in hand before she raised questioning eyes up to him. "What took you so long?" she asked quietly. "I thought you would have been here before now."

"It's your brother's fault, actually," Jasper began. "Took me forever to track down his whereabouts. I finally found him up at his manor in Saltford."

"You asked for his blessing?"

"Yes." Jasper stole another kiss before they continued their stroll. "You told me I had to."

"And are you going to tell me his answer?"

"He gave it after I told him that there would never be another man who would love you as deeply as I love you," Jasper answered, taking her hand and kissing the inside of her wrist.

"You love me," she sighed, tears forming in her eyes.

He leaned down to whisper in her ear. "This is the part where you tell me you love me too, *ma petite.*"

"Oh Jasper! I do love you, more than you'll ever know," she exclaimed, and, for the first time in her life, she knew what it was to be truly happy.

"Then would you do me the honor of becoming my wife?" he asked, pulling out a ring from his jacket.

Miranda stared at the square cut emerald surrounded by tiny diamonds. "Yes, Jasper," she replied. "I would be honored to become your wife."

He placed the ring upon her finger. Brushing the tears that began to run down her cheeks, he once more placed his lips upon her own. "I hope those are happy tears, *mon amour*," Jasper replied.

"Of course, they are. I'm only saddened thinking of the months we'll spend apart while you travel and I'm left on shore," Miranda answered, trying not to cloud this moment she had been waiting for all her life.

"Leave you on shore? You must be crazy if you think I'll leave you on shore when I can have my lovely wife with me each and every day," Jasper declared before lifting her up and swinging her around again.

"You mean I can travel with you?" she asked, while bursts of happiness poured from her eyes.

"I wouldn't have it any other way, my lovely lady. Life with you, Miranda, will be one hell of an adventure!" Jasper laughed before kissing her again.

When they entered Grace's home and Nicholas poured champagne to celebrate their announcement, Miranda could only stare in wonder at the man who had changed her world. Thanks to him, she had opened her eyes to see the person, not the title or the money, and finally fallen in love. Jasper was right... she'd never have a dull moment as long as Jasper was her husband. She would look forward to their journey through the rest of their lives together.

EPILOGUE

The Caribbean Sea
One Year Later

Jasper held his tiny infant son in his arms while he made his way to the bow of his ship. His beautiful wife stood there much as she had done over a year ago in London, before she was his. This time, though, her black hair was free of its normal restraints and floated on the ocean breeze in a heavenly display of curls. She was meant for life at sea and the whole world awaited them as they traveled to new locations in order to fulfill their thirst for new discoveries.

Miranda must have felt his presence, for she turned and opened her arms inviting Jasper and their son to join her at the rail. The crystal-clear blue-green water of the ocean sparkled like diamonds, much like Miranda's eyes did each day they were together.

"He just woke up?" she asked, holding out a finger for the baby to play, only to find the child closing his eyes to doze off again.

"Obviously, he didn't care for my sparkling conversation," Jasper replied, before his mother came over to take the child to coo over him.

He didn't mind. It gave him the extra opportunity to be alone with his wife.

"I never knew I could be so happy, Jasper," Miranda murmured, turning in his arms to face him. "I adore our life together."

"Before I found you, Miranda, I had never met anyone whom I thought would make me truly happy. You changed all that from the very first moment I saw you upon the dance floor. I know you felt it, too, even though you were too stubborn to admit it."

"You're not trying to pick a fight with me, are you, my darling husband?" she teased with twinkling eyes.

"I would never dare," he laughed, bringing her closer and kissing the top of her head.

"I tried to deny what had been happening between us, Jasper," she confided with a warm smile. "I was so blinded all those years and wasted so much time looking for a titled gentleman to wed, but none of them would have made me happy."

"You were just waiting for me, *mon amour*," he whispered. "I adore you."

"Yes, I was. I'm so glad you found me, Jasper. You must know how very much I love you," she murmured.

"Show me," he said, as he began nibbling at her ear.

"In the middle of the day?" she gasped out, before looking around the deck. For once, the crew seemed to have vanished—including Jasper's parents, much to his delight.

A chuckle escaped him when he saw how embarrassed she appeared. "Has that ever stopped us before?"

She giggled. "Well... now that you mention it, it hasn't. What did you have in mind?"

"I'm certain you will think of something, my beautiful wife," he replied with a roguish grin, as he led her down to their cabin.

And she did... on that day and for many years to come Miranda showered Jasper with so much love he never once regretted making her his wife. Something this strong would surely last beyond this lifetime and extend until the end of time itself. For Jasper, he couldn't ask for anything more from the love he shared with his wife. Life with Miranda was indeed a grand adventure!

THE END

Miranda made her first appearance in *A Kiss For Charity* followed by *The Earl Takes A Wife*. As her character developed, I knew it would take a special hero for her to learn what truly mattered in life. I believe Jasper was just who she needed. You can learn more about these two novellas along with my other Regency, medieval, and time travel stories on my website at https://www.sherryewing.com/books.

SOCIAL MEDIA FOR SHERRY EWING

You can learn more about Sherry Ewing at these social media links:

Amazon Author Page: http://amzn.to/1TrWtoy
Bookbub: www.bookbub.com/authors/sherry-ewing
Facebook: www.Facebook.com/SherryEwingAuthor
Goodreads: www.Goodreads.com/author/show/8382315.Sherry_Ewing
Instagram: https://instagram.com/sherry.ewing
Pinterest: www.Pinterest.com/SherryLEwing
Twitter: www.Twitter.com/Sherry_Ewing
YouTube: http://www.youtube.com/SherryEwingauthor
Newsletter: http://bit.ly/2vGrqQM
Facebook Street Team:
www.facebook.com/groups/799623313455472/
Facebook Official Fan page: https://www.facebook.com/groups/356905935241836/

ABOUT SHERRY EWING

Sherry Ewing picked up her first historical romance when she was a teenager and has been hooked ever since. A bestselling author, she writes historical and time travel romances to awaken the soul one heart at a time. When not writing, she can be found in the San Francisco area at her day job as an Information Technology Specialist.

Learn more about Sherry at:
Website: www.SherryEwing.com
Email: Sherry@SherryEwing.com

SCANDAL IN THE OLD WING

Dearest Reader,

The rustic seaside town of Fenwick on Sea is not as sleepy as one might think, especially with the travelers stranded by what might truly be called the Storm of the Century.

A Scotsman has arrived at the Queen's Barque, his well-made coats soaked and his fine boots caked with mud. A tall, handsome specimen of our northern cousins, he claims the status of gentleman. And yet, dear Reader, he arrived with a local woman, with whom he plans to shelter in the inn's oldest wing —alone!

Is she, in truth, a titled lady, as some say? She goes about in men's trousers, is said to be not averse to a midnight sail, and often visits the inn with a tub or two in hand! Though, on this occasion, it was her companion thus encumbered, so perhaps he truly is a gentleman after all.

THE COMTESSE OF MIDNIGHT

ALINA K. FIELD

The Comtesse of Midnight
Alina K. Field

A Scottish Earl on a quest for the elusive Comtesse de Fontenay rescues a French lady smuggler from the surf during a devastating storm, and takes shelter with her. As the stormy night drags on, he suspects his companion knows the woman he's seeking, the one who holds the secret to his identity. When she admits she is, in fact, the Comtesse Fontenay, just not the one he's seeking, she dashes all his hopes—and promises him new ones.

CHAPTER 1

Malcolm Comyn gripped the reins and clamped his other hand to his hat as a gust of horizontal rain shot straight from the North Sea.

Damnation. The rain struck like pellets of ice blasted from a shotgun.

The gelding he'd borrowed from the White Hart in Blythburgh snorted and ducked his head. A sure-footed animal, he'd managed the journey north on the coast road and then inland on Maresrow Road briskly enough. That was before they reversed course to head east again, back to the coast road. The worst of the rainstorm had caught up with them and now, the poor fellow flagged, picking his way along the verge of the flooded road.

"Soon, lad," he told the steady beast. But a few minutes more and they'd turn north and head onward to Lowestoft.

His morning mission a failure, he'd decided to push on to the Blue Boar where he could wait out the storm while puzzling out his next step. *If* they could make it, and he prayed they could. They'd passed no public lodgings on the morning ride. They would just have to plunge ahead.

Three weeks he'd been searching, to no avail. 'Twas now the first day of April, the country in uproar over grain costs and Bonaparte's escape, the weather gods wrathful as well. There'd be no hurrying back to London, neither by land nor by sea, even if he wished to give up his quest for the woman. And he didn't.

And he wouldn't.

At the end of Maresrow Road, he steered his mount left. The road north climbed above the marshes, traversing sheer cliffs that, to his right, loomed above a raging sea. To his left, a manor perched atop a slight rise, lights gleaming in the sparkling windows.

Hope sparked and just as quickly died. This manor house could not be his destination. Bloodmoor Hill Manor was not on the coastal road. He might stop here and seek directions, or even shelter.

On the other hand, making inquiries of the local gentry might raise more questions from them than he was willing to answer. Better to pick the brain of another publican or passing traveler in a cozy tap room.

Though it must still be afternoon, the churning clouds darkened the sky to late evening, and the rain sheeted the path ahead. He rode on in the diminishing light, his mount growing twitchier and twitchier. Squinting, he pulled up on the reins.

His heart pounded fiercely. The coast road ahead, the road that led to Lowestoft and shelter, had completely vanished.

"Steady boy," he said, more for himself than for the good-humored gelding. Had he put his horse into a gallop, he'd have ridden straight into the abyss, traversing that road where it now lay, hundreds of feet below on the rocky beach. Traversing it as a ghost, as 'twas sure that he'd be dead. The matter of who was the rightful Earl of Menteith would be settled.

Damn, but wouldn't that fit his enemy's plan to a tee?

Another bone-rattling sheet of rain pelted him. The full force of his predicament overcame him, and he let out a stream of oaths. Today's quest for Bloodmoor Hill Manor had been another fool's errand. With no sure direction, he might have missed the road; he might have passed directly by an overgrown lane leading to the manor.

Or the manor might be a phantasm of someone's imagination, or, more likely, a false lead planted by the villain plaguing him.

"What now?" he asked aloud.

The horse looked back at him with a snort.

"I'm as miserable as ye are, fellow. Come. Let's find the both of us shelter."

Turning back south, he eyed the lighted windows of the lonely manor. Asking for shelter there was an option.

But a branch of the coastal road continued south, and he recalled that, at the intersection with Maresrow Road, a stone post had stood, leaning as if pushed by the sea winds. He hadn't bothered to read the name carved upon it. He rode on, hoping to find a nearby village, preferably one with an inn. He would make one last foray for anonymous shelter before inquiring at the manor.

His mount stalled abruptly, ears flicking. A shout and an equine squeal carried on the wind, the animal's cry mixing with the crashing of waves. This distance south of the cliffs, the road fronted a field that sloped gently to a rocky beach studded with boulders. A beached vessel rested there with figures circling around it, their shouts carrying his way.

He nudged the gelding off the road. The beast tediously picked his way through the gorse, and boulders, and rain-induced streams, while Malcolm prayed that the ground would hold.

Finally reaching the beach, he saw white cloth puddled around the broken mast of the small sloop. A train of laden donkeys stumbled off to the north, two men guiding their precarious steps, while another man remained behind. He disappeared under sailcloth and came out with a cask, depositing it on the rocky shore. The wind swirled and sent a wave that threatened to claim the cargo, and the man dove for it, scooting it higher on the beach.

These were free traders, and this was a foolish one to battle Neptune over a cask of spirits. The next wave could very well take him as well as the cargo.

"Halloo," Malcolm called.

The man scrambled to his feet. Short and slight, his oilcloth coat tented over him. He was otherwise dripping wet, a knit cap clinging down to his eyebrows.

He dove under the sail again and came back with another cask.

Either he hadn't heard or he was ignoring the greeting. "Do you need help?" Malcolm called.

The man spun around, a scowl on his young face, and shook his head.

Another wave swamped him, the sea tugging at his boots and legs. He fell back, unsteady and struggling against the pull of the wave, still clutching his cargo.

Malcolm dismounted, tossed the reins around a stout boulder, and waded into the surf. He reached a hand and pulled the delicate lad up, swept the cask out of his loosening grip, and fought his way back up the beach with the lad in tow.

Eyes flashed up at him. Gray, or green, or blue—the color was uncertain in this dim light, but the lashes framing them were long, the lips full, the face a smooth heart shape filled with annoyance.

Feminine annoyance.

He swept a gaze over the coats and trousers, confirming the curves below. Almost confirming.

And if confirmed, it would be the first bit of intrigue unrelated to his earldom that he'd had in months.

He whisked the smuggler up under his free arm, swallowing a chuckle, ignoring the unmistakably female howl of protest.

✦

Merde. With fingers numb from fighting the storm, holding onto the casks was proving nigh impossible. And the man oughtn't to be here.

The hand reaching out was large, the arm it was attached to a strong one, and the stranger was a full head taller. He wasn't a revenue agent though, or not a known one. They'd all be snug in their beds in a storm like this, which is where the crew would be very soon. As soon as the men stowed the barrels and the landlord of the Queen's Barque received this delivery.

The man was not with the government, yet his scrutiny was a close one.

"Nooo." The scold came unbidden because he'd plucked a body tight up against him, juggling the cask in his other arm.

The devil he was, and too damned presumptuous. "Put me down. You oughtn't to be here. Go see to your horse. The animal will have the reins free in moments."

"Ungrateful brat." Still cradling the cask, he slogged back to the horse, soothing the creature with a gentle touch that quite impressed. Except, that he still held the cask that wasn't his.

"You. That's mine."

"Aye, and I'm carryin' it for ye. Come." He beckoned. "Get yourself out of the surf."

That was probably wise. Whether the sloop would be there in the morning was anyone's guess. A pity that. Nothing about this run had been easy.

This was usually a task for the midnight hour, completed by dawn. But the storm had changed everything. They were lucky to be alive.

"That cask is mine, and I'll have it now."

He picked up the other one. "I'll carry the both. Ye'll lead the horse."

The beast rolled his eyes and snorted with only mild annoyance. This was a fine creature to be only a bit discomposed by his day's work and the weather.

"Fine, then. I will lead him."

When the man turned with the casks and stomped off toward the embankment a sharp whistle checked him.

"Not that way. We will follow the beach. It will be faster and less treacherous than taking that hillside."

"Aye. Unless a wee wave comes and sweeps us away. And where would it be that we're going?"

And there it was, a guess before, but now, *certainement*: a Scots accent, one that sent a slither of fear up the spine. And why would *another* finely dressed Scotsman be visiting these parts?

Courage. "I am going as far as the village. Then you may give me my casks, and I will give you your horse, and you may go your own way."

"There's a village?" he asked.

"Yes, but of course. Fenwick on Sea." A sweet outpost of decent people in this pitiless land. "You are a stranger, I see." The crew had seen many strange people descending on Fenwick on Sea seeking refuge from the weather. It was wise to be wary of strangers. "Where are you coming from? Scotland?"

He blinked. "Not as far as all that. I've traveled from Blythburgh."

"And where were you going today that you didn't know of Fenwick on Sea?"

He quirked a lip. Water poured off the brim of his hat and coursed over a strong nose and firm jaw, yet he looked of a sudden incredibly cheerful.

"If you are thinking to take up trading in these parts—"

"No." He shook his head, spraying water like Hector, the great beast of a dog that guarded the village inn. "I'm seeking shelter, for me and for this poor fellow. Is there an inn in this village?"

How inconvenient. They were seeking the same destination. Nevertheless, seeing a horse suffer was unbearable.

"Most certainly there is an inn. The Queen's Barque."

They walked on in silence for a time, reaching the part through the dunes that led to the road that became the village's Market Street. Already, lights gleamed in the windows of the inn and the village's other shops and cottages, though it was likely not yet five of the clock.

They stopped at the entrance to the inn's courtyard. He might lead his horse and enter there.

"Give me my casks now, and I'll be on my way." The casks were better carried through the stable entrance and left in the brewhouse for the spirits to be let down.

He eyed the lighted windows of the inn. "It looks to be crowded. I can sleep in the stable if need be. Where are you taking these?"

That question was better ignored. "A gentleman who'll sleep in a stable? Hah."

He turned away from the inn and moved closer. Too close. "A lady who'll smuggle gin?" His lips stretched into a slow grin that matched his teasing tone.

There was no point correcting him, and, anyway, Marielle Plessiers was almost to the end of her ruse. Once the casks were delivered, she, like the men in the crew, would disappear, and eventually find the way home. This weather would not continue forever.

And this one... Yes, he was handsome and he knew it. And he was younger than she'd first thought, certainly younger than herself, and likely to think himself a stallion in bed. Young handsome men were a rarity in her world, and the ones she'd encountered could never be trusted. As for the bed skills... pah. The Comte de Fontenay had taught her to be skeptical of men bragging too much.

"It is not gin. It is a very fine brandy. Now be the gentleman you appear to be and give me my casks."

"Come along. I assume these are for the innkeeper. Perhaps they'll help me negotiate a better bed than the hayloft."

She ought to crack open his thick Scottish head.

He turned to enter the inn's courtyard. Spluttering, she hurried to catch up, and grabbed his arm. "Not this way." She yanked him along to the stable entrance.

CHAPTER 2

Malcolm swallowed a chuckle and went along like a dutiful packhorse. In the stable yard, carriages and wagons crowded the cobbled space. A groom hailed them and ran out, eying him closely before shifting his gaze back to the lady.

"We were *that* worried," he said.

She gave her head a little shake. "This man is looking for shelter."

A boy raced out and joined the other fellow. "You can't mean me to saddle your mare," he cried. "The coast road is gone."

She chewed her luscious lip.

"He's right," Malcolm said. "I was headed that way. The whole road is at the bottom of the cliff. With the rain falling this hard, I wouldn't risk trying to go around through the marshland."

She shrugged. "I see. Well, I mustn't subject the dear girl to this weather. Please see that this fellow is dry and well fed." She handed over the reins.

"And fetch me the bag attached to my saddle." Malcolm turned to the lady. "And where do these go?"

She rolled her eyes and led Malcolm over to the covered carriageway that led to the inn's courtyard.

A tall, lean man popped out of the inn door, followed by a woman in an apron. She scurried behind the building, but the man crossed the courtyard and joined them. Mayhap this anxious looking fellow in shirtsleeves was the innkeeper.

"Thank heavens." He tucked a bar towel away in his waistband. "We were worried. Ryman." He beckoned the groom who'd first greeted them. "Take these."

Malcolm glanced at the lady smuggler, who nodded permission. He handed over the precious cargo.

The innkeeper cast Malcolm a curious glance, and then turned a questioning gaze on the lady.

"Mr. Brewster, this gentleman needs shelter."

"Every room is taken, m—"

A quick shake of her head coincided with the lad delivering his bag, both actions interrupting a declaration of her name.

Ah, well. More delicious mystery.

Brewster frowned and went on. "The road north is washed out. All the others are flooded. We've had castaways washed ashore. There's talk of ships foundering at the point. The last carriage limped in only an hour ago. I've had to put the wounded wherever I had space, despite the state the south wing is in, and the east wing is even worse."

"The stables will do," Malcolm said.

"It's overflowing with coachmen and grooms."

"Well then, if ye've a dry blanket, I'll take a bench in the taproom." Malcolm turned to the lady. "Allow me to buy ye dinner."

An indecipherable look passed over the landlord's face. "That won't do."

"Why not?" Perhaps there was a riding officer in the taproom. He wanted to hear the man say it.

He cleared his throat. "There's a, er, reporter hereabouts. From one of those London scandal sheets, the Teatime Tattler. Wife heard someone whispering about it. We don't know who it is."

A reporter for a scandal sheet? That was infinitely worse than a riding officer.

Three weeks of grueling travel and uncomfortable inns had him fighting unending fatigue. He'd been trying to get ahead of a looming scandal, one that threatened everything dear to him, including his very identity. He'd been undecided whether to publish the story himself or try to conceal it.

Damnation. He needed more time to finish his quest, more time to decide on the best course of action.

The lady pressed her lips together while the innkeeper stood silently. These villagers were a cagey lot. They guarded their tongues and, where the lady was concerned, names.

He must do the same—if anyone could smoke out a peer of the realm it was a London reporter.

"What of your ancient wing?" she asked.

"I've barely begun on the Maiden's Wing. Fixed the roof in the upper rooms, so they'll be dry, but... I'll need the revenue from that large south wing to do her up right."

"The Maiden's Wing," Malcolm mused. "After Bess, I presume."

"Aye, and dating to her visit here, and not much touched since. 'Twill be an elegant suite of rooms for distinguished visitors when we are finished."

"Are there lower rooms there?"

"Only one. It's our smallest wing. The ground floor has naught but a furnished parlor. But there's no bed."

He was damnably tired of the wet. "If there's a hearth and some fuel, you may bring in..." He glanced at the lady. She was dodging the scandalmongers as well. "You may bring in pallets for us, or at the very least, blankets."

She blinked, the flutter of feminine eyelashes a silent expression of discord. "Us?"

He paused, eyeing her. He wasn't a man given to whims, especially where women were concerned. And it might be a damned foolish thing, risking sleep in the same room with a woman who wore trousers and smuggled spirits. And then there'd been that robbery attempt by an ugly fellow at an inn outside Clacton-on-Sea.

On the other hand, she might know the way to Bloodmoor Hill Manor. And from what he could see, she was pretty.

"If there's only the one room available and no bed, we might as well share the parlor. I'm dead on my feet, mayhap ye are as well after your... exertions. I'll not molest ye, my word as a gentleman, and this good man as witness." He swallowed another chuckle. Given those casks of brandy, how good Brewster was might be in question. "And I also would rather not appear in some London tattle sheet." For, he had a feeling the lady was not some local smuggler's woman, but a lady of quality. He was going on gut instinct perhaps, or the tone of her speech, genteel with a hint of something foreign.

Or she could be a London ladybird retired to the sea coast. If he wasn't so bluidy tired, perhaps that would be all right.

Telling them to wait while he fetched the key, Brewster turned for the door. As he passed into the courtyard, they heard him bellow. "What're you doing here, Alice? There's rooms needing cleaning."

The aproned woman appeared from behind the building and cast a curious glance his way. He sent her a challenging frown, the hair on his neck quivering. Nosy maids and scandal sheet scribes—the sooner he left the Queen's Barque, the better.

⚜

Key in hand, the lady led him through the courtyard, past the outbuilding she said was the brewhouse, around the back of the taproom and along another covered passage to a sagging door.

"Allow me." The lock creaked and resisted, the metal threatening to bend. He mumbled a curse and tried again. This time the mechanism screeched and opened.

A stairway led up from the entry. To the right was another door, this one with no lock. When he pushed the door open, faint scurrying noises told him they wouldn't be entirely alone. The room smelled of mice and damp but appeared dusty and otherwise reasonably clean. A table held the middle of the room with a few chairs placed neatly about, and near the fireplace was a threadbare sofa and two worn wing chairs, all upholstered in an aging brocade that might once have been striped in blue.

"It's not as bad as I feared," he said. "Ye may have the sofa."

Her shrug was quite elegant. "It is used upon occasion by... local people. When the other parlors are taken," she added.

It was used for stowing goods, in other words.

Not that he cared. The exploits of the free traders had naught to do with him, and having his own small distillery, he was no friend to the King's gaugers.

"Do they also use the rooms above?"

"No."

"I'll just run up and make sure the ceiling won't fall in on us." And check that they truly were alone. Since seeing his cousin assaulted in London by paid thugs, and fending off that inn thief, he'd grown warier, if one didn't count the whole madness of this expedition.

And a night spent with a lady smuggler? The foolishness of it made him smile, but needs must. If she was less intriguing, he'd bump a coachman into the taproom and sleep with his horse.

Waving him away, she walked to the hearth where a lamp and tinderbox sat upon the mantel.

He pocketed the key and navigated the dark stairs carefully, making a quick survey of the upper rooms. The ceilings were streaked with water stains, and, in various places, wood paneling had warped, but the buckets and tubs placed in strategic spots sat empty. The floors, and therefore the ceiling above the parlor, seemed dry and solid enough. The bed ropes held no mattresses, and only a few scattered chairs and tables littered the rooms. Even the vermin might have abandoned this floor for the cozier regions below.

He reached the foot of the stairs just as Brewster arrived with a scuttle of coal, blankets, and two servants carrying buckets of hot water and a massive covered tray. The innkeeper left, promising to send over clean pallets.

A good thing, since the sofa might have other occupants nestling in the comfortable upholstery.

Eyes averted, the male servant silently went to work making a fire while the maid set out their dinner. When they'd left, Malcolm draped his damp overcoat on a chair and helped the lady out of her oilskin.

Underneath, she wore another coat that failed even more miserably than the oilskin at hiding her womanly figure.

"Your cap is soaking." His fingers itched to snatch it off of her head, to get a look at what was hidden there. "If you wish to remove it—"

"No," she said with enough haughtiness to pass for a duchess.

"Very well." He pulled out a chair for her, and she seated herself gracefully.

Uncertain about the appetite of a lady smuggler, he defaulted to good manners and filled a plate for her with lady-sized morsels. The innkeeper had provided enough food for two or three men, so perhaps lady smugglers didn't stint on their meals.

Outside, a howl rattled the window as the storm surged and grew fiercer, the rain pounding the east-facing window.

"We haven't been properly introduced," he said, filling his plate. They might forgo titles, his, and hers if she had one. "My name is—"

"There is no need," she said.

The sheer ferocity of the statement intrigued him. "Why?"

"When the storm ends, you will go your way, and I will go mine."

She ate then, in silence and quickly, like a schoolboy needing to finish before the dishes were removed. Or, since she took a second helping, perhaps like someone unsure of her next meal. But her table manners were otherwise impeccable.

Not having eaten since a quick breakfast that morning, Malcolm hurried through his meal as well before venturing again to begin a conversation.

"The ale is decent," he said. "A home brew?"

"As I pointed out, the Queen's Barque has a brewhouse."

A knock at the door brought a cheerful lad burdened by two straw-stuffed pallets. He was accompanied by a massive beast.

The dog cast Malcolm a curious gaze, and then went to the lady, tail wagging furiously.

"Hector." She knelt to receive slobbery kisses from the brindled mastiff, or, given the droopy ears and gloriously plumed tail, part mastiff. The dog stood a full yard at the shoulder and, when done kissing, grinned at her through its jowls.

"He hasn't forgot you, my lady," the boy said.

She plucked a scrap from the tray and handed it to the dog.

"Was all well tonight, my lady? Mam was worried about..."

He froze, noticing Malcolm's interest.

"Everyone is well," she said. "Finishing up and returning home."

"Ah good, thank you, my lady. I'll be going then. Hector?"

"Hector is busy making my acquaintance," Malcolm said, for indeed the dog was sniffing his trousers and hands, and allowing his massive head to be fondled. "Ye're a fine fellow," he said. "Let him rest here a bit."

The boy looked a question at the lady and then shrugged. "He'll look after you then, my lady."

The dog was here to guard her from Malcolm? He laughed. Very well. But who would guard Malcolm from her?

When the door closed, she bustled about covering the food. *My lady*, the lad had called her, not once but four times. If she was a lady, what the devil was she doing out in trousers running cargo?

She hefted a bucket of water and went to the dark corner of the room.

In the light of the lamp, he'd seen that her eyes were blue, and her eyebrows were a dark shade of blond. A few freckles spotted the bridge of her nose, and delicate frown lines etched the space between her eyebrows. She was older, but not yet old.

She was far too young to be the lady he was seeking.

When she returned to the light, he saw that she'd finally shed the ugly cap, revealing shoulder length hair in a dark shade of blond, hair that shimmered in the lamplight and made his fingers itch to explore.

A sudden flash of light streaked through the grimy windows. The storm gods had added lightning to their repertoire. The crack of thunder that followed evoked a whine and sent the massive dog pacing.

He beckoned, and the dog came and laid its head on his lap, adding slobber to the mud splattered on his only pair of trousers. He rubbed the loose skin and scratched behind a floppy ear.

"There'll be no sleeping soundly until the storm eases, I fear," she said. "Hector will make sure of it."

"Should I send him away, poor fellow?"

"No."

Whether she wished Hector to stay for her own safety or the dog's, he couldn't be sure, but her decisiveness pleased him. She wasn't a dithering sort of female. "As long as the building around us holds."

"It's withstood these storms for some three hundred years, they say.

We must hope for the best." She went to a cabinet and returned with a bottle. "Brandy?"

"I've something better." He retrieved his flask from his bag. "Good whisky. The last of it. Share it with me?"

She nodded and accepted the glass he poured. "You are Scottish."

"Aye. Have ye ever seen a Scotsman before?" he joked.

"Where is your plaid, your... your kilt?"

"I've left it at home."

Her gaze narrowed on him. She clinked her glass to his, said "cheers," and took a tentative sip. "It's good."

"Aye. Are there many Scots here about?"

"I fear I don't know."

"But ye've kenned that I'm Scottish, and ye're from these parts. Ye would know were there others of my countrymen here."

She dipped her head. "No. I am not from these parts."

He heard it then—*non*, not *no*. She'd swallowed the *n* on the end of the word, the faint trace of an accent he'd noticed earlier and couldn't pin down. She was French. A French lady who'd recognized him as a Scotsman.

His hopes rose. *My lady*, the boy had called her. She wasn't from around here, she said, but neither was the lady he was seeking, the Comtesse de Fontenay. Mayhap this lady was her young sister, or a cousin, or some fellow émigré who might have once met the Earl of Menteith. She would know where another French lady was residing.

Yet she was a wary one, as wary as himself. She had no reason to trust him, and, for his part, he might be risking having his throat cut— quite decisively.

More thunder crashed, and Hector raised his head again, howled and threw himself upon the lady. The dog's regard for her eased Malcolm's worries about her character.

More fool him.

He refilled both their glasses with the very last of the whisky and picked up the brandy bottle. "Come," he said. "I'll take one of those chairs by the fire. If ye like, stretch out on the sofa or one of those pallets."

She seated herself in the opposite chair, and they drank, silently. Hector settled himself on one of the pallets, making Malcolm laugh.

"I'm bluidy tired myself," he said.

"Go to sleep."

He studied her over the top of the tumbler. What had he been thinking, to share a chamber with this woman?

"You fear me, that I'll cut your throat in the middle of the night," she said. "I won't. Nor will I rob you."

Thunder boomed and Hector leapt up, looking between the both of them. She beckoned the beast, and he went to her for another head rub.

"Are ye giving me yer word as a lady?" he asked.

"Something like that."

"The boy called ye *my lady*."

She shrugged. "A mere courtesy."

The thoughtless arrogance of that tiny gesture spoke volumes. She might be an actress pretending to act the role of a noblewoman, but he didn't think so.

He would stay awake. A Scotsman could hold his liquor better than any mere lass, noble or not.

CHAPTER 3

T he handsome young Scotsman drank freely and deeply, refilling
her glass, and she could see that he was willing himself to stay
awake.

He did not appear to be a naïve man, or one of the countless frib-
bles that populated aristocratic circles. Perhaps he wasn't an aristocrat
at all, but just some wealthy man of trade's sprout trained up to the air
of command that was bred into the nobility.

No matter. Whatever his station in life, he was younger, and she
was older. She had played this game more often, and, like any woman
in a man's world, for higher stakes. What one lacked in muscle, one
must make up for in cleverness, including the skill of holding one's
liquor.

Besides, after spending yesterday morning diligently going through
the Comte's dun letters, deciding who might be paid and who she
might tell to go to the devil when she left for France, she'd had a very
long afternoon nap, anticipating a call to help offload the lugger. The
perilous weather meant all hands had been needed. She was not so very
tired.

The Scotsman, however, was dead on his feet. She could almost feel
sorry for him. He was far from home, and had been traveling for

several days. His neckcloth was limp, his cuffs soiled, his coat wrinkled. His boots, well and carefully crafted, if not by Hoby then by some equally fashionable bootmaker in Edinburgh, had not been properly polished in the last few days.

He'd shaved though, probably very early that morning, because a delicious dark stubble had sprouted along his strong jaws.

Did he have a razor in his interesting valise? She wouldn't molest him, unless he thought to do the same to her. If it came to that, and she prayed that it wouldn't, she would use her own blade and not some unfamiliar shaving instrument.

"Is this one of yer imports?" he asked, swirling the amber liquid. "It's very good."

His words stirred her out of her imaginings about handsome young men, and she realized she must manage the conversation else she'd slip into sleep, or perhaps something more inconvenient, without thinking.

The Comte had always succumbed to sleep when they'd conversed, no matter the topic. She must soothe this fine-looking and very fatigued man the same way.

Outside, the thunderstorm had moved on, and the rain pounded in a comforting downpour. With the warm fire, and the heavy blankets, and the sleeping dog, it was quite cozy.

But what to talk about? Most certainly not the free trade. It would be far too diverting to put him to sleep. Besides, she had no idea what he would do with the knowledge.

The countryside? She might slip and drop a hint about her home at Bloodmoor Hill.

She thought back to her time on the fringes of a London society that she'd found unbearably dull.

The weather.

"I am glad you are enjoying the brandy," she said. "But I daresay you are not liking this weather. It is quite the worst storm in many seasons, people are saying. Normally at this time of year the sea has quietened." A lie, of course, but how would he know?

He sipped his drink, eyeing her over the glass.

Oh. Given that it might remind him of her activities that evening and spark questions, the sea was an inappropriate topic, whether or not one was fudging a weather report. "Winters, however are generally mild."

He yawned, and she went on, discussing the number of rainstorms in March and going back to February, and then January, and making up the story as she went along, until his eyes drooped and the empty glass fell into his lap and lodged itself next to his fall.

Warmth uncurled in her. His trousers were tight in the usual fashion for gentlemen, outlining masculine endowments that sparked her interest far too much. Retrieving the fallen tumbler was out of the question.

She set down her own glass and fought the urge to join him in slumber.

Malcolm woke to a sense of unsettling awareness, eyes opening, the rest of him motionless. He was at yet another bluidy inn—ah yes, the road north had collapsed. He was with a fetching lady smuggler wearing trousers.

He'd fallen asleep in a chair and his neck ached like the devil, and... the chair opposite was empty, as was the sofa.

A steady gurgling snore came from the floor in front of him where the massive dog lay, and the rain still pounded. All else was silent.

The lamp on the mantel emitted a low light, as did the fire.

He carefully swiveled his head. A candle sat atop the dining table, next to his open travel bag. The woman bent close to the dim light, studying a paper.

In three silent strides he was on her. She squeaked, startled, while he gripped her around the waist and yanked her back into him.

This close she smelled of a floral soap and her hair tickled his nose. Her curves tickled other parts of him. He eased his grip on her, and she huffed out a quiet breath.

"I believe that's mine. What are ye doing, my lady?"

She turned her head to look up at him and shrugged. "Satisfying my curiosity, *my lord*."

Hot anger flared in him, warring with a begrudging acknowledgement that, if he'd lulled her to sleep first, and if she'd been carrying a bag to search, he'd have done the same.

And there was her distracting femininity, so close, so enticing, stirring a different kind of heat. He'd not had a woman since he broke with a Highland widow before traveling to London in February.

"Mayhap ye'd like me to satisfy aught else," he whispered.

She froze and then scoffed, relaxing into apparent indifference.

On the table next to where her hand lay was his sheathed razor. If she knew where his mind was traveling, she'd have every right to use it upon him.

He released her and backed away. "There's little of value there. If ye're looking for my weapons or my money, it's my person ye'll want to peruse."

She looked back at him again, her gaze traveling over him, her bowed lips curving up. "I am not in need of money," she said.

"A smuggler not in need of money. I don't think I believe ye." He fought the urge to grin back at her. "In any case, those are my things. It's rude to go through a gentleman's belongings unless ye're his valet. Or perhaps his wife. Kindly put everything back."

She left everything as it was and faced him. "Knowledge, my lord, is sometimes more valuable than money. *You* are no mere gentleman. *You* are an earl."

He had two documents in his bag, a letter addressed to him from an unfortunately anonymous sender, and the declaration of a witness to his birth.

She perched her hands on her shapely hips. "Who is threatening you?"

She'd been reading the letter.

He stared into glowing eyes, wondering about her interest. Wondering if he might trust her. "Why? Will ye help me find the sender?"

Her gaze traveled over him again, head to foot and then back up again. It had been assessing, not amorous. She frowned. "You are young. Perhaps...three and twenty?"

The skin on his neck quivered. "Precisely." He glanced at the bag and the few contents littering the table. The other document was less accessible, wrapped in an oilskin in an inner compartment. He felt certain she hadn't yet found it. "And ye know this how?"

"I know nothing."

She'd spoken too quickly. "Ye know that I am Scottish, that I am an earl, the Earl of Menteith, and ye know my age. What else do ye know, my lady?"

"Nothing." She pushed past him, skirted the snoring dog, and stood by the warm hearth.

He followed and loomed over her, propping a hand on the carved wood of the mantel.

She seemed unsettled, perhaps because her search had been interrupted. She was a lady who liked to be in control.

His blood stirred. It was time to match wits with her.

"Shall I tell ye what *I* know?" He brushed a lock of hair from her cheek and her eyes flashed something between anger and fear.

Malcolm folded his arms over his chest. He'd given his promise as a gentleman that he wouldn't molest her. And he wouldn't.

However, if she were willing...

She lifted her chin. "You know nothing."

"I know ye are French."

A slim hand fluttered, dismissively. "There are many French *émigrés* in England."

"French and a lady. A noble lady? Or perhaps related to a noble lady... a *comtesse* perhaps."

Her gaze held steady.

"A *comtesse* who resides at Bloodmoor Hill Manor."

She blinked.

"Aye. Ye are a relative, or perhaps a friend of the Comtesse de Fontenay."

Her mouth opened and then closed, firming into a mulish line.

"What do you want with her?" she asked.

His heart lifted, excitement thrumming. *Finally*. After months of pondering since the letter arrived, after weeks of dreary searching, chasing about from Devon to Hastings, to Clackton-on-Sea, finally he'd found someone who knew the Comtesse—and he was sure this lady smuggler did know her.

"Will ye take me to her?" he asked.

A long thoughtful pause ensued. The bowed lips closed into an expression that was neither a pout nor a smile. The gaze revealed nothing—not curiosity, not fear, not suspicion.

A duchess who'd condescended to allow his introduction had worn the same haughty bland expression just before cornering him privately to express her interest in *something more*.

And he needed to stop thinking about the *something more*. His goal was in sight, and the goal was not swiving this lady, no matter how appealing.

"Why?" she asked, finally. "You must tell me why."

"Because..."

A reporter for a London rag sheltered next door in the inn. She might say she didn't need money, yet this tidbit of news he'd been protecting would bring someone a few coins.

He let out a breath. If need be, he had the scandal of a lady smuggler to barter. "She is my mother. My true mother."

Her mouth dropped, her eyes widened, and softened. Her hand floated up and her palm cradled his cheek.

"It *is* you then. So handsome you are. Young, and yet not young. You have old eyes, Lord Menteith, and, I can see, a weary heart. And I confess, I am quite smitten."

Smitten? She was smitten? They might have an entirely more pleasant evening together than what had transpired so far. But first he must secure a promise. "Will ye take me to her?"

She lifted her hand away and shook her head slowly. "Yes, but no, Lord Menteith."

She'd moved close, her hands smoothing along his shoulders down to his elbows, her eyes full of a warm emotion that he couldn't quite discern.

A lady smuggler entirely too close and too warm. His good sense ought to kick in, but his mind was too jumbled, his male parts on high alert.

"Yes, but no?" he repeated dumbly.

"Lord Menteith, *I* am the *Comtesse* de Fontenay. And I am most assuredly *not* your mother."

"Ye're..." His mind stuttered over the facts as she'd stated them. "My mother..." He rubbed at his forehead.

"I am *not* your mother." She took him into her arms—'twas the only way to explain it—in an embrace that was maternal, but... oh what did he know about maternal affection? The woman he'd thought was his mother had died when he was a babe.

He became aware of the breasts crushed against him and the hands stroking his shoulders, and all of his male parts stirred. He swept a hand down the back of her sturdy wool coat, down to the shapely swell of her trousers.

And froze. She'd quite handily distracted him. He ought to be asking more questions.

"When did she die?" he asked, still holding her close. A handful of woman this fine was worth holding onto, even if she might be lying. "Or..." His cousin had divorced *his* wife. Perhaps Malcolm's mother still lived. "Did he put her aside? Where is the Comte? When did ye marry him?"

Another thought struck him. He had no certainty about who had sent the letter. This lady might be the anonymous correspondent.

CHAPTER 4

Marielle clutched him to her bosom, taking comfort from his great brawn and his masculine strength. For he was strong, this young man with the old eyes. In his long-limbed height, he put her in mind of her first lover, a lieutenant home recovering from wounds, a clumsy, ungainly fellow growing into his manhood, as unskilled as herself, but delightful and funny, able to distract her from thoughts of her country. When their affair was uncovered, her aunt had quietly married her off to the widowed Comte de Fontenay, an old roué with few teeth, a bald head that he draped with an old-fashioned wig, and dwindling abilities in the bedchamber.

Still, having learned from his past, the Comte had a sense of honor about his young wife's satisfaction and, from him, she'd learned things about men and about herself.

She had a sense of honor as well, and so, though Gaspar had kindly declared that she was free to take lovers, she'd been faithful to him until his death the previous autumn. And, been too picky about men since to enjoy her widowed state.

She felt certain the Comte would understand the heat stirring in her now.

Yet Menteith had many questions that first must be answered

before any thoughts of an amorous congress. Marielle gathered her wits and stepped back from him.

First the unasked question she sensed was simmering within him. "I am not the letter-writer. That would *certainement* be another Scotsman, Giles Banquo."

His achingly handsome jaw dropped. "How—"

"We will come to that." Oh yes, he knew Banquo. His eyes had flared at the mention of a name that never failed to stir anger in her. "Your mother, who was the Comtesse de Fontenay before me, died in the Vendee, in the *populicide,* the revolutionaries' attempt to wipe out everything that was the old France."

Rage born of terrible memories and bitter despair flared in her, emotions that Gaspar had urged her to abandon lest they eat away her heart. She had mostly managed to constrain them within a firm cage of cynicism. But not entirely.

"The good and noble *citoyennes* turned out to be tyrannical and destructive beasts. It is an abomination that the son of this so-called revolution, Bonaparte, has been allowed to escape... to... to spread more death."

She took in a breath, squeezing her eyes against the emotion that overcame her whenever she thought about the chaos and tyranny and destruction of France. It had been five and twenty years since the Bastille fell, and still France was a cancer upon the world.

When she opened her eyes, she found him staring at her with something that looked like concern. He blinked, and his demeanor changed, and he again became the self-contained aristocrat gathering facts. "How exactly did she die? When? Where?"

"When and where, I don't know, but the Comte said she died by the guillotine." She shook her head. "So much death. It angers me so. They murdered the royals, they killed the nobles and priests, and then they devoured the bourgeoisie." Including her father, a doctor, and her mother, both executed after sending Marielle off to the country with an aunt. "And in the Vendee, they killed on a grander scale."

She'd been no more than a child when she sought refuge at her aunt's home in the Vendee. Before their narrow escape, she'd seen bloodshed that no child should ever witness.

She squeezed her eyes shut again on the visions. After a moment, she became aware of his hands, large and warm, cupping her shoulders. She lifted his hands away and took a breath, bringing herself into the present. "It was years before the Comte received proof of her death. They had come here, you see, quite prudently, after the Bastille fell, but she... she left him. She fell in love."

Menteith's gaze finally turned away from her as he looked into an unseen past.

"I had this story from the Comte himself."

He bit his lip. This news was a burden for him, but she must continue on.

"After your birth, she saw that there was no future with her lover. She returned to the Comte and soon after left to fight in the Royalist cause."

That Comtesse had left him, this handsome and noble son. How *could* she have done so?

"I might be the Comte's son."

His matter-of-fact tone belied a turmoil she sensed rising within him.

"No. He never fathered a child, not on your mother, not on me, nor on any lovers. Gaspar—the Comte—died last autumn. He knew of your birth, though I don't believe he sent that threatening letter to you either. However, before he died, he had a visit from Giles Banquo."

"I see." He walked to the table and poured another drink. Outside, the rain surged again, reminding them both of its power and its presence, the wind howling like the uneasy guilt eating away at her heart. It was Gaspar's guilt, yet he had left it to her as part of her meager inheritance.

"On his deathbed, he told me that he sold the story of your birth to Banquo for a price. He had little to leave me, you see. We had come here to this last lonely outpost because an old friend was engaged in the free trade. Gaspar had contacts in France and had done some business out of Devon and Kent. His heart was failing, and he was far too old for the endeavor, but he went out anyway and wore himself out. Then, last year, when he was ailing, he told me that Giles Banquo had advanced him money for the story and promised a grand sum if he could but find proof."

"And he never did?"

"Pay money? Or find proof?"

"Either. Both."

"The money advanced was spent on Gaspar's care." As for proof... was there proof? She had no idea. "And to my knowledge there is no proof. And it is no matter. I don't wish for his blood money."

"How did he come to know Banquo?"

"I don't know how Banquo came to visit us. But Banquo's wife was French, and Gaspar knew her family."

"I see."

He studied her for an uncomfortable moment while she straightened her spine and gazed directly back until the shame flooding her made her drop her eyes. What a dreadful inheritance Gaspar had left her.

"And so," he said, lifting her chin with two fingers, "you've taken up the Comte's smuggling." He reached for her, his eyes warm with unaccountable forgiveness and drew her into his arms. "Surely you cannot continue in the free trade?"

The kindness unsettled her. What sort of young man was this?

"I only help when needed. I am returning to France."

"What will you do there?"

"I will fight Bonaparte. I know, I cannot perhaps, take up arms like the infantry, but I can help in other ways. I can tend wounds, or pass information. And meanwhile, I will see about reclaiming my family home."

"My lady, it is twenty years gone."

"Yes. I know. I was a child of five when I left there. But I at least want to try if I may. Perhaps the new owner will rise for Bonaparte and be struck down with him, and then I may bring a lawsuit. It is worth the attempt. My parents were well off, but your mother, my lord, she was very rich. She was the sole heir of a large estate near La Roche-sur-Yon." Bile rose in her. "After they'd killed all the *Yonnais*, they changed the name of the town to Napoleon-sur-Yon."

Heart pounding, she leaned back and looked up at him. She had been alone for too many months now. She was a widow. She might take a lover if she wished. And she did wish. "Come with me to France."

His dark gaze burned down at her.

"At the manor, there are some things of your mother's that Gaspar kept. They mean little to me, and I haven't known what to do with them. I read the newspapers. The world is mobilizing against Bonaparte. We will not be alone in making our way to the Continent. Banquo..." She huffed out a breath remembering another reason she wished to disappear from Suffolk. "Is he following you?"

"No. Or I don't think so."

"He might show up anywhere, even in this terrible storm. We might find him in France, although what side he'll be fighting on is unclear."

His steady gaze sent goosebumps jumping along her back.

"We'll leave for Bloodmoor Hill Manor at first light," he said. "About the rest..." He traced a finger along her cheek, and under her neckcloth, and then went to work single-handed untying the knot.

The skilled touch sent shivers through her. The neckcloth fell away, as did the opening of the linen shirt.

She'd bound her breasts, as she always did. He dipped a finger under the cloth, watching her.

"Ye're certain we're not related?" he asked.

"I am certain. Your blood is much higher than mine, my lord."

"What is your name?"

"Marielle Plessiers. And you are Malcolm?"

"Yes. And for now, we're just a man and a woman."

She went up on her toes and their lips met. The storm picked that moment to rage harder, the wind howling again like the need boiling inside her.

He was virile, and strong, and a man in the prime of his mating years. Oh, how she wanted him.

CHAPTER 5

Her soft lips tasted like brandy. Malcolm clasped her more closely, inhaling her scent of fresh sea air and soap while she trembled against him, as if the soul-baring tales of both his mother's suffering and her own had been true. His good sense told him to hold back trust. His heart said to comfort her. His base nature said she was his for the taking, and his base nature won out.

He pulled the tails of her shirt from her loose trousers and searched for the tie of the cloth binding her breasts, the need to see them, to touch them driving him mad. He found the knot, and unable to loosen it, ripped it, while his tongue dueled with hers and the cloth fell away.

Her loose coat slipped off easily, and he stepped back to look. The gaping shirt bared the tops of her breasts, a sight more alluring than all the bursting bosoms he'd seen at society events.

He inched the shirt hem up and slid his palm over the bare skin at her midriff to her waistband. "A dress on a lady is much more convenient than trousers."

She set a hand to his waist. "While a gentleman finds the trousers oh so *very* convenient."

Her blue gaze intent, she slid her palm down the front of his trousers and took in a sharp breath.

Malcolm watched her, reining in the urge to toss her down on the sofa and rip every stitch from her. He set his hand upon hers, and lifted it away. "Not yet," he said, easing a hand up to fondle her breast.

At his touch, her eyes closed and her head tilted back. "You are a patient lover, Malcolm Menteith?"

"Malcolm Comyn."

"What?"

"My surname is Comyn, Marielle."

He took her lips again and led her to the sofa, settling her back on the cushions, pushing her shirt up. He needed this. He needed her.

Voices outside made him look up. Hector jerked out of his slumber and lifted his nose in the air.

"Someone is coming," she said.

He muttered a curse. He'd failed to lock the outside door, and this door had no lock.

Marielle sprang to her feet and found her coats, while he went to the door and pressed his ear to the panel.

He recognized the innkeeper's voice and opened the door a crack. Lantern in hand, the innkeeper escorted a lady attired in a dark water-logged carriage gown. Another lady just as drenched followed behind carrying a valise.

"Begging your pardon, sir," said the innkeeper, spotting him.

Malcolm opened the door wider.

"We've more refugees from the storm. Husband and sons are helping fetch the fuel and the mattresses. We'll just get you upstairs then, madam, and we'll have you set up in a wink."

"Thank you," she said, her voice shaky, her relief obvious.

If they were only just arriving by carriage, they must have endured a terrible journey in this storm.

Hector pushed up next to him, Marielle following. She'd tucked her long hair into the damp cap, playing a boy again.

"Bring them in here to wait," Malcolm said. "I peeked in upstairs earlier. It's dry, but quite chilly. You may warm up at our hearth while your fire is made and your beds are set up."

The innkeeper nodded his thanks and hurried out, promising to send hot drinks.

Merde. What had she been thinking?

Marielle hustled about, fetching brandy for the two women while Malcolm took their wet wraps and set the warm blankets about their shoulders as if he were tending to his own mother or aunt.

Her eyes filled and she blinked, carrying the glasses over and silently handing them to the women.

They were soaked to the bone, their teeth chattering, and there were at least two feet of mud on the hems of their skirts. What once might have been lace on the older woman's gown now looked like spun mud. The ladies must have walked for a good part of their journey.

"What happened?' she asked, risking them recognizing that she was a woman.

She'd managed to fumble her coats closed and tie a loose knot on her neck cloth, but the cloth that had bound her breasts lay on the pallet. Fortunately, Hector had decided to retire again, and stretched himself over all but a wee bit of cloth. Sadly, she was well-enough endowed that her coats might not provide the right silhouette for the young man she was pretending to be.

She crossed her arms over her chest.

The maid—for Marielle was convinced the thin, more plainly dressed woman was a maid—sipped her drink and choked.

"It's brandy," Malcolm said, coming to stand next to Marielle. "A fine one, for those who are used to the taste. Sip it. It will help to warm you."

The older lady unclenched her chattering teeth long enough for a sip. "We thank you. It's very good."

"What happened?" Marielle asked again. She really needed to know the state of the roads. While the storm still raged, they would wait; but at the first sign of the weather easing, they must be off. She would like to depart for France before Banquo decided to pay a call. "Were you coming from Lowestoft?"

The road from Lowestoft had collapsed, but despite what Malcolm had said about the marshland, they might have made their way around on foot.

"No, we were traveling north on the coast road," the maid said, launching into a tale of woe.

Marielle stepped into the shadows, listening.

Bloodmoor Hill Manor stood to the south and west of Lowestoft. The road was impassable, but in normal times, she could find her way through the marshes and fields. They might also take the westerly road and pick their way north. However, if that road was impassable, if the path through the marshes was flooded, she still didn't wish to remain in Fenwick on Sea. She didn't wish to remain in England at all. As soon as the downpour eased, she must make the attempt to leave.

And Malcolm would be with her. Though he didn't know the land hereabouts, she would not be alone. That knowledge made her braver.

The ladies had finished their tale and had begun asking questions that Malcolm was amiably deflecting, while sounding like a Mayfair fribble, hiding most of the clipped and inflected Scottishness of his speech. Which accent was true? Could she trust him?

From her chair in the dark corner of the room, she watched and listened. Malcolm was hiding from the scandal sheet reporter as was she. Like herself, he didn't have a good face for dissembling, and he'd taken himself off to the shadows as well. Though no lady with blood in her veins would forget that handsome profile.

Malcolm Comyn, the handsome young Earl of Menteith—the letter she'd perused in his bag had claimed to have proof that he was not the true earl. And she felt certain she'd seen that handwriting before in a letter Banquo had sent her mere weeks ago.

Malcolm's father ought not to have put him through this. If one could not trust one's own father...

She sighed. Life was precarious and there were always battles to be fought over property and money. And trust... *pah.* Trust was a rare commodity.

She'd trusted the Comte, though he wasn't entirely a good man, and rarely a law-abiding one. But what were men's laws? They changed with the government or one's social standing. Good character was something more basic.

Having watched Malcolm comfort Hector and tend to the ladies, she decided he was altogether a good man. It was perhaps too impulsive, but she'd also decided she must find a way to convince him to come with her to France. He hadn't actually agreed to go any farther than Bloodmore Hill.

Malcolm escorted the ladies up the stairs and returned to find the lamp doused and the fire low. As he entered, Marielle stepped out of the shadows. She'd taken the cap off and was brushing her hair—with his brush.

He laughed. "Searching again?"

"Only for this. And thank you for the use of it."

He shoveled more coal into the fire. "What do ye think? Can we find our way to Bloodmoor Hill tomorrow?"

Outside the storm picked that moment to blast rain at the window.

"Not if this downpour continues. But if it slows in the morning, we may try, I think." She came to stand next to him. "Tonight, we must sleep."

"How do I know ye won't leave without me? This fellow here," he pointed at Hector who was again fast asleep, "won't warn me."

"Do you mean to bind me to you?" she asked in a teasing tone.

His male parts stirred and he touched her shoulders. "Would ye like that? I've better means of persuasion than that."

She laughed. "No, my dear young Earl of Menteith. We will sleep tonight. However, I shall make sure you accompany me when I leave, because at Bloodmoor Hill Manor, there is a very comfortable bed."

She moved behind him, helping him out of his coat, and tugging his hand to join her on the remaining pallet. "We shall not disturb Hector. If there are fleas, they will visit his bed and not ours."

Malcolm laughed, allowing himself to be led. She was unaccountably trusting to bed down with a lusty young man. "Where is yer blade, madame Comtesse?"

"In my boot, which I will leave on in case there are unwelcome arrivals this night."

Something—or someone—worried her. Perhaps Banquo.

She stretched next to him and rolled on her side, facing the fire, her delectable bottom flush against him.

How could he possibly sleep? This was torture.

Nevertheless, he shut his eyes and tried.

"Malcolm," she said softly "tell me how you know Giles Banquo."

"That is a topic sure to squash any romance. He's a distant cousin."

"And he would inherit if you are illegitimate?"

"There is another cousin before him, Finnley Macbeth." He shifted the scratchy blanket they were using as a pillow. "Shall I tell ye the tale, Comtesse?"

Was there a risk trusting her? He wasn't sure that he gave a damn, not anymore.

"Will it put me to sleep?"

He chuckled. "I'm weary to death of it, Comtesse, so perhaps it will."

She rolled over to face him, a hand tucked under her head. Close enough to kiss.

"Tell it," she said.

Glad for the unexpected intimacy, he dropped a kiss on her forehead and draped an arm over her. "Once upon a time, there was a Scottish lord, the Thane of Menteith, who had three wives. He put the first one aside, and then the second as well, and then took a third. Each wife bore him at least one son, but 'twas the son of the second marriage who the title passed down to, his mother having been his favorite, and him having regretted divorcing her." He touched a finger to her cheek. "Your eyes are still open."

"I am being polite." She smiled and shifted under him with one of her Gallic shrugs. "And I am usually awake at this time. When I'm needed to help, it is usually at midnight."

"The Comtesse of Midnight."

She smiled. "If you wish. Please go on."

"There were feuds through the centuries over the inheritance, but my ancestors held on through the generations up to my father, Duncan Comyn."

"And you."

"If I'm a bastard, the title goes to my cousin, Finnley Macbeth."

"Is he working with Banquo?"

"No. Macbeth feuded with my father over the title twenty years past, and almost killed him in a duel. A few weeks ago, in London, Macbeth was attacked by footpads. I believe Banquo was behind that attack."

"This Macbeth is alive?"

"Yes. His man and I arrived in time."

"He is alive because of you. That was very noble."

Unease threaded through him. Was Macbeth still alive? His injuries had not been life threatening, but it was possible another attempt had been made. He ought to have written to his aunt, Lady Fiona, except that he'd had no fixed address to receive a reply.

"He might have prevailed with just the help of his servant. Macbeth is a soldier. He spent the last twenty years fighting the French. The years have otherwise mellowed him—he told me the title is mine, and he's pledged me his sword."

"I see. He is noble, as well. Will he return to fight Bonaparte?"

"I don't know. He was recovering from a wound he received at Toulouse. And I left London before the news of Bonaparte's escape arrived."

"So, Banquo was in London as well?"

"Yes. That letter ye lifted out of my bag was mailed from there, and I'd gone to investigate. Macbeth was there on half pay, seeking employment. As it happened, Greer and Lucie, his wife—that is, his former wife—and his daughter had joined me in London."

She went very still.

"We were all guests of my great aunt, Lady Fiona Carlin." He touched her nose. "Ye must not be jealous. For certain, Greer has been reunited with Finnley, and Lucie is much like a sister to me. She's much like ye in that she occasionally dons trousers. Do not worry, she wouldn't have me as a spouse, and the feeling is mutual."

"I am, of course, not jealous."

He chuckled "Of course. But if ye were, I should be very flattered."

"If I flatter you, I fear that your head will swell so much you will not allow me any sleep tonight."

He laughed out loud, rousing Hector, who grumbled and set his chin on Malcolm's hip.

"The chaperon will keep me in line."

She raised up on her elbow and fondled the dog's head. "He is a good boy. But what is this about your cousin having a former wife?"

"He divorced Greer many years ago, believing she'd been unfaithful."

"Was she?"

"She was caught speaking with my father, and then later was discovered to be with child."

"The girl... Lucie?"

"Yes. And she is certainly Macbeth's. Ye've only to see them together to know it. Greer denied any affair and I believe her."

"This was the reason for the duel?"

How perceptive she was. "Yes."

"And he divorced her. I take back what I said about your cousin being noble. Perhaps he's as big a villain as Banquo."

"Perhaps, but I doubt it. In any case, he's acknowledged Lucie as his."

"Malcolm, do you suppose Banquo is still in London?"

"I don't know."

She bit her lip.

"What is it, Marielle?"

CHAPTER 6

"A letter came from him two weeks ago. He rambled on about many things. He wanted what papers Gaspar held about your mother and your birth. I can only think that Gaspar had baited him. Unbelievably, he also wrote of desiring all of the trade in these parts, which is *certainement* not mine to give. Nor was it Gaspar's. There are many players between here and Yarmouth."

She shivered and he drew her closer. "Did he threaten ye, Marielle?"

"He will give testimony against me, so he says. He claims to have influence with the Riding Officer, and undoubtedly, he does, or rather, his coins do. We all pay the man to feign blindness, but Banquo has deeper pockets than I. If it were merely a matter of being deported to France, I would not worry, but I might be transported to the end of the earth. It is another reason I want to leave England."

"Ye're French nobility."

"Only by marriage. And... there is the threat of him reporting me as a spy. I am not a spy. That is, I would never spy for France as it has been for the last five and twenty years."

Spying from bluidy Bloodmoor Hill Manor, a place so isolated and remote he hadn't been able to find it? Possibly, but her denunciation of Bonaparte had seemed genuine to him.

He remembered what she'd said about the Comte having contacts in France. "Was the Comte a spy?"

She sighed. "Not as I am aware."

"Why didn't ye leave right after the Comte's death? Bonaparte was defeated months ago."

"There was the matter of settling Gaspar's debts, selling things as I am able. I needed money for the journey, as well. I did ponder what I might give Banquo. He has plagued me with requests for more than I can give." She bit her lip. "Or will give. I want to be gone before he shows up in Suffolk."

"Has he...has he harmed ye in other ways? If he's laid a hand on ye—"

"I would put out his eyes first." She grimaced. "And other friends would take note. I am not entirely undefended. The people near Fenwick on Sea, they have been kind to both me and to Gaspar while he lived, and I return the kindness when they need extra hands. You would not have discovered me if we'd gone out at our regular time. In fact, I could not imagine there would be any travelers after the coast road washed out and the westerly road was flooded. I am astonished that more have arrived. I do hope Banquo is not among them. I fear I will have to do him harm."

"Ye will leave that task to me."

She sighed and her eyes fluttered shut, a lock of hair falling across her cheek. She looked young and vulnerable and the urge to protect her was overwhelming, even more powerful than the desire to make love to her.

One long-lashed eye opened. "You are watching me," she said.

"Tomorrow, we'll travel to Bloodmoor Hill. Then we'll gather your things and go north to Yarmouth." With troops mobilizing, the inns there might be crowded. "We'll stop first at Lowestoft. I'll need to write to my factor and send an express to my aunt and find out what has happened to Macbeth and Banquo. We'll need things—clothing, supplies. Then, we'll travel to France together." He touched his lips to hers. "Sleep now."

She set her hand atop his and studied him, eyes growing shiny. "Thank you," she whispered.

He watched as her eyes drifted closed. On one side, the fire cast a steady heat their way and on the other, the dog lay sharing his warmth.

The crackling of the fire and the dog's snoring and Marielle's quiet breathing soothed him. Upstairs, the rustling and footsteps had died, the late arrivals having settled in after a day of exhaustion.

He should do the same, but his mind was a jumble. Much as he'd have liked to have found his mother and know that undiscovered side of himself, he wasn't a bit disappointed with the *comtesse* he *had* found.

Whatever the Comte had kept of his mother's, he wanted to see it. He wanted to understand why she'd left him, her son, in the untenable position of fighting for a title that wasn't his.

And why had his father put forth the lie? That, perhaps, was the bigger question, for Father had certainly felt guilt over the deception and thus had been more than generous in helping Greer and Lucie. He only wished his father had summoned the courage to tell him the truth before he died, instead of wasting his last words relating a witch's prophecy that Macbeth and Banquo's son would each hold the title.

That was one story he'd not shared with Marielle this night. Astonishing, how much he'd confided in her, this Comtesse de Fontenay.

The question was, when the weather settled, when the skies cleared and they were able to set out for her manor, would she lead him a merry chase? Probably, he decided, at least until their common enemy, Giles Banquo, was disposed of, one way or another.

Clouds layered the horizon in shades of gray with occasional glimpses of blue sky. Yet, as they left Fenwick on Sea and rode west, the rain still fell, steady, silent, and soft, as if they were riding into a lifting mist.

Marielle reached the edge of the navigable road and reined up, deciding the best approach. Ahead, the path dipped into a newly created lake. To either side ran marshland, here and there bordering on fields that had recently been cultivated. Some farmer generations ago had labored to drain those fields, and God had laughed, turning them back into mire.

Malcolm reined up next to her. "Any crops planted will be ruined."

She glanced over at him and found him frowning with real concern. "You farm, my lord? Oh, of course you do." This serious young man wouldn't be one of those lords who merely swanned about London—or perhaps Edinburgh—having new coats made, visiting his clubs and dueling studios.

"I have a home farm and tenants. So yes, I know about this sort of loss and the lean times it might bring." He shook his head. "I *had* a home farm and tenants is more appropriate, I suppose."

He was still thinking about Banquo's threat.

"Why don't you fight for the title?" Malcolm hadn't impressed her as soft or weak. "You are still the Earl of Menteith. Will you give it all up so easily? Banquo may bring suit, but you may tie him up for years in court. Or he may die before he can make the claim." Yes, that would be preferable. "And then no one will know the truth of your maternity."

"*I* will know the truth." There was steel in his voice, and a good bit of impatience. "Now, are we able to travel farther, or must we turn back to the Queen's Barque and wait for the weather and roads to clear?"

Returning to the inn was in neither of their best interests. They'd risen early, awakened by Brewster's daughter bringing breakfast, and then Malcolm had saddled both their horses, since the ostlers were busy seeing to yet another carriage that had straggled in.

She wiped moisture from her face. "Look at those patches of blue sky. I do believe the storm is weaker to the west. Let us try to find our way through. If need be, there are some humble cottagers around who may allow us to sleep with their cow."

"Instead of their dog? Lead the way."

He laughed, sending shivery warmth through her, as if she was a lighthearted young girl again. Her comfortable bed could not come too soon.

The rain did, indeed, diminish as they navigated through the marshes, seeking higher ground, zig-zagging through the Suffolk countryside. They paused in a circle of stones laid out on high ground and ate the luncheon Mrs. Brewster had packed for them.

It was late afternoon when they reached the gently sloped wooded ground near Bloodmoor Hill Manor. They hadn't conversed much the last part of the journey. Marielle had silently worried over her horse, who deserved better treatment, and Malcolm, on his steady gelding, had seemed immersed in his own thoughts.

Still, at every path that might prove precarious, he'd insisted on going first. She'd allowed it, only because the trust he'd placed in her ought to be reciprocated. And for the sake of her horse, of course.

"How much farther?" he asked, moving up alongside her.

She reined up and patted her mount. To the left, a narrow footpath reached deep into the wood, the dense foliage around it beaten down by the rain, so that they could see a cottage beyond with its rude clearing and a boy throwing feed to a smattering of chickens.

"Not far," she said. "Those are my neighbors."

Spotting them, the boy waved and scampered through the brush toward them.

"My lady," he said, short of breath. "Da feared you were lost."

"He is safely home?"

"Aye."

"And so am I. Is all well here?"

His gaze slid to Malcolm.

"You may speak freely, Hal," she said.

"I saw someun in the woods, not more'n an hour ago."

Dread slithered through her.

Hal glanced up the path that led to the manor. "Mam said not to wake Da yet. He was up all night saving the roof."

"What did the someun look like?" Malcolm asked.

"'Twas a man. A witchy sort. Gave me goosebumps. Had hair growing back from here." He smacked his forehead. "And a streak, like the devil's touch."

Her pulse quickened, and she drew in a breath, trying to swallow her fear, reminding herself she must be brave. Banquo was here for one final attempt to bully her. And it would be final. She would not run, nor would she cower. She had found the rightful owner of the letters

Gaspar had been holding and, thanks be to God, this stalwart and brave young man had come with her.

She prayed he could fight as well as he could kiss.

Malcolm fished in a pocket and produced a coin, holding it up. "Does your da have any dry powder, Hal?"

Hal frowned up at her, seeking guidance.

"Malcolm, a poor man with a gun and powder might bring down some lord's precious game to keep his family from starving," she whispered. "A capital offense."

He frowned and nodded.

"This is Lord Menteith, Hal," she said. "We may trust him. But Malcolm, I do not think we should trouble Hal's father."

Nor did she wish to involve the poor man in what most certainly would be an ugly confrontation. Perhaps a taking of life. "Was it only the one man?" she asked. "Was there anyone else with him?"

"Not as I saw. And I followed him. He smashed out yer window. Knocked all the glass out." His eyes had gone round. Housebreaking was another serious offense.

"Very well. I'm glad he didn't disturb your family." She turned to Malcolm. "Do give him the coin, please."

"Hal," Malcolm called. "Catch it." He leaned down and let the coin drop into the boy's outstretched hand. "If the lady raises the alarm, ye must fetch your da. Understood?"

Hal eyed the coin and solemnly nodded.

"Go home now, sweetling," Marielle said. "And do not worry. I will be fine. Lord Menteith is with me."

Malcolm frowned, watching Hal scurry home.

"Hal's father was out with me yesterday. Banquo is fortunate he didn't harass them, for I would certainly have had to address *that* with him as well."

"Aye." Malcolm grimaced. "He has much to answer for. Come, Comtesse." He beckoned her, turned his mount off the path into a quiet clearing, and dismounted. "Even alone, Banquo is dangerous. Let us make a plan."

CHAPTER 7

"If ye won't wait with your neighbors," Malcolm said, "I insist I go in first."

The blasted woman had been quietly arguing with him since they dismounted in the small clearing. She refused to stay behind. She insisted she must confront Banquo.

Now, her mouth primmed into a hard line, and he sensed her ire under all that controlled detachment.

He reached for her, and she shrugged out of his grasp.

"Marielle, he's a dangerous enemy, and it's me he's after."

"And I would let you take all the risk? It's my home, Malcolm, and I insist I must go with you to face Banquo and I must confront him first."

The brush rustled, and he reached for his pistol. The man who approached through the trees had a care-worn face under a beat-up cap.

"Wythe," Marielle said. "I'm sorry Hal woke you."

"Twyla thought you might need my help. And Hal mentioned you asked about powder."

This neighbor of Marielle's might talk some sense into her where he himself was failing.

"I'd be much obliged for the powder," Malcolm said. "And if ye've a barn, mayhap the horses can rest there."

Bloodmoor Hill Manor proved to be a manor house as ancient as Malcolm's own country home, but smaller and far more decrepit. Marielle had informed him that her only servant was Hal's mother, Twyla, who came in a few times a week to cook, clean and tend to the laundry.

And it appeared there was little inside to clean. As dusk fell and they reconnoitered around peering through windows, he saw that most of the public rooms were sparsely furnished.

A small parlor at the back of the house held a table, benches, and, near the fireplace, two overstuffed wingchairs. In one of them sat Banquo. He'd made himself a crackling fire and seemed to be staring into it. His hands rested upon his lap, and, whether or not he had a pistol, Malcolm couldn't be sure.

At the back entrance, Malcolm set a hand to Marielle's arm. He must make one last attempt to make her see sense. "I'll go first."

Her eyes glittered with determination and more courage than many men had. "No."

A formidable woman was the Comtesse. He dropped a kiss on her lips. "I'm right behind you, then."

She used her key on the kitchen door, and they went through, meeting the smell of burnt toast. The coals in the hearth glowed, and a tea kettle rested on a central worktable. He set his hand to it—still warm.

He stayed on her heels as they tiptoed into a corridor. Age-old damp wood and mildewed wall coverings gave off a familiar scent, and the dust motes floating in the last glimmer of twilight attested to the shortage of both servants and the money for upkeep—for the last century probably. Marielle stopped at a door, straightened her shoulders and stepped into that back parlor.

"Banquo," she said. "What a surprise."

Banquo sat in a puddle of lamplight with his chair angled toward the fire.

"Marielle." He cleared his throat loudly. "Close the door."

"I will close it as you are leaving," she said coolly. "I feel no obligation to offer you hospitality. Do not let me detain you. Be on your way."

Banquo made a grumbling noise low in his throat and wheezed out a rattling cough. "Not leaving," he said.

Marielle took another step. "You are ill?" She laced the words with sarcasm. "You are bringing illness into my home?"

"Come. Sit, Marielle."

Malcolm heard the pain in the raspy wheezing that followed, as if the man was barely holding himself together.

She moved closer and turned to confront the unwelcome visitor. Heart pounding, Malcolm stepped through the doorway.

"I think not, Banquo," Marielle said.

"You haven't always been such a bitch. You used to enjoy my company."

Color rushed to her cheeks. "The Comte and I may have *suffered* your company," she said. "We never enjoyed it."

"Ah, Marielle. So beautiful. I had hoped—"

"Banquo." She shifted a step nearer to Malcolm. "You are holding a pistol. In my home, you are holding a pistol. Why? Is it your plan, then, to shoot me?"

"Have you come alone?" He wheezed out the words. "I saw that lad watching."

"Have *you* come alone?" she asked.

"She's not alone, Father."

The voice came from Malcolm's left. He turned in time to catch an upraised arm. Steel glimmered in the hand attached to a lad of no more than twelve or thirteen. With a quick tug, he wrenched the lad's hand and squeezed until the blade dropped.

In London, Banquo had told him he had two sons. This was one of them, too young and skinny for this task.

"It's all right, Giles," Banquo said.

Banquo leaned past the wing of the chair so that Malcolm could see the side of his face. Banquo's attention however, was on Marielle, and he'd aimed his pistol at her.

The blasted woman ought to have listened to him.

Malcolm latched the lad closer and drew his own weapon. "Ye don't want to do that, Banquo."

"Your powder's wet. Mine isn't."

"Shall ye risk it?" Malcolm asked, managing to keep his voice calm.

"Father," the boy said breathlessly.

Malcolm pressed the cold steel to the lad's temple. "Is this twig to be the next Earl of Menteith when ye unveil the scandal ye've concocted?"

"My second son." He huffed. "Has an elder brother."

Banquo appeared to be struggling for breath.

"You truly are ill," Marielle said. "Lower the pistol and I will send for the apothecary. Come, tell me what is wrong with you."

Malcolm shared a long steadying look with her. If she offered kindness, he could draw Banquo's ire his way. They hadn't got further than arguing over who would go first, but this seemed a good plan. Besides, Banquo wouldn't shoot her until he had whatever proof she was holding. He hoped.

"Lower your pistol, Banquo. Unless ye mean for this second twig of yours to be sacrificed when ye shoot the Comtesse."

She glanced at him, chin raised in haughty indignation. "Really, my lord? You mean to shoot a child?"

"If Banquo fires that weapon at ye? Aye, and straight through the lad's bluidy big ear."

The boy squirmed, and Malcolm tightened his grip, fighting back a surge of anger that was making this more than a role he was improvising.

"You'll swing if you kill me," the boy cried.

"Ye're a blasted little beggar who attacked me with a blade. I'll have shot ye in self-defense."

Marielle sent him a meaningful look, dipped her head, and he followed her gaze back to Banquo. The villain's hand trembled around the pistol, and his face glowed pale in the light.

"Let us cut to the chase," Marielle said. "Why are you here, Banquo?"

A laugh rattled out of him. "Knew you'd search, Menteith. Only had to set you on the trail. Find everything I needed. Knew you'd end up here, and she'd give you the proof. Ought to have waited another day." A great hacking cough shook him. "Damned storm."

Malcolm shuffled closer, holding the boy as a shield. "Is your brother here also, lad?"

"Father..." The boy trembled.

"Your brother," Malcolm said, pressing the barrel harder. "Where is—"

"He's in London."

"Ah. Did he go to London to finish the task of killing Lord Macbeth?"

"What?" The lad's shocked gaze slid his way.

"Lord Macbeth. He's the cousin who stands between me and your bluidy father for the title."

"Macbeth's dead," Banquo mumbled.

His breath caught. He ought to have written to Lady Fiona. He ought to have asked for news on Macbeth.

"*Certainement*, you are bluffing, Banquo," Marielle said, her nonchalant tone steadying him.

"Greer's dead too."

Pain ratcheted through him. Marielle turned a determined look his way, and then she rolled her eyes, again bringing him back to his senses.

Aye. She was right. Banquo might well be bluffing. In fact, he likely was. Lady Fiona would have scoured all of England to carry that news to him. Or he would have seen it in a newspaper. The murders of the scandalous Lord and Lady Macbeth would have earned a column between the Corn Riots and Bonaparte's escape.

He rallied his wits. "Is this your father, young sprig? A bluidy devil who goes about killing innocent ladies?"

"'S'enough." Banquo spluttered, his mouth contorting. He planted his feet and raised the pistol in both hands.

Malcolm caught Marielle's eye, and gave a jerk of his head, praying she'd know to duck. Then he shoved the boy hard, knocking him into his father.

A shot rang out. Yellowed stuffing burst from the worn damask upholstery of the opposite chair. The lad screamed and hit the floor, his father toppling upon him.

CHAPTER 8

Banquo lay still and unmoving.

"You shot him," the boy cried.

Hand trembling, Malcolm raised Marielle from the floor where she'd dropped. No blood stained her clothing, the chair, or either of the tumbled bodies.

"Lord Menteith did not fire his weapon," Marielle said, her coolness again settling his nerves. "But your father has ruined my chair." She slipped an arm around Malcolm's waist. "You wouldn't really have killed that child?"

Heart pounding, he glanced at her, the full weight of the stakes they'd been playing hitting him.

He swallowed a rising bile. Except for his bad blood, the lad was likely an innocent. Likewise, except for her smuggling, so was Marielle. He hoped.

Oh, damn, he wanted the chance to find out.

"Get off me, Father," the boy cried, shoving at the dead weight atop him.

The shiver that went through her belied her calm demeanor, and he dropped a kiss on her forehead. "I'll buy ye a new chair from Chippendales. Two new chairs, since the other one ought to be shot as well. Have ye a rope?"

"Are we hanging the boy?" she asked. "I must object."

Shocked eyes looked up at them. "I didn't do anything."

"Is your father dead?" Marielle asked. "Poke him, if you please."

He complied, and Banquo groaned.

"Search him," Malcolm said.

The boy retrieved another pistol and three daggers, and then submitted to his own pat down by Marielle.

"How long has your father been ill?" she asked.

"He has a... a festering wound. I don't know how long he's had it. He fetched me from school in Norwich a few days ago and said we were going to Yarmouth. But we stayed at an inn near my school and an apothecary came and treated him until his fever abated. He said we must come here first before Yarmouth and settle some business." He frowned, his eyes shining with tears he was valiantly fighting. "Do you know whether my brother is safe, sir? Father summoned him from school four weeks ago."

Malcolm and Marielle shared a look.

"Summoned him?"

"He sent orders and money for him to travel to London and join him there."

"And then he came to your school, wounded, pulled you out, and your brother is nowhere to be found?" The boy was right to be worried. If there'd been a fight that took both Malcolm and, God forbid, Greer, Banquo's elder son might have been killed as well.

Unless it was all part of Banquo's bluff.

"I don't know. I left London three weeks ago myself," Malcolm said. He stowed his weapon. "Come, help me get your father to a bed. I know the Comtesse has at least one bed here."

"That villain is not occupying my bed," she said. "Come along this way."

Malcolm stood in the doorway of the humble room off the kitchen where he and the boy had settled Banquo. Once a servant's bedchamber with a narrow bed that was no more than a cot, the room depended on the warmth of the cookfire seeping in through the doorway. It was likely freezing in winter.

However now, with three bodies crammed into the small space on this April evening and a fire in the kitchen hearth, only the man on the bed was shivering, delirious with fever.

He wished for the man to die, the sooner the better, and then felt a surge of guilt when he thought of the lad.

Not long after they'd shuffled Banquo into bed, Wythe and two of the other near neighbors had appeared, having heard the gunshot. With the villain already secure, Marielle had sent them to fetch hot meals from Wythe's wife, Twyla. Now the neighbors sat at the kitchen table, drinking ale and waiting to take turns guarding Banquo.

Malcolm had watched as Marielle tended Banquo's nasty wound, applying the salve provided by the apothecary in Norwich, and done what she could to help curb the fever. Though for the life of him, Malcolm couldn't see the point of trying to save the man. Except for the lad's sake, perhaps.

All this over a title, and the money and power that went with it. No one ever thought of the burdens. He had a good factor and land steward, but he couldn't go haring off to France forever. For two cents he'd hand everything over to... to whom? Macbeth, if he lived, didn't want it. This fatherless lad wasn't prepared for the task. Likely as not, his elder brother wasn't either. And if either of them proved to be chips off of Banquo's block, he'd skewer them himself. The people at home in Menteith deserved better.

Marielle rose, signaling one of her men to take her place next to the bed. "If he speaks, call us. Come with me, Malcolm."

Lantern in hand she led him through the corridor into the main hall, and then up two flights of creaky stairs to a large chamber.

A rare bit of moonlight filtered in through the uncovered windows. The room was completely devoid of furniture.

"No comfortable bed here," he said. "Not that there'll be any sleeping tonight."

She grimaced. "Such inconvenient visitors. But I don't wish to delay this task." She settled the lantern she'd carried on the mantel and pressed a bit of nearby paneling. A section of panel swung inward and she reached in. "This room was the Comte's bedchamber. He had a fine suite of furniture that was his property. The landlord accepted it for the last rent."

He joined her and peered into the small space. "No stacks of gold coins?"

She withdrew something small and closed the panel. "This is, perhaps, more valuable than gold to you. Come along."

He followed her through a different door into a connected private parlor where she settled the lamp and the items she'd withdrawn from safekeeping onto the table. "There is also a box with a few small items —a handkerchief, paste jewelry, a prayer book—that I must find for you, but these, the Comte kept hidden." She pulled out a chair. "Be seated. I will return directly."

She left through yet another door, this one on the opposite wall, and he looked around. This room had three doors, to the Comte's bedchamber, the corridor, and what must be her bedchamber. Besides the table and chair placed near the window, only a slipper chair and foot stool sat near the unlit hearth.

The shawl thrown over the back of the chair was definitely feminine. This sparsely furnished chamber was her sitting room.

'Twas true he was still a wealthy earl. She deserved so much better and, if he held onto the title, he could provide it for her.

He picked up the items she'd dropped: two letters, both seals still intact. He held the thicker one up to the light and his breath caught. The hand was his father's, addressed to the Comtesse de Fontenay.

Yet Marielle hadn't opened it?

The second was thinner, both the paper and handwriting equally delicate. *To my son, Malcolm.*

Heart pounding, he held it up to the light and then to his nose, catching the faint scent of a woman's perfume. His mother's perfume?

As he weighed each letter, deciding which tugged harder at his heart, he heard a pounding on the stairs.

"My lady," a man called.

Marielle poked her head through her bedchamber door. "See what's afoot, Malcolm."

He went to the door that led to the corridor.

Wythe stood, hat in hand. "He's come around, sir. Asking for ye."

"I'll be right down."

He tucked the letters into his coat. "Banquo is awake," he called. "Help me first."

She appeared in her doorway and his breath caught again. She'd shed her trousers and coats and donned a woman's dress, one that showed all of her womanly curves to full advantage.

"Do not gawk, Malcolm. Fasten this dress for me and quickly." She turned and lifted her hair away. "I assume you have some experience with ladies' gowns?"

"Not much, and ever clumsy."

"I doubt that."

"How do ye manage this without a maid?"

"I haven't worn this gown since before my maid left. But I knew you were here and would see to it for me."

He fastened the last hook, and let his hands slide down to her bottom, memorizing the shape of her. She turned in his arms and looked up at him. "There will be time, later. Let us see what Banquo has to say on his deathbed."

"He is dying then?"

"I doubt he will last the night." She bit her lip. "I had much experience with anticipating death while tending to Gaspar those last months."

"Ye were a good wife," he said. "Too young to have been—"

"You've never asked, but I am nine and twenty, not a young woman at all. And Gaspar wasn't unkind." She shrugged. "Come. I feel very sad for the boy. He is alone and adrift, I fear."

He followed her down the corridor and stairs, thinking about her heartfelt request that he come with her to France. With the Comte dead, Marielle was alone and perhaps adrift as well. But not any longer, if she would have him.

He caught up with her and ushered her into the sick room.

Banquo's eyelids fluttered. "Menteith," he whispered.

⚜

"Giles." Marielle caught the eye of the boy seated beside the bed and nodded to him. Tears hid behind the boy's long dark eyelashes, valiantly held back. Perhaps, with the right hand to guide him, he'd grow into a better man than his father.

A father who reappeared at the last and would be wrenched from him... She opened her mouth thinking to order him from the sick room, and decided against it. He was old enough to face this death.

"I am here, Banquo." Malcolm's harsh tone shattered the silence. "What is it ye wish to say?"

Malcolm's jaw had frozen as hard as steel. It was a wonder to her that he could speak at all.

"You're a bastard."

"And ye're dying. What scheme do ye have unfurling upon your death? Is there a solicitor somewhere who'll be unleashing a story to the scandal sheets?"

The words had been blunt and direct, and rather harsh for the boy's ears, but at least Malcolm had very admirably hidden the full malice he surely felt for this wretched man.

Banquo's laugh was strangled. "My son will be earl, she said. Not me." He squeezed his eyes shut.

Malcolm cast a concerned look at the boy and frowned down at Banquo. "Do not tell me ye were chasing after that old witch's tale? Macbeth has discounted it. Why could ye not do so?"

A witch's tale? She tried to catch Malcolm's attention, but he was focused on Banquo, whose eyes burned with an answering hatred toward the younger man. Such a shame for him to die in a state of malevolence. Perhaps she should, after all, escort the boy out.

"Macbeth shall be Earl of Menteith, and my son after him," Banquo said.

"I don't care about the title, father," the boy said. "Don't die. If you die, we will have n-no one."

Marielle hesitated, and then went to stand behind Giles, setting a hand to his shoulder. The boy didn't seem to notice.

"But ye weren't content to wait for the prophecy?" Malcolm said.

"Ye say ye killed Macbeth? Why not just attempt to kill me? Why concoct the story of my illegitimacy?"

"Not a story. It's true. Lady Fiona knows it."

The boy's shoulders shook under her touch, and she felt his silent sobbing. Tears formed in her own eyes, and she pressed them back, sighing. The evidence Banquo sought, if there was any, would be the letters she'd handed Malcolm. Thank God she would never have to share them with this villain.

Malcolm glanced at the boy. "Is your mother dead?"

Giles nodded.

"And your kin? Grandparents, uncles, aunts?"

"I have only my brother. If I have my brother."

"What arrangements have ye made for these lads?" he asked Banquo.

Banquo's eyelids fluttered and he mumbled something unintelligible.

"Ye're not alone, lad," Malcolm said gruffly. "Ye have a cousin: me." He pursed his lips. "Two cousins, me and Macbeth's daughter, Lucie. Your father hasn't claimed to have killed *her*. Providing ye don't try to stab me again ye'll come live with me and learn how to be a gentleman and if need be, an earl. I'll look after ye, your brother and Lucie as well."

"And so will I," Marielle said.

Malcolm blinked and looked up at her, his face softening. "Yes." He nodded. "We none of us will be alone. Banquo, I'm claiming this lad. The older one as well."

Banquo's eyelids fluttered again, and Marielle saw the tiniest of nods.

She let out a long breath. Perhaps Banquo was not irredeemable. And yet the world, and this boy, would be better off without him.

"Giles," Marielle whispered. "If you have anything to say to him, do so now." She squeezed the boy's shoulder.

Malcolm beckoned her out of the room, and Wythe stepped in to take over the watch.

She let herself be led into the corridor, fighting the inevitable heaviness that came with a dying.

Perhaps sensing her mood, Malcolm stopped and leaned close, his breath feathering her cheek. "'Tis not the proper time, I suppose, but I must ask: did ye just propose marriage to me, Comtesse?"

Marriage? The impulse to help the boy had been just that—an impulse of the moment.

But marriage? She clapped a hand over her mouth, fighting both a smile and sudden tears. "Is that why you said yes, Malcolm?"

He wrapped her in an embrace. "A woman who wears trousers might be so bold. But ye know, I have little to offer, being a bastard."

She shook her head against his still-damp coat. "You are the Earl of Menteith. It was sheer madness for him to think he could steal the title. I feel pity for the boy, but not for the man. Whoever stabbed him has done the world a favor."

She looked up into troubled eyes. "Do I sound too ruthless?"

"Did I?"

"No. If he were to live, we would have to summon the justice of the peace to bring charges, instead of merely recording his death."

He frowned, and emotion shone in his eyes. He was remembering the murders Banquo had confessed.

"What is Greer to you, truly?"

"A friend. A good friend. I can't think that she's dead, or Macbeth. He was always larger than life."

"You must write a letter to your aunt," she said. "I'll have a man carry it."

"I will do that directly. As soon as..." He tipped her chin up and pressed a gentle kiss to her lips. "We ought to keep watch with the lad."

She nodded. She was in grave danger of losing her heart.

Or perhaps, she already had.

CHAPTER 9

Three days later

"What will you do with me now, sir?" Giles asked as he and Malcolm rode back to Bloodmoor Hill Manor after the simple internment in the parish graveyard.

After a long night of suffering, death had finally come for Banquo Monday morning. Marielle had sent Giles home with Wythe and Twyla, and had summoned the local squire who served as both justice of the peace and coroner. The fat lazy fellow had accepted a bottle of brandy and the theory that Banquo, enroute to Yarmouth, had lost his way and, having caught a chill during the terrible storm, sought refuge at her home. 'Twas a blessing the squire liked Marielle's brandy so well. He'd found no need to inspect the body and quickly ruled that death resulted from illness, with no inquest required.

Giles had grieved quietly, likely worrying about his brother and brooding upon everything that had transpired since the older lad left him to travel to London.

"Were ye happy at school?" Malcolm asked, taking a stab at both finding an answer to the lad's question and drawing him out.

He chewed on his lower lip. "When my brother was there it was tolerable."

"I had one or two friends who made school bearable. We shall either find your brother or learn his fate. Our cousin Macbeth's as well." He'd sent an express to his Aunt Fiona, telling her of Banquo's death and asking for news of Macbeth, Greer, and Banquo's older son. "Meanwhile, ye'll travel with us to Yarmouth tomorrow, where we'll await a reply from my aunt. After that, ye may return to school, or travel to France with us." If Macbeth and Greer truly were dead, he might have to summon Lucie as well.

"Are you going to fight Bonaparte?"

Stories were trickling in that Bonaparte had won the allegiance of the French military and was planning to reestablish his empire. In Austria, Prussia, the Low Countries and England, troops were mobilizing to oppose him.

England had been at war for most of Malcolm's life. As heir to an earldom, he'd not been expected to join up.

But he was a Highlander. He ought to be fighting. He wanted to fight.

"We shall see," he said. "I'm going because the Comtesse says I must look into my mother's family's estates. Apparently, my mother was the granddaughter of a duke."

Unimpressed, the lad pursed his lips and said "I don't want to be earl."

"Perhaps fate won't require that of ye, Giles. Know that, even if we find your brother hale and hearty, I don't plan to surrender Menteith just yet. I must see what's what in France and, meanwhile, I have competent men tending to the business at home."

"You and the Comtesse might have a son."

Giles was still fashing over the earldom. "We're not married, lad."

Nor had he yet bedded her. Not for lack of desire, his or hers. They'd shared no more than a few stolen kisses.

And rightly so. A man had just died, and they couldn't make light of that man's son's grief.

She was a fine woman, the Comtesse. Efficient, self-contained, and not given to dramatic displays, Marielle was nevertheless thoughtful of the lad's pain. She'd seen to the death certificate, promised to arrange the funeral, and then packed Malcolm off to post his letters. He'd arrived in Lowestoft so late that he'd spent the night in the inn there.

The lad's grief made his own sorrows seem pale by comparison. For all of his childhood, he'd had a loving father. And now, mayhap, he'd have a loving woman.

He yearned to know Marielle better. And yes, to marry her, if she would have him.

"'Tis true though," he said. "We might have a son."

"Is she... is she quite respectable?"

"The Comtesse?"

The lad nodded.

"My chosen lady? Ye are a bold one, Giles." He shook his head. "And as to that, I'll only say, she is French."

Giles's frown made him laugh. "She's been through many trials in her life, but I believe she's honorable. Not the same, perhaps as respectable, but far more important."

After an early dinner prepared by the neighbor's wife, Marielle produced a map and they went over the plans for the next day's travel. The road to Fenwick on Sea and the Queen's Barque was said to be still flooded but, on his visit to Lowestoft, he'd scouted the local farm tracks. Wythe had offered his cart to freight Marielle's trunk, and at Lowestoft they would change to the post chaise Malcolm had arranged to carry them and their baggage onward to Yarmouth.

With all of Giles' questions answered, Marielle sent the lad off to bed and fetched a bottle of brandy, pouring two glasses and seating herself in the chair next to his.

For dinner that night, she'd donned a second fine dress, this one a deep blue like her eyes.

"And how did ye manage to fasten that dress, my lady?" he asked.

"I enlisted Twyla's help while the chickens were roasting."

"We shall have to arrange a maid for ye."

"Oh? Will we need a valet also?" Her fingers interlaced his. "Or shall we simply help each other to dress?"

"Come here." He tugged her onto his lap and spent the next few minutes *at last* ardently kissing her until she broke away, stroking his jaw.

"You shaved again."

"Yes. I'm perfectly capable of shaving and dressing myself. But ye're a *comtesse*, and we'll hire a maid for ye in Yarmouth. Or perhaps in Calais when we land. That will probably be wiser. A French maid will be less shocked about us sharing a bed." Unless they married first. He would get to that subject.

"I thought, perhaps, you might have changed your mind."

He traced a finger over her bosom. "No."

"Every night, I expected a knock on my door."

They'd spent the first night on Banquo's death watch. The second night he'd been at the inn in Lowestoft. And last night he'd found an empty guest room and collapsed.

"I arrived here in the wee hours of the morning. When I looked in on ye, ye were snoring."

She gave him a playful smack. "This will be my last night at Bloodmoor Hill Manor."

"Ye have memories here. Are ye sad to be leaving?"

"That is not my point. My point is that I told you I have a bed."

"I slept on a bed last night."

"Not my comfortable bed."

He laughed. "Giles asked me today if ye are quite respectable."

"I'm not, of course. I am a widow."

"And French."

"Yes."

"Thank heavens. Will ye marry me, Marielle?"

She cocked her head and eyed him. "Perhaps."

"Perhaps?" He settled a hand just under her breast and pulled her closer.

"I will give you an answer... after."

"After?"

She smiled her siren's smile and wiggled, trying to stand. "Come. I have been a wife already, and there were... aspects lacking. You must convince me that marrying you will offer advantages that will make up for the loss of my freedom."

He scooped her into his arms and got to his feet.

She squeaked. "There is no need to be any more dashing than you already are. And you may injure yourself."

"Ye've thrown down a challenge, my love."

"Your *love*...oh my." She chuckled against his ear. "*Très galant*, my lord. I may faint before—"

He stopped her lips with another kiss, then stomped up the stairs and down the corridor to a door, entering the empty chamber she'd first led him to.

The letters were still in his coat pocket. He'd taken them out a few times and looked at them, and then put them back unread.

Huffing, he carried her through to the sitting room, then into the chamber that Marielle had disappeared into the first night.

Eyes adjusting to the dark, he made out the ghostly shapes of chairs and tables. And a tester bed. Not one worthy of royalty but large enough for two people if they were sufficiently intertwined. That thought and the lush bundle of woman he carted brought his privy counsellor to full alert.

But he wouldn't rush his fences, not if an agreement to marry depended on his skills.

"Ye promised a big bed," he teased.

"I did not. I promised a comfortable bed. Put me down."

He took a few steps more, dropped her onto the bed and landed on his forearms, pinning her under him.

"This?" she hissed. "This is romance?"

He dipped his head and captured her lips, tasting brandy and a hint of expensive perfume. Her arms circled his neck, pulling him closer, cushioning him on her breasts. Freeing a hand, he dipped a finger into the low bodice, exploring.

With a nudge at his chest, she released him and tugged at his neck-cloth, untying it, while he slid her bodice down and fondled the tips of her breasts, wondering if her color was rising.

He had to see her.

He stood and tore off the loosened neckcloth. Marielle propped herself on her elbow.

"Candles," he said. "Light." He walked toward the mantel, stumbling against furniture with a crude oath.

"I will help you."

He heard the rustle of skirts as she hurried after him. His hand landed on the tinderbox before hers, and he caught her up to him for a quick kiss before grabbing a branch of candles and carrying them to the bedside table.

The scent of her perfume muddling him, he fumbled the tinder and flint like a schoolboy until she tenderly took everything from his hands.

"There is a lamp on a cabinet over there," she said, pointing.

The breathlessness in her voice stirred him more and he found her lips again, pressing her to him and trailing kisses over the warm pulse at her neck.

"Come to bed," she whispered.

He heard the plop of the flint as she dropped it and remembered the candles, setting her back from him. "Light the candles and I'll fetch the lamp. Ye may be the Comtesse of Midnight but I want to see all of ye."

He walked in the direction she'd pointed, being more careful of obstacles, and returned with the lamp.

The first taper of candlelight made her face glow, and the next turned her hair to spun bronze, and then another highlighted her pale breast tipped by a puckered rosebud.

He twirled her around, unhooking her dress, loosening her stays, and then pausing for another long kiss.

She shoved at him. "Let us be done with this clothing."

In a flurry, they shed clothing, watching each other until she wore only her stockings and garters.

His breath caught. She was beautiful, all womanly curves, as he'd suspected, like one of Botticelli's revelers. He reached for her, but she grasped his hand before he could touch her, and swept him with a gaze from head to foot, back up, and then down to settle on the proof of his desire.

"Are ye finding my aspects lacking?" he asked.

She smiled, and then laughed, walking into his arms. "Let us see what happens next. Perhaps I shall *have* to marry you."

As the candles burned lower, Marielle stroked the hair on Malcolm's chest, watching his slumber. He'd proved to be a more generous and far more effective lover than either her lieutenant or Gaspar.

But could she marry him? Would he, after they arrived in Yarmouth, after he heard from his aunt, would *he* want to marry *her*?

Likely not, and the thought saddened her. She felt pity for herself, certainly, because she'd be alone again, but also for Malcolm who would go on alone with so many responsibilities. And he would fulfill them, that she knew, even though, like that poor child down the hall, his world had been pulled out from under him.

The generous impulse to take charge of Giles—that had made her heart fill with love for Malcolm. With certainty that she must be with him.

Which she had quickly tried very hard to dash, of course, because she was, after all, a hardened cynic. Malcolm might feel that after tonight's interlude marriage was required as a matter of honor—and how rare a notion was that for a young man of three and twenty taking an older widow as a lover?

He wasn't a fool, and he wasn't a virgin either. Malcolm was a puzzle, an old soul in a young virile body.

Had he read the letters she'd given him yet? She'd asked him about them on Monday, and he mumbled something about reading them later, just before mounting his horse and riding off to Lowestoft.

A hand came down over hers. "Ye're awake," he said.

"I cannot sleep when my vision is filled with so much beauty."

He opened his eyes and frowned. "I didn't satisfy ye."

He had. More than once. "It has been a long time for me. I fear you will find me insatiable."

His arms snaked around her. "I am ready to rise to the occasion. However, I fear I've barely slept in the past five days."

"Then sleep now."

"Ye're fashing about aught."

"What?"

"Something's troubling ye."

She couldn't tell him her worries. The Comtesse of Midnight, as he had called her, would never fear losing a man's love, would she? "I am curious about the letters. Have you read them?"

"I've been too... too..."

"Afraid?"

He flung an arm over his eyes. "Highlanders are not afraid of wee letters."

She scuttled over him and jumped off the bed, retrieving his coat and the letters she knew would be tucked inside. He hadn't broken either seal.

She caught him watching, propped on one arm, his eyes drinking her in, his gaze making her insides melt.

"Careful," she said. "I will start making demands on you if you look at me like that." She placed the letters on his chest, moved the still-unlit lamp closer, and used one of the candles to light it.

"You must read them."

"Ye're a bossy one."

"Perhaps I am older and wiser. I know that a wound not tended will fester and never heal." She grabbed a pillow. "Sit up."

He complied, and she popped the pillow in behind him.

"I've been most curious about these letters since I found them in Gaspar's hiding place. I don't believe he gave Banquo anything more than a story. Now. I shall give you some privacy."

He grabbed her hand and tugged her on top of him. Her breasts brushed the letters while his eyes grew smoky and dark.

She put a finger to his lips and rolled off of him. "Read first. I will lie here and be silent."

He let out a long breath and then cracked the seal of the thicker letter and unfolded it. A smaller, finer piece of paper was enclosed that looked suspiciously like a bank draft. He bit his lip over that, and then turned to the letter, written on a heavy trimmed foolscap. The hand-writing was terse and inelegant, surely a man's, and the note brief—one page, with wide margins and spacing. Malcolm skimmed the words, frowning.

He broke the second seal. This was also a brief missive, but in a finer, more elegant hand.

Still frowning, he folded them both and set them aside.

"Well?" she asked, rolling to face him.

"There is a bank draft from twenty years past for five thousand pounds." His gaze went to the canopy. "Untouched."

"What did they say?"

"Everyone is sorry."

"Your mother?"

"And my father. But he told me at the end that he was sorry, along with telling me the prophecy. Though he never said precisely what he was sorry for."

She sat up, remembering the other thing she was curious about. "The witch's tale you mentioned to Banquo?"

"Do ye always remember everything?"

"Yes. Will you share it with me?"

He flung an arm over his eyes again, as if it was all finally too much for him—prophecies, letters, apologies, a madman chasing him across England.

"But only if you wish," she added.

He reached for her then and she clasped his hand.

"When they were boys, my father, Macbeth, and Banquo stumbled across an old woman at a bothy stirring a cauldron."

"A bothy?"

"A... a hut. A small cottage. Father was young, yet already he was Earl of Menteith. She told him Macbeth would be earl after him, and that Banquo's son would be earl after Macbeth."

"You weren't yet born."

"No. And my mother—his wife, I suppose she was, not my mother —couldn't give him an heir. I suppose the marriage soured, and he began an affair with my mother. When I was born, they passed me off as his son by his wife. She died when I was very young, like the last Comtesse. I didn't know her. After that, it was always only me and my father."

It was astonishing. "Scotland has divorce, does it not? Why not just divorce his wife and marry... Oh."

"Yes. There was no easy way for her to be rid of the Comte."

"Your father had more scruples than Banquo. Had he not, my fate may have changed and I would never have married the Comte, and we might never have met." She snuggled closer. "But the prophecy... We do not have to marry, my love" she said. "It will only complicate things if we have a son..."

She caught her breath. She was jumping ahead to children. Well and why not since she knew the consequences of the love-making they'd just engaged in. But, children with Malcolm... The thought filled her heart so much that she wanted to weep.

She found herself in fact weeping and in his arms, where he held her, shushing her. "If we have a son, we'll raise him together."

"Or a daughter."

"Or both." His hand moved over her back slowing and finally stopping, and his breathing became regular. The letters beckoned for her to read them, but there would be time for them. There would be time for many things, if they were lucky.

She reached over him and blew out the candles, and then nestled into his arms and slept.

EPILOGUE

"Well," Marielle asked, peering over Malcolm's shoulder.

"They are *all* alive." He whooped with uncharacteristic enthusiasm.

She was learning that her lover was a serious man, though not without kindness, and not without humor.

"Giles, ye don't have to be earl," he said. "Your brother lives, as well as Macbeth and Greer."

Giles grinned from his place at the table, where he was having his second helping of the inn's good breakfast.

They'd arrived at the Blue Boar in Yarmouth the day before, Malcolm having left instructions at the inn in Lowestoft to forward all mail with urgency. They'd been fortunate to find a suite of three rooms available and had been preparing to go out to shop for their journey when the letter arrived.

"Does it say where Fleance is?" Giles asked.

Fleance was the improbable Scottish name borne by Giles's brother, poor lad.

"He's with Macbeth and Greer, all of them still very much alive."

He and Giles shared happy smiles. Malcolm's glance her way

showed his relief. Banquo's lie had caused him a good deal of needless concern.

"They are all still in Chelsea, but will leave soon for Deal. Macbeth is to meet there and join the Highland regiment being brought over from Cork."

"Can we go there, sir?"

"Let me see." Malcolm scanned more of the letter. "He and the regiment are traveling from Deal to Ostend in a week or two." He smiled again at the boy. "He's bringing Greer, Lucie, and your brother."

Marielle saw the excitement in his eyes. She knew that Greer and Lucie had been his only family these last few years, and they would be reunited. He was also glad to have Banquo's boys reunited, and to learn that his cousin still lived. They were all his newly acquired family.

And where did that leave her? Except for her elderly husband, she'd been alone for so very long.

His arm came around her, his face suddenly serious. "The Highlanders will fight under Wellington," he said. "Greer and Lucie plan to follow the drum."

Malcolm had admitted he wished to offer his services. For all her talk about fighting Napoleon, she prayed that the army wouldn't take him.

But he was a man truly grown, and must be free to choose, and for her part, she must swallow her worries and hope that his newly acquired family might also be hers. Life might be short, and she must take whatever blessings she found. And if Malcolm was to fight, she would most certainly follow the drum as well.

"We must make sail for Ostend," she said, "and not Calais. Giles, you must have new shirts and neck cloths and I daresay smalls before we travel. Go scratch out a note to your brother, and then fetch your coat and hat, and you and I will visit the shops while Malcolm writes a longer letter and arranges our transport."

The boy loped off into his adjoining bedchamber.

"Is there any bad news?" she asked, sensing his mood.

"Only the tale of how Banquo got his wound. He tossed Greer into the Thames. She managed to stab him and pull him in with her. They thought he'd drowned."

"Oh," she said, hope rising in her. Besides being, like herself, not quite respectable, Greer was a woman of substance. "I look forward to meeting the rest of your family."

"They will be your family as well, Marielle."

He smiled and opened his arms, and she went to him.

THE END

Malcolm Comyn, Earl of Menteith, first appears in Fated Hearts, A Love After All Retelling of the Scottish Play.

Fated Hearts is part of the Tragic Characters in Classic Literature Project, wherein with complete artistic license and an abundance of hubris, a group of Regency romance authors are retelling some of the great stories of literature. We're setting our stories in Georgian England, and giving each of these tragic heroes and heroines a happily-ever-after.

Both Malcolm and the hero of *Fated Hearts*, Macbeth proceed at the end of their stories to Ostend, to join Wellington at the Battle of Waterloo. The epilogue of *Fated Hearts* wraps up both their happily-ever-afters.

You can find more information on *Fated Hearts* and all my other books, as well as buy links, at https://alinakfield.com.

SOCIAL MEDIA FOR ALINA K. FIELD

You can learn more about Alina K. Field at these social media links:

Amazon Author Page: https://www.amazon.com/Alina-K.-Field/e/B00DZHWOKY
Facebook: https://www.facebook.com/alinakfield
Twitter: https://twitter.com/AlinaKField
BookBub: https://www.bookbub.com/authors/alina-k-field
Instagram: https://www.instagram.com/alinak.field/
Goodreads:
https://www.goodreads.com/author/show/7173518.Alina_K_Field
Pinterest: https://www.pinterest.com/alinakf/
Newsletter signup:
https://landing.mailerlite.com/webforms/landing/z6q6e3

ABOUT ALINA K. FIELD

USA Today bestselling author Alina K. Field earned a Bachelor of Arts Degree in English and German literature, but prefers the much happier world of romance fiction. Though her roots are in the Midwestern U.S., after six very, very, very cold years in Chicago, she moved to Southern California, where she shares a midcentury home with her husband and a spunky, blond rescued terrier. She is the author of several Regency romances, including the 2014 Book Buyer's Best winner, *Rosalyn's Ring*. Though hard at work on her next series of romantic adventures, she loves to hear from readers!

Website: https://alinakfield.com/

SCANDAL, SMUGGLERS, AND SPIES

The Teatime Tattler

Dearest Readers,

Who is the mysterious Miss F. and how is she connected with Duke of C's heir, Captain B. G. H?

The Captain was found by Miss F. some time in the early hours of April 1st, at the very height of the storm. Why was a gently-reared young miss out in such weather at such an hour? Perhaps Miss F is not who she pretends to be.

The Captain and his friend Lord S. hired men to watch persons suspected of cooperating with the enemy. One of those suspects? Miss F.

To add to the mystery, Miss F and the vicar, one Rev. Mr. S., spent the better part of two days closeted together. We are expected to believe they were going over old church registers. Sadly, both Miss F and Captain BG departed the inn before more could be discovered.

WAIT FOR ME

RUE ALLYN

Wait for Me
Rue Allyn

Enemies by nature—Esmeralda Crobbin, aka the pirate Irish Red, and Captain, Lord Brandon Gilroy have met before.

Fate trumps nature—When a fierce storm creates a chance encounter and forced proximity, Brandon learns the pirate is a woman of serious honor and responsibility. Esmeralda discovers the captain is more than a uniform stuffed with rules and regulations. Both love the sea with boundless passion, but can they love each other?

PROLOGUE

Sunset, December 7, 1823

Black John, former first mate and acting captain of the *Éire Mist* sat against the leeward bulkhead carving a delicate scrimshaw he planned to give to his erstwhile captain for Christmas. The ship heeled gently at anchor in the island's inner harbor. For privacy, the Duke and Duchess of Cowal kept their personal paradise off most navigational charts. Only friends and trusted suppliers could find the lush Caribbean isle where the couple spent December and January of every year. He smiled recalling other holidays, when the present Duchess of Cowal had been a simple Miss, whose greatest ambition was to captain the *Éire Mist* herself. She'd done that and more.

A ruckus erupted from the direction of the ladder to the cabin deck. A pair of flame haired five-year olds tumbled from the hatchway, speeding across the deck and settling beside him.

"Black John, tell us the story." The oldest of the two red-heads tugged on his loose shirt.

He placed the scrimshaw within the soft drawstring bag where he hid other pieces intended for the Duke. Then he slid his carving blade into a sheath at his waist. "I told ye that tale at breakfast. Wouldn't ye rather hear about how we defeated that dastard Danville when he had us all but outgunned?"

Lady Marielle MacShennan lifted her chin imperiously. "No. I want *the* story." Her emphasis on the word 'the' could only mean one special story.

John turned his head and raised a questioning brow at her ladyship's brother, the younger of the two by five minutes. "And ye, ye're lordship. D'ye wish t'hear again how yer ma and da fell in love?"

The young Viscount Cairndow nodded rapidly. The child rarely spoke, but he always got his message across.

"Well then, yer ladyship, have kindness on an old sailor's bones. Run and fetch a lantern. 'Twill be long past dark e'er I'm done with this tale."

"All right." She was up and back in three shakes.

"Thank'ee yer ladyship."

"I don't mind. I can get it faster than you, and I want the story before Nurse comes to put us to bed."

"Then hush yer voices, so's I can set the scene. Remember not to laugh when I play the parts of yer ma and da."

The children stilled and gazed at him wide-eyed.

He might have wondered how they could have enjoyed the story so much if it weren't one of his own favorites.

"'Twas a marriage fated t' happen, though the parties involved would have denied it at the time. Yer mother, the famous pirate Irish Red, and yer father, a Lieutenant in His Majesty's Royal Navy, first met in 1812, during a skirmish off the island of Jamaica."

"But that's not when they fell in love," piped in Lady Marielle.

"Right y'are, m'lady, but no more interruptin', or I'll make ye tell the story to me."

The children giggled but soon fell silent.

"It was in April of the year when old Boney escaped from Elba and sought to terrorize all of Europe by going to war again. Yer da was sent on a mission to find some missing cannon, shot, and powder..."

CHAPTER 1

Dawn, Saturday, April 1, 1815

T he sheeting rain slackened for the moment, but the farm track remained a quagmire. Esme greatly resented having her best boots ruined by a thick layer of mud. Years would pass before she could get a pair that fit as well, then more years to break them in just right. She supposed fate mocked her for pretending to be a lady when she was by nature and profession a privateer.

By comparison with the mud, the drenching rain was nothing. Hell, she'd lived on shipboard most of her life; wet was normal. She would have given much to be in the Caribbean on board the *Éire Mist* with a warm breeze tickling her hair instead of the incessant chill of a North Sea storm. *Were it not for my promise to Danny Crobbin, I would be in those warm waters still. But I gave my word to the first Irish Red, the only father figure I've ever known, and I will keep it.*

A nameless stream flooded the marshy terrain to her left. At least she imagined it was a stream when not overflowing its banks with water and all manner of detritus. She'd been lucky thus far to have dodged most of the missiles the torrent tossed in her path. Her foot hit another hidden obstacle, and she pitched forward. She dropped her bag, and threw her hands out before her, praying as she went down that she could keep her face above the muck, else she might suffocate before she could clean the stuff away.

She landed with the expected splat but unexpectedly not in the mud. Whatever she'd tripped over had broken her fall and kept her breathing. The object was large, seemed to be covered in cloth, and, as she pushed up into a seated position, she discovered it was rather lumpy. It also groaned. A very human sounding groan.

Good lord. I've landed on a man. Aware of where she sat, she scrambled off, to lean over him, her knees sinking into the muck. She bent closer and peered through the soggy light, feeling with her hands to locate his head and check for injuries. She found only a shallow bump on the back of his crown. Thank heaven he lay on his back. The rain had kept his face clear of sludge, and beneath her palms his chest rose and fell. He was alive for now. But how long had he been here, and what caused him to be lying in the mud?

On that thought, his eyes opened. They were blue, though she couldn't see the exact color in the rainy dawn. They might have been gray.

The rain resumed, and he blinked rapidly. She fished in a pocket for her handkerchief. Damp as it was, it would clear his vision. With the kerchief, she swiped water from his eyes and face. She bent to place the cloth in her pocket and, when she lifted her head, his glare struck her. A very familiar glare. A glare that had haunted her for the past three years. *Now I know fate is laughing at me.* Before her lay the one man who hated her most in the world.

"Am I hallucinating? Lieutenant Gilroy?"

"Irish Red! What are you doing here? Why am I lying in this muck with you atop me like a doxy? And my rank is now Captain."

Wasn't that just like him to consider rank and rules more important than a storm. Captain or not, she wasn't atop him, but accuracy seemed irrelevant at present. To put him in his place she stood. "I might ask the same of you. I found you lying here unconscious." *He doesn't need to know I tripped over him.* "I was checking for injuries just before you woke. Had I known it was you, I would have left you to drown in the flood. However, having become completely filthy attempting to aid a supposed stranger, I might as well help you up." She extended her hand.

He lifted himself to a sitting position and looked at her mud-caked fingers.

Since the rain began to patter again, his hesitation was unreasonable. "What's the matter? My hand is no dirtier than your own." She noted his lack of uniform. The stubbornly square chin was made sharper by the black hair plastered to his skull. "You are or were a naval officer and cannot possibly be so fastidious that a bit of mud would deter you from accepting assistance."

He remained mute, but clasped her hand with his. Together they managed to get him on his feet. However, his balance was off, and she found herself pulling his arm around her shoulder, allowing him to lean on her. The irony of lending aid to a man who wished to see her hang did not escape her. A tall man, he was no lightweight. However, her sea legs served them well, and she found balance for them both.

"We need to find my horse," he grumbled in her ear.

"The lightning and thunder of this storm would frighten the calmest steed. Your beast may be miles from here."

A piercing whistle blasted her hearing, and her ears rang.

The curtain of rain parted, and a splendid gray gelding approached. She wished she didn't admire the horse, since it was his.

"There you are, Horatio, my friend." He grasped the halter and took up the reins.

"You named your horse after Admiral Nelson?" She didn't know whether to laugh or be shocked.

"No, the man I bought this fine fellow from was a fan of Shakespeare's Hamlet."

"Oh, too bad. Riding Nelson into battle would have been much more amusing."

Gilroy rolled his eyes. "Let's find shelter. When the weather is foul, I prefer my flirtations to take place indoors."

Is that what we've been doing? Flirting? She hadn't said anything she wouldn't have said to any of her crew. Though she had to admit few of them would have understood any reference to Hamlet. There was nothing save animosity between her and Gilroy anyway, so she pushed the conversation into the past.

With much groaning and swaying on his part, she helped Gilroy get his foot into the stirrup then lift himself into the saddle.

"Get up behind me." He extended his arm for her to clasp and moved his foot out of the stirrup."

Could she accept a favor from this man? Being anywhere near him was the last thing she wanted.

He stared down at her. "Now you are unreasonable."

She shook her head. "No, let me get my bag."

It took some time, but eventually she sat on the horse's rump, one arm around the captain's waist anchoring her in place, the other clutching her bag close.

They set off at a walk, and she prayed her destination was nearby. She prayed even more that he was in too great a hurry to rest very long at the same inn. Why fate had cast this man in her path was beyond fathoming. Once they found the village and inn, she'd avoid him until she completed her business and left. Lingering would only cause problems and provide him opportunity to give evidence against her. In short order, she'd find herself in prison waiting a hangman's noose. Speed was now of the essence.

🐝

That afternoon, warm and comfortable, in her room at the Queen's Barque, Esme smoothed the somewhat wrinkled skirt of her gray serge dress then tied a tiny lace cap over her dyed black hair. The dress was the driest item of clothing she owned, because it had been packed in the center of her valise. The cap was a concession to the role she played. She'd chosen the persona of a young lady of modest means, traveling with a companion to meet relatives. That last was true, even if she'd never met said relatives and was uncertain of the exact relation. Yes, her means were well beyond what could be called modest, but she'd never been a fool and only a fool let the world know of her wealth.

She turned as the door opened and Verity Walford, her chaperone, entered. "At last you're here. Tell me if I am presentable?" Esme asked of her companion and, Esme hoped, soon to be friend.

"I've been helping the local vicar give aid to some folk who were injured in a wreck last night." Verity cast an eye over Esme's appearance while circling a finger to indicate her charge should turn about. "Stand still a moment, Esmeralda, your belt is askew." Verity fumbled at Esme's back then moved away. "Perfect. You're the very image of a proper miss."

"You must remember to call me Miss Eugenia or Miss Fynlock in public."

Verity smiled in agreement. "You are correct. Perhaps I should call you Eugenia at all times, to ingrain the habit. I am far too used to listening to her Grace of Stonegreave talk of you as Esme and your adventures with Napoleon at Fontainebleau last year."

"When I finally have opportunity," Esme began. "I shall thank our mutual benefactress for her aid. As for names, I have a similar problem. I am more used to calling Her Grace, Marielle or Mademoiselle, as I did when we met in France. Your Grace and Duchess will feel strange on my tongue. Be that as it may, you've an excellent idea. On my part, I shall answer to nothing but Eugenia." She pulled on her gloves and picked up her reticule.

"Her Grace does not stand on ceremony with those she calls friends. Perhaps you'll not need to twist your tongue too much." Verity settled in a chair beside the parlor fireplace. "Eugenia, we've not had time to talk. We must make plans."

"We can talk tonight." She crossed the room to the door. "I'll want to check on our arrangements with the innkeeper."

"Probably wise, given the number of travelers who might not normally stay here. Such was not the case when I arrived three days ago, before the worst of this maelstrom. That is when I paid the innkeeper for these chambers, notified him you were expected, and received his promise to honor our privacy. That promise is all well and good, but this horrid storm could create some problems."

Verity didn't know the half of it. Her hand on the latch, Eugenia looked back at her companion. "There is more to my purpose in this village than simply meeting with you, but I've no time to explain now.

Tonight, when we are private, I will share what I can, and you may tell me how fares Her Grace of Stonegreave. Right now, I must go down and speak with the innkeeper."

"Have you enough coin to offer him incentive to discourage him from forcing us to share our quarters?"

"I've taken some of the spare cash from the compartment in my valise and can promise the man more if he'll not force us to co-habit with strangers. I assure you I'll manage." She left, crossing to the stair and descending slowly. They were somewhat rickety, but she anticipated no trouble. Climbing rigging and staying upright on a galloping deck was second nature. No, her care on the stairs was more for appearances than safety's sake.

However, her retarded pace allowed her far too much time to contemplate the man she'd rescued. Was it some sort of cosmic justice that she was now stranded at this inn with a man she'd once stranded on a Caribbean island? If he could, the captain would surely see her hanged.

The number of people in the hotel lobby had doubled, and getting to the reception desk where the innkeeper stood, with the young man assisting him, would take some skill. Eugenia paused on the bottom stair to decide the best path to take. The floor was slick with water and mud brought in by new travelers. Baggage lined the walls and filled the corners to just below the row of paintings hung at eye level.

The innkeeper was doing a valiant job to maintain order and keep his guests happy. A maid with a tray of steaming mugs emerged from the direction of the public room. Many in the crowd rushed in her direction, and abruptly the path to the desk was clear. Eugenia was about to leave the stairs when her ever-moving glance met that of a man leaning against the opposite wall. He smiled at her and gave a nod of acknowledgement. *Milo Cosistas. He knows me despite my changed hair-color. That is inconvenient.* Quickly she shifted her gaze, as if offended by a stranger's notice.

She was not surprised to see the well-to-do chandler and fence of stolen goods. Fenwick on Sea was within the area where he conducted business both legitimate and furtive. Her captaincy of the *Éire Mist* gave her occasion to have both types of dealings with the man. He knew how to keep a secret—a necessity in his secondary line of work. She must be certain he would keep silent about her. Not now, however, among so many people, where anyone might hear a conversation no matter how quietly voiced.

She made her way to the reception desk and waited patiently to speak with the innkeeper. His assistant became available first.

"How may I help you, Miss?"

"Miss Fynlock. Several days ago, my traveling companion, Miss Walford, arrived in advance of me and took two rooms on the second floor—a bedchamber and a private parlor. Given the increase in the number of your guests," she said and cast a glance around the room. "I wish to ensure that our original agreement remains in place. My privacy is exceedingly important to me, and I will not allow you to place a stranger or strangers in my chambers."

The young man swallowed, looked at the crowded lobby, and bobbed his head. "I understand Miss Fynlock. However..." He looked over to the innkeeper who'd begun to watch. "I... I am not certain. That is, given the circumstances..."

The innkeeper placed a hand on the young man's shoulder. "Take my place here, Timmy, and assist Mr. Cosistas. He'll have his usual room."

The assistant switched places with the innkeeper. "Welcome to the Queen's Barque, Miss Fynlock, I'm Brewster." The older man smiled.

She placed a few coins on the counter top, pushing them toward the innkeeper. "I explained to your assistant."

"Timmy's my eldest girl's intended, and he's learning the business right quick." The man puffed out his chest as he placed a palm over the money. He pulled the coins off the counter and deposited them somewhere below. "I heard what you said to him. I am delighted to assure you that we will make no changes to your accommodations. The inn is quite large, and I am certain we have sufficient chambers for all our guests. Although some of them may find the Barque a mite less comfortable than normal, since we will be compelled to assign chambers that are currently in the final stage of renovation. Also, some of the servants may have to sleep over the stables. An inconvenience, I know, but necessary, given the storm."

"Not my companion," Eugenia insisted.

"Of course not. She is already accommodated with a trundle in your parlor, is she not?"

Eugenia nodded. "And the services we requested? A private breakfast in my parlor, unless we arrange otherwise, as well as a basket of pastries to nibble on throughout the day?"

"As long as supplies last, all will be as promised to your companion."

"Then I thank you, sir. Should service continue to be satisfactory, I will be certain to recommend your fine establishment to my friends and acquaintances."

The man beamed at her. "I am very grateful for your kindness. If you require assistance of any kind, please call for me."

"Thank you again, Mr. Brewster." The crowd had returned, and she decided not to attempt going to the public room. The stairs were closer. Resting for the remainder of the day might help her clear her mind and discover solutions to some problems. Fate certainly did not want her search for her mother's marriage lines to be easy. First Captain Gilroy, then Cosistas. What obstacle might fate toss her way next?

❦

After dinner, Eugenia declined her host's general invitation to all ladies for tea in the upper parlor and retired for the evening. She was weary but still had much to do, and she paced her chambers, impatient for Verity to return. Worry about the potential for interference with her plans kept her afoot.

Finally, the door opened. Eugenia sat and composed herself, waiting while Verity deposited items on a side table.

"How many days do you think will see your business here concluded?" asked Miss Walford. "I should send a message to Her Grace as to when she may expect us."

"One or two days should suffice to complete my business, but this storm may have us stranded here for longer."

"True. I'll send my note at the first opportunity."

"Speaking of notes, I need to communicate discreetly with a Mr. Cosistas who is staying at the inn. Could you pen a missive to him for me setting a meeting time at a discreet location? Also direct him how to reply. I dare not write the note myself, lest someone recognize my handwriting. I wish no one to know I am even slightly acquainted with the man. Once the note is ready, please give it to a servant to pass to Cosistas."

Verity's brows rose. "I gather this is one of the many things Her Grace warned me not to question you about."

"Correct. Will you do it?"

"I see no harm in passing a message for you."

After the note was written, they sat in silence punctuated by rumbles of thunder and flashes of lightning. Verity bent to some mending. Esme pretended to read, but in truth wrestled with the problem of Captain Gilroy. She doubted avoidance would work, given they were stranded at the same inn, but it was worth attempting. Her mind continued to circle without resolution. She sighed and stood, moving toward the bedchamber. "I'm exhausted and wish to retire."

"I'll get your nightrail."

"You know you needn't wait on me, Verity. Your presence here is only for show."

"I think of my job here the way you think of your name. If we continue in private as we wish to be seen in public, we are much less likely to falter and make mistakes."

"Very well. While I change, tell me, how is Her Grace of Stonegreave?"

Behind Eugenia, Verity released the buttons of the dress. "She is very happy and expecting her first child."

Eugenia smiled and stepped out of her skirts to let Verity deal with ties and tapes. "And her new husband, Captain Campion, is he happy as well?"

"Over the moon with love for Her Grace and walking on air, as if becoming a papa is something only he has accomplished."

Eugenia rolled her eyes. "Men. They are so predictable."

Verity's voice held a happy lilt as she let Eugenia's underthings drop to the floor then lifted the voluminous nightrail over her head. "Truer words were never spoken. For some reason, a man always seems to think that creating a child is an accomplishment worthy of much bragging and chest puffing. But it is the woman who bears the brunt of bringing life into the world."

"I agree," said Eugenia. She gathered her skirts and sat on the turned-down bed. "Thank you for your help. Please arrange for a bath to be brought up after breakfast tomorrow. Once I've bathed, we'll go down to the public room and wait for an opportunity to pass our note to Cosistas through a servant."

"Excellent." Verity gathered the soiled clothing and left.

Eugenia put out the candle on her bedside table, but she lay awake a long time. *Captain Brandon Gilroy.* She recalled him well despite three years passing. He'd given his crew the same respect they gave him. He'd been a staunch defender of King, Country, crew and ship. He saw it as his duty to eradicate every pirate and privateer in the Caribbean. The man haunted her dreams for far too long.

When the seas were quiet and naught on the *Éire Mist* required her immediate attention, she'd wondered what had happened to him. The island where she'd stranded him with the part of his crew who chose not to join her in privateering had plenty of water and ample food. That is, if he knew how to hunt and forage. She'd left him a cache of weapons at the far end of the island. She'd never intended to abandon him and his crew without any defenses.

How long, she mused, had it taken for him to signal a ship and be retrieved from that island? What had he done to earn his promotion? Where had he been? Did he miss the sea as much as she when ashore? *And why in the world am I keeping myself from sleep with all these questions about a man who could very well put me in prison or see me hanged?* She shifted onto her side, punched her pillow, then forced her mind to blank and her body to relax.

CHAPTER 2

Sunday morning, Brandon made a slow careful descent of the inn's ancient stairs. His head still ached, but he suffered nothing like the pounding dizziness of yesterday. The vicar, who was also the village's healer, had warned him the headaches might recur for the next week, but they should subside with time. Brandon believed a good solid English breakfast would put him to rights sooner than any bedrest. He aimed for the public room, which was still crowded at mid-morning. Pausing in the doorway for a few moments, he spotted an acquaintance. His friend saw him, waved at him, and indicated an empty chair nearby.

"Good morning, Russell! May I join you?"

"By all that's holy, Brandon. I've not seen you since Eton." Russell Downey, sixth Earl of Stanton stood, clapped Brandon on the shoulder, and gestured to the chair opposite his. "Sit, sit. How have you been? How are Clan MacShennan and your uncle His Grace of Cowal? We've years to catch up on."

"There have been a few changes since we last met, but I'd prefer to order my breakfast first," Brandon broke in. "I'm famished. I've had nothing but broth for the past day, and little before that."

"Broth?" Russell's black brows met. "Ah, you're the fellow rescued by the mysterious young lady. I believe I heard Brewster address her as Fynlock. Can't say as I recall anyone in the *ton* by that name. But rumor says a reporter from that rag, *The Teatime Tattler*, is skulking about. If she's an imposter that reporter will uncover it. Unless she herself is the dastard. Whoever the reporter is will likely want to know your story as much as I do. How came you to be unconscious beside a stream in one of the worst storms of the century? And how came she to be out there to find you? Now that I think on it, no self-respecting purveyor of tittle-tattle would be out in such weather. Miss Fynlock must have had some other reason, hmmm?"

So Red is calling herself Fynlock. Brandon shrugged to indicate he thought the questions unimportant. Until he knew more of Russell's business here, he'd keep what he knew about Irish Red to himself. "I'd just emerged from fording a swollen stream when lightning struck very close and frightened my horse. Surprised us both so much I got thrown and must have hit my head on something hard."

A servant arrived to take Brandon's order as well as Stanton's request for a fresh pot of coffee.

"Whatever it was must have been very hard. As I recall you've the stubbornness of granite," Russell joked.

Brandon smiled. "I prefer to think myself determined and dedicated."

"A good thing, too, or from what I hear you might not have returned from the Caribbean alive," his friend remarked.

"I had plenty of help from the loyal members of my crew." Embarrassed at the reminder of his defeat at Irish Red's hands, Brandon waved the compliment away then leaned closer, lowering his voice for Russell's ears alone. "However, I must change the subject and ask you not to call me by my rank. While I'm not hiding my identity, I introduce myself as Mister Brandon Gilroy. I prefer to keep my association with the Navy and my relationship to the Duke of Cowal private for a number of reasons."

One of Russell's eyebrows rose. as he leaned closer "Such as?"

Brandon nodded. "None I am at liberty to discuss in public, but I am aware of your work for the Government and think we should talk privately."

"Hmmm."

They waited while Brandon's meal was served and the coffee was poured.

"I could not obtain a private parlor, with so many guests at the inn," Brandon continued. "However, the innkeeper informed me that the chambers in one of the oldest wings of the inn remain unoccupied. His intention is to renovate, but the rooms in that wing need so much work, he could not possibly use them to accommodate even desperate guests."

"That's excellent. Should anyone notice, we could say we asked Brewster's permission to satisfy our curiosity about the history of this place and explore the rest of the inn," Russell stated.

"When do you want to meet? I am available at any time. This storm has left my schedule in tatters."

"How about after dinner, today?" suggested Stanton.

His mouth full of ham, Brandon nodded.

Stanton pushed back his chair and stood. "Perfect. Now I regret that..."

Brandon slapped a hand on Russell's arm. "Wait."

Stanton resumed his seat. "What is it?"

"That man standing by the door. I know him. Do you?"

Russell turned his head making a slow perusal of the room without seeming to notice any one in particular. "No."

"Good. Perhaps you might befriend him. He is a chandler among other things, and has had dealings with the Navy on occasion."

"Interesting."

"More than you may think. I'll give you details when we meet later."

"Well enough." His friend rose once more and clapped Brandon's shoulders again. "It is very good to see you, old friend, but I must go. I promised my wife I would assist her with nursing some of the sick and injured survivors from the storm."

"You are wed?"

Russell smiled, with a glint to his eyes "To the sweetest woman in the world. Days ago."

Brandon grinned back. "Then I wish you both happy. I'll see you after dinner if not before."

He used his friend's departure to observe the chandler's destination. The man pulled out a chair at a table beside a pair of ladies. Brandon recognized the woman facing him as Miss Walford, who attended him with the vicar the previous day. The other woman had her back to him, so he could only see her dark hair and the dull gray cloth of her dress. Modest pearls adorned her earlobes, and shiny metal glimmered at her temples. Did she wear spectacles?

She couldn't be the woman responsible for his rescue. *I'd know that she-devil anywhere. I wonder where she's gone to?* Not far, he supposed, not in this weather. He'd thank Miss Walford for her care of him, then find an opportunity to question the innkeeper about the women guests. Irish Red had to be among them. He could not see that proud beauty taking the role of servant, even temporarily.

He waved over a serving girl, paid his shot and stood. He'd taken only one step toward the two women when a second lass carrying a teapot stopped at their table and refilled their cups. Brandon continued walking. Not to do so would draw unwanted attention. With the tea poured, Miss Walford passed an envelope to the girl, who continued around to the rest of the occupied tables providing fresh tea to whomever wished it. *Odd. Vails weren't usually given in envelopes.*

As the server neared Brandon, he noted the stains on the lass's apron. In and of themselves, stains on an apron were not remarkable, but ink stains? He had just enough time as she brushed by to observe similar stains on her fingers. Most servants were not educated and could neither read nor write, but some were. Finding a serving wench who could likely do both, in a backwater such as Fenwick on Sea was peculiar to say the least. He filed the information away for later examination and proceeded on to greet the ladies at their table.

"Good morning, Miss Walford," Brandon said.

The older woman smiled. "Good morning, Mr. Gilroy. Allow me to introduce my traveling companion, Miss Eugenia Fynlock."

"A pleasure, Miss Fynlock."

"Likewise, Mr. Gilroy." She kept her head bowed slightly so he could not see her face well, and she did wear spectacles. However, something about her was familiar. Then it struck him, her voice was a pleasing contralto with a tiny rasp, such as he'd heard from only one woman.

"Might I join you for a moment?" Brandon looked between the two women.

"Certainly," Miss Walford responded.

"We are nearly finished." Miss Fynlock's head came up.

As he sat, Brandon fought to force words past a throat gone suddenly dry. "Thank you, Miss Walford." He blinked twice, then smiled as if greeting a total stranger. Irish Red might imagine changing her hair color, using spectacles, and wearing staid clothing would hide her identity, but she could not hide her voice. Not from him.

Dressed as a pirate, Irish Red, despite her criminal profession, was as stunning as her voice was musical. Even her current disguise could not hide that fact completely. She was not beautiful precisely, but arrestingly attractive. Though she was seated, Brandon knew she was taller than most women. He suspected the ill-fitting gray dress that showed nothing of her figure was designed to make her appear shorter when standing. He had a very clear memory of her clothed in snug black leather britches and a form-fitting black doublet. Her naturally red hair—now dyed a dull ebony—was pulled tightly away from her oval face, revealing high cheekbones and forehead. Her mouth was a tad too broad, though her lips were rosy and full. Behind the spectacles that sat on her straight nose, startlingly brilliant and familiar sea-green eyes flashed. What was a flame-haired pirate who roamed the Caribbean doing in Fenwick on Sea masquerading as a modest miss?

In the seconds he took to catalogue her features, she ducked her head again as if she were shy. *Ha! She's anything but shy.*

He angled his chair so he was sitting closest to Miss Walford, improving his view of Irish Red, and, from his peripheral vision, Mr. Cosistas. Was it an accident that a pirate and a known fence of stolen goods were in the same obscure village at the same time? *Doubtful.*

"I wish to thank you for assisting the vicar yesterday." He spoke to Miss Walford, but his gaze refused to leave Miss Fynlock. *Lift your head again; I need to see your face, your eyes.*

"I would do the same for anyone under similar circumstances," Miss Walford demurred.

"Most likely, but you aided me. Hence, I will thank you."

"You are most welcome."

"I gather, Miss Fynlock, that I have you to thank for my rescue. However did you manage it?" *And what was a pirate doing wandering the English coastlands alone at dawn amid a downpour?*

"You are mistaken, sir. I arrived here before you. It is Miss Walford who rendered you aid with the vicar. However, a blow to the head might explain your confusion." She sipped her tea.

He finally tore his gaze away to look at Miss Walford. "I suppose I might have the details confused." But he knew differently. However, acting as if he believed himself in error could put Red at ease enough for her to let down her guard and allow him to discover her purpose here.

"Who rescued you, sir, is unimportant. How you came to be unconscious in a marsh is more worthy of notice," murmured Irish Red.

Brandon supposed he should think of her as Eugenia, just to keep her believing she'd deceived him, but he knew that to be impossible.

"I was fording a stream, the water rising rapidly. My horse and I were barely clear of the ford when lightning struck and my mount panicked. Even with gloves, my grip on the reins was slick, and I was thrown. I remember that much but little else until I arrived here. I recall nearly fainting as I dismounted. Whoever rescued me was most definitely a woman. She was good enough to get the innkeeper and see that I was taken to a chamber immediately. I need to discover my rescuer's whereabouts, so I may thank her and reimburse her for any costs incurred in acquiring a room for me."

Did Red pale a bit when he mentioned finding his savior?

"I... I do not think the woman stayed here. I recall Verity telling me that the landlord searched your belongings for sufficient funds to pay for your room and your care. She said also that he was watched as he did so to ensure nothing else was taken."

That was probably so, since the dispatches he carried were still sewn into the lining of his one piece of baggage.

"Thank you for that information, Miss Fynlock. I hope you will permit me to invite you and Miss Walford both to dine with me while we are stranded here."

"I'm not certain that would be proper."

He'd never heard a stern melody before, and found Miss Fynlock's voice fascinating. "I enlist your aid, Miss Walford. Surely two ladies may dine publicly with a single gentleman without rousing gossip."

"I suppose. But dinner only."

"Certainly. Then we are agreed. Miss Fynlock? Shall we say seven o'clock tonight?"

Miss Walford nodded. "Eugenia?"

Miss Fynlock lifted those sea-green eyes briefly. The animosity in her stare was unmistakable.

She issued an impatient sigh. "I suppose it would be rude to decline."

The maid with the teapot was making another circuit of the room. He offered tea to the ladies. Miss Walford declined for them both and stood. Miss Fynlock followed suit.

Brandon rose too.

The women said their farewells, and he echoed the polite sentiments.

They moved off just as he saw the serving lass stop at Cosistas's table. With one hand, the girl filled the man's cup. With the other she pulled a familiar envelope from the pocket of her ink-stained apron and placed it on the corner of the table. Cosistas palmed the envelope, and it disappeared within his coat.

Why would Miss Walford send notes to Cosistas? If they knew each other, why not simply stop and converse? Was it something which she wished to hide from Miss Fynlock? Or was Miss Walford aiding Red? What did a pirate need with a companion anyway? Exactly what was the relationship between these two women? Given what Brandon knew of Cosistas' dealings in stolen goods, Miss Walford's actions were highly suspicious. He must keep an eye on the chaperone and Irish Red. In all probability they were conniving together.

Once in the privacy of their chambers, Eugenia, rounded on Verity. "I thought we agreed that I should have as little contact with Gilroy as possible."

"What in the world were you thinking to claim I told you that pack of tarradiddles about the innkeeper searching Mr. Gilroy's belongings?" Verity countered, standing arms akimbo. "You have forced me into a lie, Eugenia, and I do not like it."

"My name, my appearance, even my supposed purpose for being at the Queen's Barque are all lies. You do not seem to object to those." She crossed her arms and tapped a foot.

Verity straightened. "I was informed ahead of time and was given the option to decline. I accepted out of love and respect for Her Grace of Stonegreave. She has done much for me and my family. Acting as your companion and chaperone is a small thing by comparison with what I owe her."

Eugenia moved to sit in one of the chairs flanking the fireplace. "At least we agree on that. I love her too and owe her as much as you, perhaps more. But what am I to do about this dinner? I can't face Gilroy across a table for an hour or more." *I could. It isn't as if he doesn't know who I really am. Why am I reluctant to spend any time in his company? Because he's dangerous to me. That's the only reason.*

"You could claim a headache. It's a lie but a polite one," Verity suggested.

"Possibly, but it's a much too obvious move—cowardly as well, and I've never played the coward. No, I need to turn this to my advantage." She stared into the flames, seeing Gilroy's angry face as he and his crew were forced onto that deserted island. His fury when she disarmed him and held him at sword point. She'd not forgotten those storm-blue eyes that absorbed every detail at a glance. She might never forget them. He'd surrendered, but she'd seen the fire there, the determination to even the score. She'd seen cunning too. She'd wager he could recall every box, bale, line and gun placement of the *Éire Mist*. No, any length of time in his company and she was sure to reveal more than she wished. It was more risk than she would take.

An idea began to form. "What time and place did you set for the encounter with Milo Cosistas?"

Standing on the other side of the fireplace, Verity's jaw dropped, and she covered her mouth. Clearly dismayed, she removed her hand to reveal pursed lips. "Seven tonight in the wing beyond the brew-house, which is not being used to house anyone. I'd forgotten all about that meeting. How could I?"

Eugenia smiled. "Perfect."

Verity's brows met. "Truly?"

"Yes." Eugenia leaned forward. "I'll go down with you to dinner and pretend the wine makes me ill. I'll retire with apologies, but instead of going to our rooms, I'll keep the meeting with Cosistas."

"You'll be late."

"He'll wait. He's always profited from our business dealings. He no doubt thinks I have a similar project in mind."

"And if he wants money for keeping his silence?"

"Then I'll have to pay him. It will only be once. As soon as possible after I conclude my business we'll leave. Miss Eugenia Fynlock will disappear. I'll put on another guise for my journey north."

"Leaving dinner might work." Verity sounded doubtful. "But the timing would have to be carefully orchestrated. You wouldn't want to be seen following Mr. Cosistas."

Eugenia smiled. "None shall."

She felt significantly better with a plan of action in place, and she'd have another chance to show up Captain Gilroy. Even if only she knew of it, besting him had been one of the high points of her adventures. She knew herself well enough to recognize the excitement that thrummed in her blood. Gilroy was a challenging man, albeit an inconvenient one right now. Nonetheless, she did love a challenge.

Later, after her small disagreement with Verity, Eugenia became restless. She wanted to be striding the deck of her ship instead of pacing the confines of a parlor. *Enough! I've no need to sequester myself. I'll take a light luncheon in the public room.* A young lady might not normally eat alone in a public room. However, given the circumstances of the storm it could be forgiven, especially if she kept to herself, which she was more than happy to do. She'd already encountered two men from her past. If any more familiar faces appeared, she'd think fate was intent on ruining her hopes.

Once in the public room, she took a seat in an isolated corner at one of the two empty tables, ordered a beef pie, hot tea, and a plate of biscuits for herself, then requested the same be sent up to Verity. She settled back and opened her book, pretending to read while she considered the problems the storm had brought her.

A servant brought her meal, and Eugenia put away her book so she could eat. She had yet to resolve the problem of Captain Gilroy. She'd barely begun to think about him when she was interrupted.

"Excuse me, miss. Do you mind if we join you?"

Eugenia looked up. Two young ladies with very hopeful expressions stood beside her table. A quick glance around the room showed all the other tables were fully occupied.

"Please do." She smiled and gestured to the table's remaining chairs. To refuse would be seen as churlish and would draw unwanted attention.

"Thank you so very much. This is Lady Stanton." The pretty brunette gestured to her companion as the woman sat. "I am Miss de Courtenay, but please call me Miranda." She, too, took a seat."

"Miss Eugenia Fynlock." Eugenia extended her hand, shaking with each woman in succession.

A serving girl came and took the ladies' orders.

"Lady Stanton and I just met in the lobby and decided to dine together, as this room is so crowded," Miranda chattered on when the girl had left.

"I, for one, am very hungry," Lady Stanton stated. "I've been assisting Mr. Somerville, the vicar, with caring for storm-stricken guests and have not eaten since very early this morning."

Eugenia listened as the lady and Miss de Courtenay exchanged comments about the various disasters that had stranded so many folk at the inn. It was clear they hoped she would share her own stranding story, but she preferred to keep silent. Instead, she filled pauses with questions such as the likelihood of meeting friends and acquaintances at a backwater like Fenwick on Sea. The consensus seemed to be that anything was possible.

Then Lady Stanton remarked. "I heard that a reporter from that nasty *Teatime Tattler* has taken up residence inside this very inn."

Miranda's eyes went wide, and she scanned the space. Her gaze rested briefly on a handsome man in a dark booth across the room.

Eugenia smiled. "I'll bet that came from Brewster. Our host is quite the conversationalist. A necessary skill when frequently dealing with strangers. Nonetheless, he does tend to look out for his customers' privacy."

"Best be careful of your reputations, ladies," the younger woman warned. "You don't want to end up as the latest tittle-tattle for all of Society to learn about."

"The information about the reporter is troubling. Perhaps what is needed is a plan to get out of this inn and away from prying eyes and ears," Eugenia suggested, a kernel of a plan forming as she spoke.

"Interesting," Lady Stanton said. "What do you have in mind?"

"I'd love to escape this inn for a time," Miranda exclaimed. "But the weather is hardly conducive to excursions."

"Agreed," Eugenia said and peered out the window at the pelting rain. "What if we plan to take an excursion on the first good day? With luck that might be as early as tomorrow afternoon."

"But where?" Lady Stanton inquired.

"I'm told by Mrs. Brewster," Miranda announced, "that the village church is a fine example of Norman architecture and was visited by Queen Elizabeth. The stained-glass window of the church is supposedly a gift from that noble monarch."

"That is an excellent idea," Eugenia smiled then glanced at Lady Stanton. "My travelling companion is acquainted with the vicar as well. She also has assisted him with the injured from this storm. She could ask Somerville if he would guide us through the church."

"Would your friend be Miss Walford?" Lady Stanton asked.

"She is."

"She and I met while helping the vicar. She has a very tender heart."

"Thank you, I agree. Shall I ask her to speak with Somerville? I'm sure she'll want to get out of the inn as much as all of us."

"That would be wonderful, Eugenia," Miranda replied.

For some odd reason the young woman blushed, but Eugenia had better things to do than wonder about a stranger's peculiarities. "Then we are in accord. I will send notes to you both via Mr. Brewster when I know the details of our visit to the stained-glass church."

"Excellent," Miranda stated.

Her luncheon arrived at that moment, and Eugenia began eating while the ladies enjoyed their tea.

Of a sudden, a distant bell rang with the violence that could only signal an alarm. Then a man rushed into the room drenched from the rain. "Been another wreck... " he started to say while gasping for breath. "This time it's past the dunes and fishing harbor. Stuck on the rocky shoal, it is. They've got casualties!"

A servant brought the man a warm drink. He gulped it down.

Men and some women began rising from their tables to lend aid. Eugenia kept eating. She wanted to help, but knew she would try to direct the efforts and use her strength and knowledge to best effect. All of that would raise questions about how a modest maiden could be possessed of such knowledge and strength. She would have to pray that those who did attend the rescue knew what they were about.

"What's the name of the ship?" someone asked the man who'd brought the news of the wreck.

"*The Legacy*," he replied, before taking another gulp of his brew. "Never been here before, and it's not going anywhere for a spell until repairs are done."

Miranda leapt to her feet, almost sending her chair to the floor when the ship's name was announced. "Good heavens... Jasper!"

Miss de Courtenay was poised to flee the inn when her arm was taken by the handsome man from across the room. Eugenia recognized him as a fellow ship's captain. His reputation among sailors was such that she'd never wanted any closer association. If all she'd heard was correct, Danville wasn't a man she wished to cross paths with. Should she warn Miss de Courtenay? *Before I say anything, I'll consult Verity. She'll know best how to deal with a flighty chatter-box like de Courtenay.*

"Why, Miss de Courtenay," Danville was saying. He smiled as if quite happy with something. An odd reaction to news of a shipwreck.

"I must apologize, Lord Danville, but you will have to excuse me." Miranda wrenched her arm from his grasp then ran from the public room.

No wonder none of the muck Danville is credited with has stuck to him. I wonder how long he's been masquerading as a lord?

The man no longer smiled. His gaze searched the room. Before it could light on her, Eugenia bent her head and lifted her teacup. From the corner of her eye, she saw him march off.

Lady Stanton stood, recalling Eugenia to her ladyship's presence. "A shipwreck! How horrible. I should alert the vicar and Mr. Brewster that we are likely to receive more patients."

Eugenia concurred. "You must do so with all possible speed," she suggested. "You will hear from me when the details of our visit to the church are arranged."

"Good day, then, Miss Fynlock. It was a pleasure to meet you." She left in a hurry to find Brewster and the vicar.

Eugenia finished her tea, picked up her book and stood, then returned to her rooms. Verity was out, so Eugenia settled in a chair beside the fireplace and pursued the problem of Captain Gilroy. If anyone could ruin her entire enterprise, it was her rescued Captain. *No, no, he is not, never was, never could be mine in any way. Caution is needed where he is concerned, and I must remember that.*

He'd already recognized her, despite the fact that they'd met only once before. But what an encounter. She smiled at the memory. *No man forgets a woman who defeats him in battle then strands him on an island.*

She sobered. She must avoid him whenever possible. That might prove difficult until the storm abated. She'd manage. She was fairly good at thinking on her feet. A drop of regret settled in her chest. She enjoyed challenges, and to date none had been as difficult and intriguing to overcome as this man. That was probably the reason she remembered him after three years.

"I am delighted you could join me this evening ladies." Captain Gilroy seated Eugenia then Verity. "I've taken the liberty of ordering for us."

Eugenia bent her head. She was supposed to be a modest young miss, but she knew that modesty would not permit her to avoid

Gilroy's attention even for the short time until the wine was served and she could pretend illness.

"It is our pleasure," Verity said.

"I couldn't agree more." Eugenia looked up and smiled.

Gilroy tilted his head to the side, and his brows met. He straightened as he sat. "You have a lovely voice, Miss Fynlock. That slight raspiness combined with such a melodic contralto is quite unusual."

Her cheeks heated. "You are too kind, Mr. Gilroy."

"Not at all," he assured her. "Given the circumstances of our meeting, perhaps the two of you would do me the kindness of calling me Brandon." He glanced from Verity to Eugenia where he fixed his gaze "I will enjoy listening to you all the more."

"I am not certain such a reduction in formality is entirely appropriate," Verity protested.

Is he flirting with me again? How odd and definitely unexpected. It must be a ploy to distract me and get me to lower my defenses. "If it would please you." Eugenia replied, fluttering her lashes, Eugenia spoke over Verity. Two can play the distraction game.

A quick blink was the only indication she might have surprised him.

"Very well, Brandon." Verity conceded. She gave Eugenia a reproving glare.

Brandon acted as if he'd not seen the glare. "I've no wish to pry, so, if it is not too personal, please tell me what brought you to Fenwick on Sea and the Queen's Barque?" His blue-gray, sea-change gaze bored into Eugenia, alight with curiosity and something else she could not name. Something shadowed.

She used her blushes as an excuse to lower her lashes. "I am on my way to visit relatives and, like most of the current guests, the storm prevents any progress."

The wine arrived. Gilroy approved the vintage, and the server poured, leaving the bottle when he departed.

"I toast your good sense." Beaming, he lifted his glass. "And my good fortune in meeting two such lovely ladies."

Good fortune, bah! He's glad he'll have the opportunity to arrest me for piracy. The English do not look kindly on privateer captains who cannot produce legitimate letters of marque. Curse Danny Crobbin for leaving the documents ashore then dying before he could tell me where to find them. I'll let Gilroy continue thinking he's about to have me cornered, but his confidence is misplaced.

Verity and Eugenia echoed Brandon's toast with their own about a courageous gentleman.

"However," he continued. "I am now even more curious how you came to be alone in the coastlands at that hour of the morning in the height of a storm."

"You accused me of that action this morning. I denied it then, and I deny it now." She looked around the room crowded with diners, then fixed him with a steady gaze.

Verity raised a brow, her gaze flicking between Eugenia and Brandon.

Brandon lowered his voice for their ears alone. "I understand the need for discretion, Miss Fynlock. No proper young lady would admit to wandering about alone at such an hour, especially in a storm. However, you and I both know you are the person who rescued me. So, between the three of us." He acknowledged Verity with a glance. "I see no reason to dissemble."

What could she say? Eugenia sipped some wine, giving herself time to think. Her face grew warmer. *He'll think I'm a ninnyhammer, if I continue to blush at every word he utters. And that's a bad thing because...?* She gave a tiny shake of her head. "You force me to confess my horrible secret, sir."

Across the table, Verity's eyes went wide.

"I've no wish to distress you, Miss Fynlock. Please keep your secrets." His tone belied his words, inviting her to reveal all.

"I... uh..."

"Mr. Gilroy, Brandon, has said he wishes to respect your privacy," stated Verity.

"No, it's all right. It might be a good thing if Mr. Gilroy knows I walk in my sleep."

"Really?" The interest in his eyes strengthened. "I've heard of people who experience nocturnal perambulations, but I've never met one. Do you know what causes it?"

"The doctors I've spoken with believe I am acting out dreams. If true, I certainly do not recall those dreams. Whatever the cause, the condition is annoying and potentially dangerous, since my sleep-walking is not limited to interior spaces. The morning I found you, I had experienced an episode. Fortunately, stumbling over you woke me up. So, you might say we saved each other." Eugenia paused to sip more wine. "Verity had noticed I was missing and came to find me."

Gilroy looked at Verity. "I'm surprised you were able to determine which direction Miss Fynlock took?"

Verity all but glared at Eugenia. "My charge has an affinity for the sea. I chose to look in the direction of the surf which I knew would attract her."

"You've known each other for a long time, then."

Now Verity blushed. "We've become quite close."

Eugenia groaned. "Oh dear. I am unwell.

"Is it the wine?" the chaperone asked.

"Wine?" Brandon queried.

Eugenia stood, a hand to her stomach. "I'm afraid so. I knew better than to take more than one or two sips, but the vintage is so pleasant. Please excuse me."

"Let me assist you." Brandon rose and reached for her hand.

She shook her head. "Thank you, but I've no wish to disturb your meal. I shall be fine, if I can only lie down.

"She is right," Verity said. "Please sit, sir. I will check on her after we eat. For right now, nothing can be done. When I go up, I'll take her some clear broth to settle her stomach. I shall see you anon, Eugenia."

She nodded. "Thank you." Then she turned away, heading for the lobby entrance. Two steps from Brandon, she slapped a hand over her lips, issued a small moan, and began to hurry. She could feel him watching her back and wished she could see his expression to determine if he believed her or not. Verity would tell her later.

Finally, in the lobby, and out of view of the public room, she rested against the oaken wall panels and smiled. The sleepwalking lie was genius. Now she had an excuse for being about in the night should the need arise—though she hoped it would not. She stood, shook out her skirts, and patted her hair, tucking away any loose strands. Next, she marched down the hallway to her meeting with Cosistas. She heard footsteps crossing the lobby, but they did not follow her. The only person who truly gave her worry was occupied with Verity.

⚜

The hallway of the old wing was strewn with buckets and construction tools, so despite being late for her meeting, Eugenia took care where she stepped. She could see a door standing open at the far end.

A man's head appeared. He peered into the corridor. She was close enough now to identify Cosistas and waved him back into the room. He went and she followed, closing the door behind her.

"My dear Captain, I must admit I was surprised to see you. Doesn't the *Éire Mist* sail the Caribbean this time of year?" Cosistas showed his teeth in a smile that did not reach his eyes.

Eugenia grabbed his arm, drawing him away from the door to the room's opposite side. All the furniture had been pushed to the center of the floor and lay beneath heavy dust covers. "The location of my ship is none of your concern. I asked for this meeting to warn you not to call me by name. Best for both of us if you act like you never met me."

His teeth disappeared into a *moue*. "That is a shame. I always enjoy our exchanges. They are quite profitable for me."

"I'll pay you for your silence, but not until I leave Fenwick on Sea."

"And when might that be?" He leaned back against a wall, his arms crossed before him.

"As soon as the roads are clear enough for me to make my way south, to London." There, if Cosistas betrayed her and informed someone—like Brandon Gilroy—about her, he'd be looking in the wrong direction.

"Is that where you plan to meet the *Éire Mist*?"

"You already know more than you need about my movements."

"I suppose you're worried about Captain Gilroy." Cosistas uncrossed his arms and studied his fingernails.

"Gilroy is of no import to me. What is important, and what will get you paid, is your silence as to my identity. Do I have your word to treat me as you would any stranger?"

"Yes." He nodded.

"Good." She believed him. If he broke his word, he knew she had enough information about him to serve him an equally bad turn. "Now, I have other places to be. Wait five minutes before you leave."

He pulled out his pocket watch. "Will do."

Eugenia left, hurrying along the corridor, through the lobby and up to her rooms. The encounter with Cosistas relieved her of one worry. Now all she had to do was avoid prolonged encounters with Brandon. Pray heaven the roads would be cleared soon. She couldn't wait much longer. She needed to be in the Highlands soon, or the Duke of Cowal might die before she could speak with him. He'd been ailing for years, with some sort of wasting sickness. She had to get to him before he died. He could confirm the truth of the evidence about her parentage she would acquire here. With speed in mind, she sat at the writing desk and penned a note to Mr. Somerville at the church. Then she wrote another note to the ladies wishing to visit the church with the reply Verity had received.

Their dinner finished, Brandon followed Verity into the lobby.

From the corner of one eye, he saw Russell, Lord Stanton, rise from his seat on a shadowed bench and give a slight nod. Without taking his focus from Miss Walford, Brandon returned an even slighter nod.

"Thank you again for dinner, Mr. Gilroy, Brandon." She extended her hand.

Brandon bowed over her fingers. "It was my pleasure, Miss Verity."

"I am sorry that Eugenia fell ill and was forced to leave."

"I am as well. Please let me know how she is doing and, if I can help in anyway, do not hesitate to call on me." He hoped the offer would encourage Miss Walford to confide in him, should Red attempt to embroil the woman in any crime.

"You are too kind, sir. I'd best go and see if the broth I ordered for her has arrived. Goodnight."

"Goodnight, Miss Verity."

Russell had remained in the shadows, so Brandon joined him there.

"Brewster approved our tour of the south wing," stated Russell. "Let us go now."

They turned and went down the corridor being renovated. Skirting around the buckets and construction tools, they stopped when they reached the last doors on either side. One stood slightly open, the other was locked. They entered the open room and proceeded to the corner farthest from the door and any windows.

"We should be very private here," Russell remarked. "What kept you so long? You are not usually tardy."

"I had the opportunity to dine with Miss Fynlock and Miss Walford. Miss Fynlock left part way through the meal, claiming that the wine had disagreed with her. I used the rest of the meal to question Miss Walford about Miss Fynlock. Miss Walford is either a very skilled liar, or more likely knows very little about her traveling companion."

"Do you still consider Miss Walford to be a co-conspirator with Miss Fynlock?"

Brandon shook his head. "No, it is evident that she has no knowledge of any of Miss Fynlock's activities."

"Excellent," Russell opined. "One less person to watch. We are spread too thin, trying to divine who among all the guests here are villains and who are not."

"I agree. We can probably hire help, once we narrow the possibilities," Brandon offered. "But first tell me what you have learned and were you able to befriend Cosistas?"

"Cosistas now regards me as a pleasant acquaintance for passing the time, but he never goes beyond the point of casual conversation. I doubt an intimate friendship will be possible before the roads clear and he leaves."

"It is enough that he perceives you as no danger and might relax in your presence when he is with others," Brandon said.

"True. The person I have seen him converse with most is Danville."

"That is useful knowledge. The Navy has suspected Danville of piracy and smuggling for some time. However, solid evidence is difficult to obtain, so nothing is proven."

"With luck you'll get your proof soon. Cosistas's other companion of note is Miss Fynlock, as you suspected," Russell offered.

"The two have been at pains to behave as if they are not acquainted," Brandon said.

"And have probably succeeded in deceiving everyone but us. I heard you and Miss Walford discussing Miss Fynlock's indisposition at dinner tonight. I can tell you that she most definitely was not indisposed."

Brandon's brows rose. "I suspected she was giving an excuse, but what makes you confirm my suspicions?"

"About quarter past seven, I saw Cosistas take the very same path we just traveled. Not five minutes later, I witnessed Miss Fynlock leave the Public Room then follow where Cosistas had just gone."

"So you can stand witness to their secret meeting?" *Why am I not delighted to gain proof that Cosistas and Red are collaborating?*

"After waiting a moment or two, I followed them to this very room. The door is so badly warped, I had no difficulty hearing the conversation."

"What did they say?"

"By the time I arrived, they'd already begun speaking. However, I heard enough to know that Miss Fynlock was very concerned that Cosistas act as if they are strangers. So much so, that she was willing to pay him, but not before she completes her business here."

"That, along with her refusal to give him any details implies her business is not with Cosistas," Brandon reasoned. "Otherwise they would have discussed it and the details would have been an important part.

"If she isn't conspiring with Cosistas, what could she possibly want here?" Russell wondered.

"Did she say when she planned to leave?" Brandon raised his brows and rocked on his feet. He wanted to know how soon Irish Red thought to escape the storm-locked village.

"As I recall, her words were 'as soon as the roads are clear through to London.'"

Even better, thought Brandon. *Once in London, she'll head for the docks. I now know her destination and can follow easily if need be.*

Russell continued. "The moment I heard footsteps, I hurried to duck into one of the other open rooms."

"So that was all you learned?" Brandon asked.

Russell nodded confirmation.

"Blast. I was hoping for specific details as to their plans. Now I must wonder if there aren't two plots afoot. One involving Cosistas and Danville. The other involving Miss Fynlock."

"I agree." Russell commiserated.

"Since you represent the Home Office, I may tell you that I am here investigating the disappearance of munitions for the Master General of Ordnance," Brandon explained. "A large number of cannon and many barrels of powder departed Woolwich destined for Great Yarmouth to supply ships currently guarding the Channel coast. Some of the armaments were intended for delivery to the Army in Brussels. The munitions never arrived, and the various captains have complained."

"So that's what the courier from the Home Office was babbling about. He kept going on about French spies, cannon, smuggling, and stolen messages. He caught a fever, riding through all this rain and wind. I only learned of the message through my wife, who was tending him along with the rest of the sick and injured. I made haste to locate the man's belongings but could not find whatever message he'd been carrying. If, as seems to be the case, some spy has pilfered the message, I hope the thing was in code or, better yet, was never committed to paper at all."

"Do you think the Home Office would approve of us working together? I am tasked with discovering where the munitions are now and who was involved in the theft, as well as recovering the stolen items and arresting everyone involved."

"A large job for one man," Russell stated. "So, regardless of the Home Office's wishes, working together makes sense. I came to Fenwick on Sea in support of my wife and her father who pass information to the Home Office through their business contacts on the Continent. That affair is complete, but since information and spying were involved, I'd say I've acquired a new task."

"I have an entire investigative team at my disposal. We were to meet at the Naval Yard in Great Yarmouth when this storm delayed me, and possibly others of my team."

"As long as I am here, I am happy to help in any way." Russell's eyes narrowed, then he raised a finger. "I have a man with me. Quite by accident to have him along, but we can employ his talents. And once the courier is recovered—my wife did say he was on the mend—we could employ him as well."

"The Navy will pay any costs involved."

Russell waved a hand in dismissal. "I can do that. However, hired help will be needed because these criminals are wily. But also, as you may know, I am newly-wed, and wish to spend some time with my wife. I want her safe, which is even more reason to hire trusted men. She and I have already had our own challenges here with intelligence agents and these storms. I'm sure you've heard of the death of a woman earlier today. That I am not at liberty to discuss, of course. But my wife's business and mine here is concluded and once the roads are open again, we will leave."

"I apologize for intruding on your honeymoon."

Russell waved off the apology. "You have not intruded. My wife and I had a mystery to solve and the clues led us here. Indeed, we've had no honeymoon yet. But we will go west to my country home near Bury St. Edmonds as soon as we can. Our stay at the Queen's Barque is a small delay. In the meantime, I am glad to see some action."

"I suspect we shall see plenty of action before this business is concluded. The Master General of Ordnance believes all the missing munitions—both for the Army and the Navy—were stolen to supply Napoleon's forces. When the Bourbons fled Paris, much of the national treasury went with them, so Napoleon lacks funds to equip the army he can barely afford to pay."

"I'm aware of the state of Napoleon's finances."

"In addition, British cannon and powder are of superior quality. Without them, Napoleon is at a distinct disadvantage. And Wellington will need every possible advantage over the Corsican," Brandon concluded.

"There is a man here," Russell stated, "who claims to have been on the Ostend ship that was wrecked, but there is no record of him on the manifest, nor did any of the other survivors recognize him when I questioned them. I've seen this man in conversation with both Cositas and Danville. If my information is correct, he goes by the name of Sutherland, though I doubt he is any relation to that noble family. I cannot help but wonder if he might be Napoleon's agent come to arrange for delivery of the missing munitions."

"It would make sense that Napoleon would send someone to assure the safe delivery of much needed supplies. We must include this Sutherland among our watched suspects." Brandon said.

"I'll see to it."

"Then we are agreed on a course of action. Watch our four main suspects as carefully as possible and learn all we can about their connection with the missing supplies. I will concentrate on Miss Fynlock, for I believe she is the weakest link of the three who interest me." Brandon thought nothing of the sort. Irish Red was a clever and determined foe. However, he could not explain that to Russell unless he wished his friend to know exactly who Miss Fynlock was. Brandon's reluctance to rip aside her disguise was something he could not explain, even to himself. Until he could, he would keep his own counsel. "Your two men could keep an eye on Sutherland and Cositas."

"Which would leave me to concentrate on Danville," Russell added. "We should arrange a signal in case one of us discovers information that should be shared immediately."

"A note sent via one of the servants should suffice. If the matter is urgent, offer a bonus vail upon completion. That should ensure the servant returns to let you know the message was received."

Russell tapped a finger against his lips. "Very well. In addition to their other duties, the servants seem to be occupied with delivering notes to almost every traveler here. One or two more would be unremarkable.

"Excellent. If we've covered all contingencies, I'm for bed. I intend to be up at dawn to check the state of the roads and beaches."

"Excellent idea. We'll have advance notice, if any of our suspects attempts to leave."

"Precisely."

"I am determined to join my wife in our rooms. We've spent entirely too much time apart today."

"Then you leave first. If I linger here a bit, 'twill make little difference to my bed."

Russell grinned and slapped Brandon on the shoulder. "Good night, and good hunting, my friend."

"The same to you, Russell. Give my regards to Lady Stanton."

Russell nodded and left.

Brandon waited, considering what business had brought Red to Fenwick on Sea. If that business did not involve Cosistas and the stolen munitions, then what else was possible?

Three years ago, he'd thought he understood her. A woman in pirate's clothing was unusual, but she'd behaved as every other pirate captain he'd ever heard of. She'd offered a place on her crew to any sailor who wanted it. The rest of the defeated crew, him included, had been stranded on an island. When he'd fought with her, she'd smiled broadly and all but taunted him to attempt to defeat her. She'd beaten him, and gloried in it. His memory of her in that moment was of a woman most proud, shining with accomplishment. It confused him that he'd admired her in the same moment that rage at his own defeat nearly caused him to vow her destruction.

He'd not seen that proud woman during the few days here at the Queen's Barque. She'd not been the glorious adventurer, but instead attempted a mousy, shy demeanor. Why? What could that possibly gain her?

CHAPTER 3

Monday afternoon, Eugenia perused the note from Lady Stanton stating she would accompany the party visiting the church. Verity had arranged for the ladies to gather in the inn's reception room. The vicar would escort them from there. As a local, he would know the driest pathway to their destination.

"Verity, we need to dress for the outing to the church."

Her companion looked up from the book she was reading. "Must I accompany you? I've just begun the part where Miss Bennet rejects Darcy's proposal."

"I wish you would come with me. As I told you earlier, I need to speak with Mr. Somerville privately. It would be helpful to have you there to distract others from that conversation." She moved to the armoire and removed her dark blue serge walking ensemble. Dull as it was, it would be perfect for this outing.

Verity joined her at the armoire. "That blue is an excellent choice. For my part, I'll wear this copper brown dress. I love the sheen of the material, yet it is muted enough to be appropriate for daytime."

In short order, they were ready and descended to the reception room, where they found the other ladies assembled.

"I am delighted you could join us." Miranda, Miss de Courtenay, enthused. "Allow me to introduce Lady Felicity Belvoir." She gestured to the young woman standing at her side. "We wait only for Mr. Somerville to arrive before departing."

Eugenia curtsied then waved toward Verity. "Permit me to introduce you both to Miss Verity Walford." She is my traveling companion."

Lady Felicity nodded. "Pleased to meet you, Miss Walford. I do hope you are planning to join our excursion."

Miranda followed suit.

"If it isn't too much trouble on such short notice, and please, call me Verity."

"I will call you Verity, if you will call me Felicity. If I remember correctly, Lady Stanton said you assisted in planning this outing, so of course you are welcome. It is I who am the late-comer. My brother Hythe seems to think the fact that we were shipwrecked just yesterday is reason enough for me to keep to my chambers, but I told him he should know me to be made of sterner stuff."

A chorus of empathy and questions filled the space. Then the door opened and two men entered. From his conservative attire, one was clearly Somerville. The other was Brandon, much to Eugenia's dismay.

Brandon gave her a brief nod, beamed at Miranda, took her hand, and bowed over it. "Ah, Miss de Courtenay what a pleasure to meet you again. You and your friends are about to visit the church, or so Mr. Somerville tells me."

Miranda fluttered her lashes and all but preened. "We are, sir."

"It is vastly unfair that Somerville alone is to enjoy the company of so many fair damsels. Might I be your escort as well?" He offered his arm to Miranda and Verity.

"By all means," said Verity.

The smiles he exchanged with the two women nearly turned Eugenia's stomach, they were so sweet. She frowned. *What is he so happy about?* Her mind rolled its metaphorical eyes. *Why do I care? Brandon's a handsome man. Any woman would be flattered by his attention.*

Not me. Eugenia spun and turned to the vicar. "I am eager to see the church and learn its history."

Nodding politely to Eugenia, the man offered his arm to

Lady Stanton and extended his other to Lady Felicity. "I'm honored by the interest of all of you ladies. Some local folk believe our church's greatest claim to fame is, like the Queen's Barque, a visit by Her Majesty Queen Elizabeth. However, it is also of great interest to scholars of history for another reason. With the exception of the Queen's window, the building is almost entirely Norman—one of the finest examples of a Norman church that has retained nearly all of its original features. I'll explain more when we arrive at the sanctuary. Ladies, are you all ready to depart?"

Consent was given by all, and they soon entered a beautifully preserved example of Norman architecture. Eugenia was grateful to be in the rear of the party. Slipping away would be all that much easier.

Mr. Somerville led the group to the center of the main sanctuary and had them turn around. "The stained-glass rosette window was the gift of Queen Elizabeth. You'll note, from the Queen's coat of arms, the lion and dragon rampant in the two lower corners of the glass framing the rosette as well as the triple *fleur de lis* and lions supine in the upper corners."

Eugenia slipped away from the main group, aiming for the church register, which she'd observed in an alcove at the far end of the entry nave. Behind her the conversation continued.

"It is beautiful," Lady Felicity admired.

"The sun has blessed us by shining so that we can see the true skill of the artist," the vicar said.

"I agree," Verity commented. "Is the artist known?"

"No, I am sorry to say. However, the workmanship is of excellent quality. We've even had mention of our window in one or two guide-books to this part of Suffolk," Somerville replied. "Now, if you look up to the top of the side walls of the sanctuary, you can see one of our Norman features."

Brandon's tones rumbled forth, but Eugenia was out of hearing distance and could not determine his exact words. She was glad he was distracted. A light breeze from the open church doorway ruffled her skirts. Somerville had left it open to allow fresh air to enter the church. Two oriel windows on either side of the alcove let in sufficient light to read the register, but she was glad for the additional illumination from the open door. Stepping up to the lectern that held the register, she quickly paged through the thick tome to the earliest entries. She needed to find marriage lines from decades before. She was now twenty-three, so her mother would have married in 1791 or earlier.

She found January 1791 entries on the first pages of the book. As she read, she ran her finger down the page. There must have been ten marriages registered that month. Finding the entries among the tiny script describing, births, deaths, confirmations and other parish events was not easily or quickly done. She skimmed through January and February with as much speed as the light and miniscule lettering permitted. There was only one wedding in March, then an entire half page toward the end of April and on into May. She was partway through those when a shadow dimmed the light coming from behind her.

She cast a glance over her shoulder. *Brandon*! He stood hat in hand about one yard distant.

"You were studying that register with great intent, Eugenia." His tone was warm and only a little wry. "I'm surprised I got this close before you noticed me."

She shrugged, as much to dispel the pleasure his tone encouraged as to cause him to think she cared little for his opinions. However, she did not bother feigning surprise at a statement that would be peculiar, if addressed to a real young miss. She was no such thing, and they both knew it. They were alone for the moment, so why pretend?

"I would not have expected churches in general nor their registers in particular to be an item of interest to Irish Red," he continued.

Is he baiting me? To what purpose? "Shhh," she hissed. "You are mistaken if you imagine you can prove I've any connection with that person, so I'll thank you not to talk of him in my presence."

"As proof, I have my word as a naval officer, and Irish Red is no man," Brandon muttered low.

"And any accusation would be your word against mine. I can conjure some very powerful support from among the peerage."

His left eyebrow rose, and he stepped forward. "And you think I cannot? There are things you don't know about me."

Dismayed, she retreated involuntarily to the far side of the lectern.

"I know more about you than I need or care to," she said with a bravado she didn't feel.

He masked his reaction.

"I will add that you know much less of me than you may think," she continued.

"I would like to know more." The warmth had returned to his voice and his gaze. He followed her into the shadows beyond the windows.

Another backward step would place her against the wall with no room for escape. She didn't know what he was after, but she stood her ground. "That is unlikely to happen."

He placed his hat atop the open register and took her hand. "Possibly." His thumb stroked across her gloved fingers. "However, you have secrets that you are paying to keep private. If you told me what your purpose is with Danville and Cosistas, I might be persuaded to maintain my silence as to those secrets. Were you to assist me with thwarting whatever criminal enterprise those two are embarked upon, I would speak on your behalf, should you be arrested for piracy."

Anger rose at his words but was undermined by the shivers traveling the length of her arm and farther. She snatched her hand from his grip and glared into his gray-blue gaze. She could not read his thoughts. "You think to blackmail me into dishonorable actions, sir. Even among thieves there is honor. I may have been a privateer in the past, but you cannot prove piracy. Nor can you prove that I am still such."

"Privateer, pirate. 'Tis a legal quibble for which you have never shown documents in support of your privateer claim. You have been an enemy of the British government in the past and, with Napoleon gathering troops for war, there is no telling what nefarious purpose has brought you here."

"My presence in this village has nothing to do with Napoleon or the British government."

"So you say." He continued to hold her gaze. "I am simply offering you the opportunity to mitigate the punishment you are destined to receive for your crimes."

She almost laughed in his face. She would be gone long before he could arrange for her arrest. "Any argument is pointless. However, you are most definitely wrong. Now, if you will excuse me, I would like to continue perusing the register."

He didn't move.

"In private." She attempted to skirt around him to the front of the lectern.

His hand on her arm halted her. Heat burned through her sleeve from his palm. "Wait. Please."

"Why?" Their gazes locked once more. This time she saw an unnameable emotion of such heat that it could have frightened her. He'd always been cold with her before; perhaps she should be frightened.

"I... I'm not..."

An unidentifiable racket interrupted, but she could not look away. Then an unseen force pushed her in Gilroy's direction. His arms closed about her as a storm of activity surrounded them.

"Ooof."

Eyes wide she tilted her head and stared past his shoulder. At full speed, Hector, the dog from the inn, fled out the open church door with a stream of boys trailing after him. She straightened and found herself smiling into Brandon's face. He smiled back.

She could not have said how the kiss happened, or who broke away first. She found herself with her back against the wall, fingers to her mouth, astonished at the sensations the brief meeting of lips caused.

Gilroy seemed equally surprised. He did an about face and fled, moving as if Napoleon's entire army were on his heels.

What in the world? Her lips still tingled, and confusion swirled below her stomach. In front of her, the register stood forgotten. She'd never experienced anything like that. She'd kissed men before but had never wished the activity had gone on for hours.

"Are you well, Miss Fynlock?"

She blinked and finally noticed Mr. Somerville standing a few feet beyond where Brandon had been moments before.

"Quite well."

"I am sorry for the disturbance from the boys and the dog."

She smiled. "No apology needed, sir. They've been cooped up for days, and chasing a dog is a perfectly innocent way to burn off some energy."

"It is kind in you to be so understanding," he said.

"It's nothing. However, I do have a favor to ask of you." Eugenia spoke tentatively, as she imagined a well-bred young miss might when requesting a favor of a man whom she did not know well.

"How may I be of assistance?"

"I am trying to locate my parents' marriage lines."

"Are you certain they were wed here? Fenwick on Sea isn't exactly on the main throughfare and hasn't been for close on one hundred years."

"So I have been told. However, I've only been able to peruse register entries for the first few months of 1791. I was born in early 1792, so my parents would have married in the first months of that year or earlier."

"This register," he gestured toward the book, "begins in January 1791. Older registers are preserved in the vicar's library next to the church offices. I could take you there. You certainly have my permission to search for as long as you like."

"Thank you. You are very kind. However, my time here is limited."

"Pardon me if this question is, er, indelicate, but would the marriage be recorded under the Fynlock name?"

"You perceive my main difficulty sir. One of the reasons I need the marriage lines is to discover exactly who my parents were. I was adopted at an early age and have only recently been made aware that my parentage is different than I thought it to be."

He shook his head. "If you don't know the names, how will you know which lines are your parents'?"

"I have a sample of my mother's hand writing, and I was told by those who raised me, her name might have been Mary or Katherine." She withdrew her mother's diary from the large reticule she carried. "I hoped to match it with a signature in the registry."

"That could take some time. I could perhaps help."

"Oh, would you? I would be ever so grateful. In fact, I have the means to make a, um, a donation to the church."

His eyes lit, though with amusement rather than fervor. "Donations are always welcome. Maintaining a structure as old as this is a costly endeavor."

"It would be my pleasure to make a donation whether we find the marriage lines or not." She knew she could afford more than he could imagine he needed.

"Do you wish me to do the work alone? I fear I have other commitments that require much of my time."

"A shared task is completed much more quickly, sir. I need the lines fairly soon and don't have a great deal of time to devote to this."

He grinned at her. "Excellent, Miss Fynlock. I will make you free of my library."

"Splendid, then perhaps you won't mind writing a letter attesting to the existence and veracity of the lines, should we find them."

"If we find them, I will happily do so." Somerville gave a small nod of courtesy.

"Even better. Shall I return after luncheon to help you begin the search?"

"That would be satisfactory. If you are comfortable leaving the diary with me, I can start as soon as all the ladies have finished looking over the church, and I have retrieved my baby niece from the inn."

She blinked. "Are some of the ladies still here? I'm sorry if I've kept you from your charges."

"Not at all." He waved away her concern. "Most have left. However, Miss Walford and Lady Felicity were so intrigued by some of the older features of the stonework that they remained. Shall we go and find them?" He extended his arm.

She accepted it. "By all means."

Eugenia was glad of the distraction. Left to her own devices she might have remained frozen by that kiss until past midnight. Why had Brandon done it? Had he? *Or did I?* It's all the fault of that horrid dog. *Hector isn't really horrid. He's quite dear.* Unlike Captain Brandon Gilroy, who was at best confusing and at worst exceedingly dangerous. Thank heaven for Somerville's help. *I'll be away from here as soon as the roads are passable. And I'll be happy to be gone. Yes, I will.*

CHAPTER 4

B randon rose with the dawn on April fourth, broke his fast, and rode out once more to assess the possibility of travel. He was pleased to discover that no one would be able to go far from Fenwick on Sea before having to turn back. Bridges had either been washed away or were still submerged, and a grounded ship still blocked access to and from the nearest harbor.

He returned in mid-afternoon, having missed his luncheon. Handing his horse over to a groom, he aimed for the inn with a pint of its excellent porter in mind. However, he halted at the sight of Cosistas and a woman in a dull, rather shapeless frock walking toward the far end of the inn's pleasure garden. Was the woman Irish Red?

If it were, so what? A man and a woman could walk out in public view with perfect innocence. Innocence and Irish Red were an ill-suited pair, more so when in the company of a fence like Cosistas.

Almost without volition, Brandon's feet changed direction. He took a circuitous route keeping within the shadows of the trees that bordered the garden until he was directly behind the vine covered arbor where the couple stood.

"You dare to threaten me!" Though outraged, the musicality of the woman's voice identified her unmistakably as Irish Red.

"Such harsh terms, Miss Fynlock," Cosistas protested. "I'm simply offering you an opportunity to avoid an embarrassing encounter with officers of the law."

"Ha! Embarrassing is a mild word for it. The British authorities may consider my activities to be criminal, but I have always operated honestly under letters of marque from the United States."

What opportunity, wondered Brandon? *Can you not be more explicit, Cosistas? I need to know what villainous endeavors are planned, and how deeply Irish Red is involved. Though why I should give a tinker's damn about the fate of a pirate is beyond knowing.*

"Now that Britain and my adopted country are at peace," she continued. "What you ask would indeed be criminal, and I'll not be coerced into such action."

Good for you, Red. Stick to your guns.

"It is, of course, your decision."

Brandon heard the implied warning ooze from Cosistas' lips.

"However, as I suspect it will be another day or so before departing this place is possible," the fence said. "I'll permit you to consider the consequences until word arrives that the roads are clear. By then you must agree to do as I ask or I will inform on you." The man's warning was impossible to mistake.

"You'll be waiting much longer than that. I'll remind you that I can cause as much trouble for you as you imagine you can cause for me."

"I know you think so, but you've no idea of the connections I have in Great Yarmouth." His tone was boastful. "I am much better protected now than in the past. You would find it difficult to cause me any harm. Whereas, you have no resources in Great Yarmouth, and I guarantee that is where you would be arrested, tried, and hanged for your crimes."

"You could be right. But you do not know all there is to know about me. I, too, have powerful friends and, in a contest of authority, I'll bet on my connections over yours every time."

"Really? Who might these influential people be?"

Eugenia laughed, a full throaty noise that Brandon recalled well. In the past, as now, his body had vibrated in concert with the sound. In that moment he longed both to throttle her and make love to her.

"You can't imagine I'm fool enough to give you that kind of information. You'll simply have to do your worst and find out when I set the law on you."

"My offer of time to change your mind stands. May I escort you back to the inn?"

"No, thank you. When you invited yourself to join me, I was on my way here to enjoy some solitude and a picnic in the sunshine, so I prefer to remain in the garden. Miss Walford knows where to find me."

"Then I'll bid you good day, Miss Fynlock."

Brandon peered around the corner of the arbor and watched Cositas walk away, then waited for Red to follow. He could not think of her as Eugenia, and Miss Fynlock was hardly better. To his mind she was Red and always would be. One of the most exciting and challenging females he'd ever met. She rivaled the sea in that regard. Would she remain in the arbor alone, or did she intend another meeting, perhaps with that villain, Danville? If so, Russell might wish to know what the two discussed.

As he returned to hiding behind the arbor, the scent of aged cheddar and apples assailed him. He'd not eaten since early morning, and the shadows were lengthening toward evening. His stomach protested his neglect rather more loudly than he wished.

"Captain Gilroy. Would you care to share my repast?" Her words lilted beyond the arbor's leaves.

Betrayed by my stomach. How mortifying. Nonetheless, the practical thing to do is to accept her kindness. Enjoying Red's company has naught to do with anything. Besides, if she chose to invite him to interrupt her solitude who was he to decline?

"By all means, Miss Fynlock. Thank you." He walked round to face her where she sat on the bench.

"Such formality is unnecessary when we are alone, don't you think?" She scooted over to one side and gestured to the other.

"I agree, but Eugenia hardly suits you, and I really shouldn't call you Irish Red." He sat, and she placed her cheese and apples between them.

"I give you permission to address me as Esmeralda, or Esme."

"Is that your true name?"

"It is the only name I've ever known," she stated dismissively. Then she leaned over, inserting her arm between the bench and the vines. When she retrieved her arm, she held a bottle of wine.

"Would you do the honors, sir?" She took a corkscrew from a pocket of her dress and handed it to him along with the bottle. "I was unable to obtain any glasses or mugs, so we will have to share. Should you prefer not to, I will enjoy the wine while you go thirsty." She grinned.

"I have no objection," he stated, and accepted the proffered items, continuing to speak as he worked. "I would be surprised at your preparedness, did I not know you to be an extremely practical woman who anticipates much."

She smiled at him. "And you are not surprised that I knew you were listening to my conversation with Cosistas?"

He lowered his eyelids a moment. "Not so much surprised as dismayed. I thought myself quite cleverly discreet in my approach."

"As far as Cosistas is concerned, I believe you went unnoticed, else he would not have issued his threats in your hearing. As for me, when you give it a moment's thought, you'll acknowledge that remaining hidden from the sight of an experienced seaman is decidedly difficult."

"True, but that you admit to the experience does surprise me." He captured her shining sea-green gaze with his.

She laughed. "Come now, Brandon. We both know I never fooled you as I have many others who might know of me but have no experience of me."

He pushed aside the wish to make her laugh again. He wanted information. Entertaining her had purpose only if it gained him that. "Is Miss Walford aware of your chosen profession?"

"No. She knows I am not who I pretend to be, but we both believe that she is better not knowing much of my past."

He nodded. "It is good of you to protect her from prosecution by giving her the ability to deny she knows anything of your, er, activities."

Red stared toward the inn chewing then swallowing. "Verity has been all that is kind to me and deserves better than I can give at present."

More surprises. What else could he get her to reveal. He took a swig from the bottle and passed it to her, chewing on a bite of apple as he watched her lips cover the place where his had been moments before. Thought of her lips recalled the instant of that kiss at the church. It had taken him most of that day to gain control over the lust that raged through him. *Get your mind back on business and out from under her skirts, man.* He'd avoided her for nearly an entire day, though he'd kept watch of her movements, seeing her go to and from the church several times. What was that all about? Did it connect to her business with Cosistas? If so, how? Somerville did not appear to have criminal tendencies, but stranger things happened. A female pirate for instance.

"So, you would like to be generous with Miss Walford?"

She handed him the wine. "I would like to be generous with all my friends and acquaintances. I'd like to establish a charitable foundation for orphans." Her expression sobered, and she fell silent for a moment then brightened. "I'd also like to fly. But that too is impossible."

As she spoke, the longing in her eyes struck a chord. He'd gone to sea, not simply because it was a family tradition, but because restless yearning had driven him there. He'd found many sailors, though few officers, who shared the unsettling feeling.

He sipped and handed the bottle back. "I find it is best to concentrate on what is possible, and leave the impossible to fate."

She tilted her head, those green eyes studying him. "You are a fatalist?"

"I am a realist. Reality is that we have very little control over our lives. Sailing the ocean should teach you that." In between bites and conversation, the bottle continued to change hands.

"True, but the challenge of confronting that over which we have no control is impossible to resist."

She understood. He'd found no one, not even his best friends, who comprehended the lure of challenging limitless power.

"What did Cosistas want you to do?" The words slipped out before he thought. He held his breath and waited. Would she confide in him? She had no reason to do so.

"It would be dishonorable of me to tell you."

"Would it? I would think that dishonor lay in not exposing a criminal plot?"

"Yes, but I do not believe Cosistas has done anything criminal. Proving differently would be difficult."

"I don't like that he threatens you."

She grabbed her middle and laughed.

Baffled, Brandon stared at her, both pleased and embarrassed. *I wanted to make her laugh, but I'm uncertain that offering concern is what I intended as humorous.* "I don't see the humor in being threatened by such as Cosistas."

Eventually, she regained her breath and could speak. "Oh, I agree, threats are nothing to laugh about. However, that you should be concerned about me is worth hours of humor. So much so that, come what may, I'll smile for the next month. Less than two days past, you too issued implied threats to me, yet you worry about Cosistas—a man by far less dangerous to me than you. Can you not appreciate the irony of such concerns?"

He wanted to preen that she thought him a more dangerous man than the fence. At the same time, he could comprehend the contradiction of his statement. What was clear to him was that he did not understand Irish Red nor his own reactions to her.

He looked at the wine bottle. "I offer you the last swallow."

"Thank you." She accepted the bottle, drank, then emptied the dregs onto the ground.

He set about collecting the remnants of cheese and apples into a napkin and tying the whole into a bundle.

She stood, smoothing the fabric of her plain dress.

He stood as well. The action brought him much too close to her. The fresh lemon-grass scent of her filled his nostrils. "I'll apologize later, for I cannot seem to resist."

As he spoke, she came into his arms. Their lips met, and the world dissolved. Desire burst through him like cannon fire. Whether they fell or sat, he couldn't say how they ended reclining on the bench, her body atop his, her arms clasping his head, fingers in his hair, her lips yielding, tongues dueling. A moan of surrender followed his hands to the swell of her breast.

"Let me," he begged.

"Please," she pleaded in answer.

In all his experience, her "please" was the sweetest of words.

A female voice rang out. "Eugenia. Eugenia?"

A North Sea storm could not have chilled his ardor as quickly as the sound of Miss Walford's voice.

"Go," urged Red, straightening her bodice and patting her hair. "Behind the arbor. Verity and I will depart in moments."

The sun had begun to set, so he disappeared into the darkness behind the structure.

"There you are, Eugenia. I know you said you wished for some solitude but night is falling. It is not wise to remain out of doors much longer." Miss Walford was quite close now.

"Thank you for fetching me. I'm afraid I dozed off; the sun was so warm and welcome. I relaxed as I had not in weeks."

"I am delighted for you. Now take my arm. Together we'll find our way back to the inn."

Their voices continued, fading as they left the arbor behind. When he could hear them no longer, Brandon emerged from hiding and slowly made his way to his chamber. He'd kissed her. Deliberately. And she'd wanted more. The idea that a captain of His Majesty's Navy and a pirate could be lovers was insane. Duty alone demanded he see her arrested and tried. If she could produce the letters of marque she claimed to have, she might escape hanging. But even the possibility of her dead, no longer defiant against her enemies, nor laughing in the face of challenge near broke his heart. *That's ridiculous. I don't even know the woman. How could she possibly break my heart?* Yet, he knew what he felt. Deception, whether of himself or others, was not his habit.

So, what do I want? To give her a slip on the shoulder in exchange for my silence? Disgust at the idea soured in his mouth. That action would dishonor them both. Duty demanded one thing, his heart another, and he could not resolve the two. Would waiting for events to unfold help? Did he have any choice? The mess the storm had made of the roads prevented any decisive action. He had two days, three at the most, to figure out what to do about loving a pirate.

CHAPTER 5

Eugenia, spent most of the night tossing and turning, sleeping only in snatches populated with disturbing dreams. Every time her eyelids lowered, she drifted again within the strength of her captain's arms. Her lips throbbed as if they still kissed. Her entire being ached with a longing to go to him and share the splendor she knew would be theirs together.

Her eyes would pop open on the image of their naked bodies tangled in bedsheets, her face and torso flushed, and her breathing erratic. She'd wanted men before, but never like this. Never with so strong a compulsion to throw every care aside and surrender completely to a man's embrace.

She rose and dressed on Wednesday when night grayed into a fog-shrouded dawn. Moving quietly so as not to wake Verity, Eugenia took her cloak and left the room. She needed exercise to work off this irritating restlessness. She avoided the garden, simply to get a change of scenery, she told herself, ignoring the fact that little scenery was visible through the thick mist. Sticking to the driest part of the still muddy lane, she aimed in the direction of the church.

Somerville would not be up at this hour, but asking him about the progress of the search for her mother's wedding lines was not Eugenia's purpose. No, she needed respite from the thoughts and images that pursued her like a man-o-war pursues a fully-loaded galleon. She'd visit the cemetery on the far side of the church. Reading the names, dates and final obits of the dead would surely push Brandon Gilroy from her thoughts.

Dew soaked her shoes as she walked the grassy paths of the grave-yard. She did not mind though, for the words and dates fascinated her.

There were entire families buried together with the same month and year of death. That must have been a plague year. She found soldiers, sailors, and heroes who'd lost their lives rescuing others from storm-wrecked ships.

She began to tire and considered returning to the cozy warmth of the Queen's Barque when a simple headstone caught her eye. Someone had placed a knot of spring violets tied with a plaid ribbon at the base of the memorial. She knew that plaid like she knew her own ship. The colors and pattern belonged to the Duke of Cowal. She believed the current Duke was her grandfather, her mother's father. Who would put such a posy in this place, and who was the deceased person for whom this gesture was made?

She approached, forcing herself forward, surprised to find herself fearful of what she might discover. Fear was best conquered quickly with action.

The stone read, "Here lies a wayfarer, whose kindness shall ne'er be forgotten." The flowers blocked the rest of the carved words, so Eugenia knelt and lifted them away. "M. K. MacShennan. Daughter, wife and mother. July 7, 1772 — June 12, 1792. May she rest at peace in God's embrace.

The chill that crept down Eugenia's spine had nothing to do with the surrounding icy fog that obscured all sights and muffled all sounds other than the flowers and her own breathing.

What had Danny Crobbin said when, at about the age of nine, Eugenia had asked about her mother?

"Oh, dinna fash yers'el 'bout that."

"But I want to know." She'd poured him a mug of grog, aware from their years together that he became talkative with drink.

After several mugs of the liquid, he'd said, "'Twas in spring of 1792, a woman brought ye to me. Said she was maid to yer mother. A woman she called Mary Katherine MacTavish." *But this gravestone reads MacShennan. Which is it? And is this 'M. K.' my mother? I don't know her name for sure.* But the feeling of certainty settling in her chest claimed otherwise.

"So that's my mother's name?" Esme had asked her adoptive father.

Crobbin shook his head. "I dinna know. I half suspect that the woman who brought ye to me was yer true mother."

"What was her name? What did she look like? Like me? How old was she? Where did she come from?"

Crobbin held up a hand. "Cease now. I'll tell y' what I remember. I canna tell y' more."

She'd had to bite her tongue, literally, to keep from interrupting him.

"She called herself Analise Morton, and I met her when the *Éire Mist* was lying off the coast a bit south of Great Yarmouth. She was outside a tavern, trying to fend off three gents determined to have their way with her."

"What does that mean? Having their way?" Esme blurted, unable to contain her curiosity longer.

Crobbin raised a brow. "Never you mind. 'Tis enough to know that Analise was in trouble. I decided to help. Took only a couple of blows from me fists to send those curs packing. After Analise stopped weeping and thanking me, I asked if I could escort her to her destination. She confessed she didn't know where she should go. That's when ye with y'r lusty lungs made yerself known."

Eugenia recalled sitting up straighter, proud that even as a babe she'd been sticking up for herself.

"Analise said the babe belonged to her mistress who was dying. She had charged Analise with taking the babe home to Scotland but had never been able to tell her where in Scotland. To keep ye and herself from getting the same sickness as her mistress. Analise left, hoping she would find someone to help her.

"She found you."

"Aye. I told her I was a sea captain, but I couldna promise to take her to Scotland. Ye ken why I'll ne'er go back there."

"Aye," she had nodded sagely, having heard his stories but never fully understanding the risk to him until a year or more after he passed away.

"When did you find my mother's diary?"

"Analise and I were happy for about seven years, then she got sick and died. I found the book when I was going through her things t' give away what I could t' charity. Ye know how much trouble I have with reading and writing. But I saved the book for ye."

"That's when you insisted I go to the Sisters of Mercy school."

He'd put more grog in his mug. "That's right. I ne'er had learning, so I knew how much better yer life would be if ye could read and write.

I learned a great deal more, and, while I appreciate it now, at the time, I hated every moment of sitting still and not being on shipboard.

She knelt in the wet grass and leaned forward, running her fingers over the stone and the words that were most likely about her mother. She'd wanted desperately to believe that her mother was a woman who had servants, the unknown Mary Katherine. But where had her family been? Why had she died alone in this tiny village? If this grave were indeed hers. Where was the husband, Eugenia's own father, who should have cared for their babe? Crobbin had never been able to tell her more, nor had she found the answers in the diary. The unresolved questions had gnawed at her, until she'd finally decided she could take the time from her ship and crew to discover who she really was.

She put the bouquet back in its place and was about to stand when voices came to her through the fog. Clear and easily identified, Cosistas and Danville spoke as if they stood just to her left. She dared not move.

"What insane notion seized you to have this meeting here of all places and at this hour. I'm chilled to the bone," whined Cosistas.

"I told both of you I'm being watched."

Both of you? Were there three men present or two? I only heard two voices.

"Between Lord Stanton and that navy captain you pointed out to me, I can't make a move unseen," Danville growled. "I'm seaman enough to know there would be a fog this morning. Between that and the isolation of this churchyard, we can finalize our plans in complete safety."

"I still don't like it," Milo grumbled.

"What you prefer is not what you are being paid for. *Le petit general* desperately needs the munitions you promised. When and where will they be delivered?"

Eugenia did not recognize the voice with the slight French accent in the rolling 'r's of prefer and promised.

"I'm working on a solution," Cosistas said.

"What is it?" French Accent demanded.

The voices moved back and forth on the opposite side of Mary Katherine's headstone, as if the men paced or circled each other.

"I have a hold over another captain, whom I am certain will see the advantages of assisting me with delivery of the munitions," Cosistas explained.

"Oh? Other than me?" Hugo questioned. "You've no hold over me. However, I'd no idea of this captain's presence."

"Nor I," French Accent announced. "I assume he's close by or you'd not be making use of him."

"The captain is staying at the Queen's Barque. Running into her here was an amazing stroke of good fortune."

"Her? I only know one female captain of any repute," Hugo muttered.

"Indeed, it is Irish Red."

"What brought her here?" Danville queried. "She's never far from the *Éire Mist*, and that ship is always in the Caribbean at this time of year."

"I am well acquainted with Irish Red and her sailing habits," the chandler explained. "But that is neither here nor there. She is here, which means the *Éire Mist* cannot be too far away. She'll have a means of contacting them quickly, so the ship can be at the Great Yarmouth docks within a few days. Once loaded, two days will see your munitions delivered at Calais."

"*Le Corsaire Rouge* is reputed to be a stubborn independent *putain*. Are you sure she'll cooperate?" French Accent asked.

Eugenia would have liked to run the man through for his insults but knew she'd learn more if she kept quiet.

"Unless she wishes to visit the hangman, she'll load those munitions and take them exactly where I tell her." Cosistas sounded confident.

Too bad I can't tell him right now that he's mistaken, but the more I know the better I'll be able to double cross him, the dirty dog.

"Excellent," Danville's voice all but smiled. "Let her know that the *Acacia* will meet her off the French coast at Calais. We'll shift the cargo from the *Éire Mist* to the *Acacia* at sea. Tell her she'll be handsomely rewarded."

"That's not necessary," Cosistas muttered.

"I know that, my friend," Danville agreed. "The reward I have in mind will leave Irish Red as dead as the fools in this graveyard, and the *Éire Mist* will become the second ship in my fleet. When word gets out about who rid the seas of Irish Red, I'll be a hero. Who knows, perhaps the King of England will make me a duke out of gratitude."

French Accent laughed.

"Hmm." Cosistas's words came out carefully. "Stranger things have happened. *Monsieur*, all shall be arranged as we have agreed."

Hell, why couldn't he have used the man's name?

"See that you do," French Accent ordered.

"Have I ever played you false, or you Danville?"

"No, and that's the one reason you are still alive."

"I am most grateful for your magnanimity."

Could Danville hear the mockery in Cosistas's tone? Probably not. *If Danville imagines he can defeat the* Éire Mist, *even without her captain in charge, he's too stupid to recognize mockery when it lands in his ears.*

"Gentlemen, I am for breakfast and a warm fire," Cosistas announced. "Don't follow until you are certain no one will think we met."

"I'm not stupid," Danville growled.

Moments passed.

"You will see to Mister Cosistas's silence, as we agreed?" French Accent asked.

"It will be my great pleasure." The smile was back in Danville's voice.

So Cosistas would be silenced. Dead or shanghaied did not matter to her. His intent to double-cross her indicated he deserved whatever fate he received. Her one regret was that she would not be at hand to serve up that fate. She was headed to Scotland. Her first mate, Black John, would captain the *Éire Mist* until Eugenia resolved her affairs in Scotland and returned to the Caribbean. She'd signal her contacts to have her ship meet her north of Yarmouth and then speak with Black John. She had an idea how she could use this plot to bait her own trap for Cosistas, Danville, his ship and possibly the anonymous Frenchman. But Black John would be the one to spring the trap.

Long after both men had left, when the fog was beginning to burn off, Eugenia stopped at the church and left word for the vicar. She wanted to ask him if the M. K. in the graveyard might have been her mother? If so, the search for the marriage lines should proceed more quickly now. She then returned to the Queen's Barque public room. Within the hour as she prepared to ascend the stairs, Brewster called her over to the reception desk and handed her a note. It was Somerville, stating he believed he'd found what she was looking for, and inviting her to come to the church offices after luncheon.

Excellent. She'd be able to leave tomorrow, given clear roads. Which meant she had a fair number of loose ends to secure, as well as making plans with Verity for the first stage of her journey. *Finally, some action.* She was heartily sick of sitting idle constrained by weather and her chosen disguise. She was fairly dancing as she approached the stairs, and might have burst into song, had Brandon Gilroy not been blocking her way.

CHAPTER 6

Fascinated, Brandon watched Red approach. He'd seen her furious, flushed with victory in battle, and eyes agleam with anticipated passion. The sheer happiness he witnessed as she'd read her note touched him more deeply than he wanted. He knew the ardent wish to give her cause for such happiness on a daily basis. He lowered his brow. That was a pipe-dream. He wasn't even certain she shared his feelings, though their garden kiss confirmed she desired him.

"What has you so pleased, Miss Fynlock." He remained standing on the last stair, preventing her passage.

A frown formed on her beautiful face. "You are in my way, sir."

"Aye." He almost moved aside just to see her smile again, but he had more pressing needs. Duty to king and country demanded he spike her guns before she had a chance to conclude whatever piracy had brought her here. "Come with me," he spoke for her ears only then gripped her elbow. "I've asked for Miss Walford to arrange luncheon for us in your private parlor."

He'd said a great deal more to the older woman, explaining to her that he was concerned about Miss Fynlock and asking Miss Walford to be present. However, he'd also asked her to leave on his signal, for her own safety, should he believe that remaining might cause her legal difficulties. She'd been alarmed and confessed to some concern for her companion as well, but she only promised to leave if she believed Eugenia would be completely safe with him.

He'd offered reassurances, but Miss Walford insisted she make up her own mind as events unfolded.

Beyond Red, he saw the young man tending the reception desk step away into the public room.

"How dare you," she responded. "A gentleman would never presume to give rise to gossip by dining in private with a lady. Let alone announce those arrangements in public."

The irony of a pirate lecturing him on propriety did not escape him. Yet he resisted the urge to laugh, frowning instead. "Stifle your outrage. It is you announcing our meeting to the world, though thankfully no one is present to hear you. Miss Walford will be present, so all is proper and above board."

She glanced around the lobby, and her lips thinned. Clearly, she was miffed that he was in the right.

"Let me pen a short note, then we shall get this over with. I've an important appointment with the vicar after we eat."

He wanted to follow her, read what she wrote over her shoulder, and prevent an attempt to escape dining with him, but some perverse need to trust her, even though he knew he should not, kept him on the stairs. She'd not get far if she tried evasion, and he'd prefer she tell him voluntarily the subject of her mysterious note.

Minutes later they entered her parlor, where Verity stood directing the servants in laying out the meal.

"Put all the food on the side board," she said. "We shall serve ourselves. But pour the wine. We would like to converse before we eat."

When the servants left and Brandon had helped the ladies to sit before taking his own seat, Eugenia cleared her throat.

"Now, Brandon," she began. "You insisted on dining in private, so please tell us what this luncheon is all about?" She sipped her wine.

"By all means, Miss Eugenia. I am concerned that you may be

getting into very deep waters and involving yourself in illegal activities."

"How...?"

He could see her struggle to remain calm yet show how offensive she found his words. She wasn't half as good at deception as she imagined. Even when she'd defeated him then stranded him on an island, he'd admired her forthrightness.

"Are you accusing me of being a criminal?"

"Not at present." They both knew he could, but he was uncertain what Miss Walford knew. "However, on more than one occasion, you have been seen conversing with Mr. Cosistas, a known fence. You've also been seen visiting the church alone at all hours. By itself, visiting the church raises little suspicion. However, in light of your conversations with Mr. Cosistas, visiting the church alone and at odd hours does cause speculation as to your purpose. And if you think I believe that tarradiddle about sleep-walking, you are mistaken."

"Mr. Cosistas is no more than an acquaintance made during the forced proximity of the past two days. As for my business at the church, that is none of your affair." She shifted her head to look at Miss Walford. "Verity, I assume you consented to participate in this discussion to maintain propriety. As you can see, nothing about Brandon's conversation is proper. In fact, he's implying that I disregard the rules of propriety for nefarious reasons, yet he presents no evidence of such." Turning back, her glare found him.

Verity cleared her throat. "I agreed, Eugenia, because I too am concerned about your movements when folk are normally abed or otherwise occupied. At dawn this morning, despite your attempts at silence, I heard you go out. Our window fronts the street, so despite the fog, I was able to see you leave the inn and disappear into that mist going toward the church. What could possibly have taken you there at such an hour?"

Red's jaw dropped for a moment. "I was restless, and hoped some exercise would permit me to sleep when I returned."

"Yet you did not return for several hours. In fact, not until shortly before I encountered you on the stairs, correct?" Brandon interrogated. Where had she been?

Her chin came up. "What of it? I am an adult and entitled to behave as I wish."

"True." He clasped his hands together atop the table and held her gaze. "But as an officer in His Majesty's service, I am entitled to ask questions of anyone whom I deem is acting suspiciously."

Verity, who had been fiddling with the timepiece pinned to her bodice, stood abruptly. "Oh dear. I promised to meet with Miss de Courtenay and Mrs. Brewster at two o'clock, and it is already quarter past the hour. "Eugenia, I trust Captain Gilroy to take every care of you and behave with the utmost propriety, else I would postpone this meeting for another time. I'll return as quickly as possible."

She was out the door so fast Red could do no more than utter a desperate sounding, "But..." Brandon watched his pirate's gaze narrow and her lips form a straight line.

"All right, Brandon. Now that we are alone, let's have the gloves off and get to your true purpose. I have other business that I must be about."

"Besides yourself and Cosistas there is at least one other person at this inn whom I believe has criminal intentions." Before his eyes her face paled.

"So why not arrest us all?" Color leaked slowly back into her complexion.

"Because I have no solid proof yet. I had hoped you might be willing to tell me what you know."

"You've stated before that I might find leniency by acting dishonorably. I refused then and wish to refuse now."

He lifted his left brow. "Dare I imagine that you are less resolved in your decision than the first time I broached this subject."

She stood and paced to the window where she stopped, shoulders squared, back ramrod straight, her hands laced together behind her. 'Twas a stance taken by the captains of every ship he'd served with when scenting the wind and deciding how best to guide ship and crew.

"You are correct that I am in somewhat of a pickle."

That was probably an understatement. Men like Cosistas and Danville were the scum of the earth. Brandon knew from experience that Cosistas would sell his grandmother for tuppence profit. From what Russell told him, Danville was of the same stamp. Then there was the possibility of a French spy's involvement.

"And the nature of this pickle is such that you are willing to forego your honor?" He hoped she'd say no. Troublesome as it was, he respected her more for maintaining her principles in the face of personal advantage. Nonetheless, he needed whatever information she could provide.

"I wish I could claim differently. First, let me ask if your mission here involves discovering what happened to certain Naval munitions that never arrived at their designated destination?"

"How...? Never mind. I needn't ask how. You found out about the missing ordnance from Cosistas."

"In a manner of speaking." She continued to gaze out the window. "I overheard him talking with Danville and another man earlier today. Cosistas wants me to deliver the munitions to Danville's ship. In exchange Milo promises not to report me to the magistrate."

A tear of disappointment fell from Brandon's heart. He left his seat to stand behind Red but did not touch her.

"Who was the other man?"

"I don't know. The fog prevented me from seeing any of them. I only knew Cosistas and Danville by their voices. This third man had a very faint French accent. The conversation made it fairly clear that the munitions are intended for Napoleon's army."

"Where and when are you to meet with Danville?" Brandon pressed for as much information as he could get.

"Cosistas has yet to confirm my cooperation, though he has approached me. However, the conversation I overheard made clear that he intended to approach me again and attempt to blackmail me, if I refused to cooperate. I will only be a little reluctant when he puts his proposal to me. He would expect some resistance. Once I know the details, I'll send the information to my crew and have them contact you. At present, I only know the *Éire Mist* is to meet Danville's ship off the coast of Calais and make the transfer of the munitions at sea."

"So, you are willing to assist the navy in catching Danville in the act of receiving stolen goods by allowing Cosistas to load the ordnance on the *Éire Mist*?"

"'Tis what I intended, and why I'm telling you. That and the fact that Danville imagines he can capture the *Éire Mist* away from me."

"With your ship approaching his willingly and unsuspecting of betrayal, he might accomplish that."

"But I do suspect treachery. Even did I not, I keep my ear to the waves and know the quality of his crew. They are vicious but weak-willed at heart. Not a man among them would stand in the face of better fighters. His crew will turn tail and run faster than minnows from a whale." Her pride in her own crew was unmistakable.

Brandon dared to place a comforting hand on her shoulder. She continued to stand rigid and strong. "Has the *Éire Mist* attacked a British ship since the recent peace with the former colonies was declared?"

She shook her head then turned, seating herself on the window sill, arms braced on either side. "No, I've been occupied by other concerns. Besides, British ships and crews fight almost as well as Americans. British enemies, with the possible exception of France, make much easier pickings." She smiled. "I've no wish to lose any more crewmen in a fight than necessary."

She was close enough to kiss. All he had to do was reach out and pull her up then take her lips. The kiss would be sweet at first then grow fierce enough to burn them both to cinders. But he kept his hands to himself. Now was not the time. Much as he wanted Red's passion, he wanted to understand her more.

"So, you'll lend the navy your aid, to get revenge on a fellow pirate?" *Please let her motive not be revenge. What then? Loyalty to Britain? She's an American by adoption if not birth. Love? Hardly.* But what exactly he wished her motive to be he couldn't have said.

She snorted. "You think me so petty that I would revenge an action as yet untaken and impossible to take in the first place."

"No, you're right. You'd not do that. So why help the navy when we've hunted you without mercy in the past?"

"To teach Danville a lesson in humility. The man has a bloated concept of his own excellence. He deserves to have that pricked, and it pleases me greatly for the *Éire Mist* to do the job. And you might just be grateful enough to grant the crew of the *Éire Mist* amnesty from past actions against Britain. I'll warn my first mate to get that amnesty in writing before the *Éire Mist* does anything for you."

"You do not ask amnesty for yourself."

"True, but did I ask that, my motives would be tainted by self-interest."

"Ah." He smiled. "So not bloodlust, but education and unsullied forgiveness motivates you to lend the navy assistance."

"Something like that." She smiled back at him, reached for his lapels, hauled him forward then downward, and placed her lips smack against his.

The kiss ended almost before it began. She slipped around his left side. He was still blinking away his surprise when he heard a door shut and the click of a key being turned. She'd wanted to kiss him so badly that she'd acted on the impulse. Then she'd run, locked herself in her bedchamber. He'd been playing hide and seek with the desire she inspired in him for the past five days. He doubted she would have any more success in hiding than he. His smile broadened. Perhaps when this business with the missing munitions was concluded, he and Red could spend some pleasant days together. God knew he could use a respite before leaving the navy and going to Scotland to attend on his father and uncle.

CHAPTER 7

Between Midnight and Dawn
Thursday, April 6, 1815

W hat possessed her to kiss Brandon? Telling him of Cosistas and Danville's plot had been the right thing to do, but she hadn't intended to do so until much later, just before she left the Queen's Barque for good. She planned to offer the services of the *Éire Mist* to the Navy in exchange for amnesty for her crew, and she'd informed Brandon of that requirement. Hopefully Black John would see the amnesty written and signed. She listened to Brandon's footsteps cross the parlor and the door to that room click open then shut. She found her cloak and left for the church; the uneaten food in the parlor forgotten.

Returning from her errand, she locked her bedchamber door for the second time that day. She leaned back against the wooden panel and held the precious documents to her chest, savoring the thrill of knowing she'd found her mother's marriage lines. Her father's name was Henry, Henry Bowen MacTavish, esq. That made her Esmeralda MacTavish and legitimate.

"I always thought you might be Analise's child and she'd just made up the tale about leaving her mistress to die." Esme shoved away the memory of Crobbin's words.

It couldn't be true. She wouldn't permit it to be true. She'd travel to Cowal in the highlands and present herself as the Duke's long-lost relative. The marriage lines and the vicar's witnessed statement would make that true. It didn't matter that another man had been vicar when her parents wed. What mattered was that the lines existed and could not be denied. The duke would have to confirm she was his granddaughter.

She walked over to the dressing table, placed the missive and her reticule containing her mother's diary on the surface then draped her cloak over the chair. She opened the armoire and took her valise from inside. Placing it on the bed, she began to pack.

Someone knocked on the bedroom door.

"Verity?"

"Yes."

Esme unlocked the door and opened it.

Verity entered, closed the portal, and took in the scene. "You're packing."

"Yes, I've completed my business here successfully and am ready to move on."

"Have you eaten?"

Esme looked up from closing her carpet bag and blinked. "No, now that you mention it. I've eaten very little today. I'm famished."

"I had the servants leave some of the things from luncheon. I didn't know when you'd return and suspected you'd be hungry. Let's adjourn to the parlor table. I'll sip some cider while you feast."

"Excellent idea. We can discuss our plans for meeting up with our transportation."

They were soon settled comfortably, and Esme devoured her meal.

"I arranged for Mr. Englewirth, Her Grace of Stonegreave's coachman, to wait for us at the Traveler's Rest in Upper Fenwick. The town is to the west between here and Great Yarmouth. I hear that many of the farm tracks are navigable and, since we are going west, we should be able to find fordable places when we must cross water. It isn't too far to walk in one day if we leave early."

Pushing away her empty plate, Esme took a swallow of cider. "We'll leave before sunup," she said. "But we'll not walk. I've plenty of cash to hire horses and pay a posting lad at the Traveler's Rest to bring the steeds back to The Queen's Barque. You do ride, do you not?"

Verity sighed. "Yes, not well, but I should be able to manage a short distance on a mild-mannered hack. Most inns have such beasts for ladies. I even packed a habit should the need arise."

"Excellent. I would appreciate it if you would speak with Brewster before you retire for the night."

Verity tilted her head. "Of course."

"Remind him how much I value my privacy and stress that his silence about us is important. I want to delay anyone knowing of our departure for as long as possible. I will give you money to give to him for our shot and some extra as incentive for keeping mum about our departure as well as sufficient to hire the horses and have them ready for us before dawn."

Verity shrugged. "That seems a great deal more secretive than necessary. However, Her Grace said I should accommodate you as I would her, so I shall do as you ask."

"Thank you. Now I'll help you pack. Then I have some letters to write while you visit with Brewster. Be sure to thank him for all his work in taking care of us and so many others. Let him know that I am very satisfied with my visit to the Barque and will certainly recommend it."

Verity nodded. "Of course. Now let me get my own valise."

⬨

"Brandon, Brandon."

Something jostled his shoulder.

"Get up man."

Lord Stanton stood beside the bed. "By Davy Jones's beard, Russell. It's the middle of the night."

"Yes, and we need to be about, quickly. Danville and Cosistas have taken to the road."

"Why did you not say so?" Brandon leapt from his bed and pulled on his clothing. "When did you learn of this?"

"Moments ago. I paid the head groomsman to notify me if either man requested a horse. He took note of their direction. They are headed to Great Yarmouth."

"That won't be an easy ride in the dark." Brandon finished putting on his boots. The timing couldn't have been worse. He had unfinished business with a certain red-haired pirate. Standing, he bent over his chamber's desk grabbing pen and paper.

"What are you doing?" Russell sounded irritated.

"I must leave a note for someone." He wrote as he spoke.

"We've no time for your billet-doux to a serving wench."

"Go order the horses made ready. By the time they are, I'll be waiting to get into the saddle."

"Suit yourself," Russell said and left.

There was no time to ponder the wording. *Dearest Eugenia.* He could not risk anyone accidentally seeing a note addressing Irish Red. *I am called to Great Yarmouth on an urgent matter. We have much to settle between us. I will return with all possible speed. Wait for me.*

BG

He left the missive along with a generous vail with the lad keeping watch at the desk for the night. "Deliver this to Miss Fynlock immediately."

"Aye sir."

The lad was running up the stairs as Brandon rushed out the door.

He'd no idea what he would say to Red when he returned, but he could figure that out on the way back from Great Yarmouth. For now, he must focus on keeping track of the men who would eventually lead him to the stolen munitions. He mounted his horse and took the reins from the groom. *Wait for me Red. Please wait for me.*

When all was ready for Esme's departure, save the last-minute tasks that could not be taken care of before morning, Verity left to speak with Brewster, and Esme sat at the parlor desk. Her first note was to

Black John on the *Éire Mist*, giving instructions on how to contact Captain Gilroy in Great Yarmouth and to assist him in every way the captain requested. She warned her mate to get in writing the amnesties due the *Éire Mist*'s crew for lending this assistance. Then she explained the situation with Danville, charging her crew with teaching that mariner a much-needed lesson. Finally, she regretted not being able to join the crew in this adventure, but her business necessitated a trip north to Scotland. Black John could expect another message some time before December with details about where and when to meet her so she could at last rejoin the *Éire Mist* and the crew she greatly missed.

She sanded, folded and sealed that epistle, then drew another sheet of paper out of the desk's drawer.

Dearest Captain Gilroy,

She crossed out the words. Yes, he was becoming dear to her, and he probably knew it. But she recognized if he did not that they had no future together. She had the novel experience of feeling her chest tighten and tears brim in her eyes. She swept those away before they could fall, took a deep breath, and wrote.

> *Captain Gilroy,*
>
> *By the time you receive this, I will be gone beyond your reach. I regret that I cannot be the person to instruct Danville as to his proper place in the world and assist the navy in retrieving its munitions. However, Black John, first mate of the Éire Mist, will contact you within the week at the Great Yarmouth naval yard.*
>
> *My business in Fenwick on Sea is completed, and my presence is demanded elsewhere. I wish you all the best.*
>
> *E*

She could not bring herself to lie directly as she had to Cosistas, and tell Brandon that she was headed south. Her conscience hurt at the idea of lying to him by omission. However, the more her feelings for him grew, the stronger her conviction they could never be together. He would never marry a pirate, and she would not be a mistress. The sea was in her blood, and the sea bowed to no man.

She reviewed what she had written. It was the best she could do under the circumstances. She copied the letter onto a clean sheet of paper and threw the blotted original in the fire. Sanded, folded and sealed, she set the letters side by side on her dressing table. She would send them by separate couriers from Upper Fenwick.

She dressed and retired to bed. She heard Verity come in and move about the parlor. Then all was silent, save for the shift of an occasional log in the banked fire. She lay there with her jumbled thoughts in the dark of night waiting for sleep. It never came. As the sky turned from black to gray, she rose to dress. Her eyes dampened. She patted them dry with a kerchief. *I'll not cry. I'll miss him, but I'll not permit myself to weep. He is the past, and I must look to my future.*

A soft knock came from the direction of the parlor door. "Are you ready, Esme?"

She picked up her valise, looped the train of her habit over her arm, and opened the door. "Aye, are you?"

Verity nodded. "Oh, by the way, Brewster's son delivered this note for you after you had retired. I didn't want to disturb your sleep, so I kept it until now."

Esme took the sealed paper. Only the name Eugenia graced the outside, written in a bold slashing hand. The writing was unfamiliar, but she could only imagine one person who might send her a note. She tore at the seal and read. "Verity, if you do not mind, please take my valise with you to the stable. I will meet you there in two minutes.

"As you wish." She took the valise from Esme and left.

Esme hurried to the parlor escritoire, sat, and drew out paper and pen. The dear foolish man. He should know better, but if there was any chance for them, she must let him know how she felt.

Brandon,

I cannot delay to wait for you, and I am uncertain any conversation between us would be of use. However, if you still wish to involve yourself with me, I will return to The Queen's Barque in a year and a day, April 6, 1816. I will wait here three days. If I do not see or hear from you by April 9, 1816, I'll know you've come to your senses. With all my heart I wish you everything that is best in the world.

E.

She sanded, folded and sealed the note and addressed the outside to Mister Gilroy. Her earlier missive, she tossed in the flames. Then placing her two letters in her reticule she descended the stairs. Fortunately, Brewster was alone at the reception desk. "Mr. Brewster, I wish to thank you one last time for your kindness to me and Miss Walford. Would you please see this note delivered to Mr. Gilroy as discreetly as possible?"

"The good man has already left, Miss Fynlock."

"I know, but he informed me he would return. I cannot wait for him, so please, give him this note."

Brewster took the letter. "I'll keep it safe for him."

"One last item." She paused hesitant to commit herself this far in the future.

"Yes?" Brewster offered helpfully.

"I wish to reserve the same rooms for April sixth through April ninth of next year."

The innkeeper beamed. "We'll be delighted to have you return, Miss Fynlock."

"Thank you, Brewster. All the best to you and your family."

"Likewise to you, Miss."

Esme turned her back on her past and walked into her future.

EPILOGUE

Well past dark, December 7, 1823

I n the flickering lantern light, Black John kept a guardian hand on each of the two flame-haired children whose heads lay pillowed on his long thighs.

From the direction of the bow came the murmur of voices. Two figures emerged arm in arm from the darkness there.

"Ho there, Black John. Are you weary of playing nursemaid yet?" The Duke of Cowal's deep tones carried a note of laughter.

"We've sent for Nurse," stated the Duchess's contralto. "Thank you for entertaining them."

"'Tis niver a problem, Yer Graces."

"No," the duke said. "I imagine not half the problem that Russell is when he decides to visit the crow's nest without asking permission."

"Nor when Marielle decides to order the crew to weigh anchor just because she doesn't like the look of the dawn sky."

"Aye," agreed Black John. "She's an early riser that one. And will be a right fine cap'n someday."

"We're going to have to build another ship, so each of them may have their own. I've no wish to hear the squabbles of my two children when each tries to captain the same ship at the same time," the duke murmured.

Her Grace grinned at her husband. "I fear you must order two new ships built, my love."

"Are you telling me you are expecting again?"

She nodded. A more graceful imitation of her son's earlier consent to hearing the story.

"Then what say you we set sail for Barbados in the morning. I've had word that a number of ship builders from Massachusetts are convening there for a meeting about their trade."

"A splendid idea. We'll need to decide who will crew these vessels while our children grow into them."

The duke looked at Black John, speculatively. "I think I know just the man to captain Marielle's ship."

Black John dropped his jaw. "Now, now Yer Grace, what have I ever done that ye'd want to punish me so."

The duke batted his lashes with feigned innocence. "Are you suggesting my daughter is not well behaved."

"Yer daughter is the image of yer duchess, Yer Grace."

"And the best captain you've ever known," the duke suggested.

"Aye, sir. She is that."

Her Grace of Cowal rolled her eyes, and spying the approach of Nurse, sighed with relief.

THE END

A note to readers. Brandon and Esme are destined to meet again in a future novel where they will, after much tribulation, achieve their lasting happily ever after. That book is tentatively titled The Pirate Duchess. Look for it this year. Discover more about Rue Allyn's books at https://rueallyn.com/booksnew/

SOCIAL MEDIA FOR RUE ALLYN

You can learn more about Rue Allyn on these social media links:

Facebook: https://www.facebook.com/RueAllynAuthor
Twitter: https://twitter.com/RueAllyn
Amazon: https://www.amazon.com/Rue-Allyn/e/B00AUBF3NI/

ABOUT RUE ALLYN

Award winning author, Rue Allyn learned story telling at her grandfather's knee and has been weaving her own tales ever since. She and her husband of more than four decades (try living with the same person for more than forty years—that's a true adventure) have retired and moved south. When not writing, enjoying the nearby beach or working jigsaw puzzles, Rue travels the world and surfs the internet in search of background material and inspiration for her next heart melting romance. She loves to hear from readers, and you may contact her at Rue@Rue-Allyn.com. She can't wait to hear from you.

Learn more about Rue at:
Website: https://RueAllyn.com

THE VICAR'S ILLICIT LIAISON

The Teatime Tattler

Dear Reader,

The village of Fenwick has been shaken to its core by the discovery that its revered curate, Mr. S., has feet—nay, entire limbs—of clay.

First, he allowed his nephew, a bold impertinent boy, to insult our own beloved Mrs. F. Second, as noted in a previous report, he spent much time alone with a female visitor to the village.

But now he has taken up with another female, a visitor's maid. Said maid has been staying all day at the presbytery, purportedly nursing Mr. S.'s wards through the influenza.

Today, she sunk so far in depravity as to stay overnight on the pretext that Mr. S. is now ill. This is unlikely to end well.

A DREAM COME TRUE

JUDE KNIGHT

A Dream Come True
By Jude Knight

The tempest that batters Barnaby Somerville's village is the latest but not the least of his challenges.

Vicar to a remote parish, he stretches his tiny stipend to adopt his orphaned niece and nephew and his time to offer medical care as well as spiritual. A wife is a dream he cannot afford.
But the storm sweeps into his life a surprising temptation—a charming young woman who lavishes her gentle care upon his wards—and him. God knows, he will forever be richer for having known her, even if he must let her go.

CHAPTER 1

Barnabas Somerville sat at the great battered desk with his head in his hands. The discarded note from the manor shifted under his elbow, the damp edges—where the driving rain had seeped through the messenger's oiled coat—disintegrating into a paste. Mrs. Fullerton, whose note it was, was the housekeeper who ruled Morpeth Manor in the absence of its owner, and the parish's self-appointed leader of pious and proper women.

After Sunday service this morning, he had been delayed in the sacristy. Mrs. Fullerton must have thought he had left already to make a noon meal for his two-year-old niece and her thirteen-year-old brother. Until today, the sour gossip had been careful to insult Barney's nephew and cast aspersions on Barney's sister out of her vicar's hearing.

But he stood for a full minute just inside the doorway from the nave, listening to her spread her venom, a drowsy Annabelle snuggled into his shoulder, a fuming Daniel beside him. As Barney stepped out of hiding, the carriage from the manor pulled up in front of the church. Mrs. Fullerton hurried away through the rain and her listeners scattered like alarmed hens, absconding before he could master his anger enough to say a word. "I will deal with it," he told Daniel. "But first, I had better get Annie her lunch."

He would walk up to the manor and confront her, he told himself. But Daniel had begged permission to lend a hand at the stables at The Queen's Barque inn. No one else was in the house; he'd not seen Mrs. Withers for days, even though she was meant to come every day to cook and clean. She'd been absent since the rain started and the little village of Fenwick on Sea began to fill with visitors.

Instead, Barney retreated to his study when Annie went down for her afternoon sleep, his mind teeming with words for a sermon on the proper treatment of strangers and orphans, keen to get down at least the gist of it. Then the message came from the manor house. Now the words had been blown asunder as if the wind that howled in from the North Sea had ripped them from his skull and tossed them over the treetops and the inlet beyond.

Now he knew where Daniel had gone. The message was an assumption couched as fact. Mrs. Fullerton had no evidence that Daniel had crept into her private chamber and spread Indian ink on the flannel that waited for her pre-prandial wash. It might not be him.

Of course, it was him. Not another boy in twenty miles would imagine such a prank, let alone have the fortitude to carry it out. Barney suppressed both a grin and a groan. It was unbecoming in an ordained minister to be amused by the imagined vision of Mrs. Fullerton, face all stained with ink.

Blackface. Daniel's revenge had been tailored to the offence. More than once, according to Mrs. Withers, the manor's housekeeper had mused aloud about the wicked habits and immoral ways of blackamoor half-breeds, and the risk such imps from hell might pose to the village.

She had also expressed doubt that Barney's poor dead sister had ever been wed, calling into evidence that the children had different fathers, and speculating that no decent man would marry a woman with a black son.

Daniel was quite right to take exception to the slight against his mother. Barney should have been firmer a week ago when he reprimanded Mrs. Fullerton for her lack of charity and for bearing false witness. Apparently, his words washed past her without any effect. She had treated him with a toxic combination of pity and smugness. She denied everything, said she had been misunderstood, was hurt that he would take up against her. She had only been trying to help. Of course, no one expected a vicar to be worldly, and it was to his credit that he wanted to believe the best of his sister, and her poor little daughter. As for the boy, he should be sent to school, if any school would have such a one. There was one in Yarmouth, she said, that would know what to do with such an imp from hell.

Barney could not make a single dent in her self-righteous conviction that she was right and he was wrong. She even pointed out that she had raised her own niece, so might be expected to have expertise he lacked, since he had only known of the children's existence a short while before they arrived on his doorstep a mere six weeks ago after the death of their mother.

Barney had also made Daniel write a letter apologizing for being rude. The boy had called Mrs. Fullerton, to her face and in front of others, an ugly old besom, a bully, and a liar.

Daniel had barely spoken to him since, and clearly had no faith in Barney's ability to stop Mrs. Fullerton's persecution. He must have run straight up to the manor to take his revenge after what they heard at the church this morning. Understandable, but naughty beyond belief. Barney sighed. Doubtless, the village would focus on the boy's sin, rather than the adult's.

Lacking the wisdom of Solomon, Barney had no idea what to do. Perhaps Daniel might benefit from school, though not one where they beat the children. The Academy for the Formation of Young Gentlemen, a short ride up the coast, had a good reputation and a kindly proprietress. Would Miss Abney take Daniel as a day pupil? Though, by all accounts, the school was in ruins, driving Miss Abney and her boarders to take refuge at the local inn.

He smoothed the note to read again the strident demands for a beating at the least and exile to an orphanage for preference. He should have spoken to her again this week, when it became clear that she hadn't stopped her vicious remarks. Now the parish would take sides. Already, Daniel had been in several fights, jumped on by other boys for the crime of being singled out as different by an adult.

Barney's head jerked up as his misery was interrupted by the sudden clanging of the church bell. He was halfway to the door, one arm in his jacket and the other searching for the armhole when the miscreant of the moment burst in the door.

"Mr. Somerville, there's a ship ashore at the harbor mouth. You'll be needed, Mr. Dursley says."

He'd been fighting again. One eye was puffy above a split cheek, and his shirt was torn. No time to worry about that now. "Annie is asleep, Daniel. I'll need you to stay with her." As he spoke, Barney was taking his satchel from the corner and shrugging into the jacket that hung from the back of the door. He'd need bandages, probably some laudanum—other things, too. And his oiled coat. A muffler, perhaps. It would keep the rain from seeping down inside his clothes, at least for a while.

His mental list of things to collect from around the house was interrupted. "Please, Uncle Barney. I can help. 'Every able-bodied man', Mr. Dursley says. Let me come, too."

Barney stopped, halfway through the doorway. Daniel would be a help, at that. He was tall for his thirteen years and—though his slender frame suggested frailty—all courage and muscle. Besides, in the six weeks since the boy had arrived, sullen and grieving, this was the first time he had addressed Barney as 'Uncle'.

Barney spoke over his shoulder as Daniel followed him into the kitchen. "Run next door and see if one of the girls there can sit with Annie. Tell them what's going on, and that I need you. Be quick, Daniel."

The kitchen door banged behind the boy before Barney had finished his sentence. He slipped the strap of the satchel over his shoulder and hurried upstairs to look in on Annie. The child was asleep in a nest of blankets, her knees tucked underneath her body and her thumb in her mouth. Barney bent over the cot to tuck the blanket over her. "Sleep well, little one," he whispered.

Daniel met him at the foot of the stairs, shaking his head to scatter the rain from his hair. "Janet is coming."

Barney nodded. "My old oil cloth great coat is hanging on the back of the kitchen door. Wear that, Daniel. Follow me when she arrives."

He didn't wait for agreement or argument, hurrying out into the lane to join the others answering the tolling bell. Men, mostly, but some women and boys, singly and in clumps, allowed the wind to speed their steps through the village and along the path that led through fields and then the sand dunes that sheltered the long channel leading to the village's fishing harbor.

The wind was too strong for much conversation, but Barney noted that their numbers had been swelled by some of the inn's guests. Good. If the ship was where he thought, they'd need all the help they could get.

As they left the fields for the dunes, Daniel fell into step beside him, hood-covered head down against the rain, recognizable only by the distinctive patch on the shoulder of the older coat. "Good man," Barney told him, and was rewarded with a flash of teeth as the boy turned his face up for a moment to acknowledge the remark.

They crested the highest point of the path. Ahead, the harbor inlet was a turmoil of waves blurred by the rain. No ship. Wait! There it was, slightly to the right of where Barney expected, aground on the rocks part way up the other side of the harbor mouth.

Thad Penn, who worked the smithy, had taken charge at the near shore, where a rowboat from the ship had landed a cable and was already on its way back to the ship to fetch another.

Barney found himself on the team assigned to the cable, Daniel before him, two of a score of people trying to hold steady against the drag of wind and waves. For long minutes, all that was required of him was his physical effort, as Penn hammered a long spike deep into the ground to anchor the cable, and the first row boat was joined by a couple of local skiffs, each braving the tossing sea to take anchor lines in different directions.

Barney's team continued to brace against the pull as another group waited for the second cable. It had arrived by the time the fishermen had tied Barney's cable firmly to Penn's spike, and Penn was hammering another further down the coast. Two long fishing boats scudded before the wind up the inlet, and tacked to come about within splashing distance of men who waited to cross the inlet, presumably to secure cables from the other side of the ship. Barney rolled off one glove to examine his hand for blisters.

"How are your hands, Daniel?" he asked. Below them, the first boat was away again, ploughing heavily laden through the waves with the insouciance of a working craft that regularly plied the North Sea for a harvest.

Daniel held up two undamaged palms. "Held the rope through my sleeves," he explained. Barney wished he'd had the sense to do the same.

"Right. Let's see what else we can do to help."

Another skiff was crossing from the stranded ship. From the patches of color he could see through the rain, this one carried a female or two. Passengers, probably. Barney patted his satchel absent-mindedly as he hurried down to the water. He and the midwife were the closest the village had to medical expertise, and his was limited, though he'd studied a bit under a physician before being ordained.

Daniel darted ahead to help hold the prow of the skiff steady as it rode a wave up onto the first line of pebbles at the half-tide mark, and men spilled over the side. Barney had been right about the women; two of them. One was a splash of color in the rain, her hooded cape a fur-trimmed piece of practical frivolity in a rich cherry red. The other, huddled in a black cloak that was possibly blue when dry, broke away from the cherry-red lady to lean toward the side of the boat, heaving as if to be sick, but managing to produce nothing.

One of the men held out his arms to the dark-clad female. "Here, Theo. You'll be better on dry land." Sea sick, then. Barney recognized the pallor, the sunken eyes. She'd had a bad run of it, poor thing.

"Get them both ashore, my lord," commanded one of the sailors, whose voice identified him as an officer though his shapeless coat didn't. Barney met the peer on the beach and reached for the sick woman. "Is she hurt?"

"*Mal de mer.*" The peer's reply was curt. "She'll be fine now we're on land."

"I'll take her up to the fire," Barney said. The young man transferred his burden and turned back for Miss Cherry-Red, who was looking at the water as if contemplating wading ashore herself.

Barney crossed the beach toward the fire someone had managed to start under a makeshift shelter of canvas and driftwood. The woman lying inert in his arms weighed next to nothing. Her eyelids quivered as the rain struck her face. It was all he could see of her—a face too slim for beauty. He hunched over her to keep as much rain from her as he could.

Daniel skipped sideways beside him. "Is she going to be all right?"

Barney looked down and met the woman's wide eyes; green-flecked hazel and slightly out of focus. She blinked. "Yes, Daniel," he said, his words meant to reassure his patient more than his nephew. "She will."

His patient's lips curved in a tired smile. "Travel-sickness," she murmured, so softly that he had to bend his head closer to her lips to catch the words. "So foolish. Laughable."

Nothing amusing about severe travel sickness. From her sunken eyes and the way her voice rasped, she was severely in need of water, and soon. She confirmed his assessment by darting out a tongue to lick at the rain that dripped off Barney's hood.

He settled her by the fire under the shelter and called for water. Someone gave him a flask, and he checked to find it contained cold tea rather than spirits. He pressed it into her hand. "Drink," he told her. "A few mouthfuls at a time, and rest between."

He watched for a moment as she obediently sipped from the flask, pausing to gift him with another curve of the lips. "Thank you, sir."

Barney returned the smile. Had he thought her plain? Not with those fine eyes and that sweet smile.

Miss Cherry-Red arrived in a flurry of silk and sank down beside his patient, words gushing out of her in a flood. Barney reassured her that 'Theo' (what sort of name was that for a pretty woman?) would recover, with plenty to drink plus rest and food, preferably in that order.

CHAPTER 2

Theodora Conroy looked up at the ceiling, too weak to get out of bed but well enough to fret about Lady Felicity, who had insisted on managing for herself while Theo recovered.

"I didn't know seasickness could be so bad," the lady had said, with her usual bluntness. "I thought we might lose you, Theo. Mr. Somerville says you must stay in bed, sleep, and eat small amounts frequently until you are recovered. You know that, if you are with me, you will insist on doing too much."

"But who shall look after you, my lady?" Theo had wondered.

Lady Felicity laughed. "If I find myself quite incompetent to do up my own buttons and dress my own hair, I am sure one of the inn's maids will help. And if she makes a mess of it, Theo, then I shall have my just desserts for not insisting you stay in England, when I know what a bad traveler you are."

Theo hadn't the strength to argue, and had allowed Lady Felicity to tuck her into bed and feed her a few spoons of the gruel that Mr. Somerville said was all she was allowed.

Lady Felicity had no reason to blame herself; Theo had been as eager as her mistress to go to Brussels with the lady's brother, Lord Hythe, who was traveling on government business. Her stupid stomach, with its violent reaction to travel, had rebelled from the moment their ship met the choppier waters of the Thames Estuary, and had only worsened during the time they'd spent riding out the storm at sea.

The day after the rescue, her head still spun when she tried to lift it from the pillows, and she was still limited to feeding her tender digestion a few spoons of pap at a time. At least she could feed herself, propped up on the pillows, read a little from her prayer book, and even deal with her own personal needs if she took her time and had the bed or a wall to hold on to for support.

Which was easy in a room of this size. "It is tiny," Lady Felicity had apologized, "but I thought you would prefer to be on your own. It must have been a dressing room for the big chamber next door, back when this wing was in use." The room was dilapidated, but clean, and even had a small window through which she could see a patch of sky, blue changing to gray and back again as the clouds blew by.

A knock on the door brought her attention from the window, and she swallowed against the dizziness that came from turning her head. "Come in," she called.

The man who had carried her from the boat entered. Mr. Somerville. He was in charge of this scattered hospital that the village had set up in the older wings of the inn—her little room, the larger chamber next door, and other rooms scattered around the inn.

"Miss Conroy," he greeted her. "How are you today?" Without asking, he picked up Theo's arm and felt for her pulse. The firm press of his fingers sent a quiver shooting all the way to her chest, and she shifted restlessly on the pillows.

What had he said? Oh, yes. "Much better, Mr. Somerville. I am well enough to return to my duties."

Mr. Somerville looked at the mostly-full bowl of gruel and raised a brow. "Not quite, I think. Be kind to yourself, Miss Conroy. Your body has suffered an insult, and will take a little time to recover."

He spoke in the accents of a gentleman, and carried himself like one, too. A gentleman of modest means, to be sure. He was tidily dressed, though not fashionably, with none of the excesses of lace at the cuffs or ornately tied cravat. A handsome man, too, with hair that curled a little at the ends, darker brown than Theo's own mouse-fawn, and eyes of a similar shade.

How did such a man end up in a tiny village on the edge of the North Sea, many miles from the main carriage ways and harbors? That put her in mind of the other victims of this storm, including a sailor from their ship who had broken a leg when the jury-rigged mast had collapsed as they struck the rocks. "How are your other patients, doctor?" she asked.

Mr. Somerville smiled. "I am not a physician, though I have learned a little from one. I am available, however. Fortunately, Dr. Roth, who came on your ship, seems to be recovering from the injury he received during the landing. We will not be able to fetch another physician until the floods recede, so I am pleased he will soon be available to remedy any mistakes I have made in my ignorance."

If he is not a physician, what is he then? The local squire, perhaps? Or a lawyer?

Her question must have shown on her face, for he explained, "I am the vicar of this parish, as curate for my father. My poor medical skills have been more in need these past days than my pastoral ones." He twisted his mouth as if the words tasted sour, then forced a smile. "You may be sure that one of the innkeeper's daughters is looking after your Lady Felicity, and pleased to have the opportunity, so relax, Miss Conroy, and take the time to get better."

Lady Felicity had said exactly the same thing when she had visited, and—in truth—Theo was very much afraid that she might pass out if she tried to take up her normal duties. Even so, Theo grimaced.

Mr. Somerville nodded once, as if agreeing to something. "If you promise you will not try to work, I shall see about having you moved to Lady Felicity's room."

Theo smiled her agreement, and relaxed back onto her pillows.

Barney hurried away to find Lady Felicity and her brother, the Earl of Hythe. Miss Conroy could have no idea how appealing she looked, with her hair tousled from being on the pillow and a shawl over a nightgown that was surely far too fine to belong to a maid, however well paid. It set a man thinking of things he shouldn't, especially a man sworn to the service of God.

Her hair was a cloud of ashy brown around a sweet oval face, made lovely by those fine hazel eyes. Having such a pretty girl here just one doorway away from half-a-dozen men, however battered, was probably a bad idea. Men could be such dogs, and he did not exclude himself from the description.

Once Miss Conroy's removal had been arranged, Barney checked on Annie, whom he'd left in the charge of Mrs. Brewster in the inn's office. "We gave the blessed little lamb some bread and cheese, Vicar, and she is playing with Hector."

Mrs. Brewster beckoned him into a storeroom, where Annie was sitting on the inn's great mastiff, laughing as the dog shifted so that she rolled off and had to clamber on again. "Leave her be, dearie, and have something to eat yourself. Just step into the parlor, and I'll have someone bring you some stew."

"I am hungry," Barney realized. He followed the hum of conversation into the main parlor. The inn was frantically busy, every bedchamber filled with travelers marooned by the storm, and even the stable loft at capacity. They'd opened up all the disused wings that were safe to use, and Barney had been lucky to beat the late arrivals in laying claim to the chambers where his patients now recovered from their various ills.

Innkeeper Brewster had big plans for the future of Fenwick as a summer destination for the wealthy, which had worked in their favor. While only the Tudor building that formed the heart of the Queen's Barque inn was in day-to-day use at the moment, he had completed basic repairs to make the wings that had been added on over the centuries weathertight and safe.

With the influx of guests, Brewster was in his element. He'd pressed every unoccupied hand for miles into service to cope with the onslaught. One of the men behind the bar usually worked as a fisherman. The meal, so its server assured Barney, had been cooked by Mrs. Withers, which explained why she had been absent from the presbytery. The maid exchanging laughing quips with a group of gentlemen by the fireplace was on loan from the manor, no doubt so that Mrs. Fullerton would have a direct connection to any gossip.

Barney didn't want to be reminded about his unfinished business at the manor. He and Daniel had enjoyed the most amicable breakfast of their acquaintance, and Barney hadn't wanted to spoil it by mentioning the ink incident. Coward, he scolded himself.

Mrs. Fullerton had not been seen in the village since she departed the church foyer yesterday morning. Presumably, she was washing her face and hands, over and over, to get out the stains.

Barney had to ask Daniel if he'd played the trick, and he already knew what Daniel was going to say. One of the boy's virtues was his honesty. Then Barney would need to apply appropriate discipline. He had no idea what punishment might fit such a well-deserved crime.

Mrs. Fullerton had demanded a birching, at the very least. If Barney believed in the efficacy of birchings—and he'd had enough himself to know that all they engendered was resentment—he'd recommend one for Mrs. Fullerton.

"That is an uncharitable thought, Barnabas," he scolded himself, and not for the first time. As penance, he made up his mind to walk up to the manor, though he had no idea what he was going to say when he got there.

Before he could finish clearing his plate, however, a couple of the lady guests approached to remind him about their planned tour of the church. The hour they appointed meant no time for the trip to the manor and back—Mrs. Fullerton would keep.

CHAPTER 3

"**R**est," Lady Felicity commanded, when Theo tried to fetch the redingote that went with the walking gown her mistress was wearing for the proposed expedition to the church. "I do not wish to be forced to explain to that delicious-looking vicar why my maid has suffered a relapse. I wonder if there is a Mrs. Somerville?"

Theo caught back a protest. Lady Felicity was not serious. For her, it was all light-hearted flirting. She hoped Mr. Somerville took it in the same spirit, but what difference would it make to Theo if he didn't? Mr. Somerville was as far above a servant, even a lady's maid, as Lady Felicity, as the well-dowered sister of a wealthy earl, was above Mr. Somerville.

It needn't have been so. I am gentle-born. Petty-gentry, only, and not even that now, she reminded herself. Not since she had gone into service when she was only fifteen, so that her family's meager resources might be divided between her prettier sisters. It worked. They were all wed. Only Theo, scooped up by the wife of the relative whose living her father held, remained unmarried.

She should be grateful to her father's distant cousin, an irascible countess who had selected her as the plainest of the sisters and taken her home to train as a maid. She was grateful! She had a job she liked for an employer who treated her well.

In recent years, her four sisters had each offered her a home, and Papa, too, had sent for her when Mama died, but she knew what to expect if she'd gone. If she was going to do the work of a servant, she would rather be paid the wages of a servant. She knew she was too plain and too matter-of-fact to have attracted a husband even if the countess had left her at home, and all she had done the past twelve years was embroider handkerchiefs and plan menus with cook, like her sisters.

So, your confusion over Mr. Somerville is quite ridiculous. Just because he is the first handsome gentleman ever to treat you as if you were a gentlewoman. He wasn't interested in Theo. He was just being kind and polite.

Enough, she scolded, and set herself to finding some mending to take out into the garden, where she could enjoy the sun that had finally peeped through the clouds. No doubt Lady Felicity had found several things to tear or damage in the days since Theo had to lay down her duties.

The sun had tempted many of the inn's temporary residents outside. Theo found a quiet spot with a comfortable chair and settled in to combat a run in one of Lady Felicity's stockings. Before long, she had company—a large boned dog wandered amiably through the tables set in the sun, inspecting the laughing and chattering groups as he went, then dropped himself heavily at her feet, resting his head on his paws.

"You are a big fellow, are you not?" Theo said, putting out a hand. The dog raised his head and sniffed her fingers, then let it fall back onto his paws, still looking up at her with lugubrious eyes. A rub behind the ears prompted a more enthusiastic reaction. He shifted so that his weight was against Theo's legs and waved his tail in appreciation. When she stopped patting him and turned back to her darning, he gave a heavy sigh and went to sleep with his great snout on her foot.

The work was precise but required little thinking. Theo sat enjoying the sun, half dreaming and half listening to scraps of conversation that drifted her way.

The dog shifted, attracting her attention. A little girl, just past toddling age, had plumped herself down on the great patient beast and was ruffling his ears. The dog was taking it well, his eyes watching the child, his tail thumping with slow pleasure.

"And who might you be?" Theo asked. She looked around for a nursemaid, but none were in sight. Someone must be missing the child, though. She was too clean and too well dressed to be a neglected stray.

The little girl looked up at her words, tipped her head to one side, and babbled something. "Nans eky. Ig eky. I ov eky." She threw both arms as far as they would reach around the dog's huge neck and hugged him.

Theo tried to match the most frequently repeated sound to words. "Eggy?" For a moment the child's expression was eerily reminiscent of Theo's first employer, the countess. *You are being particularly stupid today, but I must be patient with you because this is all strange to you*, the expression said.

"Not 'eggy', then," Theo acknowledged.

"Hector," said a voice behind her, making her start.

Theo straightened and looked over her shoulder. "Mr. Somerville!" She frowned. "Hector?"

Mr. Somerville was holding out his arms to the little girl.

"The dog is called Hector," he told her. "Annie, my love, you mustn't bother Miss Conroy. She has not been well."

The child held on tight to the dog, ignoring the vicar's outstretched arms. "Nans eky. Ig eky. I ov eky," she repeated.

Mr. Somerville crouched on his heels. "I know you love Hector, Annie, and yes, he is big. But he is not Annie's Hector. He is Mr. Brewster's Hector."

The child pouted and glared. "Nan's Ekky."

Theo choked back a chuckle. Annie even scowled like the old countess. Mr. Somerville looked up at her, his brows raised, eyes wide and helpless. "It really is Mr. Brewster's dog," he explained. "But the only way she will let go is if I use my fingers to uncurl her hands, and Hector will take exception to that. He has decided that Annie is his to protect. I apologize on behalf of them both, Miss Conroy." He shrugged, a big competent man entirely at the mercy of the small morsel of humanity who held his heart hostage.

She pointed to the chair beside her. "Sit for a minute, Mr. Somerville. If she doesn't fear being taken from the dog, she will relax, and will be easier to distract."

Mr. Somerville obeyed. "And therefore, to extract," he agreed. He checked a watch he pulled from his pocket. "I have a little time before I have to meet the ladies I promised to show around our church. It is Norman, you know, and they have begged a tour. Are you feeling well enough to join us, Miss Conroy?"

Theo shook her head, wanting to remind him that she was a servant, and would not be welcomed by the others of the party. She couldn't think of a way to say it without it sounding like a reprimand or a complaint, so instead, she said, "Is it very interesting, your church?"

He took her cue, and started to talk about the Norman arches, the central crossing tower, and the thirteenth century paintings high up on the wall of the nave, which illustrated Christ's parables.

Theo found herself wishing she could join the tour. Perhaps, if Lady Felicity could spare her, she could make her own visit while they waited for transport out of Fenwick. She shied away from the thought of another sea voyage, and Mr. Somerville picked up on her distraction. "I am tiring you. I apologize, Miss Conroy."

"Not at all, sir. What you say has been so interesting." His enthusiasm for the history and architecture in his charge had been enthralling. But now he had stiffened, the liveliness gone from his eyes. Snuffed out by what he saw as her disinterest.

"It was a passing thought," she explained, even as the heat of a blush warmed her cheeks. "I wondered if I would have time to see the church myself before we have to leave, and then I remembered that, when I leave, I must go to sea again. Oh, Mr. Somerville, I think I shall set down roots in this garden and never travel again."

As she hoped, he smiled at that. "Be careful, Miss Conroy. If you convince me of your sincerity, I will offer to show you around the church at a day and time of your choosing." The color rose in his cheeks. "I know I give people far more detail about such matters than they care to know."

Theo leaned forward in her eagerness to reassure him. "If you really mean it, and if my lady can spare me, I would love to see your church and hear more about it. I am fascinated. I promise, and I am the daughter of a vicar, Mr. Somerville. My sainted mother would spin in her grave if I ever told an untruth, and I could never face my father again."

He chuckled with her, then sobered again as he looked down at the dog and child at their feet. Annie was sound asleep between her guardian dog's paws, one hand still clutching the hair on his great barrel chest. He sighed, and checked his pocket watch again. "I hate to wake her again. She must be tired to have dropped off so quickly after I got her up to take her home."

"Leave her here," Theo suggested. "I can watch her." Oh, but she was intruding. "I beg your pardon. I imagine Mrs. Somerville will be wondering why her daughter is so long from home."

Mr. Somerville's smile was tired. "There is no Mrs. Somerville, and I'm only Annie's uncle, not her father, though she and her brother are my wards, poor things. I plan to ask one of the neighbors to sit with her. I couldn't impose on you, Miss Conroy, and you so recently in your sickbed."

"Impose away. I am well again, I promise you." Apart from a small tendency to dizziness if she moved too quickly, easily managed.

Mr. Somerville frowned. "I will be late if I do not go. Are you sure? No. Wait a minute." He was on his feet and hurrying along the side of the inn and through a gate into the stable yard before she had time to answer. She watched the gate and in only a few moments, he was back, propelling a thin dark-haired boy by one shoulder.

"Miss Conroy, may I present my nephew, Daniel Labulo, Annie's brother?" The boy looked down at the toe he was kicking against the ground. "Daniel, Miss Conroy is going to watch Annie while she is sleeping, but I want you to stay close to take her home when she wakes up."

Theo had only heard the surname once before. "Are you related to George Labulo?" The boy's dark skin offered evidence of a connection.

Daniel's head lifted, and his startled eyes met Theo's. "You have heard of my father?"

"I have read his book and some of his pamphlets." It would be impossible to live in the Hythe household and not to at least recognize the name of one the great voices in the abolition movement, since Lord Hythe and both his sisters carried on the previous earl's commitment to that cause.

"You must be very proud of him." Theo's voice softened, as she remembered hearing that the campaigner had died not long after Parliament finally voted to abolish the slave trade. "My deepest sympathies for your loss, Master Daniel."

The boy scuffed his foot again. "Thank you, ma'am. Miss." He looked up at his uncle, who nodded.

"Yes, lad. Off you go." He smiled at Theo as the boy dashed off. "He is horse-mad, that one. If you need him, send for him in the stables. He'll be there. He's been helping with the horses. A group of boys from a school up the road has also taken refuge there, which is an added attraction."

Theo returned the smile. "We shall manage perfectly well between us, Mr. Somerville. Hurry now, or you shall keep the ladies waiting."

After he was gone, Theo sat for a while, her hands still on the mending in her lap. The vicar's sister must have married again, for little Annie was too young and too English-looking to be the daughter of the famous abolitionist. And now both children were orphans, and poor Mr. Somerville appeared completely out of his depth.

Theo felt her usual yearning to know more of the story, but it was none of her business, of course. *I would like it to be my business.* Perhaps, if she had met him while she was still in her father's house... She halted the fruitless direction of her thoughts. She was a lady's maid, and that was all she'd ever be. The plain sister, sent into service so the others would have a better start in life. The countess's words to her mother echoed in her head. "She'll not marry with a face and figure like that, so give her to me and I'll make sure she can at least support herself."

In eight years in service, she had only once had to fight off inappropriate attentions, and that from a man almost too drunk to stand up. If that didn't confirm the countess's words, she didn't know what did.

Mr. Somerville is a kind gentleman, and I am a lady's maid. And there was nothing more to be said. She checked to see that Annie was still fast asleep and bent back to her darning.

That evening, Barney had dinner with Daniel for the first time since the injured began arriving in the village. It had been their practice since the boy and his sister arrived on the vicarage doorstep, unless Barney was out on his duties. Barney remembered all too well his own boyhood. His father thought children should be invisible until they were at least sixteen. Barney ate alone in the schoolroom while his father and much older sister dined in formal splendor downstairs. Which, at that, was better than later meals eaten under his father's critical eye.

At least when he was a child, Louisa used to come and see him to wish him a good night. She would always break her fast with him in the nursery and often sneak him up a snack in the middle of the day, when the tutor went home for his own meal.

She left before Barney turned ten, disowned by her father for the crime of giving her passionate support to a cause he abhorred, a sin she compounded by marrying Daniel's father, who was not just an abolitionist but black and an ex-slave.

Barney remembered the lonely years thereafter, and was determined to give her son better memories than Barney had.

So far, it had not been a conspicuous success. Daniel answered any direct question as briefly as possible, polite but taciturn. He never offered conversation of his own, and always asked for permission to leave the table as soon as he had cleared his plate. Barney expected even more reticence tonight, since they had still not had time to address the trespass against Mrs. Fullerton.

Barney was startled, then, when Daniel volunteered a remark. "Miss Conroy is very kind."

Barney's own mind had been on Miss Conroy. Daniel couldn't possibly know his uncle's scandalous thoughts, and just as well, too.

"She is," he replied. "Annie likes her, too." He'd arrived back from the tour of the church to find Annie awake and sitting on Miss Conroy's knee, being bounced and tickled, while the lady carried on a conversation with Daniel.

"She likes Annie. And she is nice to me, too." The last sentence was more wistful than truculent. *Damn Mrs. Fullerton and the old tabbies who supported her. I must tell her that this persecution cannot continue.* If only Daniel hadn't taken his own revenge!

Daniel was pursuing another line of thought. "The earl and his sister plan to leave as soon as they can. They have to sail to the Low Countries, Miss Conroy said. The earl has been sent by the Prince Regent."

"Miss Conroy will not be here long then," Barney replied. He hardly knew the woman. His sinking feeling made no sense. Yes, she was pretty and kind and brave. From her speech and carriage, she was a lady by birth and training even if circumstances had forced her to work for a living. But nothing could come of his admiration. He was nobody. A country curate, with little income and no security—it was highly possible that taking in his sister's children would lead to his dismissal, since Mr. Somerville senior had declared them no grandchildren of his.

Daniel broke into his thoughts, a thread of pleading in his tone. "She doesn't want to go, Uncle Barney. She is afraid of being sick again."

She'd joked about setting down roots. Gallant lady. "She should tell Lady Felicity." Lady Felicity's concern for her maid appeared genuine. If she knew of Miss Conroy's fears, surely she would arrange to send the maid home.

He said as much to Daniel, who shook his head. "She gets sick in coaches, too. She should stay here, Uncle Barney."

Barney regarded Daniel suspiciously. That was two 'Uncle Barney's' in one conversation.

The boy returned a limpid look, eyes wide and innocent. "We should hire her. You need someone to look after Annie, and everyone who can be spared from cleaning up after the storm is working at the inn or taking in boarders."

Barney squelched his own immediate enthusiasm for the idea. "She has a job, Daniel, and that job will take her away in a few days." No point in explaining to Daniel the difference in status between personal maid to an aristocratic lady and nursemaid to a country curate. Not when it was more to the point that he could barely afford the shillings he paid to the neighbors for their occasional services in the nursery, let alone the full-time wages of an expensive London servant.

The boy clenched his teeth on whatever protest he was going to make and subsided, his shoulders drooping. Barney couldn't stand the dejection. "We'll find someone, Daniel. Meanwhile, we are managing, are we not?"

Daniel sniffed his disbelief. "Not in this village, we won't. Mrs. Fullerton..." He trailed off, as if suddenly conscious of a tactical error.

A thought flowered full blown, and Barney suddenly knew how to address Daniel's misbehavior. And well-overdue, too. "Mrs. Fullerton. Ah, yes. I've been meaning to talk to you about that."

Daniel's lips tightened.

"Daniel, if you had left me to deal with Mrs. Fullerton, a few of the villagers would have followed her lead, and some may have stuck by her once I and others in the community made my opinion clear. But she doesn't have as much support as she thinks she does."

The boy jutted out his chin and objected. "You weren't doing anything."

Barney sighed. "I was, but I should have realized you have no reason to trust me. If I had told you that I had met with Mrs. Fullerton privately to reprimand her, would you have trusted me to deal with her after what she said yesterday morning?"

Daniel's shoulders hunched more and he mumbled into his jacket. "Don't know."

Time to lay it on the line. *Daniel is a bright boy. He will understand what he has done if I explain it.* "Each time you do something to revenge yourself on Mrs. Fullerton, you make it harder for me to solve the problem, and harder for you and your sister to be accepted in this community."

Daniel's head came up at that, his eyes aflame. "It isn't fair, Uncle Barney!" The universal cry of those who fight for justice. His parents would be proud of him. He drooped again, into the ubiquitous wail of a child. "She started it."

Both of his statements were true, but that wasn't the point. "Your grandmother used to tell me that life is not fair, and that was all the more reason why we humans must be so. What do you think you have achieved by the tricks you have played on Mrs. Fullerton? Have you changed her mind?"

That caught Daniel's attention. He looked up and shook his head.

"Have you won the respect and support of the other adults in the community?"

Another shake, this one reluctant.

"Have you made it easier to find a nursemaid for Annie?"

Daniel shifted, uneasily. "Miss Conroy said the same. She said my cause was righteous but my strategy was all wrong and my motives were suspect."

Did she, indeed? And how interesting that Daniel had discussed the situation with the lady. Barney set his feelings about that aside to examine at another time. "Miss Conroy is right. Do you understand what was wrong with your strategy and what your motives were?"

Daniel answered the second question first. "I was mad at Mrs. Fullerton. I didn't want to change her. I wanted to embarrass and hurt her."

Barney nodded. "Like she did you. But why should you care what an ignorant old woman says, Daniel? You know your parents loved each other and you, that they were married, that you are a fine lad, and one to be proud of."

Daniel shrugged. "I haven't behaved like it, Miss Conroy says. The other boys won't let me play with them, now, and people who were nice to me when we first came look at me like I am a bad egg. Miss Conroy says a better strategy would have been to behave extra well so people could see that Mrs. Fullerton is a nasty old besom full of her own bile."

He caught the admonishment in Barney's expression and rushed in before Barney could open his mouth. "That's what Miss Conroy called her."

"Probably better not to repeat it," Barney managed. *Right though Miss Conroy is.* "What do we do now?" he asked, speaking more to himself than the boy. "There have to be consequences, Daniel."

Daniel nodded, with a deep sigh. "I need to be punished," he agreed. He hunched his shoulders again, as if to make himself smaller, his voice shrinking, too. "Will you beat me?"

Barney flung out a hand in his revulsion, shoving the idea away, and Daniel flinched. Barney softened his voice. "I won't beat you. I don't believe that beating solves anything." *Someone has beaten you, though. I recognize that flinch. Your step-father?*

Daniel shrugged. "What, then?"

What, indeed? Another inspiration, this one born of desperation. "You tell me. It needs to be something you don't want to do, that will be useful to me and the village, and that will show the village, including Mrs. Fullerton, that you are sorry. Think about it, Daniel, and let me know."

CHAPTER 4

The next day dawned fine and clear. Theo went down to the kitchen after Lady Felicity joined her brother for breakfast, and was enjoying a second cup of tea when one of the inn maids hurried in to say Lady Felicity wanted her immediately.

Up in her bedchamber, her ladyship had already pulled out one of her favorite walking gowns. "Help me change, Theo. A party is walking up the coast to see how easily the road can be cleared, and Hythe says they will leave without me if I am not down in fifteen minutes."

They did it in ten, though it took another minute to finish pinning Lady Felicity's hair up under a short-brimmed hat that tied firmly to the side of the chin. "Take the rest of the morning to yourself," Lady Felicity commanded. "We won't be back before noon." She whisked out of the room, leaving her maid to tidy away the abandoned morning dress and indoor slippers.

When they were in London, Lady Felicity changed five or six times a day, as she went from one activity to another, sweeping into her chambers in a rush at a moment's notice to prepare for the next event. "Quick, Theo, my green habit with the hussar jacket. I am going riding with the Earl of Hayhurst to see if I can persuade him to donate to Sophia's village." "Hurry, Theo. I have to leave for

Lady Hamner's ball in less than an hour. The ladies' committee ran over time." "The purple walking dress, Theo. No, the other one, with the lace collar. I am going to see a balloon ascension. What fun!"

Lady Felicity was not just a social butterfly (though she was that). She was her brother's hostess, a reformer devoted to several causes, and an inveterate writer of letters. Her energy seemed inexhaustible, but Theo's was not. She usually spent her weekly half day asleep. A few hours to herself to do as she pleased was a special gift indeed.

"I'll go take a look at the church," Theo decided. Today, she was feeling well again, free of the headache that had plagued her the previous day, but the thought of the coming travel darkened her mental horizons, casting a shadow over her enjoyment of the unaccustomed leisure to stroll through the village.

When she reached the church, the big carved front doors stood open. Theo stepped under the arch and into the cool interior. The nave was in gloom, but beams of sun from high windows sent bands of light across the nave, crossing and chancel. Mr. Somerville moved in and out of the shadows as he walked toward her from the chancel, a smile blossoming as he noticed her.

"Miss Conroy! This is an unexpected pleasure."

Her own lips curved in response to the welcome in his eyes and voice. "Good morning, Mr. Somerville."

He stopped a couple of feet from her, and Theo almost put out her hands for him to clasp, catching herself from such forward behavior just in time.

"Are you on an errand for your mistress?" The words acted as a splash of cold water. Not enjoyable, but useful in reminding her that she was a servant, and far beneath a gentleman such as Mr. Somerville.

"No, sir. Lady Felicity has gone with the expedition to test the road toward Yarmouth, and has given me the day to myself. I came to see the church."

"Let me show you, then." Mr. Somerville offered his arm, as if she was still a lady.

Theo hesitated a moment, fully aware of the risk to her hard-won equanimity. She had come to terms with being the sacrifice on the altar of her family's comfort, but Mr. Somerville reminded her of the cost she paid.

His face fell and his arm started to drop. Without allowing herself a moment longer for consideration, Theo reached out to lay her hand on the offered limb. "Thank you. I would be grateful, if you have the time to spare."

"The gratitude is on my side, Miss Conroy," Mr. Somerville insisted, as he escorted her further into the church. "Your words about what he has been up to seem to have made a profound impression on my nephew."

Theo frowned. "I wish I could make an impression on the nasty woman who has been persecuting him." The words had escaped without her thinking. She glanced up at Mr. Somerville, expecting to see censure, and was startled at his expression. Surely, he was not suppressing a grin?

"That was un-Christian," she admitted.

"I agree. Mrs. Fullerton has behaved in a most un-Christian manner, though I will admit that Daniel's response to her unkind remarks has also been wrong." They had stopped part way down the nave, and he fixed his gaze high up on the wall before continuing. "I must confess, it was only last night that I thought of suggesting that it was also poor strategy. This past two weeks and more, I have been telling him that his behavior was naughty, but apparently you realized far sooner than I that pointing out the negative results was the key to getting him to stop."

Theo shrugged. "From what he said, he was motivated by the insult to his parents and his sister. I thought to set him thinking about how his reaction hurt the very family he wanted to protect." She looked up into fine eyes shining with an appreciation that shortened her breath, so that she had to swallow before she continued. "He is a fine boy, Mr. Somerville. You must be very proud of him."

He may have said something, but she was aware only of his eyes, and of the warmth spreading through her body, until he jerked as if someone had poked him with a stick, and looked around him as if finding his bearings. "The, ah, church. Yes. We're very proud of our Norman drawings—up above the windows. They're clearer on the north, with the southern light on them, but they can be found on both sides. Those on this side tell the story of…"

Theo allowed him to escort her through the church, asking the occasional question, enjoying the fine arches and Mr. Somerville's knowledge, all the time wondering what had just happened. She was confident a man like Mr. Somerville would not try to take advantage of a servant, but what else could there be between them?

Barney lingered over showing Miss Conroy the church, reluctant to see her leave. She exclaimed over the very features of the church he liked best, and laughed when he tried a couple of feeble jests. She asked after Annie and Daniel, too. Before long, he found himself telling her about his sister. "Louisa was nine years my elder, and was a little mother to me before I went to school. She left home when I was ten, and we lost touch until only a few months ago. She had been widowed for a second time, and was already suffering the malady that killed her."

Miss Conroy didn't need to know that their father had kept him from receiving Louisa's letters, even instructing the school to burn them unopened. The Reverend Mr. Matthias Somerville had no wish for his rebellious daughter to influence the son he was raising in his own image.

"My father was—is—very conscious of appearances and reputation," he said. His father believed that the orders of society had been ordained by God, with royalty and peers of the realm at the top, Matthias Somerville and others like him a few rungs lower, and most of the rest of the population born to serve. He had never understood the burning sense of injustice that drove his daughter to campaign for better working conditions, rights for women, and the abolition of slavery.

"Mine, too," Miss Conroy said, and a few questions soon had her sharing her stories of growing up in a vicarage in the midlands, the middle daughter of five. From the sound of it, her father was clinging on to gentry status by a fingernail, a poor country parson with insufficient connections or influence to gain a living of his own, and therefore stuck with working in place of a wealthier minister with more than one parish, or with interests outside of his calling and the money to pay someone else to carry out parish obligations on his behalf.

Much like Barney, in fact, but at least he looked after one of his father's livings, and would probably inherit it when his father was gone. Provided he married the bride his father chose for him. Provided his father didn't dismiss him for the crime of taking in Daniel and Annabelle.

If Barney had to leave Fenwick on Sea, he was unlikely to find another post as a cleric. He would have to find other employment to support his wards. As if she could read his mind, Miss Conroy asked, "What made you decide to become ordained, Mr. Somerville?"

"My father always assumed I would follow in his footsteps," Barney explained. An earl's grandson, his father had a small allowance as well as several livings. But the allowance would die with Barney's father. All he had to leave his son was his influence with his own patrons so that Barney could become vicar after him.

Not that Barney had wanted, at first, to be ordained. "My greatest joy as a boy was following the physician around while he visited the sick. Indeed, I thought of being a physician myself."

But that was only a small part of the story. He wanted Miss Conroy to know the truth. He had only known her for a couple of days, but long enough. In another time and place, if he had a secure living that was not dependent on the goodwill of a man without any, she was the woman above all others that he might have courted. "When I went up to university, I studied theology as instructed and discovered a vocation. To serve a parish as pastor—this is what I was made for."

Would she smirk as some of his contemporaries had when he first spoke of his vocation? But she was herself the daughter of a vicar, and he had seen her prayer book that first night when she was in his care in the make-shift hospital at the inn. Surely, she will understand? When she nodded and smiled, he released the breath he hadn't known he was holding.

Her smile stayed with him after she hurried away, having glimpsed the returning exploratory party from the top of the tower. "What does it mean?" he asked God. "She could be my heart's desire, so why send her here now? Only you know if I will be allowed to stay in the parish, and even if I am, my stipend is barely enough to keep me and the two children, and certainly not enough to pay for the servant I need to look after them properly. I can't possibly court a woman when I can't afford a wife."

God has a plan, his tutors would have said, but it isn't given to us to know what it is. Barney shook his head and trudged next door to the vicarage to check that Daniel had everything in hand. He wasn't looking forward to his next task, but he could put off the visit to Mrs. Fullerton for no longer.

But after the slog through the mud to Morpeth Manor, the housekeeper refused to speak with him. Friends of her employer had descended on the manor seeking a refuge from the storm, and she declared herself too busy to deal with personal business. Barney left Daniel's apology letter, stopped rehearsing his own mixture of excuses and admonishments, and returned home.

If not for the blessing that was Miss Conroy, he would have fretted for the rest of the evening about his failure to resolve things with the manor's housekeeper. Instead, he found himself remembering bits of his conversation with the enchanting lady's maid, or the appealing arch of her neck as she looking up at the murals, or her laughing eyes as they shared stories about childhood mischief.

Given the circumstances, he could not with honor explore the connection between them. But how he wished circumstances were different.

As Theo helped her change out of her mud-spattered skirts, Lady Felicity reported that the road to the north had crumbled into the sea in several places and was blocked in others. "We managed to go around the first hole in the road, and over the first two landslides, but in the end, we had to turn back. The whole road is gone for fifty yards. I hope some of the other parties have had better luck."

Long locks of her ladyship's hair had slipped out of the smooth coil that fitted under the pert shako that matched the habit. She sat before the mirror so that Theo could take it all down, brush out the tangles, and redress it in a more formal style for the rest of the afternoon.

"What did you do with your morning, Theo, dear? I hope you didn't overdo things."

"I am fully recovered, my lady," Theo protested.

Lady Felicity caught her eye reflected in the mirror, and put up a hand to touch Theo's where it stilled in Lady Felicity's hair. "You worried me. I should never have dragged you off to sea when I know how sick you get when you travel."

"I chose to accompany you, my lady." Theo shrugged, and resumed combing and pinning. "I thought it would be exciting to see another country."

Lady Felicity's eyes narrowed as she frowned at herself in the mirror. "Hythe says we will probably need to leave by sea. He can't wait until the roads are fit for travel, he says. He is talking to the fishermen to see if anyone is willing to take us to Yarmouth." She grimaced even as Theo's stomach twinged at the mere thought of going back on a boat.

Lady Felicity ripped the curl Theo was pinning from Theo's hands as she turned to look directly at her maid. "Theo, Hythe and I think you should stay here until the roads open again, then make your way back to London."

I'm being dismissed? Theo blinked rapidly, her mind spinning to no purpose as she tried to process the shock. Something of that must have shown on her face, because Lady Felicity reached up to take her hands. "I am sending you to our town house in London, Theo. I thought you could completely review my wardrobe there, and then tour around the rest of our houses and review those, also. Refurbish my favorites and make lists of what needs to be replaced. Get rid of anything that is clearly never going to be worn again. Someone will find it useful."

Theo nodded, slowly. It was a task they had discussed before, but Lady Felicity was always too busy to turn her mind to it. It could wait till they returned from the Low Countries, however. Indeed, replacements would need to wait, since who knew how long Lady Felicity would be overseas and fashions might change. She should protest, rather than giving in to the sense of relief that flooded her.

Lady Felicity didn't wait for her to respond, continuing to talk even as she turned back to the mirror so that Theo could continue to dress her mistress's hair with hands made heavy by the thoughts she hadn't expressed.

"Also," her ladyship said, "we talked about updating my bedroom at Belvoir Hall? I am putting you in charge of that project. And Hythe says, while you are about that, you might as well update the Master Suite. He has made some small changes to his own chambers, but they need a complete overhaul. And the Mistress's rooms have not been redecorated since my mother did them before I was born, so it is high time to refresh everything."

More make-work, or work for the housekeeper or house steward—though Theo probably knew Lord Hythe's taste nearly as well as she knew Lady Felicity's.

"But you need a maid, my lady." Theo could overcome her fear of another sea voyage. Somehow. She couldn't leave Lady Felicity in the lurch, and—in any case—she hated the thought of someone else taking her place as the lady's handmaiden.

Lady Felicity showed no awareness of Theo's mixed feelings. "I have already spoken to the youngest daughter of the innkeeper. She did my hair and looked after my clothes while you were incapacitated, and she would love the opportunity to come with me. Her parents have agreed to let her go." She turned her head again, but by now the curls were all fixed in place so she didn't undo any of Theo's work.

"She has a lot to learn, Theo. I will need you to work with her in the next day or so."

It was decided, then. No point in arguing. "How long..." Theo had to clear her throat before she could continue. "How long before you leave, my lady?"

They were interrupted by a knock on the door. Theo opened to let Lord Hythe inside. "Fliss, Lord Glenaire has sent a yacht to take the majors to Ostend. They'll take us, too, but they won't wait. Can you be on the beach in ten minutes?" The majors were two officers stranded here in the inn when their coach had been diverted by floods.

Fortunately, Theo had kept most of Lady Felicity's things packed. Hythe directed the servants who accompanied him to carry the main trunk down while her ladyship and Theo gathered the few items left out around the room.

They hurried down the stairs to the courtyard, where the luggage was being tied onto a handcart and the innkeeper's daughter waited, bouncing on her toes with excitement, a large bag in one hand.

"Shove that on the cart and let's go," Hythe commanded her, and led the way out the back gate of the stable yard and across the garden to the path over the sand dunes. Theo followed the party, but Lady Felicity put out a hand to stop her.

"No point in coming down to the beach, Theo. Hythe has left money for you to board in the village. Several respectable women offer rooms, and you would be more comfortable than being alone at the inn, but if you wish to stay here, Mr. and Mrs. Brewster have promised to make sure you are safe."

"Hurry up, Fliss," Hythe called.

Felicity waved him off. "It may be a week or more until it is safe to travel," she continued. "Even then, I would like you to wait for one of Hythe's carriages to be sent from London. Or one of Sutton's. I'll send a letter to Sophia from Ostend and tell her what has happened."

Sophia, the Countess of Sutton, was Lady Felicity's elder sister, and had been the one to employ Theo as her maid five years ago. She'd left Theo with Felicity when she married, because of Theo's travel sickness. The Earl of Sutton traveled frequently and fast in the service of his father, the Duke of Winshire, and Sophia had needed a maid who could take the pace.

Now my stupid stomach has made me fail again.

"Think of it as a holiday, Theo," Lady Felicity insisted. "You'll have fun, dear Theo." She dropped a kiss on her maid's cheek and hurried away up the path, waving again at Hythe who was waiting for her at the top of the dune.

Theo sank onto one of the garden benches, struggling to come to terms with the unexpected changes to her future.

CHAPTER 5

O n Tuesday afternoon, some of the inn's guests were rowed
offshore to a sloop bound for Ostend. Barney saw two women
clambering aboard, identifiable in the distance only by their skirts and
bonnets. The children watching from shore knew all about it. The
large major and the limping major had gone, and so had the grand earl
and his sister. Barney continued down the beach to an isolated cottage
south of the village, swallowing the sorrow that welled in his throat
and sending up a silent request for Miss Conroy to be spared the worst
of the *mal de mer*.

He echoed that prayer from time to time as he sat through the
night by Jasper Pentney, an elderly fisherman who was dying. "Go out
with the tide, he will," said the man's daughter, who had picked her
way through the flooded marshes from an outlying farm.

"Always did," Mrs. Pentney agreed. "Always come back, afore." As
bent and wrinkled as her man, she faced this final separation with a
stoic expression and moist eyes. "This time, I'll 'ave to follow."

When the tide turned several hours before dawn, Pentney gave his
wife's hand a final squeeze and stepped out onto the eternal tide.
Barney stayed with the grieving wife and daughter. He'd see the night
out with them, and wait until family and friends came to give their

support, which wasn't going to happen while it was too dark to see the way.

As the night slowly gave way to dawn, Barney's thoughts turned more often than appropriate to Miss Conroy and her voyage, and he had to wrench them back. He fretted, too, over Daniel and Annie. They would have gone to the inn for their evening meal, and Daniel was responsible enough and capable enough to look after Annie in his absence.

He stayed for a cup of tea, made by the nearest neighbor, who arrived shortly after sunrise. One by one, others came, word of the man's death spreading by some alchemy of villages. Neighbors. Old fishing colleagues and drinking friends. Grandchildren from the marsh farm, and even a great-grandchild on his mother's hip.

Barney wouldn't be needed until the funeral, and was returning from the kitchen-living room to the single bedroom to make his farewells when the daughter gave a cry. "Ma!" Mrs. Pentney slumped forward in her chair, her hand still in her husband's, her head on the bed beside him. While others talked, she had quietly followed him into eternity.

It was nearly noon before Barney felt he could leave. Back at the vicarage, Daniel was feeding Annie in the kitchen. The floor was swept, and a pot of something stood on a trivet at the edge of the fire.

"That smells good," Barney said, as he took off his hat and bent over to kiss the top of Annie's head. Daniel's shy smile prevented Barney from making the mistake of asking whether the daily woman had made the meal. They had apparently lost her to the inn and other clients, though each time Barney saw her, she promised to be there the next day.

But Daniel had decided that part of his reparation should be looking after Annie and the house in her absence. The other part, the dignified written apology to Mrs. Fullerton that Barney had delivered the day before, had fallen into silence.

Barney had already known that Daniel knew how to look after his sister, and had a basic competence at housekeeping and simple kitchen tasks. "I used to help my mother," Daniel had explained. Like Barney, he could manage breakfasts of bacon, eggs, sausages—anything that could be cooked in a pan over the fire. But their staple diet when Mrs. Withers failed to arrive was gifts from parishioners and pies and bread from the bakery. The stew (or was it soup?) was a new departure, and welcome, since the gifts dried up once Daniel and Mrs. Fullerton began their feud.

It was stew served with bread, and delicious. Barney could compliment it with enthusiasm, and Daniel's broadening smile showed that he knew the praise was sincere.

"I don't know what I would have done without you, Daniel."

The boy shrugged. "It wasn't that hard. Just had to cut everything up and ask up at the inn how long to put it on for."

"It is very welcome after being up through the night, but I don't mean just the stew, appreciated though it is. You have done magnificently, looking after Annie by yourself and keeping the house clean. I'll tell you what. Why don't you take some time for yourself, and Annie and I will have a nap together?"

Daniel looked as if he might argue, but then his eyes lit up. "I might go back up to the inn. Mrs. Brewster is going to be making pies this afternoon, and if I help, she will teach me."

Barney widened his eyes. He had thought Daniel might want to rush off to the sand dunes with friends or hang around the stables or smithy till they let him help with the horses. "You don't have to work all the time, Daniel. You're allowed time off to have fun."

"Cooking is fun." Daniel leaned closer over the table. "I thought it was a woman's job, but Miss Conroy says that some of the most famous cooks are men. She knows a cook who married the cousin of a duchess, and he has a shop where people pay to eat their dinner. He is French, but Miss Conroy says some Englishmen are cooks, too."

He reached across the table for Barney's empty bowl to stack it with his own.

"Miss Conroy is going to have lessons, too," he said over his shoulder, as he headed for the scullery.

Barney lifted Annie from her chair and followed Daniel into the scullery. "Miss Conroy left for the Continent yesterday afternoon with her mistress and Lord Hythe."

Daniel shook his head. "No, she didn't. One of the Miss Brewsters went with the sloop to be her ladyship's maid. Miss Conroy is staying in the village until the roads reopen. She moved into a room at Mrs. Peabody's this morning."

۞

Theo knew it was forward, but she was going to do it anyway. Despite the internal voices chorusing in her ear—her mother's peevish tones almost drowned beneath the more strident demands of the countess— she was going to offer Mr. Somerville her help.

Think of your reputation, Theodora. A Teatime Tattler *reporter in the village, they say! A single man, even if he is a member of the cloth. Even for a maid, reputation is everything. You cannot think of visiting Mr. Somerville alone, let alone staying in his house without a chaperone.*

According to Mrs. Peabody, Mr. Somerville had been unable to find a nursemaid and had been abandoned by the woman who cooked and cleaned for him. He was managing his clerical duties, his household, and the care of his wards with no more help than young Daniel could provide. And assisting Dr Roth with the remaining patients at the inn.

You stupid girl. He must have done something to deserve the way the community is treating him. Let him work out his own troubles. You have enough to worry about, being left behind by your mistress. Who wants a maid who cannot travel? I have told you a hundred times, you should have more fortitude, Theodora.

Mrs. Peabody had been a fount of information. Only some of the villagers sided with Mrs. Fullerton in her campaign to evict Daniel from the village. Others were just too busy to concern themselves as long as Mr. Somerville seemed to be coping. Still more were afraid to take his part lest they lose the custom of the manor. A few, Mrs. Peabody among them, thought it their Christian duty to help the poor man out, but had not quite taken the first step that would deepen the divide between neighbors.

The voices from her girlhood continued to rant, and Theo continued to ignore them.

As soon as the roads can be traveled, you must go home and look after your father.

He had summoned her to do so just six months ago, his letter explaining that she was the only one of his daughters to have no real obligations. *Better be of use at home than gad about London as someone else's servant.*

Do as you are told, for once in your life, said her internal persecutors.

She had been an obedient daughter all her life, and a humble and loyal servant since she was fifteen. She had never thought of rebelling until her eldest sister put the idea into her head after their mother's funeral.

"If I am ever in doubt about the right thing to do," Theo had said, "I just imagine what Mother and the Countess would tell me."

Her sister had raised both brows so they disappeared into the little fringe of curls that peeked from her frivolous lace cap. "Mother? But she was of no more than modest understanding, and the countess was a bully, darling Theo. I have never forgiven them for the way they used you. Please do not continue to allow them to do so even after they are gone."

Theo had opened her mouth to disagree, then closed it again as the truth her sister had spoken settled into her consciousness.

Ever since then, though her memories of her two mentors continued to plague her with advice and admonishment, she had refused to allow them to cow her. That was why she didn't go home to care for Papa when he sent for her. That was why she was knocking on the door of the vicarage today.

What would Lady Sutton say about her behavior? She was a far greater lady than the countess; from one of England's oldest families, and married to the eldest son of a duke. Theo thought that Lady Sutton would approve.

No one was answering. Theo knocked again. Still nothing.

Perhaps Mr. Somerville is out? Theo grasped hold of the fleeting edges of her courage and squared her shoulders. She would try again later. But as she turned away, she heard a sound from within the house; a sort of whimpering moan, coming closer.

After a moment, the door opened. Mr. Somerville stood in the doorway, shrugging into his jacket while his arm on the other side supported a miserable little girl who clung to him with one cheek resting against his shoulder. Tears trickled down the side of the face that was showing, mingling with strands of hair and sticky substances better left unexamined.

Mr. Somerville patted her back, swaying to and fro. "Hush, Annie. Hush. Miss Conroy! I beg your pardon. I cannot put her down, you see. She is unwell. A minor ague, but..."

Annie rubbed at her ear and wailed louder.

Theo's doubts melted like mist in the sun. "Poor little girl. May I come in, Mr. Somerville?"

He stood for a second more, blinking as if confused, then stepped back from the doorway. "Of course. Perhaps you would step into my study? How may I help you, Miss Conroy?" His hair stood up in different directions, as if he had slept on it and failed to brush. He had dark shadows under his eyes, and the buttons on his waistcoat did not align.

"I am here to help you." Theo picked up the rug that trailed over a chair and tucked it around Annie, ignoring the tingling sensation that shot up her arm when her hand brushed Mr. Somerville's arm. "I have heard that you are having trouble finding servants, and I find myself at leisure, so I have come to do whatever you need to make you and your wards more comfortable."

"Miss Conroy! That's very kind of you, but I cannot ask you to..."

"You are not asking me, Mr. Somerville. I am offering. I can see that Annie is not feeling inclined to be comforted by anyone but you, so if you tell me what is most urgent, I will do it."

He was shaking his head, more in bewilderment than negation. "You are very kind, but..."

"No 'buts'," Theo insisted. "You and Daniel need help, Mr. Somerville, and it appears your parishioners are all too busy to be of service."

She could not resist the wry emphasis on the word busy, but Mr. Somerville did not comment. "Well." He looked around as if expecting to see a job list somewhere. "Thank you, then. Perhaps...?" He had not stopped the patting and swaying, but still Annie complained in a shrill continuous whine.

"Some soup for Annie?" Theo suggested. "Or a little honey in warm water, perhaps? What about you, sir? When did you last eat?"

Whether it was the thought of food or Theo's refusal to take 'no' for an answer, Mr. Somerville suddenly surrendered, his worried frown clearing. Even his gentle smile was tired, but it reached his eyes. "If you are to be my rescuing angel, will you not call me Barney? A little honey in water sounds like an excellent idea, and I would be grateful for some bread and cheese, if you would be so kind."

Theodora Conroy. Theodora was a pretty name, but she'd asked to be called Theo. Barney was not about to argue with a woman who had made him a cup of tea to eat with his bread and cheese. She then cleaned up the dishes Daniel had left when Barney sent him out to try to beg some willow-bark tea off anyone in the village who might have some to spare, and rummaged through the larder until she found the ingredients for the pot of soup that was now simmering on the fire.

She'd also found time to fetch warm water and a flannel so that Barney could wash Annie's face, and then a change of clothes for the little girl. "For I always feel better, when I am unwell, once I have washed and am in clean clothes."

Theo then gently rubbed a flannel over Annie's body while Barney sat in the rocking chair by the kitchen fire, turning the child so that Theo could reach every part of her. Once the lady had helped Barney dress her again in a clean nightgown and wrapped her in the cozy rug, Annie dropped off to sleep snuggled into Barney's shoulder. Barney hadn't realized how much her vocal distress had rubbed at his nerves until the noise stopped.

In the silence, he realized that Daniel had been gone for over an hour, and opened his mouth to suggest that Theo stay with Annie, so he could go and look for his nephew. At that moment, he heard someone at the kitchen door, and Daniel burst into the room.

"I'm sorry it took me so long, Uncle Barney. Dr Roth had no willow-bark left, Mrs. Brewster has used up all her supplies and so has Mrs. Peabody, and Mrs. Gatesby was on her rounds. I had to go right out to Cockerdon's farm before I caught up with her." He held out the bag he had been hugging to his chest.

"I'll take it," Theo said, and Daniel spun round, his eyes widening. "Miss Conroy. I didn't see you."

Daniel handed the bag over. "The green bottle has willow-bark extract. Mrs. Gatesby says to put no more than ten drops in warm water, and sweeten it with honey." He followed Theo to the fire as she bent to move the kettle back to the flame. "She didn't have much extract left. The Thurston children have the ague, and so do Widow Runacres and the Casham brothers. The paper bag has dried willow bark you can use to make tea or extract." He held up a brown bottle.

"This is the oil you asked for, Uncle Barney. Almond, they said at the store."

Barney continued to rock, one hand supporting Annie's buttocks and the other gently patting her back. "Well done, Daniel."

"Well done, indeed," Theo agreed. "Now, you need to get into dry clothes, warm by the fire, and have a hot drink and some of my soup, or we'll have you down with the ague, too."

Daniel shot Barney a questioning look. "Miss Conroy has offered to help us out, Daniel. For today."

"For as long as you need me," Theo shot back.

Daniel rewarded the lady with a broad smile. "Thank you, Miss Conroy."

"Thank me by getting yourself changed, young man." She smiled at Barney over Daniel's head, and his lips tugged into a smile in response. He really must discourage her from coming back tomorrow. Seeing her bustle around, looking after him and his wards, set him dreaming of things that could not be.

CHAPTER 6

By Sunday, Annie's temperature was back to normal and she was no longer rubbing at her ears, though she was still listless and inclined to sleep. Daniel, though, had woken up that morning with heavy eyes, a congested nose, and a hacking cough.

Barney was grateful he hadn't worked harder to dissuade Theo from her self-appointed ministry. After the past few days, Annie went to her as willingly as to Barney, and she had even taken to watching out the window in the morning for Theo to arrive.

Barney went off to morning service confident that he left the children in safe hands. There were gaps in the congregation, including the families Daniel had named. Barney made a mental note of the absentees so he could make a pastoral visit. A medical one, too, come to that. Annie's illness had been slight and she had recovered quickly, but knock-me-down fever, as the country-folk called the ague, could be hard, especially on the elderly.

On the steps of the church after the service, he cast a quick glance over to the vicarage. He had asked Theo to put a scarf in the window if she needed him to return immediately, but he wasn't surprised the window was empty. Theo was highly competent, and both children loved her. He loved her himself, much good it would do him.

Mrs. Peabody was the first to approach him, asking after Annie and talking loudly about her boarder's generous Christian response to the vicar's need for childcare. Barney suppressed the smile that wanted to form at the twinkle in the landlady's eye. Her warm praise for Theo was a rebuke to the other women of the parish, as she well knew.

Those who heard knew it, too, several of them coming up to join the discussion with their own enquiries about his wards, each managing to insert into the conversation the reasons why they were not available to offer their own help. "But I have baked some pies with the last of the stored apples, vicar," said one. "I shall bring one over for your lunch. It may be just the thing to tempt young Daniel's appetite."

Not to be outdone, some of the other parishioners declared their intention of feeding the vicarage. If they followed through, Barney and his household would not have to cook or even shop for a week.

He was pleased, though, when they stopped competing to prove their generosity and moved on to discussing what had been happening in the village and the wider parish during the last few days. Barney apologized for his absence, but they all assured him that they understood.

"You need a nursemaid for the little girl," Mrs. Brewster opined.

"He needs a wife," said Mrs. Peabody.

One was as impossible as the other. His income was barely adequate for himself, and stretching it to cover two children had left great gaping holes in his budget through which had dropped everything that could possibly be construed as unnecessary. He could just about pay the wages of a nursemaid on his stipend, if he gave up purchasing books and made his shirts and socks, already several years old, do for another season. Hunt as he would, he had not been able to find a woman who would live in his bachelor household and work for her keep and the pittance he could afford.

As for a wife, no woman could be expected to take on an impoverished curate. Especially one whose tenure depended on an irascible father who had never forgiven the defiance of the daughter whose children Barney had inherited.

His thoughts, which never flitted far from the lovely Theodora Conroy, mapped out a whole future for the pair of them in a series of flashes. Theo in the vicarage pew with the children either side of her. Theo on his arm greeting the parishioners after church. Theo at his table, her beautiful eyes shining as she listened to his practical problems or theological conundrums then responded with calm common sense. Theo in his bed, her smile just for him, her hair spread out on his pillow.

He wrenched his mind away from that thought so hard that Mrs. Peabody noticed. "Are you well, Mr. Somerville? This must have been a worrying time for you."

From somewhere, he dredged up a smile and a few commonplace remarks. Before long, he was able to extricate himself and head back to the vicarage, where Theo looked after his children and his house, and daily carved herself a larger and larger slice of his heart.

It was already too late to come out of this without heartbreak. He could only hope that he would retain his dignity and his moral compass. He should be praying that her promised transport back to London would arrive soon!

When the first road had opened to the outside world, Theo sent a message to Lord Hythe's London town house postponing her transport, and another to Lady Sutton, explaining the nature of the emergency. Lady Felicity had said she was to stay in the village until she felt ready to leave, and to regard her time here as a holiday. Theo intended to spend her holiday with Barney—that is, the vicar—and his wards.

Daniel was far sicker than Annie had been, but a less demanding patient, swallowing broth and his doses of willow-bark tea without complaint, and sleeping for much of the day. Annie was content in Theo's company as she moved from room to room, catching up on years of neglected cleaning and mending in between checking on her patient and preparing food and drink.

Not that her meagre skills as a cook were much tested. The parish had decided to reopen their hearts to their vicar, and not an hour went by but a knock on the door heralded another offering of food. The pantry was overflowing with baked goods and vegetables, with a good ham hock and a couple of ducks hanging in the meat safe and the stew or soup or pie of the day staying warm on the hearth.

They all asked after the vicar, but nodded and smiled when Theo explained he wasn't there. The ague had the parish in its grip, and Barney was in demand as both cleric and medic. He often left on his rounds as soon as Theo arrived in the morning, and seldom returned until after dinner, for even households struggling with the sickness were keen to feed their vicar.

As the days passed and Daniel's fever and cough lessened, Theo fought the temptation to pretend that this was her house, these her children; that it was her man for whom she cleaned window ledges, scoured doorsteps, picked spring flowers to brighten the house. That way lay heartbreak. She'd heard from a maid at the inn that Barney was the great grandson of an earl. A man like him need never look to the serving classes for a bride.

Sometimes, when he happened to be in the house at the same time she was, he looked at her with such warmth that she struggled to subdue the hopes she refused to entertain. Their paths crossed seldom, though, and that told her all she needed to know. He was grateful for her help as a gentleman should be, but his heart did not lift for her as hers did for him.

On the first day that Daniel was well enough to dress and take Annie out into the sun to play in the garden while Theo beat the carpets, Barney arrived home early, half supported by Arnie Arbuckle, the eldest son of the family that owned the smithy. Theo hurried to open the gate, curving her neck to peer at Barney's face. It was flushed and feverish.

"Near fell out of his gig at t'forge, Miss Conroy. It's old knock-me-down, right enough. He's hooly sick.

"Gracious! Bring him in, Mr. Arbuckle. I'll just turn down his bed for you."

Arnie's large smith hands were gentle as he stripped Barney out of his clothes, Theo fleeing to put on the kettle before the operation reached the point of scandal. Arnie followed her down the stairs a few moments later to report that the vicar was in a nightshirt and tucked under the blankets. "I can't stay, miss. Will you be right?"

"I can manage," Theo assured him. "Thank you for bringing him home, Mr. Arbuckle. The horse?"

"I'll put the gig away and stable the horse, miss. No worries there."

Theo let him out the front door, and turned to find Daniel and Annie in the doorway to the kitchen. She spoke to the anxious question in Daniel's eyes. "Your uncle has the ague. Don't worry. He is strong and will be well again soon."

Daniel swallowed before he spoke. "It is nearly time for you to go home, Miss Conroy. Will you show me what I need to do for my uncle?"

"I will, but you are not well yourself, yet. I will stay and help nurse him." It was the right thing to do. *You are dead,* she told her mother and the countess. *I don't need to listen to you anymore.*

⚜

As it turned out, Barney was much sicker than either of the children had been. Theo shared the nursing with Daniel, deputing during the day those personal services that might be embarrassing for both her and Barney if she performed them. They shared the other duties around the house, too.

Except at night. Theo insisted that Daniel sleep the night through in his own bed, since he was himself recovering, and was a growing lad, besides. She caught what sleep she could in a chair in Barney's room, waking frequently to sponge Barney's face and neck when he was too hot, and replace his blankets when he was too cold.

News of their vicar's condition must have spread through the community almost as fast as thought, for the next day, repeated knocks on the door kept her or Daniel running up and down the stairs. First, Mrs. Peabody called by to drop off a bag with Theo's hairbrush and a change of linen. After that visit, not thirty minutes went by without another knock, heralding wishes for Barney's fast recovery; another old family remedy to bring him back to health; another jug of soup or pot of stew or carefully-wrapped pie to feed the household. Some wanted only to help. Others had less benign intent. Alice, one of the servants from the inn, was one of those. She offered to help with the cleaning, and Theo might have accepted had it not been for the avid curiosity with which Alice peered over Theo's shoulder.

There was even a message from the manor. "Mrs. Fullerton sent a carriage to fetch Uncle Barney," Daniel reported. "She wants her niece to nurse him, the groom says. There's a note."

The note was an imperious demand, with no salutation beyond Theo's surname.

Conroy
Pack some nightshirts for Mr. Somerville and send him up to the manor, where he can get proper care to recover from his ague, and avoid the impropriety of being alone with a female.
Mrs. J. Fullerton
Morpeth Manor

Theo raised a brow. 'Conroy?' As a lady's maid, she could expect the courtesy of an honorific from those of similar standing in the servants' hierarchy. At least the presumptuous woman had not addressed her as Theodora.

"Can you sit with him while I pen a reply?" she asked Daniel.

She was tempted to use the housekeeper's unadorned surname as salutation, but that would be petty. She settled for:

Mrs. Fullerton
Thank you for your consideration. Mr. Somerville is too sick to move, and does not wish, in any case, to leave his wards.
Miss T. Conroy

Not that Barney was in any condition to express an opinion. Theo handed the note to the manor's groom and returned to Barney's room, where she took over the job of using a wet sponge to tenderly swab all the parts she could politely reach, in an effort to bring his temperature down.

The visits continued through the day. Mrs. Gatesby, the midwife, came by to interrogate Theo about her nursing, but would not venture into the house. "I must stay well for my clients, Miss Conroy, and will not risk possible contagion. Just continue what you are doing, my dear. Mr. Somerville is a strong young man."

"Keep the little girl away from him," she instructed. Theo nodded. She and Daniel had been doing that, taking it in turns to look after each of their charges.

Mrs. Gatesby handed over more willow bark. "Do you know how to prepare this, and the dosage to use?" Theo nodded, and the midwife continued her instructions.

"As long as the air smells clear, you might open the windows to help with cooling the poor man down." She explained that the influenza miasma had its roots in the rotting vegetation left by the receding waters of the flood. After a few more pieces of advice she released Theo to return to her nursing.

The next visitor was Mrs. Fullerton herself. Theo saw the carriage from Barney's window and left her patient to interrupt Daniel on his way down the stairs. "It's the manor again, Daniel. I'll go. Your uncle is asleep and this won't take long."

She was surprised to see the housekeeper on the doorstep, but not at all astounded by the older woman's glare. "Out of my way, Conroy. I've come to see Mr. Somerville for myself." When Theo did not move, Mrs. Fullerton stepped to one side.

Theo shifted to prevent her from sliding past. "I cannot permit that, ma'am. Mr. Somerville is asleep. Besides, you cannot wish to inhale the air of the sickroom. You must consider the wellbeing of the manor and its visitors."

Mrs. Fullerton was not passing unless she physically shoved Theo out of the way. Fortunately, she didn't try, since Theo didn't think a physical contest would fall her way. Mrs. Fullerton was taller and much larger in every dimension.

The housekeeper narrowed her eyes. "You are impertinent, Conroy. Someone should teach you your place."

Theo had not had a lot of sleep the previous night, and was, in any case, disposed to dislike the harridan who had persecuted both Daniel and Barney. "The impertinence is on your part, Mrs. Fullerton. I am lady's maid to the sister of the Earl of Hythe and not your servant. Even if I were in your master's household, which I am not, I would not be in your employ. The correct form of address is Miss Conroy, and you have no authority here. Now, if you will excuse me, I must get back to my patient."

She stepped inside, but Mrs. Fullerton put a hand on the door to prevent her from closing it. "I imagine Lady Felicity would like to know what her maid is up to in her absence: inveigling her way into the vicarage; staying the night with an unmarried man. He won't marry you, you know. A servant and the great-grandson of an earl? Ridiculous."

Theo maintained her calm façade, meeting the woman's angry eyes. "I am not entirely sure of my mistress's direction, but I imagine a letter would reach her care of her sister, the Countess of Sutton, or of her brother, the Earl of Hythe. Lady Sutton is currently in London, at the house of her father-in-law, the Duke of Winshire, and a letter to Lord Hythe might be transmitted through the Duke of Wellington. Good day, Mrs. Fullerton." She had never been fond of name dropping, but she felt an ignoble satisfaction at wielding such powerful titles at the housekeeper of a neglected manor of a minor peer.

For a moment, Theo thought she was going to have to press the door shut with Mrs. Fullerton pushing against it. But after a final glare that should have turned Theo to stone where she stood, the woman fell back. Theo had been exerting enough pressure that the door followed and the latch snicked into place.

Theo rested her forehead against it for a moment, waiting for her heart to cease pounding—and her nausea to subside.

"Miss Conroy?" Daniel's touch on her arm had her turning with a smile to reassure him and little Annie, who was perched on his hip. "Did that old... Did Mrs. Fullerton upset you, Miss Conroy?"

"A little," Theo admitted, "but only because I do not like argument."

The boy's face did not clear. "Are you going to get into trouble for helping us?" He bit at his lip. "If you could take Annie with you to Mrs. Peabody's I could look after Uncle. I don't want people to be mean to you, Miss Conroy."

What a dear lad. Theo squeezed his arm, a quick gesture of affection. "I won't be in trouble, Daniel. As long as Lady Felicity supports me, no one else matters. And she will trust my word." *I hope. She will, will she not?*

In any case, it made no difference. Daniel was not old enough to face this alone. Even as she had the thought, Theo knew she was being dishonest with herself. She was not here for Daniel, but for herself. She could not bear to be somewhere else, wondering if Barney was getting the care he needed and if he was improving.

Deep within, she was convinced that only her care could bring him alive through the illness. Because she loved him. She could admit that to herself. She loved Barnaby Somerville, even if she was a servant and far below his orbit.

CHAPTER 7

B efore he collapsed in the village, Barney had been avoiding Theo Conroy, staying out late so he didn't have to see her in his home, caring for his children. Why torture himself with visions of a future he couldn't have? Then the smith's son carried him home. Theo was waiting, and even through the daze and fatigue of the illness, Barney sensed the rightness of her presence in his home.

He'd loved puzzles when he was a boy, treasuring that moment when he moved the piece that disclosed the secret of the whole. He felt the same sense now. He saw Theo and everything fitted. He just knew that she was the secret to his happiness—and his wards'.

He captured images of her as his fever mounted. Theo in his doorway, her adorable brows creased in concern before she hurried to assist Arnie to carry him up the stairs to bed. Theo bent over his bed, sponging him with a damp cloth. Theo, her face so red that he could detect the blush by candlelight, helping him to attend to his bladder in the middle of the night. Less alarmingly, Theo's face showing above the rug she'd pulled around herself as she slept in the chair beside his bed.

He could not have said how long he was sick. Much of the time, he slept. Sometimes, he was conscious enough to smile at his ministering angel, or at Daniel, who also took a turn at his care. Sometimes, he had no idea whether he was awake or asleep, as the world around him warped in strange ways. His whole body burned in the flames that leapt around him or froze in a land of ice. Monsters crowded him, many of them with his father's face or Mrs. Fullerton's voice.

Time and again, Theo's voice and hand drew him out of a nightmare and back into the oasis of peace that surrounded her.

At last, he woke with his mind clear. His throat felt raw and his head throbbed a little and, when he tried to move, his limbs were heavy as lead, but the darkness no longer plagued him, and he was no longer aflame or freezing, but cozily warm.

Daniel sat looking out the window. The lad looked tired. Had he really been helping with the nursing? He was barely out of his own sickbed. Barney tried to make sense of his scattered memories. He didn't think Daniel had been looking after him at night; didn't remember seeing anyone other than Daniel and Theo night or day.

"Has Theo been staying here at night?"

Daniel's head whipped around at the sound of Barney's voice. "Uncle Barney!" He took two long strides across the room to grasp Barney's wrist to feel his pulse with one hand while laying the other on Barney's forehead. "No temperature, and you're awake. Auntie Theo said you were past the worst of it."

Auntie Theo, is it? Barney had no objection to that. "Where is Miss Conroy?"

"She and Annie are both sleeping, but Auntie Theo said to call her if you woke up." Daniel turned for the door, but Barney stopped him. "Let her sleep. You can catch me up on what has been happening. For a start, what day is it? How long have I been sick?"

"It is Wednesday, Uncle Barney. You have been sick for over a week."

More than a week! "And Miss Conroy... Theo? She has been here this whole time?"

Daniel nodded. "Yes. She and I have been taking turns during the day, but she wouldn't let me nurse you at night. She said I might get sick again myself, if I didn't get my sleep. Tea?" He didn't wait for an answer, but busied himself nudging a kettle closer to the fire, and measuring tea into a teapot that stood ready.

Barney absorbed that. She had moved in; nursed him every night; put her reputation on the line to keep him alive.

"The village has been keeping us fed," Daniel volunteered. "I don't think they hate me, anymore."

Barney protested. "They never hated you, Daniel. They just didn't understand you."

Daniel grimaced. "Also, Mrs. Fullerton was telling lies about Mama, and I was being childish."

"You were angry." Not just about the housekeeper's insults, but about losing his mother and his home, and being exiled to an unfamiliar village and an unknown uncle. Barney had always understood that.

"The people have been nice, Uncle Barney." Daniel wrinkled his nose. "Not Mrs. Fullerton. She hasn't come back since the second day you were sick, when Auntie Theo refused to let her take you to the manor. But the others come. They bring us food, and ask after you, and say nice things about Annie, if she is with me."

Barney would need time to think about all of that, though it was nice to know the parish had been supporting his family. And Theo had saved him from the dreadful fate of being nursed by Mrs. Fullerton and her niece! He owed Theo a lifetime of devotion for that alone.

"Barney, you are awake!"

Barney turned toward the voice, and there she was. Theo. His ministering angel. His beloved. Some part of his brain registered that her eyes were weary, her clothing rumpled, and wisps of untidy hair fell from the braids that crowned her head. He had not seen a more splendid woman in all his years. She was altogether beautiful.

Barney's recovery was slow, but surer than if Theo had not been there to scold when he pushed himself too hard. She had moved back to Mrs. Peabody's when he was out of danger, but arrived each morning in time to cook him a nourishing breakfast, and remained for the day. Some days, he was even successful in persuading her to stay and have dinner with him and Daniel.

To his great relief, she did not fall ill herself, and a few good nights' sleep restored her to her usual quiet good looks.

Barney hadn't resumed any of his parish duties, yet. Theo not only objected vociferously to the mere suggestion; she marshalled the leading lights of the village to tell him his services were not required until he was well. They visited him in a deputation in his parlor, where he was sitting with his feet up, a rug over his lap, trying to convince himself that he could do without his usual afternoon sleep.

"The worst of the ague seems to be over, and we're managing just fine with Sexton to lead the prayers. Stay home and get well," said Mr. Brewster, the innkeeper, and the others chorused agreement. Brewster had brought with him Barney's sexton, the midwife, the smith, and the district's most prominent farmer and his wife. Not, thank goodness, Mrs. Fullerton.

His nurse did allow that resuming the lessons he'd begun with Daniel would not tax his meager strength. "An hour morning and afternoon, and not a minute more," she commanded. Barney caught her hand and kissed it, which made her blush, tug the hand from his grasp, and hurry out of the room.

Embarrassing her was not well done of him, but his courtship couldn't follow the normal paths. He couldn't dance with her or take her walking after church or even bring her flowers, though he deputed that job to Daniel with some success.

They needed to have a long talk, and soon. Barney was determined to make her his own, though he hadn't yet been able to work out how to manage their future. He needed another position; one where he could keep the children with him; one that paid enough to support them and a wife. Wouldn't it be wrong to speak of his feelings and his hopes when he had no future to offer her?

Still, he had given her cause enough to know how he felt. Unless he was much mistaken, she felt the same.

❧

Theo was living in a heady dream. It was all going to come crashing down when she had to leave, and she would pay the price for these few days of pretending. But since it was too late to avoid the coming heart-break, she was going to enjoy every moment of pretending to belong with Barney and his wards.

As the village emptied of visitors, Mrs. Withers returned to her duties, turning up one morning when Theo was up to her elbows in washing the breakfast dishes, Daniel at her side with a drying cloth. Annie was sitting on the floor, stacking baking pans into towers and then knocking them down again to squeals of laughter.

The woman grunted a greeting and strolled into the pantry, where Theo could glimpse her picking up items and peering under covers. "I have the meals for today planned and prepared as far as possible," Theo called out. "What I need from you today is help with Mr. Somerville's room. Now that he is well enough to be downstairs most of the day, I want to give it a thorough going over. Change all the linen, take down the curtains and hang them in the sun, wash all the surfaces and beat the carpets."

Mrs. Withers emerged from the parlor scowling, and Theo suddenly remembered that she was an intruder, and had no right to give such orders. But the scowl must have been deep thought, for Mrs. Withers only said, "If the boy will fetch water, I will set the coppers boiling."

It was Theo's turn to scowl. "Master Daniel," she pointed out. Responding to Mrs. Withers's puzzled expression, she expanded the thought. "Mr. Somerville's nephew and ward is *Master* Daniel."

Annie abandoned her pots and tugged at Theo's apron. "I need pottie."

"I will just go and start fetching water," Daniel offered into the silence. "Leave those dishes on the rack, Auntie Theo, and I'll finish up later."

Mrs. Withers blinked once, slowly, then said, "Thankee, Master Daniel." Theo hid a smile as she scooped Annie up from the floor, nudging the pans to one side to pick up later, and carried the little girl upstairs.

Barney had been shaving in his bedroom, and he came to the door in his shirtsleeves, a towel around his shoulders and flecks of foam still decorating parts of his face. "Was that Mrs. Withers?"

"It is. She is going to help me turn out your room while we have a sunny day to air the draperies and bedding. If I bring Annie and her blocks down to the parlor, will you keep an eye on her?"

He nodded, and stepped forward to drop a kiss on Annie's cheek. "I'll finish getting dressed and be out of your way in a few minutes," he promised.

Theo smiled at the closed door even as her eyes filled with tears. Barney treated her as if she belonged; as if he had the same impossible dream as hers. She screwed her eyes shut, took a deep breath, and continued along the passage to Annie's room.

Annie touched a finger to her cheek, collecting a tear. "Teo sad," she commented.

"Theo is a silly duffer," Theo grumbled, and manufactured a bright grin for the child's sake.

By noon, Barney's bed chamber was sparkling clean, the windows open to the sun and fresh air, the curtains pegged on a long rope across the back garden and blowing in the wind.

"I'll be off to get Withers his dinner, ma'am," the daily woman said. After the first hesitation, she'd accepted Theo in her assumed role and been careful to address Daniel respectfully, as a young gentleman of the house. "I'll come back late afternoon, before the sun goes, and get them drapes back up, if it suits you. Leave the bed for me, too, lessen the vicar wants to sleep in it."

They'd held that conversation on the path outside the parlor window, and, when Theo took Barney a slice of pie and a mug of ale, he asked her about it. Confronted her, she would have said, except he was laughing. "What did you do to Mrs. Withers, and who did you get to impersonate her?"

Since Daniel had already expressed wonder at Mrs. Withers's hard work that day, Theo knew what Barney meant. "She needs direction and encouragement, Barney. If no one tells her what needs to be done, she flounders and achieves very little."

Barney reached out and caught her hand. Theo cast a quick glance at Annie, sleeping on the hearth rug, before letting him tug her closer. Was he going to kiss her at long last? But no, he lowered his voice so it carried no further than her ear. "We need you, Theodora Conroy. Would you consider staying?"

Forever, her heart said. But he didn't mean that, of course. "I can give Mrs. Withers a daily routine, so she knows just what is expected of her," she offered.

Barney shook his head and opened his mouth to speak, then sighed. "Where is Daniel?" he asked.

Theo frowned at the change of subject. "I told him he could go to the inn, to see his friends in the stables. He has been such a help, Barney, and he deserves an afternoon off." Now Barney would know how far she had overreached, making decisions about the comings and goings of his ward as if she had the right.

But Barney just nodded and tugged at her hand again, so that she sat down on the sofa beside him. "Good, because we need to talk."

CHAPTER 8

Behave, Barney told himself, as Theo landed so close that her thigh brushed his. Her delectable mouth, open in surprise, was within kissing distance, if he just leaned a little sideways and bent his head.

He could see her collect herself. She closed her mouth, swallowed, and looked down at her hand, still trapped in his. "I have overstepped," she admitted. "I should have sent Daniel to ask you."

"No!" He reached for her other hand and captured it. "You did exactly right. Theo, darling Theo, don't you know how we feel about you? Daniel has adopted you as his aunt. Annie prefers you even to Daniel when she has a bruise or is tired. And I love you."

Theo looked up at that. "You love me?"

His heart sank at the note of surprise, but he carried on. She needed to know how little he had to offer. "I am not much of a bargain. I am only my father's curate, with a very poor income, and, once my father finds out that I have taken in my sister's children, I am likely to lose even that. I will have to find another position, perhaps tutoring, or secretarial work, or assisting a physician. Will you wait for me until I have an income to support a wife? Will you be the children's aunt in truth?"

Theo was silent, tears welling in her eyes and trickling disregarded down her cheeks.

Barney's heart landed in his boots and kept falling. "My turn to overstep." He let go of her hands and shifted a few inches away from her along the sofa. "I am sorry I upset you. I thought you... Never mind. We shall pretend all of that unsaid, shall we?"

A smile was spreading across Theo's beloved face, and she retrieved Barney's hands. "Foolish man," she scolded, fondly. "Don't you know that I love you, too? I am just surprised because I never believed that dreams could come true." With that, she moved closer and tilted her head for a kiss, and brought into reality one of his most cherished dreams of the weeks since he'd met her.

How long the kiss, or perhaps the kisses, lasted, Barney could not have said. The bang of the front door followed by thudding of feet in the hall gave them a second's warning to spring apart, though anyone with eyes would have known exactly what they were doing. They had only to look at Theo's swollen lips, mussed hair and disarranged clothing. Barney assumed he looked no more reputable.

Daniel flung open the door and burst into the room. He was breathing hard. "Auntie Theo; Uncle Barney, we've got trouble."

Barney leapt to his feet. "Will I need my medical bag?"

Daniel was resting his hands on his knees and taking deep breaths, but he straightened at that. "Not that kind of trouble, sir. Visitors. I saw them at the inn having their horses stabled, and I heard them talking. Your father, Uncle Barney."

Damn. Barney had hoped for more time, so he could write to friends from university and enquire about positions.

Daniel had turned to Theo. "And a lady, Auntie Theo. The Countess of Sutton. She asked Mr. Brewster where you were to be found, and—when he said the vicarage—Mr. Somerville introduced himself. They are coming now. I ran all the way, but they will be here any minute."

"Lady Sophia?" Theo looked more thoughtful than concerned. "Lady Sutton is Lady Felicity's sister, Barney, and married to the son of the Duke of Winshire."

They had time for no more. The door sounded a loud rat-ta-tah-tat, and Annie woke, grizzling.

"I'll get it," Daniel said, as Theo crossed the room and held out her arms for Annie.

Barney ran his hands over his head and retied the neckerchief he was wearing, tucking the edges under his lounging robe. Across the room, Theo was adjusting her bodice with one hand. Hopefully the visitors would blame the baby for the locks that had escaped her hairpins.

They could hear the voices in the hall.

"I suppose you are Louisa's misbegotten get." His father, loud and harsh.

"I am Daniel Labulo, sir." Daniel, his voice calm and neutral.

"Labulo?" That was a lady's voice, cool and low. "I knew your father, I think, young sir. Your mother, too. Fine people, both of them. How delightful to meet you."

Daniel held the door open for the lady to enter, followed by Barney's father, who looked around the room, dismissed Theo and Annie as being of no account, and focused on Barney. "What do you mean by this, eh?"

"Miss Conroy? Will you introduce us, please?" The lady was as lovely as her voice. Barney didn't know much about women's fashion, but he could recognize elegance and perfect workmanship when he saw it. The reassuring smile she gave Theo settled some of his anxiety. At least his beloved was likely to come out of this with a job.

Theo managed a graceful curtsey despite the child on her hip. "Lady Sutton, may I present Barnaby Somerville, who is curate of this parish, and his wards. You met Daniel at the door, and this is his sister, Annabelle."

The Countess of Sutton stroked Annie's cheek. "You are a pretty little thing. And this gentleman, Miss Conroy, is Mr. Somerville senior, your Mr. Somerville's father."

Theo curtseyed to Barney's father, who waved an impatient hand and otherwise ignored her. "I do not wish to be rude, my lady," he proclaimed, in the sonorous tones he used for a sermon, "but I have not come to socialize, but to put a stop to a scandal. A scandal, I say, and in the midst of it this young female who has her claws into my son."

Lady Sutton shut his mouth with a look, and, with another glance, prevented the defense Barney was about to make. "If you do not wish to be rude, Mr. Somerville," she said sweetly, "then take a seat and begin again." She settled herself on a chair. "I know Miss Conroy as well as I know my own sister, and—if there is any scandal—it is not of her making. Furthermore, Mr. Barney Somerville has been highly recommended to me. I suspect we shall find that the scandal is the invention of a prurient mind."

She raised her brows as Barney's father stood gaping, and then nodded. "Ah. Of course, you cannot sit while a lady remains standing. Miss Conroy, perhaps we can trouble you for a pot of tea?"

Barney held out his arms for Annie, and Theo passed the child over before leaving the room with Daniel at her heels.

"Lady Sutton," Barney's father started again. He had clearly decided on the fatherly tone he used with the maidens of the parishes he occasionally deigned to visit. "I regret to have to inform you—and I have this on the best of authority—that your sister's maid has been living with my son." He frowned at Barney, his heavy eyebrows drawing together. "Deny it if you dare! Mrs. Fullerton herself wrote to me, and described all the goings on. Yes, and one of the London newspapers has reported the matter. Her ladyship must be shocked. Shocked, I say."

Lady Sutton raised one of those expressive eyebrows. "Say it a little less loudly, if you please, Mr. Somerville. You are frightening your granddaughter. Barnaby—if I may call you so to avoid confusion—have you been compromising my protégée? And if you have, what do you intend to do about it?"

"I have not compromised Miss Conroy, my lady," Barney assured her. "Indeed, we did not even kiss..." he paused to stand as Theo opened the door and held it for Daniel, who carried in a tray. She must have heard him, because she was blushing, but he finished his sentence anyway. "Not until today, when she accepted my proposal of marriage."

Lady Sutton beamed. "Congratulations, my dears." She took the plate of cake Theo was holding, and put it down before drawing Theo into a hug. "Felicity will be so delighted." She shook Barney's hand. "She wrote that she hoped leaving Theo here would mean your attraction had a chance to come to something."

"I forbid it," growled Barney's father, who was still sitting even though the countess was on her feet. "You cannot marry a servant, boy. What will people think? I demand that you rescind the proposal and send these children to an orphanage, where they belong. You can't afford children or a wife, not on what I am paying you, and you can be certain I'll not raise your stipend. Not for those children, or for that wife." He sat back in his chair with a smug smile, steepling his hands before his chest.

"I resign," Barney said, his mind racing as he reviewed which of his possessions he could sell to provide for his wards while he looked for a job. "I will be out of the vicarage within a week."

Lady Sutton smiled at him then turned that lethal eyebrow on his father, her head tilted in question. "Perhaps you might reconsider, Mr. Somerville? From what I have been told by your parishioners, the younger Mr. Somerville will be difficult to replace."

"An ungrateful child is sharper than a serpent's tooth," Barney's father intoned. "Honor thy father and mother. Children, obey your parents."

Lady Sutton sat again, and gestured toward the teapot. "Tea with milk, please, Daniel. Mr. Somerville, you might also remember, Fathers, do not provoke your children, lest they become discouraged. I see no objection to the match. Theodora Conroy is the daughter of a gentleman, with every qualification to be the wife of a clergyman, and Barnaby Somerville is of age." She leaned forward, her suddenly fierce glare skewering Barney's father. "And a man who understands honor and duty, since he has accepted the responsibility of your grandchildren when your daughter was no longer able to look after them."

Barney's father quailed for a moment, then stood, drawing his pride and dignity around him. "Madam, my mind is made up. Let Barnaby find out for himself that the world is an uncharitable place for those who disobey their parents and must subsist without parental support. I disown him as I disowned his sister. I have no daughter, and therefore I have no grandchildren." He nodded, his satisfied smirk confirming that he thought his argument irrefutable. "If your brother sins, rebuke him. And I do, Lady Sutton. I rebuke him. Let him repent, as his sister never repented, and then—as a Christian—I must forgive him. If he repents and obeys me by disposing of his encumbrances."

Daniel was simmering with anger; Barney knew the signs. Before the boy could erupt, Theo handed him a plate with a piece of cake on it, and marched to stand in front of Barney's father.

"Mr. Somerville, I must ask you to leave. Barney is no longer in your employ, and you have rejected us as family, so you have no place here. Daniel and Annie are ours—mine and Barney's—and I will not allow you to sit there and insult their mother in front of them. She was a wonderful woman, and she has two amazing children. We are privileged to care for them, and delighted to do so without your poisonous influence."

By the time she reached the end, Barney was standing at her side, his arm around her shoulders and Annie reaching across him to pat her face. Daniel had tucked his arm around her from the other side. She was shaking, though with anger or some other emotion Barney could not tell.

"Well!" Barney's father snarled. "I have never heard anything of the sort. Young woman, this is my vicarage, and I will have you and the children out within the hour!"

Lady Sutton interceded. "Or? If they are not out within the hour, which is a most unreasonable requirement, what will you do?"

Before Barney's father could reply, another person appeared at the door, one bizarrely costumed in a long red robe over loose black trousers, head topped by a round sheepskin hat. This man had a curved sword tucked in the bright sash that closed the robe, and a rifle in a holster slung across his back. "My lady?" This apparition said. "I heard shouting."

Lady Sutton gestured to Barney's father. "This gentleman was just leaving, Jeyhun Bey. Perhaps you would be good enough to escort him out?"

Barney drew Theo and Daniel to one side, and watched in stunned disbelief as his father meekly left, clearly cowed by the warrior, or at least by that man's hand on his sword.

He had not quite left the room when Lady Sutton said, her voice uncompromising, "Three days, and not an hour less." He paused; then his shoulders drooped and he continued on his way, Lady Sutton's henchman on his heels.

"I take it three days will be enough?" Lady Sutton asked. Barney turned from the door that closed behind his father and escort. Lady Sutton was taking a sip of her tea as if such scenes were nothing to ruffle her equanimity.

"I take it the furniture came with the vicarage," Theo commented. "It won't take long to pack the children's possessions."

"The children have a bag each and a trunk between them. I own my clothes and a few books," Barney said. "We could be out tonight." Unbelievable. An hour ago, he had not even proposed to Theo, and now he was betrothed, homeless, and unemployed. He shook his head, slowly.

Lady Sutton interrupted his thoughts. "Tomorrow will be time enough. Take a seat, please, and let us discuss your plans."

Barney let Theo chivvy him into a seat and serve him a cup of tea. His legs, still wobbly from the ague, had grown tired of holding him up. Theo fetched her own tea and sat beside him on the sofa, putting Annie down between them. Daniel sat at their feet, and the four of them faced Lady Sutton as a family.

By that time, Barney had marshalled his thoughts. Her ladyship was clearly a good person to have in support, so it made sense to share the ideas he'd had so far. Theo protested, though, when he listed the possible occupations open to him: tutor, secretary, physician's assistant. "But Barney, you have a vocation to clerical ministry."

Barney didn't see that he had a choice. "I don't have a living, though, Theo, and I can't support a wife and children on what a curate earns."

"I might be able to help you there," said Lady Sutton. "As it happens, my sister thought you might be in need of a new parish, and my husband has a village that needs a vicar. I've asked him to hold off on the appointment until he could meet you."

"But..." Why was Barney protesting when she was offering everything he wanted? Nevertheless, he continued, "I don't know you, my lady. Why would you help us?"

She didn't seem to mind. "Theo is very dear to my sister and myself, Barnaby. Also, I knew your sister a little through the abolition movement. She was a wonderful woman, and I am delighted to be able to use my influence for the benefit of her children."

Barney nodded and took another sip of tea, though he would have preferred something stronger. Events had spiraled out of his control, but they seemed to be working out better than he could have imagined in his wildest dreams. Theo as his wife. A place for his wards to grow in safety. His own parish.

Theo asked a few questions about the position, but Barney said nothing, barely listening as he began making mental lists of everything he would need to do in the next couple of days. Until she asked a question that caught his attention. "My lady, what brought you here in such a timely fashion?"

Lady Sutton laughed. "Felicity asked me to watch out for you, Theo dear. Apparently, she thought a woman called Mrs. Fullerton might try to cause trouble. I began to pack when I saw the *Teatime Tattler* article. Then I received a letter from Mrs. Fullerton making all sorts of scandalous and outrageous claims, and she mentioned that she'd also written to Barney's father, I thought I had better make haste." She raised her cup in a mocking toast. "Thank you, Mrs. Fullerton."

CHAPTER 9

They were married four weeks later in Oxfordshire. The village church that would be Barney's own was filled with his new parishioners and invited guests. On one side sat Lord and Lady Sutton and several of the Suttons' intimidating foreign retainers, who proved to be charming and friendly when Barney got to know them during the long gentle trip from Suffolk. On the other side the front pews held three of her sisters and their husbands and children, whose separate arrivals yesterday had caused his wife several bouts of happy tears.

The fourth sister was looking after her ailing father, who declared himself too frail to travel. "Too stubborn, more like," the sister had written. "He does not wish to admit he was wrong about you, Theo."

Hers was only one of the messages of joy and congratulations they received. Mrs. Peabody from Fenwick on Sea sent an effusive letter. A number of other Fenwick residents had also written or asked to have their best wishes included in the missives of more literate correspondents. Mrs. Fullerton was in disgrace with the parish, and Barney's father had been gifted with so much cold shoulder that he had fled the environs.

On this happy day, Barney could forgive them both, as long as they stayed well clear of his family.

He waited at the front of the church, with an old friend from university as his best man and Daniel at his side. "You are my true best man," Barney had told his nephew, "but I need an adult to sign as witness."

Between them and the altar stood the elderly cleric whose parish this had been. He was officiating at the wedding of his successor as his last pastoral duty. He and his wife were moving to live with their daughter and her family, and were so anxious to be gone that their baggage and belongings had trundled off to their new home this morning, and they would follow immediately after the ceremony.

Leaving the vicarage, for this one night, to Theo and Barney, for the children were staying a final night with the Suttons.

Visions of the night ahead threatened to consume Barney's mind, but a rustle as people turned to look behind them attracted his attention to the main door at the end of the aisle. There she was. There they both were, actually. Theo, on the arm of Sutton's brother, Lord Andrew Winderfield, a dream come true in a pale blue gown and a white silk bonnet, her eyes shining as she smiled down the church at him. Annie, also smiling, hand in hand with her new auntie. The child skipped as she walked, swinging the basket in her other hand so that rose petals scattered on their way down the aisle.

Then Theo was before him.

As if from a long way away, he heard the vicar begin the ceremony. "Dearly beloved, we are gathered together here, in the sight of God, and in the face of this congregation."

Barney smiled at Theo. Annie hugged Theo's leg. The vicar explained the three reasons why God had created matrimony. Barney, eager to promise to love, comfort, honor and keep Theo, waiting impatiently for the moment to say 'I will', his trained voice sounding throughout the church.

In her turn, Theo spoke, and then Lord Andrew gave Theo's hand to the vicar, who presented it to Barney. This was the moment. Barney had heard these words dozens of times since he was ordained. Did they resonate like this for other grooms? Did they resound like trumpet blasts, calling him to leap gladly into a life in matrimonial harness?

I, Barnabas Nathaniel Somerville, take thee, Theodora Conroy, to my wedded wife, to have and to hold from this day forward, for better for worse, for richer for poorer, in sickness and in health, to love and to cherish, till death us do part, according to God's holy ordinance; and thereto I plight thee my troth.

Theo repeated the vows, her voice firm, her gaze never leaving his.

Barney knew the service by heart, which was just as well, because he kept getting lost in Theo's eyes. But at last, his ring on her finger, their signatures in the register, God's blessing proclaimed by the vicar, they were on their way down the aisle to receive the good wishes of their family and friends.

Too many people wanted to talk to them. But, at last, Lady Sutton commanded that the bride and groom be allowed to climb into the open carriage ready to take them up to the manor, where refreshments awaited all the wedding guests.

Theo and Barney exchanged a glance, and he scooped Annie out of the arms of one of Theo's sisters, and called for Daniel.

"Just the two of you," Lady Sutton scolded.

"Four of us," Theo insisted. "We are family." And after Daniel helped her up into the carriage, she took Annie from Barney so that he could climb up as well.

Several of the rowdier guests set up a cheer, and ran alongside the carriage, waving. Theo, Annie, Daniel, and Barney waved back.

Daniel was looking worried. "Lady Sutton said we should let you have this time alone, and go with our new aunties."

Theo put an arm around his shoulder to give him a hug. "Lady Sutton doesn't understand. You belong with us, Daniel."

Barney's heart was too full to put words to what he felt as he watched his new bride hug his nephew with one arm while using the other to prevent his niece from clambering over the edge of the carriage. Then the words occurred to him, and he spoke them out loud.

"This, the four of us together, is my dream come true."

Theo had no hand spare to reach out, but her smile gathered him in. "We share the best dream of all."

THE END

Theo appears as Lady Sophia Belvoir's maid in *To Wed a Proper Lady*, which you can buy here: https://books2read.com/CMK-ProperLady I have no idea why I made her susceptible to travel sickness in that book, but it sure helped her happy ending in this one. *To Wed a Proper Lady* is book one of the series *The Children of the Mountain King*. For the rest of that series and others, see your favorite retailer or the book tabs on my website.

SOCIAL MEDIA FOR JUDE KNIGHT

You can learn more about Jude Knight at these social media links:

Website and blog: http://judeknightauthor.com/
Subscribe to newsletter: http://judeknightauthor.com/newsletter/
Bookshop: https://judeknight.selz.com/
Facebook: https://www.facebook.com/JudeKnightAuthor/
Twitter: https://twitter.com/JudeKnightBooks
Pinterest: https://nz.pinterest.com/jknight1033/
BookBub: https://www.bookbub.com/profile/jude-knight
Books + Main Bites: https://bookandmainbites.com/JudeKnightAuthor
Amazon author page: https://www.amazon.com/Jude-Knight/e/B00RG3SG7I
Goodreads: https://www.goodreads.com/author/show/8603586.Jude_Knight
LinkedIn: https://linkedin.com/in/jude-knight-465557166/

ABOUT JUDE KNIGHT

Jude Knight always wanted to be a novelist, but life got in the way for decades and she nearly lost the dream. She wrote a thousand beginnings, but it took a huge life event to shove her into writing an ending. That was in 2014. Eight novels and counting later, plus short stories and novellas galore, she's living her dream: writing historical fiction with a large helping of romance, more than a dash of suspense, and a sprinkling of humor.

Learn more about Jude at:
Website and blog: http://judeknightauthor.com/

facebook.com/JudeKnightAuthor

twitter.com/JudeKnightBooks

pinterest.com/jknight1033

bookbub.com/profile/jude-knight

linkedin.com/in/jude-knight-465557166

THE RUNAWAY HEIRESS AND THE BLACKSMITH

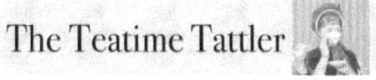
The Teatime Tattler

Dearest Reader,

Is the lady boarding with our own Mrs. P. in truth a Lady, or a Mrs. as she claims?

Those who follow the social pages suspect her of being the heiress, Lady S. W. If this is the case, why is she here in Fenwick, and not in London with her betrothed? And what is going on between her and Fenwick's blacksmith?

T. P., if that is indeed his name, is another refugee from London, although he has been here for years. Never before has he accepted a lure from a lass. At least, not a girl in Fenwick, despite expressions of interest from several local women.

Perhaps he prefers to dally with someone who is certain to move on? Or perhaps one of the pair is risking a broken heart?

A KISS BY THE SEA

GRACE BURROWES

A Kiss by the Sea
Grace Burrowes

To all the summer loves

He's not really a blacksmith, and she's not really an heiress... Can they forge a happily-ever-after anyway?

Thaddeus Pennrith finds a way to recover from multiple griefs when he accepts the blacksmith's post at Fenwick on Sea. Village life gives him a sense of belonging that Polite Society never could, though he must resume his aristocratic responsibilities soon. Along comes Lady Sarah Weatherby, refugee from an engagement gone badly awry, and Thaddeus is faced with both a compelling reason to reveal his titled antecedents, and a longing to keep them forever hidden....

CHAPTER 1

A blacksmith's job was mostly solving problems for mute beasts. The squire's morning gelding was shying at stiles. Miss Fifi's stoat of a pony was three-legged lame. Because the animals could not convey the details of their difficulties, an astute blacksmith learned to notice what was otherwise ignored.

For Thaddeus Pennrith—Thad Penn to his neighbors in Fenwick on Sea—ignoring the lady in the elegant coach would have been impossible. Her coachy, groom, and footmen had the martyred air of London servants forbidden to wear fancy livery, while the team in the traces—matched chestnuts, white stockings on all sixteen glossy legs—fairly shouted a Mayfair provenance.

When a lady's relief teams were London-fancy this far from Town, the lady herself was bound to be fancy as well.

She did not disappoint, though she did intrigue. Even climbing down from a conveyance into the muck of Fenwick's thoroughly soaked high street, she had the sort of grace that comes from years of deportment instruction. The boot that first appeared on the iron step was doubtless Hoby, and polished to a high shine. The lace peeking out from the hem of the woman's carriage dress was as frothy as summer white caps on the North Sea, and her bonnet gave the rest of the game away.

The bonnet was nearly plain, but for the green satin ribbons adorning the brim and tied under a chin charitably described as firm. A young woman chose such millinery when she wanted to go about in society without calling attention to herself. That her entire ensemble otherwise revealed her to be wealthy, pampered, and far from home had apparently escaped her notice.

Alas, great wealth and great intelligence were not always found in the same person. The lady's expression was obscured by the brim of her bonnet, but she used that firm chin to point in Thad's direction.

"Mr. MacAdams," she said, hand on the footman's arm, "please explain our situation to yonder blacksmith."

The voice was so euphonious as to make a command into a gentle request. Thad had fled the siren call of such voices five years ago, and yet, that sheer gracious warmth blended with just a hint of wrought iron still affected him.

When he should have turned his back on the fine lady and her sniffy servants, he instead waited for the coachman's approach. The fellow was older and, like many a coachman, moved gingerly as he climbed down from the box. Years of battling the elements, headstrong teams, and what passed for English roads took a heavy toll on a man's body.

"Good sir," the coachman called, splashing across the muck. "A word. Can you refashion a spring for a vehicle designed with a post undercarriage?"

An undercarriage such as the post coaches and public stages favored was unusual on a private conveyance. The design was intended to smooth out the ride on heavily laden vehicles, and unnecessarily complicated for most personal travel.

"To whom do I have the pleasure of speaking?" Thad asked.

"John MacAdams, coachman to—"

"John." The lady's quiet tone had taken on more of that wrought iron quality.

"Mrs. Winston, late of Surrey," the coachman said, drawing himself up as if that would better disguise his mendacity. "Time is of the essence and my mistress will compensate you handsomely."

Truly, the lot of them were wanting in the brainbox. "The coach road has been washed out by the storm," Thad said, not unkindly. "If the queen of the fairies magically repaired your coach by sunset, you'd still have nowhere to go."

John looked askance at Mrs. Never-in-a-century-was-she-a-Winston.

She turned to regard Thad, and, while he had expected her to be pretty, he had not expected her to be stunning.

Her eyes were the same green as her bonnet ribbons, a luminous, grassy hue offset by auburn hair. The combination was unusual in the English aristocracy, and—given her slightly too-wide mouth, and ever so gently aquiline nose—she would never be called pretty, but neither would a man easily forget the sight of her.

And she would never be mistaken for plain Mrs. Winston of Surrey, either.

Thaddeus bowed, not to the depth a London gentleman would offer a lady of high degree, but rather, as a yeoman would bob deferentially at gentry. He remained silent, for no introductions had been made, and even a bumpkin knew not to assume uninvited familiarity with the Quality.

"We are cut off from the main roads?" she asked.

The question was put directly to Thad, so he answered. "The Great Flood would have done less damage than the storm that just came through here. If you look to the water, you'll see the ocean is still showing the effects." Even Granny McClintock couldn't recall such swells in her nearly ninety years of earthly toil.

Mrs. Winston dropped the footman's arm and approached Thad. He resorted to gentlemanly euphemisms out of old habit: The lady was *well formed*, her three-quarter-length spencer showing off an abundance of curves. She was of middle height, which put the top of her head in the vicinity of Thad's shoulder.

She would be, to use less genteel parlance, a lovely armful. Not that her kind ever enjoyed *armful* status, which was a grand shame and a poor reflection on the Creator Himself.

"I grasp that inclement weather has made the roads impassable for a time," the lady said. "But I must be in a position to resume my travels at the earliest opportunity. I can pay you to make my coach repairs a priority."

"No, madam, you cannot. You are in a hurry to meet some bounder hiding from his creditors in Great Yarmouth," Thaddeus said, "but my neighbors are in a hurry to plough up destroyed fields in the hopes of replanting so we don't starve come winter. When I am the only fellow who can repair their ploughs, your naughty little tryst is of no moment. Every cart horse and cob in the village will pull a shoe in the muck this storm has left, and those animals are the difference between a midwife attending a difficult birthing or a mother suffering in agony with none to aid her. I'll have a look at your coach, but I can make no promises."

The longer he'd spoken, the more unreadable Mrs. Winston's expression had become, until her physiognomy resembled the blank face of an Elgin marble.

Then her gaze narrowed as the wind whipped the green satin ribbons against her chin. "You are not from around here." She visually inventoried him with all the dispassion of a bidder at Tatt's eyeing up a new hack. "You are public-school educated. Your proportions suggest generations of good nutrition added to Viking ancestry, and you are rude. How long ago did you leave London, and why shouldn't I alert the authorities to your whereabouts?"

Thad managed not to smile, barely. "The only authority concerned about my whereabouts is my grandmother, and I write to her each fortnight lest she have me taken up by her minions. If you can lower the tip of your nose even an inch, the innkeeper at The Queen's Barque might find a room for you while your coach awaits repairs."

She raised the tip of her nose, of course. "I can pay you."

"So you've said, but unless you can deliver a baby, provide medical care to the sick, plough under a lost crop, or otherwise do more than beautify the landscape, your coach will have to wait."

She glanced at her coachman, who was admiring the humble storm-washed prospect of a Suffolk village's high street. The Queen's Barque coaching inn was the central edifice in the hamlet, bringing the occasional eccentric traveler, news of the greater world, and the promise of escape to those longing for life beyond rural obscurity.

Thad, to his surprise, was no longer in that latter group.

"Excuse me," Thad said, honestly forgetting to bow. "Fifi, hold up a moment." He ambled across the smithy's humble forecourt, the cobbles still slick with rain and brine.

A small, muddy person whom Thad knew to be of the female persuasion glowered up at him from Mrs. Peabody's side yard.

"I can catch him, Mr. Penn. I always do."

Fifi never caught her mount. Thelwell, named for a vicar since gone to his reward, simply grazed his fill and—being the laziest equine ever to dump a child into a mudpuddle—caught forty winks until Fifi led him home.

She advanced upon her shaggy steed with all the subtlety of a game beater in high brush. Thelwell flicked a hairy ear but did not cease his efforts to trim Mrs. Peabody's yard.

"Wellie, come," Fifi crooned. "I've got a bit of carrot for you."

Wellie disdained to heed her summons. His reins trailed in the grass, and, because he was hatched from the union of a demon and a unicorn, he would surely tromp upon those reins to break them when it suited his purposes.

"Wel-lie dearest, wouldn't you like some nice scratchies?" Fifi asked, inching closer.

Thelwell sighed and toddled six feet down the hedge.

This went on for another five minutes, and all the while Mrs. Winston held her peace.

"Won't you help the child?" she said at length. "That dratted pony will founder on spring grass before she catches him."

Perhaps Mrs. Winston had ventured beyond the confines of Mayfair in her childhood.

"Fifi," Thad called. "Hold your ground. I'll have a go from the other side." He rounded the far end of the hedge and advanced on the pony.

Thelwell, having lost several arguments with Thad at the forge, snatched a few more mouthfuls of grass and went to his fate with the dignity of an affronted elder. His put-upon air said that the child had come out of the saddle through no fault of her long-suffering pony, and

GRACE BURROWES

all this grass was going to waste and looking so untidy, and truly, one grew vexed with the tedium of human incompetence.

Grandmother had the same ability to pack an entire lecture into a single sigh.

Thad tightened the girth, earning a glower from the pony, and used his handkerchief to swipe a streak of mud from Fifi's cheek.

"Don't gallop," he said, depositing the child into the saddle. Fifi was young enough to ride astride, though that would change all too soon. "The footing is rotten, and Wellie has a full tummy. You may trot, you may not canter. Do you understand me, Fiona Sweeney?"

She gathered up the reins. "Yes, sir, Mr. Penn, and thank you. Wellie says thank you, too. He really is a sweet boy." She patted the useless beast on the shoulder.

Thad took Wellie's reins close to the bit. "You've had your fun, you equine market hog. Behave on the way home or you'll wish you had. I'll toss you into the sea and let the mermaids snack on you."

Wellie turned an innocent eye on him, and—possibly—on Mrs. Winston. Fiona trotted off, bouncing gamely in rhythm with the pony's choppy gait.

"I had a whole string of Wellie's," Mrs. Winston said. "They taught me what the better schooled mounts could not."

"What was that?"

"How to deal with temperamental creatures much larger than I."

Grandmother didn't like anybody, but she would *approve* of Mrs. Winston. "I will have a look at your carriage this afternoon. I have some shoes to reset, and, as the storm damage becomes more apparent, my dance card will doubtless fill up. If the road is to become passable again, that will involve picks, shovels, and any number of tools inclined to break when they are most needed."

"I understand," she said. "I am a supplicant at the mercy of your availability. I will be at the posting inn should you need me."

Her air of utter self-possession goaded Thad into doing what he never did—explaining himself. "Storms bring on babies," he said, a truth doubtless unknown to every other earl's heir in the whole of England. "Our midwife is getting on. Mrs. Gatesby needs reliable transportation, but her gelding's right-front shoe sounded clinchy to me when she came by to visit Mrs. Peabody yesterday morning. I will stop by Mrs. Gatesby's cottage and have a look, and that means having a cup of tea... and my time is not my own."

Mrs. Winston signaled to her footman. "You are right, Mr. Penn. My concerns are trivial compared to those of others in this village. I will bide at the inn." She surveyed the high street, some emotion brewing in her emerald gaze. "If I cannot leave this place, then others cannot find me here. Enjoy your cup of tea with Mrs. Gatesby."

She strode off, as self-possessed as Boudicea on the morning of battle. And yet, as Thad gathered up his tools and made his way to Mrs. Gatesby's cottage, he was uneasy. A woman as well-heeled as Mrs. Winston ought to be traveling the major thoroughfares, not the coastal track winding through Fenwick.

She ought to have a sniffy companion and an even sniffier lady's maid traveling with her.

Her coachy, grooms, and footman should have been in livery.

And she should not have been gazing upon the lowly main thoroughfare of Fenwick with fear in her eyes.

🙰

Storms bring on babies.

Of all the lessons Lady Sarah Weatherby had learned on this ill-fated journey—and she had learned many—that was the most surprising. As she sat in her coach, waiting for MacAdams to parlay with the innkeeper, she mentally listed others.

Comfortable shoes were a greater necessity than a matching reticule and parasol. Thank God and blind chance, she'd worn her older pair of half-boots when she'd left Town.

Another lesson: Whatever she was paying MacAdams and his fellows, it wasn't enough. Sarah did not know how to raise this topic with her coachman, which reflected badly on her education. Uncle Burton claimed to have hired her the best governesses, tutors, and companions, but after five London Seasons, Sarah still had no idea what it cost to run her own household.

She had learned that Anglia was beautiful, though its roads were for the most part terrible.

She had also become aware that she should not have packed carriage dresses that fairly screamed of London's finest modistes, nor should she have brought a London coachman—dear though he was—who'd got turned around seventeen miles back, and not realized his error until the sea was before their very eyes.

But then, all of Sarah's dresses were of excellent quality, and her only other option would have been to steal from Miss Framington's wardrobe. The idea of wearing a turncoat's clothing was too repugnant to be borne.

MacAdams stalked out of the inn, his homely features set in a scowl as he approached the coach window. "No room, my—I mean Mrs. Winston. The innkeep is happy to put up the horses, and the lads and I are welcome to sleep in the stable, but for a proper lady, he has nothing to offer."

"Should we turn around?" Sarah asked.

MacAdams shook his head. "The storm has wreaked havoc all along the coast, and many of the roads are low-lying for a good distance inland. Innkeep says we are likely to find a lot of flooding and destruction and not much in the way of accommodations."

An apt metaphor for the state of her life generally.

Another lesson Sarah had learned was to make the best of bad situations. If she was stranded and without accommodations, the not-very-honorable Matthew Tewksbury likely was as well. He'd hate that, though this whole venture could be laid at his handsome, booted feet.

"I can bide in the common, I suppose."

"My la—Mrs. Winston, you cannot. The inn is a madhouse, full of all manner of folk. The innkeeper suggested we inquire at Mrs. Peabody's, for she occasionally has rooms to let."

Sarah considered the two-story Tudor cottage with the lush yard and cheerful pots of heartsease by the door. The place looked inviting, for all it sat next to the smithy. But that was the nature of an English village, with everybody living cheek by jowl, and shopkeepers dwelling above their business establishments.

"Please inquire of Mrs. Peabody, Mr. MacAdams, and you have my thanks."

Not by word or expression did MacAdams indicate that Sarah's thanks had become cold consolation, but after driving for hours through bad weather, her stalwart Scot was looking much the worse for wear.

He was nonetheless wreathed in smiles when he returned from the cottage. "Mrs. Peabody will be happy to let you a room to yourself, and that includes breakfast and dinner. Her establishment, if I might say so, is clean enough to make my sainted granny smile. I'll have the lads unload your valise, and you'll be enjoying a cup of hot tea in no time."

"Thank you, Mr. MacAdams."

And if anybody inquired for Sarah at the inn, the innkeeper could honestly say no fine London ladies answering to her description bided at his establishment.

She climbed down from the coach and took Thomas's arm to cross to the cottage. She was admitted by a cheerful maid in a clean apron and tidy white cap. The girl looked to be about fourteen, while the appreciative eye she ran over Thomas's broad shoulders was that of a grown woman.

"I'll send Mrs. P to you directly, ma'am," the girl said, when Thomas had returned to the coach, and Sarah had been shown to a parlor awash in cabbage roses and sunshine.

Whereas a London home of modest means might have adorned its guest parlor with framed cutwork or embroidered samplers done by the ladies of the house, Mrs. Peabody's parlor was dominated by a sunny landscape of a long, sandy beach, imposing headlands, and a pair of sailboats running close to the wind on a white-capped sea.

Racing, perhaps. Or perhaps the lead boat was piloted by a lady trying to outrun a devious and importunate suitor in the second vessel.

The mantel sported a collection of curiosities, including a nearly intact crab shell, some fearsome looking gray objects that vaguely resembled small caltrops, a tiny starfish with five delicate arms, various intricately spiraled whelks, and smooth lumps of cloudy green and blue glass.

"My nieces and nephews collect that lot from the beach," said a blond, softly rounded lady in a lacy mobcap and lavender day dress. "They love the fresh air and sunshine, and the ocean breeze is good for us, I say. You must be Mrs. Winston. I'm Penelope Peabody."

Of course, nobody was on hand to make introductions. Most of the world apparently gave that great awkwardness no thought whatsoever.

Sarah curtseyed. "Mrs. Peabody, a pleasure. You have a lovely home." And that was the truth rather than a polite fiction.

Mrs. Peabody reviewed the terms of room rental with brisk good cheer, even to naming the sum owed per night or per week. "Let me show you to your room, and then I'll send along a tea tray and some hot water for washing." She bustled from the parlor, leaving Sarah to follow in her wake.

"We have dinner at seven, though with the days getting longer, I'll soon be moving that back. I lock the door at ten of the clock and, I daresay, if you are abroad after that hour in Fenwick, you must be involved in the coastal trade or a darts tournament at The Queen's Barque. Neither pastime speaks well for your judgment."

She offered that conclusion with a friendly smile and a wink, suggesting the coastal trade—and the darts tournament—were in fact regarded locally with some affection.

Mrs. Peabody continued up a set of steps, the bannister of polished oak, the walls papered in green silk.

"If you are inclined to practice arias or that sort of thing, Mrs. Winston, please do so during daylight hours. Some of my tenants work long hours, and need their rest. Breakfast is on the buffet by 7 am, though we can put something together earlier if you've a mind to march out at dawn."

She took a key from her pocket and opened the door to a corner room. The space was dominated by a large, uncanopied bed set against the inside wall. The fireplace was full-sized and laid with coal, though bricks of peat were stacked in a brass bucket on the hearth. A privacy screen shielded a wash stand and mirror from the door, and a writing desk sat near the windows.

"I have a balcony?" Sarah said, peering out the French door.

"What's the use of having a view of the sea if nobody can admire it? You share a balcony with the next room, though you'll probably have it to yourself. Those of us who live here tend to take a less romantic view of the ocean. We respect it, but we know it can bring storms as well as pretty shells to our beaches."

The balcony also had a view of the smithy's yard next door. As Sarah watched, the blacksmith, Mr. Penn, strode across the cobbles with a tool box in his hand. He'd put on a coat and something resembling a neckcloth. His hat was a battered straw affair that clearly had more to do with protecting his eyes from the sun's glare than impressing anybody with his turnout.

He'd meant what he'd said, then, about tending to the midwife's gelding's loose shoe. *My time is not my own.*

His magnificent body was most assuredly his own. He strode along with a confidence that said he belonged here, and he took seriously the welfare of everybody in Fenwick from little Fifi to the aging Mrs. Gatesby and even the unborn children and their gravid mothers.

Sarah had never met such a large man, not only tall but bristling with muscle. She ought to have been intimidated, but something about Mr. Penn's demeanor spoke of a benevolent outlook on life, despite his unruly dark hair and dark eyes. He would be happy at his forge, a merry Hephaestus cheerfully fashioning Cupid's arrow and Athena's shield, and not much missing the blandishments of Olympus.

"I'll leave you now," Mrs. Peabody said, "but don't fall asleep just yet. You'll want to enjoy your tea hot."

"I am a bit fatigued," Sarah said, an understatement.

"You are fair exhausted, Mrs. Winston. Running off from Town is hard on a lady's nerves, and more than a bit tiring. If your jilted groom should come calling, what shall I tell him?"

Drat the luck. "That you never saw me."

"Precisely. I never saw you. If he's bungled matters so badly that you've fled his loving embrace, he can work a bit to win you over. Be warned though, we're not as isolated from London society as you might think. Even the maids at the Queen's Barque send and receive regular correspondence from Town, some of them nigh daily."

Mrs. Peabody pulled the door closed, leaving Sarah in blessed solitude. Matthew Tewksbury could labor until Judgement Day and Sarah would not willingly return to his far-from-loving embrace.

She returned to the French door and watched Mr. Penn's progress as he jaunted down the high street. He greeted everybody, doffed his hat to the ladies, and knelt to speak to small children. The sheer friendliness exchanged among the townsfolk made her homesick, but not for her groom's loving embrace.

Never that. Never, ever that.

CHAPTER 2

Like the flotsam and jetsam washed up on its beaches, Fenwick's citizenry tended to include curiosities among its number. Thad felt at home among them, never having dreamed that an earl's wayward heir could find welcome in an obscure coastal town. He had happy memories of boyhood summers at Grandmother's cottage, though, so to the coast he had fled.

The neighbors doubtless speculated about who or what had sent him pelting from London in high dudgeon five years ago, but they did not pry. Some of them had doubtless put the pieces together. Mrs. Peabody read two different London papers every evening, and the staff at The Queen's Barque heard all the Town gossip courtesy of the coachies and tinkers passing through.

Fenwick was obscure, but—barring roads washed out by monstrous storms—not isolated.

He tipped his hat to Martha Whyard, who was towing six-year-old Tommy by the hand. "Off to the beach?" Thad asked. Half the village was out on the sands, picking over storm-tide's offerings.

"Thomas thought to investigate by himself," Millicent said, glowering at the boy. "I woke up to find his bed empty. I never had such a fright in my life, with the roads washed out, the marshes flooded, and my only son nowhere to be found."

She sounded furious, but Fenwick knew—the whole village knew—that Thomas was the only child to survive infancy out of three babies born to the Whyard family. Thomas was as reckless a little fellow as ever kicked off his shoes and went barreling into the surf.

Thad knelt, the better to see into the soul of a lad intent on staring at the ground. "You wanted to see what the storm had tossed up, didn't you, young Thomas?"

He nodded, lower lip stuck out in a pout.

"And now you'll be among the last to have a good look, because you were forgetful."

Tommy peered at him. "What did I forget?"

"To ask mum's permission."

"Mum weren't even awake yet."

"Do you suppose, if some considerate lad had brought mum some jam and bread to start her day, she would have minded a wee tap on her door on such a glorious morning?"

"Jam and bread? With butter too?"

"Most ladies enjoy a dollop of butter with their jam and bread, but it's too late for that, lad. You must do as honor compels now."

Tommy assayed a dubious glance at his mother. "'Pologize?"

"Afraid so, my boy, but take the time to get the words right. Don't fling a few sorries at your poor mum right here on the street. You were thoughtless, but you can make it right by apologizing and doing better."

Tommy nodded, and Thad stood up.

"Has the captain's boat come in yet?" Thad asked.

Martha shook her head. "He said he'd put in at Great Yarmouth, if the weather turned foul. There's talk of shipwrecks, though, and in such a gale who could see the lighthouses?"

"If anybody could, it's Tom Whyard. He's been fishing these waters man and boy, and so has his crew. He would not be careless for the sake of one more catch. He has two very good reasons to be cautious."

Martha smoothed a hand over the boy's fair hair. "He would not let Tommy go with him yesterday."

And Tommy doubtless knew his father hadn't come home last night, and had run down to the sea searching for Papa's boat.

"Perhaps some jam and bread all around is a good idea. The road is washed out, so word from Great Yarmouth will take some time to get through, and tacking south against this wind won't be easy either."

Martha nodded tersely, then surprised Thad by wrapping him in a quick one-armed hug. "Thank you, Mr. Penn." She hurried off, the boy's hand still clutched in her firm grip.

Thad was still pre-occupied with the encounter when he knocked on Birdy Gatesby's door.

"You came," Birdy said, beaming up at him. She was graying, diminutive, and wore a pair of spectacles that gave her the inquisitive air of a wren on the kitchen windowsill. Thad would have been surprised if anybody in Fenwick knew her true given name.

"I said I would, and the day is too fair to spend entirely at the forge." He leaned down to accept a peck on the cheek.

"Bless you, my boy. I do fear you must hurry, for Socrates and I will doubtless be making calls. That was a birthing storm, mark my words."

"I can manage if you haven't finished your breakfast," Thad said. "Socrates isn't the fidgety sort." A midwife's cart horse learned patience and fortitude, like the midwife herself.

"Breakfast was hours ago, young man. Has Captain Whyard's boat put in yet?" Birdy asked, escorting Thad to the outbuilding that served as Socrates' stable. The gelding shared his quarters with a chicken coop, garden shed, hog wallow and goat pen, all neatly organized and as spotless as such a place could be.

"Not yet," Thad said, scratching behind Socrates's hairy ear. "Whyard promised the missus he'd put in at Great Yarmouth."

Birdy passed him a headstall with lead rope attached. "And you promised your grandmama you'd only bide with us for a year or two."

He'd told her that on the occasion of having been stranded at a birthing out on the marshes. Socrates had come up lame, and Birdy had prevailed upon Thad to drive her to a remote, tumbledown farm. Weather had closed in, and he'd sat the vigil out with the farmer, though Birdy had pressed the husband into service in the birthing room as well.

The experience had provoked confidences from Thad that he'd long since regretted, though Birdy had at least kept his disclosures to herself.

"Do you know," Thad said, opening the half door, and slipping the headstall onto the gelding, "my own grandmother reminds me by post, every two weeks without fail, that I was to have abandoned my life here long since. I'm to return to wenching, wagering, and waltzing, according to her, because that is my solemn duty."

He led Socrates out onto the little cobbled yard and passed Birdy the lead rope.

"Wagering," she said, "is admittedly so much nonsense, but what about the wenching and waltzing did you find so burdensome?"

Between Birdy Gatesby and Pen Peabody, Thad felt as if he had both a great-auntie and an older sister intent on stirring the cauldron of his guilt.

"The wagers came to include my bachelorhood, Miss Birdy, and I am not a horse to be auctioned off by the Mayfair hostesses. Socrates, my lad, you will need new front boots if you're to traverse the muddy roads."

Thad managed with a reset of the front shoes and did a quick trim on the hind feet for good measure.

"Keep his feet picked out," Thad said, dropping his tools back in their box. "The wet ground makes for soft soles, and that is never good for the foot." He took the lead from Birdy, though the horse had not moved other than to lift or put down a hoof at Thad's request.

"How old is he?" Thad asked, scratching Socrates about the withers.

"He's a mere lad of twelve. In a few years, he might even have some common sense. You cannot stay here forever, Thaddeus. Arbuckle's eldest is almost old enough to take over the smithy, and your granny has been patient long enough."

"I like Fenwick," Thad said, leading the horse back to his stall. "I am useful here, and Arbuckle's eldest should not have to take on the support of his entire family just because my grandmother wants to see me leg-shackled."

"Arbuckle would help the boy."

"Arbuckle would shout at the lad the live-long day, until young Arnold hopped on the London stagecoach and was never seen again. Give Arnie another few years to pop into Norwich for a spot of carousing while he finishes learning the trade."

"Your grandmother won't live forever," Birdy said, as Thad shrugged back into his jacket. "And neither will you. There are worse things than taking a wife and starting a family, Thaddeus Pennrith. You have the means."

"Starting a family takes more than means, Miss Birdy."

"I daresay you have the necessary equipment and the ability to use it too. Come in for a cup of tea."

Birdy did not invite, she commanded. Grandmother would either get into rousing battles with her or join ranks with her—if she hadn't already.

"A cup of tea sounds—"

One of the Pallant boys trotted into Birdy's stable yard. The entire family had bright red hair and prominent teeth, and each child's name began with a P. Peter, Patrick, Patricia, Posie... Thad lost track of them after that.

"Ma said to fetch ye," the boy panted. "Baby's coming. Pa said please come quick."

"I'll hitch up the horse," Thaddeus said. "Miss Birdy, you find your cloak and bag." Birdy hustled off to her cottage at a sprightly pace. "Patrick, if Miss Birdy isn't back home by suppertime, you come pen the chickens, milk the nanny goat, and feed and water the hogs. Same thing in the morning, even if she's driving back by then."

"Aye, Mr. Penn." Patrick scrubbed a hand over his face. "Petey's tending to the livestock at home. Pa were walking with Ma. Ma said it helps the pangs."

"Maybe it does, and walking also helps your father not worry so much, but don't tell him I said that."

By the time Thad had the horse hitched to the dogcart, Birdy was back, wearing her cloak and bonnet and carrying a valise that was part overnight bag and part medical kit. She popped onto the bench, took up the reins, and clattered out of the yard, Patrick up beside her.

Grandmother wanted Thad to leave this—people who cared for

one another, children who were loved by their parents, work that mattered—to resume life as Mayfair's largest fribble.

Soon, he would have to, but not yet. Not quite yet.

He ambled back to the smithy saying a silent prayer for Mrs. Pallant, and for all the Pallants. For good measure, he asked the Almighty to send word that Tom Whyard and his crew were sitting safe and snug in a Great Yarmouth tavern.

A line had formed outside the smithy, three men holding horses, two more sitting in wagons that held some piece of large, damaged equipment.

"What have you brought me, Oxborrow?" Thad asked the man in the closest wagon.

"Archimedes screw needs mendin'," Oxborrow replied. "Whole damned marsh pasture is turned into a broad."

Broads were unique to Anglia, a cross between rivers and flat, shallow lakes. The old folks said they were ancient peat cuts submerged by rising estuary levels, the young folks said they were God's gift to the mosquito population.

Without an irrigation pump to drain his marshes, Oxborrow could lose all of his spring pasture. "I'll get to it today," Thad said, "and you can pick it up tomorrow. Leave the screw with young Arnie. Spall, is that a plough bottom, I see?"

He moved down the line, mentally organizing the rest of his day, which would be quite long. More customers came, mostly with sprung and pulled horseshoes, and Arnie worked with him tirelessly to see every one of them tended to.

When the last customer had been sent on his way, his gelding wearing four brand new shoes, Thad smacked Arnie on the shoulder, then pressed a coin into his hand.

"Go have a pint at the Barque," he said, gathering up his shirt, neckcloth, and waistcoat. "Catch up on all the news. Your parents will want to know, and inquire particularly after Tom Whyard's boat."

"He made port," Arnie said, grinning. "No significant damage. Word came when Mrs. P sent over your supper."

Thad was abruptly famished. "I trust my supper did not go to waste?"

Arnie thumped his skinny belly. "You were willin' to let it get cold. Mrs. P's shepherd's pie deserved appreciatin'."

"You deserve a knock on the head. Be off with you."

Arnie trotted across the street, his energy making Thad feel elderly. Birdy was right that the lad would soon be in a position to take over his father's smithy, provided he had some help. He was only a few inches shorter than Thad and, year by year, he was growing into the muscle needed to tend a forge.

Thad went around to the side of the smithy, draped his shirt and waistcoat on hooks set into the side of the building, and worked the handle of the pump that filled the horse trough. He used his neckcloth to wash himself thoroughly, everywhere above the waist. Summer was coming, but the evening air was bracing particularly when driven by a brisk sea breeze.

Thad used his shirt as a towel and spared a thought for his supper. Pen Peabody made a delicious shepherd's pie, alas. He was scrubbing his hands through his damp hair when he happened to look up and catch sight of somebody in a long, pale dress—or night robe?—on the balcony along the back of the Peabody cottage.

A female, watching him at his ablutions. A slim, petite female, standing absolutely still in the evening shadows. If Pen Peabody were to watch him, as she often had, she'd make some bawdy remark about his physique, or wishing she were younger, though she might be all of ten years Thad's senior.

He did not know who watched him—Pen occasionally took in the overflow from the Barque and, with the storm, she'd doubtless have filled every room in the cottage.

The lady remained on the balcony, suggesting she liked what she saw. Thad had brought his height and a Corinthian's appetite for sport with him from London, but the forge had put muscle on him beyond what any London dandy could claim. The lady remained watchful on her balcony, probably never having seen a blacksmith without his shirt.

Thad smiled and waved, then went back to drying off, while two admissions claimed his attention. First, Arnie would indeed soon be ready to take over his father's business. He was old enough to enjoy a pint at the Barque with the menfolk, and skilled enough to handle all of the farriery if not all of the smithing.

Second, Thad did have the equipment necessary to start a family, *and* the ability to use it. For too long, though, he hadn't had the *opportunity* to use that equipment. That thought had him working the pump handle, and sticking his head right back under the cascade of brutally frigid water.

Village life was a revelation to Sarah—the life of this village, anyway. People in Fenwick on Sea greeted one another by name, stopped and chatted, laughed, and—this fascinated her—they touched one another.

Children were the recipients of universal affection, from a chuck under the chin to ruffling of their hair. Women touched each other's arms, men slapped one another on the back or shook hands. Sarah had even seen a pair of women hug—right on the street—and nobody passing by had thought anything of it.

She had seen the blacksmith, Mr. Penn, gently cuff the gangly young man on the shoulder, which had the young man grinning and scampering off in the direction of the posting inn. The exchange was easy, friendly, and, to Sarah, utterly novel.

The sight of Mr. Penn without his shirt so far surpassed novelty that Sarah had been unable to look away. A proper young woman would have withdrawn the instant it became obvious she was about to see a man tending to his ablutions.

But then, proper young women did not bolt from London, no lady's maid, no companion, not even a handy cousin or uncle to serve as escort.

Mr. Penn's physique was *excessively* impressive. He would have made two of Matthew Tewksbury, and Matthew considered himself a fine figure of a man. She was intrigued with Mr. Penn's sheer abundance of muscle, and even more so by the easy grace with which he moved. He'd stripped off his shirt with no hint of self-consciousness. When he'd waved to Sarah, the gesture had been purely friendly—no swagger, flirtation, or arrogance about it.

He was honestly unconcerned about being seen half-naked.

Rather than gawk at him as he resumed washing, Sarah stepped back into her room to retrieve a shawl. The sunset over the water had been amazing, but the sea air was brisk, and night coming on quickly.

When Sarah returned to her balcony, Mr. Penn was nowhere to be seen, and that was for the best. She needed time to think, to plan next steps, and to simply enjoy the rare thrill of solitude. In London, her lady's maid had slept in her dressing closet, and Sarah had often awakened to a chambermaid tending to the hearth or her lady's maid laying out the first outfit of the day.

No solitude and no privacy—except for when Matthew Tewksbury had sought privacy with her.

Sarah sank into the chair on the balcony, wrapping herself in her shawl. The last indigo streaks of the sunset painted the clouds over the horizon, and fatigue dragged at her. Still she did not want this vexing, intriguing, day to end.

A door latch clicked several yards down the balcony, and a very large shape emerged into the gloom.

"You're still here." The voice was masculine, deep, and amused.

Sarah would recognize it anywhere. "Mr. Penn, good evening."

"Mrs. Winston, greetings. Do you mind if I join you?"

He wore no jacket, only a billowing white shirt and darker waistcoat. His casual dishabille aside, for a man and a woman without a family connection to tarry in the dark alone was so far beyond the bounds of propriety as to exceed the imagination.

But not quite as far as running from a wealthy, handsome, and exceeding well placed fiancé.

"The balcony is a shared treasure," Sarah said, "based on what Mrs. Peabody said. Please do have a seat." The gathering darkness was fortunate, for Sarah blushed to offer that invitation.

Mr. Penn pulled a heavy wooden chair over—one handed—and set it a few feet away. He lowered himself with a grand sigh, stretched out his legs, and crossed his feet at the ankles.

"Storms are great for bringing coin and custom to the smithy, but they play merry hell on a man's back. I should be able to get to your coach tomorrow, though that's not a promise, and besides, the road is still washed out."

In London, one did not discuss commerce. In London, one did not use profanity before a lady. In London, one did not delight when a man broke both rules in one sentence.

Thank the merciful powers, Sarah was no longer in London. "I have enjoyed my day in Fenwick on Sea, Mr. Penn. I suspect I will find another such day equally pleasant. You need not turn aside other business to tend to my coach."

He sank lower in his chair. "Have you truly enjoyed your day in Fenwick?"

"I had never seen the ocean before, and I find it... any words I could use to describe the sea would not do it justice, like talking about God. The ocean provokes me to silence, as if I have come upon an enormous, ancient cathedral and have all to myself."

"You don't mind the sand getting everywhere?"

"I did not venture onto the beach, so no, I did not notice the sand." Sarah promised herself that tomorrow, she would start her day on the beach, and maybe even—the idea itself gave her a thrill—let the surf touch her bare toes.

"What else did you notice about our fair village?" Mr. Penn asked.

This was not small talk, or maybe it was small talk between strangers in a small village. Sarah had no way of knowing.

"I noticed that no footmen or maids trailed behind their employers, eavesdropping and looking impatient. Children were not harried by nannies and governesses, and come to that, I found it odd that children were even allowed out of their school rooms, much less permitted to go barefoot on the beach. Where was Fifi's groom? Why was the child permitted off the lead line if she can't control her pony? People shout here—raise their voices to bellow at one another across the high street. I never knew small villages made so much noise.

"And the *air*," she went on. "The air is magical. Never have I seen such clear air, almost as if the air itself embraces the sunlight. The sun on the water is nearly too bright to behold and the sunset over the marshes was proof everlasting of benevolent almighty powers."

Don't prattle, Sarah Louise. She sank back, though was it prattling to admire the Creator's handiwork?

"You are wiser than I," Mr. Penn said. "When I arrived here, on a horse going lame I might add, all I noticed was that the local speech is nigh unintelligible. The letter R runs amok in these surrounds, disappearing from its proper locations and popping up where it has no business. *Oi fell orf me hoss and hit me head s' hawd.*"

"And g's at the end of the words are a rarity," Sarah added. "*The sun is shinin' this mornin'.* I find that charming."

"I found it incomprehensible. I thought the ocean stank, the marshes reeked, and the salt air would ruin my boots. I was right about that part. Sea air will rust a pair of horseshoes almost as fast as I can reset them."

He propped his feet on the balustrade, casual as you please.

"Did you come here to ply your trade?" Sarah asked, though he was certainly well spoken for a man involved in commerce.

"I did not." He crossed his feet at the ankle, taking a moment either to get comfortable or to choose his words. "I arrived in Fenwick for a repairing lease, I suppose you might say. My horse came up lame, the farrier had nobody to hold the beast while he pulled the shoes. My gelding needed some time to recover from a stone bruise, and I had nothing better to do than make a nuisance of myself at the smithy. When an unruly mare tromped on Henry Arbuckle's foot, I became a kind of apprentice, and now here I am."

"How long ago did your horse turn up lame?"

"Five years, give or take." He said this softly, perhaps sadly. "They have been good years, too. What of you? What brings you to Fenwick on Sea?"

Over supper, Sarah had been asked the same question. She'd responded that she was on her way to visit relatives in the area, which was only a slight embellishment on the truth. A lady did not propound falsehoods, except in service to kindness or tact.

"I need a repairing lease too," she said. "I found myself engaged to marry a party who turned out to be unsuitable, and those around me were not inclined to listen when I said so. I learned that my intended was about to abduct me for an unscheduled journey north." Sarah kept the worst of it to herself: Uncle had not only approved Matthew's scheme, he'd all but authored it.

"You don't strike me as being very abduct-able."

"Is that a compliment or an insult?"

White teeth gleamed in the darkness. "Given that you are here, and your intended is not, that's a statement of the truth. I can understand why your fiancé would wish to make off with you, but what sort of man can only procure a wife by stealth and force?"

"A determined one. The gentleman is quite smitten with my settlements."

"Then he's not a gentleman. Is he an honorable?"

In for a penny... "Yes."

"They are the worst. Just enough consequence to be arrogant, not enough responsibility to grow up. Congratulations on a narrow escape." Mr. Penn spoke as if he too had had a narrow escape.

"I suspect my former intended will attempt to persuade me to resume our engagement, if he can find me. I have caused a very great scandal. No one else will have me."

Uncle had flung that observation at her with particular frequency and force. Used goods, soiled goods, a jilt... And the accusations, thanks to Matthew's charm and Sarah's stupidity, were true.

Come, Sarah. What's the point of getting engaged if you won't let me under your skirts?

Very well, but don't muss my hair.

On the half-dozen occasions when Matthew had been *under her skirts*, he'd accomplished his aims without mussing her hair. Those experiences had left Sarah increasingly unwilling to speak her vows.

"I very much doubt that no one else will have you," Mr. Penn mused. "But if so, you are free, and to be envied that rare and blessed state. Be warned though, the longer you tarry in Fenwick, the more it begins to feel like home, and that becomes a powerful anchor."

He fell silent, and Sarah found she had no need to chatter. A glow on the horizon of the vast silvery sea to the east presaged an imminent moonrise.

The conversation with Mr. Penn had been extraordinary. No talk of the weather. No malicious gossip about other women. No speculation about who would offer for whom. The whole day, from Mrs. Peabody's odd friendliness and scrumptious shepherds' pie, to the hum and bustle of the village, to the sight of Mr. Penn without his shirt, had been a revelation.

Proof that life—and good life—existed outside of Mayfair, beyond Uncle's lectures, out past Miss Framington's hypocritical sermons. People lived and loved without consulting Debrett's or etiquette manuals. They had things to do besides fittings, at homes, and calls. They cared for one another without a thought for who had large settlements or a large bosom.

The relief—the vindication—Fenwick on Sea had provided in the space of a day was as immense as the ocean.

And Mr. Penn was part of that vindication. He'd been naked before her from the waist up, and hadn't turned the moment scandalous. He was sitting alone with her in the dark, and his hands weren't wandering. He had *commended* her on breaking her engagement, and he had done her the precious courtesy of listening to her.

The first sliver of golden light broke the horizon gilding the waves and whitecaps.

"I have not watched a moonrise in too long," Mr. Penn said, "much less in such congenial company. I hope you'll tarry a while in Fenwick, Mrs. Winston."

"My maternal grandmother was Mrs. Winston. My given name is Sarah, and I am nobody's missus, thank heavens."

Another slight pause followed. Perhaps Mr. Penn was allowing Sarah a moment to give him the rest of her name, or perhaps she had shocked him.

"The locals know me as Thaddeus Penn, but my full name is Thaddeus Pennrith—at your service." He added that last with an ironic smile.

She did not say, *Your secret is safe* with me, because he had to know that, just as she knew he would not spread her confidences in the high street. His name sounded vaguely familiar—Sarah had studied Debrett's thoroughly before making her come-out—but the details refused to come to her.

The moon drifted higher until it cleared the horizon, casting silver beams on the flooded marshes as well as the endless sea. Night birds sang and, in the distance, the roar and retreat of the surf confirmed—as if the whole day had not—that Sarah was blessedly far from London.

"If I don't seek my bed now," Mr. Penn said—Mr. Pennrith, "I will fall asleep out here. Tomorrow promises to be hectic, so I'll bid you good night."

He rose and stretched, a great beast of a man with more manners and consideration than all the honorables in Mayfair combined.

"Sleep well, Mr. Pennrith."

He remained at the balustrade, the moonshine putting highlights in his dark hair. "Thaddeus."

"Sleep well, Thaddeus."

He turned to regard her. "Are you glad you left London?"

"I am now. Talking to you helped me sort that out. The night air is a bit cool, isn't it?" She made to rise and found his hand extended to her. Because the chair was low and she needed to keep her shawl about her, she accepted his assistance.

He kept her hand in his. "I am glad you've found your way here, and welcome to Fenwick, Sarah."

She realized he was asking some sort of permission or offering an invitation. Whatever he was about, it had nothing to do with getting under her skirts and everything to do with genuine welcome.

"Sweet dreams," she said, going up on her toes to brush a kiss to his cheek. "And thank you for the moonrise."

CHAPTER 3

T had should have been asleep before his head hit the pillow. He lay on his bed, his whole body aching with fatigue and the knowledge that tomorrow would be even busier. Road repair was hard on tools, sodden ground was hard on farm equipment, and mud was pure misery on shod hooves.

He would be swamped with work for at least a week, and spring was a busy time of year to begin with. Henry Arbuckle would have to be temporarily coaxed out of his advisory role if customers weren't to grumble.

Sleep eluded Thad, despite his exhaustion. He revisited his conversation with Sarah, and revisited his decision not to tell her that he too was a refugee from Mayfair's marriage madness. She'd had nothing good to say about a mere honorable, and for Thaddeus to mention his title had seemed ill-advised.

Though he really should find a way to tell her the truth before allowing any more kisses to his cheek. Rather than ponder how he'd convey his particulars, he instead imagined Sarah preparing to retire, taking down her hair, slipping out of her night robe, and climbing onto the big bed in the room next door. Thad had taken that room for his first few months in Fenwick, until this one—with a higher ceiling—had become available.

Sarah's hair was an unfashionable auburn, and, for all she wore it captured in a tidy chignon, she brought to mind the old horseman's adage, "Chestnut mare, better beware." She had apparently kicked over the traces and bolted from a proper match, and as many weary travelers bearing strange tales had, she'd washed up on Fenwick's shores.

He liked hearing her voice, particularly in the dark. Every word was a grace note, every thought dipped in ladylike elocution. She was no snob—he'd been wrong about that—and she was already ensnared in Fenwick's charm.

He had noticed her charms too. She was womanly rather than girlish, with a well-rounded fundament and generous breasts. A gentleman could note those blessings without gawking, and, when she'd kissed him goodnight, she'd briefly pressed all that luscious softness close to him.

He had friends in Fenwick, true neighbors, people with whom he could share a tankard of ale and depend on to jolly him out of a passing low mood. Fenwick's denizens were good folk, the salt of the earth, and he loved them as he'd never loved the posturing dandies at his London clubs.

But Thad had to acknowledge that he was nonetheless lonely in Fenwick. He occasionally made the trip into Norwich to pass the time with a discreet and friendly widow, and that eased the ache in his body.

It did not ease the ache in his heart. He was Thad Penn, the blacksmith with a past. Nobody here had seen him fencing at Angelo's, or accompanying some soprano as she warbled of true love and blushes at a Mayfair musicale.

Once upon a time, he'd had gentlemanly accomplishments. Once upon a time, he'd danced with the wallflowers and claimed some charm.

He did not miss the wallflowers, but did miss being known for who he truly was. Missed hearing his family name, missed—a little—the speculation in the eyes of the matchmakers. Yes, he was a big brute, but he had the title, thirty thousand acres, and an old fortune. Even if the ladies hadn't coveted his kisses, and frankly shuddered to consider the wedding night, they'd coveted the wealth and standing he could bring to a marriage.

His hand drifted down over his belly, and lower, to grasp his half-aroused manhood. He let his imagination wander idly, to questions with no answers. Just what had Sarah's fiancé done, that a genteel young lady took her chances on the King's highway? How long was her unbound hair? Would she ever hike her skirts enough to wade at low tide and allow a fellow a glimpse of trim ankles and sturdy calves?

Did she kiss on the mouth as sweetly as she pressed her lips to a man's cheek?

Desire welled from a combination of hopeless longing and hoarded joy. *She* had kissed *him*. Brought him the scent of roses. She'd laid her hand on his chest and brushed her lips over his cheek, as if he were not a prodigal heir who'd never meet proper society's standards for lordly refinement, but as if he were someone special and precious.

Thank you for the moonrise. Whoever her dimwitted *former* fiancé was, he deserved to lose her if he couldn't be bothered to share the occasional moonrise with his intended.

Satisfaction, when it came, brought a hint of joy to go with the pleasure. Had Thad met Sarah in Mayfair, he would have been properly introduced by a mutual acquaintance. He would have asked her for the honor of a quadrille or a waltz. They would have minced around a crowded dance floor together, and he would have bowed politely over her hand before leading her to her next partner.

They would not have spoken of failed engagements or repairing leases, she would never have kissed his cheek or sat conversing with him in the dark. Soon, he'd have to leave Fenwick and bow to Grandmother's increasingly querulous demands, but not quite yet.

Sarah had decided the repairs to her coach were not urgent, and that was fortunate. Maybe, before Thad sent her on her way, he and she could make a few more sweet memories here in Fenwick on Sea.

Sarah could not leave common sense so far behind that she eschewed headwear altogether, but she did accept the wide-brimmed floppy straw hat Mrs. Peabody offered rather than any of the millinery packed from London.

Beneath the late morning sun, the ocean was too bright to stare at directly, and, on such a day, it was nearly impossible to believe that a hundred miles to the east lay the coast of the Netherlands, and beyond that, France. The Corsican had escaped his island prison, the French Army was all but declaring for him, and everybody spoke of war.

Here in Fenwick, such thoughts seemed obscene.

Sarah had broken her fast in Mrs. Peabody's sunny dining parlor, equally relieved and disappointed that Mr. Pennrith did not join the other guests for his first meal of the day. She'd eaten a prodigious amount of buttered toast, eggs, and apple tart, and consumed three cups of stout black tea. Miss Framingham would be scandalized at such an appetite, but then, Miss Framingham had much to answer for.

Sarah had written a letter to Great-Aunt Fletcher explaining her situation and location, but, because the road was washed away, she'd had to inquire at The Queen's Barque for a special courier willing to carry her missive through the marshes the more than forty miles to Cromer.

The sun was directly overhead by the time she found her way to Fenwick's gleaming sandy beach. She quickly realized that trudging through the deep sand was much more work than walking closer to the water, where the tide packed the sand close. Her destination was an outcropping of rocks a hundred yards or so distant. The rocks weren't visible from the village, being partly around a bend in the shoreline.

She would sit upon those rocks, and turn her focus to the scandal she'd created, just as soon as she could pry that focus loose from the more interesting subject of Thaddeus Pennrith's hands. His hands were enormous, like the rest of him, and they were warm.

What had made Sarah aware of the chilly night air was the contrast between the brisk breeze and the enveloping warmth of Mr. Pennrith's grip around her fingers. His touch had been delicate and gentlemanly, but also strange for being without gloves, and for the abundance of his calluses.

Calluses between a man's third and fourth finger were the natural result of hours on horseback, even wearing gloves. Mr. Pennrith had calluses everywhere—fingertips, palms, the heel of his thumb. And yet, Sarah suspected his touch on a lady's person would be gentle and cherishing.

He would not bend his intended over a handy chair, ruck up her skirts, and tell her to hold still as he thumped away and the lady mentally composed a menu for her uncle's next formal dinner.

Sarah reached her destination, delighted to find that the rocks sheltered substantial depressions that were filled with sea water. Little worlds existed in the resulting tidal pools, full of strange brown and green plant life, tiny scuttling crabs, and clusters of blue-black mussels.

She perched above one particularly clear pool, fascinated with the variety of life within.

"It's a miniature world," said a deep and familiar male voice. "They have everything they need in there, and the whole vast sea remains unknown to them, like an isolated village."

Mr. Pennrith carried his boots, and sizeable boots they were too. He'd turned up the cuffs of his trousers, and his toes were covered with sand.

"I was thinking of Mayfair," Sarah said, sitting back. "Of how insular and self-absorbed most people I know are—how insular I am. Will you join me?"

He settled beside her on her rocky perch, his coat over his arm. "Do you miss it?"

"No. I ought to. It's all I know, save for a few summers spent with my great aunt, but I dread to return. I thought you were expecting a great lot of business today."

"I have been at the forge since before dawn. We are awash in sprung horseshoes, broken pickaxes, and bent blades. The work is too demanding to be done on an empty stomach for long." He held up a cloth sack that his coat had hidden. "Will you join me?"

"A picnic by the sea?" What a marvelous idea.

"More of a sandwich in the middle of the day." He opened his sack and passed her a parcel wrapped in paper. "Must you return to London?"

"Eventually. I have to live somewhere, and my uncle's home is the one available to me. Aunt Fletcher can host me for a visit, but Uncle is my trustee, and until last year he was my guardian." The sandwich was raspberry jam and clotted cream, the bread fresh.

"So purchase your own home," Mr. Pennrith said. "Your trust is doubtless written to allow the funds to be used for your basic needs, and if pretty dresses and a fancy coach meet that definition, so should keeping a roof over your head."

"I cannot maintain my own household, Mr. Pennrith. I am not yet thirty."

He glanced over at her between bites of his sandwich. "I'd put you at five-and-twenty. If you are old enough to marry and manage your husband's domicile, you're old enough to manage your own staff."

He'd guessed her age correctly, and from him it was merely a number, not significant of failed seasons and looming disaster.

"If I were a bluestocking spinster, perhaps I could establish my own household, but I am a ruined heiress. If I ever want to be received, I must accept the scolding my uncle will heap upon me. This is an exceptionally satisfying sandwich."

Mr. Pennrith dusted his hands together. "The honorable dunderhead took unpardonable liberties, didn't he?"

So much for allowing a change of subject. "He did not *take* liberties, I *permitted* him liberties." Society especially would see it in that light.

"You capitulated to stop his whining, then realized his ability to whine was reborn exactly ten minutes after he'd rebuttoned his falls."

"Twenty." When Matthew had demanded "a little encore," after their last coupling, Sarah had realized what he was about. "I suspect he was determined to get me with child, so that I could not cry off."

"No wonder you tossed him over. Are you with child?"

"That is an extraordinarily personal question." Though clearly not meant to offend.

Mr. Pennrith gazed out over the sparkling waves. "Do you know the signs of conception, Sarah?"

She did, thanks to Aunt Fletcher. "As determined as Matthew was on his objective, he was unsuccessful." Sarah told him the rest of it, though a lady never spoke of such things. "My companion abetted him, ensuring I was left alone with him at every opportunity, and that we were not disturbed. She reported to him on my... on the failure of his attempts in the direction of conception. While I might be half-way able to understand Matthew's scheming, my uncle encouraged him in it."

Mr. Pennrith was quiet for a time, perhaps shocked, though Sarah suspected it took a lot to shock him.

"How wealthy are you?"

The precisely relevant question, given her disclosures. "I am not sure. The solicitors send the reports to Uncle, but I've picked the lock in his desk drawer often enough to have a general idea of the sum." She named the figure, quietly, despite their deserted location.

"And all of that money becomes your husband's upon your marriage?"

"It isn't supposed to. Aunt says the money is to remain in trust, for me and my progeny, but I suspect Uncle has diverted a large sum into my settlements, and much of that would come under a husband's control."

Mr. Pennrith slanted a brooding glance at her. He was not a laughing god of the forge now. "You haven't signed the settlement agreements?"

"I was never asked to."

"But you are of age, and no longer under your uncle's guardianship. You would have to sign the settlements to make them binding."

"All of which suggests that Matthew's rutting was indeed an attempt to get me with child. To ensure my offspring were legitimate and well cared for, I would have signed half my fortune into Matthew's keeping and left the other half with my uncle. I never wanted a fortune anyway."

Mr. Pennrith passed her an apple tart. "I believe you, given what that fortune has cost you. Where is your auntie?"

"Cromer, twenty some miles past Norwich."

"And you cannot get to her as long as the road is washed out and your coach is unreliable. Promise me something."

"Of course."

His smile was crooked and fleeting. "You barely know me. Why promise so readily?"

"I *know* you. You've been honest with me, you trusted me with your real name but you don't ask for mine. You don't stare at my bosom, and, if we were engaged, you wouldn't bend me over the nearest writing chair and not even bother to lock the door."

"A *writing* chair?"

Perhaps the fresh sea air had addled her brain, because Sarah could not seem to stop her tirade. "A wing chair is too tall, a vanity stool too short. Matthew prefers that I hold onto a writing chair while he enjoys himself. The angle is convenient for him. He also prefers that I not wear drawers even in cold weather, and, when he is my husband, he will forbid me such scandalous underlinen."

"Did he ever speak to you of anything besides his convenience?"

"Not once we became engaged. As often as I was lectured about writing chairs, he could not be bothered to kiss me. He likes certain parts of my physique better than others, and felt the need to impress his preferences upon me."

Sarah passed the apple tart back uneaten, for Mr. Pennrith had finished his, and she abruptly had no appetite.

"They will make me marry him," she said. "He promised to give me a *jolly spanking* on my *splendid rosy bum*, to celebrate our wedding night, as if this is some great treat to look forward to, and he the master of the art. How can a spanking *be* jolly, and why would any woman marry a man who boasts of using violence on her person? He does not listen to me; he does not want me to even speak. I'm simply to bend over and hold still every twenty minutes for the rest of my life."

Mr. Pennrith passed her a handkerchief, though she hadn't realized she was crying. "They cannot make you marry him. You are of age, you have means."

"They can send me for a respite in the north until I come to my senses, Mr. Pennrith. Uncle was very clear about that. A great fortune inspires great ingenuity in those who covet it. I would give them my blasted fortune, but they want to take me prisoner too."

Mr. Pennrith was quiet for some time, a man at ease with female anger and female tears. He crumbled up her apple tart and tossed the bits onto a flat rock several yards away. Within moments, a dozen sea gulls were arguing over the feast, until the rock was picked clean.

"My family has some influence," Mr. Pennrith said. "My grandmother in particular is a force to be reckoned with. I'd like to put your situation before her without getting into specifics, and see what she recommends. May I have your permission to do that much?"

When had anybody asked Sarah's permission for anything? "Of course, but I doubt your granny can work miracles. Uncle is an earl. He inherited when my papa died without male issue—that's my fault too, that I failed to be male. I am in quite a taking, aren't I?"

Mr. Pennrith patted her arm. "You are doubtless overdue for a spectacular taking, and a temper puts roses in your cheek. I'm surprised you didn't bash Matthew over the head with one of those writing chairs."

The thought had not occurred to her, not until the coach had passed the last London turnpike and freedom had been in her hands.

"I used to like Matthew. He was funny and handsome and he said charming things as if he sincerely meant them. I was an idiot."

"You were cozened, and everybody you should have been able to trust conspired against you."

Sarah took a turn being silent, sorting through feelings, even enjoying the realization that she was angry. Not out of sorts, a bit testy, or in a mood—she was furious. Her trust and her person had been violated in an attempt to seize and carry off her future.

"If he had offered me one honest kiss," she said, "I might be able to see my way to some sort of affection, an accommodation, but he never has. He couldn't be bothered when he had a chance to toss up my skirts instead. Mrs. Matthew Tewksbury, whoever she may be, will go to her grave without having known the pleasure of one sweet, passionate, genuine kiss."

"And that woman will not be you," Mr. Pennrith said. "You are safe here in Fenwick, your aunt is barely half a day's journey away, and my grandmother will take your situation under advisement. You are not to lose hope."

"I have seen the vast ocean," Sarah said, rising and dusting off her backside. "I never thought that day would come. Hope is closer here than it was in London. Would you be scandalized if I took off my boots as you have, and let the water splash over my toes?" She had spoken to him of writing chairs and Matthew's plans for her splendid, rosy bum, and yet, she had needed to ask that question.

Mr. Pennrith gazed down at her without smiling, though his eyes held warmth and humor, possibly even approval.

"You could let the water splash you even up to your *ankles*, Miss Sarah, and I would not be scandalized."

She waded in the shockingly cold surf, letting it wet her clear up to her calves, and Mr. Pennrith waded right along beside her.

⚜

"This was all your idea," Matthew Tewksbury said for the eight-hundred-and-seventeenth time. "The whole bit, the flirtation, the engagement, the anticipating the vows, the..." he twirled a lace-draped wrist in an upward spiral. "You should have known she'd bolt."

Burton Weatherby, Earl of Bassham, did not so much as glance up from his steward's report. Reading in a moving coach was difficult enough without indulging the moods of a petulant, incompetent bridegroom.

"My dear young man, how was I to know your wooing would be so inept as to send my niece on a mad flight?"

"My wooing was enthusiastic," Tewksbury retorted, "as you insisted it be, and Lady Sarah was willing, else I should have waited for the ceremony. She never raised more than an eyebrow at me when I sought a private moment."

"Spare me the details of your bumbling. We'll catch up to her soon enough."

"You said that in Alconbury. Nobody noticed a young woman traveling alone with a coach and four, and servants in London finery."

"Of course not."

The coach hit a rut, very likely the eight-hundred-and-seventeenth of those for the day as well.

"What do you mean, of course not? Young women of good

breeding do not travel the Great North Road without proper chaper-onage, but we haven't heard a word of her."

"The Great North Road sees all manner of traffic and lots of it. I daresay Sarah's coachy and grooms are not in livery."

"I'll sack the lot of them once she marries me. Damned nerve, abetting a runaway."

Bassham gave up on his steward's report. The news was never good, and it would keep for another day.

"The coachy and grooms are loyal to her, for it is she who pays their wages. They will keep her safe for you until such time as we can bring her home. You ought to reward their loyalty."

Tewksbury scowled, and, even given his blond good looks, the expression did not flatter him. "Her solicitors pay their wages."

"And she pays the solicitors. Sarah herself might not understand all the roundaboutations, but those from society's lower strata grasp these things intuitively. She has only one possible destination, and that is my Aunt Fletcher's household in Cromer. We will doubtless find her there before the week is out."

The damned spring weather had made the going difficult, as had all the traffic heading for London. Despite the threat of renewed hostili-ties on the Continent, the London Season was already well underway.

"What if she's with child?" Tewksbury muttered. "I don't like to think of my future wife, in a delicate condition, racketing about the countryside all by herself."

"Now you turn up doting? I'm touched, Tewksbury."

"You think you know her," Tewksbury said, gaze on the rain-washed countryside of Cambridgeshire. "You think she's the meek, biddable, niece who would never gainsay you, but here we are, no Sarah and no idea where she's got off to. You should never have threatened her with a madhouse."

Much as broken clocks were accurate twice a day, Tewksbury had chanced upon a truth. "She was threatening to cry off before I mentioned a respite to settle her overwrought nerves. Your charm as a fiancé was sadly lacking and I grew impatient. You are not the only one with obligations that will go unmet if Sarah's fit of pique is indulged."

Bassham had chosen Tewksbury for three qualities. First, Tewksbury, as the younger son of a viscount, was of adequate social standing to woo a late earl's wealthy daughter. Second, Tewksbury was reported to be as randy as a four-year-old colt and had male by-blows to support that reputation. Third, he was hopelessly submerged in the River Tick. His gambling debts were part of the problem, but the true source of his misery was a father unable to check the fashionable excesses of his wife, heir, and daughters.

The whole Tewksbury family was headed for ruin in a fast chariot. Until Sarah's inheritance had come into Bassham's hands, Bassham's branch of the Weatherby family had been traveling toward the same destination.

"Why didn't that Framingham creature keep a closer eye on her?" Tewksbury muttered.

"Because the Framingham creature was told Sarah was spending the day with you."

Tewksbury's fine blond brows drew down. "Sarah told her that?"

"Left Framingham a note claiming you had invited Sarah out to Richmond for a picnic in the fresh spring air. From what Miss Framingham said, for you to tup Sarah on a blanket would have been a step up from your usual fumbling."

Tewksbury grinned. "Framingham likes to watch me? I'd happily swive her if she's been too long without. The sniffy ones always moan the loudest."

"You are, of course, free to make overtures to Miss Framingham, though I suspect you will find her less biddable than Sarah has been. Miss Framingham, unlike your handsome self, performed her duties without flaw. I'm told you had no less than a half dozen interludes with your bride in the space of three weeks, and that has proven insufficient to start a family with her."

"When Sarah and I are married, and we're not limited to two interludes a week, a baby will come along soon enough."

Bassham admitted to having committed a second error, this one more egregious than threatening Sarah with treatment for nervous hysteria.

Tewksbury was a mistake. He had all the attributes Bassham sought in a prospective husband for Sarah, but he lacked qualities that might have made him better suited to Sarah herself. Fiancés and new husbands were expected to be lusty. Their job was to be lusty, in fact. Tewksbury wasn't simply lusty; he was in thrall to his own pizzle.

Sarah was too much like her mother to find that quality appealing. She'd want weighty discussions, quiet walks in rural surrounds, tender words and all the romantic whatnot. Perhaps it wasn't too late to recruit a fellow to the campaign who had those qualities, and Tewksbury could be packed off to Rome, out of reach of his creditors.

"What if she took the coast road?" Tewksbury mused, gaze once again on the fields and farms bordering the thoroughfare. "She could have gone east from London instead of north. Taken the road through Chelmsford, traveled along the seacoast, and then angled toward Norwich."

"She has a London coachman, Tewksbury. For him it's the great north road or Town, period. The coastal route is longer, the inns humbler, and there's no reason on this earth why she'd do something so unexpected."

"No reason, except to elude you," Tewksbury said, sending Bassham a brooding look. "If Sarah thought you'd look for her along the Great North Road, she'd take a less traveled route and stand a greater chance of reaching her auntie. I keep telling you she's not stupid. She knows you'll simply marry her off to another nodcock if anything happens to me. You are the one she needs to outwit."

In that much, Tewksbury was absolutely correct. "It makes no difference to me how Sarah eventually makes her way to Cromer. When she arrives to Aunt Fletcher's home, you and I will be waiting for her with open and forgiving arms. Aunt Fletcher will see reason, as will Sarah. You will trouble yourself to be gallant and restrained for once, and all will be well."

"I can be restrained but you said the sooner—"

The coach hit another rut.

"Hold your damned tongue, Tewksbury. Recriminations get us nowhere. Sarah suffered a small attack of nerves—I was right that her disposition is a bit unsteady, wasn't I?—and she simply needs reassurances and some cosseting. Can you do that?"

"I can cosset with the best of them, as long as my bills are paid."

Most of Tewkbury's bills were paid. Bassham knew better than to pay them all before the vows were spoken.

The next few miles passed in blessed if bumpy silence, then Tewksbury spoke again.

"You ever travel along the coast, Bassham?"

"I have not had the pleasure."

"The inns are cheaper, there's less traffic. The ocean is pretty, though I don't care for the stink at low tide."

The sight of Sarah's signature on the marriage settlements would be beyond pretty. "If you don't mind, I'd like to get this report read before we turn east at Stilton."

Tewksbury slouched lower in his corner of the coach. "They get bloody awful storms along the coast. I heard they had one earlier this week. Half of Norfolk and a quarter of Suffolk flooded. Would be a shame if anything happened to Sarah."

"You are attempting to think, Tewksbury. The effort is doomed. I suggest you turn your thoughts to how you'll cosset your bride when the happy reunion takes place."

"She's not stupid," Tewksbury said again, crossing his arms and closing his eyes, "and though I adore a good romp, and I'll try to make Sarah a good husband, I am not stupid either."

CHAPTER 4

R oad repair in a time of impending war was an urgent undertaking. Farming in spring was equally urgent, as was setting a village to rights after a major spring gale. Another gale was on the way, sooner or later, and the denizens of Fenwick knew to restore order as quickly as they could while the winds blew calmly.

Thad was thus at the forge until dark, and his back, arms, and legs had passed weary long before sunset. He'd shared his lunch with Sarah, and was famished as well as tired by the time he washed off at the pump.

The pump being at the back of the smithy, and Thad being filthy, he didn't merely sluice himself off. He stripped down to his natural state and had a good if chilly top to toes wash, donning only his breeches to climb the back steps to his room at the boarding house.

He really ought to go straight to bed, for tomorrow would be equally demanding, and a tired blacksmith was a blacksmith who grew short tempered with large animals and clumsy with hot metal.

The balcony beckoned, however, and—might as well admit it—the possibility of another quiet conversation with the prodigal heiress. He donned a clean shirt and pajama trousers, and found a pair of house slippers to shove his aching feet into.

Sarah, covered from head to delectable toes in a green velvet night robe, had apparently waited for him, or so he hoped. She occupied her chair, which some obliging soul had positioned a mere six inches from Thad's. That same soul had put a cushion on Thad's seat, which in his present state loomed like a heavenly benediction.

"I saw you working," she said. "You didn't even stop for an evening meal, and I stole half your nooning."

"You did not steal anything." He sank onto the blessed comfort of the cushion, for which his tired fundament would have happily ransomed his soul. "You shared your company with a man much in need of conversation beyond, 'Hold still, there, Queenie,' and 'Give me your ruddy foot, horse.'"

"Does a lot of cursing go on in the smithy?"

He leaned his head back and closed his eyes. "It shouldn't. Most horses are willing enough to be shod if you're patient and reasonable with them. We're in a hurry to repair the road, though, and get the crops in, so patience is in short supply."

"Do you like to work so hard?"

Off to the west, the moon had already cast its silvery magic over the marshes, and a chorus of frogs sang to the night air. In the distance, the surf ebbed and flowed in a relaxing rhythm, and Thad's mind turned itself to Sarah's question.

"I do like to work hard," he said, "much to my surprise, though not as hard as we're having to go at it this week. When I arrived here, I needed the challenge. I needed to wrestle with iron all day and fall into bed each night insensate. I needed practical puzzles to solve and a list of tasks that would never end."

Sarah drew her legs up, wrapping her arms around her knees. "Were you angry?"

He'd been grieving, but he hadn't realized that. "I was angry, also sad. Both my parents and my older brother had died in the space of a year. My parents were taken by illness, but my brother... his death was stupid. A matter of honor, which is to say, drunken young men waving deadly weapons at each other."

And then Grandmother had started hounding Thaddeus to marry

the instant the mourning duties had been fulfilled. In her way, she'd been grieving too, but Thad had been unable to see it at the time.

He began arranging the words in his head to explain how the title had made the whole business of grieving more fraught, when Sarah toed off her slippers.

"I pulled weeds this afternoon," she said, her bare toes peeking from beneath her hems. "I loved it. I yanked them up by their dirty roots and tossed them into the wheelbarrow to die. Why does nobody allow young ladies the opportunity to murder weeds? We'd be ever so much more even tempered."

Murdering weeds. Thad hoped she'd filled that wheelbarrow with her ire. "What else did you do?" *And might I kiss your toes?*

"Fifi came by again, chasing her pony. I caught him up and instructed her on not allowing him to snatch the reins. I took a few turns on dear Wellie, and I do not believe that pony has been so surprised since a saddle was first strapped to his lazy back."

"In your skirts, you took a few turns on Fifi's pony? I would have liked to have seen that." Not only because the pony was overdue for a comeuppance but also because Sarah had the prettiest ankles ever to wade on an English shore.

"I also helped Cook prepare for dinner. She said many hands make light work, or I think that's what she said. One could hardly understand her, but after an hour of trying, I had the knack of peeling potatoes. I will dream of peeled potatoes, a lovely great stack of them cut up for boiling."

Dreams of kissing Sarah had figured in the idle corners of Thad's mind. As he'd watched a horse trot up, or waited for iron to heat, his fancy had also turned to a pair of elegant sandy feet, and to a lady whooping with glee at the frigid sting of the surf on her ankles. On the way back to the smithy, he'd also taken a peek inside her elegant coach, and imagined her reclining on the well-padded benches, a book in hand, her feet up on the opposite cushion.

He had not envisioned Sarah peeling potatoes, not ever. Nor pulling weeds, nor hiking her skirts to give a pony a lesson in manners.

"You enjoyed impersonating a peasant?"

"I have never had such an interesting, worthwhile day. I wasn't impersonating a peasant, Mr. Pennrith, I was being useful. Do you know how lovely it is to be useful? Fifi thanked me, Mrs. Peabody thanked me. Cook said I was welcome to help again tomorrow seeing as I didn't cut myself nor waste half the *tatties*. I think that means potatoes."

Sarah was reminding Thad of his own wonderment at adjusting to life in Fenwick. Idleness was not a virtue here, as it was in Mayfair, but rather, a privilege earned by honest labor and good fortune.

"You are proud of yourself," he said softly. "And that feels wonderful."

"Precisely. I've been thinking about what you said."

Not about another goodnight kiss? "I talk a lot. What particular bloviation inspired you to pondering?"

"About why not simply buy myself a house and take up the life of a spinster? Uncle was generous with my pin money, doubtless in hopes I would not grow curious about the rest of my funds. I had no place to spend what he gave me, and nine years of pin money is a lot of money."

"Nine years?"

"My mama's will specified that I was to have my own spending money from the age of sixteen. My come-out was delayed by deaths in the family, and I have thus arrived to the great age of five-and-twenty having had only five Seasons."

"Did you enjoy those Seasons?" He still could not envision her peeling potatoes, much less schooling Fifi's equine sluggard. Ladies did putter in the garden, but *murdering weeds* was a new perspective on that activity.

"One is supposed to enjoy one's come out," Sarah said. "One is supposed to feel special and as if life in all its sparkling potential awaits in the very next ride in the park or trip to the shops."

Thad propped his feet on the balcony. "You hated it." Very likely, nobody had known that. They'd seen the pretty heiress in the pretty ballgowns and envied her a prison made of money and family schemes.

"Wait here," she said. "One shouldn't sit in the chilly night air with wet hair. You'll develop an ague." She disappeared into her room and came out holding a shawl. "Sit forward."

Thad obeyed and she wrapped the shawl, a soft, closely woven merino, around his shoulders. The scent of roses clung to the wool, suggesting Sarah had recently worn it.

"Thank you." *I don't suppose you'd like to keep me warm by snuggling in my lap?* As tired as he was, he should not have been able to think of snuggling, but he suspected, where Sarah was concerned, only death would part him from such wayward thoughts.

Thad was arranging his shawl when a thought occurred to him. "It's fairly dark on this balcony, Sarah. How did you know my hair was wet?"

She resumed her seat, once again tucking herself into a ball. "I watched you at your ablutions. You are quite well formed. One could wish one had more than moonlight by which to admire you." She sounded as if she was complimenting somebody's skill at pall mall. All proper and polite.

Perhaps with Sarah, the more polite she sounded, the more emotion she was controlling.

"Would you like to watch me make some cheese toast? I will likely keep my clothes on, though if you ask very nicely, I might give you back your shawl."

"I couldn't really see you when you washed," she said. "Not nearly as well as I wanted to. But I knew you were down there in the yard, not a stitch on, and I envied you how casual you can be about such behavior. The sea air is making me wicked."

"The sea air is waking you up," Thad said. "It can have that effect. Shall we to the kitchen, Miss Sarah?" He rose and extended a hand to her.

She accepted his courtesy, and kept his hand in hers. "I never want to leave this place, Mr. Pennrith. Do they have fairy mounds here in Anglia, because I feel that far removed from what I believed my destiny to be in London?"

He wrapped her in a brief hug, not because he desired her—though he absolutely did—but because he knew that feeling of not wanting to leave, ever, and the sorrow that lay behind it. Ordinary people somehow made Fenwick an extraordinary place, a place worth cherishing.

"Let's raid the larder," he said, stepping back and draping the shawl around her shoulders. "And nobody is making you leave here, nor can they. You are of age, you have means, you should do as you please."

She squeezed him around the middle. "How I wish that were true. To the larders, Mr. Pennrith. Let's put the coastal trade to shame with our plundering."

Thad smiled and let her go, though if Sarah chose to plunder his personal treasures, he would not object one bit. He would volunteer, in fact, to become her prisoner for at least the duration of a few nights.

⚜

Hugging Thaddeus Pennrith was like hugging a venerable oak. He was that solid and sturdy, that formidable. Sarah hadn't been quite honest with him though.

She'd seen every detail of his wet, naked form gilded by moonlight. He was perfection on a grand masculine scale, roped in enough muscle to make the Mayfair dandies look like the prancing doddypolls they were.

Making love with Thaddeus would be a glorious, passionate under-taking, not some furtive interlude involving a writing chair. Sarah knew this by the way Thaddeus had frankly washed his parts, pausing to add a few affectionate strokes to his quiescent member, his head thrown back and the wet column of his throat exposed for her delectation.

She wanted to bathe him with her own hands, to explore his secrets and have him peel her out of her clothing, article by article. This was what came of peeling potatoes by the hour on the kitchen's sunny back steps, and of wading barefoot in the surf at high noon.

Sarah pushed those thoughts firmly aside and cast around for small talk. "Mrs. Pallant was safely delivered of a fine, healthy boy."

Mr. Pennrith paused on the landing. "What will they name this one?"

"Peregrine is among the possibilities, as well as a Percival, Parsifal, Peyton, Pompeii, Preston. Mrs. Pallant was hoping for a girl, for she did want to name the child Pandora." Not Charlotte, Elizabeth, or Georgina, as half of Mayfair was named. The girl would be called Dora and Dorie, and her husband would probably call her Adorable.

As Sarah and Thaddeus descended into the darkened kitchen, she realized she had never once considered what she might name a child conceived with Matthew. She hadn't, in fact, had much interest in bearing his child, viewing conception as simply his means of entrapping her in an increasingly distasteful union.

"Light a lamp," Thaddeus said. "And I will be about the cheese toast."

Sarah used the iron poker on the hearth to stir up the coals, touched a lit spill to the wick of the lamp on the mantel, and felt pleased with herself for mastering even such a pathetically mundane skill as lighting a lantern. She had not done even that much for herself for years.

"Shall I light another?"

"No need. I know what I'm about in this kitchen. Mrs. Peabody realized years ago that when I miss meals, I will forage."

The idea that a man knew his way around a kitchen should not surprise Sarah. The Regent's chefs were all men, most of the cooks in the military were men. But those men gave orders to underlings when it came to food preparation.

Thaddeus cut even bread slices off a half-loaf, then pared cheese from a wheel with equal precision. "The trick to perfect cheese toast is to get the cheese slices uniform." He popped a bite of cheese into his mouth, then sliced another and held it out to her.

When Sarah would have taken the cheese from his hand, he instead put it to her mouth. She took the bite, and he watched her chew.

Was this flirtation? It had nothing to do with fans, gloves, parasols, or bouquets. No poetry was involved, save for the poetry of Thaddeus's hands competently wielding kitchen utensils.

"Where are the plates?" Sarah asked.

"We're eating cheese toast," Thaddeus said. "Plates don't come into it." He arranged the bread slices on long toasting forks, and passed one to Sarah. "We'll wash this down with some lemonade, and, if you'd rather we put butter and jam on a few slices, we can do that too."

He went through a quarter of the loaf, expertly toasting the bread to golden brown, and melting the cheese just so. The result was delicious and messy, consumed sitting side by side on the warm stones of the raised hearth.

Sarah finished the last of her lemonade some moments later. She was full and happy, but not content. "That was scrumptious. Thank you."

"That," Thaddeus replied, re-banking the coals, "was barely enough to hold me until morning, but I could not ask for better company." He took their empty mugs to a dry sink, and put them in a pan of water with other dishes awaiting the scullery maid's attention. "Shall we to bed, Sarah?"

He extended a hand down to her, and grimaced. "That came out wrong. Forgive me."

Sarah took his hand, and also grabbed for her courage. "I would like to go to bed with you. If that doesn't suit, I would be pleased to share a few kisses. Matthew doesn't like to kiss, and I found that honestly a relief. I'd always thought... that is... kisses should be special, and you are special, and this place is special, so I wondered if perhaps..."

She dropped his hand, and moved away to blow out the lantern. "I have made a complete gudgeon of myself, haven't I?"

The kitchen was cast in the deep shadow, only a lit sconce on the stairs shedding any light.

Thaddeus scrubbed a hand over his face. "Let's discuss this upstairs, shall we?"

That was not a yes, not a stolen kiss, not much of anything.

But it wasn't a no, either.

Sarah, licking her fingers by the meager light of the coals and a single lantern...

Sarah, reaching for the spill jar, such that her night robe strained across a generous, unconfined bosom.

Sarah, peeking at him as he'd washed off the sweat of the forge, and very likely watching as he'd considered a quick self-indulgence and discarded the idea for being a little too improper, even for a country blacksmith in the dark of night. And now she wanted to take him to bed.

The mind of a mere mortal male boggled.

He took her to his room, because if they were to make memories, he wanted them made in his bed. He also wanted her to be able to leave if and when she took a notion to quit his company.

"Here is my dilemma," he said, closing and locking his door. "You are a lady without escort at present, and I do not want to take advantage of you as you endure a low moment."

She peered around at his room, which was a temple to quotidian male needs. A wardrobe, clothes press, and cedar chest held his entire store of clothing. The writing desk was bare but for the implements needed to send Grandmother the twice-monthly reports she demanded. The bed was big, the quilts worn soft with age, the rug equally well used.

His hearth was swept clean, a fire laid in case a spring night turned chilly, and behind the privacy screen—yes, she peered around that too —she'd find everything needed to keep a fellow reasonably tidy and clean.

"I'm not having a low moment," Sarah said, coming back around the privacy screen. "I'm having an honest moment. They are rare in my experience, though here in Fenwick you probably see more of honesty than dissembling."

The comment stung, because Thad hadn't been entirely honest with his neighbors, or with Sarah. They knew him to be a Town swell who'd been passing through and had stayed. They did not know his lineage could be traced back to the Conqueror, and his fortune was more venerable still.

He could reset a pair of front shoes on a draft team in half an hour, and that was all the good folk of Fenwick needed from him.

What did Sarah need from him?

"I do not want to take advantage of you," Thaddeus said, "but I also do not want to leave you with the impression that I am indifferent. I nearly set my pants on fire twice today at the forge, because I was daydreaming about your toes."

She opened his wardrobe and peered inside. "My toes?"

Her hand stroking over his Sunday frock coat might as well have been caressing his cock. "Your toes—bare, sandy, elegant, like your feet, ankles, and calves. I found myself wondering if your knees would be elegant too."

She faced him and looked down, and then slowly, inch by inch, hiked the skirts of her robe and nightgown. Up, past exquisite ankles, up, past surprisingly muscular calves, and *up*, over the curious join of bone and muscle known as a lady's knees.

"Are they?" she asked. "Elegant? Nobody has opined on the matter previously."

She was trying for amusement, but Thad heard the courage—and the frustration—in her question. Her dunderpated fiancé had not *made love* with her, had not bothered to see to Sarah's pleasure, had not shown her the courtesy owed any woman, much less a wife-to-be.

"Sarah, your knees are the Creator's greatest testament to beauty, but are you sure? If we go to bed together, I will withdraw, and Mrs. Peabody keeps a store of the tisanes used to prevent conception, but you must be sure." *And please might you raise those skirts to your waist?*

Sarah let her skirts drop, which was a kindness to Thad's ability to form sentences. "I was *not* sure, with Matthew, but I let him convince me. We were to be married, after all—why delay the inevitable when he would simply pester me until I capitulated?"

She paced closer to Thaddeus, and he fisted his hands at his sides.

"Then," Sarah went on, "Matthew went about the business with no more finesse than a boar rooting in the midden, and again, I was not sure. Perhaps that was simply how men go on, and the poets have been embellishing reality rather more than I'd been led to believe. I was not sure when I left London, knowing my uncle would follow, and fearing scandal would as well, but I saw no other course."

She stopped before him. "When I behold you, Thaddeus, I know my own mind and body. I am sure in my bones of my preferred course. The feeling is marvelous. I want more of that feeling, and I want it with you." She slipped her arms around his waist, and gave him her weight. "I will not beg, but I am asking to become your lover."

Thaddeus had no illusions about his charms.

He was far from handsome, but he was big and fit. Just as some men wanted to ride impressively large horses, some women wanted a roll in the hay with a man well equipped to pleasure them. If that fellow was low-born that only added to their adventure.

As far as any of the merry widows tooling through Fenwick knew, Thaddeus was simply a town blacksmith with decent manners, a flirtatious smile, and a sizeable and occasionally willing prick. Of late, he'd been less inclined to accommodate the ladies passing through because the whole exercise put him in mind of furtive couplings in Mayfair alcoves.

Sarah didn't want a furtive coupling; she did not want to feel naughty or wayward. She wanted lovemaking and cherishing, and she hoped to explore that lovely and fraught terrain with him.

Thaddeus gently wrapped his arms around her and rested his cheek against the top of her head. "What if there's a child, Sarah? I will not allow my firstborn to be raised as a cuckoo in another's nest."

"Matthew tried diligently to get me with child. He failed. I am not all that worried about conception."

"You should be. Promise me you'll tell me if there's a child. I know you won't tarry but a few days in Fenwick, and I will probably quit the town myself before too long, but a child deserves legitimacy and two loving parents."

She shifted to look up at him. "This is why I am drawn to you, Thaddeus Pennrith, because I am all but throwing myself at you, and you think about the consequences to an innocent child. You might labor all day at the forge and eat your luncheon from a sack while sitting on a sandy rock, but you are more of a gentleman than all the strutting peacocks in London combined."

She met his gaze, gave him a moment to protest, demure, or babble, then kissed him squarely on the mouth.

Before Thaddeus unwrapped the great gift Sarah had made of herself, he had the presence of mind to open the draperies so the bedroom was full of moonlight.

"I want the bed," Sarah said, as Thaddeus draped her shawl across his reading chair and undid the belt of her robe. "I want to be lying on my back, facing you when you join your body to mine. I want to touch you everywhere, not just hang onto a chair arranged at the proper height. I want... so much. I want *you,* Thaddeus, all of you."

"You will have all of me," he said, peeling her robe from her shoulders. "I promise, all of me and more. You will leave that bed knowing what you like, what pleases you, what tickles. You will have satisfaction from me such as you will never forget. Never again will a man leave you *not sure* about your due."

If he thought he was giving her something—a benchmark, a frame of reference, some truth with which to battle against the ignorance she'd been subjected to—he could more easily allow himself the great selfishness of becoming her temporary lover.

So, he gave her kisses, by turns delicate and voracious, to her mouth, her cheeks, and temple, then lower. She liked to have her neck kissed, and—thanks be—she adored having her breasts fondled. She arched into his touch like a demanding cat, until Thaddeus eased off her nightgown, and she stood panting, naked, and pale in the moonlight.

"You too," she said. "All of you."

By Saint Clement's forge, she was lovely. Also blushing.

"Undo me," Thaddeus replied, when he wanted to toss her onto the bed and commence pleasuring them both. "Undress me. I want to be skin to skin with you, and I want your hands on me everywhere."

She smiled, and if her stupid *former* fiancé and all the other witless fortune hunters distracted by her riches could have seen that smile, they'd have known her wealth was pocket change compared to the passion she possessed.

She unbuttoned Thad's shirt and pulled it over his head, then undid the drawstring of his pajama trousers and went exploring.

"Sit," she said, urging him into the reading chair angled toward the window. She retrieved her shawl from the back of the chair and draped it around her shoulders.

He kicked off his slippers, took his assigned seat, and prayed for fortitude. Sarah extracted his half-hard cock from his clothing, her touch tentative at first—but not for long. By the time she'd licked, kissed and otherwise explored the object of her curiosity, Thad was in the hands of a bold lady indeed.

"Would you like to sit in my lap?" he said, when she rested her cheek on his thigh and was using just the tip of her tongue on the tip of his cock.

"Sit in your lap?" Sarah's tongue found *that spot*, that wickedly sensitive spot...

"Sit *on* my lap, rather. We face each other, you take me inside of you, and much of how we move and pleasure each other is up to you. You could tell me to tease your nipples for example, or put my mouth on them. You might like a few kisses from me, or—"

She peered up at him and used her thumb on his wet flesh to mimic the action of her tongue. "I'd rather be on the bed. I've had enough of chairs for the moment."

"Then take me to bed, Sarah, and have your pleasure of me." The words should have been naughty, but what Thad felt as he watched emotions play across Sarah's face, was a tenderness too vast for words.

She had been manipulated and threatened by the people who should have kept her safe. She had fled everything familiar to take her chances on the unknown. For her to entrust Thad with this night of loving was to honor him deeply. He would be worthy of her trust, if it took him until dawn and broke his heart in the process.

CHAPTER 5

Lovemaking was not intended to be a hurried or furtive process. Sarah had suspected as much, as she'd become intimately acquainted with the writing chairs in her uncle's home. Her suspicions had bloomed into near certainty when Matthew had concluded his rutting with a pat and a pinch to her derriere, then a hasty rebuttoning of his falls.

His next tender gesture was usually to remove himself to the nearest mirror, where he'd apply a comb to his artfully styled curls, while Sarah fumbled beneath her skirts with a handkerchief and fumbled in her heart with dismay.

Surely *that* was not the marital act?

That hopeless indignity could not possibly be the motivation for sonnets and ballads without number?

That perfunctory awkwardness wasn't the pleasure for which many a lady had sacrificed her good name?

Beholding Thaddeus Pennrith clad in little more than moonlight and exhaustion, she knew that patience and consideration were the essence of lovemaking, and whatever Matthew had been about, nothing of love had informed his behavior.

More fool he.

"You would sit in that chair, clutching the arms until they splintered if I asked it of you, wouldn't you?" she asked.

"In another two minutes, either the chair arms will splinter with force of my grip, or I will come undone with the cleverness of yours."

Sarah wanted to keep touching him, particularly his intimate parts. The contrasts fascinated her. Hard and silky, mighty and vulnerable, hot and sensitive. She wanted to consume him, with her mouth, her hands, her body, everything.

She contented herself with more of the first, but something about the tension coiling in Thaddeus's big body warned her to desist.

"I like having you in my mouth," she said, sitting back. "I am truly becoming wanton."

"A trifle bold perhaps," he said, cradling her jaw against a callused palm. "I long to be the man with whom you become bolder still. You might like having my mouth on you too, Sarah. Shall we find out?"

She rose, not exactly sure what he was proposing. "The sheets will be cool."

"No," Thaddeus said, getting to his feet, "they will not."

His pajama trousers had been pushed down to reveal his rampant arousal—pushed down *by her*—and the silk stretched tight over his hips and buttocks. That provocative dishevelment and his complete ease with it, made Sarah want to snatch him up and toss him onto the bed.

Thaddeus stepped out of his pajamas and laid them across Sarah's robe and nightgown.

"Now what?" Sarah asked, a frisson of uncertainty threading through her anticipation. Surely Matthew had not been equipped as generously as Thaddeus was. Not nearly.

Thaddeus folded the covers back, piled pillows against the headboard, and climbed onto the bed. "Now we take up where you so mercifully left off." He patted his thighs. "Your chariot awaits."

He had described this to her: making love facing each other, her straddling his lap. The opposite of her experiences thus far. Sarah got herself onto the bed, her shawl still about her shoulders, and settled herself in Thaddeus's lap. A length of hard male flesh arrowed up along his belly, and her ignorance once again threatened to swamp her ardor.

"That goes inside me, if I recall the particulars correctly."

Thaddeus cupped her elbows and kissed her. "We'll get to that part. No need to rush." He palmed her breasts, a marvelous pleasure given the warmth and calluses of his hands, then teased at her nipples with skillful fingers and an even more skillful mouth.

Sarah winnowed her fingers through thick, damp hair, and at some point—perhaps when he'd used the rough texture of his beard on the underside of her breasts?—she began to move. She slid her sex along the thick column of male flesh between her legs, and nothing—not anything, ever—had felt as shocking or as pleasurable.

"I like this," she panted. "I like this exceedingly."

"I like it rather a lot too," Thaddeus countered. "Say when you want more, Sarah, and that will please us better still."

He was asking her something, even as he kissed her throat and sketched the contours of her back with his hands. Sarah became dimly aware that for their bodies to join intimately, somebody had to touch somebody, and Thaddeus was leaving that initiative up to her.

A battle ensued, between the part of Sarah that was having a spectacularly good time riding his arousal, and the part of her that wanted him inside her.

"I don't want to stop," she said. "I like..." She sank her weight more tightly over him. "That feeling."

"Take me inside you. We can make that feeling more intense."

Had Matthew given her that assurance, she would have scoffed. He'd made her all sorts of promises. *I'll be done in five minutes. You'll get better at it with practice. You'll learn to love it. You'll beg me for this.*

Nobody should learn to like, much less tolerate, being bent over a chair for a man's convenience. Sarah could envision no sane moment when she'd beg Matthew for anything so tedious.

Thaddeus waited, his hands on her hips, and once again his patience did what passion could not. Sarah took him in one hand and started the joining.

"Go slowly," Thaddeus said, when she had placed him snugly against her opening, and dropped her hand. "Take your time."

He was barely seated, not even truly penetrating, and she'd

expected him to start thrusting away. Apparently not. She tried a small, tentative undulation of her hips.

"Slowly," Thaddeus said again, two syllables conveying iron self-discipline.

Sarah could not help but go slowly, for Thaddeus was generously endowed and the sensations were too delicious to be rushed. She hung over him, attuned to her own body in a way that was new and fascinating.

"You were right," she said, withdrawing almost all the way before sinking back down. "This is scrumptious."

He laughed, a low rumble that Sarah could *feel* because they were so intimately connected. "Make a feast of me, Sarah. Gorge yourself on the sweetness."

His hands glided up from her hips to her breasts, where he applied a diabolical combination of caresses, pressure, kisses, and even his teeth, until Sarah's desire became as frantic as an ocean gale. The pleasure broke over her in a tempest, and when she would have gone still with shock, Thaddeus took over the rhythm of their joining.

He swept her past mere pleasure into a realm of transcendent, unimaginable sensation. The intensity of the cataclysm overpowered thought, and all Sarah could do was fling herself against Thaddeus until satisfaction battered desire into submission.

And yet, the storm was not over. Emotions flooded in even as the aftershocks of pleasure ebbed. Sarah was suffused with a joy that had no name. Perhaps the glow in her heart was simply the effect of a celebration of animal lust, for she and Thaddeus had celebrated wildly.

Behind the happiness came an urge to weep, for this moment with Thaddeus was stolen and could have so easily been missed. His hand in her hair was tenderness incarnate, his hard presence in her body a consolation for the parting to come.

He had not found satisfaction, and that he should deny himself made the tears creep closer.

"I am about to wax lachrymose," Sarah said, mashing her nose against his muscular shoulder. "I cannot credit such a thing."

"Cry if you want to," Thaddeus said quietly. "*...thy eternal summer shall not fade,*" he quoted. "*Nor lose possession of that fair thou ow'st/Nor shall* *death brag thou wand'rest in his shade/When in eternal lines to Time thou grow'st...*"

He quoted the Bard, gently implying that Sarah's interlude with him here by the sea might end, as the glories of a summer day did, but he would treasure his memories of her forever.

Thaddeus shifted them, so Sarah lay under him, sheltered by his body. She did cry then, for the foolish woman formerly engaged to a silly young man, for a family distracted by greed from what really mattered. She cried for a future she could not share with the man who had stolen her heart.

After Thaddeus had dried her tears and embroiled her in an orgy of kissing, he began to move again inside her, and Sarah moved with him. She would conjure a storm of passion for him as he had for her, and together they would glory in the gale.

Making love with Sarah had forced Thaddeus to think of his future, not in an abstract, vaguely grumbling allusion to *someday soon*, but as that future encompassed the rest of his fleeting and precious life. Did he truly want to live out his days wrestling hairy equines and sweating at the Fenwick forge? Was that truly his best option?

How much longer must his grandmother harangue him to take up the duties of his birthright?

He'd arisen from the bed he'd shared with Sarah resolved to put an end to Grandmother's waiting, and had written to her accordingly. To his surprise, she'd answered by return post that he was to join her not at her London residence, but at her girlhood home and dower property in East Runton. She'd directed him to attend her at once, and he was not to do anything foolish regarding the Errant Heiress.

Attending her *at once* would be foolish indeed. Grandmother had harangued Thaddeus for five long years, she could hold her horses for another few days.

As he'd waited for Grandmother's reply and slogged through the furious demands at the smithy, he'd also developed the habit of sleeping with Sarah. Over the past week, she'd been corresponding with her solicitors, though Thaddeus didn't pry into those details. He could draw the relevant conclusions: If her solicitors knew where she was, her uncle could find her easily enough.

She too was reconciling herself to her fate.

She did not ask Thaddeus to buy her passage to the Continent, and truly, she was safer in Britain.

"You repaired my coach springs today, didn't you?" Sarah asked, as she took Thaddeus's jacket from him.

"I did. The job took some effort, because the metal has to be tempered, but it's done. You are free to leave at any time." He'd also lingered over his inspection of her vehicle, noting the details of comfort and design, inside and out, and making certain the rest of the undercarriage was sound.

She leaned into him. "I don't want to go, but I must resolve matters with my family."

Let me resolve them for you. Except Thaddeus had his own family matters to resolve before he was free to make that offer.

"I could put you on a packet for Edinburgh," he said. "Your family won't think to look for you there."

"My funds come from London," Sarah said, stepping back. "My solicitors, much to my surprise, have been responsive to my queries, but I doubt they will withhold my location from my uncle. Here, I have an ally in Aunt Fletcher, and I need that."

"You have an ally in me," Thaddeus said. "I too have funds, Sarah. More than you'd think, and they are at your disposal. If you want a house in Scotland, I will cheerfully buy you one. Don't capitulate to your family's demands because of the money." It was on the tip of his tongue to tell her the rest of it: I have means mostly because I have a title, you see...

But that title was an earldom, and Sarah had on many occasions made scathing references to her uncle of the same rank.

She gazed up at him, her expression unreadable. "Would you come to Scotland with me?"

He was a peer of the realm, he had responsibilities, and they did not lie in Scotland, and after five years, Grandmother was out of patience.

"I could come to you there, for a time, but first... Do you recall telling me that you fled London because you did not know what else to do?"

She hung his jacket in the wardrobe and sat on the bed. "I do, and I am so very glad I did flee London."

"I fled London too, and that was the right choice for me as well. I have sorted myself out here in Fenwick on Sea. You provided me with the last bit of sorting that I needed to face a situation I ran from years ago."

Sarah unbelted her night robe and untied the bow of her night-gown's décolletage. "Does that situation involve a woman?"

"Yes, in a sense." Grandmother was female, though she was more dragon than human lady.

"Do you love her?"

"I do."

"And she has waited patiently for you all of this time?"

Thad had to focus on the question, because Sarah had raised her skirts to her hips, scooted to the edge of the bed, then spread her legs.

The view was spectacularly distracting. "She has waited," Thaddeus said, "not patiently. Sarah, what are you doing?"

She parted the fabric of her nightgown, so her breasts were all but displayed. "Saying good-bye."

"Not good-bye," Thaddeus said, crossing the room to stand between her legs. "Not that, Sarah. I must deal with matters relating to my family, as you must, and then I will beg you for an audience, if you are willing to receive me. I will come to you in London, I will call upon you at your aunt's, but please do not say good-bye."

And pray God, Sarah would not take a Cornish earl into dislike because she'd fallen in love with a Suffolk blacksmith.

"You are not engaged to another?" Sarah asked, leaning back on her elbows.

Two nights ago, Thaddeus had sat Sarah on the edge of the bed, the better to share with her the pleasures of his mouth on her sex. They had also discovered, though, that the bed was the perfect height for copulation if she lay on her back and he stood at the bedside.

Thaddeus undid the buttons of his falls. "I am not engaged to anybody. Never have been. Will you break it off with the ninnyhammer?"

"I am convinced he will break it off with me."

Thaddeus took his aroused cock in hand and stroked himself along Sarah's damp folds. "Not good enough, Sarah. Tell me you'll send him packing." Thad had no business making that demand, but his store of gentlemanly delicacy was rapidly washing out to sea.

"If he doesn't toss me over," Sarah said, jiggling on the bed a little, "I will cry off. Stop teasing me."

"When you wiggle like that, it makes your breasts bounce. I love it when your breasts bounce."

She looked him right in the eye, and began twiddling a nipple. In mere days—and nights—she'd gone from a prim and proper lady to a houri of the bedroom, and Thaddeus had the sense she was still—*still*—barely getting started on her erotic vocabulary.

He eased into her heat, more slowly than she usually liked, because he owed her the pleasure of anticipation. "Did you peel potatoes today, Sarah?"

She eyed him balefully, though this was a game they played. Small talk to make the passion flare hotter.

"I made pie crusts and jam tarts. I brought Mrs. Pallant some fabric and thread to make baby clothes. I separated irises, and planted some in the yard of your smithy."

Sarah had a surprising aptitude for village life, another reason she might prefer a blacksmith to an earl. Thad set that troubling thought aside and sent his thumbs exploring the russet curls between Sarah's legs all while he kept up an easy, relaxed rhythm.

"Sarah, if I were not a blacksmith, but some other sort of fellow, from some other station in life, would you still want me?"

"If I were not an heiress, awash in money and running from my family, would you still want me?"

He bent over her and gathered her close. "Yes, I absolutely would. I will want you to my dying day and beyond. I will cherish every moment spent with you and long to return to your side when we are parted."

The lovemaking changed, from mutual teasing to a focus on not only desire—desire was ever present between them—but on closeness. Sarah lashed her arms around his neck, and her legs around his waist. She met him thrust for thrust until the bed was creaking and Thad's thighs were burning. Still they pushed each other, straining both toward and away from the moment of completion, until Sarah began the soft panting that signaled her release.

Thaddeus held out, barely, until Sarah was once again moving in a lazy, replete rhythm. He withdrew and spent on her belly, though it nearly cost him his sanity. He would not take choices from Sarah as her family had tried to do, and foreclose her options with maternal guilt.

"I want you again," she said, when he was spooned around her in bed some minutes later. "I am still humming inside, and I want you again."

If I were an earl, would you want me? If we had to bide in London for a portion of the year while I voted my seat, would you want me?

"Shall I escort you to your aunt's home in Cromer," he asked, "or would you rather your family not realize you've formed a friendship with a village blacksmith?"

Sarah was quiet for a time, while Thaddeus once again mentally arranged ways of announcing the truth to her:

I have this little earldom in Cornwall, quite pretty, a mere 30,000 acres if you count only the Cornish properties.

There's this title I've been meaning to mention—my own, as it happens.

I realize your uncle is an earl and you probably detest all things earl-ish, but I hope you'll make an exception in my case...

"I did not know how to ask you," she said, "but I am very much afraid Aunt Fletcher will try to talk sense into me, or that Uncle will simply have me carted off to the north unless I marry Matthew by special license. I am not a coward, but I think the escort of an ally would be a prudent measure."

"We will call on your aunt first," he said, "but I'd also like to introduce you to my grandmother. She's just down along the coast from Cromer in East Runton, and she will be less uncivil if I bring a proper lady with me."

That wasn't half of the story, but Thad would take on one set of difficult relations at a time. He made love with Sarah again, slowly, tenderly, hoping it wasn't the last intimacy they'd share.

Sarah was more determined than nervous, or so she told herself, until she saw Thaddeus crossing the thoroughfare to join her beside her coach. In the sparkling morning sunshine, he looked not like the village blacksmith, but like the largest and most exquisite exponent of Bond Street's sartorial arts ever to saunter down a high street.

His boots were polished to a champagne shine, his morning attire was cut to lovingly flattering perfection, and the paisley embroidery on his waistcoat found the exact balance between extravagant needlework and elegant good taste.

"My finery is a few years out of date," Thaddeus said, bowing over her hand, "but will I do?"

He had assisted her to dress, then sent her to make her farewells to Mrs. Peabody, so his splendid turnout was a case of first impression for Sarah.

"You will dazzle Aunt Fletcher," Sarah said, fluffing the snowy lace of his old-fashioned jabot. "You dazzle me." Even Uncle would take Thaddeus seriously attired thus, which was more reassuring than a determined—but *not* nervous—woman should admit. Aunt Fletcher had sent a note warning Sarah that both Uncle and Matthew were imposing on her hospitality, and they did not intend to leave until Sarah joined them.

Thaddeus had declared that development to be a relief, for it allowed Sarah to settle matters without returning to her uncle's household.

Her uncle's household, from which Sarah could be sent, bound hand and foot, to some walled estate where hysterical women were interned with orders to *come to their senses.*

"Let's be off," Thaddeus said, tossing a valise to the footmen at the boot. "The roads will be the worse for the storm, and delays and detours are likely." He handed Sarah up, climbed in after her, and joined her on the forward-facing seat.

A sharp rap with Thaddeus's fist on the coach ceiling, and MacAdams gave the horses the office to walk on.

Because Thaddeus chose the route that turned inland toward Norwich rather than keeping the coach traveling along the coast, the going was lamentably uneventful, and the coach passed through Norwich well before noon. Sarah spent the first part of the journey dozing against Thaddeus's side, but her sleep was fitful.

"You are worried," Thaddeus said, stroking her hair. "Don't be. I won't let them bully you, Sarah. You state your terms, and your family complies with them. This is not a negotiation."

"They aren't in the habit of complying, and I am not in the habit of stating my terms."

He bent near enough to whisper. "*Touch me here, Thaddeus.... Faster... Not like that, like this.* You state your terms quite firmly, and I love it when you do."

"That's different."

"No, my love, it is not. The same woman who takes me by the hand and shows me exactly how I'm to please her can be equally clear and firm with meddling relations. In mere days, you have Fifi's disgrace to the equine species trotting docilely up and down the lane, and I see that your solicitors have been prompt responding to your queries. If you can make the lawyers attend you, a troublesome uncle will be of little moment."

"An uncle and a fiancé. I did accept Matthew's proposal."

"Crying off is a lady's prerogative. Leave me to my forge in Fenwick if you must, Sarah, but never tell me that you'll allow a man like that to call you wife."

"Do you intend to remain at your forge?" she asked, taking his hand.

"For the near term, while the Arbuckles sort out how to go on when I leave." He took Sarah's hand, and she had so often joined hands with him over the past week, she noticed that his grip felt different.

Still callused, still warm, still a pleasure... but he wore a ring. A *signet* ring.

"Why would you leave Fenwick?" Sarah asked. "You seem so happy there."

The coach slowed as he peered down at her, and then he gently kissed her. The kiss held no heat, no offer of an erotic distraction, but a wealth of tenderness.

"I have been happier in Fenwick on Sea in the past week then I thought it possible for a mortal man to be, but my grandmother will not leave me in peace until I set her straight on a few points."

"Exactly," Sarah said, "I must set my uncle straight on a few points."

"And your fiancé?"

"I pity him." Sarah could say that honestly. Matthew was a rutting boy with nothing to offer the world but charm, good looks, and bumbling skill with an unimpressive pillicock. "I watched you at the forge, yesterday. You work without your shirt."

"The forge is hot, and fabric can catch fire."

The forge was also dark, the better for a smith to assess the exact color of heated metal or hot coals, and Sarah had tarried in a shadowed corner after bringing Thaddeus his nooning. He'd been fashioning a new set of horseshoes from a straight iron bar, curving the metal blow by blow, then reheating it to bend it yet more.

Thaddeus working at the forge had stirred all manner of emotions, and not a little arousal. He was a magnificent specimen, also skilled, patient, hard-working, good-humored, kind, and determined. Sarah would never regard horseshoes, herself, or the working man in the same light as she had before leaving London.

"You toil without your shirt, but you work with your mind as well as your hands," Sarah said. "I found that impressive. I would like to work with my mind too, Thaddeus, to be of use, and not merely a means to the end of my uncle's laziness and greed."

The coach slowed further and made a turn off the road.

"Of use how?" Thaddeus asked. "Your fortune could be of great use, but perhaps that's not what you meant."

"I don't know, except that I would like to find a worthy charity or three to support. Peeling potatoes is useful, though I hope I can aspire to more than that. Schooling Fifi's pony was useful. Taking the air in Hyde Park so other ladies can criticize my bonnet and gentleman can ogle my bosom is not useful."

"We are agreed. Who are these other gentlemen?"

The coach halted, and the time for private discussions was over, which was fortunate for the gentlemen whose names she would have listed.

"We have arrived," Sarah said. "Aunt can be a dragon, but I hope she breathes her fire on Uncle rather than me. And Thaddeus?"

"My love?"

Oh, she adored his endearments. "I suspect, given the chance, you could be of even greater use to the realm than you are when serving at Fenwick on Sea's forge. When we have more time, perhaps we ought to discuss that topic as well."

Thaddeus looked pained, and as close to out of sorts as he ever became. "Agreed, but if your aunt breathes fire at you today, you simply singe her eyebrows with your own flames. Once or twice and she'll get the idea." Thaddeus preceded Sarah from the coach and handed her down.

Aunt's cottage—a rambling three-story edifice of eighteen bedrooms—sat on a rise overlooking the sea. The white columns of the front terrace were still gleaming white, and red pots of salvia still adorned the steps. The same venerable butler Sarah recalled from her childhood admitted her, and the same scent of lemon oil and sea breezes wafted through the house.

"May I take the gentleman's hat?" the butler asked.

Thaddeus passed over his hat, and Sarah noted the beat of awkwardness when no calling card accompanied the hat.

"Mr. Pennrith has kindly escorted me from Fenwick on Sea," Sarah said. "Where might we find Aunt Fletcher?"

"Madam is in the guest parlor," the butler replied, setting Thaddeus's hat on the sideboard. "Your uncle and Mr. Tewksbury are with her. Today is her day to be at home, and I am certain she will welcome you with open arms."

The butler twinkled at Sarah, then led her down the corridor past familiar paintings and a sparkling pier glass Sarah did not recall seeing before. Thaddeus paced at her elbow, silent, and oddly of a piece with the elegant surroundings.

He wasn't nervous, and Sarah borrowed from his calm as she waited for the butler to announce her.

"Lady Sarah Weatherby," the butler intoned, "and Mr. Pennrith, late of Fenwick on Sea." He bowed and withdrew.

And abruptly, Sarah was very nervous indeed.

CHAPTER 6

"Your ladyship?" Thaddeus winged an arm at Sarah, and if he was dismayed that she claimed an honorific, he hid it behind a warm, even mischievous smile.

Sarah took his arm, angled her chin up, ignored the flock of demented butterflies in her belly, and let Thaddeus escort her into the parlor.

Uncle stood near the window, his expression radiating banked annoyance. Matthew struck a pose near the piano, a cross between wronged suitor and eager lover. He kept one hand on the lid of the piano, and half-turned toward her, as if forces beyond his control kept him from going to her.

Or perhaps common sense did that, when he caught sight of Thaddeus at Sarah's side.

"My darling girl." Aunt Fletcher, tinier than ever, came out of her seat. "I have been so worried about you. And here you are, quite in the pink and on the arm of as impressive a fellow as ever graced my parlor. The gentleman bears a resemblance to your grandson, Sephronia. Isn't Pennrith an old Cornish name?"

Aunt addressed another older woman, who reposed in a rose velvet wing chair near the unlit hearth.

"Unless I mistake myself, which I almost never do, that is my wayward grandson. Thaddeus make your bow."

Good heavens. *That* was Thaddeus's grandmother? She rose from her wingchair with all the dignity of a grieving queen, and extended a beringed hand to him. He moved forward and some perverse impulse led Sarah to keep her hand entwined with his arm.

Even as he bowed to his grandmother, Sarah did not let him go.

"Thaddeus," Sarah said, "might you introduce us?"

The older woman glowered down her nose at Sarah. On Thaddeus that nose was splendid. On his grandmother, the effect was not nearly as attractive.

Aunt Fletcher rang a little bell that chimed merrily enough to be heard in the corridor. "Introductions are hardly necessary, Sephronia. You know my Sarah and I know your Thaddeus, though I do believe he was frolicking naked in the surf when last I met him, and an exasperated nursemaid or three was begging him to come back to shore. We will need a fresh pot of a certainty. Mr. Tewksbury, shut your mouth, lest you catch flies, and Bassham, do stop pouting by the window. Our Sarah is here, safe and sound, and we rejoice to see her."

"Bassham?" Thaddeus said. "Earl of?"

Uncle bowed. "At your service, and you would be?"

"Thaddeus Pennrith. And this must be the *honorable* Mr. Matthew Tewksbury."

Matthew mustered a bow. "At your service. Sarah you are looking none the worse for your ordeal. You will be pleased to know I brought a special license. We can return to London as a married couple, and nobody need know that you indulged in a mad flight due to your bridal nerves."

Matthew smiled, and the kindly promise of forgiveness in that smile, the smug confidence, lit the fire of Sarah's temper. He was graciously offering to bend her over an endless procession of writing chairs, while setting her abigail to spy on her, and spending her money on stupid wagers.

"I have made arrangements to give away my fortune, Matthew. Are you still interested in returning to London as my husband?"

The only sound was the soothing rhythm of the distant surf, breaking on the beach far below the windows.

"You are mad," Uncle said. "Clearly, unequivocally mad."

"I might be," Sarah replied, as Thaddeus rested his hand over the fingers she'd wrapped around his arm, "but I am well within the terms of the trust when I make that decision. Mother gave generously to charities, and I merely intend to follow her example. I have also reviewed an accounting of all disbursements made from my funds since you became the trustee. You are either excessively greedy or a very poor manager. The solicitors have been scolding you for years because you waste my money."

"Sarah," Matthew began, taking a step toward her. "You must be reasonable. In times of war, investing is uncertain, and I'm sure Lord Bassham has done his best to preserve—"

"Whatever he has preserved," Sarah said, "I am giving the bulk of it away. Injured soldiers strike me as a worthy cause. Life boats appeal to me, as do widows and orphans. If you have any self-respect to your name, Matthew, you will take yourself off for a repairing lease in the West Riding and never blight my day with your presence again. Uncle paid a number of your gambling debts, and you provided *nothing* of value in return."

Thaddeus's posture shifted subtly. He went from quietly standing at Sarah's side to *looming*. Matthew retreated to the piano.

"You're crying off," Matthew said, nodding once, and glowering at Uncle. "A gentleman does not argue with a lady."

"I am not crying off," Sarah said, "I am casting you into the nearest muddy ditch like the rubbish you are. Aunt, Mr. Tewksbury will not be staying the night."

Thaddeus' grandmother harrumphed. "Be off with you, puppy. Thaddeus has a taste for a good brawl, I am ashamed to say. In this case, one is inclined to indulge his unfortunate proclivities."

"But Sarah," Matthew said, sounding genuinely bewildered, "*why?* I'm reasonably good looking, of suitable station, and I would have let you buy all the fripperies you cared to buy. I could keep Bassham from being too big of a pest, and give you some babies to spoil. Why throw that away and a fortune as well?"

Sarah did drop Thaddeus's arm. "You would have *let me buy fripperies*, and I am supposed to be grateful for that? When it's my money I'd be spending—while you fornicate the afternoon away with my lady's maid? What woman in her right mind would choose that future when she can instead make a difference throughout her day and share a bed at night with a man who thrives on honest work? I could slap you."

"Why don't you?" Thaddeus's grandmother asked.

"Because," Thaddeus replied, calmly, "to slap him, she'd have to touch him, and Sarah decided before she left London that Tewksbury isn't worth even her anger."

Sarah felt as if she'd been about to trip, but a strong hand had prevented her from stumbling. "Exactly," she said. "Away with you."

Matthew jerked down his waistcoat and marched from the parlor, though his show of affronted dignity was undermined by the speed with which he scampered past Thaddeus.

"We are well rid of him," Uncle said, "though I had hoped to avoid the scandal of a broken engagement. I will take you back to London, Sarah, and we will sort out your funds to your satisfaction. To disburse a fortune—and it remains a sizable fortune—in a display of pique is not the behavior a rational woman."

The exhilaration of casting Matthew aside collapsed into cold dread. "I will not return to London with you, Uncle. I refuse to."

Aunt remained silent in the face of that declaration, when Sarah very much needed her to speak up.

"Nonsense," Uncle replied. "You were foolish, but I agree that Tewksbury lacked the intellectual stature to keep you amused. We'll find you another fellow, one willing to overlook a broken engagement in light of your means, and this will all be forgotten."

Thaddeus did not cross the room so much as he rolled forth like a storm making landfall from the North Sea.

"Shut your stupid mouth," he said, stopping two paces from Uncle's place by the window. "Sarah is of age. You are no longer her guardian, and if her Aunt will not provide a home for her, *she can provide a home for herself*. You have offered her nothing but a gilded cage and selfish manipulation. You turned a rutting bounder lose on her in a further attempt to steal from her. Tewksbury is pathetic, but you are disgusting."

And Thaddeus was absolutely lovely. Sarah's resolve had slipped with Uncle's threats, her courage had flagged. Thaddeus was simply pointing out the truth, though. Uncle was no longer her guardian, and he had stolen from her.

"Who the hell are you, sir," Uncle sneered, "to be insulting a peer of the realm? I have no doubt you've been sniffing around Sarah's skirts in an attempt to get your own brutish hands on her money. I will take her back to London, and she will thank me for sparing her from your advances."

The old women were exchanging a glance that to Sarah looked quietly amused.

"Uncle, hush," Sarah said, not amused in the least. "You have pilfered the last coin from my coffers. I would rather be a blacksmith's wife in Fenwick on Sea than your niece in Mayfair. I am happy to sever relations with you if you insist on clinging to your arrogance."

"The arrogance," Uncle snapped, "is yours, my girl. Those damned solicitors had clear instructions, and—"

"And lately, they have obeyed them," Thaddeus said, "because those instructions came from Sarah, and her mother, their clients, while you are a parasite and a disgrace to the peerage. You either apologize to Sarah or run along back to London to explain to your glovemaker, coalman, mistress, and jeweler, that you have no legal means of paying your bills."

The very calm with which Thaddeus offered those options settled something inside Sarah that had needed settling.

"I do not want to see you ruined, Uncle," Sarah said. "I will bring your accounts up to date, but then you must manage within your means. I expect you will quit London and let out the town house at least for a few years."

"Burtie," Aunt Fletcher said, "you'd best take that offer, for I have neither the means nor the inclination to bail you out."

Uncle looked down his nose at Sarah, using an attitude of disdain that would have turned her knees to blanc mange only a few short weeks ago.

"And you will rusticate in some seaside swamp with this, this..."—he waved a hand at Thaddeus—"jumped up stable boy?"

Thaddeus was watching Sarah, his eyes conveying his admiration for her, and something else, something that reminded her of his pained expression in the coach.

"I will gladly become the wife of the Fenwick on Sea blacksmith, and spend my days weeding our garden and raising our children rather than subject myself to an earl's high-handed meddling."

Uncle strode for the door. "That you would make such a choice proves that the last of your wits have gone begging. Marrying a blacksmith. For shame, Sarah. I can assure you that Chancery will see me re-appointed as guardian of your property the moment I inform the courts of your proposed folly. And to think, I took you in, when you hadn't a roof over your head or a—"

Thaddeus had shifted during this tirade to block the door. "And what if, instead of marrying a lowly blacksmith, the young lady is planning to marry an earl?"

"I am the only earl foolish enough to endure this company," Uncle said, "and I can easily remedy that sad state of affairs." He swanned out the door, and Sarah frankly never cared if she saw him again.

To think his approval had ever meant anything, when in fact, he ought to have been earning Sarah's respect. The comfort of that insight was fleeting, however, when she grasped the significance of Thaddeus's words.

"Thaddeus," she said, "what are you going on about? I want nothing to do with earls or honorables or even baronets. I shall have my blacksmith, if he will have me."

Thaddeus should have given her a broad, mischievous smile, maybe even a wink. Instead he looked a bit sheepish.

"I blush to inform you, Lady Sarah, that your plan to marry a village blacksmith has become slightly problematic."

"Quite," Grandmother said, as Thaddeus searched for the words that would explain his situation to Sarah without making him sound like another manipulative, untrustworthy, titled male.

"You cannot expect a peer of the realm," Grandmother went on, "the sole male exponent of the earldom's line, to marry a hoyden who goes racketing about the countryside because she's lost her patience with a strutting dandy and his dollymops. Dollymops are a fact of married life, and I am surprised that Eudora Fletcher's great-niece would quibble over such a detail."

"Grandmother," Thaddeus said as gently as he could for a man who wanted to clap his hand over a querulous old woman's mouth, "please hush."

"Sephronia,"—Mrs. Fletcher chose a tea cake from the tray—"your grandson has apparently done a fair bit of racketing himself."

Grandmother thumped her cane. "Men are always racketing. That's most of what they are good for, but the least Thaddeus can do is take twenty minutes to speak his vows and secure the succession. I have made a list, a carefully researched list, and now that he's done with Frolic on Sea, he will subject himself to my guidance—"

Thaddeus might have let Grandmother's temper blow itself out, but across the room Sarah was looking again like the bewildered young woman whose coach had pulled up on damaged springs outside The Queen's Barque.

"Grandmother, if you do not cease prattling, I will take Lady Sarah by the hand, quit this parlor, and never open another letter from you."

"I never prattle."

Thaddeus reached for Sarah's hand and she caught him in a firm grip. The effect was the same as if his spine had been a length of iron glowing with the heat of the forge, then plunged into cool water for tempering. Every strength he possessed became focused on the same end, casting mere determination into the shade.

"Sarah met me as I labored at the Fenwick on Sea forge, where I have earned a wage these past five years. She did not disdain me because I labored with my hands, but she might well disdain me for allowing you to berate me as you did my brother. There is more to life than securing the blighted succession."

Another grandmother might have resorted to tears, or at least made a dignified retreat.

"Had your brother listened to me, my lord, I would have seen him married to a decent young woman whose steadying influence would have prevented his lamentable excesses. I would have great-grandsons by now, and you would be free to dirty your hands all you pleased."

Sarah slipped her arm around Thaddeus's waist, and her silent support—without hearing Thaddeus's apologies or explanations—reminded him of the families he knew in Fenwick on Sea. They loved one another, they accepted one another. They argued and fumed and pouted, but they found their way back to high, sunny ground when the domestic storms moved on.

Respect was evident in those families, as it had not been in Grandmother's dealings with Thaddeus.

"Grandmother," Thaddeus said, tucking an arm around Sarah's shoulders, "had you not carped at my brother so ceaselessly to marry the biddable cipher of your choosing, he might not have been driven to those excesses in the first place. Your days of pestering and shaming and haranguing me are over. If you ever want to know your great-grandchildren, you will cease meddling *now*."

Sarah leaned against him. "When Thaddeus uses that tone of voice, I daresay draft horses ten times his size know better than to argue. God willing, he will be papa to any number of darling children. I'm sure he would hate for them to have no idea *at all* who their great-grandmother is."

Grandmother inhaled through her nose. "You are comparing me to a *beast?*"

Mrs. Fletcher munched on her tea cake. "You are as stubborn as a mule, Sephronia. You'd best listen to your grandson."

Grandmother rose. "Send for my coach," she snapped at the footman. "There is no good company to be found here."

She made an exit worthy of Mrs. Siddons when upstaged by the ingenue, while Mrs. Fletcher poured herself another cup.

"Sephronia drove your poor father to eloping, my lord," Mrs. Fletcher said, dropping a lump of sugar into her tea. "Best thing that could have happened. Inbreeding invariably results in feeblemind-edness and weak nerves, as my late husband often observed."

"My parents eloped?" That was news to Thaddeus.

"Sephronia fumed about it until your brother showed up. Once you came along, the match was very nearly Sephronia's idea, despite your mother's people being *in trade*. Owning half a dozen foundries isn't exactly the same as selling posies on a street corner, but Sephronia thrives on being affronted. Will you have some tea, my dears?"

"Sarah?" Thaddeus wanted to hear more from Mrs. Fletcher about his parents' courtship, but his own courtship matters had become pressing. "Will you walk with me by the water before we sit down to tea?"

"Take a parasol," Mrs. Fletcher said. "The sea air is fine for invigo-rating the animal spirits, but a lady must protect her complexion."

Sarah gave Thaddeus a measuring look. "Are you truly an earl?"

"I am afraid so. Are you truly parting with your fortune?"

"Most of it."

"My title wasn't making me happy, but I could not escape it entirely. If your fortune is making you miserable, then toss it into the sea for all I care."

"You mean that?"

He offered her his arm. "With all my heart. Let's enjoy some fresh air, Lady Sarah, for there's more I would say to you."

Sarah did take a parasol, because the sun on the water was fierce. "I will pay off my uncle's immediate debts, but are you horrified that I'd give away my fortune?"

"Are you horrified that I'm an earl?"

The beach was a wide expanse of fine white sand, but here too, the shore turned to rocks a hundred yards on. Sarah headed for the rocks, because she and Thaddeus could sit and talk there, and because they'd be out of sight of the cottage.

"You told me you were a London dandy, and those fellows tend to come from a notably few well set-up families. I did see the finery in your wardrobe but I was too interested in seeing more of you at the time to puzzle over your clothing. Your diction is public school, and your size is also indicative of aristocratic breeding."

"My size is indicative of Viking blood blending with my Norman antecedents. I didn't mean to lie to you Sarah. I am sorry for that, but discretion has become my habit. What I have in Fenwick on Sea has saved my sanity, and I protect it instinctively."

That dear, decent Thaddeus had sought refuge by the sea as Sarah had sought refuge, suggested he'd been in dire straits indeed.

"I did not exactly announce my lineage to you when I climbed into your bed either, Thaddeus. I thought you would run from the room in dismay, gentleman blacksmith that you are."

He took her hand. "Your coach sat in the innyard for days, Sarah. I had a closer look at the springs and also noticed the turned crests. I also saw the solicitors' letter to you, and being solicitors, they addressed their mail properly."

"You knew I was the daughter of a peer?"

"I figured that out eventually, but you deserved to be just yourself for a few days in Fenwick on Sea. I'd had that privilege for five years. I wasn't anybody's *lucky spare*, I wasn't a nob. I was simply Thaddeus Penn, a competent hand at the forge. I'd earned some respect with hard work, honest dealings, and skill. That was balm to the soul of a man who'd been raised to be a reproductive insurance policy dangling idly from the family tree."

"Can we be honest with each other going forward, Thaddeus? We had reasons for guarding our privacy before, but I don't want to keep secrets from you."

He stopped walking and faced her, their hands still joined. "You want to go forward with me? I will understand if I was simply a means of blasting your future free of the course your uncle had set for you."

The breeze whipped his dark hair about his shoulders, and his grip was the same warm, firm, callused grip Sarah adored.

"Thaddeus, I will *not* understand if you merely wanted a farewell frolic with a willing woman in Fenwick on Sea. I'm glad we met without family trappings—or traps, to use the more accurate word. I'm glad you took me to bed on the terms I set for myself, glad you were willing to come to me simply as Thaddeus Pennrith, the real man rather than the title. I will treasure the memories of our early days for all my life, and I want that life to be shared with you."

He looped his arms around her shoulders and held her in a loose embrace. They were still visible from the cottage, and Sarah did not give a hearty damn who saw her in the arms of her beloved.

"I love you," Thaddeus said. "I wish I could say, I will be anybody you want me to be. The village blacksmith, an Anglian country squire, a Cornish earl, a London swell... but the more I saw of village life in Fenwick on Sea, the more I realized that the labor of people like the Arbuckles and Pallants is what drives this land, and their needs and priorities should be heard in Parliament."

Sarah leaned into him and slipped her arms around his waist. "And your earldom?"

"I miss Cornwall. I miss my home, I miss being able to visit the graves of my family, Sarah. I love Fenwick on Sea in part because it reminded me so much of home. For five years, I've contented myself with the reports of stewards and factors, but the land deserves more from me. The Corsican will not wreak havoc forever, and adjusting to peace will take ingenuity and tenacity. I have those qualities. You have them too, and I want us to be part of forging a better future for Britain."

"I am not to have my marriage to the village blacksmith, then?"

"And I am not to become the adoring spouse of a wealthy heiress. I will adjust to my changed circumstances as long as I can still be married to you. Will you have me, Sarah?"

She closed her eyes and let the sound of the sea merge with the steady beat of Thaddeus's heart. "I would like to have you right here on the beach, Thaddeus. To cast off our clothes and get sand in inconvenient places and then wash off frolicking naked in the surf. I will settle for a kiss—for now."

He kissed her with all the tenderness and passion she could have wished for, and they sat on the rocks for a long time, talking of summers in Cornwall, an annual honeymoon in Fenwick on Sea, and how to forge a future for their homeland as happy as the future they envisioned sharing with each other.

THE END

To my dear readers,

I hope you enjoyed Thaddeus and Sarah's happily ever after!

I spent a lot of childhood summers on the Southern California coast, and my parents ended up living by the sea for more than forty years. I know how the ocean can define the land and communities adjoining it, but I'd never had a chance to write a seaside romance until the Bluestocking Belles dreamed up the *Stranded* anthology. (Thanks, Belles!)

If you'd like to see what else I have coming out this spring, please do drop by my **website**, or follow me on **BookBub**. The BB folks will let you know when a title goes up for pre-order, releases, or is discounted as a Bookbub deal. I also put out a periodic **newsletter** highlighting a new release or blathering on about works in progress. I never, ever sell, swap, give away, or otherwise let your email addie out of my sight, and unsubscribing is easy-peasy.

And finally, I **blog** every Sunday, and do a weekly giveaway of some sort in conjunction with those posts, so please do stop by and join the conversation!

Happy reading (by the sea or elsewhere)!

Grace Burrowes

PS: My most recent full-length release is *How to Catch A Duke*, the story of how Lord Stephen Wentworth finds his future duchess—and true love too, of course! **Order your copy here**: https://graceburrowes.com/bookshelf/how-to-catch-a-duke/#order

SOCIAL MEDIA FOR GRACE BURROWES

You can learn more about Grace Burrowes at these social media links:

Website: https://graceburrowes.com/
BookBub: https://www.bookbub.com/authors/grace-burrowes
Newsletter: https://graceburrowes.com/contact/
Blog: https://graceburrowes.com/blog/

ABOUT GRACE BURROWES

Grace Burrowes believes in love, and believes that writing happily evers after is the best job on the planet. She's a recovering foster care attorney, and USA Today and NYT bestselling author of both historical and contemporary romances. She loves to hear from readers and can be reached through her website at graceburrowes.com.

Newsletter: https://graceburrowes.com/contact/
Blog: https://graceburrowes.com/blog/

The Teatime Tattler

Dear Reader,

Samuel Clemens Esquire, editor and proprietor of THE TEATIME TATTLER, invites you to enjoy More News about Society and its goings on twice a week at

https://bluestockingbelles.net/category/teatime-tattler/

We bring you SCANDAL from across the fictionsphere, from the pens of any historical author whose characters' activities need to be EXPOSED to the view of the discerning public. Authors may apply at the Tattler.

With the deepest respect, I remain your faithful scribe,

S. Clemens

The Teatime Tattler, published twice weekly since 2015. For links, see the Bluestocking Belles address page at the end of this collection.

THE BELLES WOULD LIKE YOUR HELP!

Book reviews help readers to find books, and authors to find readers. Please consider writing a review for *Storm & Shelter*, even a couple of sentences telling people what you liked (or didn't like) about the stories. Reviews can be posted on Goodreads and on most eRetailers websites. For links to this book on those sites, see the *Storm & Shelter* page on the Belles' website: https://bluestockingbelles.net/belles-joint-projects/storm-shelter/

Malala Fund
The Bluestocking Belles have chosen the Malala Fund as the charity they support, and to which they donate some of their royalties. Periodically, they take on projects intended to directly support this cause, which exemplifies their personal values and intentions: the right of girls and women to do whatever they choose with their lives.
How can you help?
Make a donation to our Team Page at https://www.classy.org/team/89502

OTHER BOOKS BY THE BLUESTOCKING BELLES

Find buy links and story blurbs for all the following books on our website at https://bluestockingbelles.net/belles-joint-projects/

25% of proceeds on the following books benefit the Malala Fund.

Holiday Escapes (2020)

Holidays, relatives, pressure to marry—sometimes it is all too much. Is it any wonder a woman may need to escape? The heroines in this collection of stories aren't afraid to take matters into their own hands when they've had enough.

These stories are republished here at 20% of the cost of collecting them all from each individual author.

Two bonus short stories round out the collection.

Fire & Frost (2020)

In a winter so cold the Thames freezes over, five couples venture onto the ice in pursuit of love to warm their hearts.

Love unexpected, rekindled, or brand new—even one that's a whack on the side of the head—heats up the frigid winter. After weeks of fog and cold, all five stories converge on the ice at the 1814 Frost Fair when the ladies' campaign to help the wounded and unemployed veterans of the Napoleonic wars culminates in a charity auction that shocks the high sticklers of the ton.

In their 2020 collection, join the Bluestocking Belles and their heroes and heroines as The Ladies' Society For The Care of the Widows and Orphans of Fallen Heroes and the Children of Wounded Veterans pursues justice, charity, and soul-searing romance.

Valentine's From Bath (2019)

The Master of Ceremonies announces a great ball to be held on Valentine's Day in the Upper Assembly Rooms of Bath.

Ladies of the highest rank—and some who wish they were—scheme, prepare, and compete to make best use of the opportunity.

Dukes, earls, tradesmen, and the occasional charlatan are alert to the possibilities as the event draws nigh.

But anything can happen in the magic of music and candlelight as couples dance, flirt, and open themselves to romantic possibilities. Problems and conflict may just fade away at a Valentine's Day Ball.

Follow Your Star Home (2018)

Forged for lovers, the Viking star ring is said to bring lovers together, no matter how far, no matter how hard.

In eight stories, covering more than half the world and a thousand years, our heroes and heroines put the legend to the test. Watch the star work its magic, as prodigals return home in the season of good will, uncertain of their welcome.

Never Too Late (2017)

Eight authors and eight different takes on four dramatic elements selected by our readers—an older heroine, a wise man, a Bible, and a compromising situation that isn't.

Set in a variety of locations around the world over eight centuries, welcome to the romance of the Bluestocking Belles' 2017 Holiday and More Anthology.

It's Never Too Late to find love.

Holly and Hopeful Hearts (2016)

When the Duchess of Haverford sends out invitations to a Yuletide house party and a New Year's Eve ball at her country estate, Hollystone Hall, those who respond know that Her Grace intends to raise money for her favorite cause and promote whatever love-matches she can. Seven assorted heroes and heroines set out with their pocketbooks firmly clutched and hearts in protective custody. Or are they?

Eight assorted heroes and heroines find more than they've bargained for when they set out for Hollystone Hall for a charity ball.

MEET THE BLUESTOCKING BELLES

The Bluestocking Belles (the "BellesInBlue") are seven very different writers united by a love of history and a history of writing about love. From sweet to steamy, from light-hearted fun to dark tortured tales full of angst, from London ballrooms to country cottages to the sultan's seraglio, one or more of us will have a tale to suit your tastes and mood.

Learn more about the Bluestocking Belles at:
Website: www.BluestockingBelles.net/
Newsletter: http://eepurl.com/dAJU_9
Teatime Tattler twice-weekly gossip magazine: https://bluestockingbelles.net/category/teatime-tattler/
Free books: https://bluestockingbelles.net/teatime-tattler-free-books/

facebook.com/BellesinBlue

twitter.com/BellesInBlue

pinterest.com/bellesinblue

instagram.com/bellesinblue

www.ingramcontent.com/pod-product-compliance
Lightning Source LLC
Chambersburg PA
CBHW020224110726
47898CB00004B/1131